HOWARD CRUSE

STUCK RUBBER BABY

:01
First Second
NEW YORK

For Kim,
for Pam,
and
(as always)
for Eddie.

Howard Cruse
1944–2019

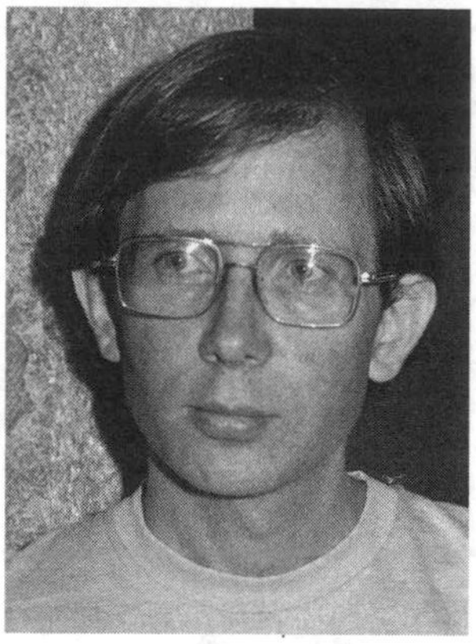

Cruse

I grew up in New York City. I'm a born skeptic. So when a cute guy I'm flirting with in 1979 tells me he's an artist, my thought balloon reads: "Yeah, right. This city is full of people who claim to be an artist. We'll see."

I saw.

Eventually (nervously, he later told me) he showed me his latest project—"Hell Isn't All That Bad," destined for *Snarf #9*—and my skeptic's protective shield melted. Howard wasn't just an artist; he was a damned skilled artist writing complexly about real life, outer and inner. By then we had already been discovering how much we had in common, this Alabama P.K. (preacher's kid) and this fast-talking Jew from New York: We had both identified strongly with the counter-culture movement of the 1960s and still held the belief that this world could be a hell of a lot nicer place to live in if only we let ourselves be ruled by peace and love. By then we both had tempered our naivete but not our idealism. We both had learned that the world doesn't heal (*tikkun olam* in my tradition) unless you do something to heal it. Art was his vehicle. In 1979 I was still looking for mine.

Thinking back now over our forty years together and the many traits, beliefs, and loves we had in common, I realize we had one more, very significant, thing in common. We were both community organizers.

Over the decades, with Howard always firmly behind me, I became an actual community organizer, working for queer rights, human rights, and against hate crimes. He felt fine about my earning practically nothing in order to start a queer senior center—one in Queens, NY, and one where we eventually settled in Berkshire County, MA—because all he wanted was for me to feel useful and fulfilled. And he felt *almost* fine about being the spouse of the political candidate when I ran for New York State Senate, smiling distractedly behind me while I made a speech. But by agreement, he only had to do it on special occasions.

Howard's community organizing was more intuitive, less formal, and was immensely successful. He took what felt like a career risk, coming out professionally as he put together the first issue of *Gay Comix* in 1980. He just knew there were queer comics creators out there, many of them lying low and doing great work that had nothing to do with their lives as queers. And of course there were the millions of us who grew up queer without ever seeing ourselves in the funny pages.

No one can claim sole credit for a major social change, and certainly polite Southern boy Howard never would. A lot has changed for American queers in general over these past four decades. But the comics artists who first gathered in the pages of *Gay Comix*, and took risks of their own to continue creating and publishing, also found each other—and their fans—at comic cons and then queer comic cons, until . . .

I mean . . . Have you *been* to the biennial Queers and Comics Conference? Holy crap, is that ever a community! Howard was a keynote speaker at the inaugural conference in 2015. He was so moved to see the hundreds and hundreds of queer cartoonists and their fans, joyously gathering as a community—owning their place in a world they helped heal.

Ed Sedarbaum
December 2019

Previous Page: Howard Cruse at the 1980 San Diego Comic-Con. Photo by Jackie Estrada
Above: Howard Cruse and his husband, Eddie Sedarbaum (left), during the first year of their relationship at New York's 1979 Gay Pride March. Photo by David Hutchison

INTRODUCTION

A few days after turning in my text for this introduction to *Stuck Rubber Baby*—a slight updating of the one I'd written for the 2010 edition, I learned that Howard Cruse had died. I'd known he was sick, but things took a turn, and at 75, he was suddenly gone. I felt hollowed out with a particular kind of grief I hadn't felt before. Losing a mentor has some similarities to losing a parent. Howard had in many ways made my life as a cartoonist possible, thanks to his trailblazing career. And I was lucky enough to have a warm personal relationship with him over the years. But I didn't spend much time in Howard's actual presence. What I'd spent time with was his work. And now there would be no more of it.

In light of this, I've revised the introduction once more, to encompass not just Howard's masterwork, but his legacy. A key part of that legacy is something that may not withstand the test of time as well as the work itself, so I want to mention it first: Howard's personal kindness. His compassion, generosity, and lack of ego permeate his work, too. But I have run across very few artists or writers who in person are anywhere near as *nice* as this guy was.

Howard was born a preacher's kid, which perhaps explains some of his gentle amiability. (His first cartoons were published in *The Baptist Student*!) He grew up in the South in the 1950s, dreaming of being a syndicated cartoonist and struggling to quash his desire for other boys. The tensions of growing up gay in that time and place are illustrated succinctly in a later cartoon in which an anxious, brush-cut teenager flips through *A Pocket Guide to Loathsome Diseases* at a newsstand, next to a rack of books from "Devotional Fatuousity Press" that includes *Jesus's Favorite Recipes*.

It took Howard a while to come to terms with his sexuality—on the way, he tried going straight, which resulted in an accidental pregnancy. (He and his girlfriend put the baby up for adoption. Later in life, their daughter would track Howard down and they'd enjoy a warm connection.) By the 1970s, the humor comics Howard had grown up emulating were beginning to disappear, and the underground scene was taking off. He began drawing his philosophical and psychedelically infused strip *Barefootz*, which would eventually include a gay character.

In 1979, the comics publisher Denis Kitchen invited Howard to edit a new comic book of work by gay cartoonists. Howard had to weigh what this might mean for his career—would coming out consign him permanently to the margins? Fortunately for all of us, he accepted the challenge—and then some. Howard was adamant that the contributions of men and women to *Gay Comix* be fifty-fifty, even though at that time lesbian cartoonists were much fewer and further between than gay ones.

I happened to stumble onto *Gay Comix* No. 1 in a gay bookstore in the Village practically the moment I moved to New York City after college. This would prove to be a conjunction as fruitful for me (I like to think) as was Howard's own happenstance encounter with the Stonewall riots one night a decade earlier when he was tripping on LSD. Here were comics by gay men and lesbians about their regular, everyday lives, including Howard's moving, hilarious, and magnificently drawn *Billy Goes Out*. I was inspired by this to start drawing my own cartoons, and I was not the only one. As Justin Hall, editor of *No Straight Lines: Four Decades of Queer Comics*, puts it, Howard is "the godfather of queer comics."

The founding premise of *Gay Comix*—that gay people are "regular human beings"—was carried over by Howard into his next project. *Wendel*, the serialized strip he wrote throughout the 1980s for *The Advocate*, was not just a witty and densely detailed tale of gay life, but a record of the Reagan administration's virulent homophobia as the nation was grappling with AIDS. Our collective memory is already beginning to forget this recent past, so *Wendel* is now an important chronicle of the lived experience of those years.

Howard's next act would be his most ambitious yet: to write a graphic novel based loosely on his own coming of age in the Jim Crow South. It would take on racism and homophobia, with the idea of truth telling at its core. A country that wouldn't admit, let alone confront, its own racism was telling a lie. The secretive life that many pre-Stonewall LGBT people were forced to live constituted a different kind of lie, but one equally destructive of integrity and connection.

I had the honor of receiving a visit from Howard during the time he was drawing *Stuck Rubber Baby*. He and his partner, Eddie, were in Vermont for a little vacation, though of course it was a working vacation for Howard, and he'd brought pages along to ink. After we'd visited a bit, he went out to the car to get some of them to show me.

This was over twenty-five years ago but my memory of the scene is very clear. As Howard came back inside with a large flat box, time seemed to slow down. I won't claim that I could see his aura, or that the artwork vibrated in my hands as I examined it. But there was an energy emanating from these sheets of Bristol board that could not be accounted for merely by the exquisitely designed, lettered, and inked details that met my eyes.

I expect that I was experiencing a reverberation of the intense effort—mental, emotional, and physical—that Howard had invested, and would continue to invest for some time, in this drawn world. The formal virtuosity of *Stuck Rubber Baby*, its ambitious historic sweep, its rich characters, its unflinching look at sex, race, violence, hate, and love, make it an immersive, truly novelistic reading experience in a way that's still uncommon for graphic narrative to achieve.

I identify uncomfortably with the young Toland Polk, the archetypal nice person. A white southerner who grew up steeped in the casual as well as institutional racism of Jim Crow, he wouldn't intentionally hurt anyone—but then again, he doesn't intentionally do much of anything at all. He's drifting along, equally disengaged from himself and from the world. But inevitably, he's caught up in the forces of change sweeping past him, and as his engagement builds, so does ours.

This is not a revisionist fantasy in which the white hero flings himself wholeheartedly into the civil rights movement. Toland's transformation is tentative, conflicted, alternately self-flagellating and self-serving—it's a scathingly honest portrayal.

He's surrounded by more active participants in the struggle, as finely drawn as Toland is. The patient, simmering Reverend Pepper. His wife, Anna Dellyne, the ex-jazz singer who now only sings hymns and freedom songs. Their gay son, Les, who turns from party boy to preacher's kid "at the flick of a switch." The flamboyant, wounded Sammy. And the brave but exacting Ginger Raines, the woman Toland convinces himself he's in love with. Ginger is a curious pivot for Toland, leading him toward the truth of civil rights activism, but also affording him the false front of heterosexuality.

What complicates and expands this story like a fifth dimension is Toland's growing acceptance of his desire for other men. I suspect this also complicated the reception of *Stuck Rubber Baby* when it was first published in 1995. The parallels Cruse establishes between racism and homophobia were perhaps just a little too ahead of their time to allow the broad mainstream embrace the book should have received.

The "fag bar," the Rhombus, is Toland's first encounter with a roomful of gay men and lesbians, but it's also the first racially integrated space he's been in. The black drag queen Esmereldus does Doris Day, singing "When I was just a little girl, I asked my mother, 'What will I be?'" In simple scenes like this, without ever resorting to rhetoric, Cruse deftly deconstructs race and gender more effectively than a shelf full of theory. In a way, *Stuck Rubber Baby* is an equal and opposite reaction to the vicious bombing at the center of its narrative. Cruse lays bare the mechanics of oppression like an explosives expert taking apart and defusing a ticking lethal device.

Clayfield is a thinly disguised version of racially riven Birmingham in the early 1960s. The pivotal episodes of violence and protest in the book are based on real events. And although the characters and story are made up, Cruse doesn't shy away from the fact that he has drawn readily from his personal experience, notably his "encounter with unintended fatherhood." This blend of documentary and fiction yields the best of both worlds—the suspense of a carefully crafted plot and the vivid immediacy of an eyewitness account.

Although the story is told by a middle-aged Toland looking back on his life, and is thus, strictly speaking, a first-person narrative, his take on the events is panoramic and omniscient. It was risky for a white author to write about African-American characters, particularly ones who are actively engaged in the civil rights movement, but Howard nimbly clears the bar. He's done his homework, yes, but like any good writer he pushes himself to explore his various characters' subjectivities as far as it's possible to go.

The image of Reverend Pepper's wife, Anna Dellyne, standing at the edge of the crowd at the jazz club Alleysax is one of my favorite moments in the book. She's aloof, regal, and wistful, half in the light, half in dense black shadow, a distillation of all the opposing tensions that push and pull this book along.

This brings me at last to the drawing. I know it took Howard years to draw this book, but even so, I don't see how one human being could possibly lay down this much ink in that span of time, even if they never stopped to eat or sleep. Many of the pages are so finely cross-hatched that they appear to have a nap—as if they'd feel like velvet if you ran your hand over them.

One stunning thing this technique affords is a very rich palette of skin tones. White and black characters alike are shaded with loving nuance. Indeed, everything in the book is drawn with manifest love and a profound generosity. Howard recreates the visual details of life in the South during "Kennedytime" with a staggering archival fidelity. In less skilled hands, this could be obtrusive. But the painstakingly rendered parking meters, textile patterns, vintage appliances, and record sleeves are woven into a meticulous backdrop that allows us to believe in and surrender to the story completely.

I should point out that this feat was accomplished long before there was such a thing as Google Image Search. Howard gathered references not with a few mouse clicks, but by digging around in library picture files, hitting the street with a camera and sketchbook, and by engaging in god knows what other time-consuming analog practices.

It's always tempting to cheat when drawing, to gloss things over. Like a crowd scene, for example. But look at the people gathered outside the funeral at the opening of Chapter 14. The back of each infinitesimal head is never a mere oval, but always a particular person's head. Howard's benevolent Rapidograph achieves transcendence here.

Despite the sometimes microscopic level of detail, this book is always eloquently legible. Howard is fluent with so many comics conventions that these too could threaten to intrude on the story. But his innovative page layouts and panel shapes, the bleeds and fades, the fragmented breakdown of crucial scenes—all these things combine to transmit a multilayered story with seamless coherence.

Stuck Rubber Baby is a story, but it's also a history—or perhaps more accurately a story about how history happens, one person at a time. What does it take to transcend our isolation and our particular internalized oppressions to touch—and change—the outside world? As Toland Polk begins to engage truthfully with his inner self, his outer self is able to connect with others more authentically and powerfully. Actually, it's just as accurate to put this the other way around, because those two actions are inextricable from one another.

Toland lives in a place and time where not just black people but "white niggers" are routinely terrorized, and where being a "nigger loving queer" has dire consequences. In a 2009 version of this introduction, I waxed eloquent about how dramatically things had changed—we had an African-American president, and support was rapidly building for marriage equality, things I'd never imagined seeing in my lifetime.

In 2019, things have changed dramatically again. White supremacists, neo-Nazis, and anti-Semites have scuttled out from under their rocks and into the public square. The Trump administration is trying its hardest to roll back LGBTQ rights under the claim of "religious freedom." Immigrants, Muslims, and women are under attack. The arc of the moral universe apparently bends like a corkscrew.

I've thought a lot over the years about how the progressive gay culture of Weimar Berlin was wiped out by the Nazis. Could the remarkable advances made by the civil rights and LGBTQ movements be likewise reversible? For a long time I assured myself that no, they couldn't. The roots of social justice have gone too deep.

Lately, on bad days, I feel less certain of this. But on good days I remind myself of the astonishing achievements of movements like Black Lives Matter and #MeToo. The everyday activism of principled people is an ongoing redemptive force in this country.

In an interview in the mid-1990s, after the first edition of *Stuck Rubber Baby* came out, Howard said, "this is a book people can live with and revisit and find new subtleties in, find issues that are contemporary even though the story happened thirty years ago. It's about issues I care a lot about: Is this country going to be a generous country or a mean-spirited country? This is very much on my mind these days." Now, almost another three decades out, that question could not be more stark or more consequential.

Howard Cruse's visceral account of America's recent past contributes with grace and force to the vision of a just world. And it makes an equally vital contribution to the power of graphic narrative to reflect life back to us—in this case the conflict and exhilaration of social change—in all its glorious chaos.

Alison Bechdel
December 2019
Vermont

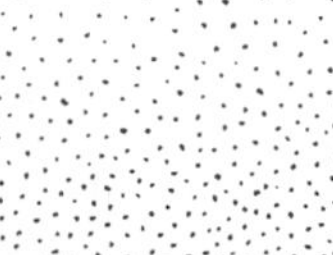

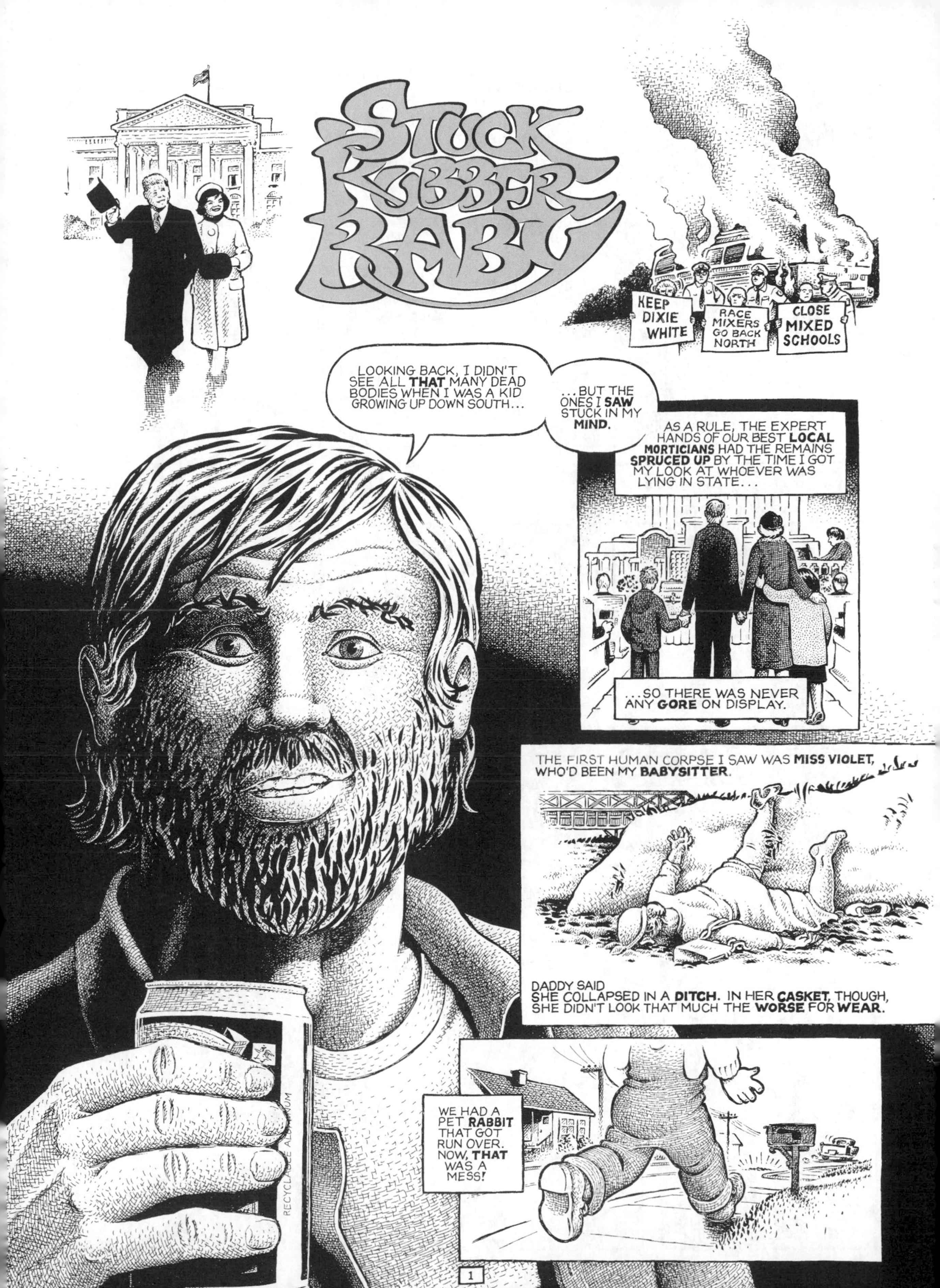

STUCK RUBBER BABY
KEEP DIXIE WHITE
RACE MIXERS GO BACK NORTH
CLOSE MIXED SCHOOLS
LOOKING BACK, I DIDN'T SEE ALL THAT MANY DEAD BODIES WHEN I WAS A KID GROWING UP DOWN SOUTH...
...BUT THE ONES I SAW STUCK IN MY MIND.
AS A RULE, THE EXPERT HANDS OF OUR BEST LOCAL MORTICIANS HAD THE REMAINS SPRUCED UP BY THE TIME I GOT MY LOOK AT WHOEVER WAS LYING IN STATE...
...SO THERE WAS NEVER ANY GORE ON DISPLAY.
THE FIRST HUMAN CORPSE I SAW WAS MISS VIOLET, WHO'D BEEN MY BABYSITTER.
DADDY SAID SHE COLLAPSED IN A DITCH. IN HER CASKET, THOUGH, SHE DIDN'T LOOK THAT MUCH THE WORSE FOR WEAR.
WE HAD A PET RABBIT THAT GOT RUN OVER. NOW, THAT WAS A MESS!
RECYCLABLE ALUMINUM

AS A DUMB **KID**, THOUGH, I CONVINCED MYSELF THAT HUMAN BEINGS WERE **DIFFERENT** FROM ANIMALS.

THE **FUNERALS** I ATTENDED LEFT ME REASSURED THAT, WHATEVER TOLL GOT TAKEN ON MY **OTHER** BODY PARTS, MY **HEAD** WOULD SURVIVE DYING **INTACT**.

THEN MY FRIEND BO WISED ME UP.

WANNA SEE SOMETHIN' **GROSS**, TOLAND?

SURE.

I FOUND A NIGGER MAGAZINE IN A TRASH CAN DOWNTOWN. LOOK AT THIS **PICTURE**....

IT WAS A CLOSE-UP PHOTOGRAPH OF A **DEAD BLACK PERSON** WHOSE **SKULL** WAS ALL CAVED IN.

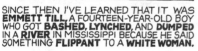

I LIKE THE MAN   JET

SINCE THEN I'VE LEARNED THAT IT WAS **EMMETT TILL**, A FOURTEEN-YEAR-OLD BOY WHO GOT **BASHED, LYNCHED**, AND **DUMPED** IN A **RIVER** IN MISSISSIPPI BECAUSE HE SAID SOMETHING **FLIPPANT** TO A **WHITE WOMAN**.

SOMETHING IN MY BRAIN PERMANENTLY BLEW A **FUSE** WHEN I SAW THAT PICTURE.

I HAD **NIGHTMARES**.

I WAS WORRIED ABOUT MY **SKULL**.

DADDY, IS THERE ANY **DIFFERENCE** BETWEEN **NEGRO SKULLS** AND **WHITE PEOPLE'S SKULLS**?

HOW D'YA **MEAN**, SON?

ARE WHITE PEOPLE'S SKULLS **HARDER** THAN NEGRO SKULLS?

OH, I **DOUBT** IT, TOLAND. I DOUBT IT **SERIOUSLY**.

IF **ANYTHING**, NEGRO BONES ARE PROBABLY **TOUGHER**, SINCE COLORED FOLKS ARE CLOSER TO THE **ANIMAL STATE** THAN WE ARE AND HAVE GOTTEN **STRONGER** FROM HAVIN' TO GET BY IN THE **WILD**.

2

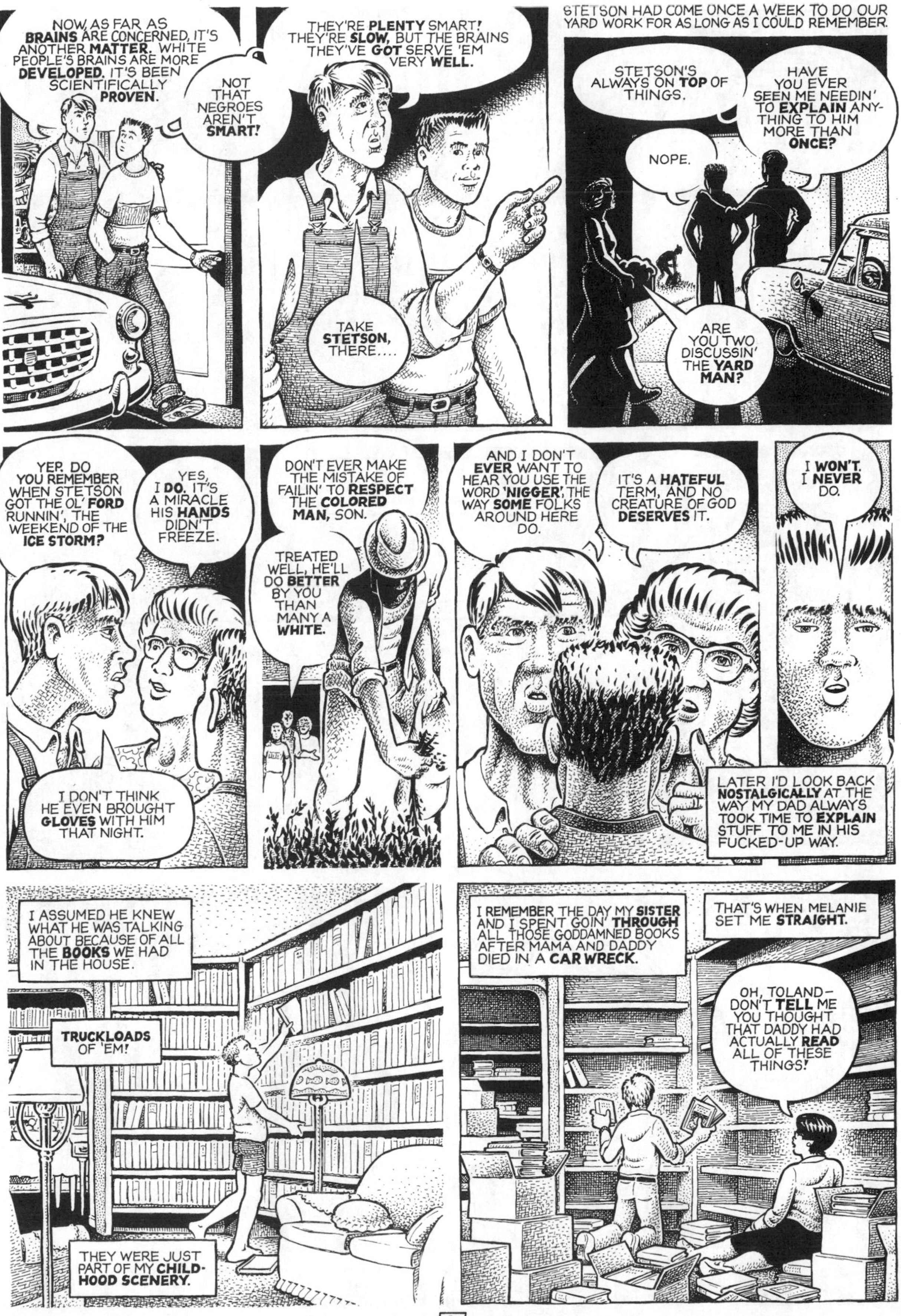
NOW, AS FAR AS BRAINS ARE CONCERNED, IT'S ANOTHER MATTER. WHITE PEOPLE'S BRAINS ARE MORE DEVELOPED. IT'S BEEN SCIENTIFICALLY PROVEN.
NOT THAT NEGROES AREN'T SMART!
THEY'RE PLENTY SMART! THEY'RE SLOW, BUT THE BRAINS THEY'VE GOT SERVE 'EM VERY WELL.
TAKE STETSON, THERE....
STETSON HAD COME ONCE A WEEK TO DO OUR YARD WORK FOR AS LONG AS I COULD REMEMBER.
STETSON'S ALWAYS ON TOP OF THINGS.
HAVE YOU EVER SEEN ME NEEDIN' TO EXPLAIN ANYTHING TO HIM MORE THAN ONCE?
NOPE.
ARE YOU TWO DISCUSSIN' THE YARD MAN?
YEP. DO YOU REMEMBER WHEN STETSON GOT THE OL' FORD RUNNIN', THE WEEKEND OF THE ICE STORM?
YES, I DO. IT'S A MIRACLE HIS HANDS DIDN'T FREEZE.
I DON'T THINK HE EVEN BROUGHT GLOVES WITH HIM THAT NIGHT.
DON'T EVER MAKE THE MISTAKE OF FAILIN' TO RESPECT THE COLORED MAN, SON.
TREATED WELL, HE'LL DO BETTER BY YOU THAN MANY A WHITE.
AND I DON'T EVER WANT TO HEAR YOU USE THE WORD 'NIGGER', THE WAY SOME FOLKS AROUND HERE DO.
IT'S A HATEFUL TERM, AND NO CREATURE OF GOD DESERVES IT.
I WON'T. I NEVER DO.
LATER I'D LOOK BACK NOSTALGICALLY AT THE WAY MY DAD ALWAYS TOOK TIME TO EXPLAIN STUFF TO ME IN HIS FUCKED-UP WAY.
I ASSUMED HE KNEW WHAT HE WAS TALKING ABOUT BECAUSE OF ALL THE BOOKS WE HAD IN THE HOUSE.
TRUCKLOADS OF 'EM!
THEY WERE JUST PART OF MY CHILDHOOD SCENERY.
I REMEMBER THE DAY MY SISTER AND I SPENT GOIN' THROUGH ALL THOSE GODDAMNED BOOKS AFTER MAMA AND DADDY DIED IN A CAR WRECK.
THAT'S WHEN MELANIE SET ME STRAIGHT.
OH, TOLAND— DON'T TELL ME YOU THOUGHT THAT DADDY HAD ACTUALLY READ ALL OF THESE THINGS!

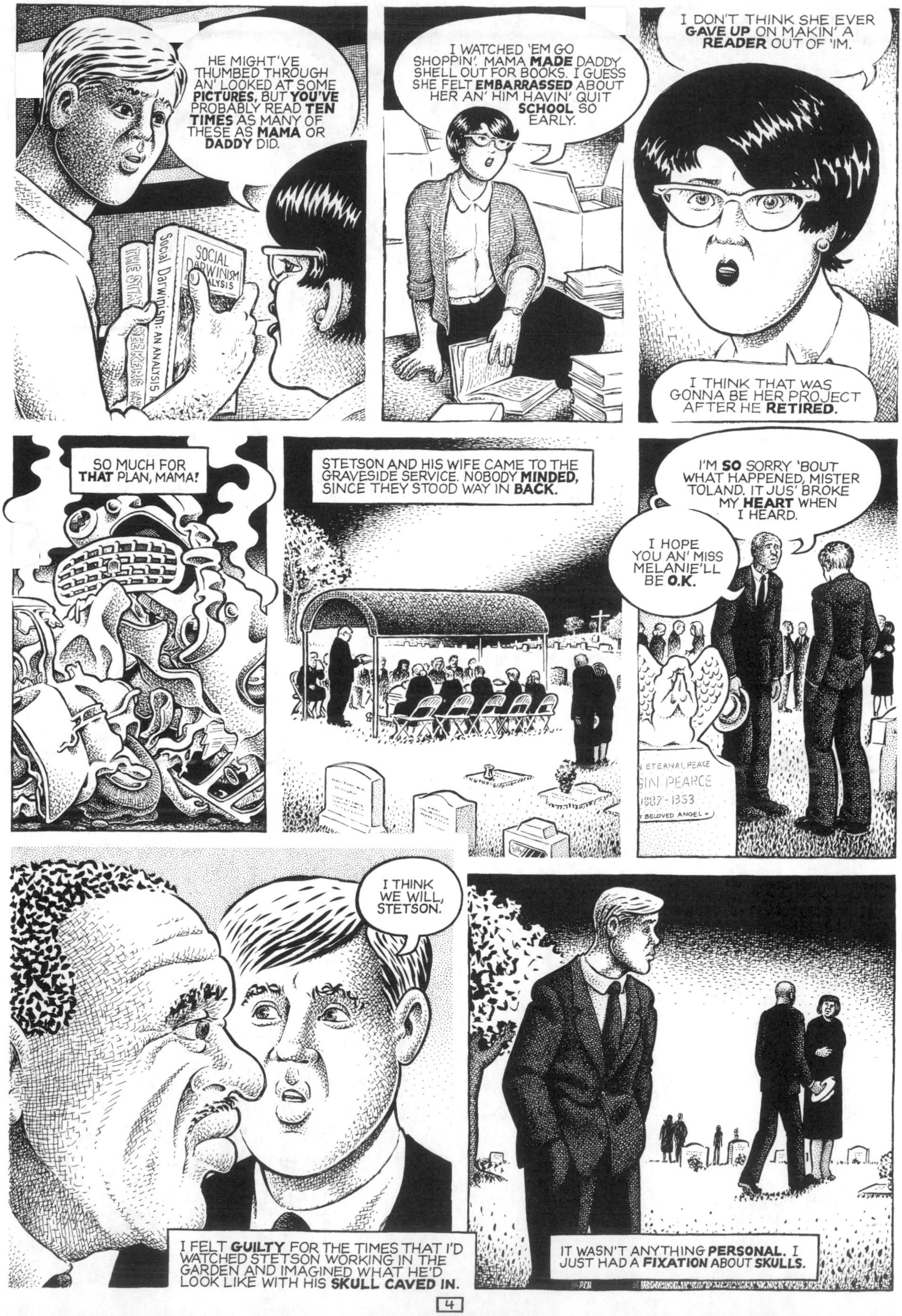
HE MIGHT'VE THUMBED THROUGH AN' LOOKED AT SOME **PICTURES**, BUT **YOU'VE** PROBABLY READ **TEN TIMES** AS MANY OF THESE AS **MAMA** OR **DADDY** DID.
SOCIAL DARWINISM
Social Darwinism: An Analysis
I WATCHED 'EM GO SHOPPIN'. MAMA **MADE** DADDY SHELL OUT FOR BOOKS. I GUESS SHE FELT **EMBARRASSED** ABOUT HER AN' HIM HAVIN' QUIT **SCHOOL** SO EARLY.
I DON'T THINK SHE EVER **GAVE UP** ON MAKIN' A **READER** OUT OF 'IM.
I THINK THAT WAS GONNA BE HER PROJECT AFTER HE **RETIRED**.
SO MUCH FOR **THAT** PLAN, MAMA!
STETSON AND HIS WIFE CAME TO THE GRAVESIDE SERVICE. NOBODY **MINDED**, SINCE THEY STOOD WAY IN **BACK**.
I'M **SO** SORRY 'BOUT WHAT HAPPENED, MISTER TOLAND. IT JUS' BROKE MY **HEART** WHEN I HEARD.
I HOPE YOU AN' MISS MELANIE'LL BE **O.K.**
I THINK WE WILL, STETSON.
I FELT **GUILTY** FOR THE TIMES THAT I'D WATCHED STETSON WORKING IN THE GARDEN AND IMAGINED WHAT HE'D LOOK LIKE WITH HIS **SKULL CAVED IN**.
IT WASN'T ANYTHING **PERSONAL**. I JUST HAD A **FIXATION** ABOUT **SKULLS**.

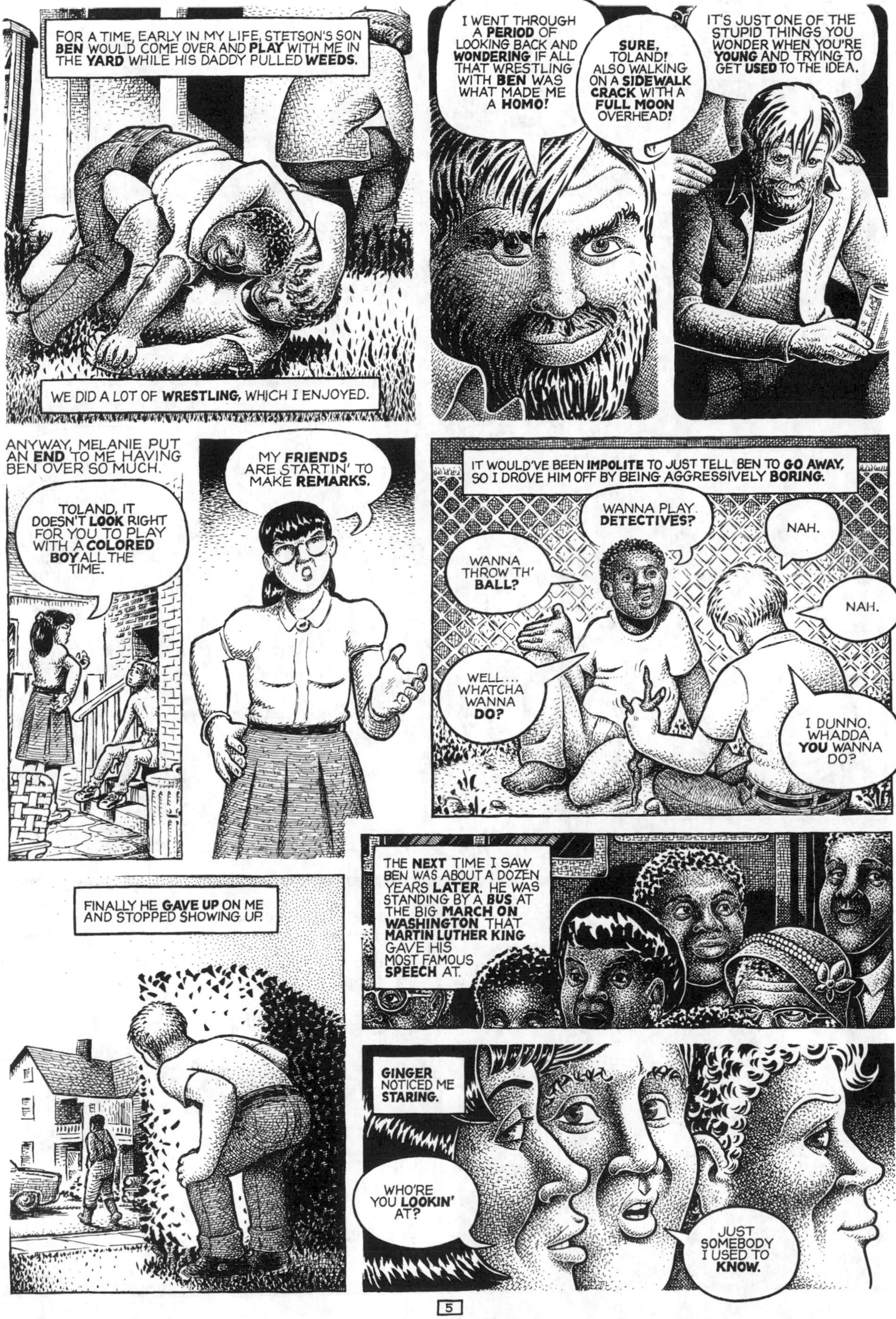

FOR A TIME, EARLY IN MY LIFE, STETSON'S SON BEN WOULD COME OVER AND PLAY WITH ME IN THE YARD WHILE HIS DADDY PULLED WEEDS.
WE DID A LOT OF WRESTLING, WHICH I ENJOYED.
I WENT THROUGH A PERIOD OF LOOKING BACK AND WONDERING IF ALL THAT WRESTLING WITH BEN WAS WHAT MADE ME A HOMO!
SURE, TOLAND! ALSO WALKING ON A SIDEWALK CRACK WITH A FULL MOON OVERHEAD!
IT'S JUST ONE OF THE STUPID THINGS YOU WONDER WHEN YOU'RE YOUNG AND TRYING TO GET USED TO THE IDEA.
ANYWAY, MELANIE PUT AN END TO ME HAVING BEN OVER SO MUCH.
TOLAND, IT DOESN'T LOOK RIGHT FOR YOU TO PLAY WITH A COLORED BOY ALL THE TIME.
MY FRIENDS ARE STARTIN' TO MAKE REMARKS.
IT WOULD'VE BEEN IMPOLITE TO JUST TELL BEN TO GO AWAY, SO I DROVE HIM OFF BY BEING AGGRESSIVELY BORING.
WANNA PLAY DETECTIVES?
NAH.
WANNA THROW TH' BALL?
NAH.
WELL... WHATCHA WANNA DO?
I DUNNO. WHADDA YOU WANNA DO?
FINALLY HE GAVE UP ON ME AND STOPPED SHOWING UP.
THE NEXT TIME I SAW BEN WAS ABOUT A DOZEN YEARS LATER. HE WAS STANDING BY A BUS AT THE BIG MARCH ON WASHINGTON THAT MARTIN LUTHER KING GAVE HIS MOST FAMOUS SPEECH AT.
GINGER NOTICED ME STARING.
WHO'RE YOU LOOKIN' AT?
JUST SOMEBODY I USED TO KNOW.

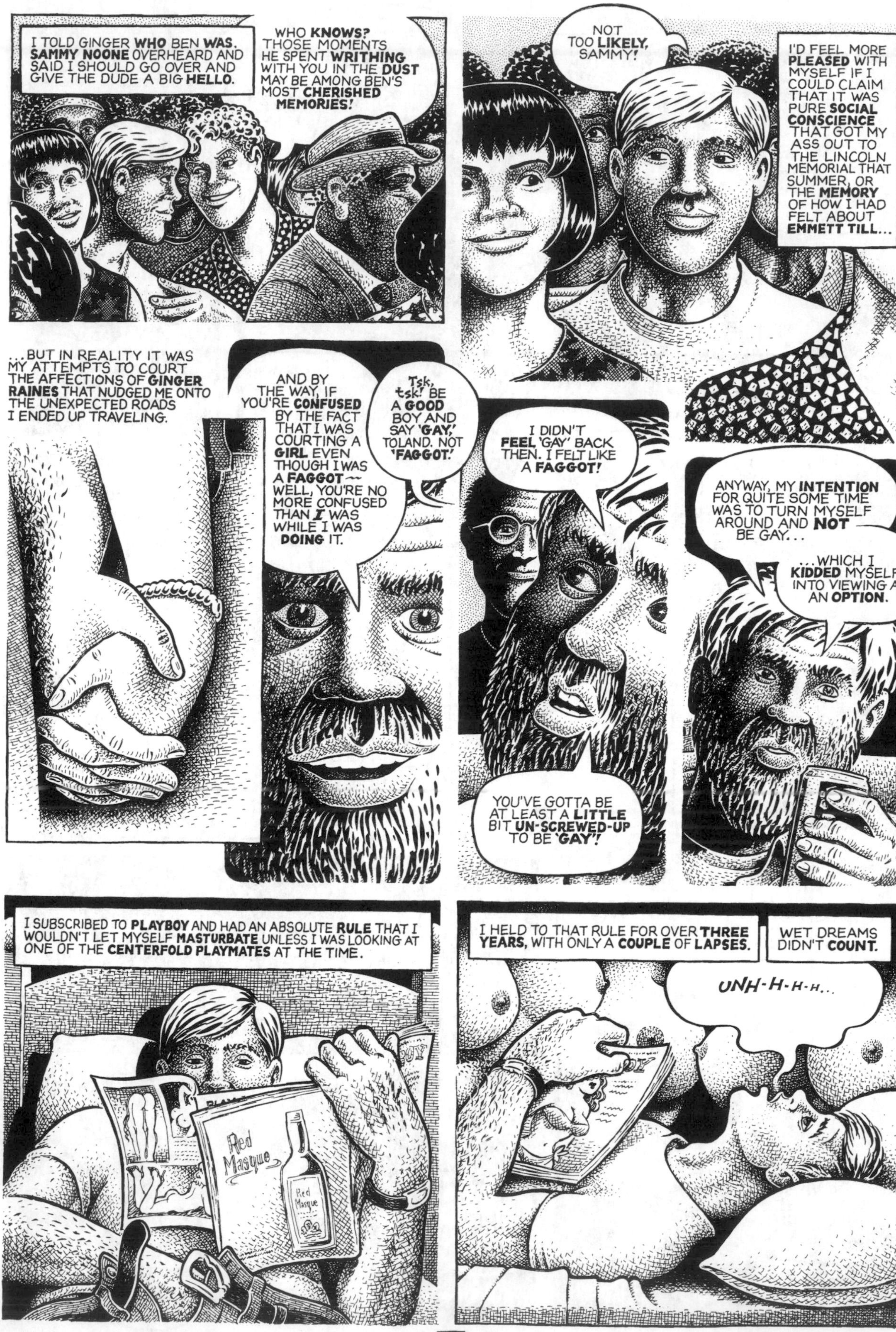

I TOLD GINGER WHO BEN WAS. SAMMY NOONE OVERHEARD AND SAID I SHOULD GO OVER AND GIVE THE DUDE A BIG HELLO.
WHO KNOWS? THOSE MOMENTS HE SPENT WRITHING WITH YOU IN THE DUST MAY BE AMONG BEN'S MOST CHERISHED MEMORIES!
NOT TOO LIKELY, SAMMY!
I'D FEEL MORE PLEASED WITH MYSELF IF I COULD CLAIM THAT IT WAS PURE SOCIAL CONSCIENCE THAT GOT MY ASS OUT TO THE LINCOLN MEMORIAL THAT SUMMER, OR THE MEMORY OF HOW I HAD FELT ABOUT EMMETT TILL...
...BUT IN REALITY IT WAS MY ATTEMPTS TO COURT THE AFFECTIONS OF GINGER RAINES THAT NUDGED ME ONTO THE UNEXPECTED ROADS I ENDED UP TRAVELING.
AND BY THE WAY, IF YOU'RE CONFUSED BY THE FACT THAT I WAS COURTING A GIRL EVEN THOUGH I WAS A FAGGOT~ WELL, YOU'RE NO MORE CONFUSED THAN I WAS WHILE I WAS DOING IT.
Tsk, tsk! BE A GOOD BOY AND SAY 'GAY,' TOLAND. NOT 'FAGGOT.'
I DIDN'T FEEL 'GAY' BACK THEN. I FELT LIKE A FAGGOT!
YOU'VE GOTTA BE AT LEAST A LITTLE BIT UN-SCREWED-UP TO BE 'GAY'!
ANYWAY, MY INTENTION FOR QUITE SOME TIME WAS TO TURN MYSELF AROUND AND NOT BE GAY...
...WHICH I KIDDED MYSELF INTO VIEWING AS AN OPTION.
I SUBSCRIBED TO PLAYBOY AND HAD AN ABSOLUTE RULE THAT I WOULDN'T LET MYSELF MASTURBATE UNLESS I WAS LOOKING AT ONE OF THE CENTERFOLD PLAYMATES AT THE TIME.
Red Masque
I HELD TO THAT RULE FOR OVER THREE YEARS, WITH ONLY A COUPLE OF LAPSES.
WET DREAMS DIDN'T COUNT.
UNH-H-H-H...

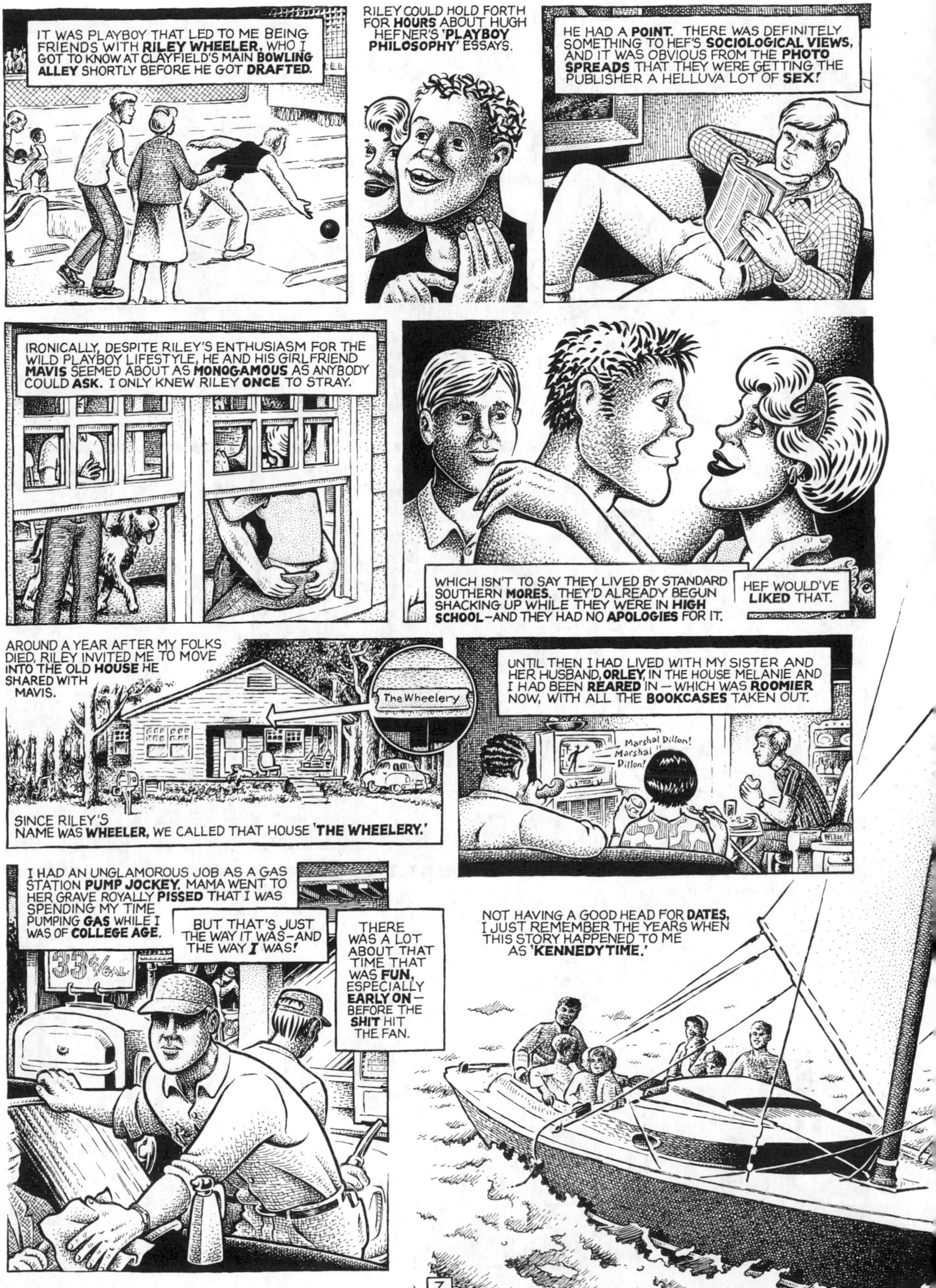
IT WAS PLAYBOY THAT LED TO ME BEING FRIENDS WITH RILEY WHEELER, WHO I GOT TO KNOW AT CLAYFIELD'S MAIN BOWLING ALLEY SHORTLY BEFORE HE GOT DRAFTED.
RILEY COULD HOLD FORTH FOR HOURS ABOUT HUGH HEFNER'S 'PLAYBOY PHILOSOPHY' ESSAYS.
HE HAD A POINT. THERE WAS DEFINITELY SOMETHING TO HEF'S SOCIOLOGICAL VIEWS, AND IT WAS OBVIOUS FROM THE PHOTO SPREADS THAT THEY WERE GETTING THE PUBLISHER A HELLUVA LOT OF SEX!
IRONICALLY, DESPITE RILEY'S ENTHUSIASM FOR THE WILD PLAYBOY LIFESTYLE, HE AND HIS GIRLFRIEND MAVIS SEEMED ABOUT AS MONOGAMOUS AS ANYBODY COULD ASK. I ONLY KNEW RILEY ONCE TO STRAY.
WHICH ISN'T TO SAY THEY LIVED BY STANDARD SOUTHERN MORES. THEY'D ALREADY BEGUN SHACKING UP WHILE THEY WERE IN HIGH SCHOOL—AND THEY HAD NO APOLOGIES FOR IT.
HEF WOULD'VE LIKED THAT.
AROUND A YEAR AFTER MY FOLKS DIED, RILEY INVITED ME TO MOVE INTO THE OLD HOUSE HE SHARED WITH MAVIS.
The Wheelery
SINCE RILEY'S NAME WAS WHEELER, WE CALLED THAT HOUSE 'THE WHEELERY.'
UNTIL THEN I HAD LIVED WITH MY SISTER AND HER HUSBAND, ORLEY, IN THE HOUSE MELANIE AND I HAD BEEN REARED IN — WHICH WAS ROOMIER NOW, WITH ALL THE BOOKCASES TAKEN OUT.
Marshal Dillon! Marshal Dillon!
I HAD AN UNGLAMOROUS JOB AS A GAS STATION PUMP JOCKEY. MAMA WENT TO HER GRAVE ROYALLY PISSED THAT I WAS SPENDING MY TIME PUMPING GAS WHILE I WAS OF COLLEGE AGE.
BUT THAT'S JUST THE WAY IT WAS—AND THE WAY I WAS!
THERE WAS A LOT ABOUT THAT TIME THAT WAS FUN, ESPECIALLY EARLY ON—BEFORE THE SHIT HIT THE FAN.
33¢/GAL.
NOT HAVING A GOOD HEAD FOR DATES, I JUST REMEMBER THE YEARS WHEN THIS STORY HAPPENED TO ME AS 'KENNEDY TIME.'

I SHOULD MENTION HOW I GOT BROUGHT OUT OF THE **CLOSET** BY THE UNITED STATES **ARMY.**

... AND HOW YOU BROKE ALL **RECORDS** TRYING TO SCRAMBLE BACK **IN!**

THAT WAS BACK WHEN MY **FOLKS** WERE STILL **ALIVE.** I HAD RECENTLY TURNED **EIGHTEEN,** AND **UNCLE SAM** WAS KEEPING **TRACK.**

SOMETHIN' FOR YOU FROM **SELECTIVE SERVICE.**

plop!

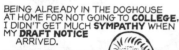

BEING ALREADY IN THE DOGHOUSE AT HOME FOR NOT GOING TO **COLLEGE,** I DIDN'T GET MUCH **SYMPATHY** WHEN MY **DRAFT NOTICE** ARRIVED.

MAYBE THE ARMY WILL HELP GIVE YOUR LIFE MORE **DIRECTION,** SON.

SURE, MA.

READY FOR A FEW **PUSH-UPS?**

I TOOK IT IN **STRIDE.** I VIEWED THE **MILITARY** BACK THEN AS A MODERATELY ANNOYING MIXTURE OF **CALISTHENICS** AND **HARASSMENT** THAT I WAS PROBABLY GONNA HAVE TO **PUT UP WITH** ONE WAY OR **ANOTHER.**

IT COULD EVEN BE **FUN,** JUDGING FROM 'SGT. **BILKO'** ON **TV.**

Hide, everybody! Colonel Hall's coming!

But we can't leave Pvt. Doberman dressed up like a pineapple!

Ha ha ha heh ha ha ha ha heh heh ha ha ha

I SHOWED UP AT THE **RECRUITMENT CENTER** AS INSTRUCTED AND GOT HAULED WITH THE OTHER DRAFTEES OFF TO THE **CENTRAL ARMORY** FOR MY **INDUCTION PHYSICAL.**

MY MOMENT OF **TRUTH** CAME WHEN A COUPLA HUNDRED OF US, STILL ALL BUT **NAKED** FROM GETTING INSPECTED FOR **LICE** AND **HEMORRHOIDS,** GOT HERDED INTO A BIG, SWEATY HALL FULL OF **SCHOOLROOM CHAIRS** AND TOLD TO FILL OUT LONG MEDICAL-HISTORY **QUESTIONNAIRES...**

...WHEREUPON, THE KID SITTING **NEXT** TO ME, FOR REASONS KNOWN ONLY TO **HIM,** GOT A **HARD-ON.**

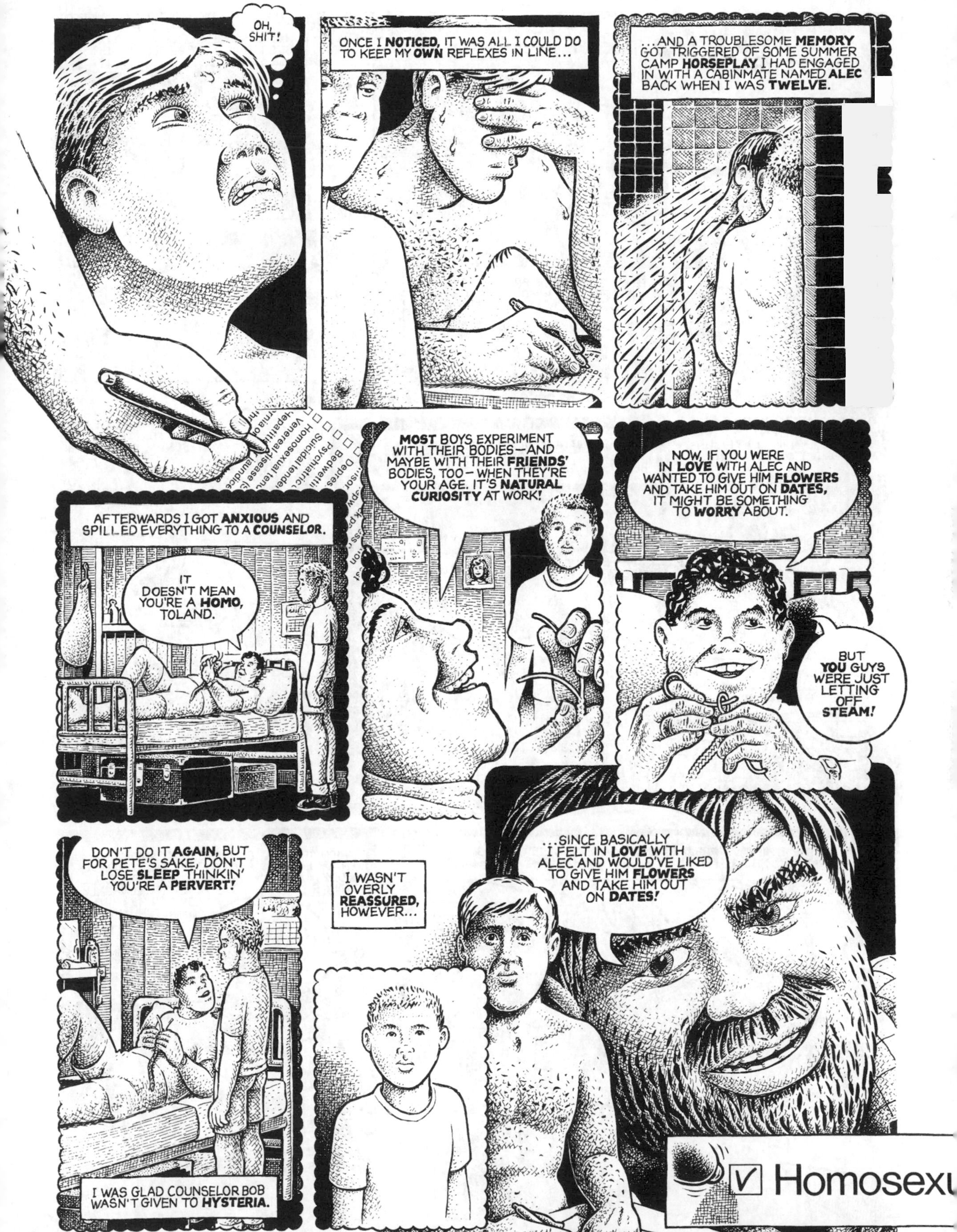
OH, SHIT!
ONCE I NOTICED, IT WAS ALL I COULD DO TO KEEP MY OWN REFLEXES IN LINE...
...AND A TROUBLESOME MEMORY GOT TRIGGERED OF SOME SUMMER CAMP HORSEPLAY I HAD ENGAGED IN WITH A CABINMATE NAMED ALEC BACK WHEN I WAS TWELVE.
AFTERWARDS I GOT ANXIOUS AND SPILLED EVERYTHING TO A COUNSELOR.
IT DOESN'T MEAN YOU'RE A HOMO, TOLAND.
MOST BOYS EXPERIMENT WITH THEIR BODIES—AND MAYBE WITH THEIR FRIENDS' BODIES, TOO—WHEN THEY'RE YOUR AGE. IT'S NATURAL CURIOSITY AT WORK!
NOW, IF YOU WERE IN LOVE WITH ALEC AND WANTED TO GIVE HIM FLOWERS AND TAKE HIM OUT ON DATES, IT MIGHT BE SOMETHING TO WORRY ABOUT.
BUT YOU GUYS WERE JUST LETTING OFF STEAM!
DON'T DO IT AGAIN, BUT FOR PETE'S SAKE, DON'T LOSE SLEEP THINKIN' YOU'RE A PERVERT!
I WAS GLAD COUNSELOR BOB WASN'T GIVEN TO HYSTERIA.
I WASN'T OVERLY REASSURED, HOWEVER...
...SINCE BASICALLY I FELT IN LOVE WITH ALEC AND WOULD'VE LIKED TO GIVE HIM FLOWERS AND TAKE HIM OUT ON DATES!
✓ Homosexu

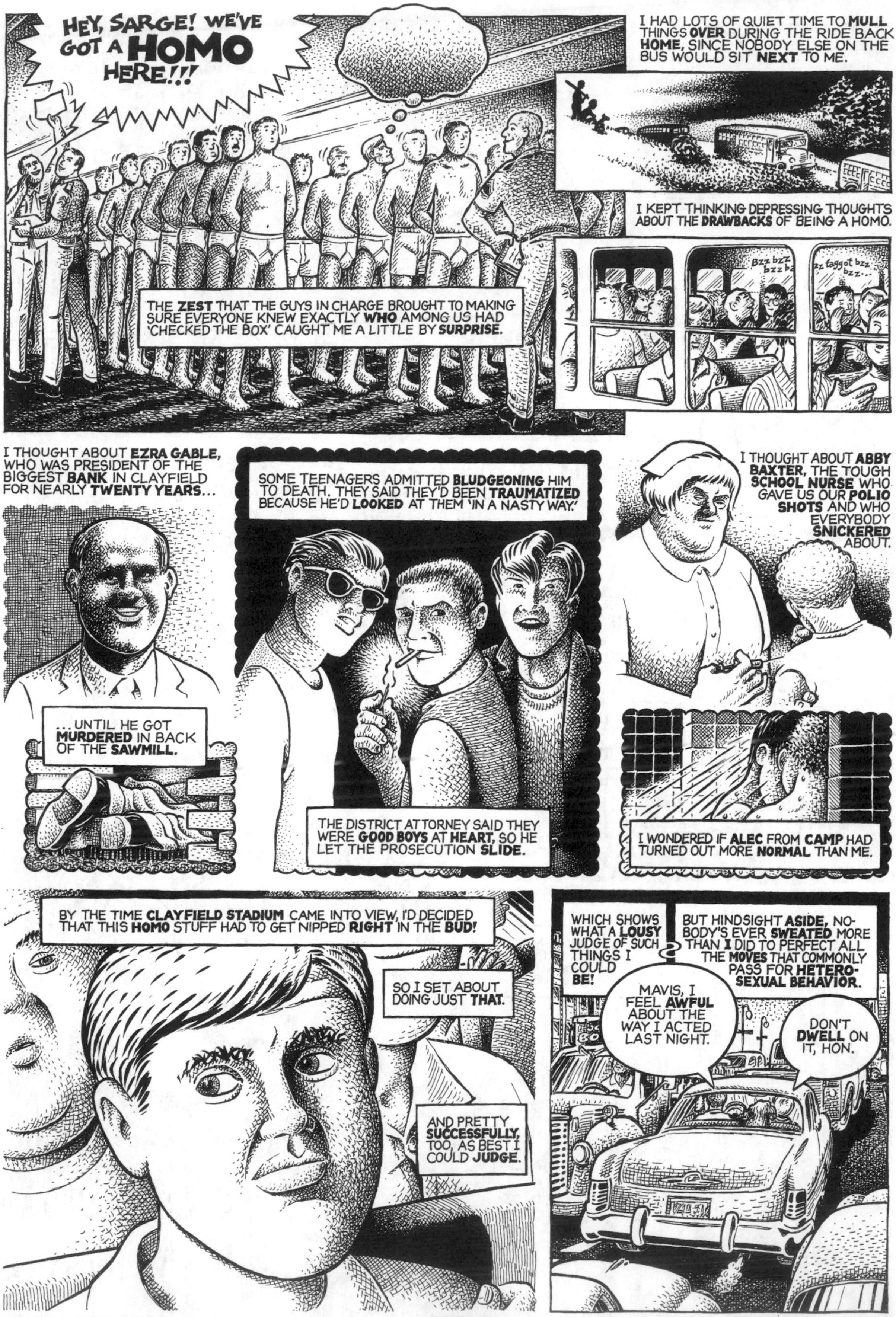
HEY, SARGE! WE'VE GOT A HOMO HERE!!!
I HAD LOTS OF QUIET TIME TO MULL THINGS OVER DURING THE RIDE BACK HOME, SINCE NOBODY ELSE ON THE BUS WOULD SIT NEXT TO ME.
THE ZEST THAT THE GUYS IN CHARGE BROUGHT TO MAKING SURE EVERYONE KNEW EXACTLY WHO AMONG US HAD 'CHECKED THE BOX' CAUGHT ME A LITTLE BY SURPRISE.
I KEPT THINKING DEPRESSING THOUGHTS ABOUT THE DRAWBACKS OF BEING A HOMO.
bzz bzz bzz bz
zz faggot bzz bzz...
I THOUGHT ABOUT EZRA GABLE, WHO WAS PRESIDENT OF THE BIGGEST BANK IN CLAYFIELD FOR NEARLY TWENTY YEARS...
...UNTIL HE GOT MURDERED IN BACK OF THE SAWMILL.
SOME TEENAGERS ADMITTED BLUDGEONING HIM TO DEATH. THEY SAID THEY'D BEEN TRAUMATIZED BECAUSE HE'D LOOKED AT THEM 'IN A NASTY WAY.'
THE DISTRICT ATTORNEY SAID THEY WERE GOOD BOYS AT HEART, SO HE LET THE PROSECUTION SLIDE.
I THOUGHT ABOUT ABBY BAXTER, THE TOUGH SCHOOL NURSE WHO GAVE US OUR POLIO SHOTS AND WHO EVERYBODY SNICKERED ABOUT.
I WONDERED IF ALEC FROM CAMP HAD TURNED OUT MORE NORMAL THAN ME.
BY THE TIME CLAYFIELD STADIUM CAME INTO VIEW, I'D DECIDED THAT THIS HOMO STUFF HAD TO GET NIPPED RIGHT IN THE BUD!
SO I SET ABOUT DOING JUST THAT.
AND PRETTY SUCCESSFULLY, TOO, AS BEST I COULD JUDGE.
WHICH SHOWS WHAT A LOUSY JUDGE OF SUCH THINGS I COULD BE!
BUT HINDSIGHT ASIDE, NOBODY'S EVER SWEATED MORE THAN I DID TO PERFECT ALL THE MOVES THAT COMMONLY PASS FOR HETEROSEXUAL BEHAVIOR.
MAVIS, I FEEL AWFUL ABOUT THE WAY I ACTED LAST NIGHT.
DON'T DWELL ON IT, HON.

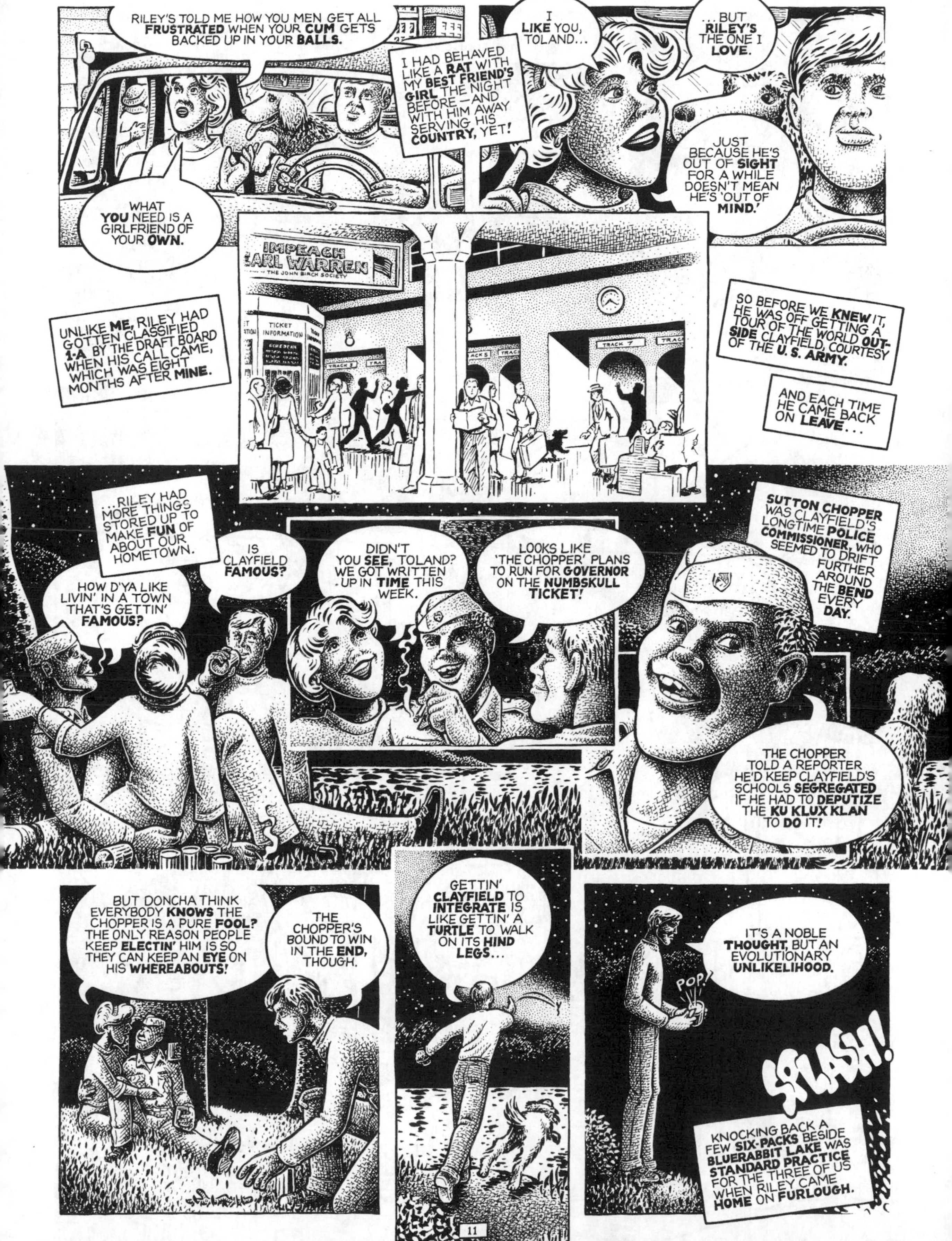
RILEY'S TOLD ME HOW YOU MEN GET ALL FRUSTRATED WHEN YOUR CUM GETS BACKED UP IN YOUR BALLS.
WHAT YOU NEED IS A GIRLFRIEND OF YOUR OWN.
I HAD BEHAVED LIKE A RAT WITH MY BEST FRIEND'S GIRL THE NIGHT BEFORE—AND WITH HIM AWAY SERVING HIS COUNTRY, YET!
I LIKE YOU, TOLAND...
...BUT RILEY'S THE ONE I LOVE.
JUST BECAUSE HE'S OUT OF SIGHT FOR A WHILE DOESN'T MEAN HE'S 'OUT OF MIND.'
UNLIKE ME, RILEY HAD GOTTEN CLASSIFIED 1-A BY THE DRAFT BOARD WHEN HIS CALL CAME, WHICH WAS EIGHT MONTHS AFTER MINE.
IMPEACH EARL WARREN
THE JOHN BIRCH SOCIETY
TICKET INFORMATION
TRACK 7
SO BEFORE WE KNEW IT, HE WAS OFF GETTING A TOUR OF THE WORLD OUTSIDE CLAYFIELD, COURTESY OF THE U. S. ARMY.
AND EACH TIME HE CAME BACK ON LEAVE...
...RILEY HAD MORE THINGS STORED UP TO MAKE FUN OF ABOUT OUR HOMETOWN.
HOW D'YA LIKE LIVIN' IN A TOWN THAT'S GETTIN' FAMOUS?
IS CLAYFIELD FAMOUS?
DIDN'T YOU SEE, TOLAND? WE GOT WRITTEN UP IN TIME THIS WEEK.
LOOKS LIKE 'THE CHOPPER' PLANS TO RUN FOR GOVERNOR ON THE NUMBSKULL TICKET!
SUTTON CHOPPER WAS CLAYFIELD'S LONGTIME POLICE COMMISSIONER, WHO SEEMED TO DRIFT FURTHER AROUND THE BEND EVERY DAY.
THE CHOPPER TOLD A REPORTER HE'D KEEP CLAYFIELD'S SCHOOLS SEGREGATED IF HE HAD TO DEPUTIZE THE KU KLUX KLAN TO DO IT!
BUT DONCHA THINK EVERYBODY KNOWS THE CHOPPER IS A PURE FOOL? THE ONLY REASON PEOPLE KEEP ELECTIN' HIM IS SO THEY CAN KEEP AN EYE ON HIS WHEREABOUTS!
THE CHOPPER'S BOUND TO WIN IN THE END, THOUGH.
GETTIN' CLAYFIELD TO INTEGRATE IS LIKE GETTIN' A TURTLE TO WALK ON ITS HIND LEGS...
IT'S A NOBLE THOUGHT, BUT AN EVOLUTIONARY UNLIKELIHOOD.
POP!
SPLASH!
KNOCKING BACK A FEW SIX-PACKS BESIDE BLUERABBIT LAKE WAS STANDARD PRACTICE FOR THE THREE OF US WHEN RILEY CAME HOME ON FURLOUGH.

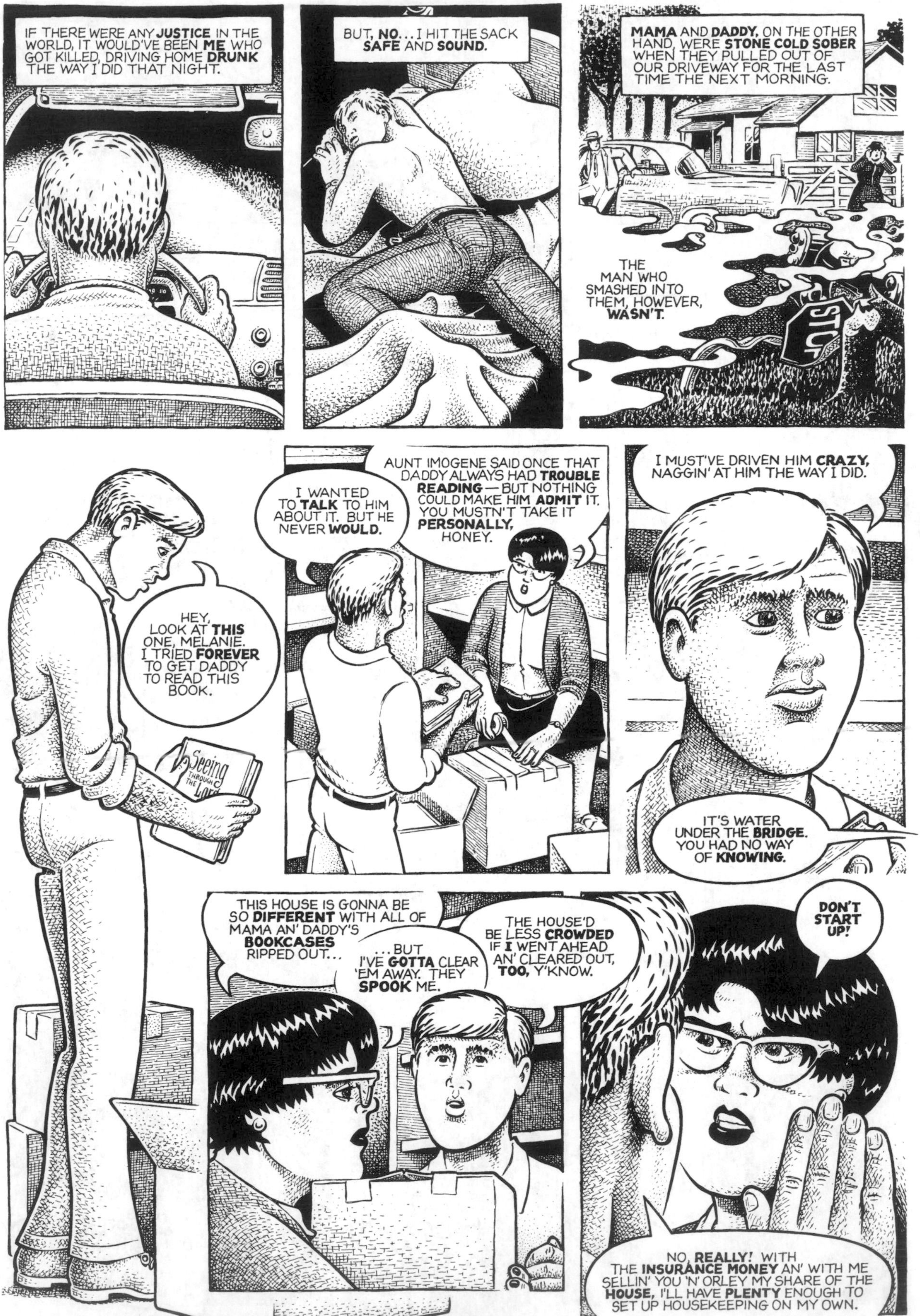
IF THERE WERE ANY JUSTICE IN THE WORLD, IT WOULD'VE BEEN ME WHO GOT KILLED, DRIVING HOME DRUNK THE WAY I DID THAT NIGHT.
BUT, NO... I HIT THE SACK SAFE AND SOUND.
MAMA AND DADDY, ON THE OTHER HAND, WERE STONE COLD SOBER WHEN THEY PULLED OUT OF OUR DRIVEWAY FOR THE LAST TIME THE NEXT MORNING.
THE MAN WHO SMASHED INTO THEM, HOWEVER, WASN'T.
STOP
HEY, LOOK AT THIS ONE, MELANIE. I TRIED FOREVER TO GET DADDY TO READ THIS BOOK.
Seeing THROUGH THE Lord
I WANTED TO TALK TO HIM ABOUT IT. BUT HE NEVER WOULD.
AUNT IMOGENE SAID ONCE THAT DADDY ALWAYS HAD TROUBLE READING — BUT NOTHING COULD MAKE HIM ADMIT IT. YOU MUSTN'T TAKE IT PERSONALLY, HONEY.
I MUST'VE DRIVEN HIM CRAZY, NAGGIN' AT HIM THE WAY I DID.
IT'S WATER UNDER THE BRIDGE. YOU HAD NO WAY OF KNOWING.
THIS HOUSE IS GONNA BE SO DIFFERENT WITH ALL OF MAMA AN' DADDY'S BOOKCASES RIPPED OUT...
...BUT I'VE GOTTA CLEAR 'EM AWAY. THEY SPOOK ME.
THE HOUSE'D BE LESS CROWDED IF I WENT AHEAD AN' CLEARED OUT, TOO, Y'KNOW.
DON'T START UP!
NO, REALLY! WITH THE INSURANCE MONEY AN' WITH ME SELLIN' YOU 'N' ORLEY MY SHARE OF THE HOUSE, I'LL HAVE PLENTY ENOUGH TO SET UP HOUSEKEEPING ON MY OWN.

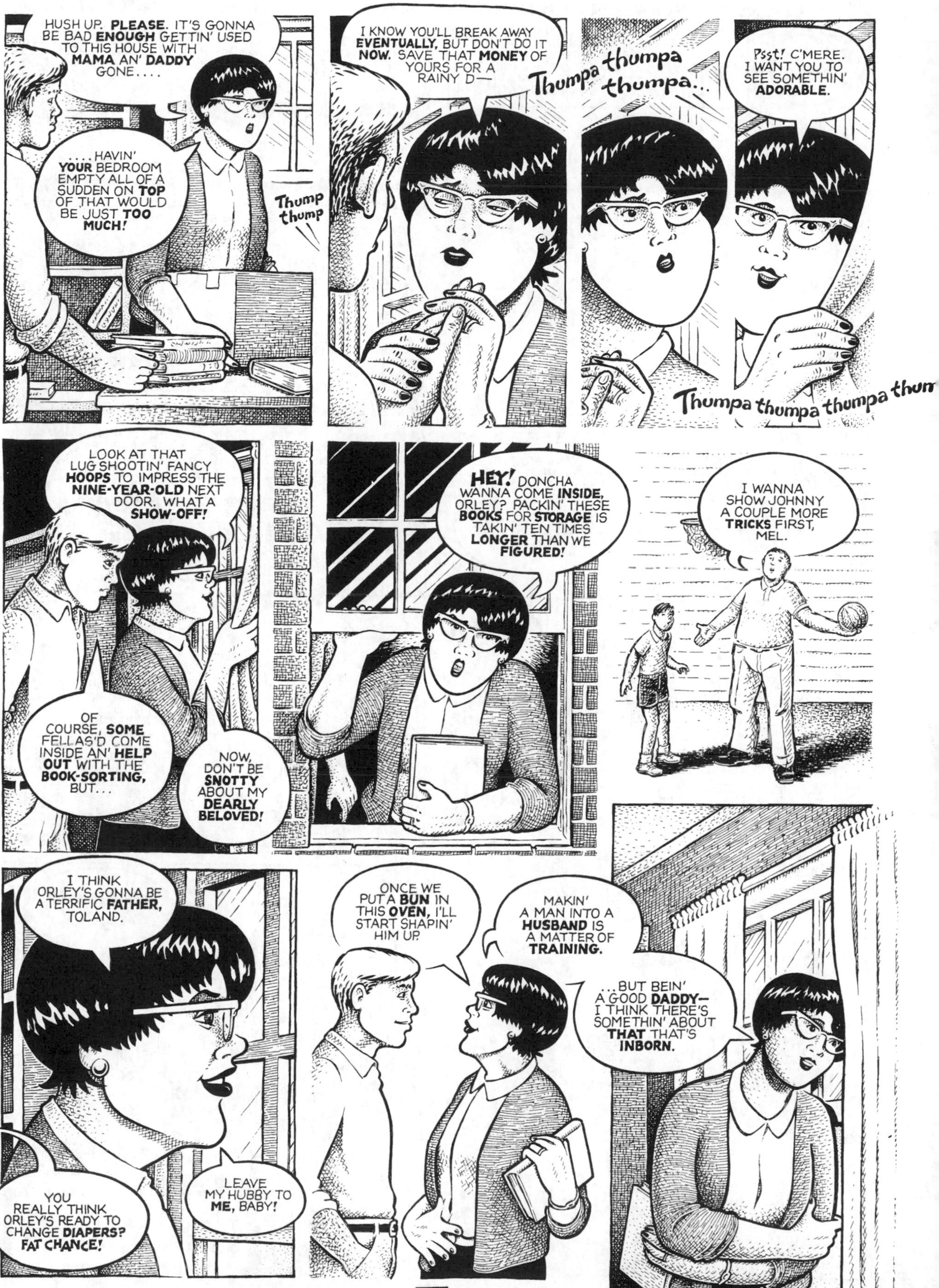
HUSH UP. PLEASE. IT'S GONNA BE BAD ENOUGH GETTIN' USED TO THIS HOUSE WITH MAMA AN' DADDY GONE....
...HAVIN' YOUR BEDROOM EMPTY ALL OF A SUDDEN ON TOP OF THAT WOULD BE JUST TOO MUCH!
Thump thump
I KNOW YOU'LL BREAK AWAY EVENTUALLY, BUT DON'T DO IT NOW. SAVE THAT MONEY OF YOURS FOR A RAINY D—
Thumpa thumpa thumpa...
Pssst! C'MERE. I WANT YOU TO SEE SOMETHIN' ADORABLE.
Thumpa thumpa thumpa thum
LOOK AT THAT LUG SHOOTIN' FANCY HOOPS TO IMPRESS THE NINE-YEAR-OLD NEXT DOOR. WHAT A SHOW-OFF!
OF COURSE, SOME FELLAS'D COME INSIDE AN' HELP OUT WITH THE BOOK-SORTING, BUT...
NOW, DON'T BE SNOTTY ABOUT MY DEARLY BELOVED!
HEY! DONCHA WANNA COME INSIDE, ORLEY? PACKIN' THESE BOOKS FOR STORAGE IS TAKIN' TEN TIMES LONGER THAN WE FIGURED!
I WANNA SHOW JOHNNY A COUPLE MORE TRICKS FIRST, MEL.
I THINK ORLEY'S GONNA BE A TERRIFIC FATHER, TOLAND.
YOU REALLY THINK ORLEY'S READY TO CHANGE DIAPERS? FAT CHANCE!
LEAVE MY HUBBY TO ME, BABY!
ONCE WE PUT A BUN IN THIS OVEN, I'LL START SHAPIN' HIM UP.
MAKIN' A MAN INTO A HUSBAND IS A MATTER OF TRAINING.
...BUT BEIN' A GOOD DADDY— I THINK THERE'S SOMETHIN' ABOUT THAT THAT'S INBORN.

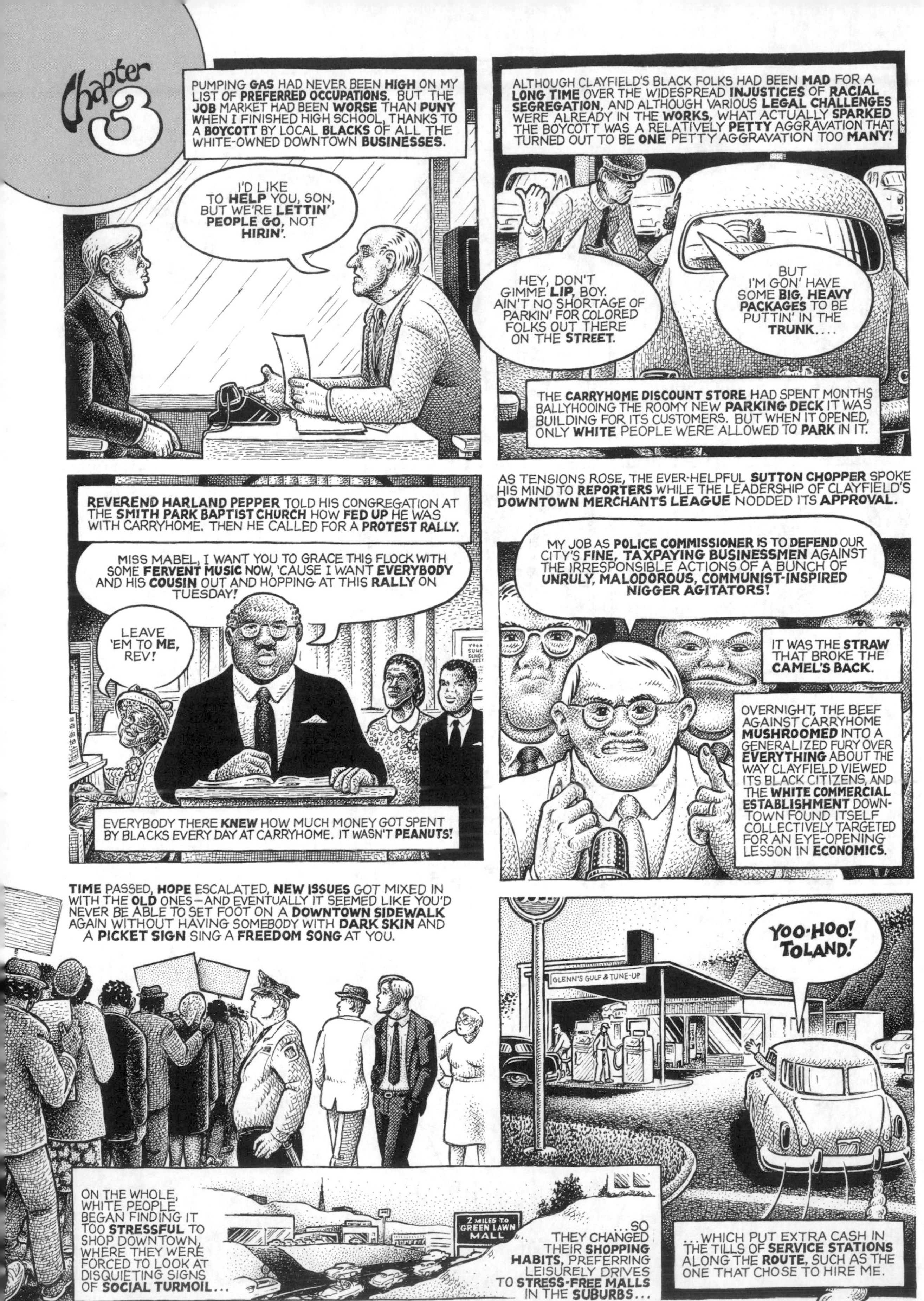

Chapter 3
PUMPING GAS HAD NEVER BEEN HIGH ON MY LIST OF PREFERRED OCCUPATIONS. BUT THE JOB MARKET HAD BEEN WORSE THAN PUNY WHEN I FINISHED HIGH SCHOOL, THANKS TO A BOYCOTT BY LOCAL BLACKS OF ALL THE WHITE-OWNED DOWNTOWN BUSINESSES.
I'D LIKE TO HELP YOU, SON, BUT WE'RE LETTIN' PEOPLE GO, NOT HIRIN'.
ALTHOUGH CLAYFIELD'S BLACK FOLKS HAD BEEN MAD FOR A LONG TIME OVER THE WIDESPREAD INJUSTICES OF RACIAL SEGREGATION, AND ALTHOUGH VARIOUS LEGAL CHALLENGES WERE ALREADY IN THE WORKS, WHAT ACTUALLY SPARKED THE BOYCOTT WAS A RELATIVELY PETTY AGGRAVATION THAT TURNED OUT TO BE ONE PETTY AGGRAVATION TOO MANY!
BUT I'M GON' HAVE SOME BIG, HEAVY PACKAGES TO BE PUTTIN' IN THE TRUNK....
HEY, DON'T GIMME LIP, BOY. AIN'T NO SHORTAGE OF PARKIN' FOR COLORED FOLKS OUT THERE ON THE STREET.
THE CARRYHOME DISCOUNT STORE HAD SPENT MONTHS BALLYHOOING THE ROOMY NEW PARKING DECK IT WAS BUILDING FOR ITS CUSTOMERS. BUT WHEN IT OPENED, ONLY WHITE PEOPLE WERE ALLOWED TO PARK IN IT.
REVEREND HARLAND PEPPER TOLD HIS CONGREGATION AT THE SMITH PARK BAPTIST CHURCH HOW FED UP HE WAS WITH CARRYHOME. THEN HE CALLED FOR A PROTEST RALLY.
MISS MABEL, I WANT YOU TO GRACE THIS FLOCK WITH SOME FERVENT MUSIC NOW, 'CAUSE I WANT EVERYBODY AND HIS COUSIN OUT AND HOPPING AT THIS RALLY ON TUESDAY!
LEAVE 'EM TO ME, REV!
EVERYBODY THERE KNEW HOW MUCH MONEY GOT SPENT BY BLACKS EVERY DAY AT CARRYHOME. IT WASN'T PEANUTS!
AS TENSIONS ROSE, THE EVER-HELPFUL SUTTON CHOPPER SPOKE HIS MIND TO REPORTERS WHILE THE LEADERSHIP OF CLAYFIELD'S DOWNTOWN MERCHANTS LEAGUE NODDED ITS APPROVAL.
MY JOB AS POLICE COMMISSIONER IS TO DEFEND OUR CITY'S FINE, TAXPAYING BUSINESSMEN AGAINST THE IRRESPONSIBLE ACTIONS OF A BUNCH OF UNRULY, MALODOROUS, COMMUNIST-INSPIRED NIGGER AGITATORS!
IT WAS THE STRAW THAT BROKE THE CAMEL'S BACK.
OVERNIGHT, THE BEEF AGAINST CARRYHOME MUSHROOMED INTO A GENERALIZED FURY OVER EVERYTHING ABOUT THE WAY CLAYFIELD VIEWED ITS BLACK CITIZENS, AND THE WHITE COMMERCIAL ESTABLISHMENT DOWN-TOWN FOUND ITSELF COLLECTIVELY TARGETED FOR AN EYE-OPENING LESSON IN ECONOMICS.
TIME PASSED, HOPE ESCALATED, NEW ISSUES GOT MIXED IN WITH THE OLD ONES—AND EVENTUALLY IT SEEMED LIKE YOU'D NEVER BE ABLE TO SET FOOT ON A DOWNTOWN SIDEWALK AGAIN WITHOUT HAVING SOMEBODY WITH DARK SKIN AND A PICKET SIGN SING A FREEDOM SONG AT YOU.
GLENN'S GULF & TUNE-UP
YOO-HOO! TOLAND!
ON THE WHOLE, WHITE PEOPLE BEGAN FINDING IT TOO STRESSFUL TO SHOP DOWNTOWN, WHERE THEY WERE FORCED TO LOOK AT DISQUIETING SIGNS OF SOCIAL TURMOIL...
2 MILES TO GREEN LAWN MALL
...SO THEY CHANGED THEIR SHOPPING HABITS, PREFERRING LEISURELY DRIVES TO STRESS-FREE MALLS IN THE SUBURBS...
...WHICH PUT EXTRA CASH IN THE TILLS OF SERVICE STATIONS ALONG THE ROUTE, SUCH AS THE ONE THAT CHOSE TO HIRE ME.

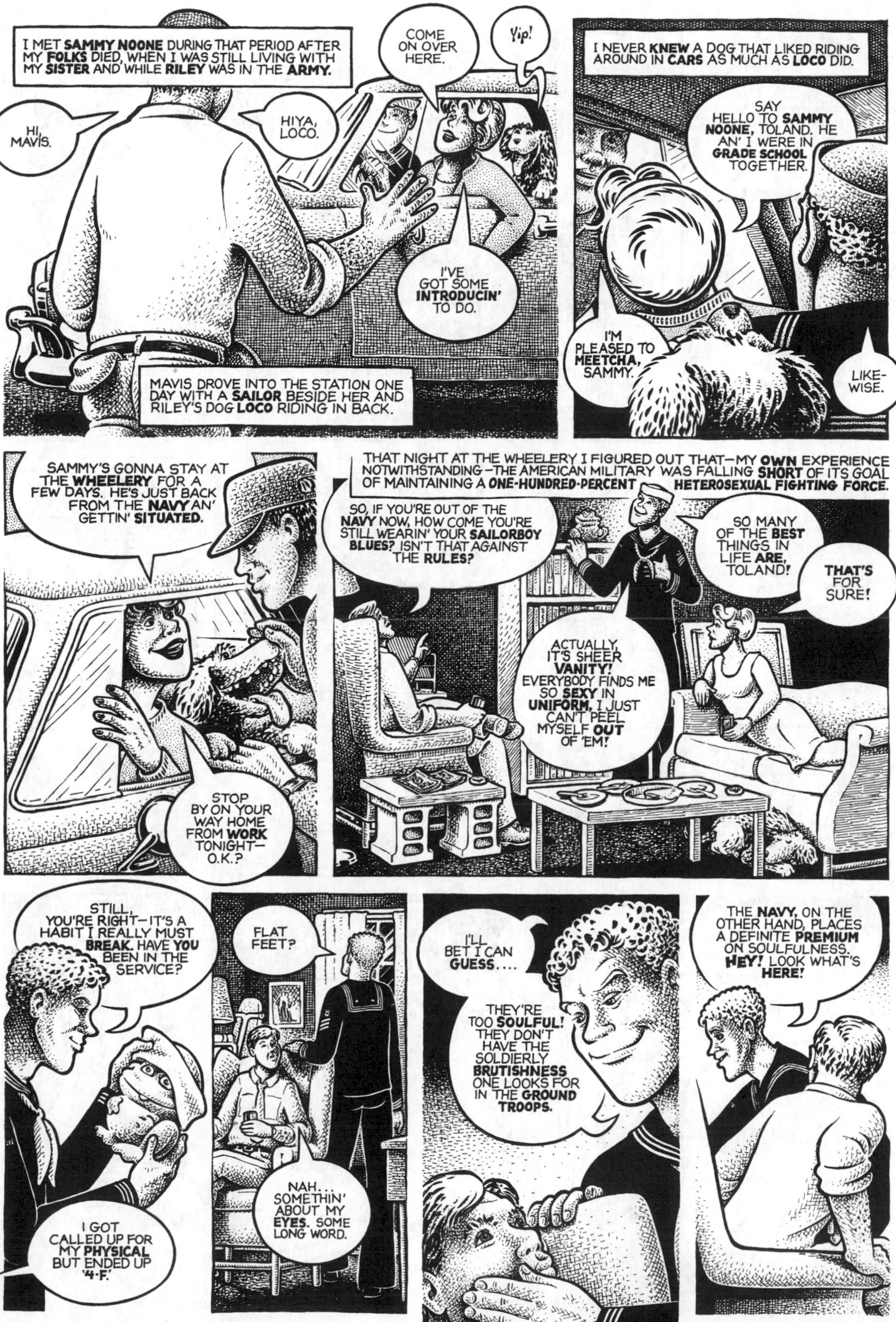

I MET SAMMY NOONE DURING THAT PERIOD AFTER MY FOLKS DIED, WHEN I WAS STILL LIVING WITH MY SISTER AND WHILE RILEY WAS IN THE ARMY.
COME ON OVER HERE.
Yip!
HI, MAVIS.
HIYA, LOCO.
I'VE GOT SOME INTRODUCIN' TO DO.
MAVIS DROVE INTO THE STATION ONE DAY WITH A SAILOR BESIDE HER AND RILEY'S DOG LOCO RIDING IN BACK.
I NEVER KNEW A DOG THAT LIKED RIDING AROUND IN CARS AS MUCH AS LOCO DID.
SAY HELLO TO SAMMY NOONE, TOLAND. HE AN' I WERE IN GRADE SCHOOL TOGETHER.
I'M PLEASED TO MEETCHA, SAMMY.
LIKE-WISE.
SAMMY'S GONNA STAY AT THE WHEELERY FOR A FEW DAYS. HE'S JUST BACK FROM THE NAVY AN' GETTIN' SITUATED.
STOP BY ON YOUR WAY HOME FROM WORK TONIGHT— O.K.?
THAT NIGHT AT THE WHEELERY I FIGURED OUT THAT—MY OWN EXPERIENCE NOTWITHSTANDING—THE AMERICAN MILITARY WAS FALLING SHORT OF ITS GOAL OF MAINTAINING A ONE-HUNDRED-PERCENT HETEROSEXUAL FIGHTING FORCE.
SO, IF YOU'RE OUT OF THE NAVY NOW, HOW COME YOU'RE STILL WEARIN' YOUR SAILORBOY BLUES? ISN'T THAT AGAINST THE RULES?
SO MANY OF THE BEST THINGS IN LIFE ARE, TOLAND!
THAT'S FOR SURE!
ACTUALLY, IT'S SHEER VANITY! EVERYBODY FINDS ME SO SEXY IN UNIFORM, I JUST CAN'T PEEL MYSELF OUT OF 'EM!
STILL, YOU'RE RIGHT—IT'S A HABIT I REALLY MUST BREAK. HAVE YOU BEEN IN THE SERVICE?
I GOT CALLED UP FOR MY PHYSICAL BUT ENDED UP '4-F.'
FLAT FEET?
NAH... SOMETHIN' ABOUT MY EYES. SOME LONG WORD.
I'LL BET I CAN GUESS....
THEY'RE TOO SOULFUL! THEY DON'T HAVE THE SOLDIERLY BRUTISHNESS ONE LOOKS FOR IN THE GROUND TROOPS.
THE NAVY, ON THE OTHER HAND, PLACES A DEFINITE PREMIUM ON SOULFULNESS. HEY! LOOK WHAT'S HERE!

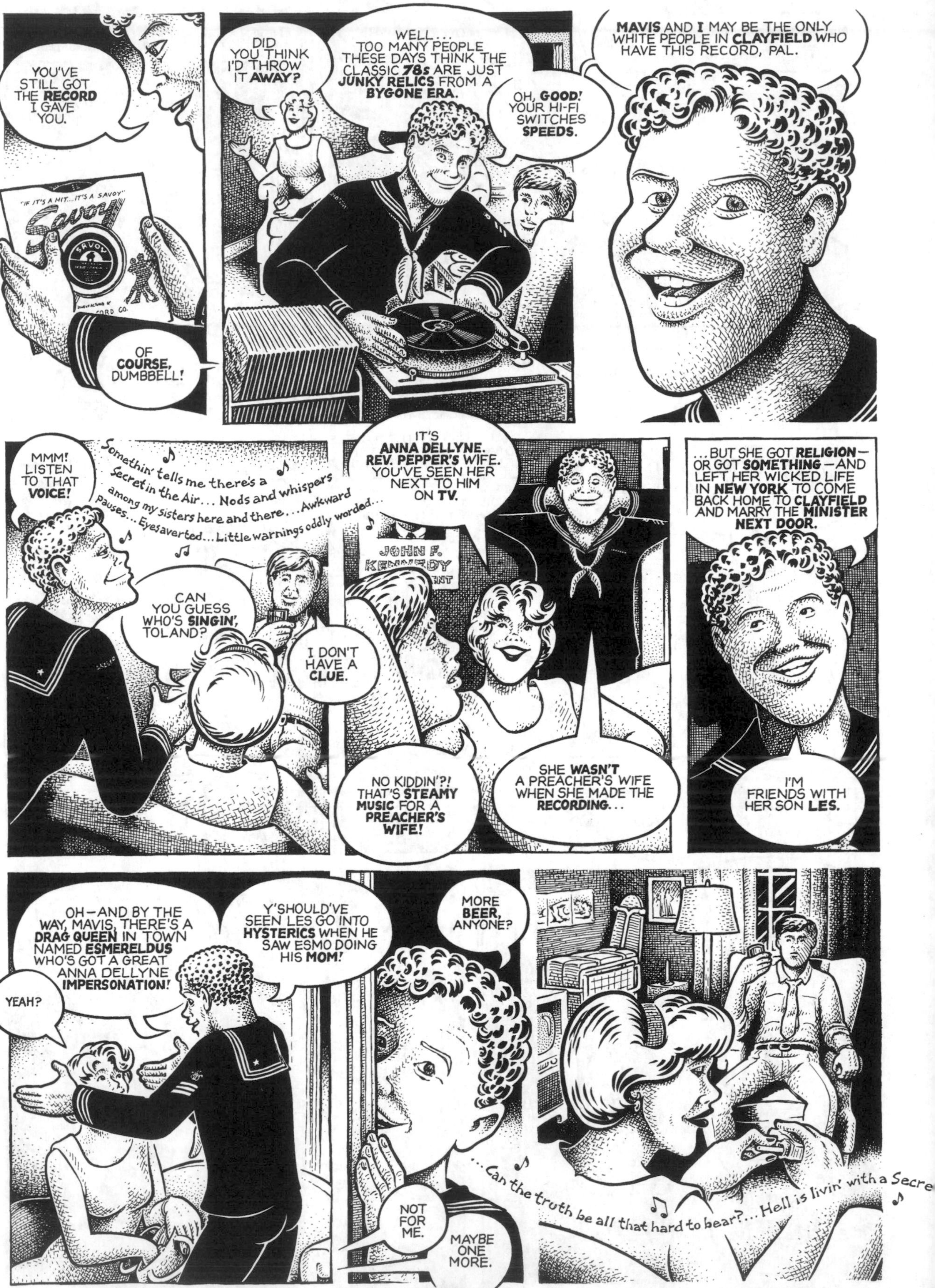
YOU'VE STILL GOT THE RECORD I GAVE YOU.
"IF IT'S A HIT... IT'S A SAVOY"
Savoy
SAVOY
OF COURSE, DUMBBELL!
DID YOU THINK I'D THROW IT AWAY?
WELL... TOO MANY PEOPLE THESE DAYS THINK THE CLASSIC 78s ARE JUST JUNKY RELICS FROM A BYGONE ERA.
OH, GOOD! YOUR HI-FI SWITCHES SPEEDS.
MAVIS AND I MAY BE THE ONLY WHITE PEOPLE IN CLAYFIELD WHO HAVE THIS RECORD, PAL.
MMM! LISTEN TO THAT VOICE!
Somethin' tells me there's a Secret in the Air... Nods and whispers among my sisters here and there... Awkward pauses... Eyes averted... Little warnings oddly worded...
CAN YOU GUESS WHO'S SINGIN', TOLAND?
I DON'T HAVE A CLUE.
IT'S ANNA DELLYNE. REV. PEPPER'S WIFE. YOU'VE SEEN HER NEXT TO HIM ON TV.
JOHN F. KENNEDY
NO KIDDIN'?! THAT'S STEAMY MUSIC FOR A PREACHER'S WIFE!
SHE WASN'T A PREACHER'S WIFE WHEN SHE MADE THE RECORDING...
...BUT SHE GOT RELIGION—OR GOT SOMETHING—AND LEFT HER WICKED LIFE IN NEW YORK TO COME BACK HOME TO CLAYFIELD AND MARRY THE MINISTER NEXT DOOR.
I'M FRIENDS WITH HER SON LES.
OH—AND BY THE WAY, MAVIS, THERE'S A DRAG QUEEN IN TOWN NAMED ESMERELDUS WHO'S GOT A GREAT ANNA DELLYNE IMPERSONATION!
YEAH?
Y'SHOULD'VE SEEN LES GO INTO HYSTERICS WHEN HE SAW ESMO DOING HIS MOM!
MORE BEER, ANYONE?
NOT FOR ME.
MAYBE ONE MORE.
...Can the truth be all that hard to bear?... Hell is livin' with a Secre

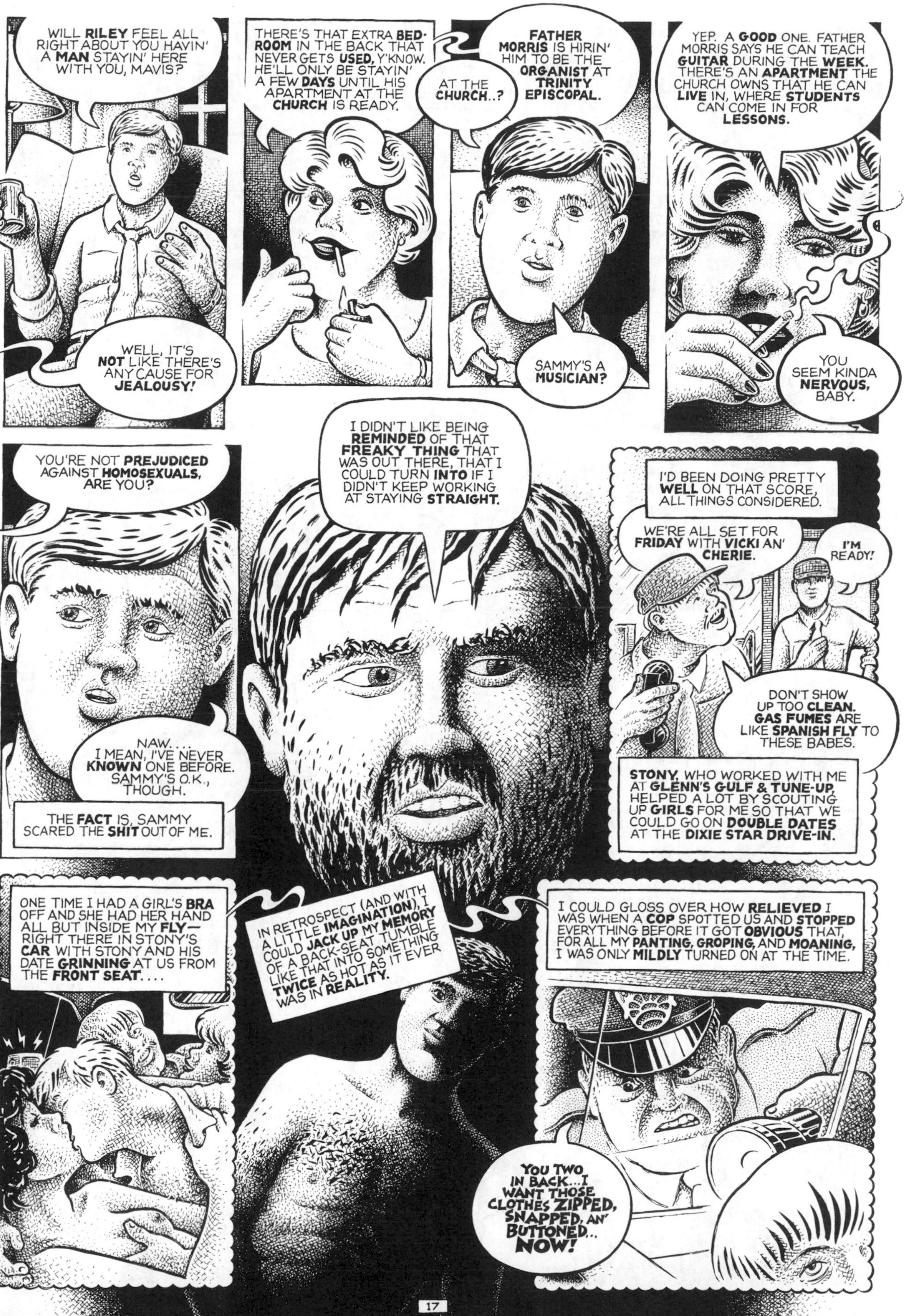

WILL RILEY FEEL ALL RIGHT ABOUT YOU HAVIN' A MAN STAYIN' HERE WITH YOU, MAVIS?
WELL, IT'S NOT LIKE THERE'S ANY CAUSE FOR JEALOUSY!
THERE'S THAT EXTRA BED-ROOM IN THE BACK THAT NEVER GETS USED, Y'KNOW. HE'LL ONLY BE STAYIN' A FEW DAYS UNTIL HIS APARTMENT AT THE CHURCH IS READY.
AT THE CHURCH..?
FATHER MORRIS IS HIRIN' HIM TO BE THE ORGANIST AT TRINITY EPISCOPAL.
SAMMY'S A MUSICIAN?
YEP. A GOOD ONE. FATHER MORRIS SAYS HE CAN TEACH GUITAR DURING THE WEEK. THERE'S AN APARTMENT THE CHURCH OWNS THAT HE CAN LIVE IN, WHERE STUDENTS CAN COME IN FOR LESSONS.
YOU SEEM KINDA NERVOUS, BABY.
YOU'RE NOT PREJUDICED AGAINST HOMOSEXUALS, ARE YOU?
NAW. I MEAN, I'VE NEVER KNOWN ONE BEFORE. SAMMY'S O.K., THOUGH.
THE FACT IS, SAMMY SCARED THE SHIT OUT OF ME.
I DIDN'T LIKE BEING REMINDED OF THAT FREAKY THING THAT WAS OUT THERE, THAT I COULD TURN INTO IF I DIDN'T KEEP WORKING AT STAYING STRAIGHT.
I'D BEEN DOING PRETTY WELL ON THAT SCORE, ALL THINGS CONSIDERED.
WE'RE ALL SET FOR FRIDAY WITH VICKI AN' CHERIE.
I'M READY!
DON'T SHOW UP TOO CLEAN. GAS FUMES ARE LIKE SPANISH FLY TO THESE BABES.
STONY, WHO WORKED WITH ME AT GLENN'S GULF & TUNE-UP, HELPED A LOT BY SCOUTING UP GIRLS FOR ME SO THAT WE COULD GO ON DOUBLE DATES AT THE DIXIE STAR DRIVE-IN.
ONE TIME I HAD A GIRL'S BRA OFF AND SHE HAD HER HAND ALL BUT INSIDE MY FLY— RIGHT THERE IN STONY'S CAR WITH STONY AND HIS DATE GRINNING AT US FROM THE FRONT SEAT....
IN RETROSPECT (AND WITH A LITTLE IMAGINATION), I COULD JACK UP MY MEMORY OF A BACK-SEAT TUMBLE LIKE THAT INTO SOMETHING TWICE AS HOT AS IT EVER WAS IN REALITY.
I COULD GLOSS OVER HOW RELIEVED I WAS WHEN A COP SPOTTED US AND STOPPED EVERYTHING BEFORE IT GOT OBVIOUS THAT, FOR ALL MY PANTING, GROPING, AND MOANING, I WAS ONLY MILDLY TURNED ON AT THE TIME.
YOU TWO IN BACK... I WANT THOSE CLOTHES ZIPPED, SNAPPED, AN' BUTTONED... NOW!

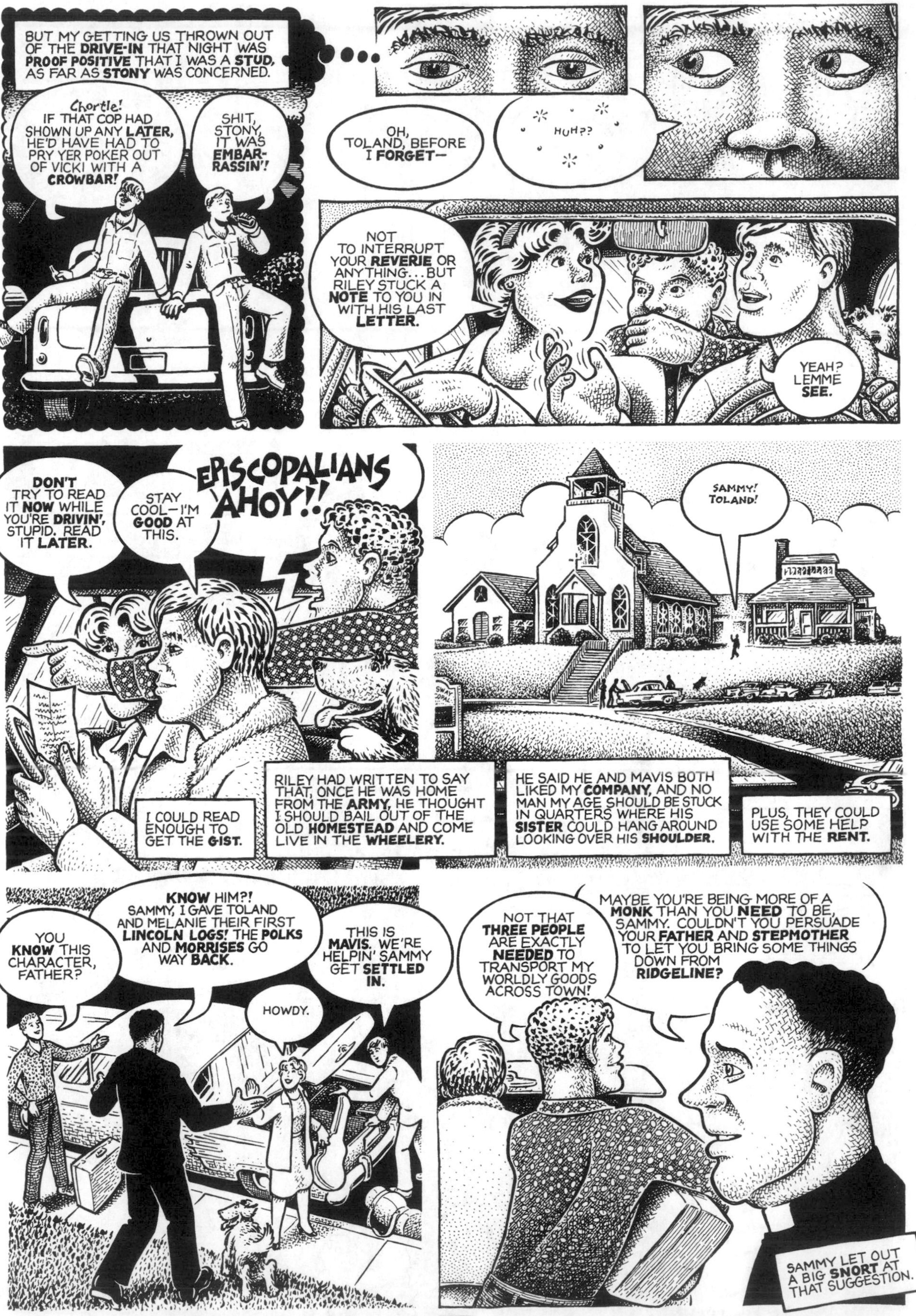

BUT MY GETTING US THROWN OUT OF THE DRIVE-IN THAT NIGHT WAS PROOF POSITIVE THAT I WAS A STUD, AS FAR AS STONY WAS CONCERNED.
Chortle! IF THAT COP HAD SHOWN UP ANY LATER, HE'D HAVE HAD TO PRY YER POKER OUT OF VICKI WITH A CROWBAR!
SHIT, STONY, IT WAS EMBAR-RASSIN'!
OH, TOLAND, BEFORE I FORGET—
HUH??
NOT TO INTERRUPT YOUR REVERIE OR ANYTHING... BUT RILEY STUCK A NOTE TO YOU IN WITH HIS LAST LETTER.
YEAH? LEMME SEE.
DON'T TRY TO READ IT NOW WHILE YOU'RE DRIVIN', STUPID. READ IT LATER.
STAY COOL—I'M GOOD AT THIS.
EPISCOPALIANS AHOY!!
SAMMY! TOLAND!
I COULD READ ENOUGH TO GET THE GIST.
RILEY HAD WRITTEN TO SAY THAT, ONCE HE WAS HOME FROM THE ARMY, HE THOUGHT I SHOULD BAIL OUT OF THE OLD HOMESTEAD AND COME LIVE IN THE WHEELERY.
HE SAID HE AND MAVIS BOTH LIKED MY COMPANY, AND NO MAN MY AGE SHOULD BE STUCK IN QUARTERS WHERE HIS SISTER COULD HANG AROUND LOOKING OVER HIS SHOULDER.
PLUS, THEY COULD USE SOME HELP WITH THE RENT.
YOU KNOW THIS CHARACTER, FATHER?
KNOW HIM?! SAMMY, I GAVE TOLAND AND MELANIE THEIR FIRST LINCOLN LOGS! THE POLKS AND MORRISES GO WAY BACK.
THIS IS MAVIS. WE'RE HELPIN' SAMMY GET SETTLED IN.
HOWDY.
NOT THAT THREE PEOPLE ARE EXACTLY NEEDED TO TRANSPORT MY WORLDLY GOODS ACROSS TOWN!
MAYBE YOU'RE BEING MORE OF A MONK THAN YOU NEED TO BE, SAMMY. COULDN'T YOU PERSUADE YOUR FATHER AND STEPMOTHER TO LET YOU BRING SOME THINGS DOWN FROM RIDGELINE?
SAMMY LET OUT A BIG SNORT AT THAT SUGGESTION.

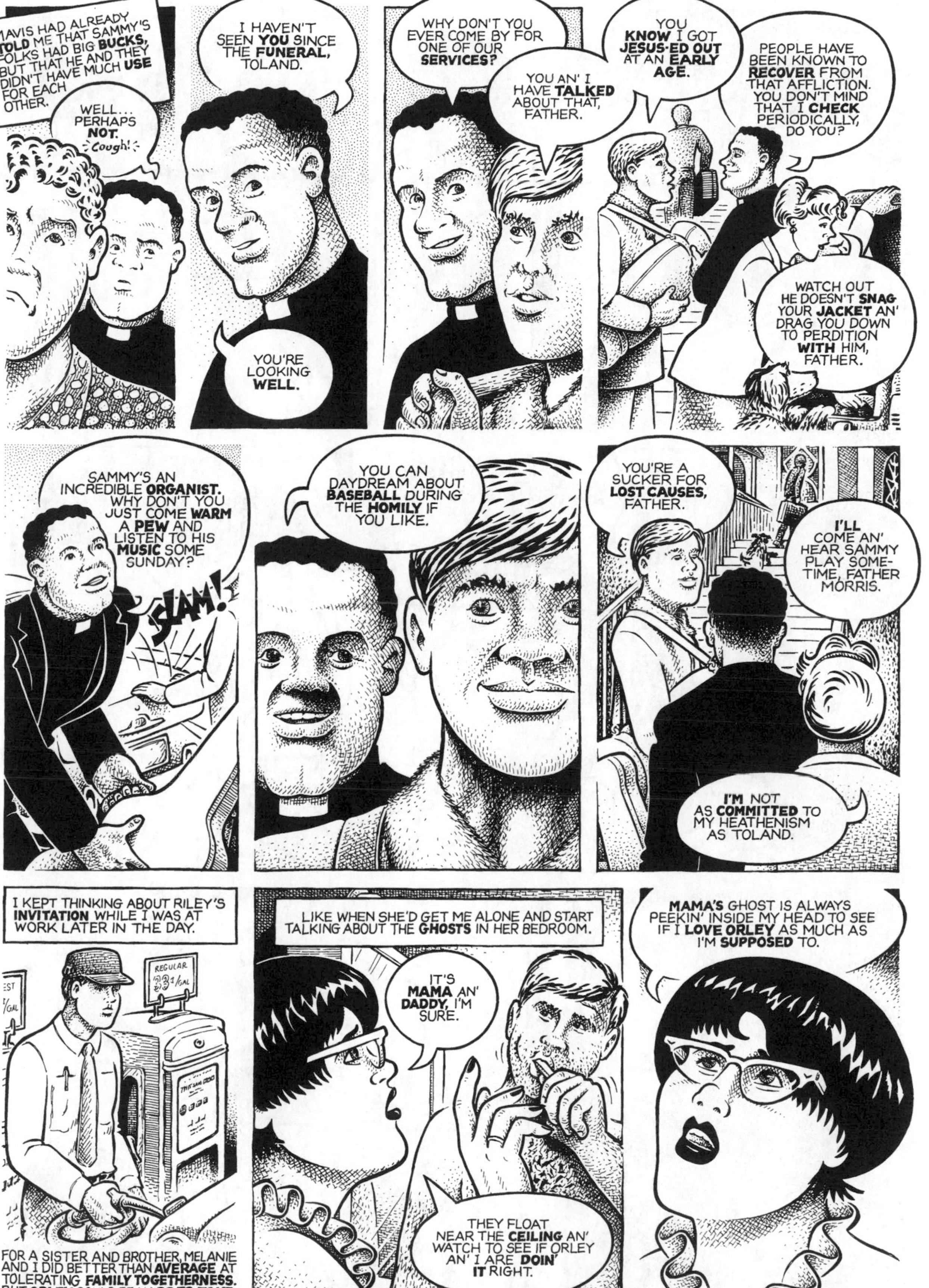

MAVIS HAD ALREADY TOLD ME THAT SAMMY'S FOLKS HAD BIG BUCKS, BUT THAT HE AND THEY DIDN'T HAVE MUCH USE FOR EACH OTHER.
WELL... PERHAPS NOT. Cough!
I HAVEN'T SEEN YOU SINCE THE FUNERAL, TOLAND.
YOU'RE LOOKING WELL.
WHY DON'T YOU EVER COME BY FOR ONE OF OUR SERVICES?
YOU AN' I HAVE TALKED ABOUT THAT, FATHER.
YOU KNOW I GOT JESUS-ED OUT AT AN EARLY AGE.
PEOPLE HAVE BEEN KNOWN TO RECOVER FROM THAT AFFLICTION. YOU DON'T MIND THAT I CHECK PERIODICALLY, DO YOU?
WATCH OUT HE DOESN'T SNAG YOUR JACKET AN' DRAG YOU DOWN TO PERDITION WITH HIM, FATHER.
SAMMY'S AN INCREDIBLE ORGANIST. WHY DON'T YOU JUST COME WARM A PEW AND LISTEN TO HIS MUSIC SOME SUNDAY?
SLAM!
YOU CAN DAYDREAM ABOUT BASEBALL DURING THE HOMILY IF YOU LIKE.
YOU'RE A SUCKER FOR LOST CAUSES, FATHER.
I'LL COME AN' HEAR SAMMY PLAY SOME-TIME, FATHER MORRIS.
I'M NOT AS COMMITTED TO MY HEATHENISM AS TOLAND.
I KEPT THINKING ABOUT RILEY'S INVITATION WHILE I WAS AT WORK LATER IN THE DAY.
REGULAR
FOR A SISTER AND BROTHER, MELANIE AND I DID BETTER THAN AVERAGE AT TOLERATING FAMILY TOGETHERNESS. BUT ORLEY COULD BE HARD TO TAKE, AND EVEN SIS GOT INTENSE SOMETIMES.
LIKE WHEN SHE'D GET ME ALONE AND START TALKING ABOUT THE GHOSTS IN HER BEDROOM.
IT'S MAMA AN' DADDY, I'M SURE.
THEY FLOAT NEAR THE CEILING AN' WATCH TO SEE IF ORLEY AN' I ARE DOIN' IT RIGHT.
MAMA'S GHOST IS ALWAYS PEEKIN' INSIDE MY HEAD TO SEE IF I LOVE ORLEY AS MUCH AS I'M SUPPOSED TO.

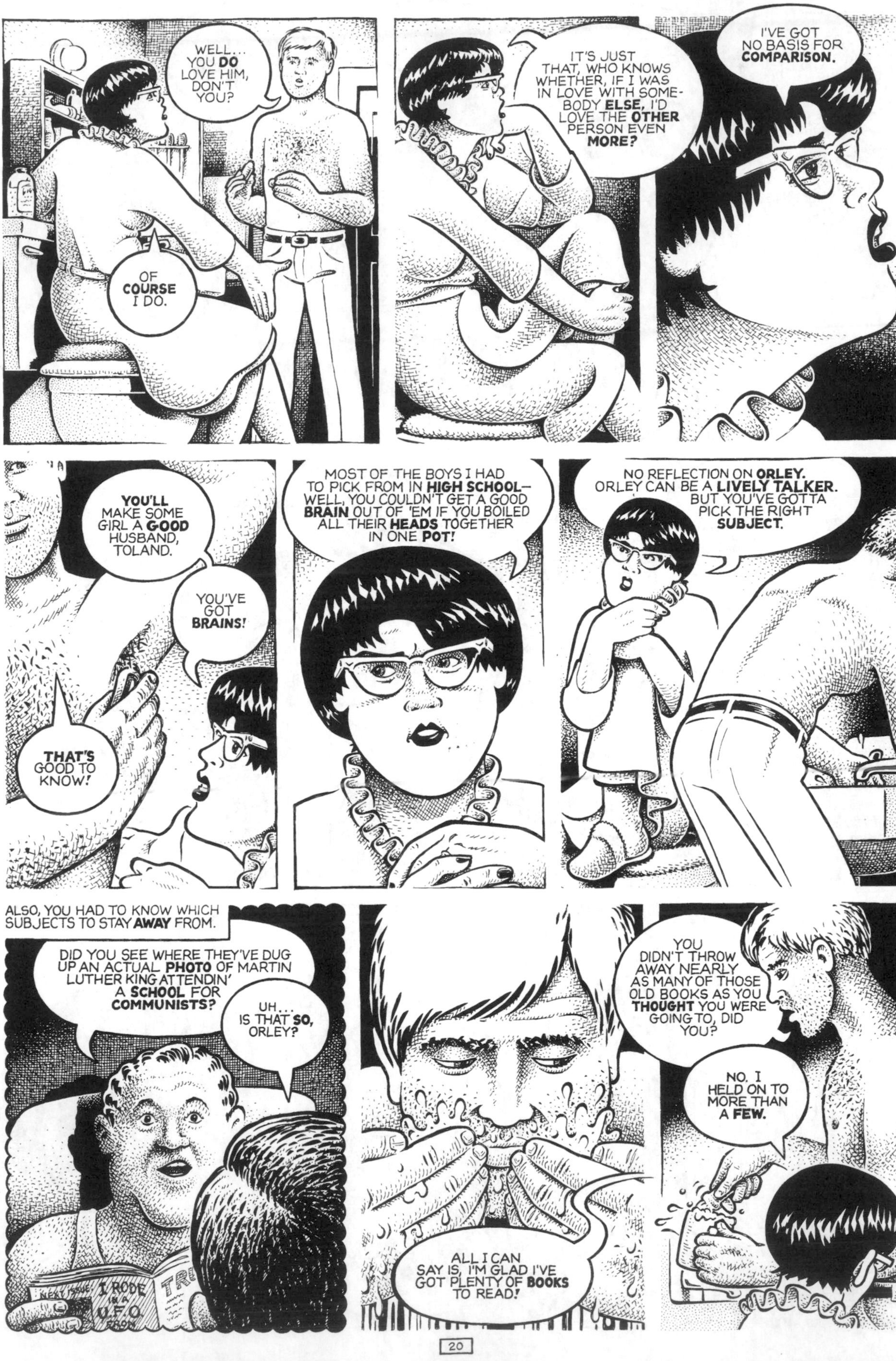
WELL... YOU DO LOVE HIM, DON'T YOU?
OF COURSE I DO.
IT'S JUST THAT, WHO KNOWS WHETHER, IF I WAS IN LOVE WITH SOMEBODY ELSE, I'D LOVE THE OTHER PERSON EVEN MORE?
I'VE GOT NO BASIS FOR COMPARISON.
YOU'LL MAKE SOME GIRL A GOOD HUSBAND, TOLAND.
YOU'VE GOT BRAINS!
THAT'S GOOD TO KNOW!
MOST OF THE BOYS I HAD TO PICK FROM IN HIGH SCHOOL— WELL, YOU COULDN'T GET A GOOD BRAIN OUT OF 'EM IF YOU BOILED ALL THEIR HEADS TOGETHER IN ONE POT!
NO REFLECTION ON ORLEY. ORLEY CAN BE A LIVELY TALKER. BUT YOU'VE GOTTA PICK THE RIGHT SUBJECT.
ALSO, YOU HAD TO KNOW WHICH SUBJECTS TO STAY AWAY FROM.
DID YOU SEE WHERE THEY'VE DUG UP AN ACTUAL PHOTO OF MARTIN LUTHER KING ATTENDIN' A SCHOOL FOR COMMUNISTS?
UH... IS THAT SO, ORLEY?
ALL I CAN SAY IS, I'M GLAD I'VE GOT PLENTY OF BOOKS TO READ!
YOU DIDN'T THROW AWAY NEARLY AS MANY OF THOSE OLD BOOKS AS YOU THOUGHT YOU WERE GOING TO, DID YOU?
NO. I HELD ON TO MORE THAN A FEW.

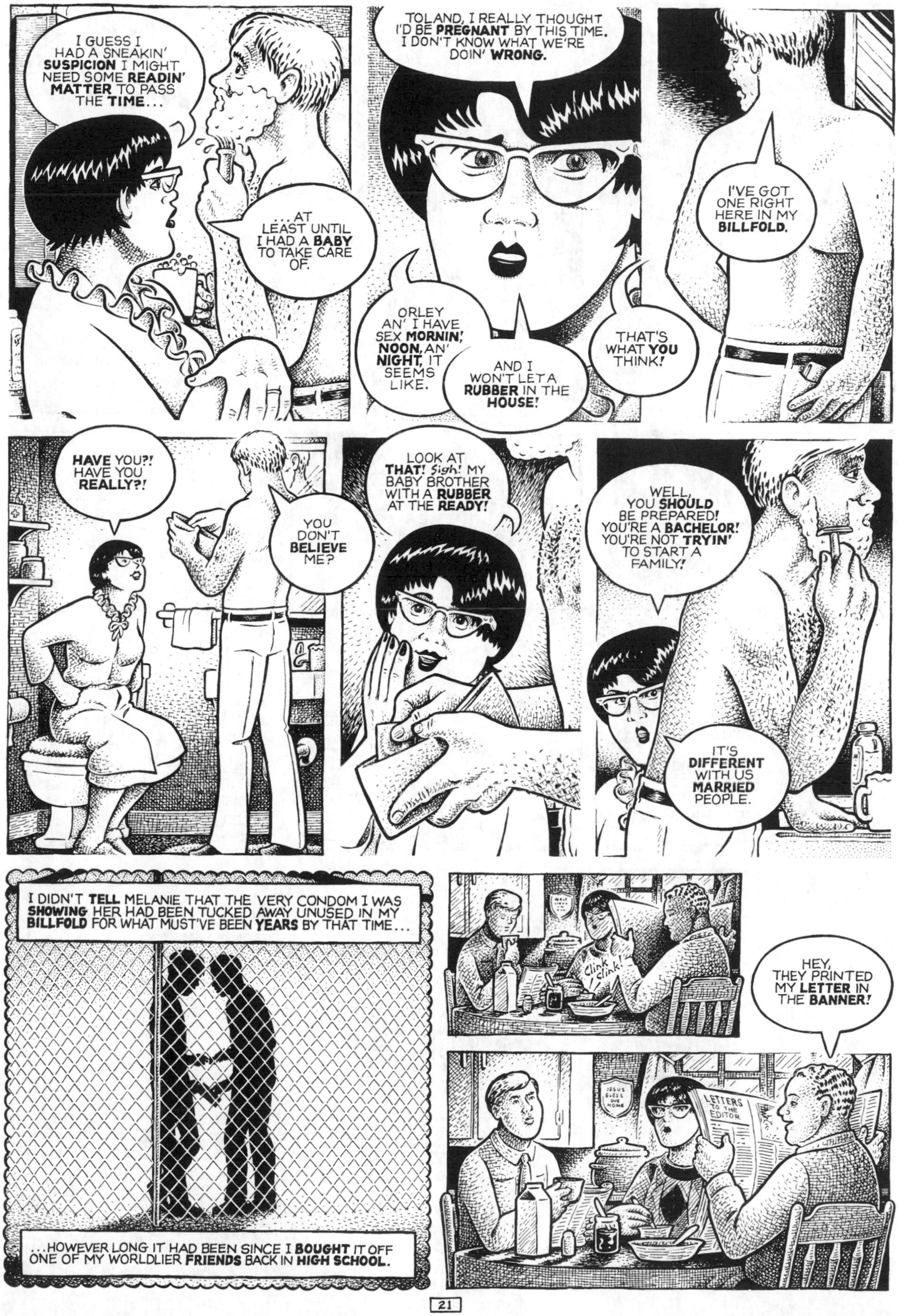

I GUESS I HAD A SNEAKIN' **SUSPICION** I MIGHT NEED SOME **READIN' MATTER** TO PASS THE **TIME**...
...AT LEAST UNTIL I HAD A **BABY** TO TAKE CARE OF.
TOLAND, I REALLY THOUGHT I'D BE **PREGNANT** BY THIS TIME. I DON'T KNOW WHAT WE'RE DOIN' **WRONG**.
ORLEY AN' I HAVE SEX **MORNIN', NOON,** AN' **NIGHT,** IT SEEMS LIKE.
AND I WON'T LET A **RUBBER** IN THE **HOUSE!**
THAT'S WHAT **YOU** THINK!
I'VE GOT ONE RIGHT HERE IN MY **BILLFOLD.**
HAVE YOU?! HAVE YOU **REALLY?!**
YOU DON'T **BELIEVE** ME?
LOOK AT **THAT!** *Sigh!* MY BABY BROTHER WITH A **RUBBER** AT THE **READY!**
WELL, YOU **SHOULD** BE PREPARED! YOU'RE A **BACHELOR!** YOU'RE NOT **TRYIN'** TO START A FAMILY!
IT'S **DIFFERENT** WITH US **MARRIED** PEOPLE.
I DIDN'T **TELL** MELANIE THAT THE VERY CONDOM I WAS **SHOWING** HER HAD BEEN TUCKED AWAY UNUSED IN MY **BILLFOLD** FOR WHAT MUST'VE BEEN **YEARS** BY THAT TIME...
...HOWEVER LONG IT HAD BEEN SINCE I **BOUGHT** IT OFF ONE OF MY WORLDLIER **FRIENDS** BACK IN **HIGH SCHOOL.**
Clink Clink!
HEY, THEY PRINTED MY **LETTER** IN THE **BANNER!**
JESUS BLESS OUR HOME
LETTERS TO THE EDITOR

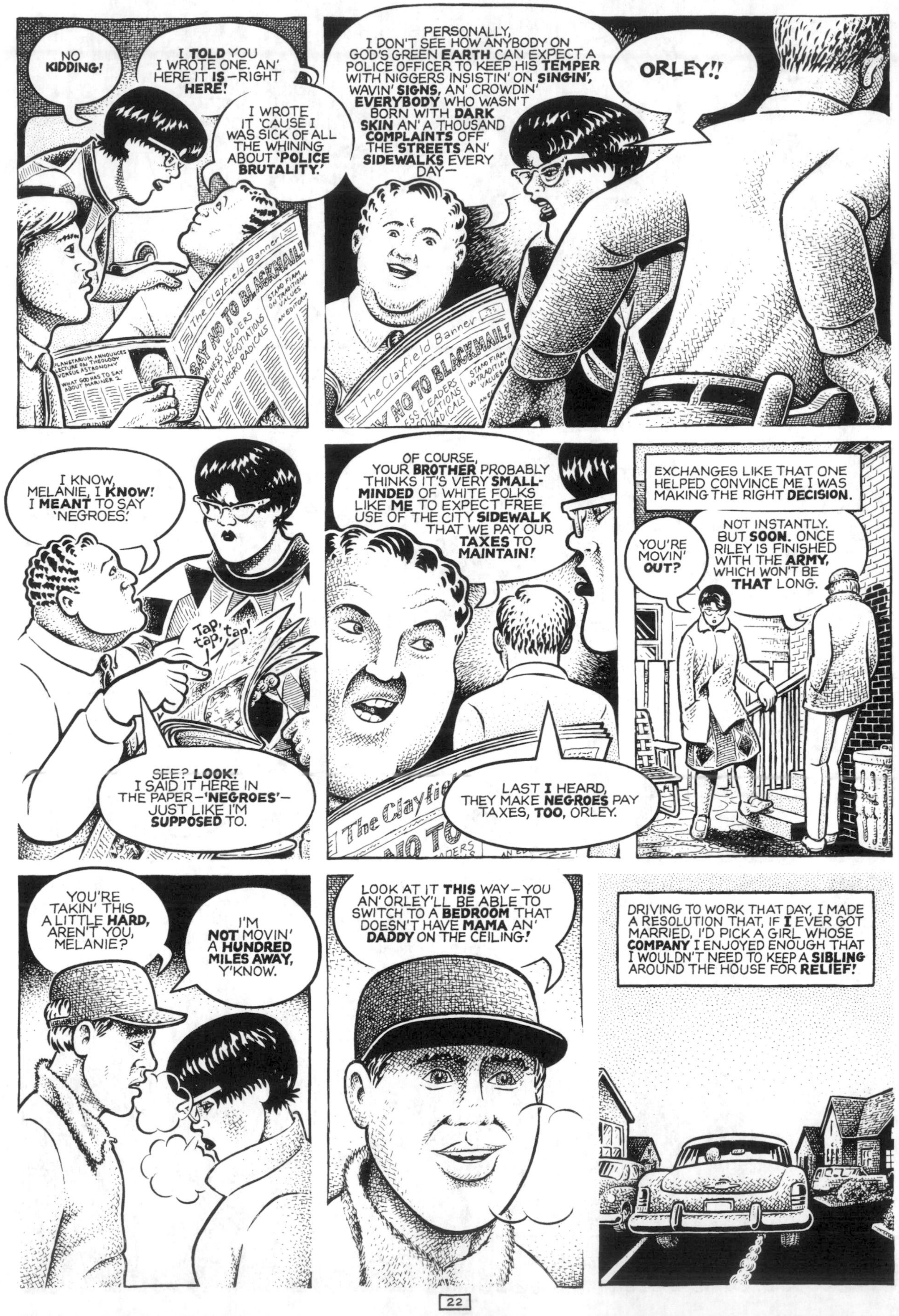
NO KIDDING!
I TOLD YOU I WROTE ONE. AN' HERE IT IS—RIGHT HERE!
I WROTE IT 'CAUSE I WAS SICK OF ALL THE WHINING ABOUT 'POLICE BRUTALITY.'
The Clayfield Banner
SAY NO TO BLACKMAIL!
BUSINESS LEADERS REJECT NEGOTIATIONS WITH NEGRO RADICALS
STAND FIRM ON TRADITIONAL VALUES
AN EDITORIAL
PLANETARIUM ANNOUNCES LECTURE ON THEOLOGY VERSUS ASTRONOMY
WHAT GOD HAS TO SAY ABOUT MARINER 2
PERSONALLY, I DON'T SEE HOW ANYBODY ON GOD'S GREEN EARTH CAN EXPECT A POLICE OFFICER TO KEEP HIS TEMPER WITH NIGGERS INSISTIN' ON SINGIN', WAVIN' SIGNS, AN' CROWDIN' EVERYBODY WHO WASN'T BORN WITH DARK SKIN AN' A THOUSAND COMPLAINTS OFF THE STREETS AN' SIDEWALKS EVERY DAY—
ORLEY!!
I KNOW, MELANIE, I KNOW! I MEANT TO SAY 'NEGROES.'
Tap, tap, tap!
SEE? LOOK! I SAID IT HERE IN THE PAPER—'NEGROES'—JUST LIKE I'M SUPPOSED TO.
OF COURSE, YOUR BROTHER PROBABLY THINKS IT'S VERY SMALL-MINDED OF WHITE FOLKS LIKE ME TO EXPECT FREE USE OF THE CITY SIDEWALK THAT WE PAY OUR TAXES TO MAINTAIN!
LAST I HEARD, THEY MAKE NEGROES PAY TAXES, TOO, ORLEY.
EXCHANGES LIKE THAT ONE HELPED CONVINCE ME I WAS MAKING THE RIGHT DECISION.
YOU'RE MOVIN' OUT?
NOT INSTANTLY. BUT SOON. ONCE RILEY IS FINISHED WITH THE ARMY, WHICH WON'T BE THAT LONG.
YOU'RE TAKIN' THIS A LITTLE HARD, AREN'T YOU, MELANIE?
I'M NOT MOVIN' A HUNDRED MILES AWAY, Y'KNOW.
LOOK AT IT THIS WAY—YOU AN' ORLEY'LL BE ABLE TO SWITCH TO A BEDROOM THAT DOESN'T HAVE MAMA AN' DADDY ON THE CEILING!
DRIVING TO WORK THAT DAY, I MADE A RESOLUTION THAT, IF I EVER GOT MARRIED, I'D PICK A GIRL WHOSE COMPANY I ENJOYED ENOUGH THAT I WOULDN'T NEED TO KEEP A SIBLING AROUND THE HOUSE FOR RELIEF!

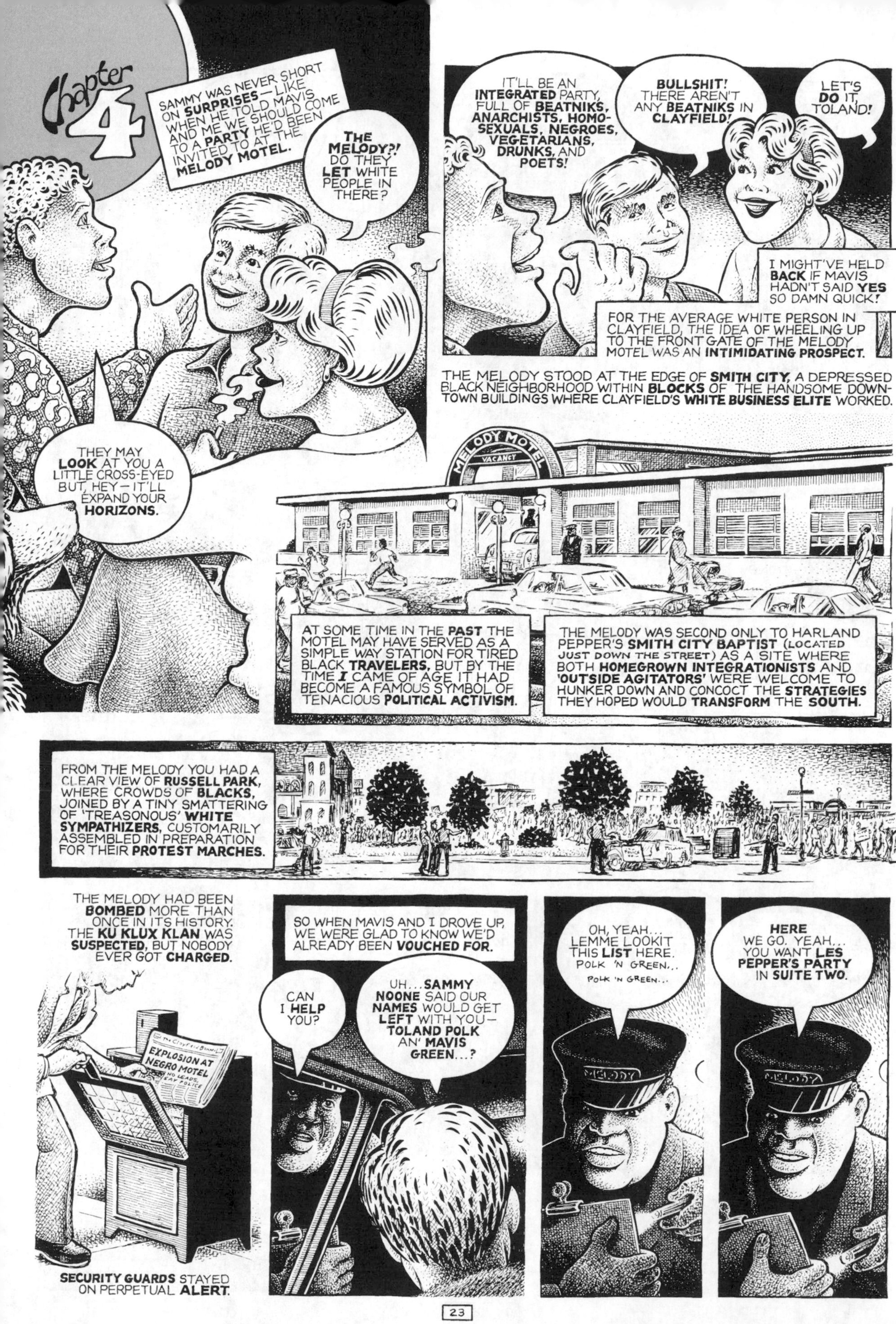

Chapter 4
SAMMY WAS NEVER SHORT ON SURPRISES — LIKE WHEN HE TOLD MAVIS AND ME WE SHOULD COME TO A PARTY HE'D BEEN INVITED TO AT THE MELODY MOTEL.
THE MELODY?! DO THEY LET WHITE PEOPLE IN THERE?
THEY MAY LOOK AT YOU A LITTLE CROSS-EYED BUT, HEY — IT'LL EXPAND YOUR HORIZONS.
IT'LL BE AN INTEGRATED PARTY, FULL OF BEATNIKS, ANARCHISTS, HOMOSEXUALS, NEGROES, VEGETARIANS, DRUNKS, AND POETS!
BULLSHIT! THERE AREN'T ANY BEATNIKS IN CLAYFIELD!
LET'S DO IT, TOLAND!
I MIGHT'VE HELD BACK IF MAVIS HADN'T SAID YES SO DAMN QUICK!
FOR THE AVERAGE WHITE PERSON IN CLAYFIELD, THE IDEA OF WHEELING UP TO THE FRONT GATE OF THE MELODY MOTEL WAS AN INTIMIDATING PROSPECT.
THE MELODY STOOD AT THE EDGE OF SMITH CITY, A DEPRESSED BLACK NEIGHBORHOOD WITHIN BLOCKS OF THE HANDSOME DOWNTOWN BUILDINGS WHERE CLAYFIELD'S WHITE BUSINESS ELITE WORKED.
MELODY MOTEL
VACANCY
AT SOME TIME IN THE PAST THE MOTEL MAY HAVE SERVED AS A SIMPLE WAY STATION FOR TIRED BLACK TRAVELERS, BUT BY THE TIME I CAME OF AGE IT HAD BECOME A FAMOUS SYMBOL OF TENACIOUS POLITICAL ACTIVISM.
THE MELODY WAS SECOND ONLY TO HARLAND PEPPER'S SMITH CITY BAPTIST (LOCATED JUST DOWN THE STREET) AS A SITE WHERE BOTH HOMEGROWN INTEGRATIONISTS AND 'OUTSIDE AGITATORS' WERE WELCOME TO HUNKER DOWN AND CONCOCT THE STRATEGIES THEY HOPED WOULD TRANSFORM THE SOUTH.
FROM THE MELODY YOU HAD A CLEAR VIEW OF RUSSELL PARK, WHERE CROWDS OF BLACKS, JOINED BY A TINY SMATTERING OF 'TREASONOUS' WHITE SYMPATHIZERS, CUSTOMARILY ASSEMBLED IN PREPARATION FOR THEIR PROTEST MARCHES.
THE MELODY HAD BEEN BOMBED MORE THAN ONCE IN ITS HISTORY. THE KU KLUX KLAN WAS SUSPECTED, BUT NOBODY EVER GOT CHARGED.
EXPLOSION AT NEGRO MOTEL
NO LEADS, SAY POLICE
SECURITY GUARDS STAYED ON PERPETUAL ALERT.
SO WHEN MAVIS AND I DROVE UP, WE WERE GLAD TO KNOW WE'D ALREADY BEEN VOUCHED FOR.
CAN I HELP YOU?
UH... SAMMY NOONE SAID OUR NAMES WOULD GET LEFT WITH YOU — TOLAND POLK AN' MAVIS GREEN...?
OH, YEAH... LEMME LOOKIT THIS LIST HERE. POLK 'N GREEN... POLK 'N GREEN...
MELODY
HERE WE GO. YEAH... YOU WANT LES PEPPER'S PARTY IN SUITE TWO.

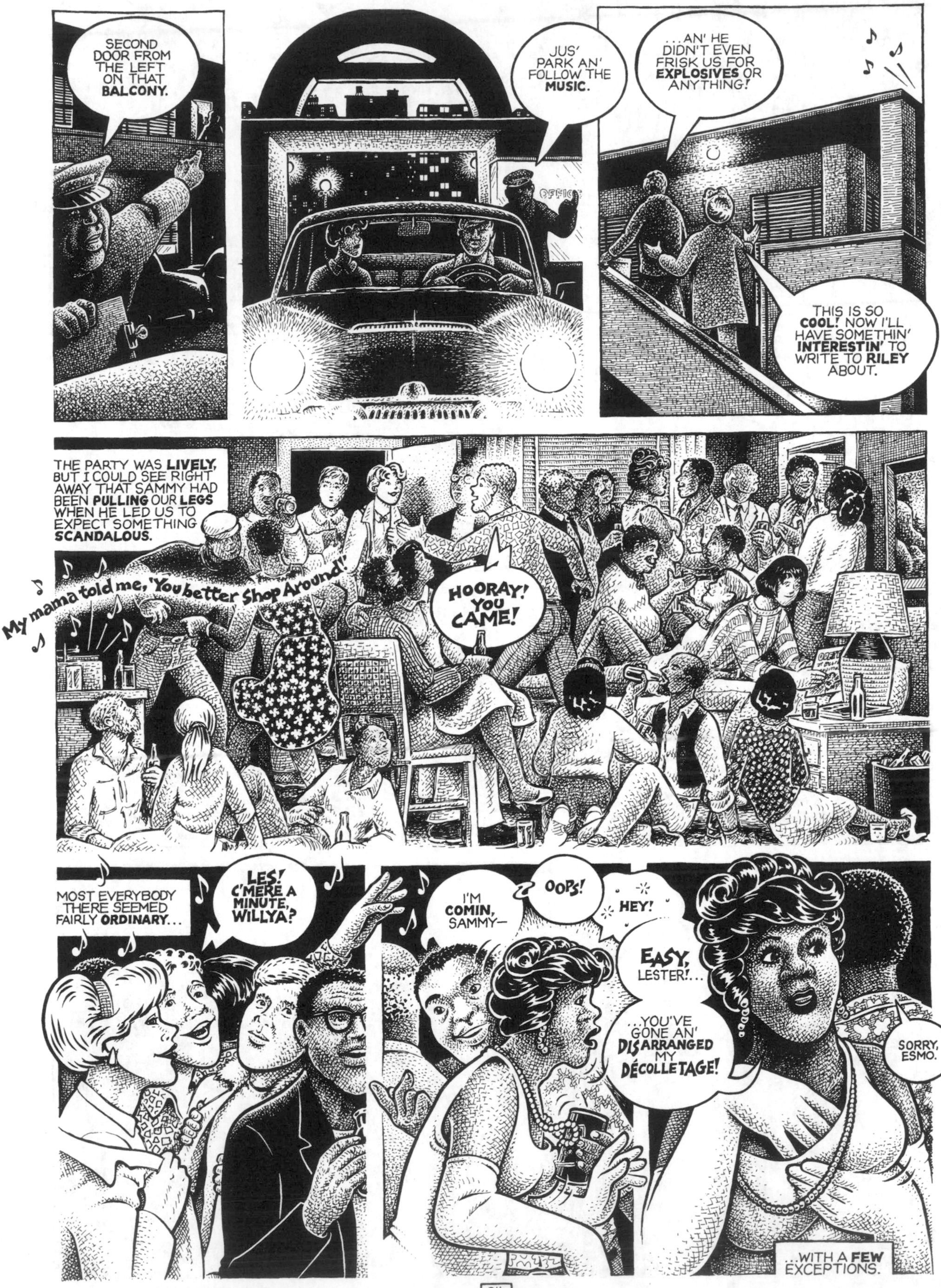
SECOND DOOR FROM THE LEFT ON THAT BALCONY.
JUS' PARK AN' FOLLOW THE MUSIC.
OFFICE
...AN' HE DIDN'T EVEN FRISK US FOR EXPLOSIVES OR ANYTHING!
THIS IS SO COOL! NOW I'LL HAVE SOMETHIN' INTERESTIN' TO WRITE TO RILEY ABOUT.
THE PARTY WAS LIVELY, BUT I COULD SEE RIGHT AWAY THAT SAMMY HAD BEEN PULLING OUR LEGS WHEN HE LED US TO EXPECT SOMETHING SCANDALOUS.
My mama told me, 'You better Shop Around!'
HOORAY! YOU CAME!
MOST EVERYBODY THERE SEEMED FAIRLY ORDINARY...
LES! C'MERE A MINUTE, WILLYA?
I'M COMIN, SAMMY—
OOPS!
HEY!
EASY, LESTER!...
...YOU'VE GONE AN' DISARRANGED MY DÉCOLLETAGE!
SORRY, ESMO.
...WITH A FEW EXCEPTIONS.

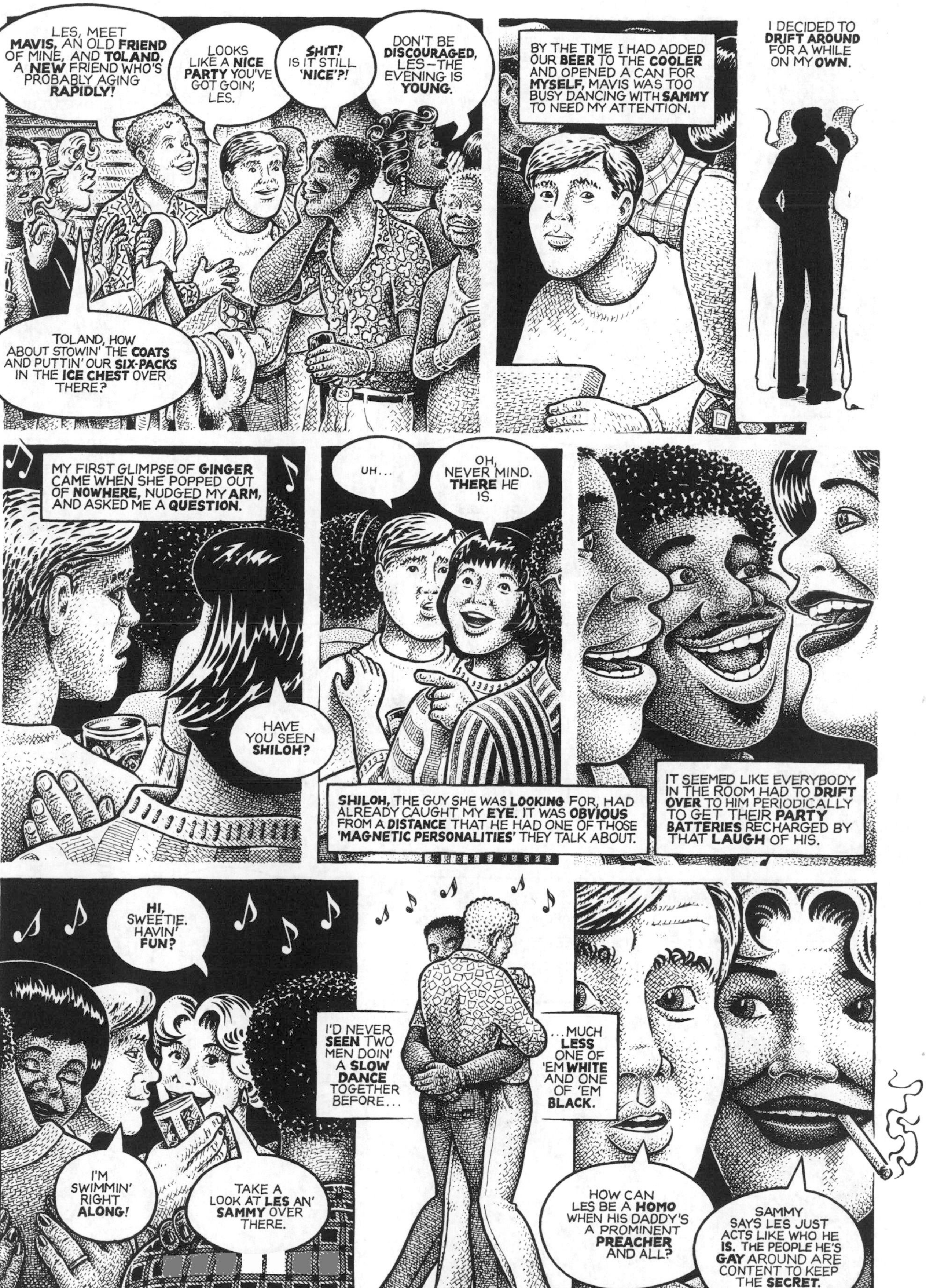
LES, MEET MAVIS, AN OLD FRIEND OF MINE, AND TOLAND, A NEW FRIEND WHO'S PROBABLY AGING RAPIDLY!
LOOKS LIKE A NICE PARTY YOU'VE GOT GOIN', LES.
SHIT! IS IT STILL 'NICE'?!
DON'T BE DISCOURAGED, LES—THE EVENING IS YOUNG.
TOLAND, HOW ABOUT STOWIN' THE COATS AND PUTTIN' OUR SIX-PACKS IN THE ICE CHEST OVER THERE?
BY THE TIME I HAD ADDED OUR BEER TO THE COOLER AND OPENED A CAN FOR MYSELF, MAVIS WAS TOO BUSY DANCING WITH SAMMY TO NEED MY ATTENTION.
I DECIDED TO DRIFT AROUND FOR A WHILE ON MY OWN.
MY FIRST GLIMPSE OF GINGER CAME WHEN SHE POPPED OUT OF NOWHERE, NUDGED MY ARM, AND ASKED ME A QUESTION.
HAVE YOU SEEN SHILOH?
UH...
OH, NEVER MIND. THERE HE IS.
SHILOH, THE GUY SHE WAS LOOKING FOR, HAD ALREADY CAUGHT MY EYE. IT WAS OBVIOUS FROM A DISTANCE THAT HE HAD ONE OF THOSE 'MAGNETIC PERSONALITIES' THEY TALK ABOUT.
IT SEEMED LIKE EVERYBODY IN THE ROOM HAD TO DRIFT OVER TO HIM PERIODICALLY TO GET THEIR PARTY BATTERIES RECHARGED BY THAT LAUGH OF HIS.
HI, SWEETIE. HAVIN' FUN?
I'M SWIMMIN' RIGHT ALONG!
TAKE A LOOK AT LES AN' SAMMY OVER THERE.
I'D NEVER SEEN TWO MEN DOIN' A SLOW DANCE TOGETHER BEFORE...
...MUCH LESS ONE OF 'EM WHITE AND ONE OF 'EM BLACK.
HOW CAN LES BE A HOMO WHEN HIS DADDY'S A PROMINENT PREACHER AND ALL?
SAMMY SAYS LES JUST ACTS LIKE WHO HE IS. THE PEOPLE HE'S GAY AROUND ARE CONTENT TO KEEP THE SECRET.

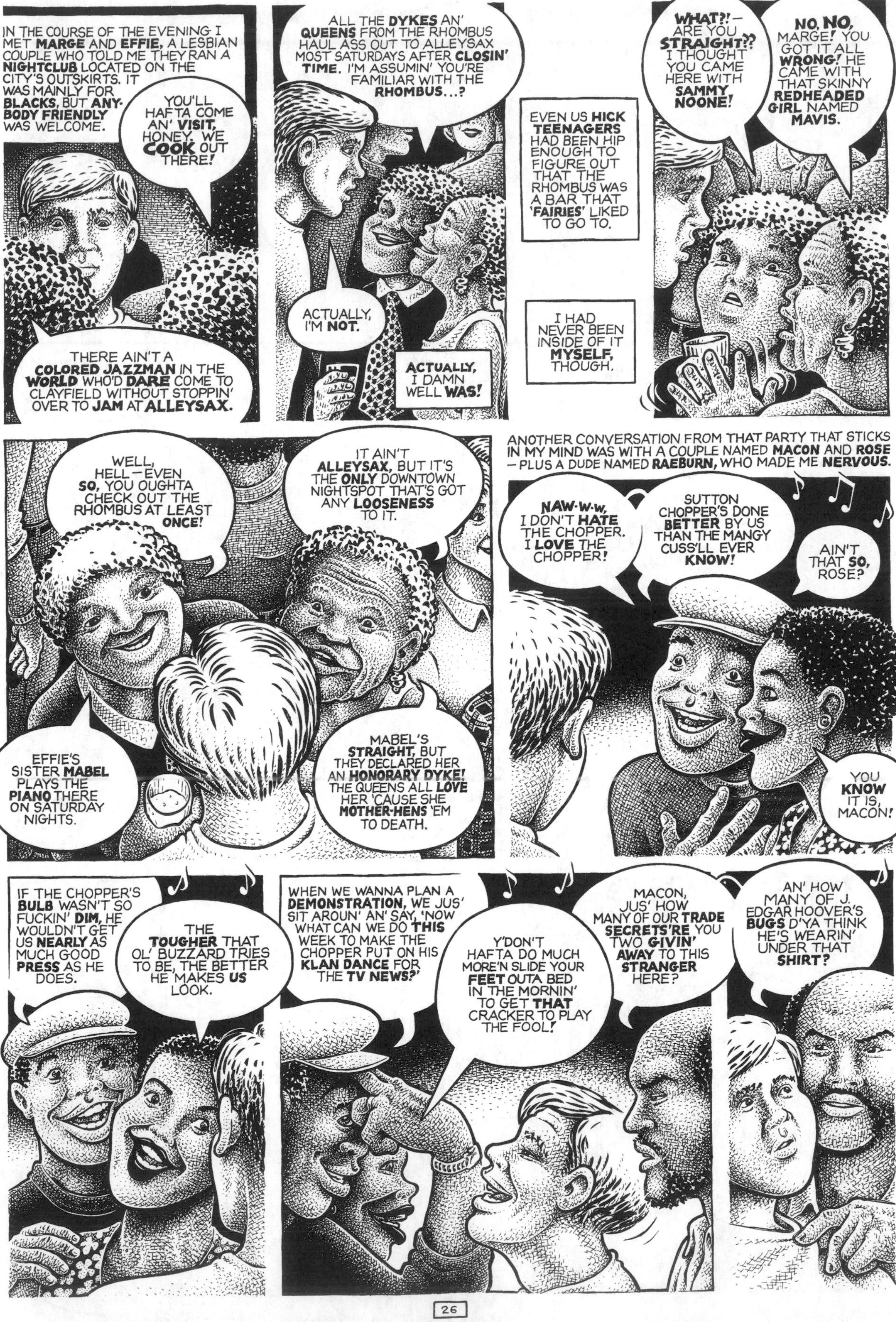

IN THE COURSE OF THE EVENING I MET MARGE AND EFFIE, A LESBIAN COUPLE WHO TOLD ME THEY RAN A NIGHTCLUB LOCATED ON THE CITY'S OUTSKIRTS. IT WAS MAINLY FOR BLACKS, BUT ANYBODY FRIENDLY WAS WELCOME.
YOU'LL HAFTA COME AN' VISIT, HONEY. WE COOK OUT THERE!
THERE AIN'T A COLORED JAZZMAN IN THE WORLD WHO'D DARE COME TO CLAYFIELD WITHOUT STOPPIN' OVER TO JAM AT ALLEYSAX.
ALL THE DYKES AN' QUEENS FROM THE RHOMBUS HAUL ASS OUT TO ALLEYSAX MOST SATURDAYS AFTER CLOSIN' TIME. I'M ASSUMIN' YOU'RE FAMILIAR WITH THE RHOMBUS...?
ACTUALLY, I'M NOT.
ACTUALLY, I DAMN WELL WAS!
EVEN US HICK TEENAGERS HAD BEEN HIP ENOUGH TO FIGURE OUT THAT THE RHOMBUS WAS A BAR THAT 'FAIRIES' LIKED TO GO TO.
I HAD NEVER BEEN INSIDE OF IT MYSELF, THOUGH.
WHAT?! — ARE YOU STRAIGHT?? I THOUGHT YOU CAME HERE WITH SAMMY NOONE!
NO, NO, MARGE! YOU GOT IT ALL WRONG! HE CAME WITH THAT SKINNY REDHEADED GIRL NAMED MAVIS.
WELL, HELL — EVEN SO, YOU OUGHTA CHECK OUT THE RHOMBUS AT LEAST ONCE!
IT AIN'T ALLEYSAX, BUT IT'S THE ONLY DOWNTOWN NIGHTSPOT THAT'S GOT ANY LOOSENESS TO IT.
EFFIE'S SISTER MABEL PLAYS THE PIANO THERE ON SATURDAY NIGHTS.
MABEL'S STRAIGHT, BUT THEY DECLARED HER AN HONORARY DYKE! THE QUEENS ALL LOVE HER 'CAUSE SHE MOTHER-HENS 'EM TO DEATH.
ANOTHER CONVERSATION FROM THAT PARTY THAT STICKS IN MY MIND WAS WITH A COUPLE NAMED MACON AND ROSE — PLUS A DUDE NAMED RAEBURN, WHO MADE ME NERVOUS.
NAW-W-W, I DON'T HATE THE CHOPPER. I LOVE THE CHOPPER!
SUTTON CHOPPER'S DONE BETTER BY US THAN THE MANGY CUSS'LL EVER KNOW!
AIN'T THAT SO, ROSE?
YOU KNOW IT IS, MACON!
IF THE CHOPPER'S BULB WASN'T SO FUCKIN' DIM, HE WOULDN'T GET US NEARLY AS MUCH GOOD PRESS AS HE DOES.
THE TOUGHER THAT OL' BUZZARD TRIES TO BE, THE BETTER HE MAKES US LOOK.
WHEN WE WANNA PLAN A DEMONSTRATION, WE JUS' SIT AROUN' AN' SAY, 'NOW WHAT CAN WE DO THIS WEEK TO MAKE THE CHOPPER PUT ON HIS KLAN DANCE FOR THE TV NEWS?'
Y'DON'T HAFTA DO MUCH MORE'N SLIDE YOUR FEET OUTA BED IN THE MORNIN' TO GET THAT CRACKER TO PLAY THE FOOL!
MACON, JUS' HOW MANY OF OUR TRADE SECRETS'RE YOU TWO GIVIN' AWAY TO THIS STRANGER HERE?
AN' HOW MANY OF J. EDGAR HOOVER'S BUGS D'YA THINK HE'S WEARIN' UNDER THAT SHIRT?

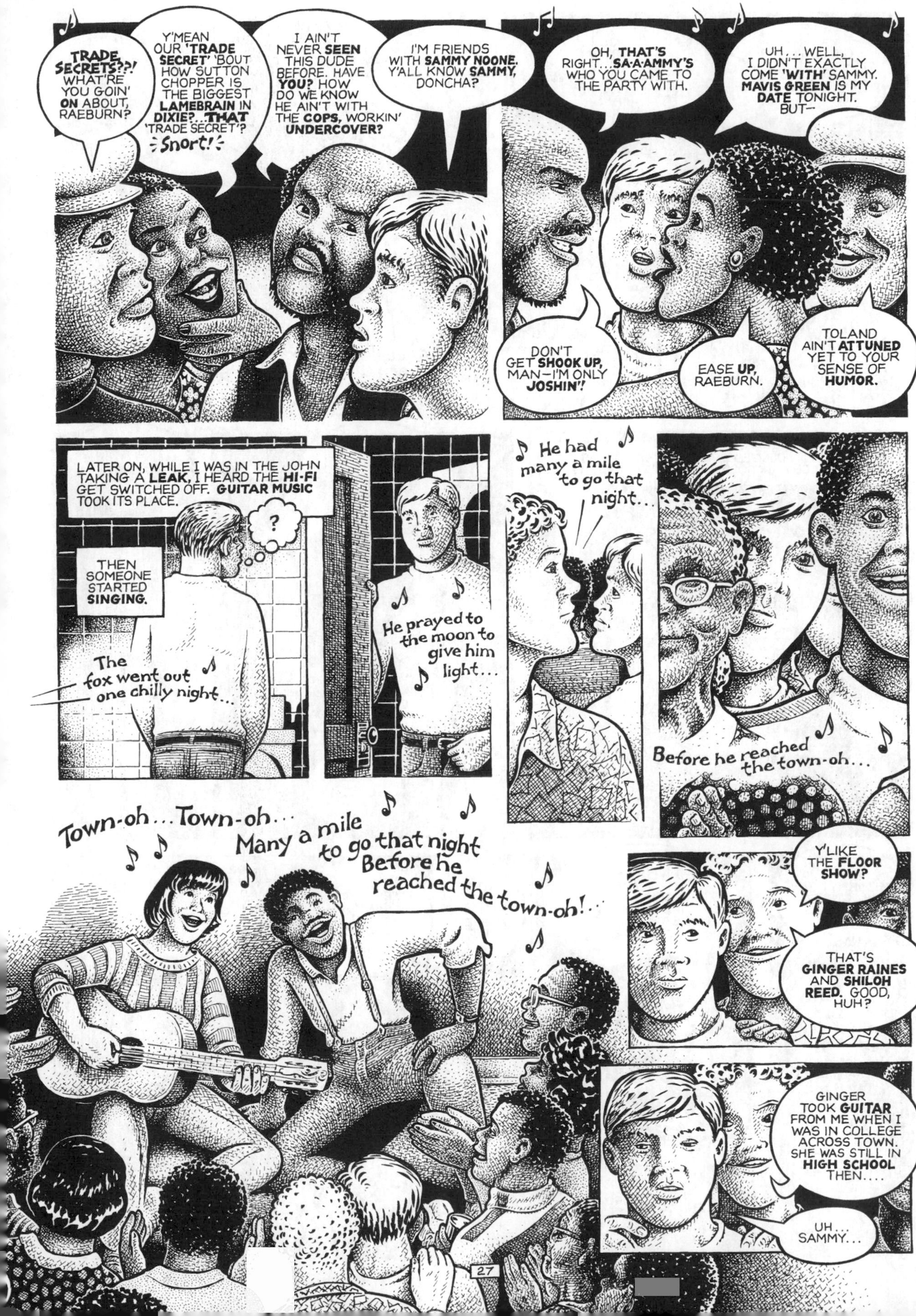
TRADE SECRETS??! WHAT'RE YOU GOIN' ON ABOUT, RAEBURN?
Y'MEAN OUR 'TRADE SECRET' 'BOUT HOW SUTTON CHOPPER IS THE BIGGEST LAMEBRAIN IN DIXIE?...THAT 'TRADE SECRET'? Snort!
I AIN'T NEVER SEEN THIS DUDE BEFORE. HAVE YOU? HOW DO WE KNOW HE AIN'T WITH THE COPS, WORKIN' UNDERCOVER?
I'M FRIENDS WITH SAMMY NOONE. Y'ALL KNOW SAMMY, DONCHA?
OH, THAT'S RIGHT... SA-A-AMMY'S WHO YOU CAME TO THE PARTY WITH.
UH... WELL, I DIDN'T EXACTLY COME 'WITH' SAMMY. MAVIS GREEN IS MY DATE TONIGHT. BUT—
DON'T GET SHOOK UP, MAN—I'M ONLY JOSHIN'!
EASE UP, RAEBURN.
TOLAND AIN'T ATTUNED YET TO YOUR SENSE OF HUMOR.
LATER ON, WHILE I WAS IN THE JOHN TAKING A LEAK, I HEARD THE HI-FI GET SWITCHED OFF. GUITAR MUSIC TOOK ITS PLACE.
?
THEN SOMEONE STARTED SINGING.
The fox went out one chilly night...
He prayed to the moon to give him light...
He had many a mile to go that night...
Before he reached the town-oh...
Town-oh... Town-oh... Many a mile to go that night Before he reached the town-oh!...
Y'LIKE THE FLOOR SHOW?
THAT'S GINGER RAINES AND SHILOH REED. GOOD, HUH?
GINGER TOOK GUITAR FROM ME WHEN I WAS IN COLLEGE ACROSS TOWN. SHE WAS STILL IN HIGH SCHOOL THEN....
UH... SAMMY...

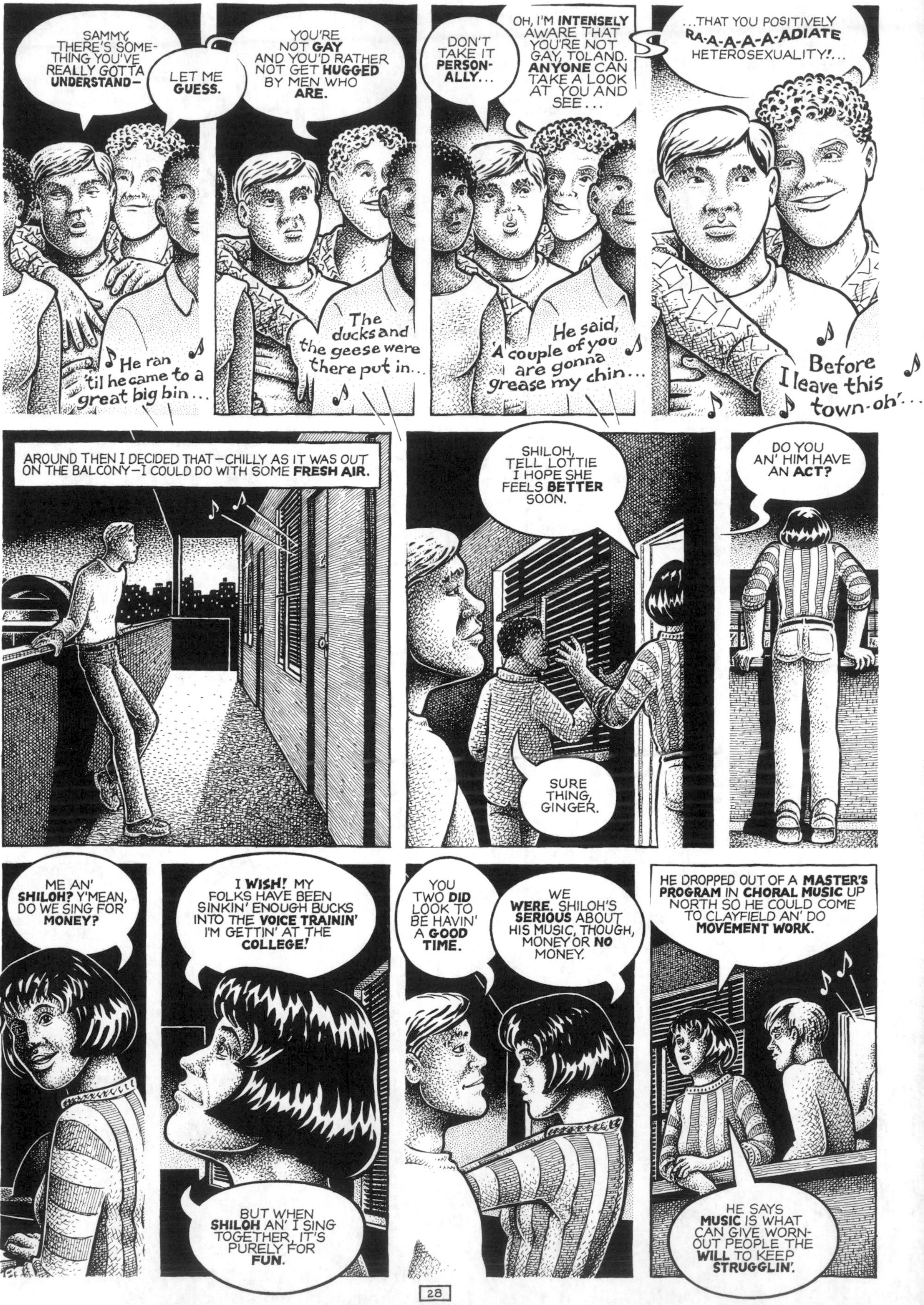
SAMMY, THERE'S SOMETHING YOU'VE REALLY GOTTA UNDERSTAND—
LET ME GUESS.
He ran 'til he came to a great big bin...
YOU'RE NOT GAY AND YOU'D RATHER NOT GET HUGGED BY MEN WHO ARE.
The ducks and the geese were there put in...
DON'T TAKE IT PERSONALLY...
OH, I'M INTENSELY AWARE THAT YOU'RE NOT GAY, TOLAND. ANYONE CAN TAKE A LOOK AT YOU AND SEE...
He said, 'A couple of you are gonna grease my chin...
...THAT YOU POSITIVELY RA-A-A-A-A-ADIATE HETEROSEXUALITY!...
Before I leave this town-oh'...
AROUND THEN I DECIDED THAT—CHILLY AS IT WAS OUT ON THE BALCONY—I COULD DO WITH SOME FRESH AIR.
SHILOH, TELL LOTTIE I HOPE SHE FEELS BETTER SOON.
SURE THING, GINGER.
DO YOU AN' HIM HAVE AN ACT?
ME AN' SHILOH? Y'MEAN, DO WE SING FOR MONEY?
I WISH! MY FOLKS HAVE BEEN SINKIN' ENOUGH BUCKS INTO THE VOICE TRAININ' I'M GETTIN' AT THE COLLEGE!
BUT WHEN SHILOH AN' I SING TOGETHER, IT'S PURELY FOR FUN.
YOU TWO DID LOOK TO BE HAVIN' A GOOD TIME.
WE WERE. SHILOH'S SERIOUS ABOUT HIS MUSIC, THOUGH, MONEY OR NO MONEY.
HE DROPPED OUT OF A MASTER'S PROGRAM IN CHORAL MUSIC UP NORTH SO HE COULD COME TO CLAYFIELD AN' DO MOVEMENT WORK.
HE SAYS MUSIC IS WHAT CAN GIVE WORN-OUT PEOPLE THE WILL TO KEEP STRUGGLIN'.

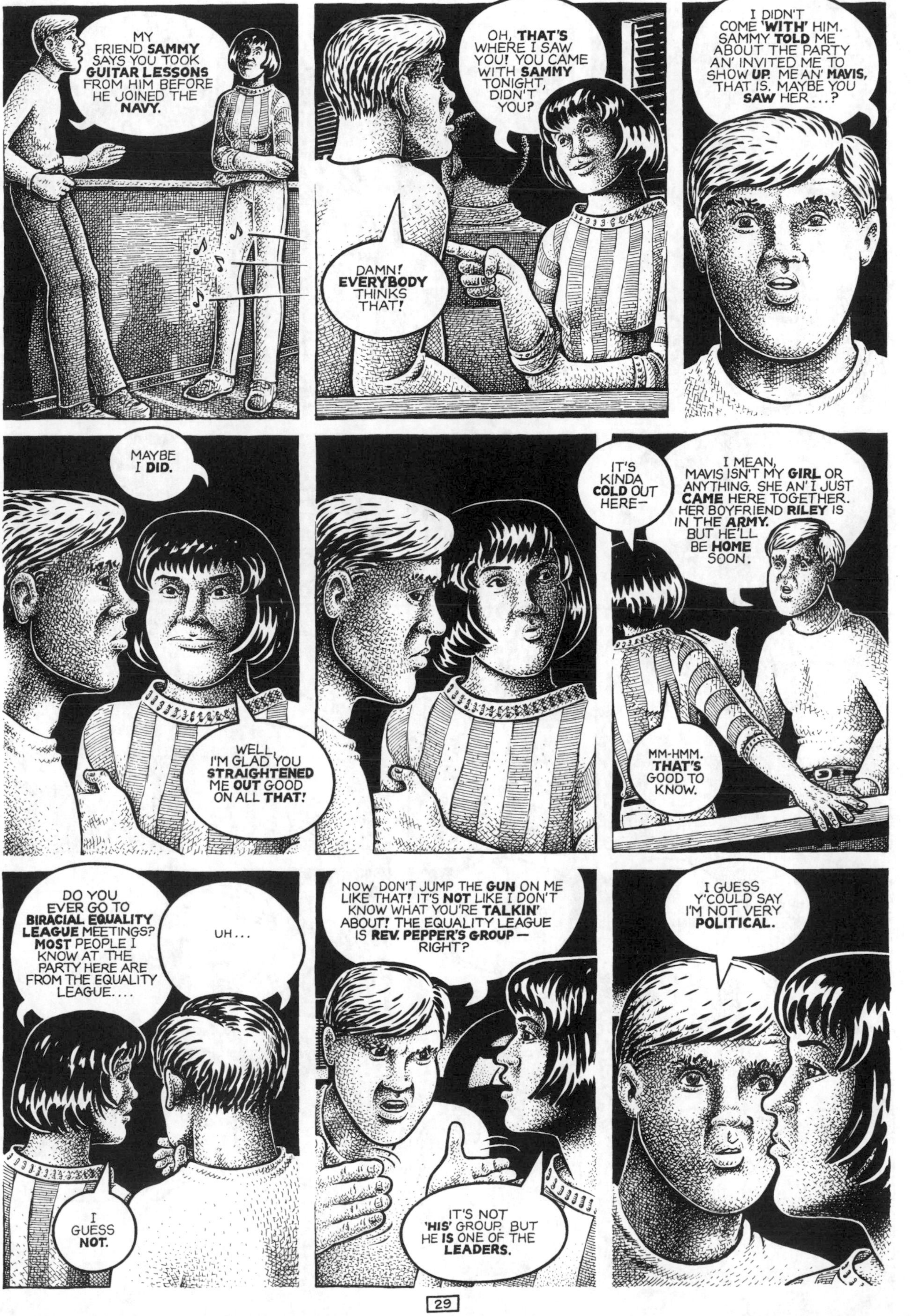

MY FRIEND **SAMMY** SAYS YOU TOOK **GUITAR LESSONS** FROM HIM BEFORE HE JOINED THE **NAVY.**
OH, **THAT'S** WHERE I SAW YOU! YOU CAME WITH **SAMMY** TONIGHT, DIDN'T YOU?
DAMN! **EVERYBODY** THINKS THAT!
I DIDN'T COME **'WITH'** HIM. SAMMY **TOLD** ME ABOUT THE PARTY AN' INVITED ME TO SHOW **UP.** ME AN' **MAVIS,** THAT IS. MAYBE YOU **SAW** HER...?
MAYBE I **DID.**
WELL, I'M GLAD YOU **STRAIGHTENED** ME **OUT** GOOD ON ALL **THAT!**
IT'S KINDA **COLD** OUT HERE—
I MEAN, MAVIS ISN'T MY **GIRL** OR ANYTHING. SHE AN' I JUST **CAME** HERE TOGETHER. HER BOYFRIEND **RILEY** IS IN THE **ARMY.** BUT HE'LL BE **HOME** SOON.
MM-HMM. **THAT'S** GOOD TO KNOW.
DO YOU EVER GO TO **BIRACIAL EQUALITY LEAGUE** MEETINGS? **MOST** PEOPLE I KNOW AT THE PARTY HERE ARE FROM THE EQUALITY LEAGUE....
UH...
I GUESS **NOT.**
NOW DON'T JUMP THE **GUN** ON ME LIKE THAT**!** IT'S **NOT** LIKE I DON'T KNOW WHAT YOU'RE **TALKIN'** ABOUT! THE EQUALITY LEAGUE IS **REV. PEPPER'S GROUP**— RIGHT?
IT'S NOT **'HIS'** GROUP. BUT HE **IS** ONE OF THE **LEADERS.**
I GUESS Y'COULD SAY I'M NOT VERY **POLITICAL.**

NOT TO **PUT DOWN** THE EQUALITY LEAGUE OR ANYTHING...

...BUT THESE **MARCHES** AN' **DEMONSTRATIONS** COME **ONE** ON TOP OF THE **OTHER** FOR MONTHS ON END —AND WHAT REALLY GETS **ACCOMPLISHED?**

PEOPLE ARE JUST AS **SCREWED UP** AN' **HATEFUL** TO EACH OTHER AS THEY'VE **EVER** BEEN, AS FAR AS I CAN TELL.

OH. WELL, MAYBE WE OUGHT TO STOP **DOIN'** IT, THEN.

WE CAN LEAVE THINGS THE WAY THEY **ARE** AN' PUT OUR ENERGIES INTO SOME-THIN' **USEFUL.**

I'LL BRING THAT UP AT THE NEXT **MEETING.**

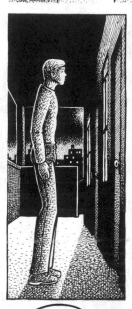

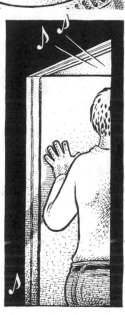

I'M **SLEEPY,** TOLAND. CAN YOU TAKE ME **HOME?**

I'LL BE READY IN JUST A **MINUTE,** MAVIS.

EXCUSE ME... I DON'T **MEAN** TO BE A **NUISANCE**—

—BUT IF YOU'RE NOT EVEN GONNA **ARGUE** WITH ME, WHAT'S THE POINT IN MY BOTHERIN' TO SAY SOMETHIN' **ASININE?**

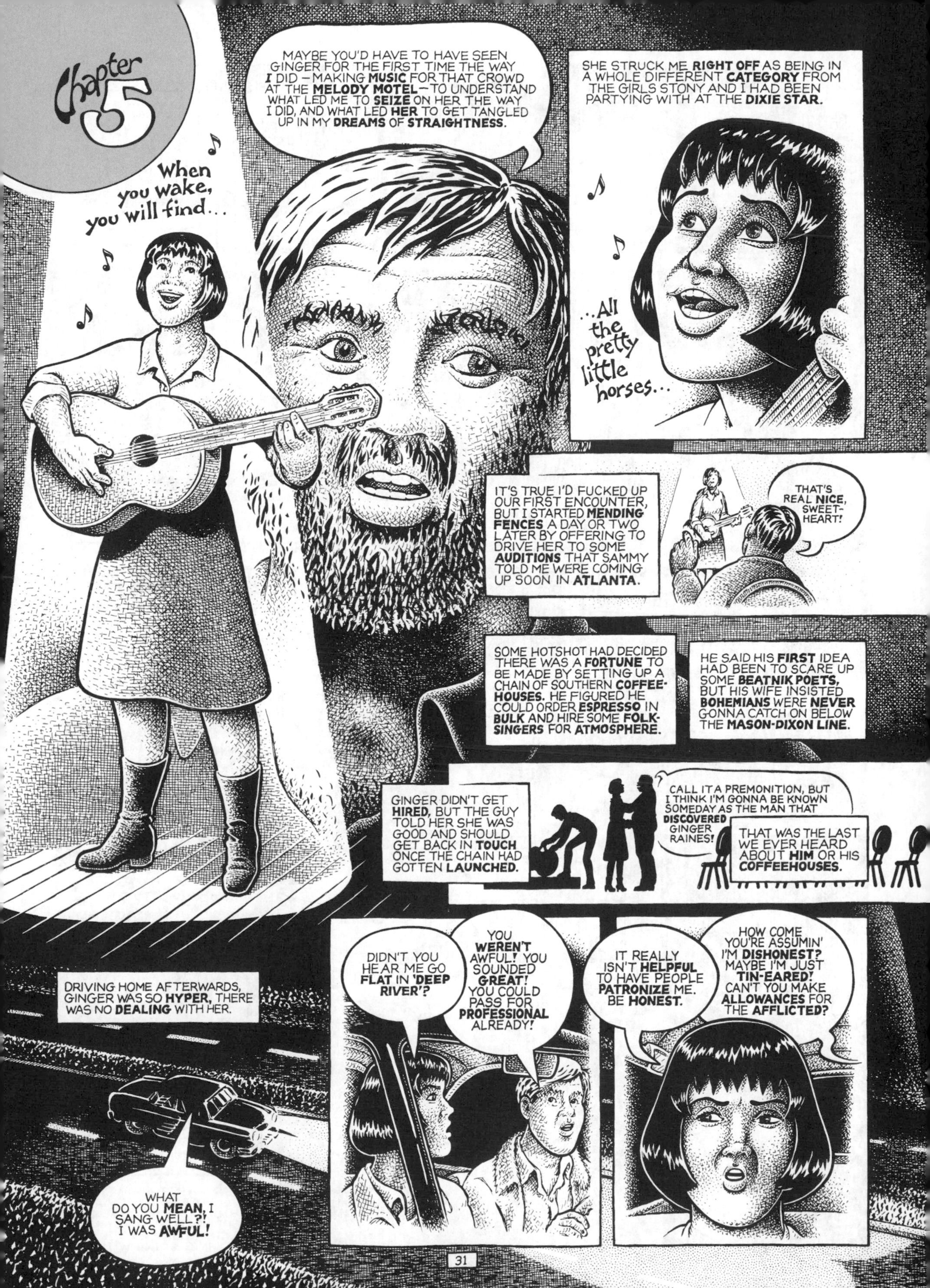

Chapter 5
When you wake, you will find...
MAYBE YOU'D HAVE TO HAVE SEEN GINGER FOR THE FIRST TIME THE WAY I DID — MAKING MUSIC FOR THAT CROWD AT THE MELODY MOTEL — TO UNDERSTAND WHAT LED ME TO SEIZE ON HER THE WAY I DID, AND WHAT LED HER TO GET TANGLED UP IN MY DREAMS OF STRAIGHTNESS.
SHE STRUCK ME RIGHT OFF AS BEING IN A WHOLE DIFFERENT CATEGORY FROM THE GIRLS STONY AND I HAD BEEN PARTYING WITH AT THE DIXIE STAR.
...All the pretty little horses...
IT'S TRUE I'D FUCKED UP OUR FIRST ENCOUNTER, BUT I STARTED MENDING FENCES A DAY OR TWO LATER BY OFFERING TO DRIVE HER TO SOME AUDITIONS THAT SAMMY TOLD ME WERE COMING UP SOON IN ATLANTA.
THAT'S REAL NICE, SWEET-HEART!
SOME HOTSHOT HAD DECIDED THERE WAS A FORTUNE TO BE MADE BY SETTING UP A CHAIN OF SOUTHERN COFFEE-HOUSES. HE FIGURED HE COULD ORDER ESPRESSO IN BULK AND HIRE SOME FOLK-SINGERS FOR ATMOSPHERE.
HE SAID HIS FIRST IDEA HAD BEEN TO SCARE UP SOME BEATNIK POETS, BUT HIS WIFE INSISTED BOHEMIANS WERE NEVER GONNA CATCH ON BELOW THE MASON-DIXON LINE.
GINGER DIDN'T GET HIRED, BUT THE GUY TOLD HER SHE WAS GOOD AND SHOULD GET BACK IN TOUCH ONCE THE CHAIN HAD GOTTEN LAUNCHED.
CALL IT A PREMONITION, BUT I THINK I'M GONNA BE KNOWN SOMEDAY AS THE MAN THAT DISCOVERED GINGER RAINES!
THAT WAS THE LAST WE EVER HEARD ABOUT HIM OR HIS COFFEEHOUSES.
DRIVING HOME AFTERWARDS, GINGER WAS SO HYPER, THERE WAS NO DEALING WITH HER.
WHAT DO YOU MEAN, I SANG WELL?! I WAS AWFUL!
DIDN'T YOU HEAR ME GO FLAT IN 'DEEP RIVER'?
YOU WEREN'T AWFUL! YOU SOUNDED GREAT! YOU COULD PASS FOR PROFESSIONAL ALREADY!
IT REALLY ISN'T HELPFUL TO HAVE PEOPLE PATRONIZE ME. BE HONEST.
HOW COME YOU'RE ASSUMIN' I'M DISHONEST? MAYBE I'M JUST TIN-EARED! CAN'T YOU MAKE ALLOWANCES FOR THE AFFLICTED?

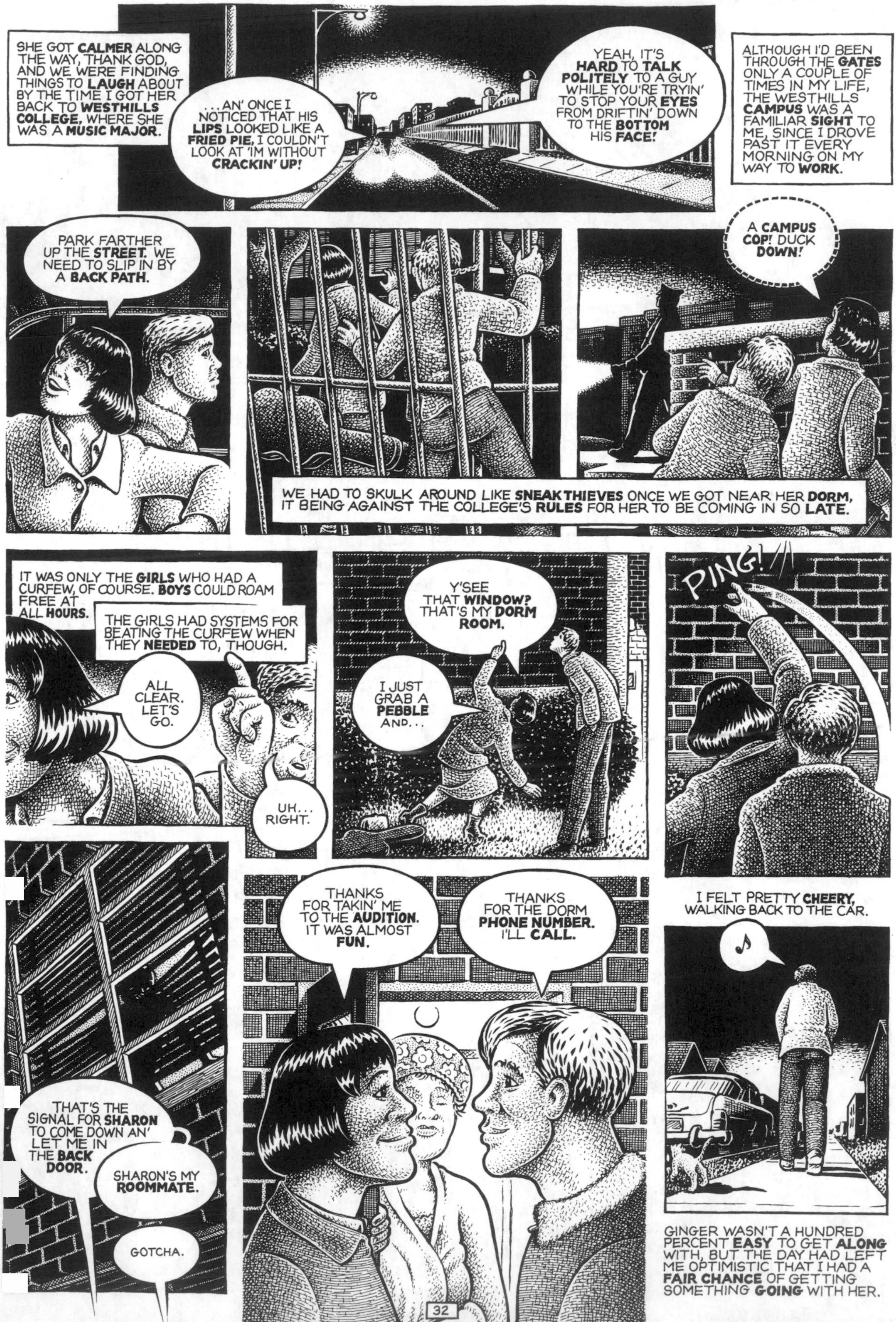

SHE GOT CALMER ALONG THE WAY, THANK GOD, AND WE WERE FINDING THINGS TO LAUGH ABOUT BY THE TIME I GOT HER BACK TO WESTHILLS COLLEGE, WHERE SHE WAS A MUSIC MAJOR.
. . . AN' ONCE I NOTICED THAT HIS LIPS LOOKED LIKE A FRIED PIE, I COULDN'T LOOK AT 'IM WITHOUT CRACKIN' UP!
YEAH, IT'S HARD TO TALK POLITELY TO A GUY WHILE YOU'RE TRYIN' TO STOP YOUR EYES FROM DRIFTIN' DOWN TO THE BOTTOM HIS FACE!
ALTHOUGH I'D BEEN THROUGH THE GATES ONLY A COUPLE OF TIMES IN MY LIFE, THE WESTHILLS CAMPUS WAS A FAMILIAR SIGHT TO ME, SINCE I DROVE PAST IT EVERY MORNING ON MY WAY TO WORK.
PARK FARTHER UP THE STREET. WE NEED TO SLIP IN BY A BACK PATH.
A CAMPUS COP! DUCK DOWN!
WE HAD TO SKULK AROUND LIKE SNEAK THIEVES ONCE WE GOT NEAR HER DORM, IT BEING AGAINST THE COLLEGE'S RULES FOR HER TO BE COMING IN SO LATE.
IT WAS ONLY THE GIRLS WHO HAD A CURFEW, OF COURSE. BOYS COULD ROAM FREE AT ALL HOURS.
THE GIRLS HAD SYSTEMS FOR BEATING THE CURFEW WHEN THEY NEEDED TO, THOUGH.
ALL CLEAR. LET'S GO.
UH... RIGHT.
Y'SEE THAT WINDOW? THAT'S MY DORM ROOM.
I JUST GRAB A PEBBLE AND...
PING!
THAT'S THE SIGNAL FOR SHARON TO COME DOWN AN' LET ME IN THE BACK DOOR.
SHARON'S MY ROOMMATE.
GOTCHA.
THANKS FOR TAKIN' ME TO THE AUDITION. IT WAS ALMOST FUN.
THANKS FOR THE DORM PHONE NUMBER. I'LL CALL.
I FELT PRETTY CHEERY, WALKING BACK TO THE CAR.
♪
GINGER WASN'T A HUNDRED PERCENT EASY TO GET ALONG WITH, BUT THE DAY HAD LEFT ME OPTIMISTIC THAT I HAD A FAIR CHANCE OF GETTING SOMETHING GOING WITH HER.

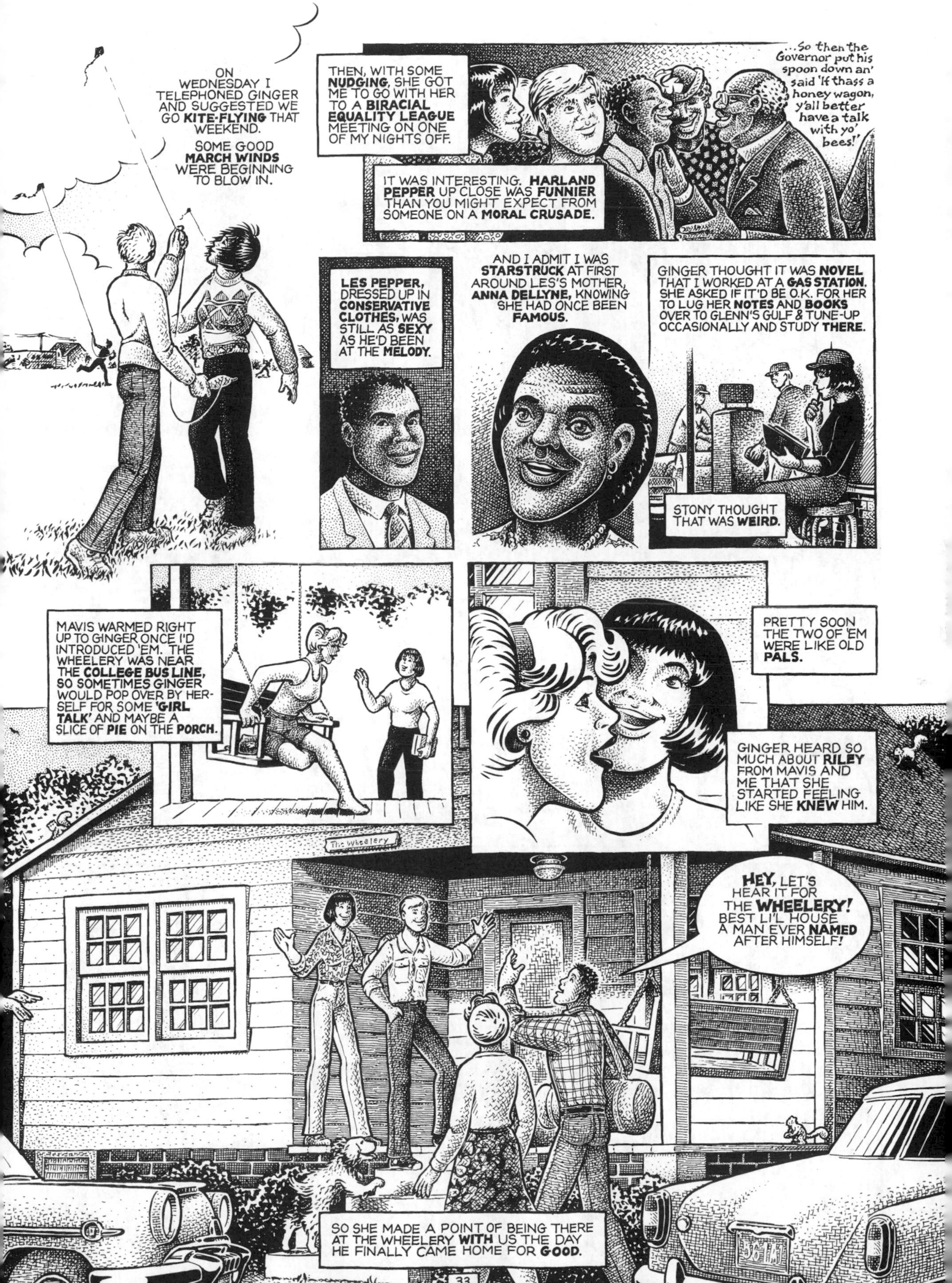
ON WEDNESDAY I TELEPHONED GINGER AND SUGGESTED WE GO KITE-FLYING THAT WEEKEND.
SOME GOOD MARCH WINDS WERE BEGINNING TO BLOW IN.
THEN, WITH SOME NUDGING, SHE GOT ME TO GO WITH HER TO A BIRACIAL EQUALITY LEAGUE MEETING ON ONE OF MY NIGHTS OFF.
...So then the Governor put his spoon down an' said 'If thass a honey wagon, y'all better have a talk with yo' bees!'
IT WAS INTERESTING. HARLAND PEPPER UP CLOSE WAS FUNNIER THAN YOU MIGHT EXPECT FROM SOMEONE ON A MORAL CRUSADE.
LES PEPPER, DRESSED UP IN CONSERVATIVE CLOTHES, WAS STILL AS SEXY AS HE'D BEEN AT THE MELODY.
AND I ADMIT I WAS STARSTRUCK AT FIRST AROUND LES'S MOTHER, ANNA DELLYNE, KNOWING SHE HAD ONCE BEEN FAMOUS.
GINGER THOUGHT IT WAS NOVEL THAT I WORKED AT A GAS STATION. SHE ASKED IF IT'D BE O.K. FOR HER TO LUG HER NOTES AND BOOKS OVER TO GLENN'S GULF & TUNE-UP OCCASIONALLY AND STUDY THERE.
STONY THOUGHT THAT WAS WEIRD.
MAVIS WARMED RIGHT UP TO GINGER ONCE I'D INTRODUCED 'EM. THE WHEELERY WAS NEAR THE COLLEGE BUS LINE, SO SOMETIMES GINGER WOULD POP OVER BY HER-SELF FOR SOME 'GIRL TALK' AND MAYBE A SLICE OF PIE ON THE PORCH.
PRETTY SOON THE TWO OF 'EM WERE LIKE OLD PALS.
GINGER HEARD SO MUCH ABOUT RILEY FROM MAVIS AND ME THAT SHE STARTED FEELING LIKE SHE KNEW HIM.
The Wheelery
HEY, LET'S HEAR IT FOR THE WHEELERY! BEST LI'L HOUSE A MAN EVER NAMED AFTER HIMSELF!
SO SHE MADE A POINT OF BEING THERE AT THE WHEELERY WITH US THE DAY HE FINALLY CAME HOME FOR GOOD.

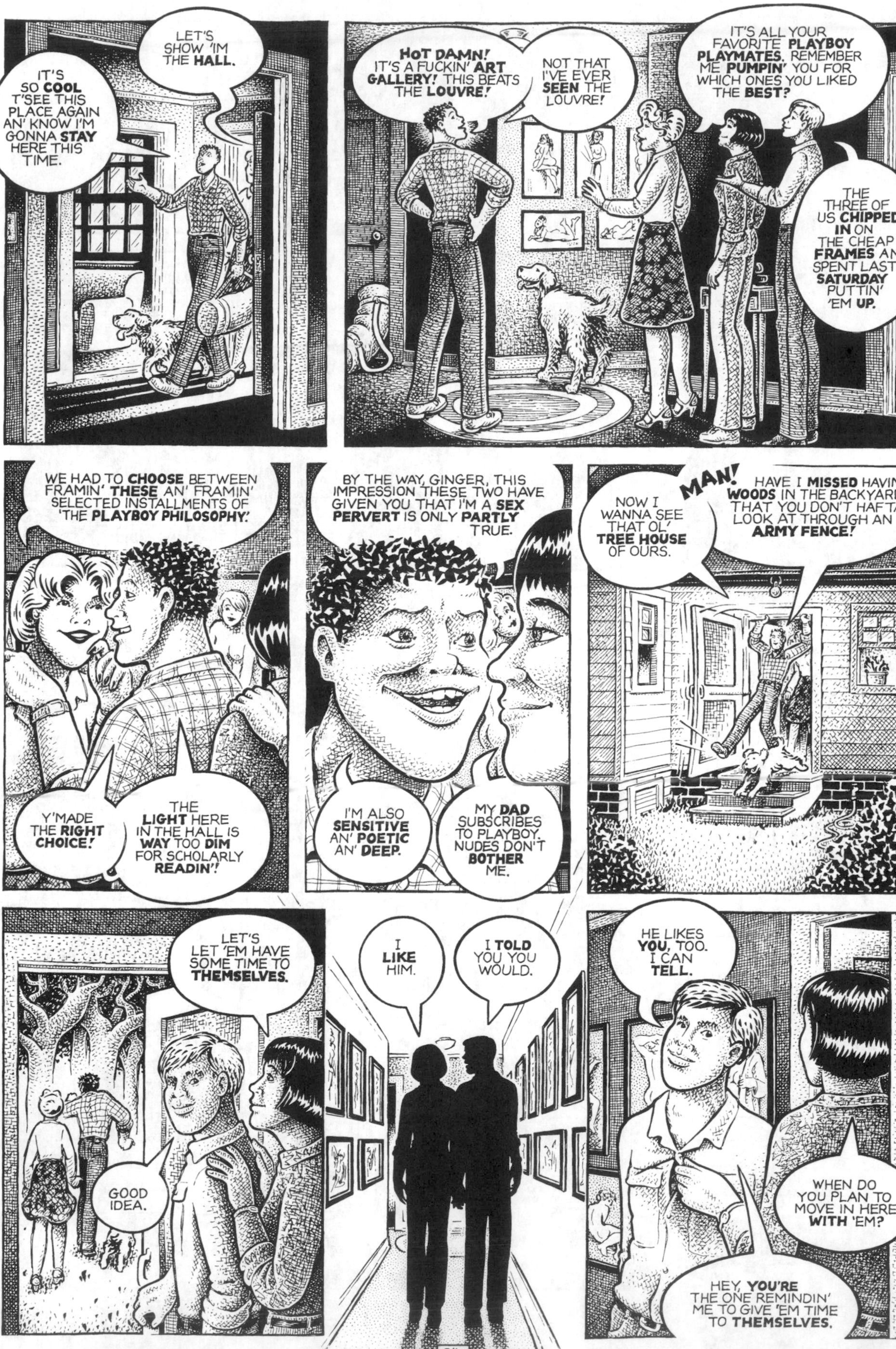

LET'S SHOW 'IM THE HALL.
IT'S SO COOL T'SEE THIS PLACE AGAIN AN' KNOW I'M GONNA STAY HERE THIS TIME.
HOT DAMN! IT'S A FUCKIN' ART GALLERY! THIS BEATS THE LOUVRE!
NOT THAT I'VE EVER SEEN THE LOUVRE!
IT'S ALL YOUR FAVORITE PLAYBOY PLAYMATES. REMEMBER ME PUMPIN' YOU FOR WHICH ONES YOU LIKED THE BEST?
THE THREE OF US CHIPPED IN ON THE CHEAP FRAMES AN' SPENT LAST SATURDAY PUTTIN' 'EM UP.
WE HAD TO CHOOSE BETWEEN FRAMIN' THESE AN' FRAMIN' SELECTED INSTALLMENTS OF 'THE PLAYBOY PHILOSOPHY.'
Y'MADE THE RIGHT CHOICE!
THE LIGHT HERE IN THE HALL IS WAY TOO DIM FOR SCHOLARLY READIN'!
BY THE WAY, GINGER, THIS IMPRESSION THESE TWO HAVE GIVEN YOU THAT I'M A SEX PERVERT IS ONLY PARTLY TRUE.
I'M ALSO SENSITIVE AN' POETIC AN' DEEP.
MY DAD SUBSCRIBES TO PLAYBOY. NUDES DON'T BOTHER ME.
MAN!
NOW I WANNA SEE THAT OL' TREE HOUSE OF OURS.
HAVE I MISSED HAVIN' WOODS IN THE BACKYARD THAT YOU DON'T HAFTA LOOK AT THROUGH AN ARMY FENCE!
LET'S LET 'EM HAVE SOME TIME TO THEMSELVES.
GOOD IDEA.
I LIKE HIM.
I TOLD YOU YOU WOULD.
HE LIKES YOU, TOO. I CAN TELL.
WHEN DO YOU PLAN TO MOVE IN HERE WITH 'EM?
HEY, YOU'RE THE ONE REMINDIN' ME TO GIVE 'EM TIME TO THEMSELVES.

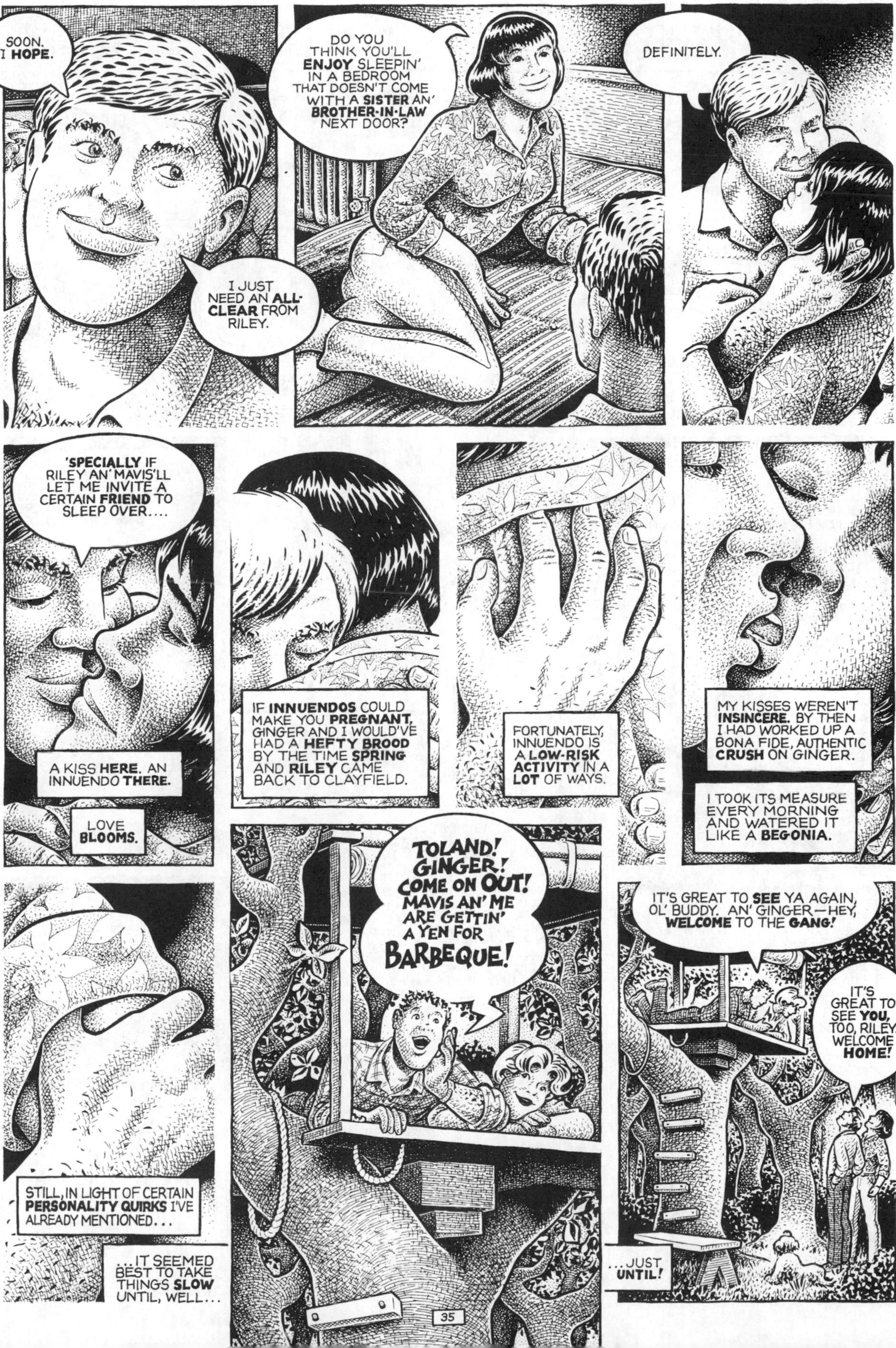
SOON. I HOPE.
I JUST NEED AN ALL-CLEAR FROM RILEY.
DO YOU THINK YOU'LL ENJOY SLEEPIN' IN A BEDROOM THAT DOESN'T COME WITH A SISTER AN' BROTHER-IN-LAW NEXT DOOR?
DEFINITELY.
'SPECIALLY IF RILEY AN' MAVIS'LL LET ME INVITE A CERTAIN FRIEND TO SLEEP OVER....
A KISS HERE. AN INNUENDO THERE.
LOVE BLOOMS.
IF INNUENDOS COULD MAKE YOU PREGNANT, GINGER AND I WOULD'VE HAD A HEFTY BROOD BY THE TIME SPRING AND RILEY CAME BACK TO CLAYFIELD.
FORTUNATELY, INNUENDO IS A LOW-RISK ACTIVITY IN A LOT OF WAYS.
MY KISSES WEREN'T INSINCERE. BY THEN I HAD WORKED UP A BONA FIDE, AUTHENTIC CRUSH ON GINGER.
I TOOK ITS MEASURE EVERY MORNING AND WATERED IT LIKE A BEGONIA.
STILL, IN LIGHT OF CERTAIN PERSONALITY QUIRKS I'VE ALREADY MENTIONED...
...IT SEEMED BEST TO TAKE THINGS SLOW UNTIL, WELL...
TOLAND! GINGER! COME ON OUT! MAVIS AN' ME ARE GETTIN' A YEN FOR BARBEQUE!
IT'S GREAT TO SEE YA AGAIN, OL' BUDDY. AN' GINGER—HEY, WELCOME TO THE GANG!
IT'S GREAT TO SEE YOU, TOO, RILEY. WELCOME HOME!
...JUST UNTIL!

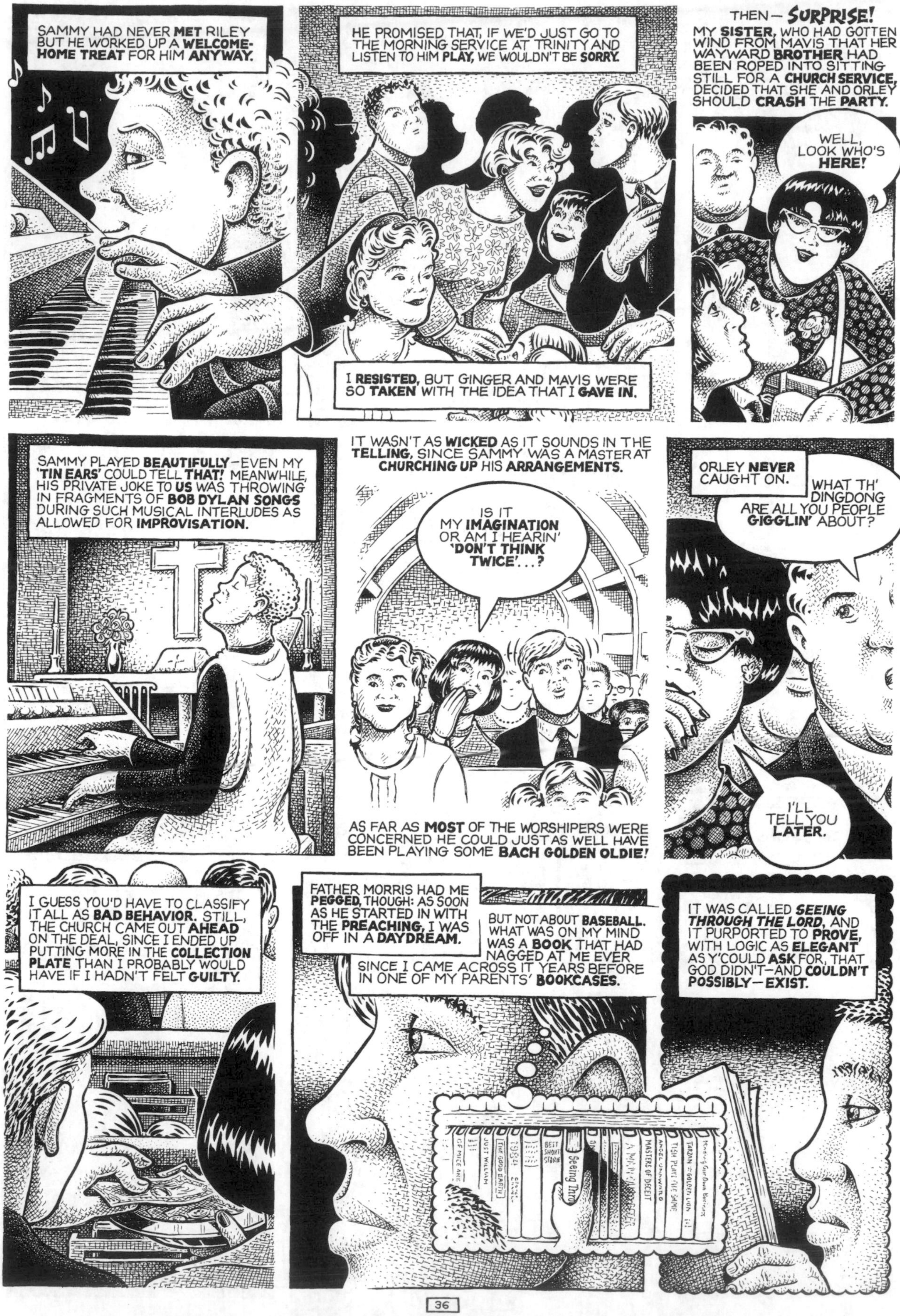
SAMMY HAD NEVER MET RILEY BUT HE WORKED UP A WELCOME-HOME TREAT FOR HIM ANYWAY.
HE PROMISED THAT, IF WE'D JUST GO TO THE MORNING SERVICE AT TRINITY AND LISTEN TO HIM PLAY, WE WOULDN'T BE SORRY.
I RESISTED, BUT GINGER AND MAVIS WERE SO TAKEN WITH THE IDEA THAT I GAVE IN.
THEN — SURPRISE!
MY SISTER, WHO HAD GOTTEN WIND FROM MAVIS THAT HER WAYWARD BROTHER HAD BEEN ROPED INTO SITTING STILL FOR A CHURCH SERVICE, DECIDED THAT SHE AND ORLEY SHOULD CRASH THE PARTY.
WELL, LOOK WHO'S HERE!
SAMMY PLAYED BEAUTIFULLY — EVEN MY 'TIN EARS' COULD TELL THAT! MEANWHILE, HIS PRIVATE JOKE TO US WAS THROWING IN FRAGMENTS OF BOB DYLAN SONGS DURING SUCH MUSICAL INTERLUDES AS ALLOWED FOR IMPROVISATION.
IT WASN'T AS WICKED AS IT SOUNDS IN THE TELLING, SINCE SAMMY WAS A MASTER AT CHURCHING UP HIS ARRANGEMENTS.
IS IT MY IMAGINATION OR AM I HEARIN' 'DON'T THINK TWICE'...?
AS FAR AS MOST OF THE WORSHIPERS WERE CONCERNED HE COULD JUST AS WELL HAVE BEEN PLAYING SOME BACH GOLDEN OLDIE!
ORLEY NEVER CAUGHT ON.
WHAT TH' DINGDONG ARE ALL YOU PEOPLE GIGGLIN' ABOUT?
I'LL TELL YOU LATER.
I GUESS YOU'D HAVE TO CLASSIFY IT ALL AS BAD BEHAVIOR. STILL, THE CHURCH CAME OUT AHEAD ON THE DEAL, SINCE I ENDED UP PUTTING MORE IN THE COLLECTION PLATE THAN I PROBABLY WOULD HAVE IF I HADN'T FELT GUILTY.
FATHER MORRIS HAD ME PEGGED, THOUGH: AS SOON AS HE STARTED IN WITH THE PREACHING, I WAS OFF IN A DAYDREAM.
BUT NOT ABOUT BASEBALL. WHAT WAS ON MY MIND WAS A BOOK THAT HAD NAGGED AT ME EVER SINCE I CAME ACROSS IT YEARS BEFORE IN ONE OF MY PARENTS' BOOKCASES.
IT WAS CALLED SEEING THROUGH THE LORD, AND IT PURPORTED TO PROVE, WITH LOGIC AS ELEGANT AS Y'COULD ASK FOR, THAT GOD DIDN'T — AND COULDN'T POSSIBLY — EXIST.

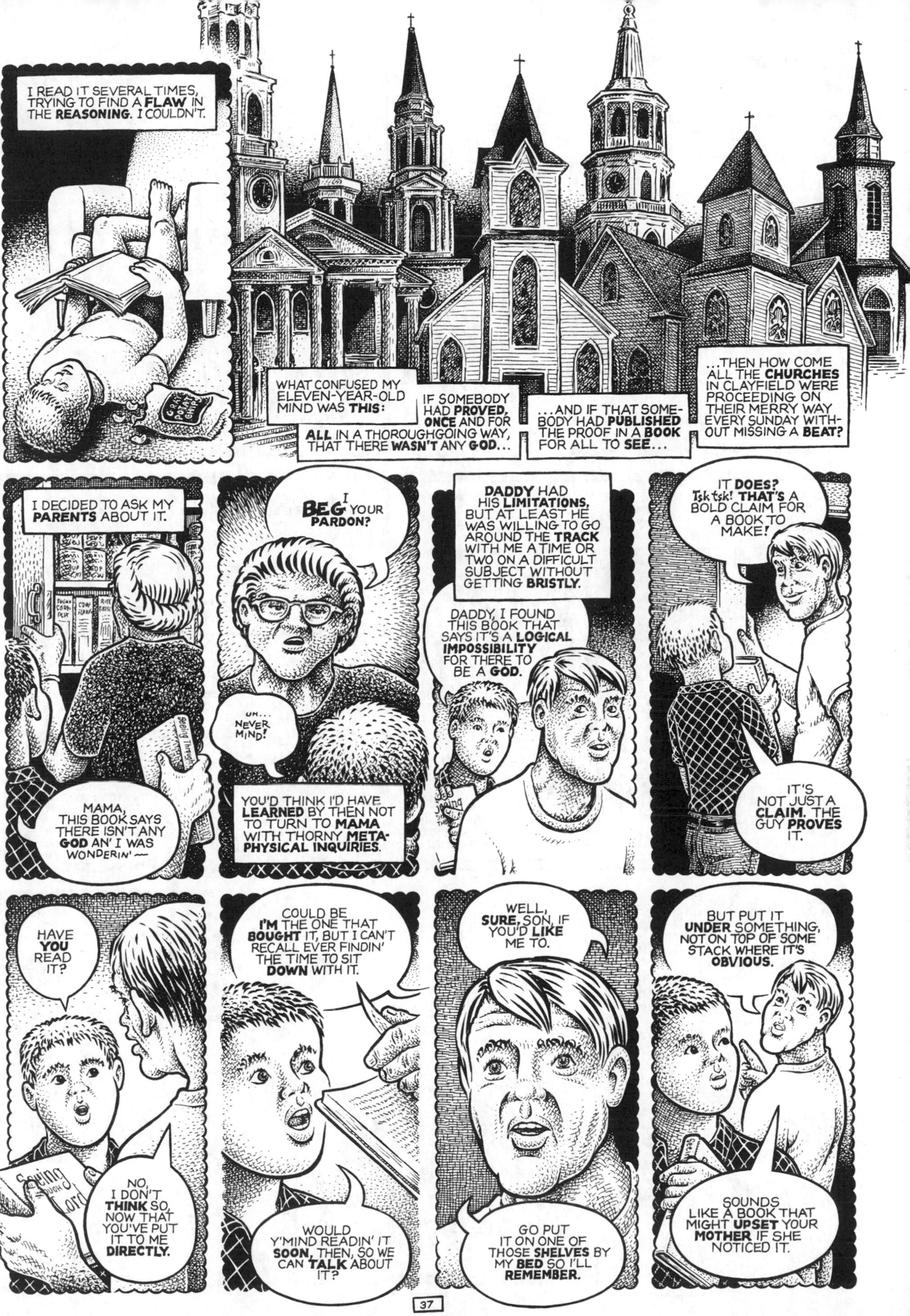
I READ IT SEVERAL TIMES, TRYING TO FIND A FLAW IN THE REASONING. I COULDN'T.
WHAT CONFUSED MY ELEVEN-YEAR-OLD MIND WAS THIS:
IF SOMEBODY HAD PROVED, ONCE AND FOR ALL IN A THOROUGHGOING WAY, THAT THERE WASN'T ANY GOD...
...AND IF THAT SOMEBODY HAD PUBLISHED THE PROOF IN A BOOK FOR ALL TO SEE...
...THEN HOW COME ALL THE CHURCHES IN CLAYFIELD WERE PROCEEDING ON THEIR MERRY WAY EVERY SUNDAY WITHOUT MISSING A BEAT?
I DECIDED TO ASK MY PARENTS ABOUT IT.
MAMA, THIS BOOK SAYS THERE ISN'T ANY GOD AN' I WAS WONDERIN'—
I BEG YOUR PARDON?
UH... NEVER MIND!
YOU'D THINK I'D HAVE LEARNED BY THEN NOT TO TURN TO MAMA WITH THORNY METAPHYSICAL INQUIRIES.
DADDY HAD HIS LIMITATIONS, BUT AT LEAST HE WAS WILLING TO GO AROUND THE TRACK WITH ME A TIME OR TWO ON A DIFFICULT SUBJECT WITHOUT GETTING BRISTLY.
DADDY, I FOUND THIS BOOK THAT SAYS IT'S A LOGICAL IMPOSSIBILITY FOR THERE TO BE A GOD.
IT DOES? Tsk tsk! THAT'S A BOLD CLAIM FOR A BOOK TO MAKE!
IT'S NOT JUST A CLAIM. THE GUY PROVES IT.
HAVE YOU READ IT?
NO, I DON'T THINK SO, NOW THAT YOU'VE PUT IT TO ME DIRECTLY.
COULD BE I'M THE ONE THAT BOUGHT IT, BUT I CAN'T RECALL EVER FINDIN' THE TIME TO SIT DOWN WITH IT.
WOULD Y'MIND READIN' IT SOON, THEN, SO WE CAN TALK ABOUT IT?
WELL, SURE, SON, IF YOU'D LIKE ME TO.
GO PUT IT ON ONE OF THOSE SHELVES BY MY BED SO I'LL REMEMBER.
BUT PUT IT UNDER SOMETHING, NOT ON TOP OF SOME STACK WHERE IT'S OBVIOUS.
SOUNDS LIKE A BOOK THAT MIGHT UPSET YOUR MOTHER IF SHE NOTICED IT.

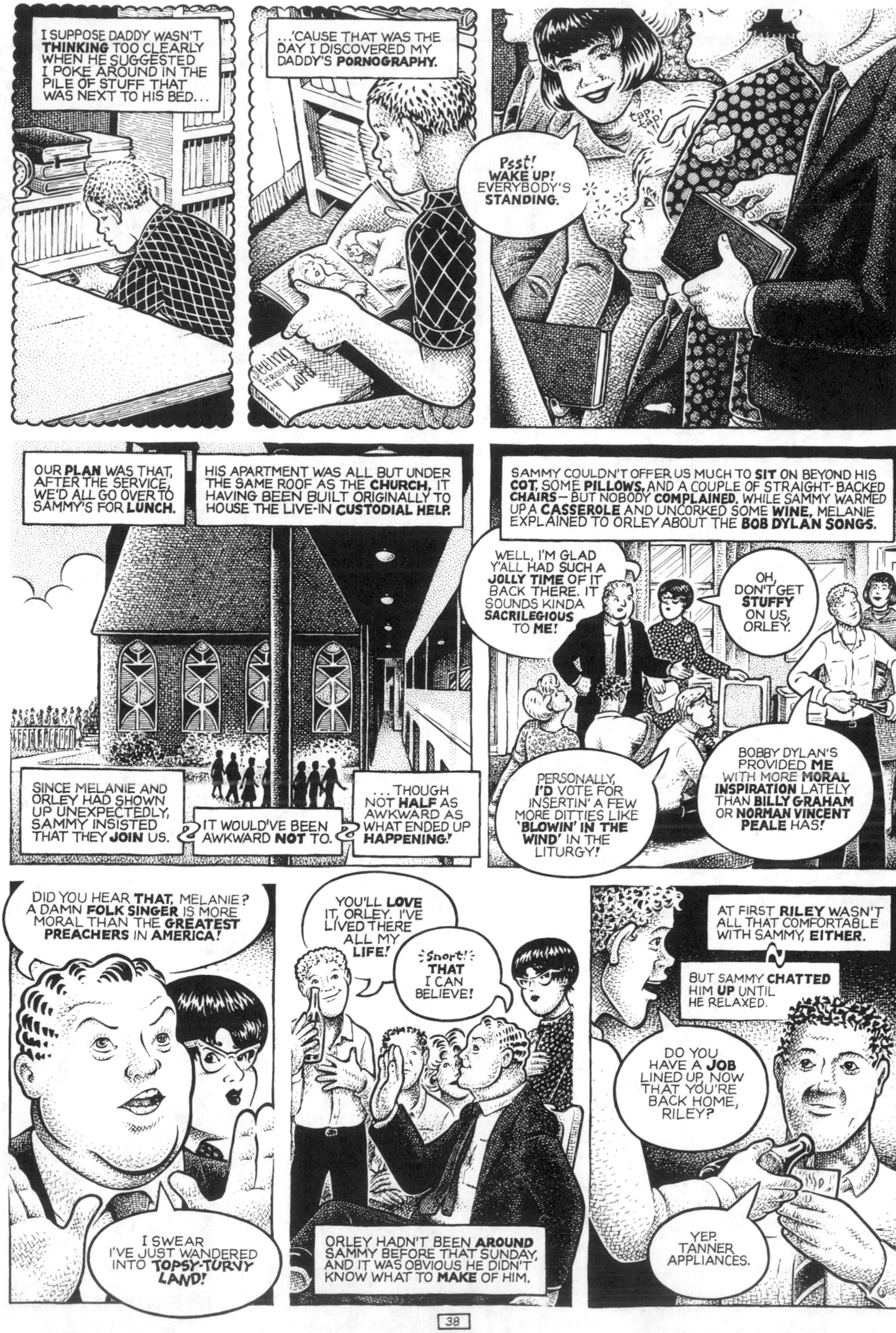

I SUPPOSE DADDY WASN'T THINKING TOO CLEARLY WHEN HE SUGGESTED I POKE AROUND IN THE PILE OF STUFF THAT WAS NEXT TO HIS BED...
...'CAUSE THAT WAS THE DAY I DISCOVERED MY DADDY'S PORNOGRAPHY.
Psst! WAKE UP! EVERYBODY'S STANDING.
tap, tap!
OUR PLAN WAS THAT, AFTER THE SERVICE, WE'D ALL GO OVER TO SAMMY'S FOR LUNCH.
HIS APARTMENT WAS ALL BUT UNDER THE SAME ROOF AS THE CHURCH, IT HAVING BEEN BUILT ORIGINALLY TO HOUSE THE LIVE-IN CUSTODIAL HELP.
SINCE MELANIE AND ORLEY HAD SHOWN UP UNEXPECTEDLY, SAMMY INSISTED THAT THEY JOIN US.
IT WOULD'VE BEEN AWKWARD NOT TO.
...THOUGH NOT HALF AS AWKWARD AS WHAT ENDED UP HAPPENING.
SAMMY COULDN'T OFFER US MUCH TO SIT ON BEYOND HIS COT, SOME PILLOWS, AND A COUPLE OF STRAIGHT-BACKED CHAIRS — BUT NOBODY COMPLAINED. WHILE SAMMY WARMED UP A CASSEROLE AND UNCORKED SOME WINE, MELANIE EXPLAINED TO ORLEY ABOUT THE BOB DYLAN SONGS.
WELL, I'M GLAD Y'ALL HAD SUCH A JOLLY TIME OF IT BACK THERE. IT SOUNDS KINDA SACRILEGIOUS TO ME!
OH, DON'T GET STUFFY ON US, ORLEY.
PERSONALLY, I'D VOTE FOR INSERTIN' A FEW MORE DITTIES LIKE 'BLOWIN' IN THE WIND' IN THE LITURGY!
BOBBY DYLAN'S PROVIDED ME WITH MORE MORAL INSPIRATION LATELY THAN BILLY GRAHAM OR NORMAN VINCENT PEALE HAS!
DID YOU HEAR THAT, MELANIE? A DAMN FOLK SINGER IS MORE MORAL THAN THE GREATEST PREACHERS IN AMERICA!
I SWEAR I'VE JUST WANDERED INTO TOPSY-TURVY LAND!
YOU'LL LOVE IT, ORLEY. I'VE LIVED THERE ALL MY LIFE!
Snort! THAT I CAN BELIEVE!
ORLEY HADN'T BEEN AROUND SAMMY BEFORE THAT SUNDAY, AND IT WAS OBVIOUS HE DIDN'T KNOW WHAT TO MAKE OF HIM.
AT FIRST RILEY WASN'T ALL THAT COMFORTABLE WITH SAMMY, EITHER.
BUT SAMMY CHATTED HIM UP UNTIL HE RELAXED.
DO YOU HAVE A JOB LINED UP, NOW THAT YOU'RE BACK HOME, RILEY?
YEP. TANNER APPLIANCES.

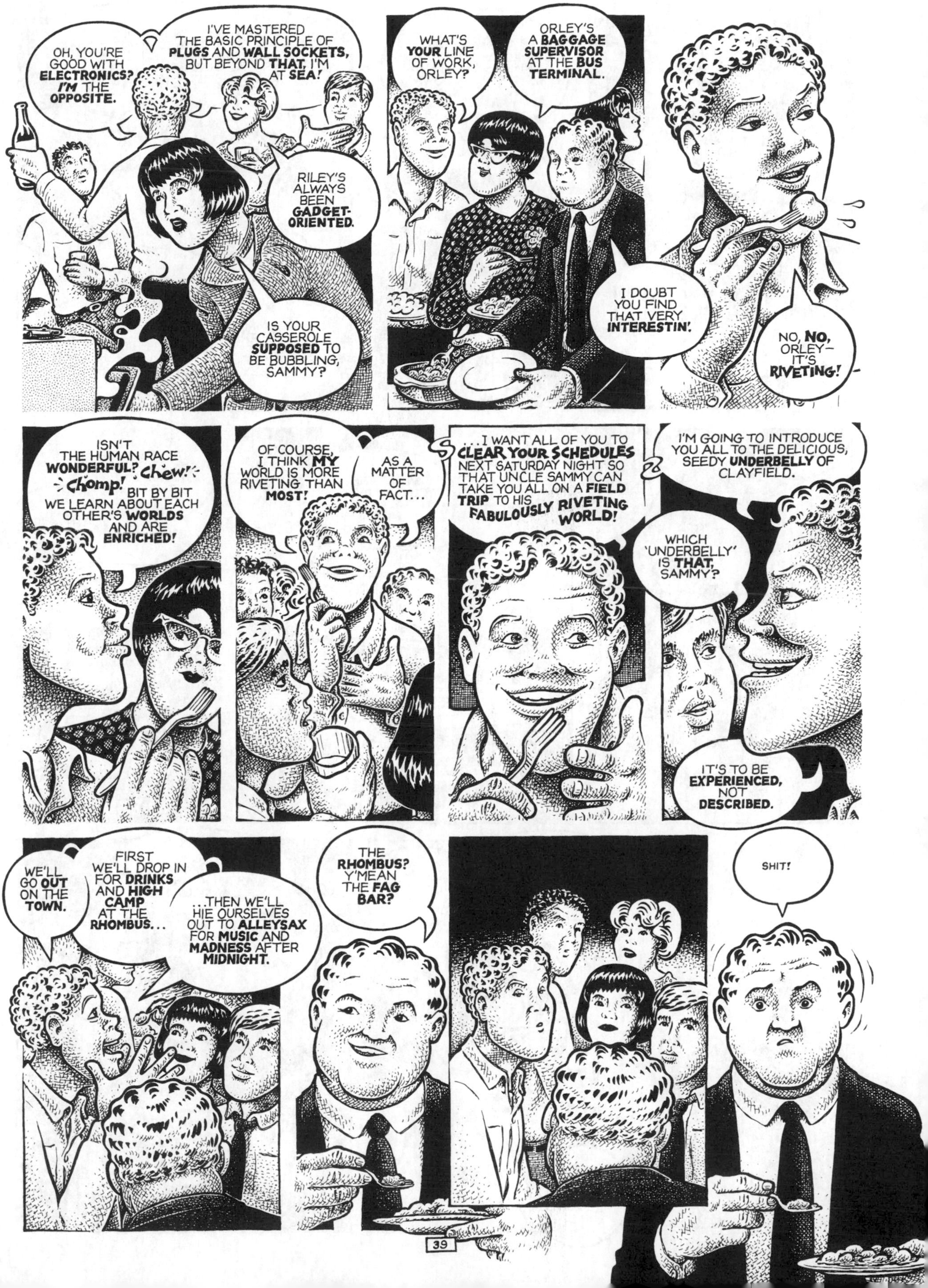

OH, YOU'RE GOOD WITH ELECTRONICS? I'M THE OPPOSITE.
I'VE MASTERED THE BASIC PRINCIPLE OF PLUGS AND WALL SOCKETS, BUT BEYOND THAT, I'M AT SEA!
RILEY'S ALWAYS BEEN GADGET-ORIENTED.
IS YOUR CASSEROLE SUPPOSED TO BE BUBBLING, SAMMY?
WHAT'S YOUR LINE OF WORK, ORLEY?
ORLEY'S A BAGGAGE SUPERVISOR AT THE BUS TERMINAL.
I DOUBT YOU FIND THAT VERY INTERESTIN'.
NO, NO, ORLEY— IT'S RIVETING!
ISN'T THE HUMAN RACE WONDERFUL? Chew! Chomp! BIT BY BIT WE LEARN ABOUT EACH OTHER'S WORLDS AND ARE ENRICHED!
OF COURSE, I THINK MY WORLD IS MORE RIVETING THAN MOST!
AS A MATTER OF FACT...
...I WANT ALL OF YOU TO CLEAR YOUR SCHEDULES NEXT SATURDAY NIGHT SO THAT UNCLE SAMMY CAN TAKE YOU ALL ON A FIELD TRIP TO HIS FABULOUSLY RIVETING WORLD!
I'M GOING TO INTRODUCE YOU ALL TO THE DELICIOUS, SEEDY UNDERBELLY OF CLAYFIELD.
WHICH 'UNDERBELLY' IS THAT, SAMMY?
IT'S TO BE EXPERIENCED, NOT DESCRIBED.
WE'LL GO OUT ON THE TOWN.
FIRST WE'LL DROP IN FOR DRINKS AND HIGH CAMP AT THE RHOMBUS...
...THEN WE'LL HIE OURSELVES OUT TO ALLEYSAX FOR MUSIC AND MADNESS AFTER MIDNIGHT.
THE RHOMBUS? Y'MEAN THE FAG BAR?
SHIT!

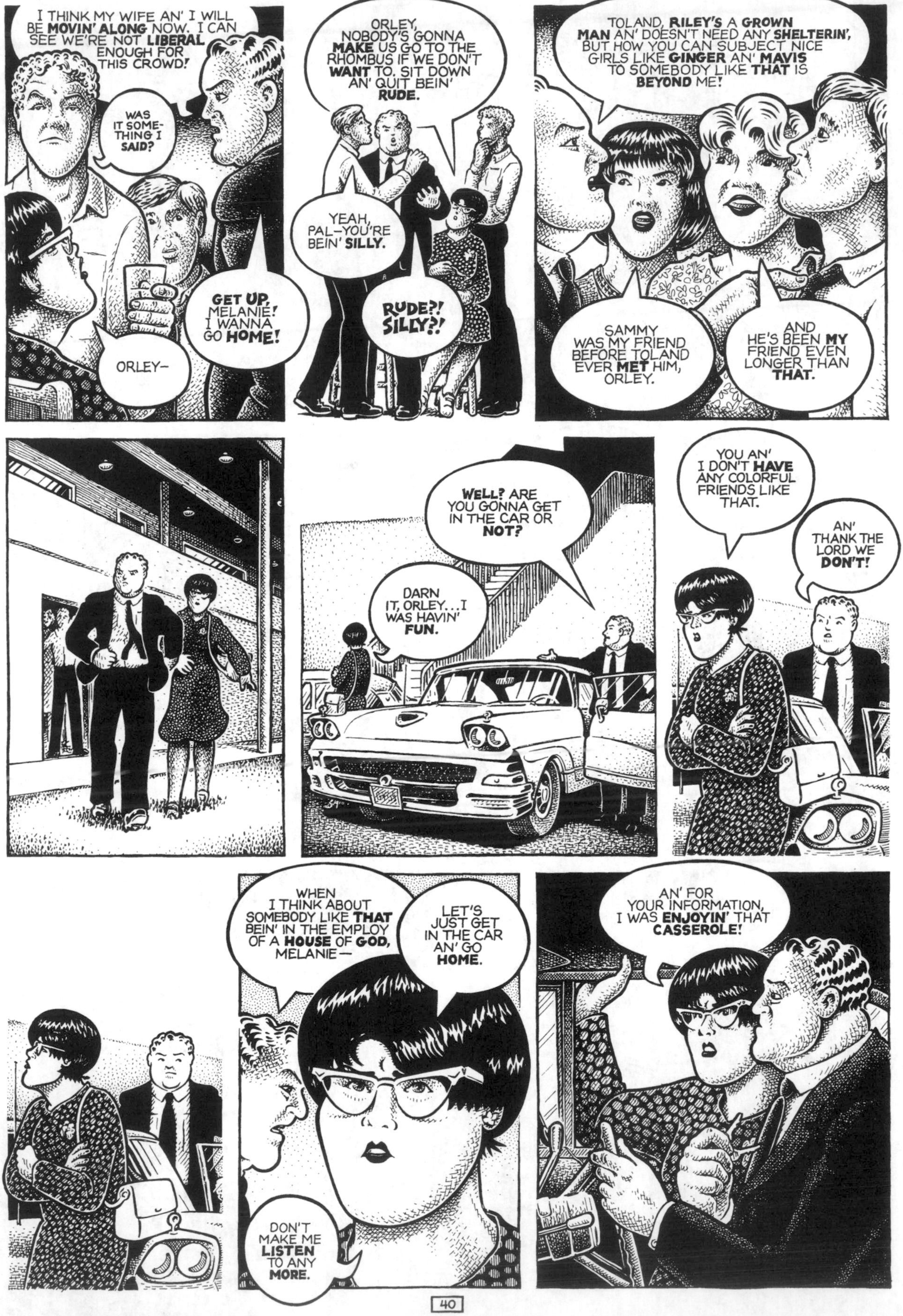

I THINK MY WIFE AN' I WILL BE MOVIN' ALONG NOW. I CAN SEE WE'RE NOT LIBERAL ENOUGH FOR THIS CROWD!
WAS IT SOMETHING I SAID?
GET UP, MELANIE! I WANNA GO HOME!
ORLEY—
ORLEY, NOBODY'S GONNA MAKE US GO TO THE RHOMBUS IF WE DON'T WANT TO. SIT DOWN AN' QUIT BEIN' RUDE.
YEAH, PAL—YOU'RE BEIN' SILLY.
RUDE?! SILLY?!
TOLAND, RILEY'S A GROWN MAN AN' DOESN'T NEED ANY SHELTERIN', BUT HOW YOU CAN SUBJECT NICE GIRLS LIKE GINGER AN' MAVIS TO SOMEBODY LIKE THAT IS BEYOND ME!
SAMMY WAS MY FRIEND BEFORE TOLAND EVER MET HIM, ORLEY.
AND HE'S BEEN MY FRIEND EVEN LONGER THAN THAT.
WELL? ARE YOU GONNA GET IN THE CAR OR NOT?
DARN IT, ORLEY... I WAS HAVIN' FUN.
YOU AN' I DON'T HAVE ANY COLORFUL FRIENDS LIKE THAT.
AN' THANK THE LORD WE DON'T!
WHEN I THINK ABOUT SOMEBODY LIKE THAT BEIN' IN THE EMPLOY OF A HOUSE OF GOD, MELANIE—
LET'S JUST GET IN THE CAR AN' GO HOME.
DON'T MAKE ME LISTEN TO ANY MORE.
AN' FOR YOUR INFORMATION, I WAS ENJOYIN' THAT CASSEROLE!

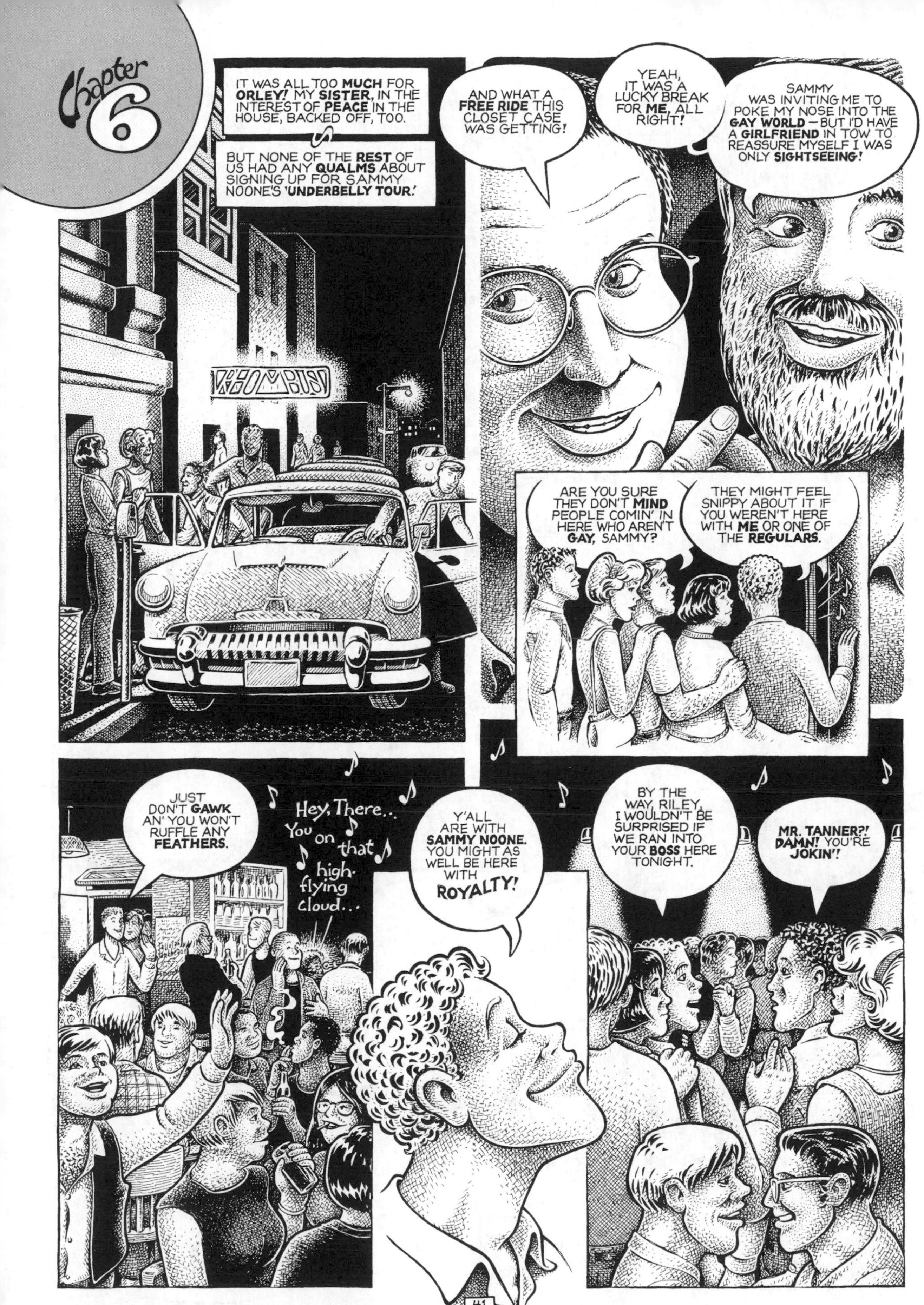
Chapter 6
IT WAS ALL TOO MUCH FOR ORLEY! MY SISTER, IN THE INTEREST OF PEACE IN THE HOUSE, BACKED OFF, TOO.
BUT NONE OF THE REST OF US HAD ANY QUALMS ABOUT SIGNING UP FOR SAMMY NOONE'S 'UNDERBELLY TOUR.'
AND WHAT A FREE RIDE THIS CLOSET CASE WAS GETTING!
YEAH, IT WAS A LUCKY BREAK FOR ME, ALL RIGHT!
SAMMY WAS INVITING ME TO POKE MY NOSE INTO THE GAY WORLD — BUT I'D HAVE A GIRLFRIEND IN TOW TO REASSURE MYSELF I WAS ONLY SIGHTSEEING!
ARE YOU SURE THEY DON'T MIND PEOPLE COMIN' IN HERE WHO AREN'T GAY, SAMMY?
THEY MIGHT FEEL SNIPPY ABOUT IT IF YOU WEREN'T HERE WITH ME OR ONE OF THE REGULARS.
JUST DON'T GAWK AN' YOU WON'T RUFFLE ANY FEATHERS.
Hey, There.. You on that high-flying cloud...
Y'ALL ARE WITH SAMMY NOONE. YOU MIGHT AS WELL BE HERE WITH ROYALTY!
BY THE WAY, RILEY, I WOULDN'T BE SURPRISED IF WE RAN INTO YOUR BOSS HERE TONIGHT.
MR. TANNER?! DAMN! YOU'RE JOKIN'!

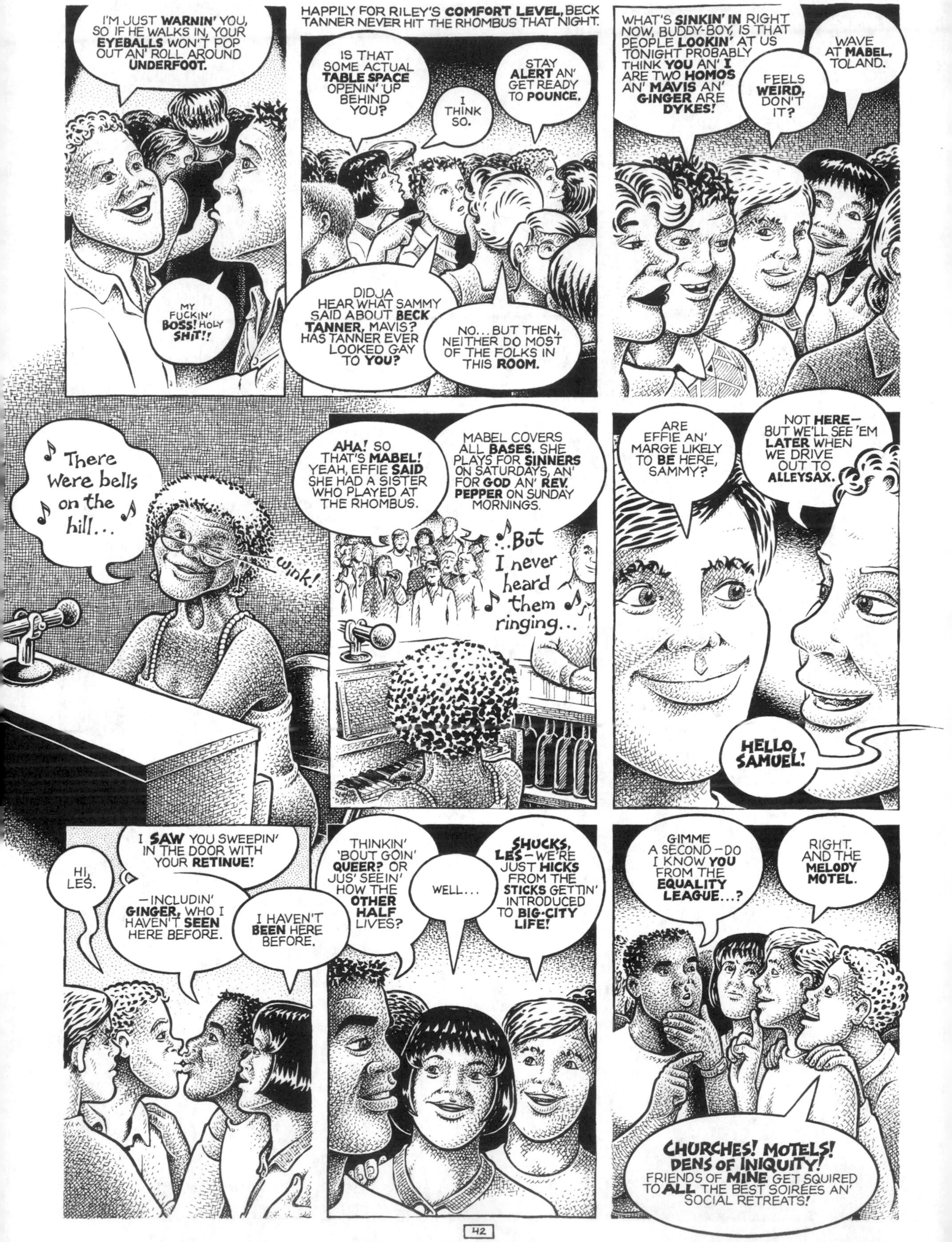

I'M JUST WARNIN' YOU, SO IF HE WALKS IN, YOUR EYEBALLS WON'T POP OUT AN' ROLL AROUND UNDERFOOT.
MY FUCKIN' BOSS! HOLY SHIT!!
HAPPILY FOR RILEY'S COMFORT LEVEL, BECK TANNER NEVER HIT THE RHOMBUS THAT NIGHT.
IS THAT SOME ACTUAL TABLE SPACE OPENIN' UP BEHIND YOU?
I THINK SO.
STAY ALERT AN' GET READY TO POUNCE.
DIDJA HEAR WHAT SAMMY SAID ABOUT BECK TANNER, MAVIS? HAS TANNER EVER LOOKED GAY TO YOU?
NO... BUT THEN, NEITHER DO MOST OF THE FOLKS IN THIS ROOM.
WHAT'S SINKIN' IN RIGHT NOW, BUDDY-BOY, IS THAT PEOPLE LOOKIN' AT US TONIGHT PROBABLY THINK YOU AN' I ARE TWO HOMOS AN' MAVIS AN' GINGER ARE DYKES!
FEELS WEIRD, DON'T IT?
WAVE AT MABEL, TOLAND.
♪ There were bells on the hill... ♪
wink!
AHA! SO THAT'S MABEL! YEAH, EFFIE SAID SHE HAD A SISTER WHO PLAYED AT THE RHOMBUS.
MABEL COVERS ALL BASES. SHE PLAYS FOR SINNERS ON SATURDAYS, AN' FOR GOD AN' REV. PEPPER ON SUNDAY MORNINGS.
♪ But I never heard them ringing... ♪
ARE EFFIE AN' MARGE LIKELY TO BE HERE, SAMMY?
NOT HERE— BUT WE'LL SEE 'EM LATER WHEN WE DRIVE OUT TO ALLEYSAX.
HELLO, SAMUEL!
HI, LES.
I SAW YOU SWEEPIN' IN THE DOOR WITH YOUR RETINUE!
—INCLUDIN' GINGER, WHO I HAVEN'T SEEN HERE BEFORE.
I HAVEN'T BEEN HERE BEFORE.
THINKIN' 'BOUT GOIN' QUEER? OR JUS' SEEIN' HOW THE OTHER HALF LIVES?
WELL...
SHUCKS, LES—WE'RE JUST HICKS FROM THE STICKS GETTIN' INTRODUCED TO BIG-CITY LIFE!
GIMME A SECOND—DO I KNOW YOU FROM THE EQUALITY LEAGUE...?
RIGHT. AND THE MELODY MOTEL.
CHURCHES! MOTELS! DENS OF INIQUITY! FRIENDS OF MINE GET SQUIRED TO ALL THE BEST SOIRÉES AN' SOCIAL RETREATS!

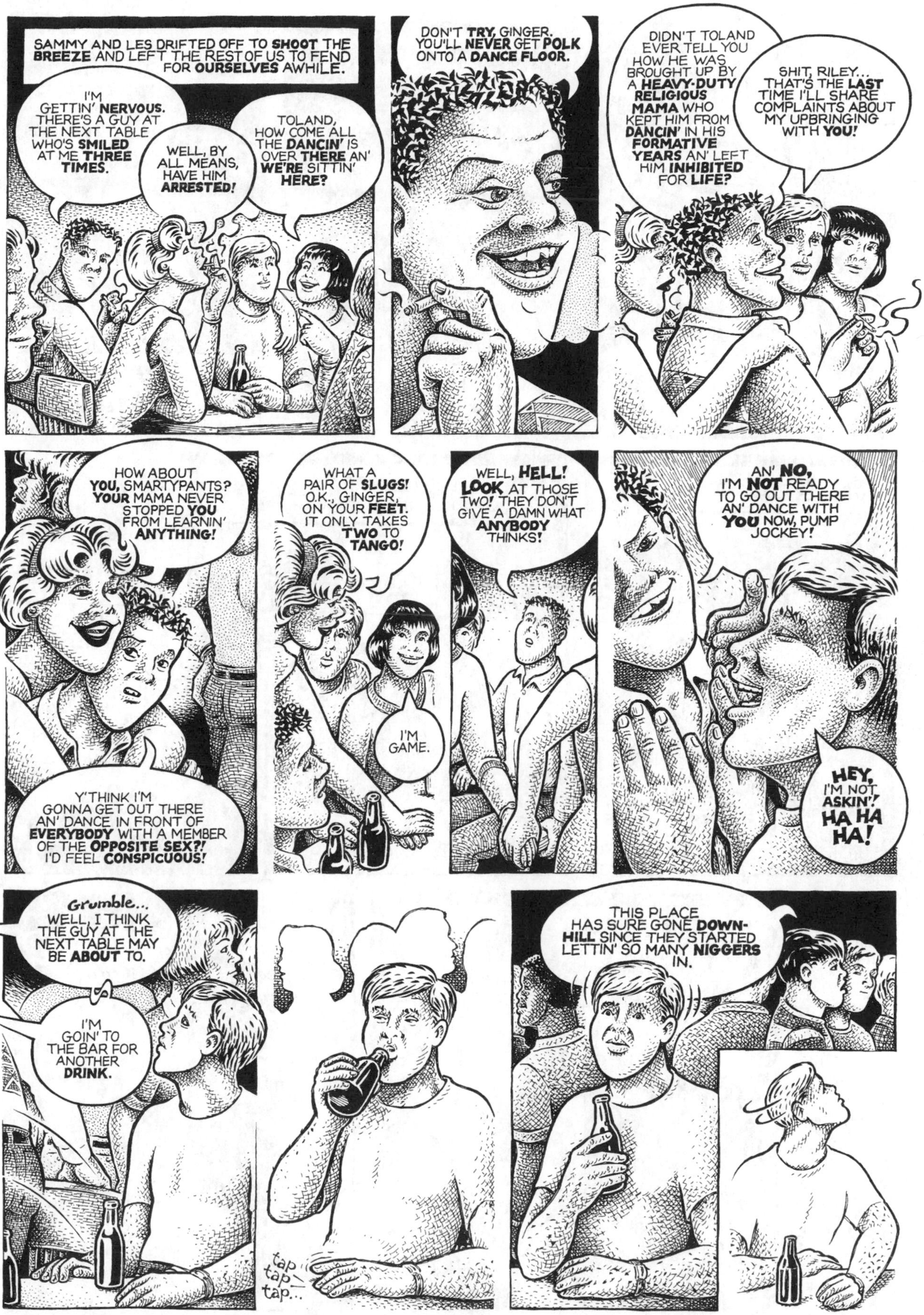
SAMMY AND LES DRIFTED OFF TO SHOOT THE BREEZE AND LEFT THE REST OF US TO FEND FOR OURSELVES AWHILE.
I'M GETTIN' NERVOUS. THERE'S A GUY AT THE NEXT TABLE WHO'S SMILED AT ME THREE TIMES.
WELL, BY ALL MEANS, HAVE HIM ARRESTED!
TOLAND, HOW COME ALL THE DANCIN' IS OVER THERE AN' WE'RE SITTIN' HERE?
DON'T TRY, GINGER. YOU'LL NEVER GET POLK ONTO A DANCE FLOOR.
DIDN'T TOLAND EVER TELL YOU HOW HE WAS BROUGHT UP BY A HEAVY-DUTY RELIGIOUS MAMA WHO KEPT HIM FROM DANCIN' IN HIS FORMATIVE YEARS AN' LEFT HIM INHIBITED FOR LIFE?
SHIT, RILEY... THAT'S THE LAST TIME I'LL SHARE COMPLAINTS ABOUT MY UPBRINGING WITH YOU!
HOW ABOUT YOU, SMARTYPANTS? YOUR MAMA NEVER STOPPED YOU FROM LEARNIN' ANYTHING!
Y'THINK I'M GONNA GET OUT THERE AN' DANCE IN FRONT OF EVERYBODY WITH A MEMBER OF THE OPPOSITE SEX?! I'D FEEL CONSPICUOUS!
WHAT A PAIR OF SLUGS! O.K., GINGER, ON YOUR FEET. IT ONLY TAKES TWO TO TANGO!
I'M GAME.
WELL, HELL! LOOK AT THOSE TWO! THEY DON'T GIVE A DAMN WHAT ANYBODY THINKS!
AN' NO, I'M NOT READY TO GO OUT THERE AN' DANCE WITH YOU NOW, PUMP JOCKEY!
HEY, I'M NOT ASKIN'! HA HA HA!
Grumble... WELL, I THINK THE GUY AT THE NEXT TABLE MAY BE ABOUT TO.
I'M GOIN' TO THE BAR FOR ANOTHER DRINK.
tap tap tap...
THIS PLACE HAS SURE GONE DOWN-HILL SINCE THEY STARTED LETTIN' SO MANY NIGGERS IN.

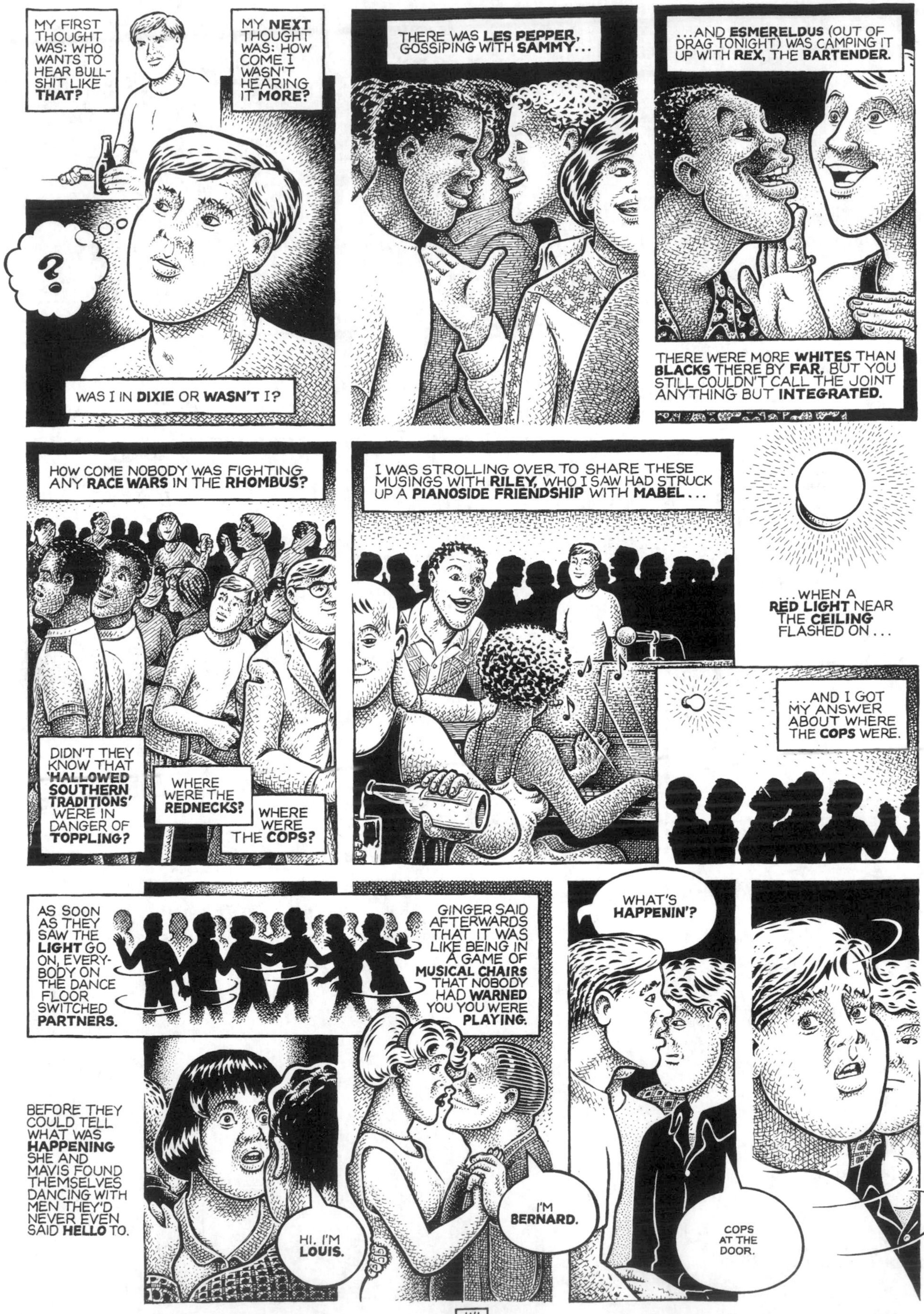
MY FIRST THOUGHT WAS: WHO WANTS TO HEAR BULL-SHIT LIKE THAT?
MY NEXT THOUGHT WAS: HOW COME I WASN'T HEARING IT MORE?
?
WAS I IN DIXIE OR WASN'T I?
THERE WAS LES PEPPER, GOSSIPING WITH SAMMY...
...AND ESMERELDUS (OUT OF DRAG TONIGHT) WAS CAMPING IT UP WITH REX, THE BARTENDER.
THERE WERE MORE WHITES THAN BLACKS THERE BY FAR, BUT YOU STILL COULDN'T CALL THE JOINT ANYTHING BUT INTEGRATED.
HOW COME NOBODY WAS FIGHTING ANY RACE WARS IN THE RHOMBUS?
DIDN'T THEY KNOW THAT 'HALLOWED SOUTHERN TRADITIONS' WERE IN DANGER OF TOPPLING?
WHERE WERE THE REDNECKS?
WHERE WERE THE COPS?
I WAS STROLLING OVER TO SHARE THESE MUSINGS WITH RILEY, WHO I SAW HAD STRUCK UP A PIANOSIDE FRIENDSHIP WITH MABEL...
...WHEN A RED LIGHT NEAR THE CEILING FLASHED ON...
...AND I GOT MY ANSWER ABOUT WHERE THE COPS WERE.
AS SOON AS THEY SAW THE LIGHT GO ON, EVERY-BODY ON THE DANCE FLOOR SWITCHED PARTNERS.
GINGER SAID AFTERWARDS THAT IT WAS LIKE BEING IN A GAME OF MUSICAL CHAIRS THAT NOBODY HAD WARNED YOU YOU WERE PLAYING.
BEFORE THEY COULD TELL WHAT WAS HAPPENING SHE AND MAVIS FOUND THEMSELVES DANCING WITH MEN THEY'D NEVER EVEN SAID HELLO TO.
HI. I'M LOUIS.
I'M BERNARD.
WHAT'S HAPPENIN'?
COPS AT THE DOOR.

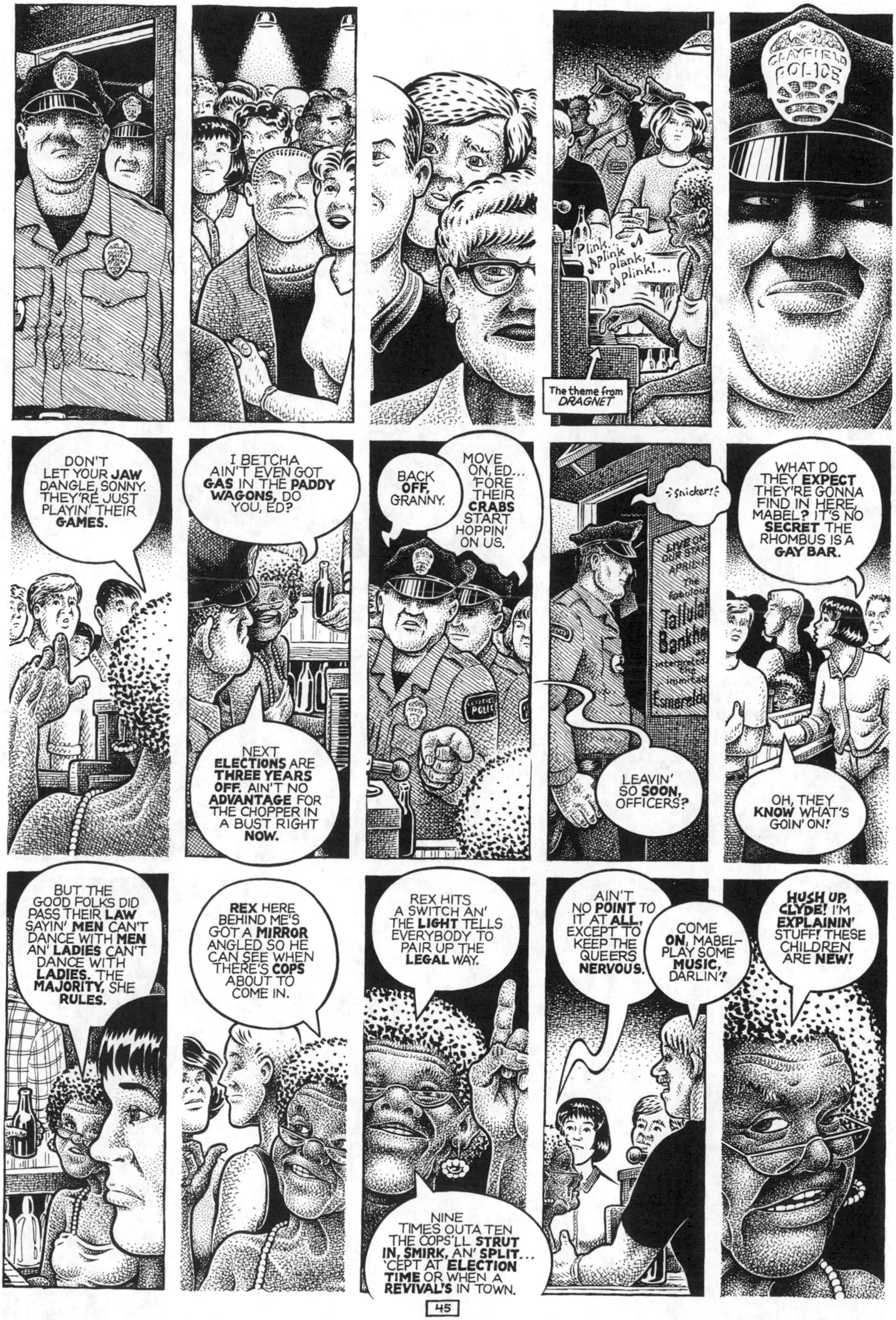
GRAYFIELD POLICE
Plink plink plank, plink!...
The theme from DRAGNET
DON'T LET YOUR JAW DANGLE, SONNY. THEY'RE JUST PLAYIN' THEIR GAMES.
I BETCHA AIN'T EVEN GOT GAS IN THE PADDY WAGONS, DO YOU, ED?
NEXT ELECTIONS ARE THREE YEARS OFF. AIN'T NO ADVANTAGE FOR THE CHOPPER IN A BUST RIGHT NOW.
BACK OFF, GRANNY.
MOVE ON, ED... 'FORE THEIR CRABS START HOPPIN' ON US.
-Snicker!-
LEAVIN' SO SOON, OFFICERS?
WHAT DO THEY EXPECT THEY'RE GONNA FIND IN HERE, MABEL? IT'S NO SECRET THE RHOMBUS IS A GAY BAR.
OH, THEY KNOW WHAT'S GOIN' ON!
BUT THE GOOD FOLKS DID PASS THEIR LAW SAYIN' MEN CAN'T DANCE WITH MEN AN' LADIES CAN'T DANCE WITH LADIES. THE MAJORITY, SHE RULES.
REX HERE BEHIND ME'S GOT A MIRROR ANGLED SO HE CAN SEE WHEN THERE'S COPS ABOUT TO COME IN.
REX HITS A SWITCH AN' THE LIGHT TELLS EVERYBODY TO PAIR UP THE LEGAL WAY.
NINE TIMES OUTA TEN THE COPS'LL STRUT IN, SMIRK, AN' SPLIT... 'CEPT AT ELECTION TIME OR WHEN A REVIVAL'S IN TOWN.
AIN'T NO POINT TO IT AT ALL, EXCEPT TO KEEP THE QUEERS NERVOUS.
COME ON, MABEL- PLAY SOME MUSIC, DARLIN'!
HUSH UP, CLYDE! I'M EXPLAININ' STUFF! THESE CHILDREN ARE NEW!

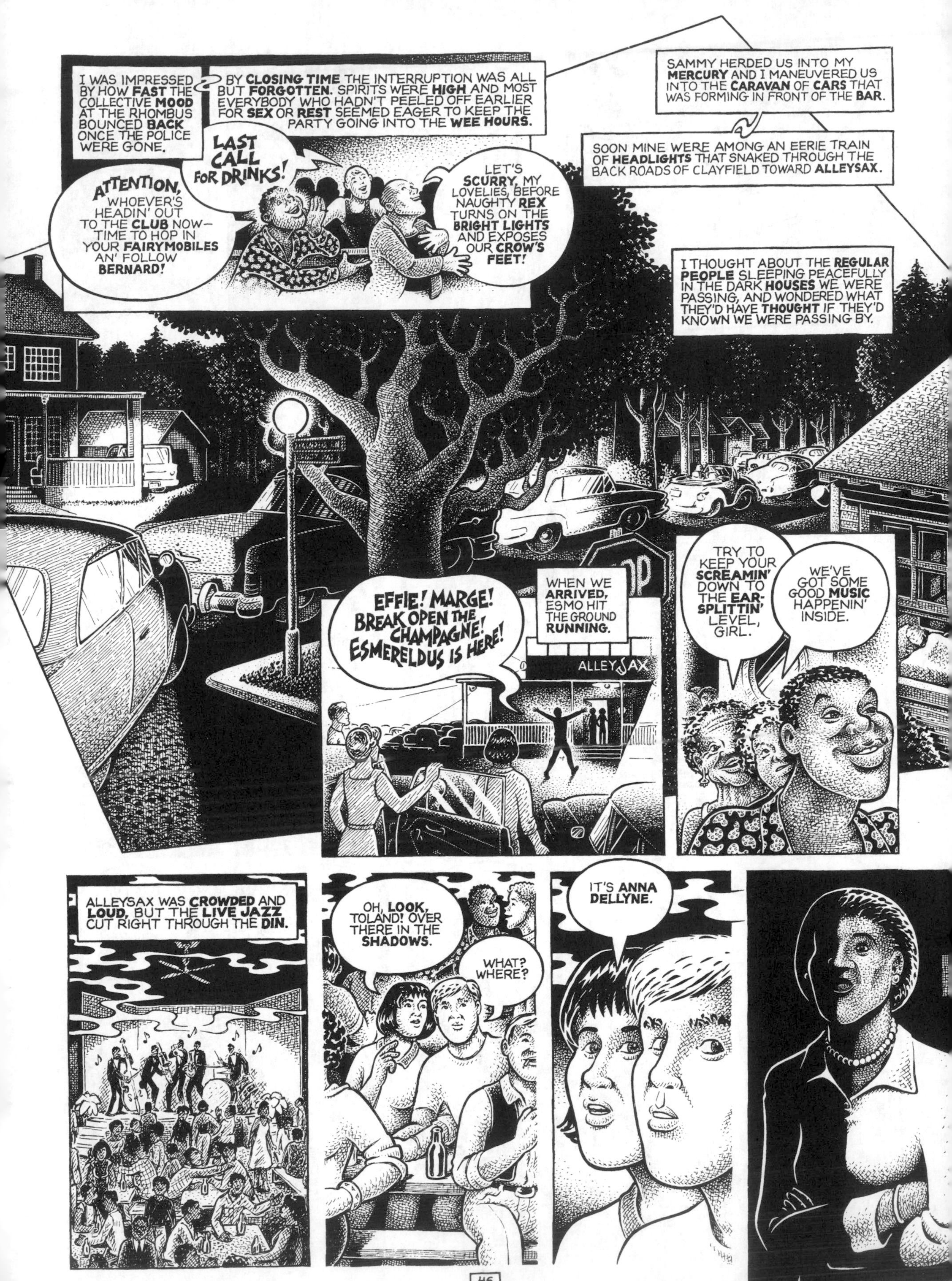
I WAS IMPRESSED BY HOW FAST THE COLLECTIVE MOOD AT THE RHOMBUS BOUNCED BACK ONCE THE POLICE WERE GONE.
BY CLOSING TIME THE INTERRUPTION WAS ALL BUT FORGOTTEN. SPIRITS WERE HIGH AND MOST EVERYBODY WHO HADN'T PEELED OFF EARLIER FOR SEX OR REST SEEMED EAGER TO KEEP THE PARTY GOING INTO THE WEE HOURS.
ATTENTION, WHOEVER'S HEADIN' OUT TO THE CLUB NOW— TIME TO HOP IN YOUR FAIRYMOBILES AN' FOLLOW BERNARD!
LAST CALL FOR DRINKS!
LET'S SCURRY, MY LOVELIES, BEFORE NAUGHTY REX TURNS ON THE BRIGHT LIGHTS AND EXPOSES OUR CROW'S FEET!
SAMMY HERDED US INTO MY MERCURY AND I MANEUVERED US INTO THE CARAVAN OF CARS THAT WAS FORMING IN FRONT OF THE BAR.
SOON MINE WERE AMONG AN EERIE TRAIN OF HEADLIGHTS THAT SNAKED THROUGH THE BACK ROADS OF CLAYFIELD TOWARD ALLEYSAX.
I THOUGHT ABOUT THE REGULAR PEOPLE SLEEPING PEACEFULLY IN THE DARK HOUSES WE WERE PASSING, AND WONDERED WHAT THEY'D HAVE THOUGHT IF THEY'D KNOWN WE WERE PASSING BY.
EFFIE! MARGE! BREAK OPEN THE CHAMPAGNE! ESMERELDUS IS HERE!
WHEN WE ARRIVED, ESMO HIT THE GROUND RUNNING.
ALLEY SAX
TRY TO KEEP YOUR SCREAMIN' DOWN TO THE EAR-SPLITTIN' LEVEL, GIRL.
WE'VE GOT SOME GOOD MUSIC HAPPENIN' INSIDE.
ALLEYSAX WAS CROWDED AND LOUD, BUT THE LIVE JAZZ CUT RIGHT THROUGH THE DIN.
OH, LOOK, TOLAND! OVER THERE IN THE SHADOWS.
WHAT? WHERE?
IT'S ANNA DELLYNE.

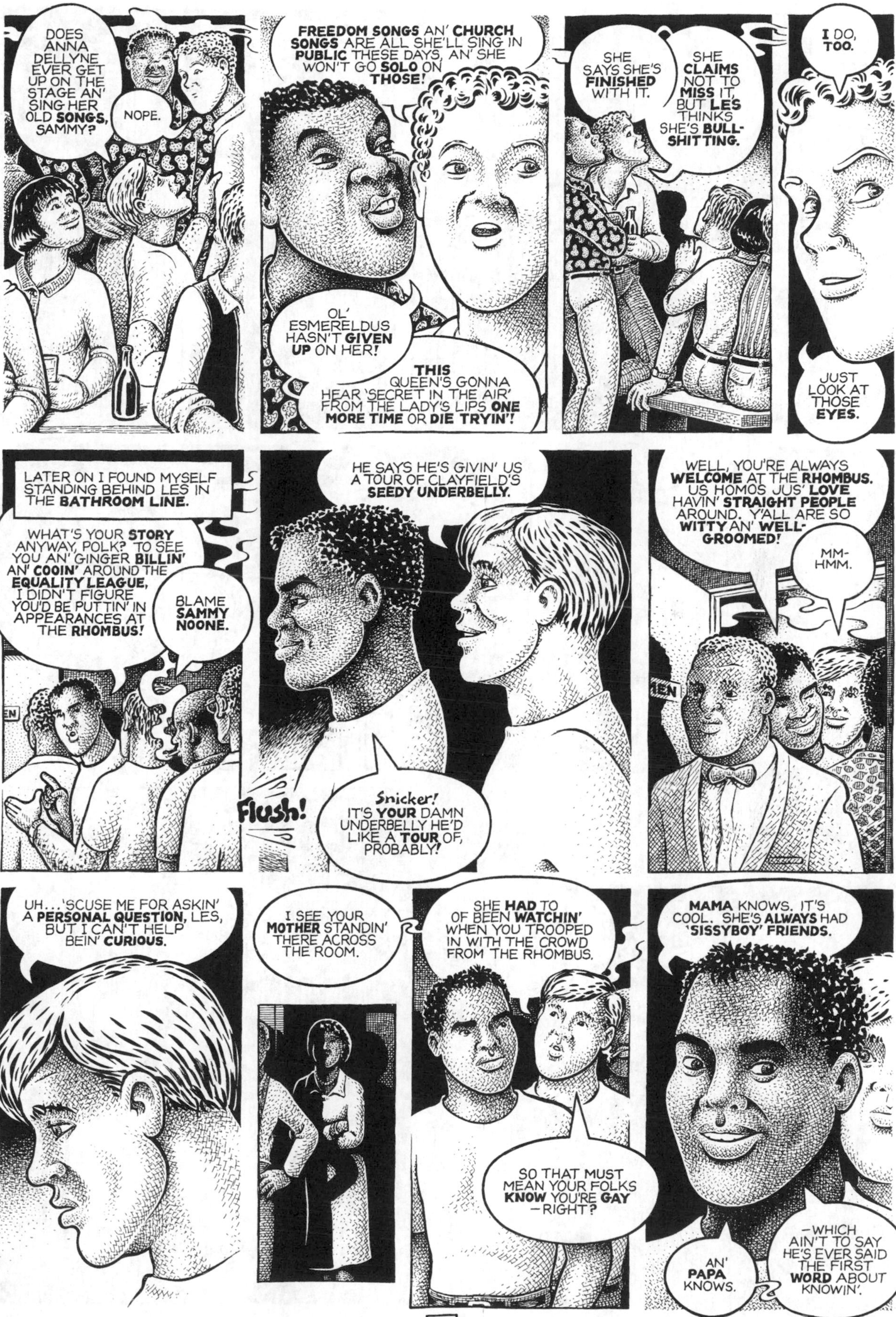
DOES ANNA DELLYNE EVER GET UP ON THE STAGE AN' SING HER OLD SONGS, SAMMY?
NOPE.
FREEDOM SONGS AN' CHURCH SONGS ARE ALL SHE'LL SING IN PUBLIC THESE DAYS, AN' SHE WON'T GO SOLO ON THOSE!
OL' ESMERELDUS HASN'T GIVEN UP ON HER!
THIS QUEEN'S GONNA HEAR 'SECRET IN THE AIR' FROM THE LADY'S LIPS ONE MORE TIME OR DIE TRYIN'!
SHE SAYS SHE'S FINISHED WITH IT.
SHE CLAIMS NOT TO MISS IT, BUT LES THINKS SHE'S BULL-SHITTING.
I DO, TOO.
JUST LOOK AT THOSE EYES.
LATER ON I FOUND MYSELF STANDING BEHIND LES IN THE BATHROOM LINE.
WHAT'S YOUR STORY ANYWAY, POLK? TO SEE YOU AN' GINGER BILLIN' AN' COOIN' AROUND THE EQUALITY LEAGUE, I DIDN'T FIGURE YOU'D BE PUTTIN' IN APPEARANCES AT THE RHOMBUS!
BLAME SAMMY NOONE.
HE SAYS HE'S GIVIN' US A TOUR OF CLAYFIELD'S SEEDY UNDERBELLY.
FLUSH!
Snicker! IT'S YOUR DAMN UNDERBELLY HE'D LIKE A TOUR OF, PROBABLY!
WELL, YOU'RE ALWAYS WELCOME AT THE RHOMBUS. US HOMOS JUS' LOVE HAVIN' STRAIGHT PEOPLE AROUND. Y'ALL ARE SO WITTY AN' WELL-GROOMED!
MM-HMM.
UH... 'SCUSE ME FOR ASKIN' A PERSONAL QUESTION, LES, BUT I CAN'T HELP BEIN' CURIOUS.
I SEE YOUR MOTHER STANDIN' THERE ACROSS THE ROOM.
SHE HAD TO OF BEEN WATCHIN' WHEN YOU TROOPED IN WITH THE CROWD FROM THE RHOMBUS.
SO THAT MUST MEAN YOUR FOLKS KNOW YOU'RE GAY —RIGHT?
MAMA KNOWS. IT'S COOL. SHE'S ALWAYS HAD 'SISSYBOY' FRIENDS.
AN' PAPA KNOWS.
—WHICH AIN'T TO SAY HE'S EVER SAID THE FIRST WORD ABOUT KNOWIN'.

HE USED TO PUSH ME TO GET **MARRIED,** BUT HE'S LEARNED **THAT** AIN'T IN THE **CARDS.**

PAPA'S THE **PREACHER** IN THE FAMILY AN' **I'M** THE **FAGGOT.**

MARTIN LUTHER KING **HIMSELF** COULD WALK UP AN' SAY TO ME, 'LES, YOU GOTTA **QUIT** BEIN' **GAY!'**...

...AN' I'D SAY TO HIM, '**SURE THING,** DR. KING—

—JUST AS SOON AS **YOU** STOP BEIN' **NEGRO!'**

Flush!

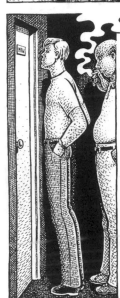

Flush!

I BEG YOUR PARDON...IF **YOU'RE** NOT READY TO USE THE **ROOM** THERE, I THINK MAYBE **I'D** LIKE TO.

OH. SORRY.

WELCOME BACK FROM THE **ARMY,** HON.

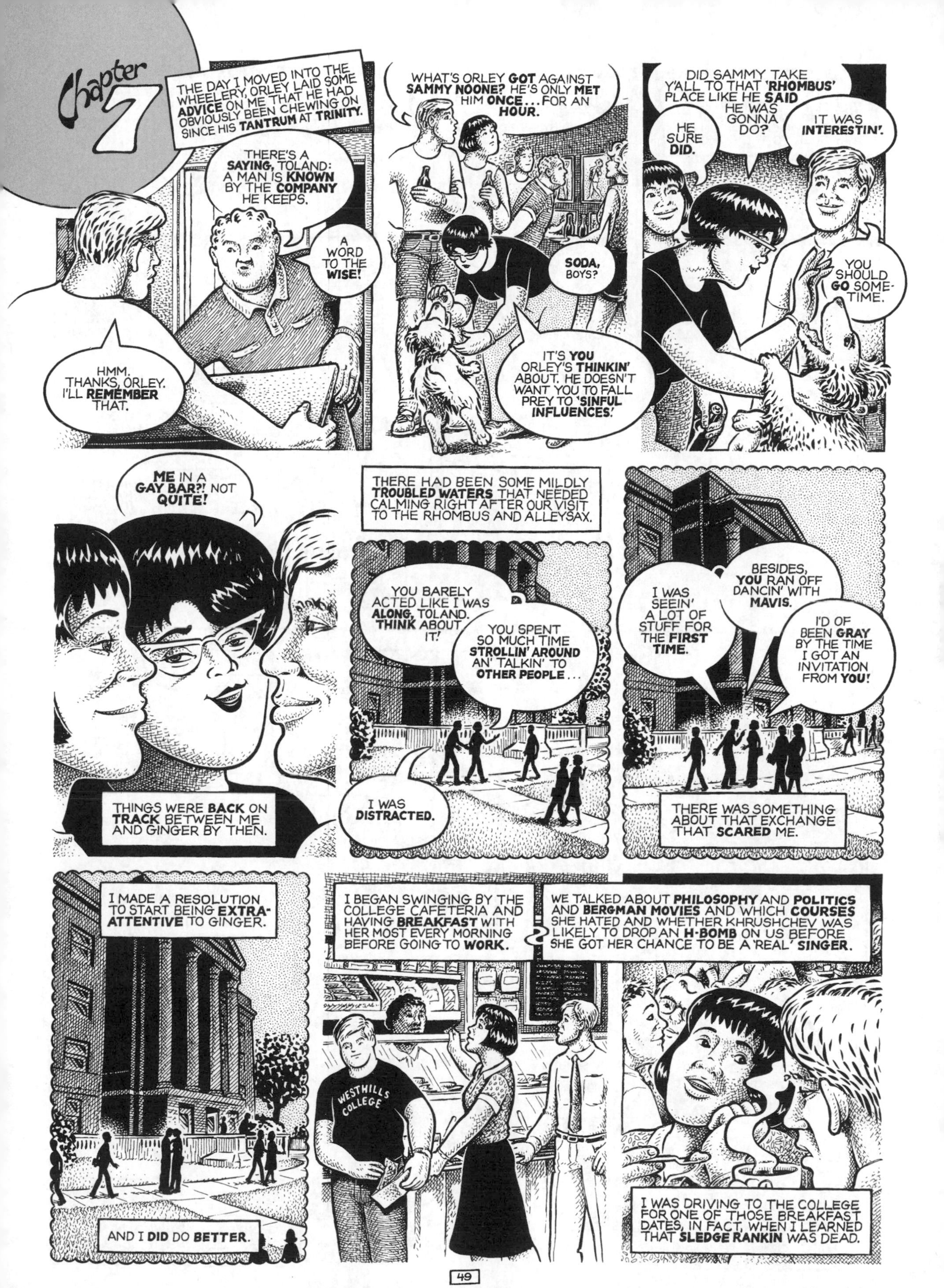
Chapter 7
THE DAY I MOVED INTO THE WHEELERY, ORLEY LAID SOME ADVICE ON ME THAT HE HAD OBVIOUSLY BEEN CHEWING ON SINCE HIS TANTRUM AT TRINITY.
THERE'S A SAYING, TOLAND: A MAN IS KNOWN BY THE COMPANY HE KEEPS.
A WORD TO THE WISE!
HMM. THANKS, ORLEY. I'LL REMEMBER THAT.
WHAT'S ORLEY GOT AGAINST SAMMY NOONE? HE'S ONLY MET HIM ONCE... FOR AN HOUR.
SODA, BOYS?
IT'S YOU ORLEY'S THINKIN' ABOUT. HE DOESN'T WANT YOU TO FALL PREY TO 'SINFUL INFLUENCES.'
DID SAMMY TAKE Y'ALL TO THAT 'RHOMBUS' PLACE LIKE HE SAID HE WAS GONNA DO?
HE SURE DID.
IT WAS INTERESTIN'.
YOU SHOULD GO SOMETIME.
ME IN A GAY BAR?! NOT QUITE!
THINGS WERE BACK ON TRACK BETWEEN ME AND GINGER BY THEN.
THERE HAD BEEN SOME MILDLY TROUBLED WATERS THAT NEEDED CALMING RIGHT AFTER OUR VISIT TO THE RHOMBUS AND ALLEYSAX.
YOU BARELY ACTED LIKE I WAS ALONG, TOLAND. THINK ABOUT IT!
YOU SPENT SO MUCH TIME STROLLIN' AROUND AN' TALKIN' TO OTHER PEOPLE...
I WAS DISTRACTED.
I WAS SEEIN' A LOT OF STUFF FOR THE FIRST TIME.
BESIDES, YOU RAN OFF DANCIN' WITH MAVIS.
I'D OF BEEN GRAY BY THE TIME I GOT AN INVITATION FROM YOU!
THERE WAS SOMETHING ABOUT THAT EXCHANGE THAT SCARED ME.
I MADE A RESOLUTION TO START BEING EXTRA-ATTENTIVE TO GINGER.
AND I DID DO BETTER.
I BEGAN SWINGING BY THE COLLEGE CAFETERIA AND HAVING BREAKFAST WITH HER MOST EVERY MORNING BEFORE GOING TO WORK.
WESTHILLS COLLEGE
WE TALKED ABOUT PHILOSOPHY AND POLITICS AND BERGMAN MOVIES AND WHICH COURSES SHE HATED AND WHETHER KHRUSHCHEV WAS LIKELY TO DROP AN H-BOMB ON US BEFORE SHE GOT HER CHANCE TO BE A 'REAL' SINGER.
I WAS DRIVING TO THE COLLEGE FOR ONE OF THOSE BREAKFAST DATES, IN FACT, WHEN I LEARNED THAT SLEDGE RANKIN WAS DEAD.

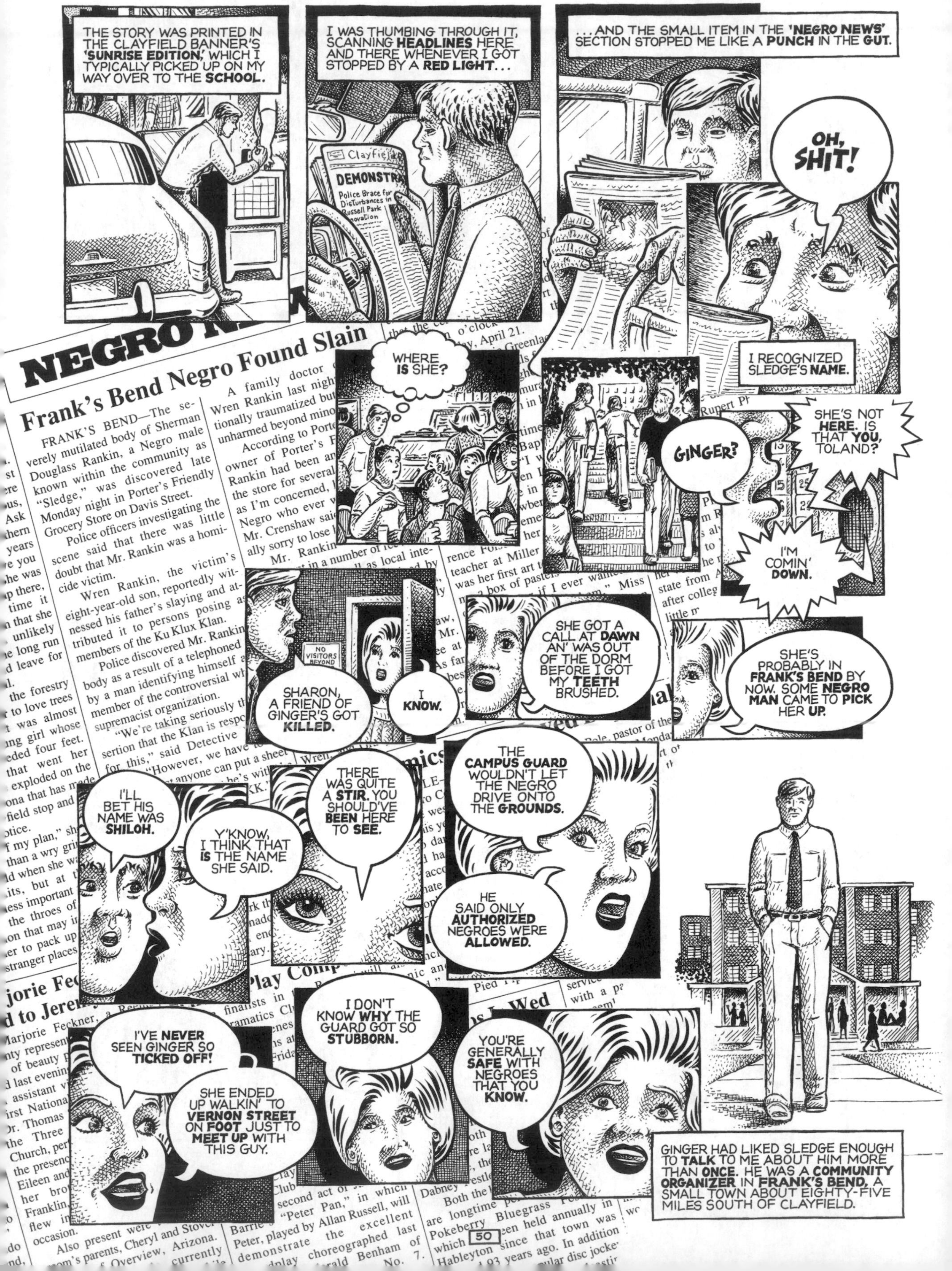
THE STORY WAS PRINTED IN THE CLAYFIELD BANNER'S 'SUNRISE EDITION,' WHICH I TYPICALLY PICKED UP ON MY WAY OVER TO THE SCHOOL.
I WAS THUMBING THROUGH IT, SCANNING HEADLINES HERE AND THERE WHENEVER I GOT STOPPED BY A RED LIGHT...
DEMONSTRA
Police Brace for Disturbances in Russell Park Renovation
...AND THE SMALL ITEM IN THE 'NEGRO NEWS' SECTION STOPPED ME LIKE A PUNCH IN THE GUT.
OH, SHIT!
I RECOGNIZED SLEDGE'S NAME.
NEGRO N
Frank's Bend Negro Found Slain
FRANK'S BEND—The severely mutilated body of Sherman Douglass Rankin, a Negro male known within the community as "Sledge," was discovered late Monday night in Porter's Friendly Grocery Store on Davis Street.
Police officers investigating the scene said that there was little doubt that Mr. Rankin was a homicide victim.
Wren Rankin, the victim's eight-year-old son, reportedly witnessed his father's slaying and attributed it to persons posing as members of the Ku Klux Klan.
WHERE IS SHE?
GINGER?
SHE'S NOT HERE. IS THAT YOU, TOLAND?
I'M COMIN' DOWN.
NO VISITORS BEYOND
SHARON, A FRIEND OF GINGER'S GOT KILLED.
I KNOW.
SHE GOT A CALL AT DAWN AN' WAS OUT OF THE DORM BEFORE I GOT MY TEETH BRUSHED.
SHE'S PROBABLY IN FRANK'S BEND BY NOW. SOME NEGRO MAN CAME TO PICK HER UP.
I'LL BET HIS NAME WAS SHILOH.
Y'KNOW, I THINK THAT IS THE NAME SHE SAID.
THERE WAS QUITE A STIR. YOU SHOULD'VE BEEN HERE TO SEE.
THE CAMPUS GUARD WOULDN'T LET THE NEGRO DRIVE ONTO THE GROUNDS.
HE SAID ONLY AUTHORIZED NEGROES WERE ALLOWED.
I'VE NEVER SEEN GINGER SO TICKED OFF!
SHE ENDED UP WALKIN' TO VERNON STREET ON FOOT JUST TO MEET UP WITH THIS GUY.
I DON'T KNOW WHY THE GUARD GOT SO STUBBORN.
YOU'RE GENERALLY SAFE WITH NEGROES THAT YOU KNOW.
GINGER HAD LIKED SLEDGE ENOUGH TO TALK TO ME ABOUT HIM MORE THAN ONCE. HE WAS A COMMUNITY ORGANIZER IN FRANK'S BEND, A SMALL TOWN ABOUT EIGHTY-FIVE MILES SOUTH OF CLAYFIELD.

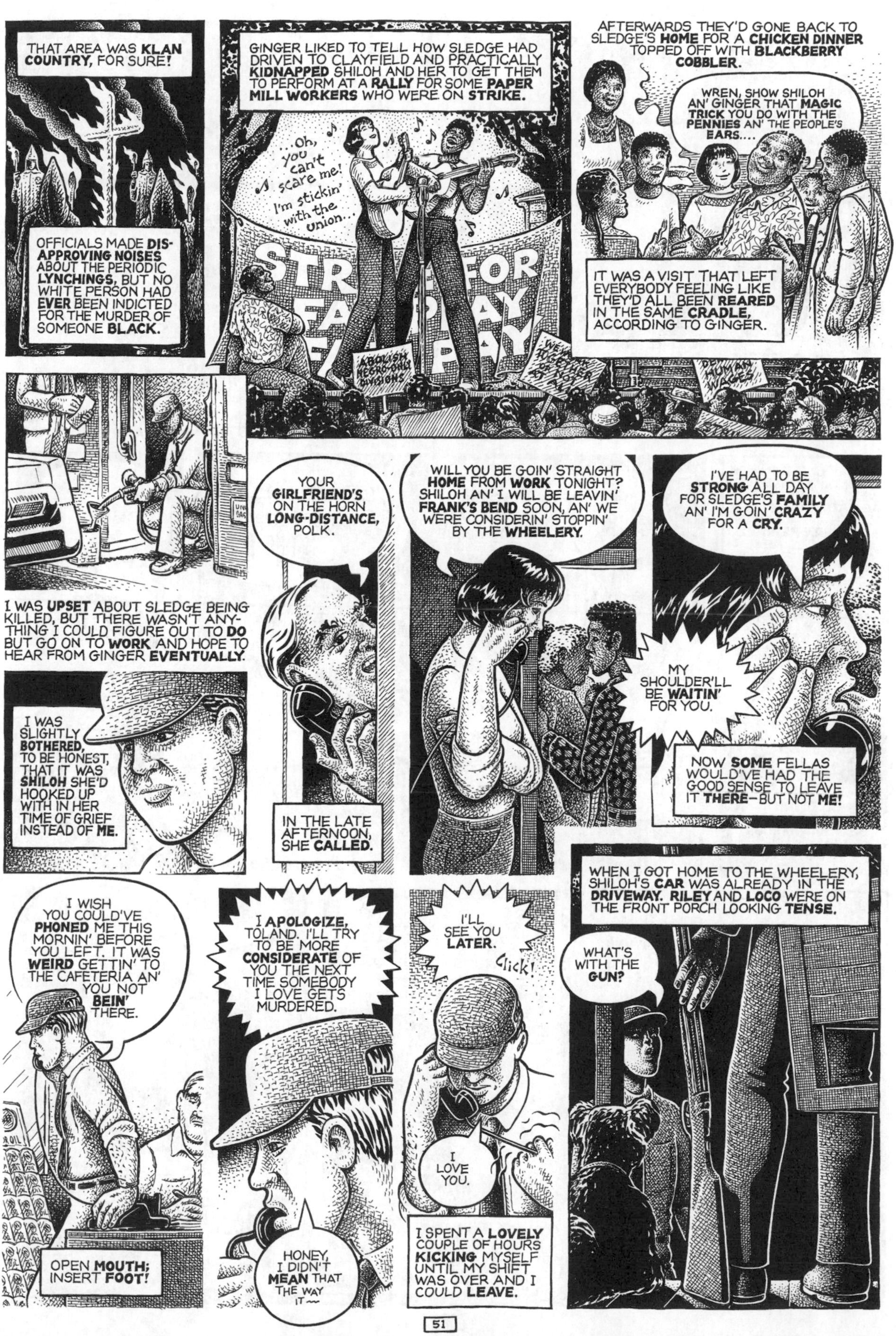
THAT AREA WAS KLAN COUNTRY, FOR SURE!
OFFICIALS MADE DISAPPROVING NOISES ABOUT THE PERIODIC LYNCHINGS, BUT NO WHITE PERSON HAD EVER BEEN INDICTED FOR THE MURDER OF SOMEONE BLACK.
GINGER LIKED TO TELL HOW SLEDGE HAD DRIVEN TO CLAYFIELD AND PRACTICALLY KIDNAPPED SHILOH AND HER TO GET THEM TO PERFORM AT A RALLY FOR SOME PAPER MILL WORKERS WHO WERE ON STRIKE.
...Oh, you can't scare me! I'm stickin' with the union...
ABOLISH NEGRO-ONLY DIVISIONS
AFTERWARDS THEY'D GONE BACK TO SLEDGE'S HOME FOR A CHICKEN DINNER TOPPED OFF WITH BLACKBERRY COBBLER.
WREN, SHOW SHILOH AN' GINGER THAT MAGIC TRICK YOU DO WITH THE PENNIES AN' THE PEOPLE'S EARS....
IT WAS A VISIT THAT LEFT EVERYBODY FEELING LIKE THEY'D ALL BEEN REARED IN THE SAME CRADLE, ACCORDING TO GINGER.
I WAS UPSET ABOUT SLEDGE BEING KILLED, BUT THERE WASN'T ANYTHING I COULD FIGURE OUT TO DO BUT GO ON TO WORK AND HOPE TO HEAR FROM GINGER EVENTUALLY.
I WAS SLIGHTLY BOTHERED, TO BE HONEST, THAT IT WAS SHILOH SHE'D HOOKED UP WITH IN HER TIME OF GRIEF INSTEAD OF ME.
YOUR GIRLFRIEND'S ON THE HORN LONG-DISTANCE, POLK.
IN THE LATE AFTERNOON, SHE CALLED.
WILL YOU BE GOIN' STRAIGHT HOME FROM WORK TONIGHT? SHILOH AN' I WILL BE LEAVIN' FRANK'S BEND SOON, AN' WE WERE CONSIDERIN' STOPPIN' BY THE WHEELERY.
I'VE HAD TO BE STRONG ALL DAY FOR SLEDGE'S FAMILY AN' I'M GOIN' CRAZY FOR A CRY.
MY SHOULDER'LL BE WAITIN' FOR YOU.
NOW SOME FELLAS WOULD'VE HAD THE GOOD SENSE TO LEAVE IT THERE—BUT NOT ME!
I WISH YOU COULD'VE PHONED ME THIS MORNIN' BEFORE YOU LEFT. IT WAS WEIRD GETTIN' TO THE CAFETERIA AN' YOU NOT BEIN' THERE.
OPEN MOUTH; INSERT FOOT!
I APOLOGIZE, TOLAND. I'LL TRY TO BE MORE CONSIDERATE OF YOU THE NEXT TIME SOMEBODY I LOVE GETS MURDERED.
HONEY, I DIDN'T MEAN THAT THE WAY IT~
I'LL SEE YOU LATER.
Click!
I LOVE YOU.
I SPENT A LOVELY COUPLE OF HOURS KICKING MYSELF UNTIL MY SHIFT WAS OVER AND I COULD LEAVE.
WHEN I GOT HOME TO THE WHEELERY, SHILOH'S CAR WAS ALREADY IN THE DRIVEWAY. RILEY AND LOCO WERE ON THE FRONT PORCH LOOKING TENSE.
WHAT'S WITH THE GUN?

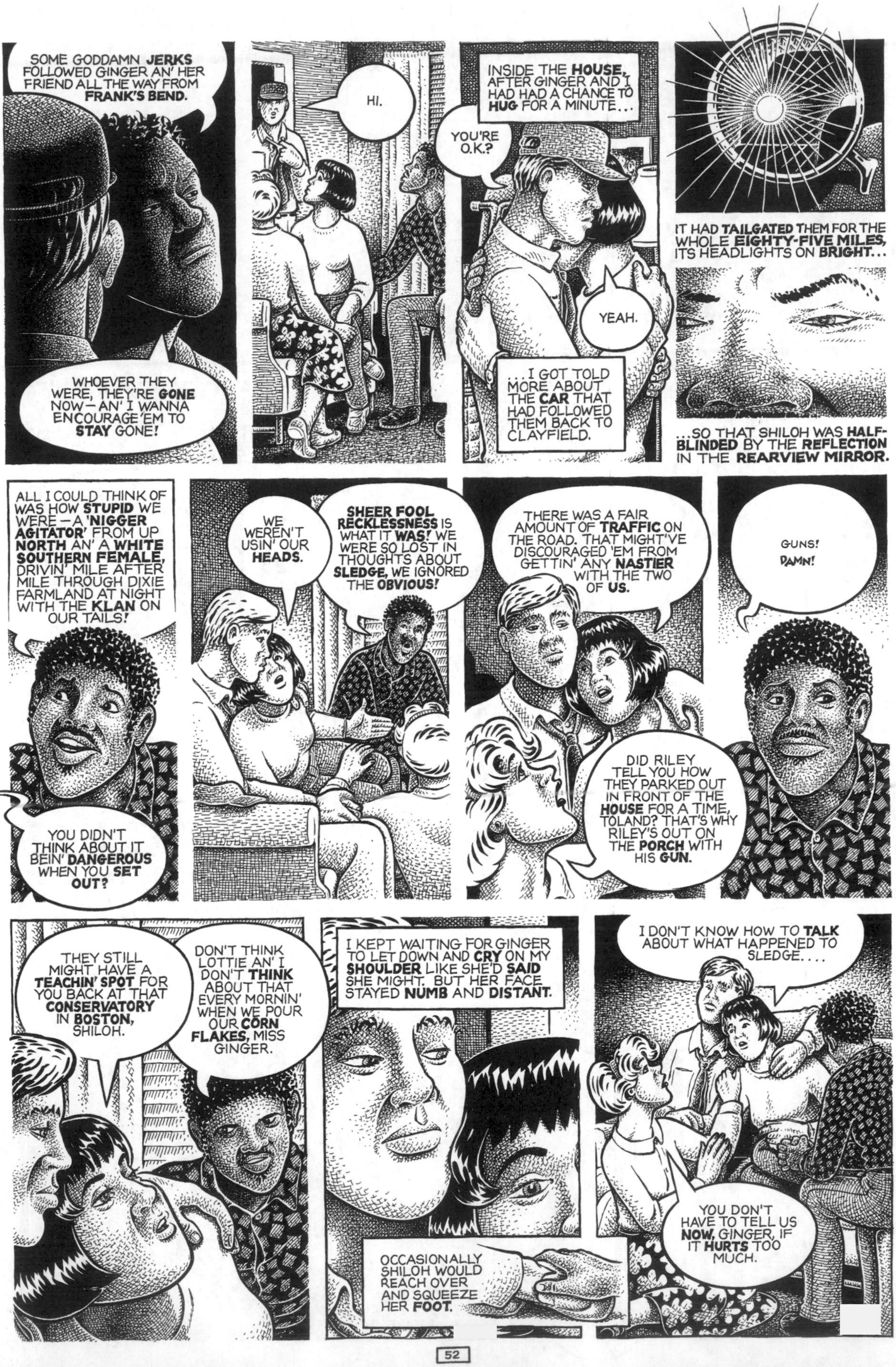
SOME GODDAMN **JERKS** FOLLOWED GINGER AN' HER FRIEND ALL THE WAY FROM **FRANK'S BEND.**
WHOEVER THEY WERE, THEY'RE **GONE** NOW—AN' I WANNA ENCOURAGE 'EM TO **STAY** GONE!
HI.
YOU'RE O.K.?
INSIDE THE **HOUSE,** AFTER GINGER AND I HAD HAD A CHANCE TO **HUG** FOR A MINUTE...
YEAH.
...I GOT TOLD MORE ABOUT THE **CAR** THAT HAD FOLLOWED THEM BACK TO CLAYFIELD.
IT HAD **TAILGATED** THEM FOR THE WHOLE **EIGHTY-FIVE MILES,** ITS HEADLIGHTS ON **BRIGHT...**
...SO THAT SHILOH WAS **HALF-BLINDED** BY THE **REFLECTION** IN THE **REARVIEW MIRROR.**
ALL I COULD THINK OF WAS HOW **STUPID** WE WERE—A **'NIGGER AGITATOR'** FROM UP **NORTH** AN' A **WHITE SOUTHERN FEMALE,** DRIVIN' MILE AFTER MILE THROUGH DIXIE FARMLAND AT NIGHT WITH THE **KLAN** ON OUR TAILS!
YOU DIDN'T THINK ABOUT IT BEIN' **DANGEROUS** WHEN YOU **SET OUT?**
WE WEREN'T USIN' OUR **HEADS.**
SHEER FOOL RECKLESSNESS IS WHAT IT **WAS!** WE WERE SO LOST IN THOUGHTS ABOUT **SLEDGE,** WE IGNORED THE **OBVIOUS!**
THERE WAS A FAIR AMOUNT OF **TRAFFIC** ON THE ROAD. THAT MIGHT'VE DISCOURAGED 'EM FROM GETTIN' ANY **NASTIER** WITH THE TWO OF **US.**
DID RILEY TELL YOU HOW THEY PARKED OUT IN FRONT OF THE **HOUSE** FOR A TIME, TOLAND? THAT'S WHY RILEY'S OUT ON THE **PORCH** WITH HIS **GUN.**
GUNS! DAMN!
THEY STILL MIGHT HAVE A **TEACHIN' SPOT** FOR YOU BACK AT THAT **CONSERVATORY** IN **BOSTON,** SHILOH.
DON'T THINK LOTTIE AN' I DON'T **THINK** ABOUT THAT EVERY MORNIN' WHEN WE POUR OUR **CORN FLAKES,** MISS GINGER.
I KEPT WAITING FOR GINGER TO LET DOWN AND **CRY** ON MY **SHOULDER** LIKE SHE'D **SAID** SHE MIGHT. BUT HER FACE STAYED **NUMB** AND **DISTANT.**
OCCASIONALLY SHILOH WOULD REACH OVER AND SQUEEZE HER **FOOT.**
I DON'T KNOW HOW TO **TALK** ABOUT WHAT HAPPENED TO SLEDGE....
YOU DON'T HAVE TO TELL US **NOW,** GINGER, IF IT **HURTS** TOO MUCH.

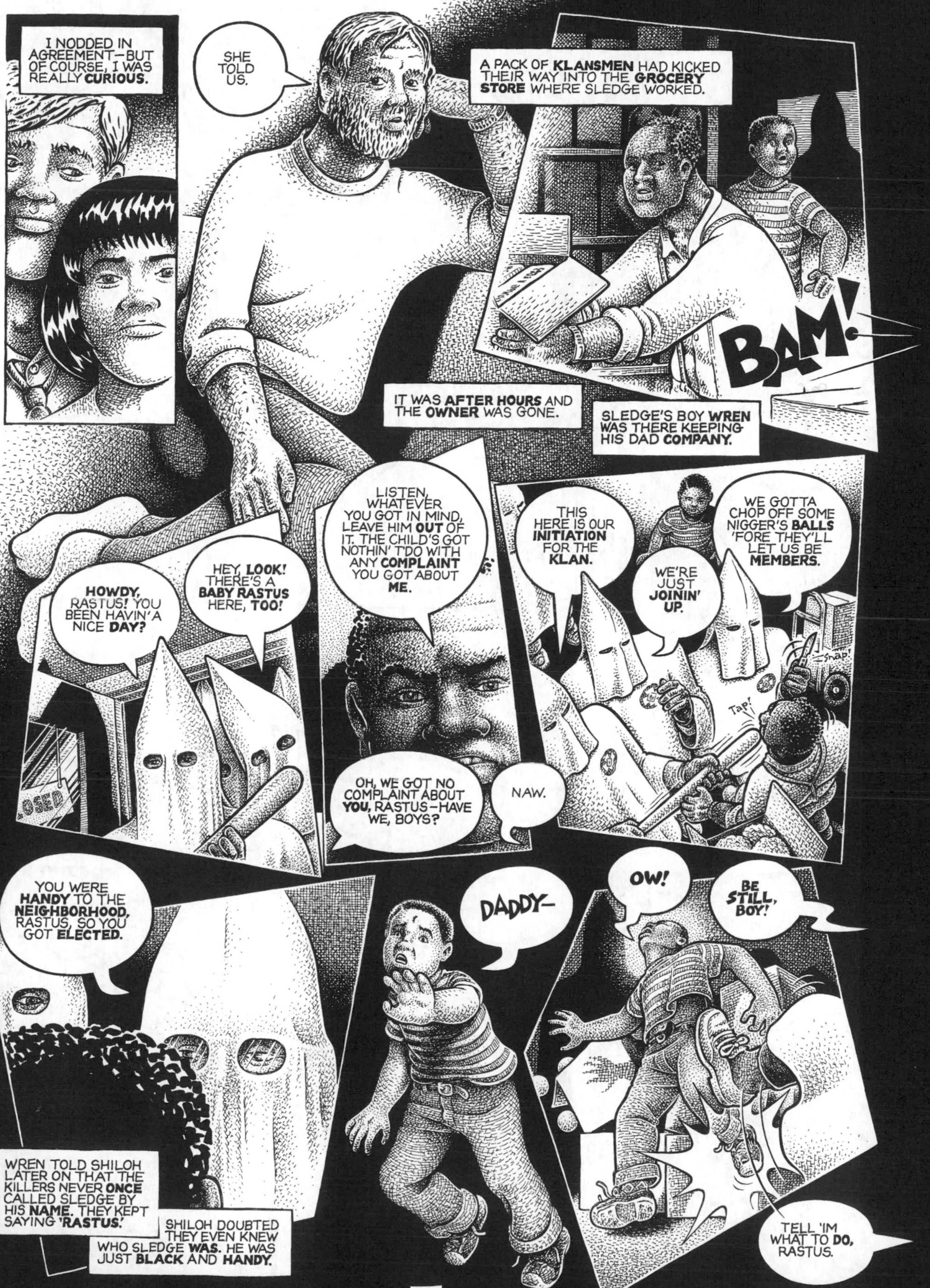

I NODDED IN AGREEMENT—BUT OF COURSE, I WAS REALLY **CURIOUS**.
SHE TOLD US.
A PACK OF **KLANSMEN** HAD KICKED THEIR WAY INTO THE **GROCERY STORE** WHERE SLEDGE WORKED.
BAM!
IT WAS **AFTER HOURS** AND THE **OWNER** WAS GONE.
SLEDGE'S BOY **WREN** WAS THERE KEEPING HIS DAD **COMPANY**.
HOWDY, RASTUS! YOU BEEN HAVIN' A NICE **DAY?**
HEY, **LOOK!** THERE'S A **BABY RASTUS** HERE, **TOO!**
LISTEN, WHATEVER YOU GOT IN MIND, LEAVE HIM **OUT** OF IT. THE CHILD'S GOT NOTHIN' T'DO WITH ANY **COMPLAINT** YOU GOT ABOUT **ME**.
OH, WE GOT NO COMPLAINT ABOUT **YOU**, RASTUS—HAVE WE, BOYS?
NAW.
THIS HERE IS OUR **INITIATION** FOR THE **KLAN**.
WE'RE JUST **JOININ'** UP.
WE GOTTA CHOP OFF SOME NIGGER'S **BALLS** 'FORE THEY'LL LET US BE **MEMBERS**.
Snap!
Tap!
YOU WERE **HANDY** TO THE **NEIGHBORHOOD**, RASTUS, SO YOU GOT **ELECTED**.
DADDY—
OW!
BE STILL, BOY!
WREN TOLD SHILOH LATER ON THAT THE KILLERS NEVER **ONCE** CALLED SLEDGE BY HIS **NAME**. THEY KEPT SAYING **'RASTUS.'**
SHILOH DOUBTED THEY EVEN KNEW WHO SLEDGE **WAS**. HE WAS JUST **BLACK** AND **HANDY**.
TELL 'IM WHAT TO **DO**, RASTUS.

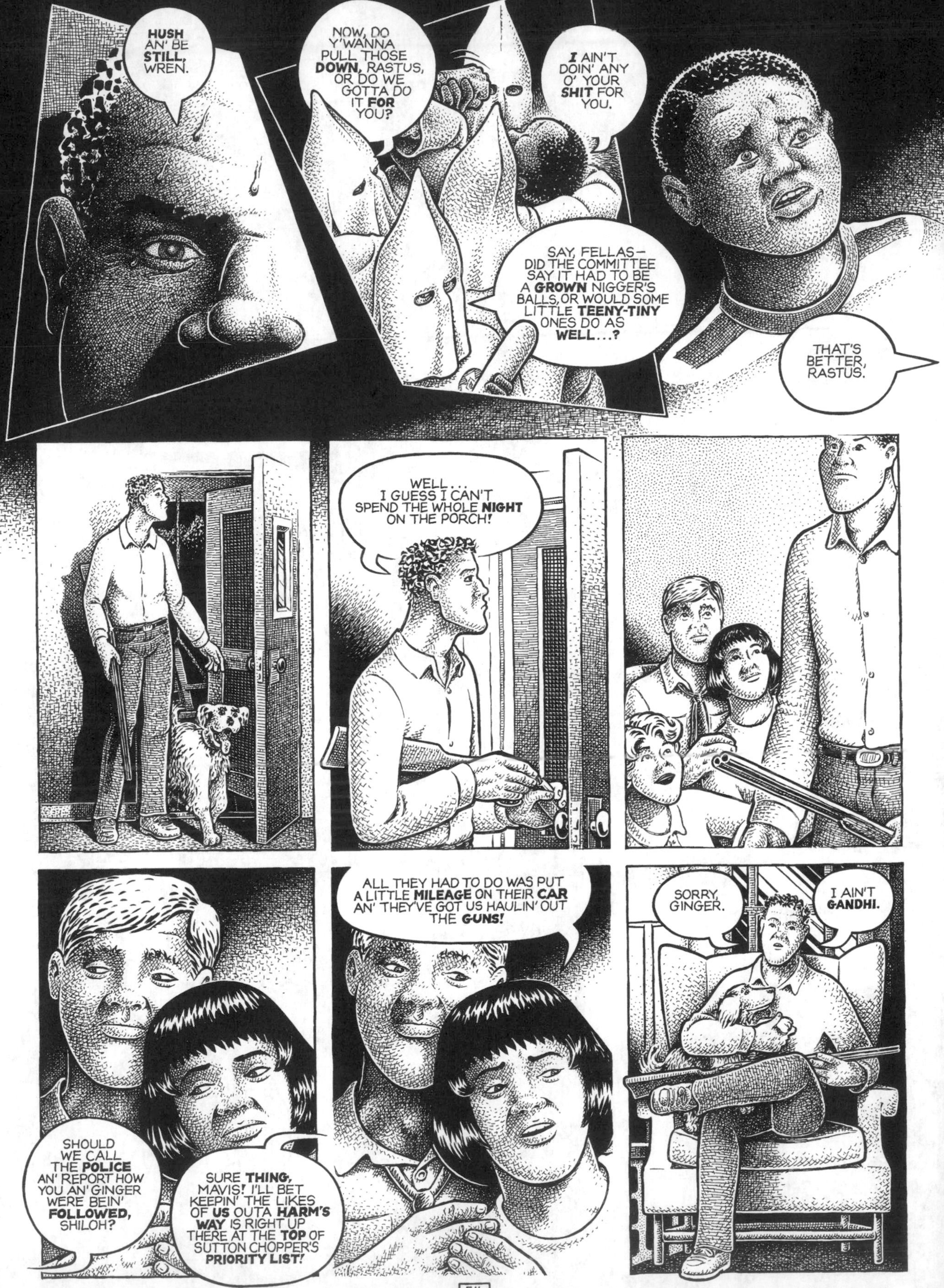
HUSH AN' BE STILL, WREN.
NOW, DO Y'WANNA PULL THOSE DOWN, RASTUS, OR DO WE GOTTA DO IT FOR YOU?
I AIN'T DOIN' ANY O' YOUR SHIT FOR YOU.
SAY, FELLAS— DID THE COMMITTEE SAY IT HAD TO BE A GROWN NIGGER'S BALLS, OR WOULD SOME LITTLE TEENY-TINY ONES DO AS WELL...?
THAT'S BETTER, RASTUS.
WELL... I GUESS I CAN'T SPEND THE WHOLE NIGHT ON THE PORCH!
SHOULD WE CALL THE POLICE AN' REPORT HOW YOU AN' GINGER WERE BEIN' FOLLOWED, SHILOH?
SURE THING, MAVIS! I'LL BET KEEPIN' THE LIKES OF US OUTA HARM'S WAY IS RIGHT UP THERE AT THE TOP OF SUTTON CHOPPER'S PRIORITY LIST!
ALL THEY HAD TO DO WAS PUT A LITTLE MILEAGE ON THEIR CAR AN' THEY'VE GOT US HAULIN' OUT THE GUNS!
SORRY, GINGER.
I AIN'T GANDHI.

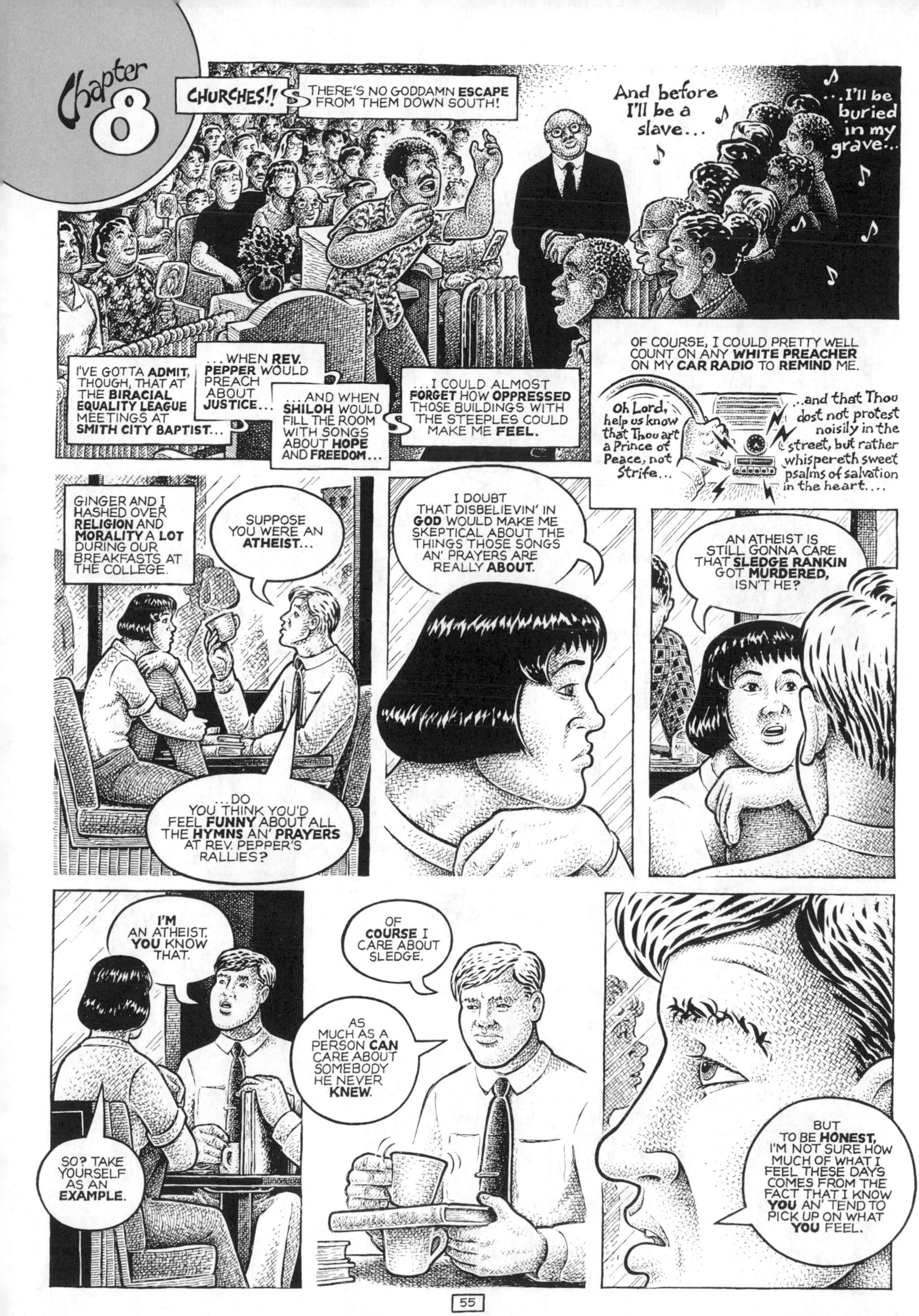
Chapter 8
CHURCHES!!
THERE'S NO GODDAMN ESCAPE FROM THEM DOWN SOUTH!
And before I'll be a slave...
...I'll be buried in my grave...
I'VE GOTTA ADMIT, THOUGH, THAT AT THE BIRACIAL EQUALITY LEAGUE MEETINGS AT SMITH CITY BAPTIST...
...WHEN REV. PEPPER WOULD PREACH ABOUT JUSTICE...
...AND WHEN SHILOH WOULD FILL THE ROOM WITH SONGS ABOUT HOPE AND FREEDOM...
...I COULD ALMOST FORGET HOW OPPRESSED THOSE BUILDINGS WITH THE STEEPLES COULD MAKE ME FEEL.
OF COURSE, I COULD PRETTY WELL COUNT ON ANY WHITE PREACHER ON MY CAR RADIO TO REMIND ME.
Oh Lord, help us know that Thou art a Prince of Peace, not Strife...
...and that Thou dost not protest noisily in the street, but rather whispereth sweet psalms of salvation in the heart....
GINGER AND I HASHED OVER RELIGION AND MORALITY A LOT DURING OUR BREAKFASTS AT THE COLLEGE.
SUPPOSE YOU WERE AN ATHEIST...
...DO YOU THINK YOU'D FEEL FUNNY ABOUT ALL THE HYMNS AN' PRAYERS AT REV. PEPPER'S RALLIES?
I DOUBT THAT DISBELIEVIN' IN GOD WOULD MAKE ME SKEPTICAL ABOUT THE THINGS THOSE SONGS AN' PRAYERS ARE REALLY ABOUT.
AN ATHEIST IS STILL GONNA CARE THAT SLEDGE RANKIN GOT MURDERED, ISN'T HE?
I'M AN ATHEIST. YOU KNOW THAT.
SO? TAKE YOURSELF AS AN EXAMPLE.
OF COURSE I CARE ABOUT SLEDGE.
AS MUCH AS A PERSON CAN CARE ABOUT SOMEBODY HE NEVER KNEW.
BUT TO BE HONEST, I'M NOT SURE HOW MUCH OF WHAT I FEEL THESE DAYS COMES FROM THE FACT THAT I KNOW YOU AN' TEND TO PICK UP ON WHAT YOU FEEL.

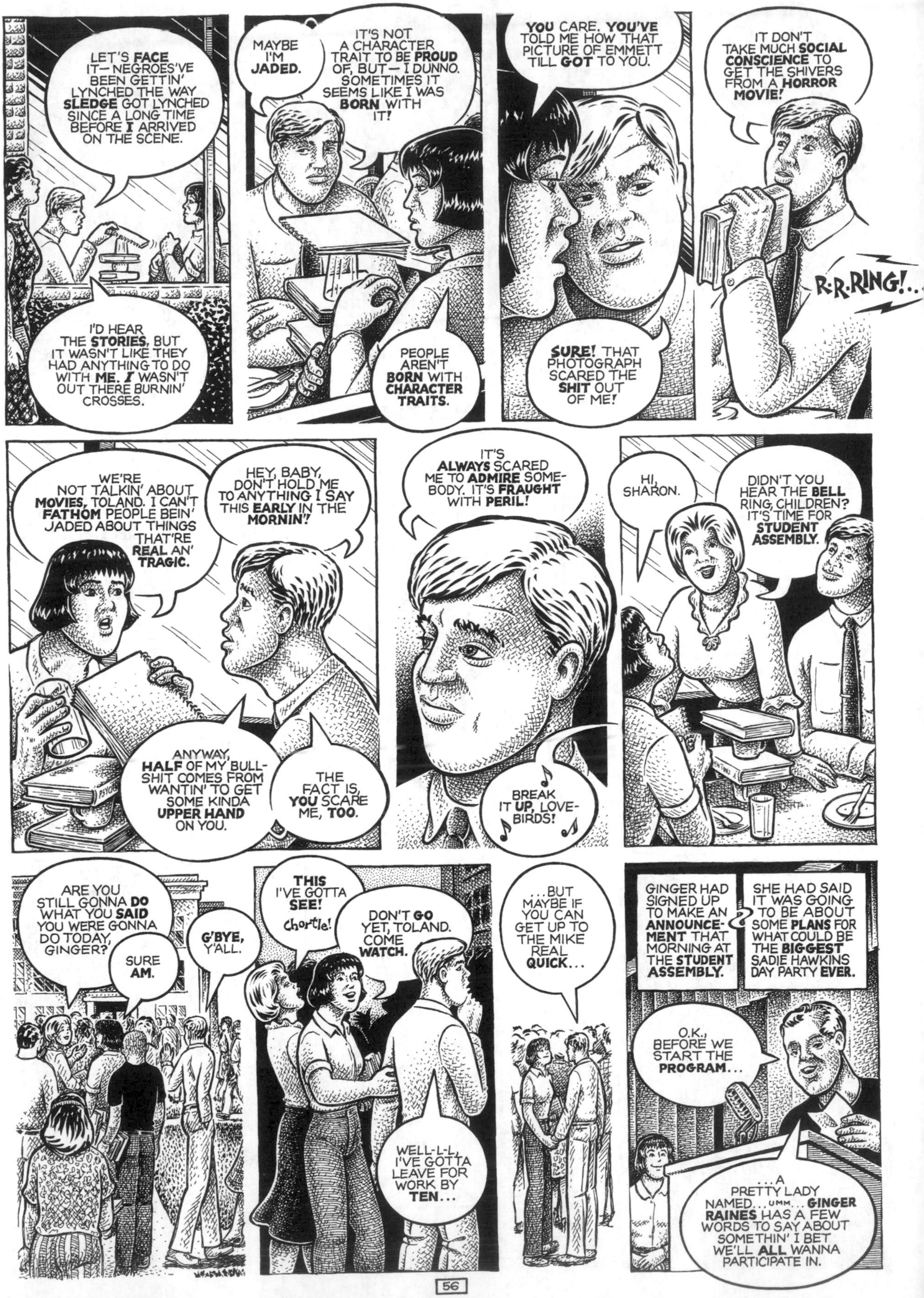
LET'S FACE IT— NEGROES'VE BEEN GETTIN' LYNCHED THE WAY SLEDGE GOT LYNCHED SINCE A LONG TIME BEFORE I ARRIVED ON THE SCENE.
I'D HEAR THE STORIES, BUT IT WASN'T LIKE THEY HAD ANYTHING TO DO WITH ME. I WASN'T OUT THERE BURNIN' CROSSES.
MAYBE I'M JADED.
IT'S NOT A CHARACTER TRAIT TO BE PROUD OF, BUT— I DUNNO. SOMETIMES IT SEEMS LIKE I WAS BORN WITH IT!
PEOPLE AREN'T BORN WITH CHARACTER TRAITS.
YOU CARE. YOU'VE TOLD ME HOW THAT PICTURE OF EMMETT TILL GOT TO YOU.
SURE! THAT PHOTOGRAPH SCARED THE SHIT OUT OF ME!
IT DON'T TAKE MUCH SOCIAL CONSCIENCE TO GET THE SHIVERS FROM A HORROR MOVIE!
R-R-RING!..
WE'RE NOT TALKIN' ABOUT MOVIES, TOLAND. I CAN'T FATHOM PEOPLE BEIN' JADED ABOUT THINGS THAT'RE REAL AN' TRAGIC.
HEY, BABY, DON'T HOLD ME TO ANYTHING I SAY THIS EARLY IN THE MORNIN'!
ANYWAY, HALF OF MY BULL-SHIT COMES FROM WANTIN' TO GET SOME KINDA UPPER HAND ON YOU.
THE FACT IS, YOU SCARE ME, TOO.
IT'S ALWAYS SCARED ME TO ADMIRE SOME-BODY. IT'S FRAUGHT WITH PERIL!
BREAK IT UP, LOVE-BIRDS!
HI, SHARON.
DIDN'T YOU HEAR THE BELL RING, CHILDREN? IT'S TIME FOR STUDENT ASSEMBLY.
ARE YOU STILL GONNA DO WHAT YOU SAID YOU WERE GONNA DO TODAY, GINGER?
SURE AM.
G'BYE, Y'ALL.
THIS I'VE GOTTA SEE!
Chortle!
DON'T GO YET, TOLAND. COME WATCH.
WELL-L-L, I'VE GOTTA LEAVE FOR WORK BY TEN...
...BUT MAYBE IF YOU CAN GET UP TO THE MIKE REAL QUICK...
GINGER HAD SIGNED UP TO MAKE AN ANNOUNCE-MENT THAT MORNING AT THE STUDENT ASSEMBLY.
SHE HAD SAID IT WAS GOING TO BE ABOUT SOME PLANS FOR WHAT COULD BE THE BIGGEST SADIE HAWKINS DAY PARTY EVER.
O.K., BEFORE WE START THE PROGRAM...
...A PRETTY LADY NAMED... UMM... GINGER RAINES HAS A FEW WORDS TO SAY ABOUT SOMETHIN' I BET WE'LL ALL WANNA PARTICIPATE IN.

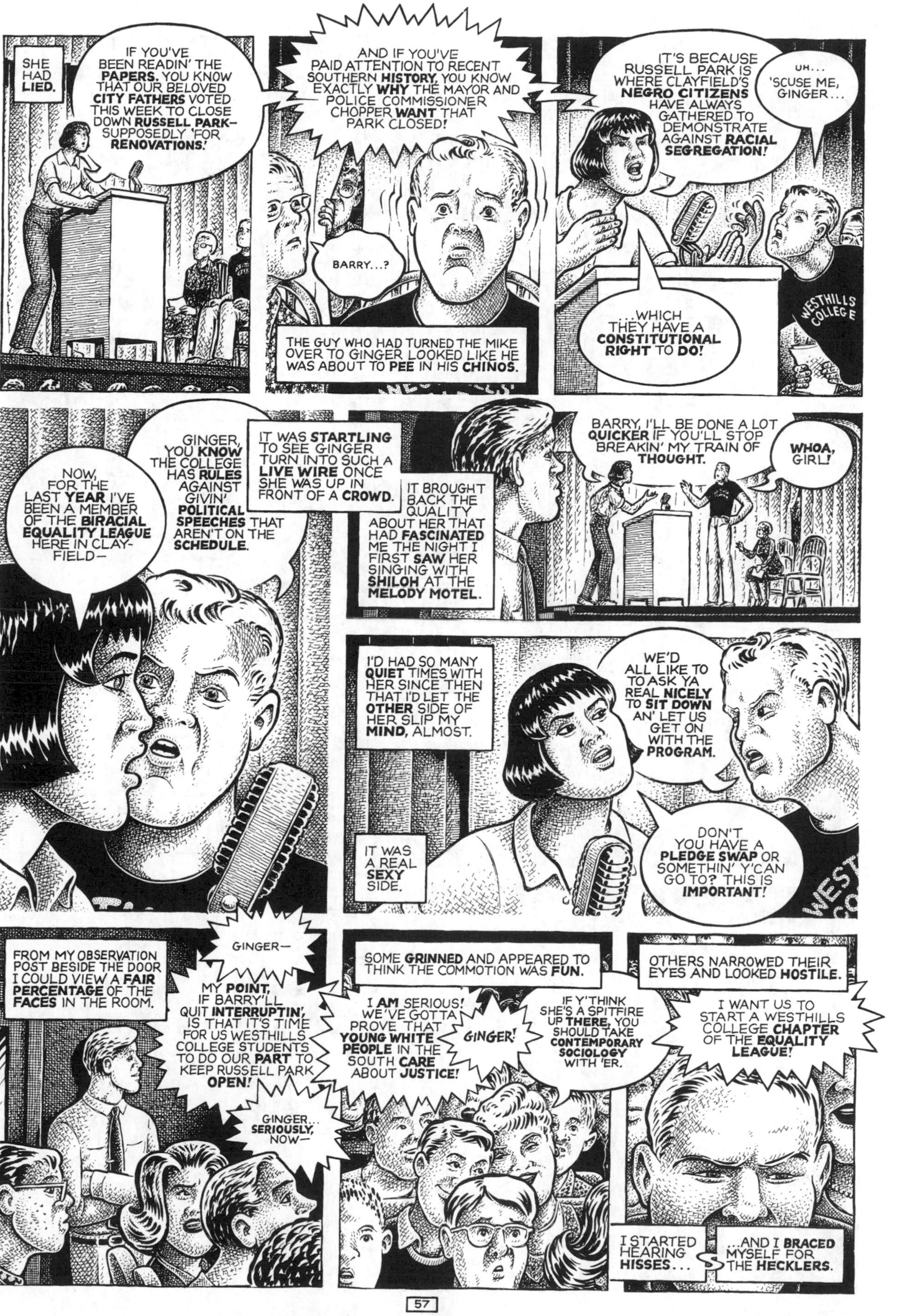
SHE HAD LIED.
IF YOU'VE BEEN READIN' THE PAPERS, YOU KNOW THAT OUR BELOVED CITY FATHERS VOTED THIS WEEK TO CLOSE DOWN RUSSELL PARK-SUPPOSEDLY 'FOR RENOVATIONS.'
AND IF YOU'VE PAID ATTENTION TO RECENT SOUTHERN HISTORY, YOU KNOW EXACTLY WHY THE MAYOR AND POLICE COMMISSIONER CHOPPER WANT THAT PARK CLOSED!
BARRY...?
THE GUY WHO HAD TURNED THE MIKE OVER TO GINGER LOOKED LIKE HE WAS ABOUT TO PEE IN HIS CHINOS.
IT'S BECAUSE RUSSELL PARK IS WHERE CLAYFIELD'S NEGRO CITIZENS HAVE ALWAYS GATHERED TO DEMONSTRATE AGAINST RACIAL SEGREGATION!
UH... 'SCUSE ME, GINGER...
...WHICH THEY HAVE A CONSTITUTIONAL RIGHT TO DO!
WESTHILLS COLLEGE
NOW, FOR THE LAST YEAR I'VE BEEN A MEMBER OF THE BIRACIAL EQUALITY LEAGUE HERE IN CLAY-FIELD—
GINGER, YOU KNOW THE COLLEGE HAS RULES AGAINST GIVIN' POLITICAL SPEECHES THAT AREN'T ON THE SCHEDULE.
IT WAS STARTLING TO SEE GINGER TURN INTO SUCH A LIVE WIRE ONCE SHE WAS UP IN FRONT OF A CROWD.
IT BROUGHT BACK THE QUALITY ABOUT HER THAT HAD FASCINATED ME THE NIGHT I FIRST SAW HER SINGING WITH SHILOH AT THE MELODY MOTEL.
BARRY, I'LL BE DONE A LOT QUICKER IF YOU'LL STOP BREAKIN' MY TRAIN OF THOUGHT.
WHOA, GIRL!
I'D HAD SO MANY QUIET TIMES WITH HER SINCE THEN THAT I'D LET THE OTHER SIDE OF HER SLIP MY MIND, ALMOST.
WE'D ALL LIKE TO TO ASK YA REAL NICELY TO SIT DOWN AN' LET US GET ON WITH THE PROGRAM.
IT WAS A REAL SEXY SIDE.
DON'T YOU HAVE A PLEDGE SWAP OR SOMETHIN' Y'CAN GO TO? THIS IS IMPORTANT!
FROM MY OBSERVATION POST BESIDE THE DOOR I COULD VIEW A FAIR PERCENTAGE OF THE FACES IN THE ROOM.
GINGER—
MY POINT, IF BARRY'LL QUIT INTERRUPTIN', IS THAT IT'S TIME FOR US WESTHILLS COLLEGE STUDENTS TO DO OUR PART TO KEEP RUSSELL PARK OPEN!
GINGER... SERIOUSLY, NOW—
SOME GRINNED AND APPEARED TO THINK THE COMMOTION WAS FUN.
I AM SERIOUS! WE'VE GOTTA PROVE THAT YOUNG WHITE PEOPLE IN THE SOUTH CARE ABOUT JUSTICE!
GINGER!
IF Y'THINK SHE'S A SPITFIRE UP THERE, YOU SHOULD TAKE CONTEMPORARY SOCIOLOGY WITH 'ER.
OTHERS NARROWED THEIR EYES AND LOOKED HOSTILE.
I WANT US TO START A WESTHILLS COLLEGE CHAPTER OF THE EQUALITY LEAGUE!
I STARTED HEARING HISSES...
...AND I BRACED MYSELF FOR THE HECKLERS.

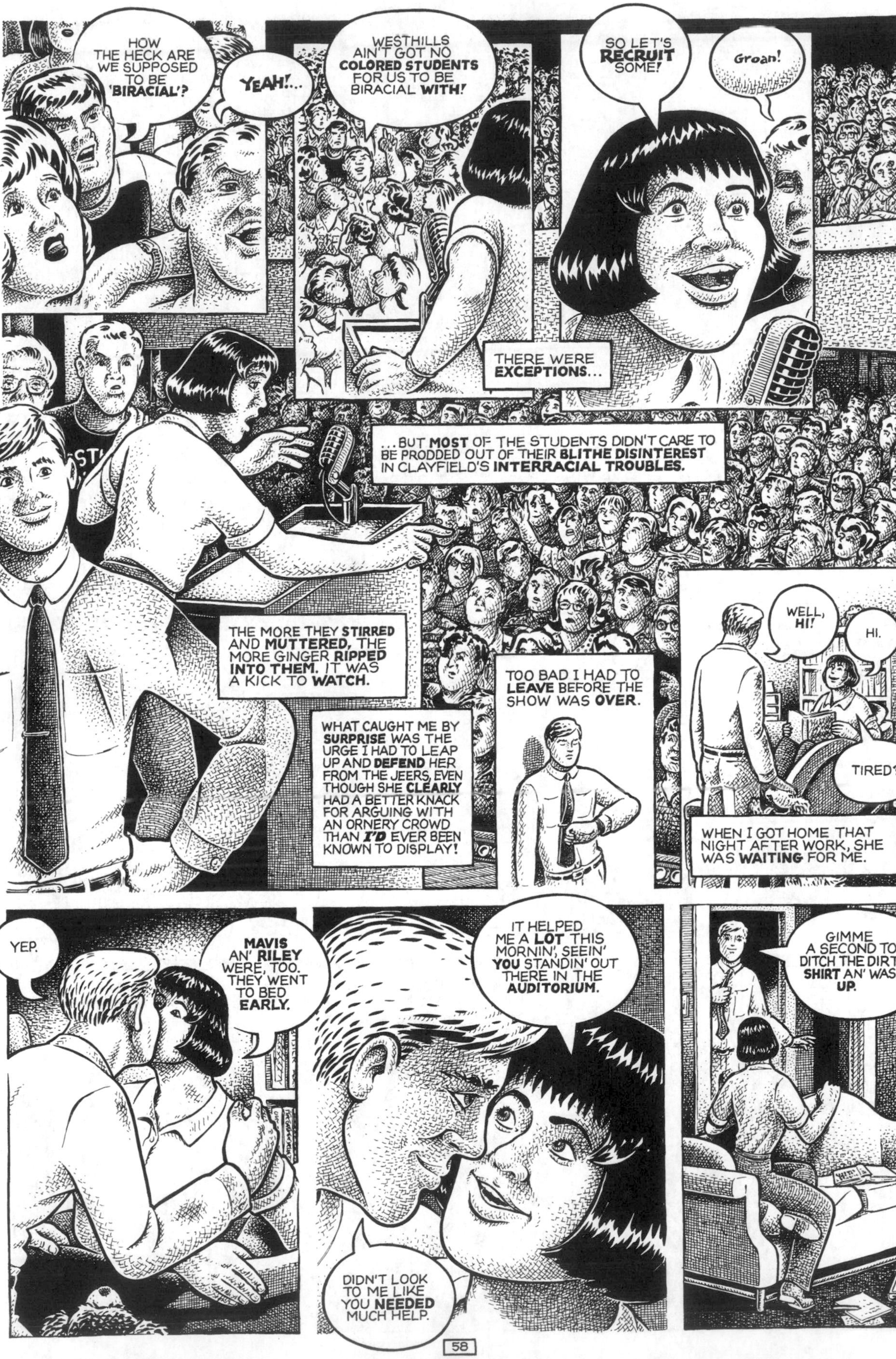

HOW THE HECK ARE WE SUPPOSED TO BE 'BIRACIAL'?
YEAH!...
WESTHILLS AIN'T GOT NO COLORED STUDENTS FOR US TO BE BIRACIAL WITH!
SO LET'S RECRUIT SOME!
Groan!
THERE WERE EXCEPTIONS...
...BUT MOST OF THE STUDENTS DIDN'T CARE TO BE PRODDED OUT OF THEIR BLITHE DISINTEREST IN CLAYFIELD'S INTERRACIAL TROUBLES.
THE MORE THEY STIRRED AND MUTTERED, THE MORE GINGER RIPPED INTO THEM. IT WAS A KICK TO WATCH.
WHAT CAUGHT ME BY SURPRISE WAS THE URGE I HAD TO LEAP UP AND DEFEND HER FROM THE JEERS, EVEN THOUGH SHE CLEARLY HAD A BETTER KNACK FOR ARGUING WITH AN ORNERY CROWD THAN I'D EVER BEEN KNOWN TO DISPLAY!
TOO BAD I HAD TO LEAVE BEFORE THE SHOW WAS OVER.
WELL, HI!
HI.
TIRED?
WHEN I GOT HOME THAT NIGHT AFTER WORK, SHE WAS WAITING FOR ME.
YEP.
MAVIS AN' RILEY WERE, TOO. THEY WENT TO BED EARLY.
IT HELPED ME A LOT THIS MORNIN', SEEIN' YOU STANDIN' OUT THERE IN THE AUDITORIUM.
DIDN'T LOOK TO ME LIKE YOU NEEDED MUCH HELP.
GIMME A SECOND TO DITCH THE DIRTY SHIRT AN' WASH UP.

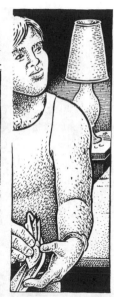

WINE?

ALL MY **INSTINCTS** WERE TELLING ME THAT GINGER FELT THE SAME WAY **I** DID.

TONIGHT WAS THE NIGHT.

YOU WERE PURE **DYNAMITE** AT THAT **ASSEMBLY** TODAY.

Wurf!

DID YOU GET ANY OF YOUR FELLOW **STUDENTS** SIGNED UP FOR THE **EQUALITY LEAGUE**?

A FEW SAID THEY **WISHED** THEY COULD HELP, BUT THEY'RE **SCARED**.

Whimper!

THERE'S PRESSURE ON THE SCHOOL TO **SUSPEND** ANY-BODY WHO GETS INVOLVED IN **SOCIAL UNREST**!

I'D LIKELY BE LONG GONE **MYSELF** IF THE DEAN'S **COUSIN** WASN'T A **BUSINESS PARTNER** OF MY **DAD'S** UP IN OHIO.

AREN'T COLLEGE STUDENTS SUPPOSED TO HAVE FREEDOM OF **SPEECH** AN' FREEDOM OF **ASSEMBLY** AN'—

TOLAND, THIS IS THE **SOUTH**! WHERE DO YOU THINK YOU **ARE**, ANY-WAY — IN **AMERICA**?!

POLITICAL TALK. NOT SO **EROTIC**.

IT CAN BE **TOUGH** TO SWITCH GEARS.

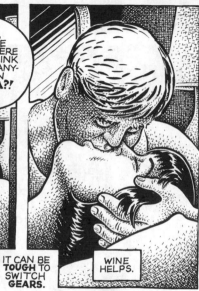

WINE HELPS.

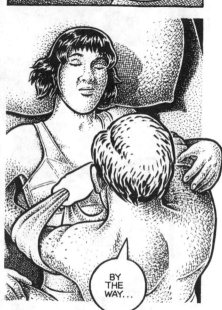

BY THE WAY...

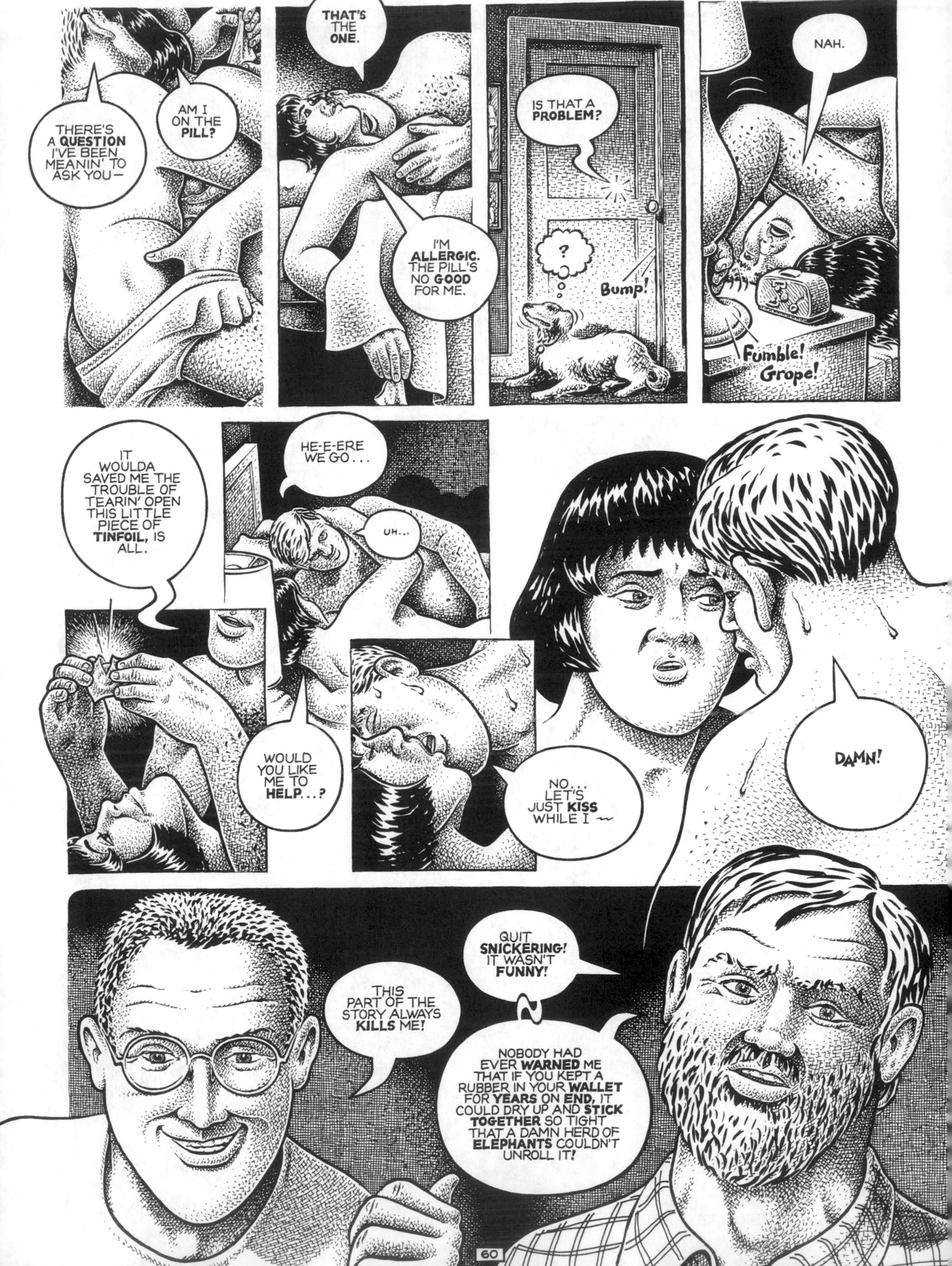
THERE'S A **QUESTION** I'VE BEEN MEANIN' TO ASK YOU—
AM I ON THE **PILL?**
THAT'S THE **ONE**.
I'M **ALLERGIC.** THE PILL'S NO **GOOD** FOR ME.
IS THAT A **PROBLEM?**
?
Bump!
NAH.
Fumble! Grope!
IT WOULDA SAVED ME THE TROUBLE OF TEARIN' OPEN THIS LITTLE PIECE OF **TINFOIL,** IS ALL.
HE-E-ERE WE GO...
UH...
WOULD YOU LIKE ME TO **HELP**...?
NO... LET'S JUST **KISS** WHILE I ~
DAMN!
THIS PART OF THE STORY ALWAYS **KILLS** ME!
QUIT **SNICKERING!** IT WASN'T **FUNNY!**
NOBODY HAD EVER **WARNED** ME THAT IF YOU KEPT A RUBBER IN YOUR **WALLET** FOR **YEARS ON END,** IT COULD DRY UP AND **STICK TOGETHER** SO TIGHT THAT A DAMN HERD OF **ELEPHANTS** COULDN'T UNROLL IT!

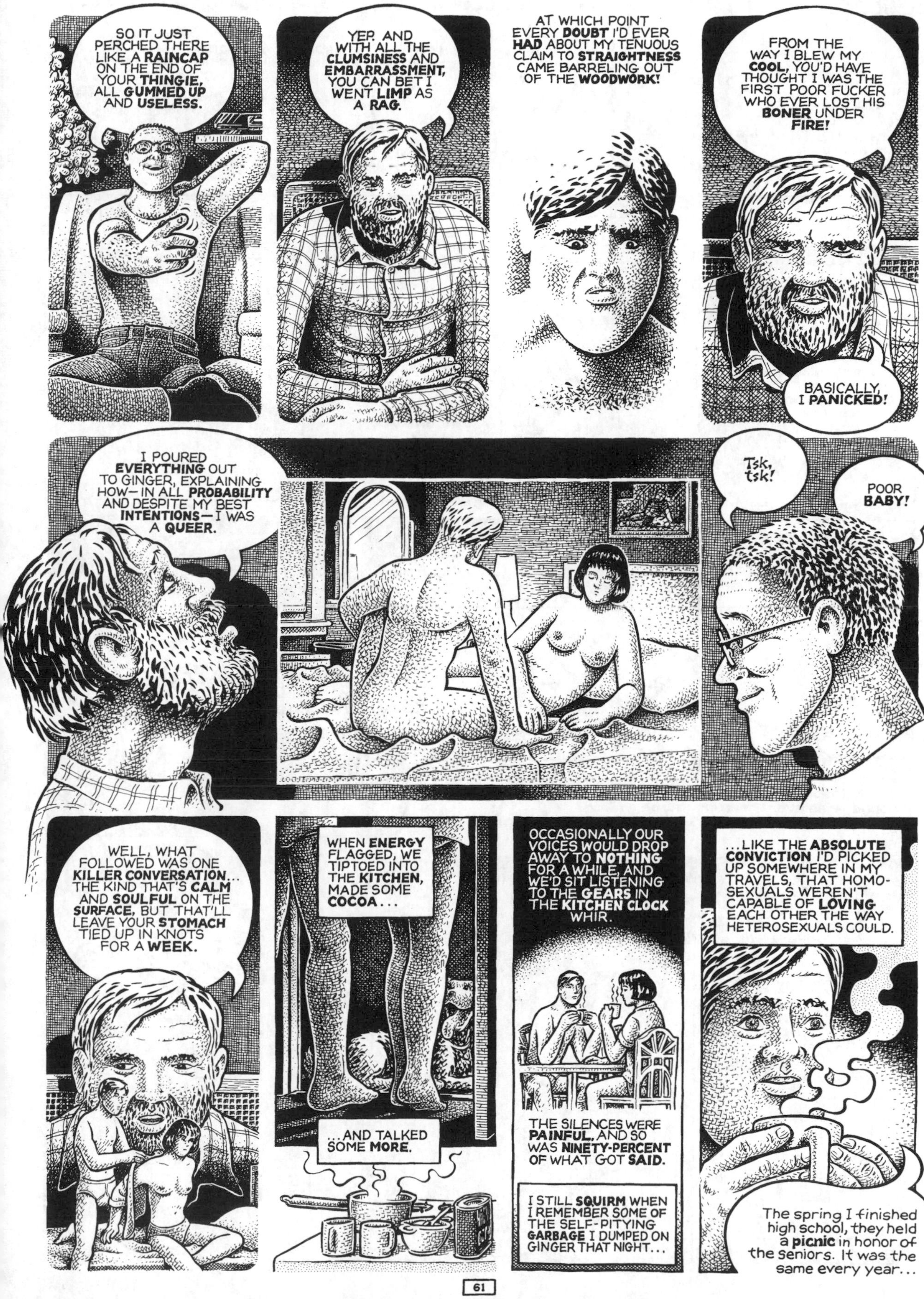

SO IT JUST PERCHED THERE LIKE A RAINCAP ON THE END OF YOUR THINGIE, ALL GUMMED UP AND USELESS.
YEP. AND WITH ALL THE CLUMSINESS AND EMBARRASSMENT, YOU CAN BET I WENT LIMP AS A RAG.
AT WHICH POINT EVERY DOUBT I'D EVER HAD ABOUT MY TENUOUS CLAIM TO STRAIGHTNESS CAME BARRELING OUT OF THE WOODWORK!
FROM THE WAY I BLEW MY COOL, YOU'D HAVE THOUGHT I WAS THE FIRST POOR FUCKER WHO EVER LOST HIS BONER UNDER FIRE!
BASICALLY, I PANICKED!
I POURED EVERYTHING OUT TO GINGER, EXPLAINING HOW— IN ALL PROBABILITY AND DESPITE MY BEST INTENTIONS— I WAS A QUEER.
Tsk, tsk!
POOR BABY!
WELL, WHAT FOLLOWED WAS ONE KILLER CONVERSATION... THE KIND THAT'S CALM AND SOULFUL ON THE SURFACE, BUT THAT'LL LEAVE YOUR STOMACH TIED UP IN KNOTS FOR A WEEK.
WHEN ENERGY FLAGGED, WE TIPTOED INTO THE KITCHEN, MADE SOME COCOA...
...AND TALKED SOME MORE.
OCCASIONALLY OUR VOICES WOULD DROP AWAY TO NOTHING FOR A WHILE, AND WE'D SIT LISTENING TO THE GEARS IN THE KITCHEN CLOCK WHIR.
THE SILENCES WERE PAINFUL, AND SO WAS NINETY-PERCENT OF WHAT GOT SAID.
I STILL SQUIRM WHEN I REMEMBER SOME OF THE SELF-PITYING GARBAGE I DUMPED ON GINGER THAT NIGHT...
...LIKE THE ABSOLUTE CONVICTION I'D PICKED UP SOMEWHERE IN MY TRAVELS, THAT HOMO-SEXUALS WEREN'T CAPABLE OF LOVING EACH OTHER THE WAY HETEROSEXUALS COULD.
The spring I finished high school, they held a picnic in honor of the seniors. It was the same every year...

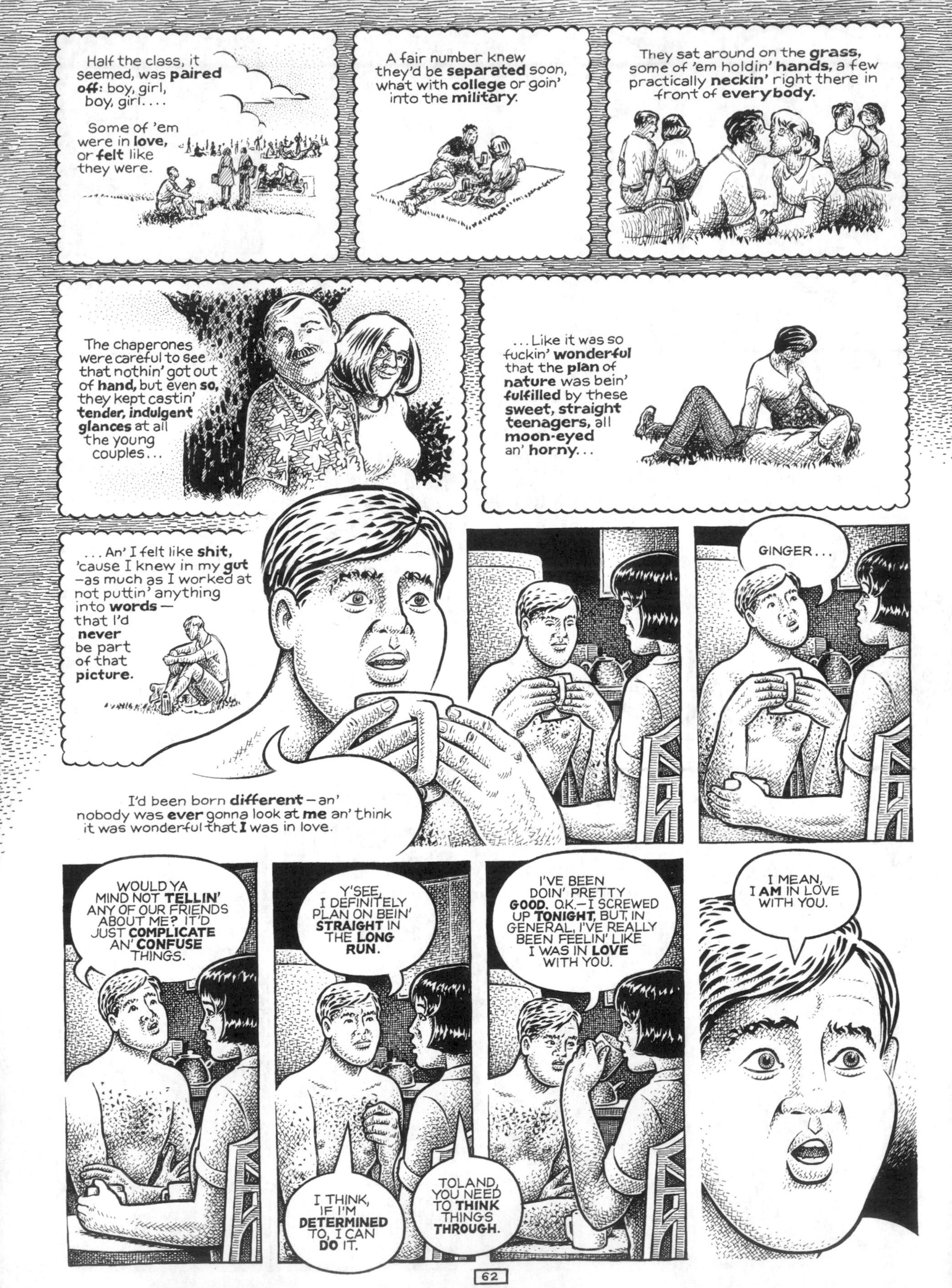

Half the class, it seemed, was paired off: boy, girl, boy, girl....
Some of 'em were in love, or felt like they were.
A fair number knew they'd be separated soon, what with college or goin' into the military.
They sat around on the grass, some of 'em holdin' hands, a few practically neckin' right there in front of everybody.
The chaperones were careful to see that nothin' got out of hand, but even so, they kept castin' tender, indulgent glances at all the young couples...
...Like it was so fuckin' wonderful that the plan of nature was bein' fulfilled by these sweet, straight teenagers, all moon-eyed an' horny...
...An' I felt like shit, 'cause I knew in my gut —as much as I worked at not puttin' anything into words— that I'd never be part of that picture.
I'd been born different—an' nobody was ever gonna look at me an' think it was wonderful that I was in love.
GINGER...
WOULD YA MIND NOT TELLIN' ANY OF OUR FRIENDS ABOUT ME? IT'D JUST COMPLICATE AN' CONFUSE THINGS.
Y'SEE, I DEFINITELY PLAN ON BEIN' STRAIGHT IN THE LONG RUN.
I THINK, IF I'M DETERMINED TO, I CAN DO IT.
TOLAND, YOU NEED TO THINK THINGS THROUGH.
I'VE BEEN DOIN' PRETTY GOOD. O.K.—I SCREWED UP TONIGHT, BUT, IN GENERAL, I'VE REALLY BEEN FEELIN' LIKE I WAS IN LOVE WITH YOU.
I MEAN, I AM IN LOVE WITH YOU.

I'VE BEEN GETTIN' THAT WAY MORE AN' MORE EVERY **DAY**...

...AN' FROM WHAT I COULD TELL, **YOU'VE** BEEN IN LOVE WITH **ME**, TOO.

HAVEN'T YOU?

I GUESS I SHOULDN'T EXPECT YOU TO SAY ANYTHING ABOUT THAT RIGHT **NOW.**

I'M **WORN OUT** AN' MY **HEAD'S** THROBBIN' AN' I DON'T KNOW WHAT SOMEBODY IN MY SHOES IS **SUPPOSED** TO SAY.

GINGER, YOU'RE THE ONLY GIRL I'VE EVER BEEN CONVINCED I **COULD** BE IN LOVE WITH. YOU'RE MY **LIFELINE.**

I'M **NOT** YOUR 'LIFELINE.' I DIDN'T SIGN UP TO BE **ANYBODY'S** LIFELINE!

EVENTUALLY GINGER ASKED ME TO DRIVE HER BACK TO THE **DORM, LATE** AS IT **WAS.**

WE KISSED GOODNIGHT IN THE **USUAL** WAY...

...ACTED LIKE NOTHING OF ANY IMPORTANCE HAD **CHANGED.** MEANWHILE, SOMETHING INSIDE OF ME STOOD **APART** FROM IT ALL AND **WATCHED**...

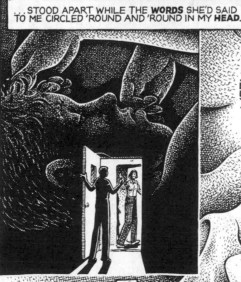

...STOOD APART WHILE THE **WORDS** SHE'D SAID TO ME CIRCLED 'ROUND AND 'ROUND IN MY **HEAD.**

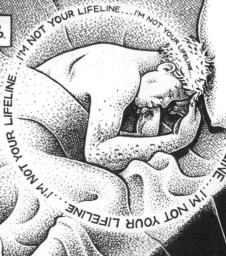

I'M NOT YOUR LIFELINE...I'M NOT YOUR LIFELINE...I'M NOT YOUR LIFELINE...I'M NOT YOUR LIFELINE...I'M NOT YOUR LIFELINE...A LIFELINE...I'M NOT YOUR LIFELINE

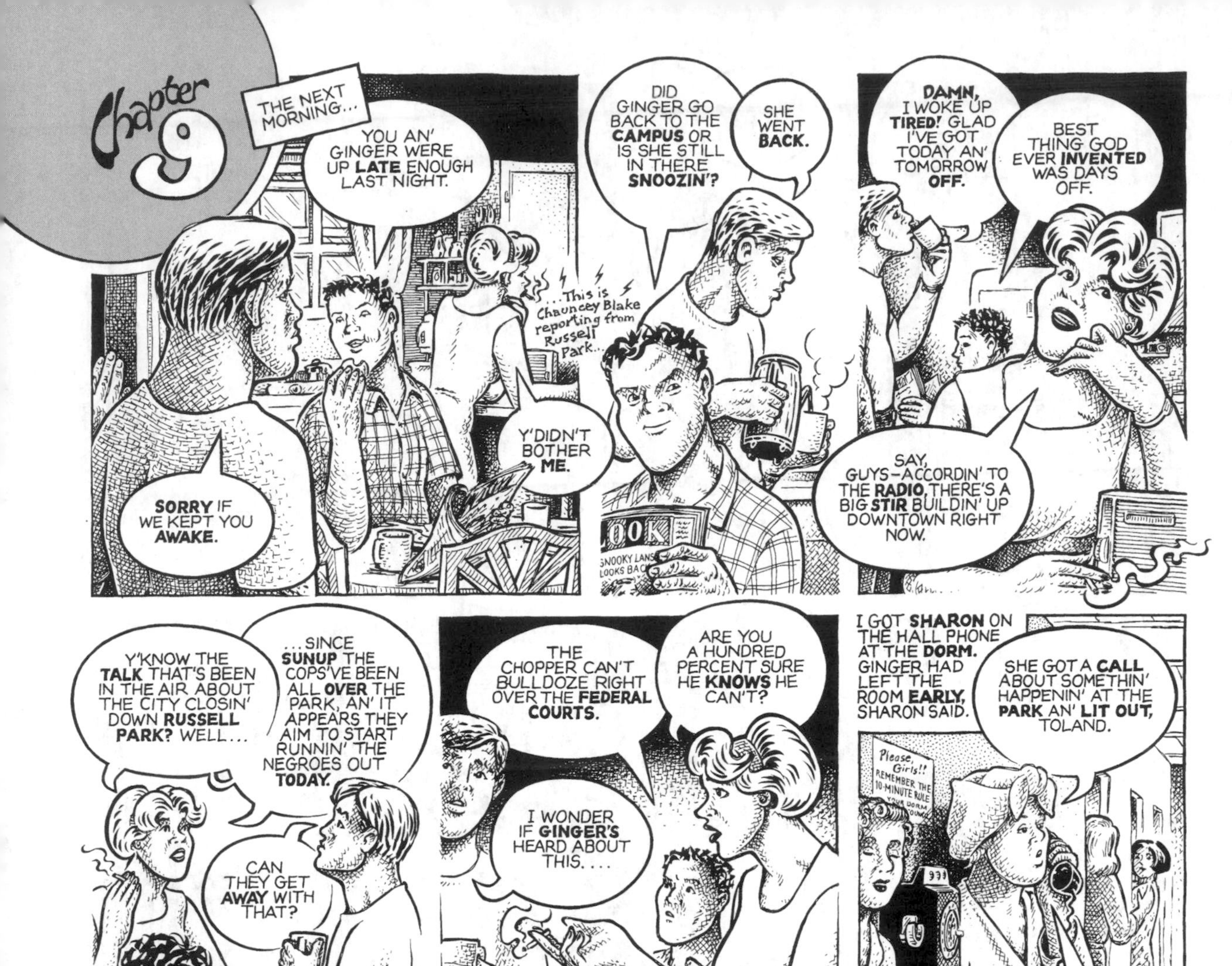
Chapter 9
THE NEXT MORNING...
YOU AN' GINGER WERE UP LATE ENOUGH LAST NIGHT.
SORRY IF WE KEPT YOU AWAKE.
...This is Chauncey Blake reporting from Russell Park...
Y'DIDN'T BOTHER ME.
DID GINGER GO BACK TO THE CAMPUS OR IS SHE STILL IN THERE SNOOZIN'?
SHE WENT BACK.
LOOK
SNOOKY LANS LOOKS BACK
DAMN, I WOKE UP TIRED! GLAD I'VE GOT TODAY AN' TOMORROW OFF.
BEST THING GOD EVER INVENTED WAS DAYS OFF.
SAY, GUYS—ACCORDIN' TO THE RADIO, THERE'S A BIG STIR BUILDIN' UP DOWNTOWN RIGHT NOW.
Y'KNOW THE TALK THAT'S BEEN IN THE AIR ABOUT THE CITY CLOSIN' DOWN RUSSELL PARK? WELL...
...SINCE SUNUP THE COPS'VE BEEN ALL OVER THE PARK, AN' IT APPEARS THEY AIM TO START RUNNIN' THE NEGROES OUT TODAY.
CAN THEY GET AWAY WITH THAT?
I THOUGHT THERE WAS AN INJUNCTION IN FORCE TO PREVENT THAT KIND OF STUNT.
THE CHOPPER CAN'T BULLDOZE RIGHT OVER THE FEDERAL COURTS.
ARE YOU A HUNDRED PERCENT SURE HE KNOWS HE CAN'T?
I WONDER IF GINGER'S HEARD ABOUT THIS. . . .
I GOT SHARON ON THE HALL PHONE AT THE DORM. GINGER HAD LEFT THE ROOM EARLY, SHARON SAID.
SHE GOT A CALL ABOUT SOMETHIN' HAPPENIN' AT THE PARK AN' LIT OUT, TOLAND.
Please, Girls!! REMEMBER THE 10-MINUTE RULE
YOU TWO DON'T PUT MUCH STOCK IN LONG HOURS OF SLEEP THESE DAYS, DO YOU!
MAVIS AN' I ARE GONNA DRIVE DOWNTOWN AN' WATCH SOME OF THE EXCITEMENT. WANNA COME?
SURE. WHY NOT?
JUST LEMME FIND SOME EATS TO TAKE ALONG. Y'ALL HAVE HAD BREAKFAST; I HAVEN'T.
NO, NO, LOCO!...YOU CAN'T RIDE IN THE CAR THIS TIME. CIVIL UNREST MAKES YOU NERVOUS.
LET'S GO! LET'S GO!
GRAB THE DONUTS. THEY'RE PORTABLE.
Wurf!
WE PILED INTO RILEY'S CAR AND HEADED DOWNTOWN.

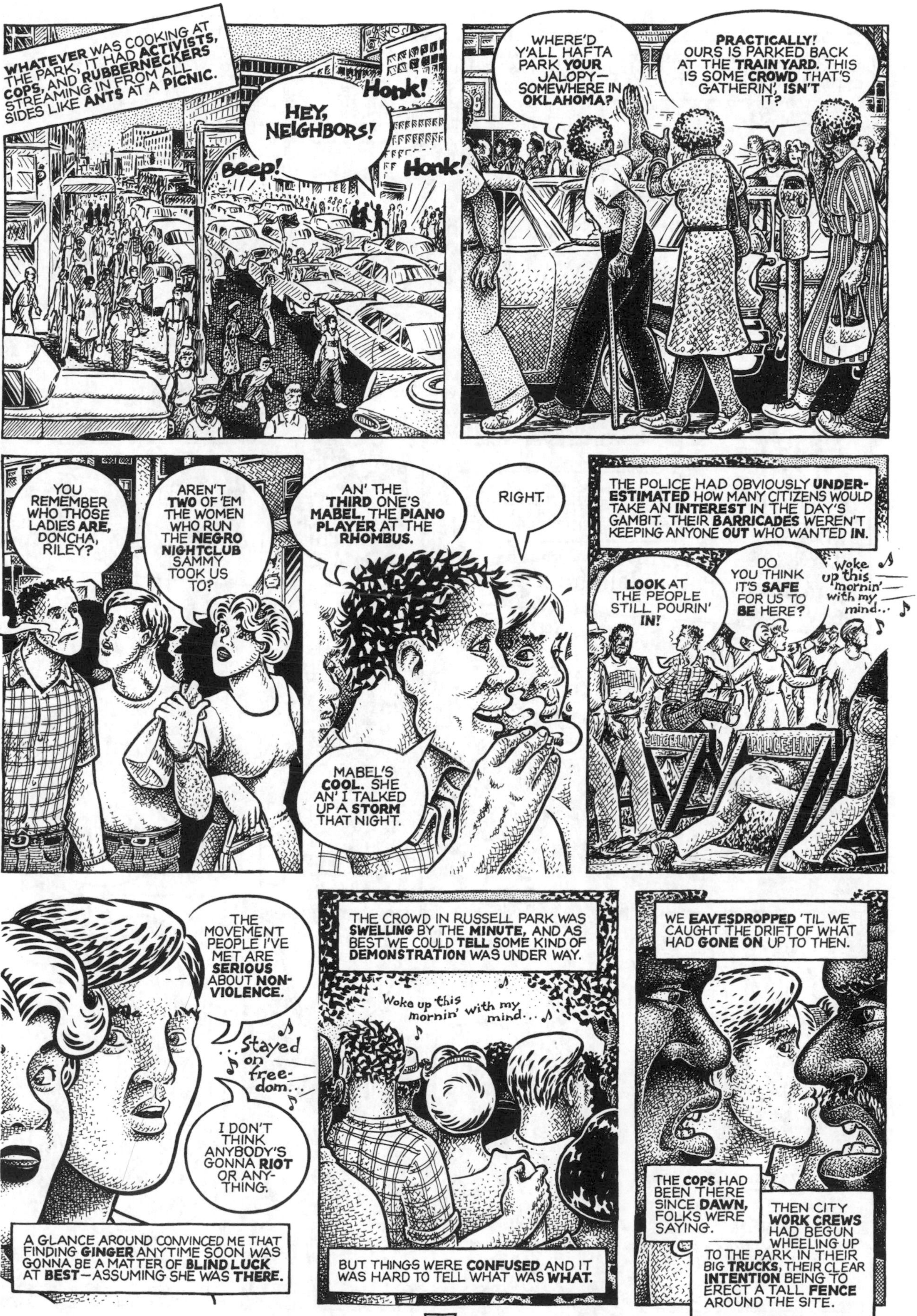

WHATEVER WAS COOKING AT THE PARK, IT HAD ACTIVISTS, COPS, AND RUBBERNECKERS STREAMING IN FROM ALL SIDES LIKE ANTS AT A PICNIC.
HEY, NEIGHBORS!
Honk!
Beep!
Honk!
WHERE'D Y'ALL HAFTA PARK YOUR JALOPY—SOMEWHERE IN OKLAHOMA?
PRACTICALLY! OURS IS PARKED BACK AT THE TRAIN YARD. THIS IS SOME CROWD THAT'S GATHERIN', ISN'T IT?
YOU REMEMBER WHO THOSE LADIES ARE, DONCHA, RILEY?
AREN'T TWO OF 'EM THE WOMEN WHO RUN THE NEGRO NIGHTCLUB SAMMY TOOK US TO?
AN' THE THIRD ONE'S MABEL, THE PIANO PLAYER AT THE RHOMBUS.
RIGHT.
MABEL'S COOL. SHE AN' I TALKED UP A STORM THAT NIGHT.
THE POLICE HAD OBVIOUSLY UNDER-ESTIMATED HOW MANY CITIZENS WOULD TAKE AN INTEREST IN THE DAY'S GAMBIT. THEIR BARRICADES WEREN'T KEEPING ANYONE OUT WHO WANTED IN.
LOOK AT THE PEOPLE STILL POURIN' IN!
DO YOU THINK IT'S SAFE FOR US TO BE HERE?
Woke up this mornin' with my mind...
POLICE LINE
POLICE LINE
THE MOVEMENT PEOPLE I'VE MET ARE SERIOUS ABOUT NON-VIOLENCE.
Stayed on free-dom...
I DON'T THINK ANYBODY'S GONNA RIOT OR ANY-THING.
A GLANCE AROUND CONVINCED ME THAT FINDING GINGER ANYTIME SOON WAS GONNA BE A MATTER OF BLIND LUCK AT BEST—ASSUMING SHE WAS THERE.
THE CROWD IN RUSSELL PARK WAS SWELLING BY THE MINUTE, AND AS BEST WE COULD TELL SOME KIND OF DEMONSTRATION WAS UNDER WAY.
Woke up this mornin' with my mind...
BUT THINGS WERE CONFUSED AND IT WAS HARD TO TELL WHAT WAS WHAT.
WE EAVESDROPPED 'TIL WE CAUGHT THE DRIFT OF WHAT HAD GONE ON UP TO THEN.
THE COPS HAD BEEN THERE SINCE DAWN, FOLKS WERE SAYING.
THEN CITY WORK CREWS HAD BEGUN WHEELING UP TO THE PARK IN THEIR BIG TRUCKS, THEIR CLEAR INTENTION BEING TO ERECT A TALL FENCE AROUND THE SITE.

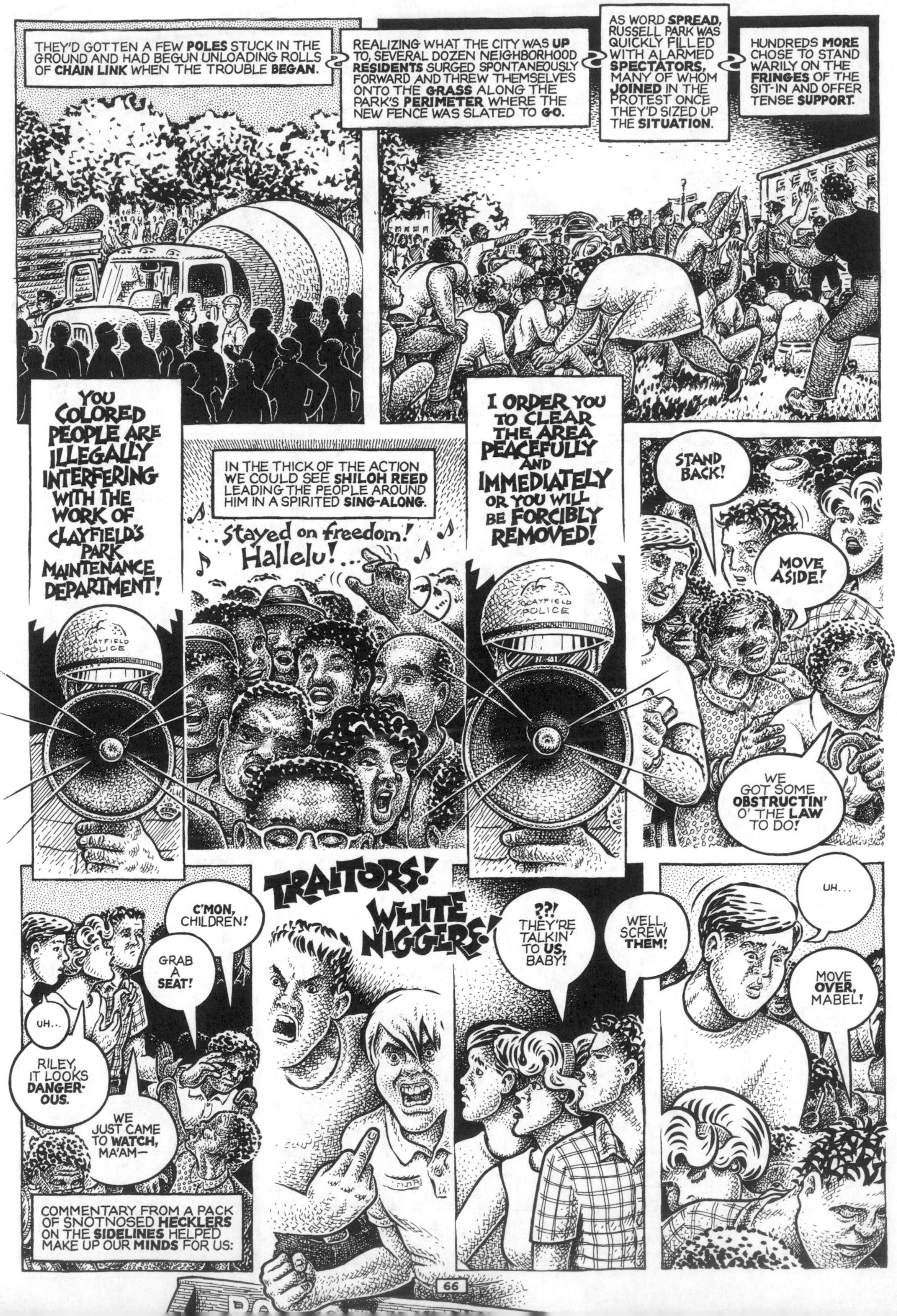
THEY'D GOTTEN A FEW POLES STUCK IN THE GROUND AND HAD BEGUN UNLOADING ROLLS OF CHAIN LINK WHEN THE TROUBLE BEGAN.
REALIZING WHAT THE CITY WAS UP TO, SEVERAL DOZEN NEIGHBORHOOD RESIDENTS SURGED SPONTANEOUSLY FORWARD AND THREW THEMSELVES ONTO THE GRASS ALONG THE PARK'S PERIMETER WHERE THE NEW FENCE WAS SLATED TO GO.
AS WORD SPREAD, RUSSELL PARK WAS QUICKLY FILLED WITH ALARMED SPECTATORS, MANY OF WHOM JOINED IN THE PROTEST ONCE THEY'D SIZED UP THE SITUATION.
HUNDREDS MORE CHOSE TO STAND WARILY ON THE FRINGES OF THE SIT-IN AND OFFER TENSE SUPPORT.
YOU COLORED PEOPLE ARE ILLEGALLY INTERFERING WITH THE WORK OF CLAYFIELD'S PARK MAINTENANCE DEPARTMENT!
CLAYFIELD POLICE
IN THE THICK OF THE ACTION WE COULD SEE SHILOH REED LEADING THE PEOPLE AROUND HIM IN A SPIRITED SING-ALONG.
...Stayed on freedom! Hallelu!...
I ORDER YOU TO CLEAR THE AREA PEACEFULLY AND IMMEDIATELY OR YOU WILL BE FORCIBLY REMOVED!
CLAYFIELD POLICE
STAND BACK!
MOVE ASIDE!
WE GOT SOME OBSTRUCTIN' O' THE LAW TO DO!
C'MON, CHILDREN!
GRAB A SEAT!
UH...
RILEY, IT LOOKS DANGER-OUS.
WE JUST CAME TO WATCH, MA'AM—
COMMENTARY FROM A PACK OF SNOTNOSED HECKLERS ON THE SIDELINES HELPED MAKE UP OUR MINDS FOR US:
TRAITORS!
WHITE NIGGERS!
??! THEY'RE TALKIN' TO US, BABY!
WELL, SCREW THEM!
UH...
MOVE OVER, MABEL!

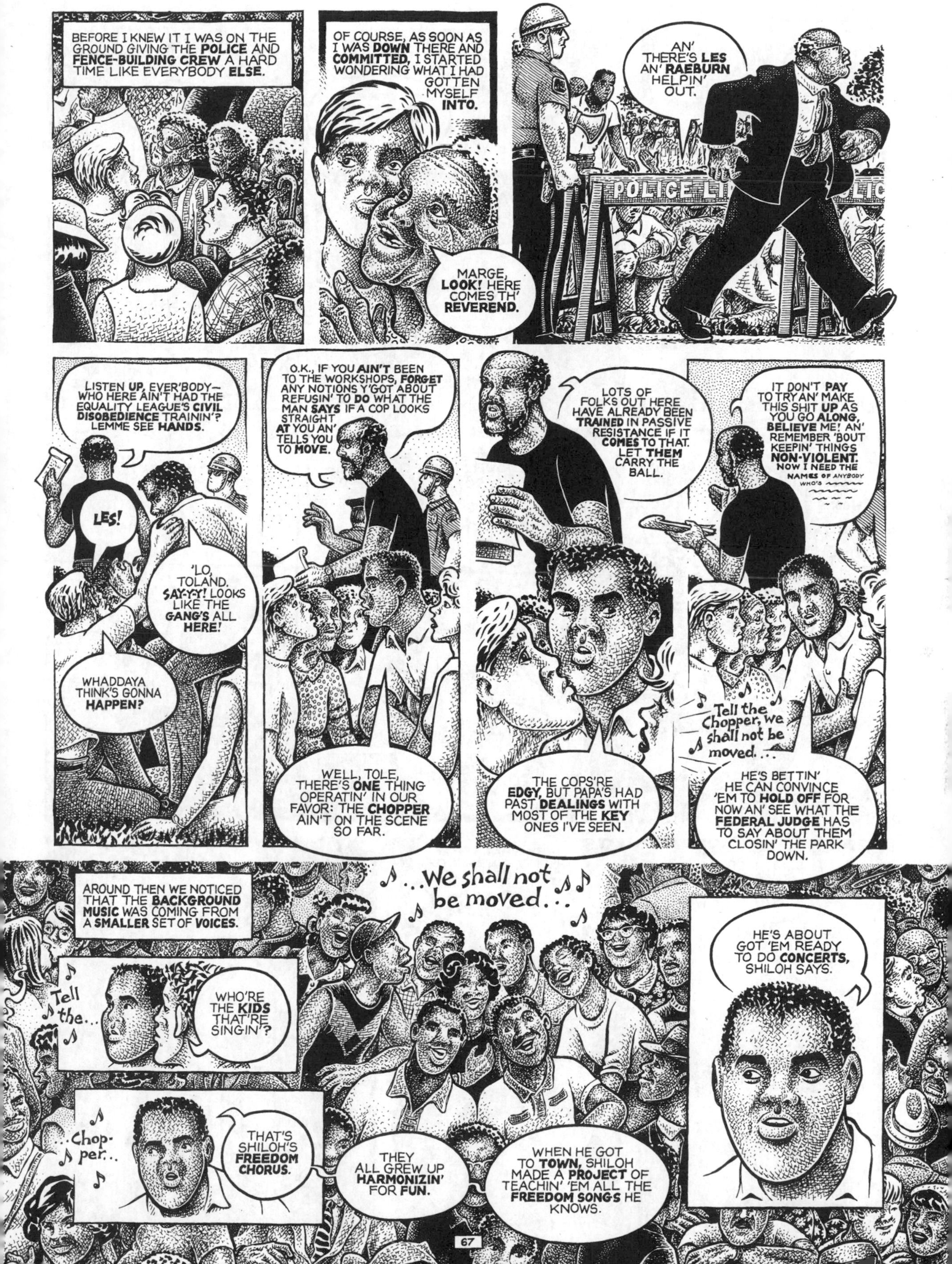

BEFORE I KNEW IT I WAS ON THE GROUND GIVING THE POLICE AND FENCE-BUILDING CREW A HARD TIME LIKE EVERYBODY ELSE.
OF COURSE, AS SOON AS I WAS DOWN THERE AND COMMITTED, I STARTED WONDERING WHAT I HAD GOTTEN MYSELF INTO.
MARGE, LOOK! HERE COMES TH' REVEREND.
AN' THERE'S LES AN' RAEBURN HELPIN' OUT.
POLICE LI
LIC
LISTEN UP, EVER'BODY— WHO HERE AIN'T HAD THE EQUALITY LEAGUE'S CIVIL DISOBEDIENCE TRAININ'? LEMME SEE HANDS.
LES!
'LO, TOLAND. SAY-Y-Y! LOOKS LIKE THE GANG'S ALL HERE!
WHADDAYA THINK'S GONNA HAPPEN?
O.K., IF YOU AIN'T BEEN TO THE WORKSHOPS, FORGET ANY NOTIONS Y'GOT ABOUT REFUSIN' TO DO WHAT THE MAN SAYS IF A COP LOOKS STRAIGHT AT YOU AN' TELLS YOU TO MOVE.
WELL, TOLE, THERE'S ONE THING OPERATIN' IN OUR FAVOR: THE CHOPPER AIN'T ON THE SCENE SO FAR.
LOTS OF FOLKS OUT HERE HAVE ALREADY BEEN TRAINED IN PASSIVE RESISTANCE IF IT COMES TO THAT. LET THEM CARRY THE BALL.
THE COPS'RE EDGY, BUT PAPA'S HAD PAST DEALINGS WITH MOST OF THE KEY ONES I'VE SEEN.
IT DON'T PAY TO TRY AN' MAKE THIS SHIT UP AS YOU GO ALONG, BELIEVE ME! AN' REMEMBER 'BOUT KEEPIN' THINGS NON-VIOLENT. NOW I NEED THE NAMES OF ANYBODY WHO'S
Tell the Chopper, we shall not be moved...
HE'S BETTIN' HE CAN CONVINCE 'EM TO HOLD OFF FOR NOW AN' SEE WHAT THE FEDERAL JUDGE HAS TO SAY ABOUT THEM CLOSIN' THE PARK DOWN.
AROUND THEN WE NOTICED THAT THE BACKGROUND MUSIC WAS COMING FROM A SMALLER SET OF VOICES.
...We shall not be moved...
Tell the...
WHO'RE THE KIDS THAT'RE SINGIN'?
...Chop-per...
THAT'S SHILOH'S FREEDOM CHORUS.
THEY ALL GREW UP HARMONIZIN' FOR FUN.
WHEN HE GOT TO TOWN, SHILOH MADE A PROJECT OF TEACHIN' 'EM ALL THE FREEDOM SONGS HE KNOWS.
HE'S ABOUT GOT 'EM READY TO DO CONCERTS, SHILOH SAYS.

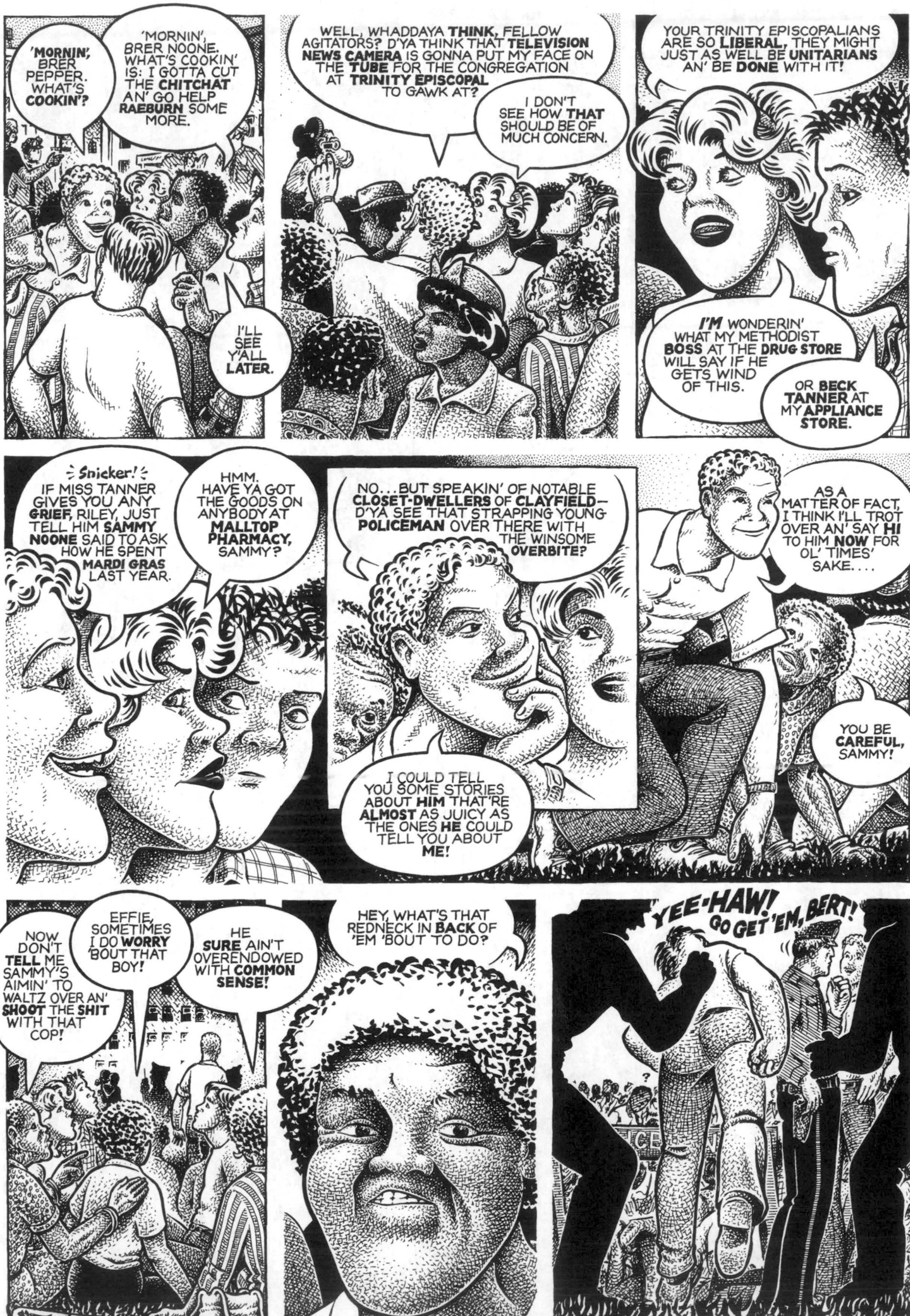
'MORNIN', BRER PEPPER. WHAT'S COOKIN'?
'MORNIN', BRER NOONE. WHAT'S COOKIN' IS: I GOTTA CUT THE CHITCHAT AN' GO HELP RAEBURN SOME MORE.
I'LL SEE Y'ALL LATER.
WELL, WHADDAYA THINK, FELLOW AGITATORS? D'YA THINK THAT TELEVISION NEWS CAMERA IS GONNA PUT MY FACE ON THE TUBE FOR THE CONGREGATION AT TRINITY EPISCOPAL TO GAWK AT?
I DON'T SEE HOW THAT SHOULD BE OF MUCH CONCERN.
YOUR TRINITY EPISCOPALIANS ARE SO LIBERAL, THEY MIGHT JUST AS WELL BE UNITARIANS AN' BE DONE WITH IT!
I'M WONDERIN' WHAT MY METHODIST BOSS AT THE DRUG STORE WILL SAY IF HE GETS WIND OF THIS.
OR BECK TANNER AT MY APPLIANCE STORE.
Snicker!
IF MISS TANNER GIVES YOU ANY GRIEF, RILEY, JUST TELL HIM SAMMY NOONE SAID TO ASK HOW HE SPENT MARDI GRAS LAST YEAR.
HMM. HAVE YA GOT THE GOODS ON ANYBODY AT MALLTOP PHARMACY, SAMMY?
NO... BUT SPEAKIN' OF NOTABLE CLOSET-DWELLERS OF CLAYFIELD— D'YA SEE THAT STRAPPING YOUNG POLICEMAN OVER THERE WITH THE WINSOME OVERBITE?
I COULD TELL YOU SOME STORIES ABOUT HIM THAT'RE ALMOST AS JUICY AS THE ONES HE COULD TELL YOU ABOUT ME!
AS A MATTER OF FACT, I THINK I'LL TROT OVER AN' SAY HI TO HIM NOW FOR OL' TIMES' SAKE....
YOU BE CAREFUL, SAMMY!
NOW DON'T TELL ME SAMMY'S AIMIN' TO WALTZ OVER AN' SHOOT THE SHIT WITH THAT COP!
EFFIE, SOMETIMES I DO WORRY 'BOUT THAT BOY!
HE SURE AIN'T OVERENDOWED WITH COMMON SENSE!
HEY, WHAT'S THAT REDNECK IN BACK OF 'EM 'BOUT TO DO?
YEE-HAW! GO GET 'EM, BERT!

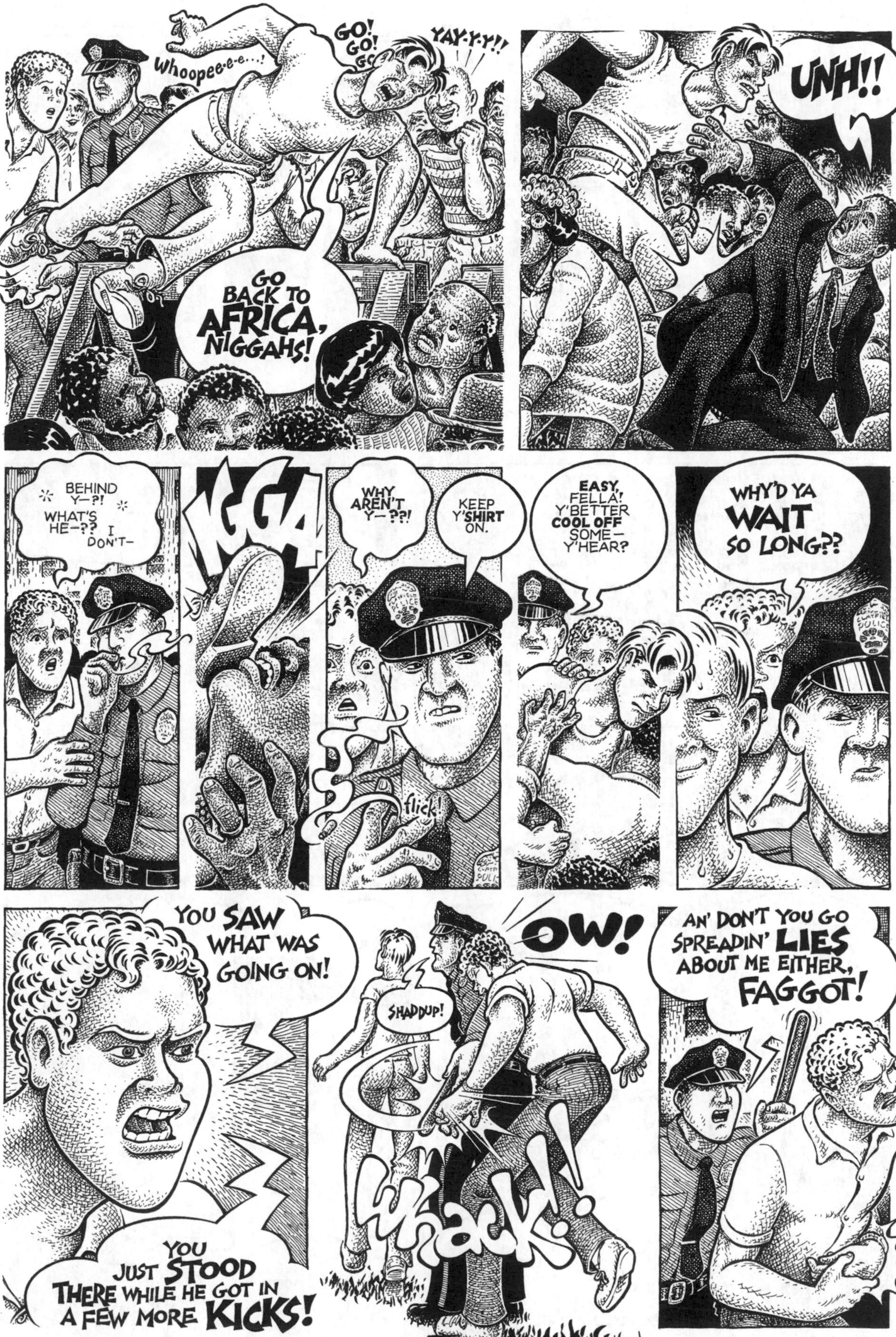

Whoopee-e-e...!
GO! GO! GO
YAY-Y-Y!!
GO BACK TO AFRICA, NIGGAHS!
UNH!!
BEHIND Y—?! WHAT'S HE—?? I DON'T—
WHY AREN'T Y—??!
KEEP Y'SHIRT ON.
flick!
EASY, FELLA! Y'BETTER COOL OFF SOME— Y'HEAR?
WHY'D YA WAIT SO LONG??
YOU SAW WHAT WAS GOING ON!
YOU JUST STOOD THERE WHILE HE GOT IN A FEW MORE KICKS!
OW!
SHADDUP!
WHACK!!
AN' DON'T YOU GO SPREADIN' LIES ABOUT ME EITHER, FAGGOT!

ARE YOU **ALL RIGHT**, SAMMY?

Groan! THE BASTARD HIT MY **HAND!** AN' HE **KNOWS** HOW I EARN MY **LIVIN'!**

DAMN COP BETTER NOT SWING AT **ME** OR I'LL KNOCK HIS BUTT CLEAR TO **BILOXI!**

DON'T TALK LIKE **THAT**, MABEL! **THAT** AIN'T THE **SPIRIT!**

Y'WANNA GO TO A **DOCTOR**, PAL?

DON'T WANNA GO **ANYWHERE** RIGHT NOW. JUST LEMME BE **STILL** HERE 'TIL IT STOPS **THROBBIN'**.

IF ASKED, I'D HAVE TOLD YOU A **RIOT** WAS GONNA BREAK OUT ONCE THE **KICKING** STARTED. BUT SOMEHOW **TEMPERS** GOT **HELD**.

COME MID-AFTERNOON, OUR ASSES WERE STILL RIGHT **THERE** ON THE **GRASS**.

IT WAS A HELL OF A WAY TO SPEND A **SATURDAY**.

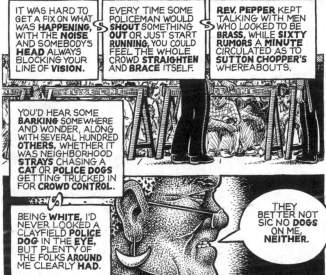

IT WAS HARD TO GET A FIX ON WHAT WAS **HAPPENING**, WITH THE **NOISE** AND SOMEBODY'S **HEAD** ALWAYS BLOCKING YOUR LINE OF **VISION**.

EVERY TIME SOME POLICEMAN WOULD **SHOUT** SOMETHING **OUT** OR JUST START **RUNNING**, YOU COULD FEEL THE WHOLE CROWD **STRAIGHTEN** AND **BRACE** ITSELF.

REV. PEPPER KEPT TALKING WITH MEN WHO LOOKED TO BE **BRASS**, WHILE **SIXTY RUMORS** A **MINUTE** CIRCULATED AS TO **SUTTON CHOPPER'S** WHEREABOUTS.

YOU'D HEAR SOME **BARKING** SOMEWHERE AND WONDER, ALONG WITH SEVERAL HUNDRED **OTHERS**, WHETHER IT WAS NEIGHBORHOOD **STRAYS** CHASING A **CAT** OR **POLICE DOGS** GETTING TRUCKED IN FOR **CROWD CONTROL**.

BEING **WHITE**, I'D NEVER LOOKED A CLAYFIELD **POLICE DOG** IN THE **EYE**, BUT PLENTY OF THE FOLKS **AROUND** ME CLEARLY **HAD**.

THEY BETTER NOT SIC NO **DOGS** ON ME, **NEITHER**.

'ROONS 'WARE!

AND THERE, TO GRATE ON **EVERYBODY'S** NERVES, WERE CARS FULL OF COCKY WHITE **TEENAGERS** THAT KEPT CIRCLING THE BLOCK WITH **REBEL FLAGS** FLAPPING FROM THEIR **RADIO ANTENNAS**.

MABEL, DO YOUR **EYES** FOR MAVIS AN' TOLAND.

AW, **HELL**, RILEY... I CAN'T JUST DO MY EYES AT THE DROP OF A **HAT**. I'VE GOTTA BE IN THE **MOOD**.

C'MON, **YOU** CAN DO IT. I WANT 'EM TO HEAR YOUR **'CRAZY NIGGER'** STORY.

LORD! YOU BEEN TELLIN' THAT STORY **AGAIN**, SISTER?

WELL... O.K.

YOU **ASKED** FOR IT.

HERE **GOES**.

YIKES!

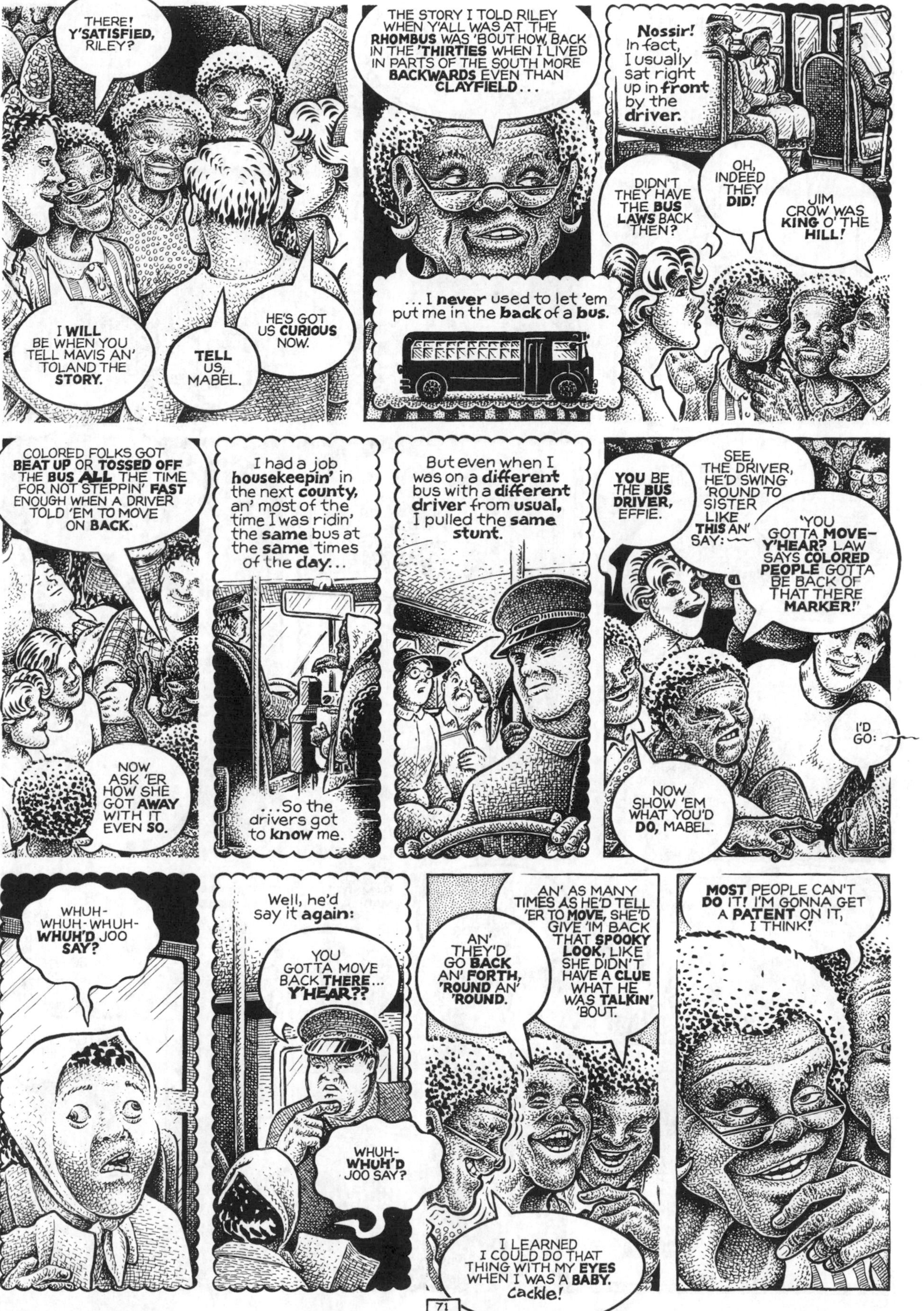
THERE! Y'SATISFIED, RILEY?
I WILL BE WHEN YOU TELL MAVIS AN' TOLAND THE STORY.
TELL US, MABEL.
HE'S GOT US CURIOUS NOW.
THE STORY I TOLD RILEY WHEN Y'ALL WAS AT THE RHOMBUS WAS 'BOUT HOW, BACK IN THE 'THIRTIES WHEN I LIVED IN PARTS OF THE SOUTH MORE BACKWARDS EVEN THAN CLAYFIELD...
...I never used to let 'em put me in the back of a bus.
Nossir! In fact, I usually sat right up in front by the driver.
DIDN'T THEY HAVE THE BUS LAWS BACK THEN?
OH, INDEED THEY DID!
JIM CROW WAS KING O' THE HILL!
COLORED FOLKS GOT BEAT UP OR TOSSED OFF THE BUS ALL THE TIME FOR NOT STEPPIN' FAST ENOUGH WHEN A DRIVER TOLD 'EM TO MOVE ON BACK.
NOW ASK 'ER HOW SHE GOT AWAY WITH IT EVEN SO.
I had a job housekeepin' in the next county, an' most of the time I was ridin' the same bus at the same times of the day...
...So the drivers got to know me.
But even when I was on a different bus with a different driver from usual, I pulled the same stunt.
YOU BE THE BUS DRIVER, EFFIE.
SEE, THE DRIVER, HE'D SWING 'ROUND TO SISTER LIKE THIS AN' SAY:
'YOU GOTTA MOVE—Y'HEAR? LAW SAYS COLORED PEOPLE GOTTA BE BACK OF THAT THERE MARKER!'
I'D GO:
NOW SHOW 'EM WHAT YOU'D DO, MABEL.
WHUH-WHUH-WHUH-WHUH'D JOO SAY?
Well, he'd say it again:
YOU GOTTA MOVE BACK THERE... Y'HEAR??
WHUH-WHUH'D JOO SAY?
AN' AS MANY TIMES AS HE'D TELL 'ER TO MOVE, SHE'D GIVE 'IM BACK THAT SPOOKY LOOK, LIKE SHE DIDN'T HAVE A CLUE WHAT HE WAS TALKIN' 'BOUT.
AN' THEY'D GO BACK AN' FORTH, 'ROUND AN' 'ROUND.
I LEARNED I COULD DO THAT THING WITH MY EYES WHEN I WAS A BABY. Cackle!
MOST PEOPLE CAN'T DO IT! I'M GONNA GET A PATENT ON IT, I THINK!

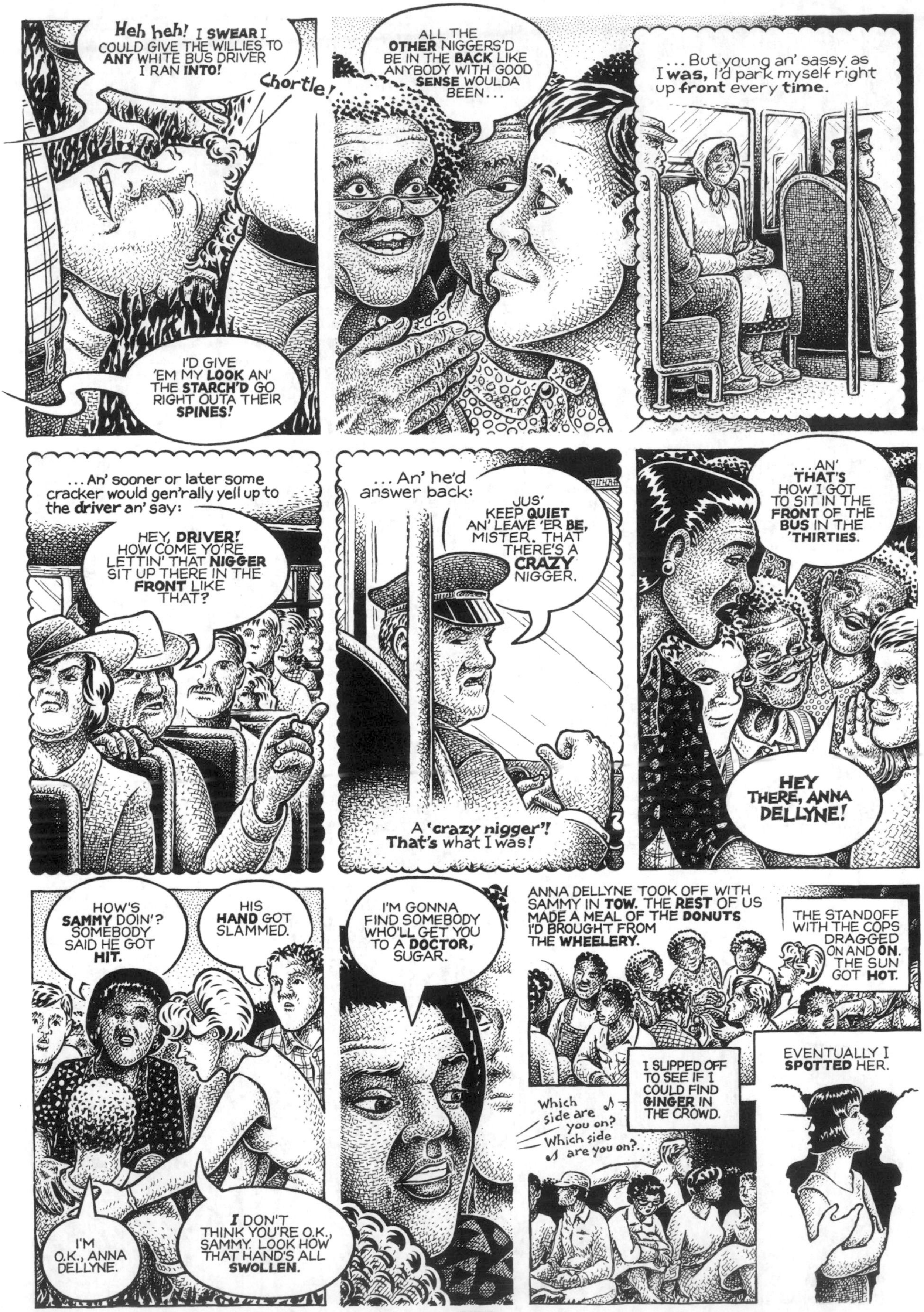
Heh heh! I SWEAR I COULD GIVE THE WILLIES TO ANY WHITE BUS DRIVER I RAN INTO!
Chortle!
I'D GIVE 'EM MY LOOK AN' THE STARCH'D GO RIGHT OUTA THEIR SPINES!
ALL THE OTHER NIGGERS'D BE IN THE BACK LIKE ANYBODY WITH GOOD SENSE WOULDA BEEN...
... But young an' sassy as I was, I'd park myself right up front every time.
... An' sooner or later some cracker would gen'rally yell up to the driver an' say:
HEY, DRIVER! HOW COME YO'RE LETTIN' THAT NIGGER SIT UP THERE IN THE FRONT LIKE THAT?
... An' he'd answer back:
JUS' KEEP QUIET AN' LEAVE 'ER BE, MISTER. THAT THERE'S A CRAZY NIGGER.
A 'crazy nigger'! That's what I was!
... AN' THAT'S HOW I GOT TO SIT IN THE FRONT OF THE BUS IN THE 'THIRTIES.
HEY THERE, ANNA DELLYNE!
HOW'S SAMMY DOIN'? SOMEBODY SAID HE GOT HIT.
HIS HAND GOT SLAMMED.
I'M O.K., ANNA DELLYNE.
I DON'T THINK YOU'RE O.K., SAMMY. LOOK HOW THAT HAND'S ALL SWOLLEN.
I'M GONNA FIND SOMEBODY WHO'LL GET YOU TO A DOCTOR, SUGAR.
ANNA DELLYNE TOOK OFF WITH SAMMY IN TOW. THE REST OF US MADE A MEAL OF THE DONUTS I'D BROUGHT FROM THE WHEELERY.
THE STANDOFF WITH THE COPS DRAGGED ON AND ON. THE SUN GOT HOT.
I SLIPPED OFF TO SEE IF I COULD FIND GINGER IN THE CROWD.
Which side are you on? Which side are you on?...
EVENTUALLY I SPOTTED HER.

♪ Wade in the water... ♪ Wade in the water, children... ♪

HAVE YOU BEEN HERE **LONG?**

SINCE MID-MORNIN'.

ME, TOO.

THE CROWD'S **THICK.** I DIDN'T **SEE** YOU.

MAVIS AN' **RILEY** ARE HERE, **TOO.** WE'VE ALL BEEN SITTIN' OVER THERE ON THE GRASS LIKE **GOOD CITIZENS** ALL MORNIN'!

I DON'T KNOW IF I'VE **EVER** FELT **SADDER** THAN I DID JUST **NOW.**

I KNOW. **REV. PEPPER** SAYS RUSSELL PARK HAS **ALWAYS—**

NO, I MEAN IT MADE ME SAD WHEN YOU LOOKED UP AN' **SAW** ME JUST NOW. YOU DIDN'T **SMILE.**

I **DIDN'T?**

I WORRIED ALL NIGHT ABOUT HOW YOU'D **FEEL** TODAY ABOUT WHAT I **TOLD** YOU. ABOUT WHETHER YOU'D STILL **LIKE** ME AND WANNA BE **FRIENDS.**

WHY WOULDN'T WE BE **FRIENDS?** I HAVE GAY FRIENDS.

I WANT **MORE.** I **LOVE** YOU.

♪ I'm gonna lay down my sword and shield Down by the riverside... ♪

TOLAND, IF THINGS WERE **NORMAL,** I'D PROBABLY HAVE SPENT SOME TIME TODAY **THINKIN'** ABOUT **YOU** AN' YOUR **PROBLEMS...**

...BUT TO TELL THE TRUTH, WITH ALL OF **THIS** HAPPENIN', **YOU** HAVEN'T BEEN ON MY MIND AT **ALL.**

♪ Down by the riverside... ♪ Down by the riverside... ♪

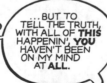

I'M NOT GOOD **COMPANY** FOR YOU TODAY, HON. MY MOOD IS **FOUL.**

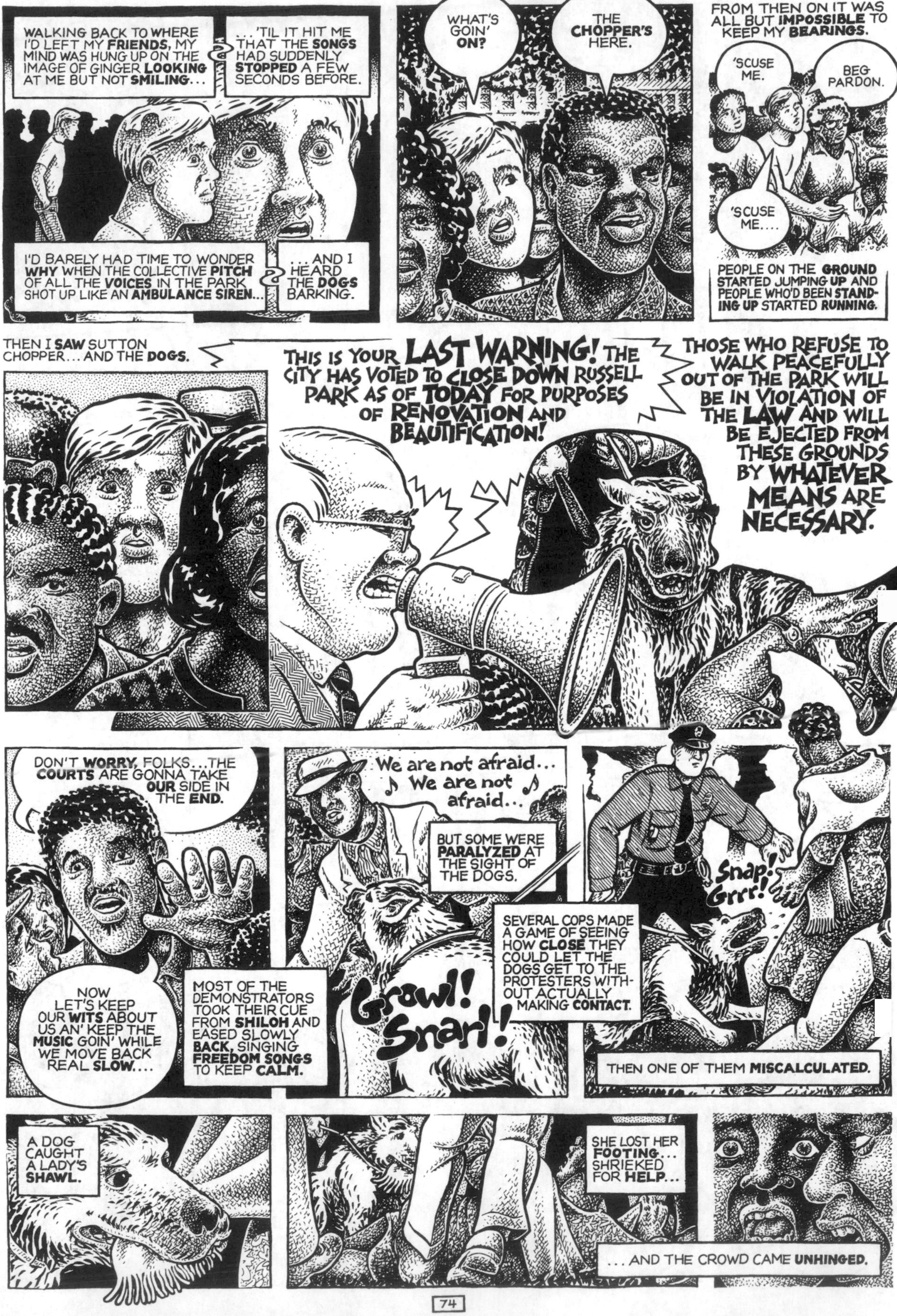

WALKING BACK TO WHERE I'D LEFT MY FRIENDS, MY MIND WAS HUNG UP ON THE IMAGE OF GINGER LOOKING AT ME BUT NOT SMILING...
...'TIL IT HIT ME THAT THE SONGS HAD SUDDENLY STOPPED A FEW SECONDS BEFORE.
I'D BARELY HAD TIME TO WONDER WHY WHEN THE COLLECTIVE PITCH OF ALL THE VOICES IN THE PARK SHOT UP LIKE AN AMBULANCE SIREN...
...AND I HEARD THE DOGS BARKING.
WHAT'S GOIN' ON?
THE CHOPPER'S HERE.
FROM THEN ON IT WAS ALL BUT IMPOSSIBLE TO KEEP MY BEARINGS.
'SCUSE ME.
BEG PARDON.
'SCUSE ME....
PEOPLE ON THE GROUND STARTED JUMPING UP AND PEOPLE WHO'D BEEN STANDING UP STARTED RUNNING.
THEN I SAW SUTTON CHOPPER... AND THE DOGS.
THIS IS YOUR LAST WARNING! THE CITY HAS VOTED TO CLOSE DOWN RUSSELL PARK AS OF TODAY FOR PURPOSES OF RENOVATION AND BEAUTIFICATION!
THOSE WHO REFUSE TO WALK PEACEFULLY OUT OF THE PARK WILL BE IN VIOLATION OF THE LAW AND WILL BE EJECTED FROM THESE GROUNDS BY WHATEVER MEANS ARE NECESSARY.
DON'T WORRY, FOLKS... THE COURTS ARE GONNA TAKE OUR SIDE IN THE END.
NOW LET'S KEEP OUR WITS ABOUT US AN' KEEP THE MUSIC GOIN' WHILE WE MOVE BACK REAL SLOW....
MOST OF THE DEMONSTRATORS TOOK THEIR CUE FROM SHILOH AND EASED SLOWLY BACK, SINGING FREEDOM SONGS TO KEEP CALM.
We are not afraid... ♪ We are not ♪ afraid...
BUT SOME WERE PARALYZED AT THE SIGHT OF THE DOGS.
Growl! Snarl!
SEVERAL COPS MADE A GAME OF SEEING HOW CLOSE THEY COULD LET THE DOGS GET TO THE PROTESTERS WITHOUT ACTUALLY MAKING CONTACT.
Snap! Grrr!
THEN ONE OF THEM MISCALCULATED.
A DOG CAUGHT A LADY'S SHAWL.
SHE LOST HER FOOTING... SHRIEKED FOR HELP...
...AND THE CROWD CAME UNHINGED.

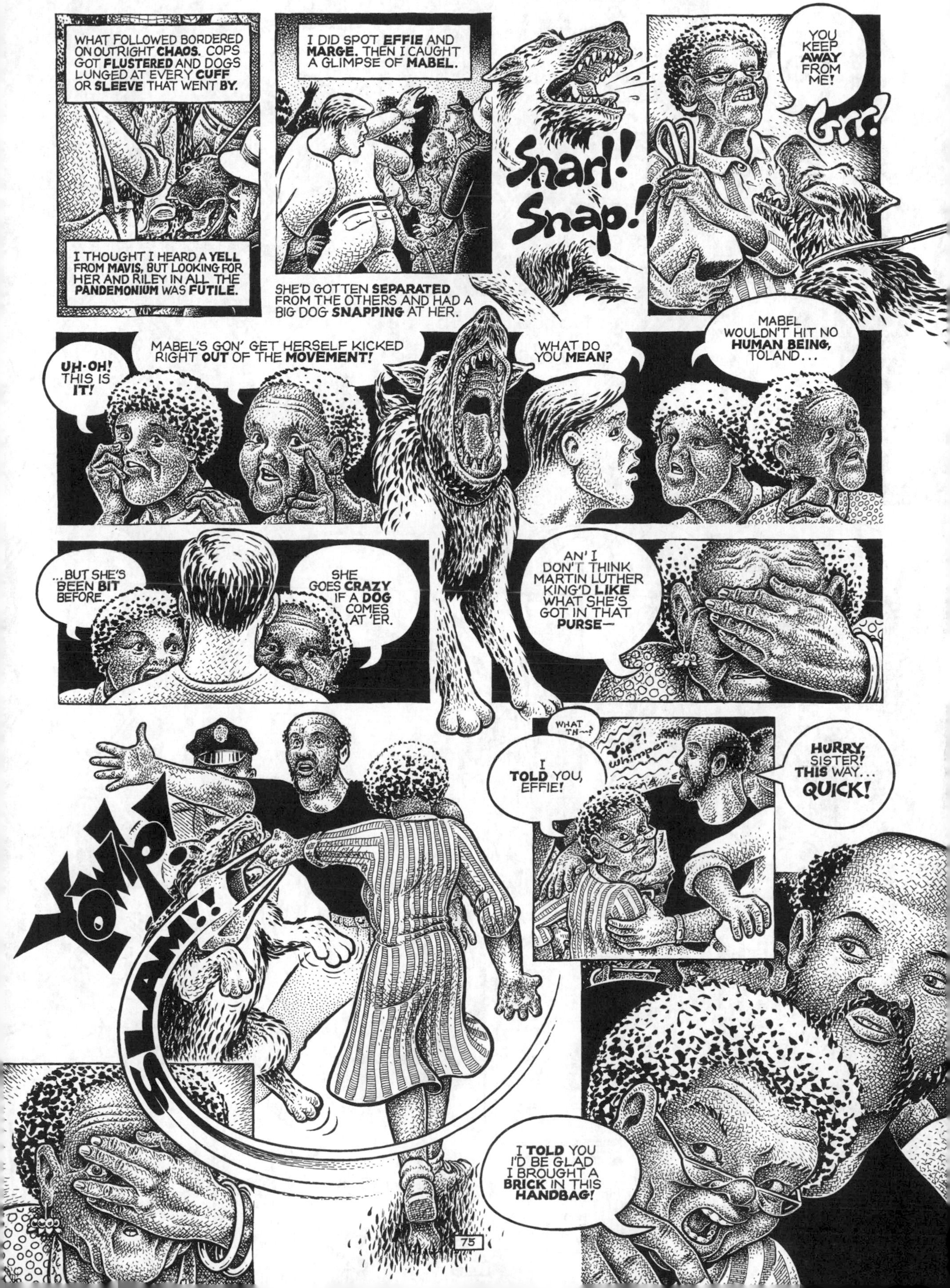
WHAT FOLLOWED BORDERED ON OUTRIGHT CHAOS. COPS GOT FLUSTERED AND DOGS LUNGED AT EVERY CUFF OR SLEEVE THAT WENT BY.
I THOUGHT I HEARD A YELL FROM MAVIS, BUT LOOKING FOR HER AND RILEY IN ALL THE PANDEMONIUM WAS FUTILE.
I DID SPOT EFFIE AND MARGE. THEN I CAUGHT A GLIMPSE OF MABEL.
SHE'D GOTTEN SEPARATED FROM THE OTHERS AND HAD A BIG DOG SNAPPING AT HER.
Snarl! Snap!
YOU KEEP AWAY FROM ME!
Grr?!
UH-OH! THIS IS IT!
MABEL'S GON' GET HERSELF KICKED RIGHT OUT OF THE MOVEMENT!
WHAT DO YOU MEAN?
MABEL WOULDN'T HIT NO HUMAN BEING, TOLAND...
...BUT SHE'S BEEN BIT BEFORE.
SHE GOES CRAZY IF A DOG COMES AT 'ER.
AN' I DON'T THINK MARTIN LUTHER KING'D LIKE WHAT SHE'S GOT IN THAT PURSE—
YOWP!
SLAM!!
WHAT TH—?
Yip?! whimper...
I TOLD YOU, EFFIE!
HURRY, SISTER! THIS WAY... QUICK!
I TOLD YOU I'D BE GLAD I BROUGHT A BRICK IN THIS HANDBAG!

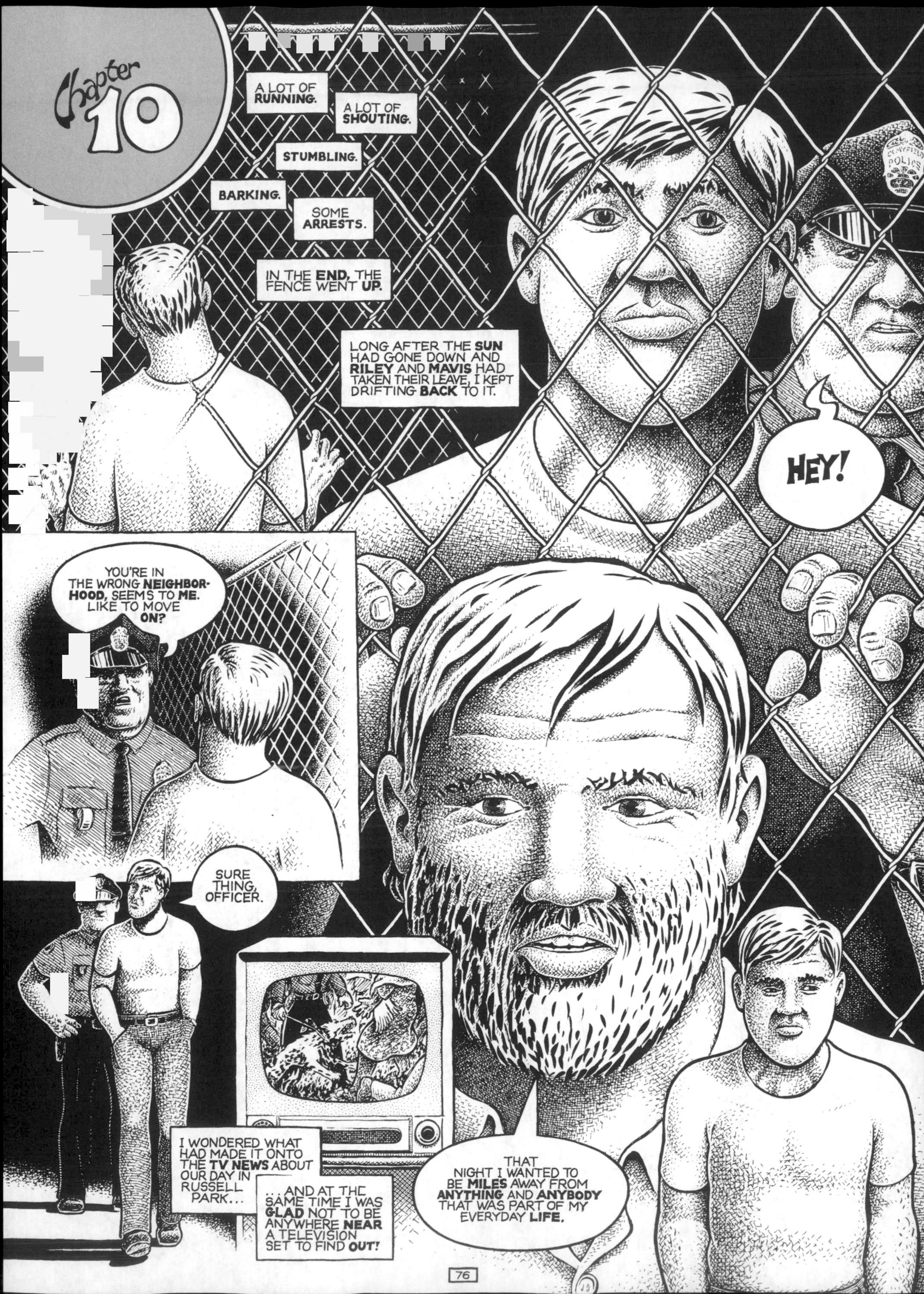
Chapter 10
A LOT OF RUNNING.
A LOT OF SHOUTING.
STUMBLING.
BARKING.
SOME ARRESTS.
IN THE END, THE FENCE WENT UP.
LONG AFTER THE SUN HAD GONE DOWN AND RILEY AND MAVIS HAD TAKEN THEIR LEAVE, I KEPT DRIFTING BACK TO IT.
HEY!
YOU'RE IN THE WRONG NEIGHBORHOOD, SEEMS TO ME. LIKE TO MOVE ON?
SURE THING, OFFICER.
I WONDERED WHAT HAD MADE IT ONTO THE TV NEWS ABOUT OUR DAY IN RUSSELL PARK...
...AND AT THE SAME TIME I WAS GLAD NOT TO BE ANYWHERE NEAR A TELEVISION SET TO FIND OUT!
THAT NIGHT I WANTED TO BE MILES AWAY FROM ANYTHING AND ANYBODY THAT WAS PART OF MY EVERYDAY LIFE.

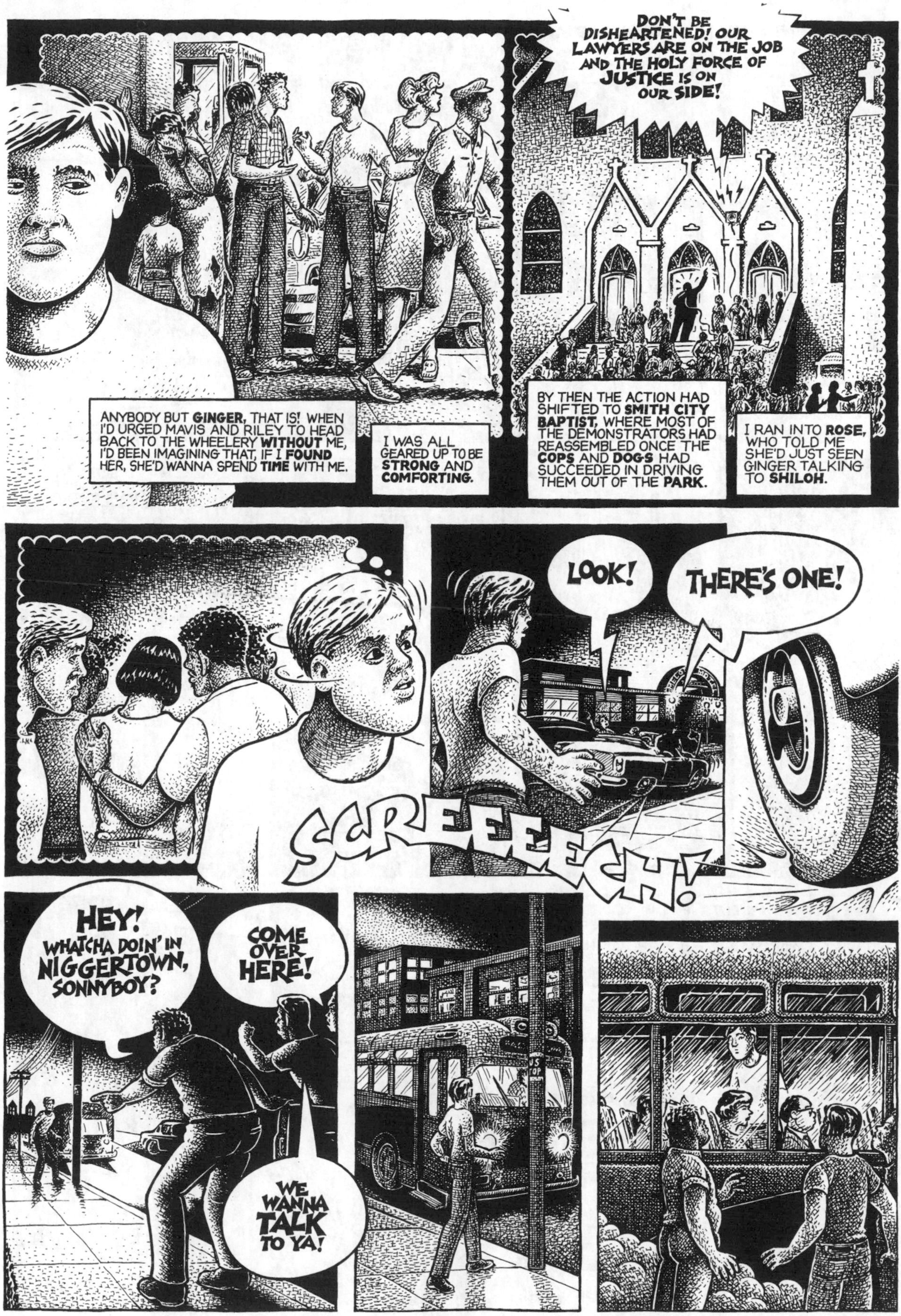
ANYBODY BUT GINGER, THAT IS! WHEN I'D URGED MAVIS AND RILEY TO HEAD BACK TO THE WHEELERY WITHOUT ME, I'D BEEN IMAGINING THAT, IF I FOUND HER, SHE'D WANNA SPEND TIME WITH ME.
I WAS ALL GEARED UP TO BE STRONG AND COMFORTING.
DON'T BE DISHEARTENED! OUR LAWYERS ARE ON THE JOB AND THE HOLY FORCE OF JUSTICE IS ON OUR SIDE!
BY THEN THE ACTION HAD SHIFTED TO SMITH CITY BAPTIST, WHERE MOST OF THE DEMONSTRATORS HAD REASSEMBLED ONCE THE COPS AND DOGS HAD SUCCEEDED IN DRIVING THEM OUT OF THE PARK.
I RAN INTO ROSE, WHO TOLD ME SHE'D JUST SEEN GINGER TALKING TO SHILOH.
LOOK!
THERE'S ONE!
SCREEEECH!
HEY! WHATCHA DOIN' IN NIGGERTOWN, SONNYBOY?
COME OVER HERE!
WE WANNA TALK TO YA!

WHEN I GOT ON THE BUS, MY **INTENTION** WAS TO TRANSFER AT EIGHTEENTH STREET TO THE **COLLEGE LINE**, WHICH WOULD HAVE TAKEN ME DIRECTLY OUT TO THE **WHEELERY**.

BUT I NEVER **TRANSFERRED**.

INSTEAD I RODE ON TO **NINTH STREET**.

YOU HAVEN'T EATEN A **BURGER** UNTIL YOU'VE EATEN A **DON BURGER**

DON'S BLACKBERRY COBBLER. FAMOUS THROUGHOUT THE SOUTH

COME AGAIN! YOU'RE ALWAYS WELCOME AT **DON'S DINER**

WE RESERVE THE RIGHT TO REFUSE SERVICE TO ANYONE AT THE DISCRETION OF THE MANAGER

DID YOU KNOW ABOUT THESE **DIXIE PATRIOTS** BEIN' STACKED THERE BY THE DOOR?

OH, **THOSE** THINGS! AREN'T THEY **AWFUL**?

SOME MAN **INSISTS** ON COMIN' AN' PUTTIN' **PILES** OF THOSE PAPERS OUT FRONT. MY **BOSS** LETS HIM DO IT. NOBODY ASKS **ME**!

THE PEOPLE THAT PUT THAT OUT **SAY** THEY'RE **CHRISTIANS**, BUT I DON'T THINK THEY **ACT** VERY CHRISTIAN... DO **YOU**?

THEY **SAY** THINGS ABOUT PEOPLE THAT DON'T SEEM CHRISTIAN TO **ME** AT ALL!

OF COURSE, I **DO** THINK THEY HAVE A **POINT** WHEN THEY SAY IT'S PROBABLY THE **COMMUNISTS** WHO'RE CONVINCIN' THE NEGROES THAT THEY'RE SO **DISSATISFIED**.

BUT IT'S THE UGLY **WAY** THEY SAY IT! **UHN-UH!!**

IT'S **WAY** TOO UNCHRISTIAN FOR **ME**!

AFTER MY **MEAL**...

I STOOD, THEN STOOD SOME **MORE**. THEN FINALLY I WENT **IN**.

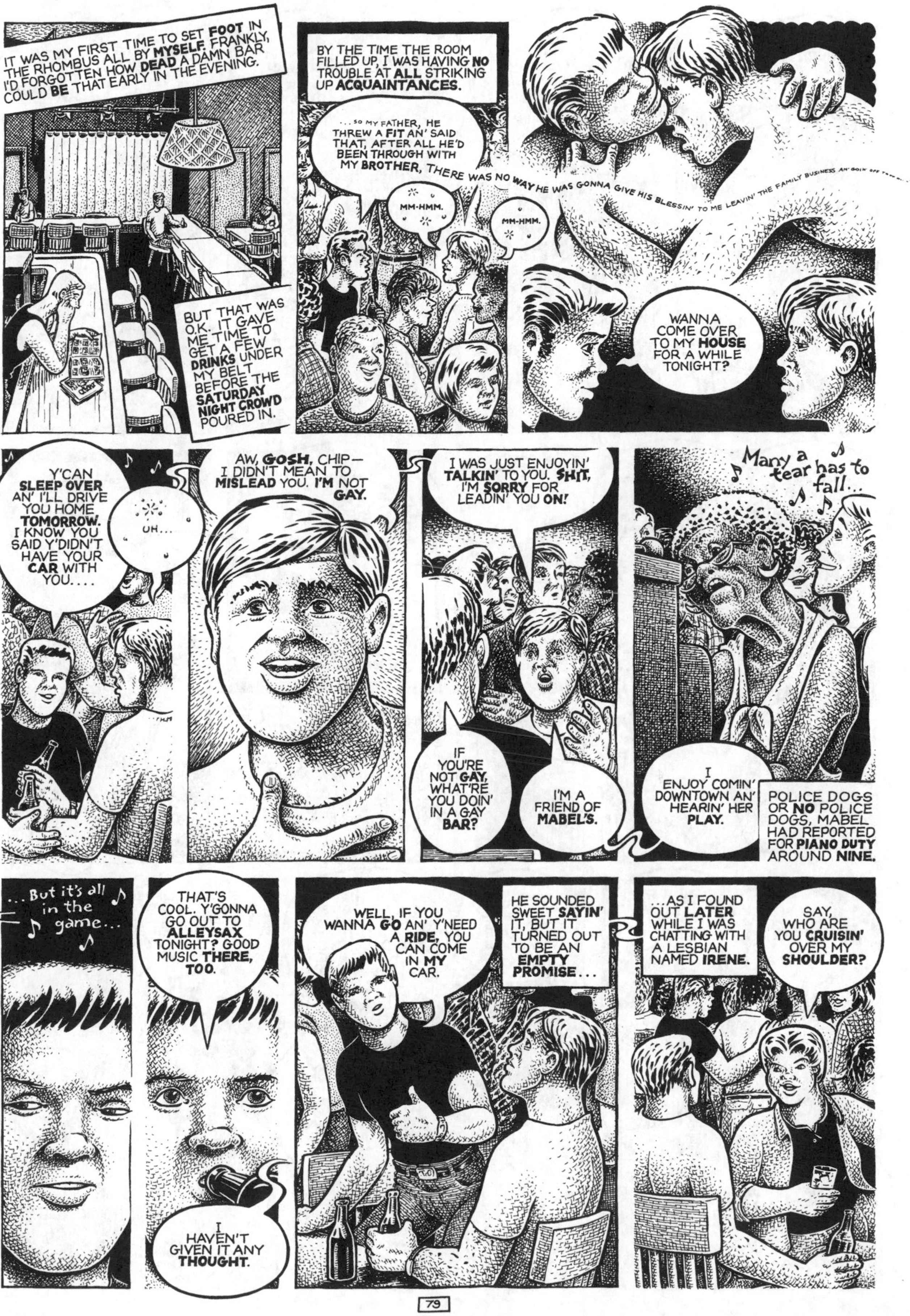
IT WAS MY FIRST TIME TO SET FOOT IN THE RHOMBUS ALL BY MYSELF. FRANKLY, I'D FORGOTTEN HOW DEAD A DAMN BAR COULD BE THAT EARLY IN THE EVENING.
BUT THAT WAS O.K. IT GAVE ME TIME TO GET A FEW DRINKS UNDER MY BELT BEFORE THE SATURDAY NIGHT CROWD POURED IN.
BY THE TIME THE ROOM FILLED UP, I WAS HAVING NO TROUBLE AT ALL STRIKING UP ACQUAINTANCES.
...SO MY FATHER, HE THREW A FIT AN' SAID THAT, AFTER ALL HE'D BEEN THROUGH WITH MY BROTHER, THERE WAS NO WAY HE WAS GONNA GIVE HIS BLESSIN' TO ME LEAVIN' THE FAMILY BUSINESS AN' GOIN' OFF
MM-HMM.
MM-HMM.
WANNA COME OVER TO MY HOUSE FOR A WHILE TONIGHT?
Y'CAN SLEEP OVER AN' I'LL DRIVE YOU HOME TOMORROW. I KNOW YOU SAID Y'DIDN'T HAVE YOUR CAR WITH YOU....
UH...
AW, GOSH, CHIP— I DIDN'T MEAN TO MISLEAD YOU. I'M NOT GAY.
I WAS JUST ENJOYIN' TALKIN' TO YOU. SHIT, I'M SORRY FOR LEADIN' YOU ON!
IF YOU'RE NOT GAY, WHAT'RE YOU DOIN' IN A GAY BAR?
I'M A FRIEND OF MABEL'S.
I ENJOY COMIN' DOWNTOWN AN' HEARIN' HER PLAY.
Many a tear has to fall...
POLICE DOGS OR NO POLICE DOGS, MABEL HAD REPORTED FOR PIANO DUTY AROUND NINE.
...But it's all in the game...
THAT'S COOL. Y'GONNA GO OUT TO ALLEYSAX TONIGHT? GOOD MUSIC THERE, TOO.
I HAVEN'T GIVEN IT ANY THOUGHT.
WELL, IF YOU WANNA GO AN' Y'NEED A RIDE, YOU CAN COME IN MY CAR.
HE SOUNDED SWEET SAYIN' IT, BUT IT TURNED OUT TO BE AN EMPTY PROMISE...
...AS I FOUND OUT LATER WHILE I WAS CHATTING WITH A LESBIAN NAMED IRENE.
SAY, WHO ARE YOU CRUISIN' OVER MY SHOULDER?

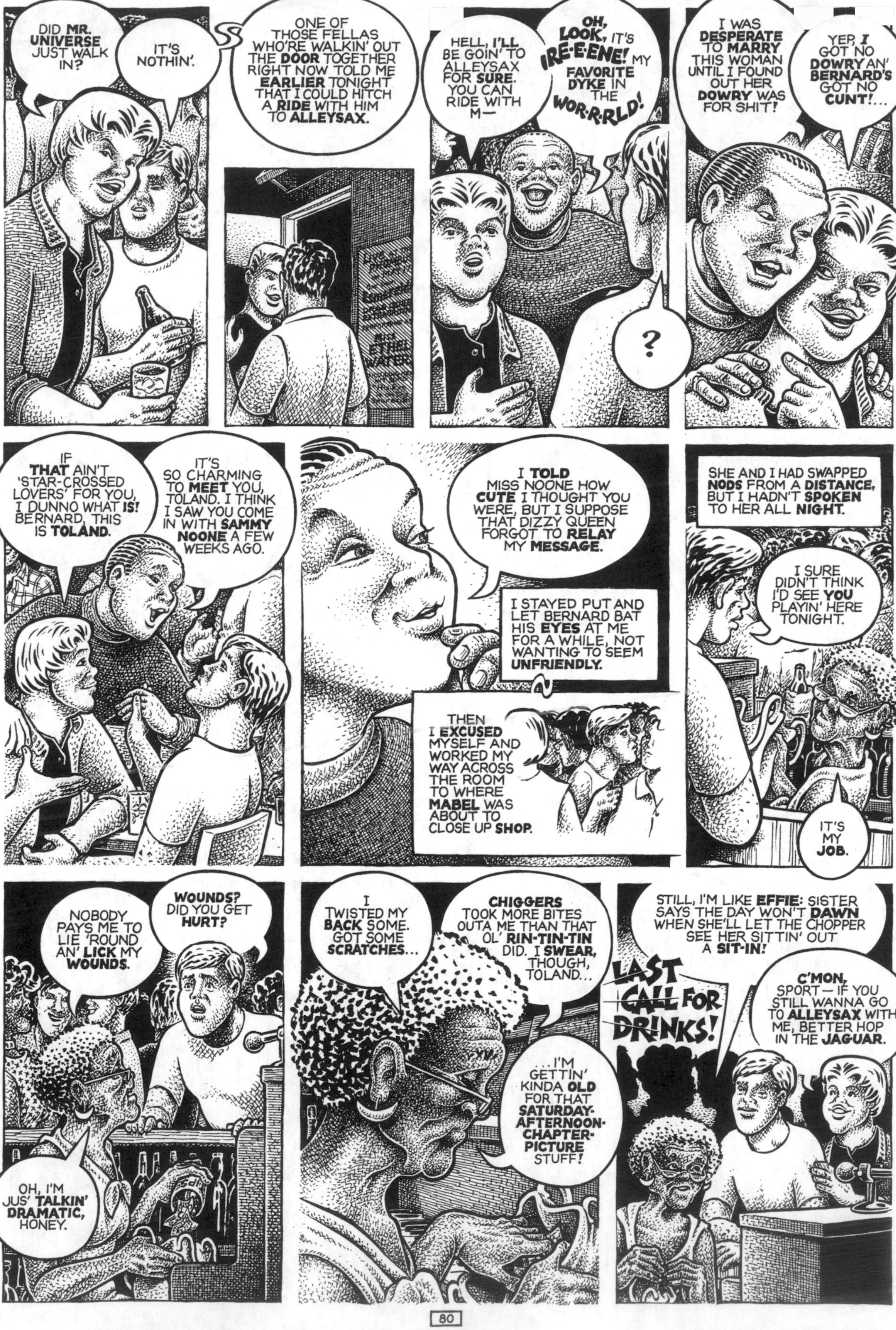

DID MR. UNIVERSE JUST WALK IN?
IT'S NOTHIN'.
ONE OF THOSE FELLAS WHO'RE WALKIN' OUT THE DOOR TOGETHER RIGHT NOW TOLD ME EARLIER TONIGHT THAT I COULD HITCH A RIDE WITH HIM TO ALLEYSAX.
HELL, I'LL BE GOIN' TO ALLEYSAX FOR SURE. YOU CAN RIDE WITH M—
OH, LOOK, IT'S IRE-E-ENE! MY FAVORITE DYKE IN THE WOR-R-RLD!
?
I WAS DESPERATE TO MARRY THIS WOMAN UNTIL I FOUND OUT HER DOWRY WAS FOR SHIT!
YEP, I GOT NO DOWRY AN' BERNARD'S GOT NO CUNT!...
IF THAT AIN'T 'STAR-CROSSED LOVERS' FOR YOU, I DUNNO WHAT IS! BERNARD, THIS IS TOLAND.
IT'S SO CHARMING TO MEET YOU, TOLAND. I THINK I SAW YOU COME IN WITH SAMMY NOONE A FEW WEEKS AGO.
I TOLD MISS NOONE HOW CUTE I THOUGHT YOU WERE, BUT I SUPPOSE THAT DIZZY QUEEN FORGOT TO RELAY MY MESSAGE.
I STAYED PUT AND LET BERNARD BAT HIS EYES AT ME FOR A WHILE, NOT WANTING TO SEEM UNFRIENDLY.
THEN I EXCUSED MYSELF AND WORKED MY WAY ACROSS THE ROOM TO WHERE MABEL WAS ABOUT TO CLOSE UP SHOP.
SHE AND I HAD SWAPPED NODS FROM A DISTANCE, BUT I HADN'T SPOKEN TO HER ALL NIGHT.
I SURE DIDN'T THINK I'D SEE YOU PLAYIN' HERE TONIGHT.
IT'S MY JOB.
NOBODY PAYS ME TO LIE 'ROUND AN' LICK MY WOUNDS.
WOUNDS? DID YOU GET HURT?
OH, I'M JUS' TALKIN' DRAMATIC, HONEY.
I TWISTED MY BACK SOME. GOT SOME SCRATCHES...
CHIGGERS TOOK MORE BITES OUTA ME THAN THAT OL' RIN-TIN-TIN DID. I SWEAR, THOUGH, TOLAND...
...I'M GETTIN' KINDA OLD FOR THAT SATURDAY-AFTERNOON-CHAPTER-PICTURE STUFF!
STILL, I'M LIKE EFFIE: SISTER SAYS THE DAY WON'T DAWN WHEN SHE'LL LET THE CHOPPER SEE HER SITTIN' OUT A SIT-IN!
LAST CALL FOR DRINKS!
C'MON, SPORT— IF YOU STILL WANNA GO TO ALLEYSAX WITH ME, BETTER HOP IN THE JAGUAR.

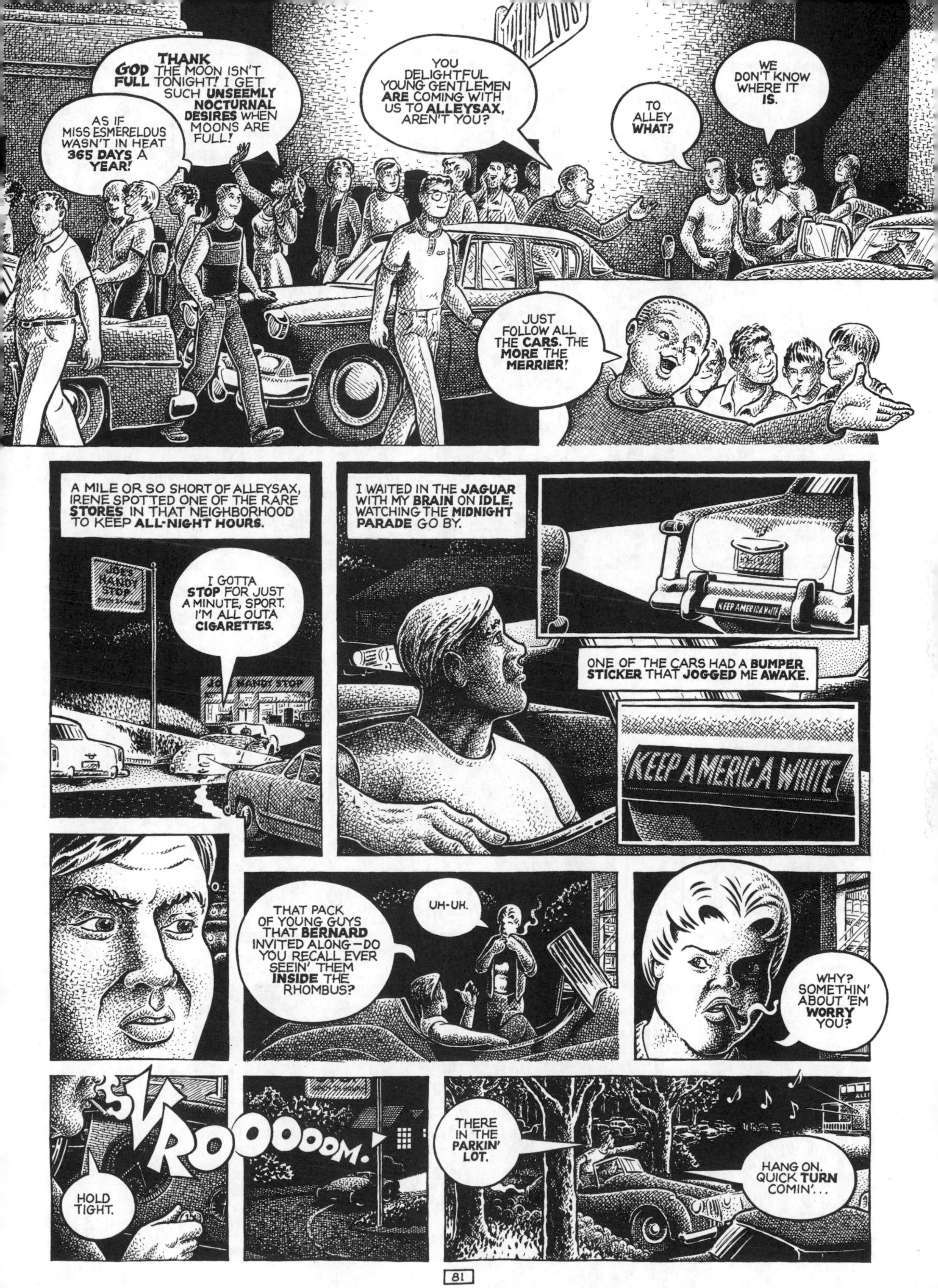
THANK GOD THE MOON ISN'T FULL TONIGHT! I GET SUCH UNSEEMLY NOCTURNAL DESIRES WHEN MOONS ARE FULL!
AS IF MISS ESMERELDUS WASN'T IN HEAT 365 DAYS A YEAR!
YOU DELIGHTFUL YOUNG GENTLEMEN ARE COMING WITH US TO ALLEYSAX, AREN'T YOU?
TO ALLEY WHAT?
WE DON'T KNOW WHERE IT IS.
JUST FOLLOW ALL THE CARS. THE MORE THE MERRIER!
A MILE OR SO SHORT OF ALLEYSAX, IRENE SPOTTED ONE OF THE RARE STORES IN THAT NEIGHBORHOOD TO KEEP ALL-NIGHT HOURS.
JOE'S HANDY STOP
I GOTTA STOP FOR JUST A MINUTE, SPORT. I'M ALL OUTA CIGARETTES.
I WAITED IN THE JAGUAR WITH MY BRAIN ON IDLE, WATCHING THE MIDNIGHT PARADE GO BY.
KEEP AMERICA WHITE
ONE OF THE CARS HAD A BUMPER STICKER THAT JOGGED ME AWAKE.
KEEP AMERICA WHITE
THAT PACK OF YOUNG GUYS THAT BERNARD INVITED ALONG—DO YOU RECALL EVER SEEIN' THEM INSIDE THE RHOMBUS?
UH-UH.
WHY? SOMETHIN' ABOUT 'EM WORRY YOU?
SVROOOOOOM!
HOLD TIGHT.
THERE IN THE PARKIN' LOT.
HANG ON. QUICK TURN COMIN'...

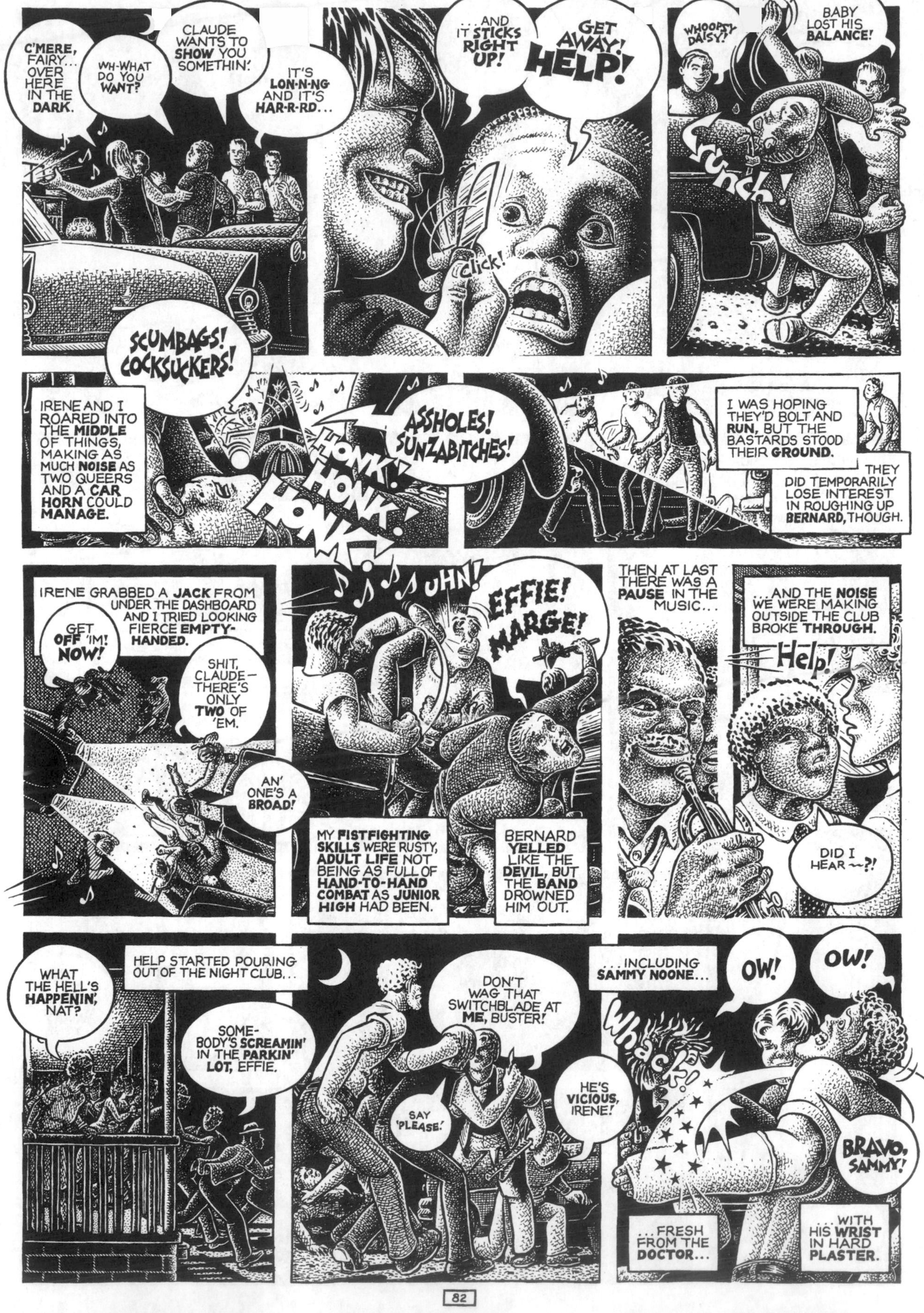
C'MERE, FAIRY... OVER HERE IN THE DARK.
WH-WHAT DO YOU WANT?
CLAUDE WANTS TO SHOW YOU SOMETHIN'.
IT'S LON-N-NG AND IT'S HAR-R-RD...
...AND IT STICKS RIGHT UP!
GET AWAY! HELP!
CLICK!
WHOOPSY DAISY!
BABY LOST HIS BALANCE!
CRUNCH!
SCUMBAGS! COCKSUCKERS!
IRENE AND I ROARED INTO THE MIDDLE OF THINGS, MAKING AS MUCH NOISE AS TWO QUEERS AND A CAR HORN COULD MANAGE.
ASSHOLES! SUNZABITCHES!
HONK! HONK! HONK!
I WAS HOPING THEY'D BOLT AND RUN, BUT THE BASTARDS STOOD THEIR GROUND.
THEY DID TEMPORARILY LOSE INTEREST IN ROUGHING UP BERNARD, THOUGH.
IRENE GRABBED A JACK FROM UNDER THE DASHBOARD AND I TRIED LOOKING FIERCE EMPTY-HANDED.
GET OFF 'IM! NOW!
SHIT, CLAUDE— THERE'S ONLY TWO OF 'EM.
AN' ONE'S A BROAD!
UHN!
EFFIE! MARGE!
MY FISTFIGHTING SKILLS WERE RUSTY, ADULT LIFE NOT BEING AS FULL OF HAND-TO-HAND COMBAT AS JUNIOR HIGH HAD BEEN.
BERNARD YELLED LIKE THE DEVIL, BUT THE BAND DROWNED HIM OUT.
THEN AT LAST THERE WAS A PAUSE IN THE MUSIC...
...AND THE NOISE WE WERE MAKING OUTSIDE THE CLUB BROKE THROUGH.
Help!
DID I HEAR ~~?!
WHAT THE HELL'S HAPPENIN', NAT?
HELP STARTED POURING OUT OF THE NIGHT CLUB...
SOME-BODY'S SCREAMIN' IN THE PARKIN' LOT, EFFIE.
DON'T WAG THAT SWITCHBLADE AT ME, BUSTER!
SAY 'PLEASE.'
HE'S VICIOUS, IRENE!
...INCLUDING SAMMY NOONE...
OW!
OW!
Whack!
BRAVO, SAMMY!
...FRESH FROM THE DOCTOR...
...WITH HIS WRIST IN HARD PLASTER.

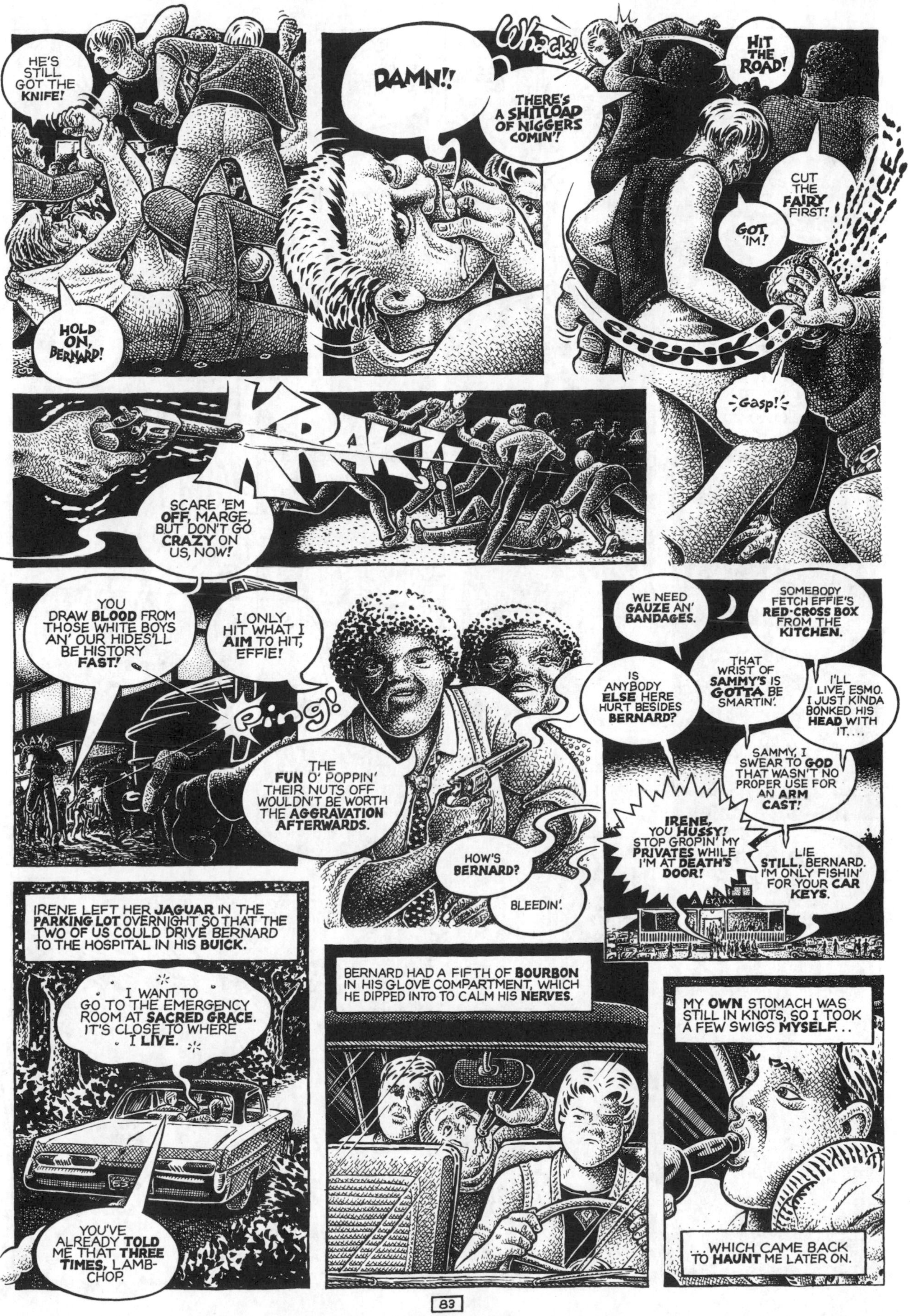

HE'S STILL GOT THE KNIFE!
HOLD ON, BERNARD!
DAMN!!
THERE'S A SHITLOAD OF NIGGERS COMIN'!
WHACK!
HIT THE ROAD!
CUT THE FAIRY FIRST!
GOT 'IM!
SLICE!!
CHUNK!!
Gasp!
KRAK!!
SCARE 'EM OFF, MARGE, BUT DON'T GO CRAZY ON US, NOW!
YOU DRAW BLOOD FROM THOSE WHITE BOYS AN' OUR HIDES'LL BE HISTORY FAST!
I ONLY HIT WHAT I AIM TO HIT, EFFIE!
Ping!
THE FUN O' POPPIN' THEIR NUTS OFF WOULDN'T BE WORTH THE AGGRAVATION AFTERWARDS.
HOW'S BERNARD?
BLEEDIN'.
WE NEED GAUZE AN' BANDAGES.
SOMEBODY FETCH EFFIE'S RED-CROSS BOX FROM THE KITCHEN.
IS ANYBODY ELSE HERE HURT BESIDES BERNARD?
THAT WRIST OF SAMMY'S IS GOTTA BE SMARTIN'.
I'LL LIVE, ESMO. I JUST KINDA BONKED HIS HEAD WITH IT....
SAMMY, I SWEAR TO GOD THAT WASN'T NO PROPER USE FOR AN ARM CAST!
IRENE, YOU HUSSY! STOP GROPIN' MY PRIVATES WHILE I'M AT DEATH'S DOOR!
LIE STILL, BERNARD. I'M ONLY FISHIN' FOR YOUR CAR KEYS.
IRENE LEFT HER JAGUAR IN THE PARKING LOT OVERNIGHT SO THAT THE TWO OF US COULD DRIVE BERNARD TO THE HOSPITAL IN HIS BUICK.
I WANT TO GO TO THE EMERGENCY ROOM AT SACRED GRACE. IT'S CLOSE TO WHERE I LIVE.
YOU'VE ALREADY TOLD ME THAT THREE TIMES, LAMB-CHOP.
BERNARD HAD A FIFTH OF BOURBON IN HIS GLOVE COMPARTMENT, WHICH HE DIPPED INTO TO CALM HIS NERVES.
MY OWN STOMACH WAS STILL IN KNOTS, SO I TOOK A FEW SWIGS MYSELF...
...WHICH CAME BACK TO HAUNT ME LATER ON.

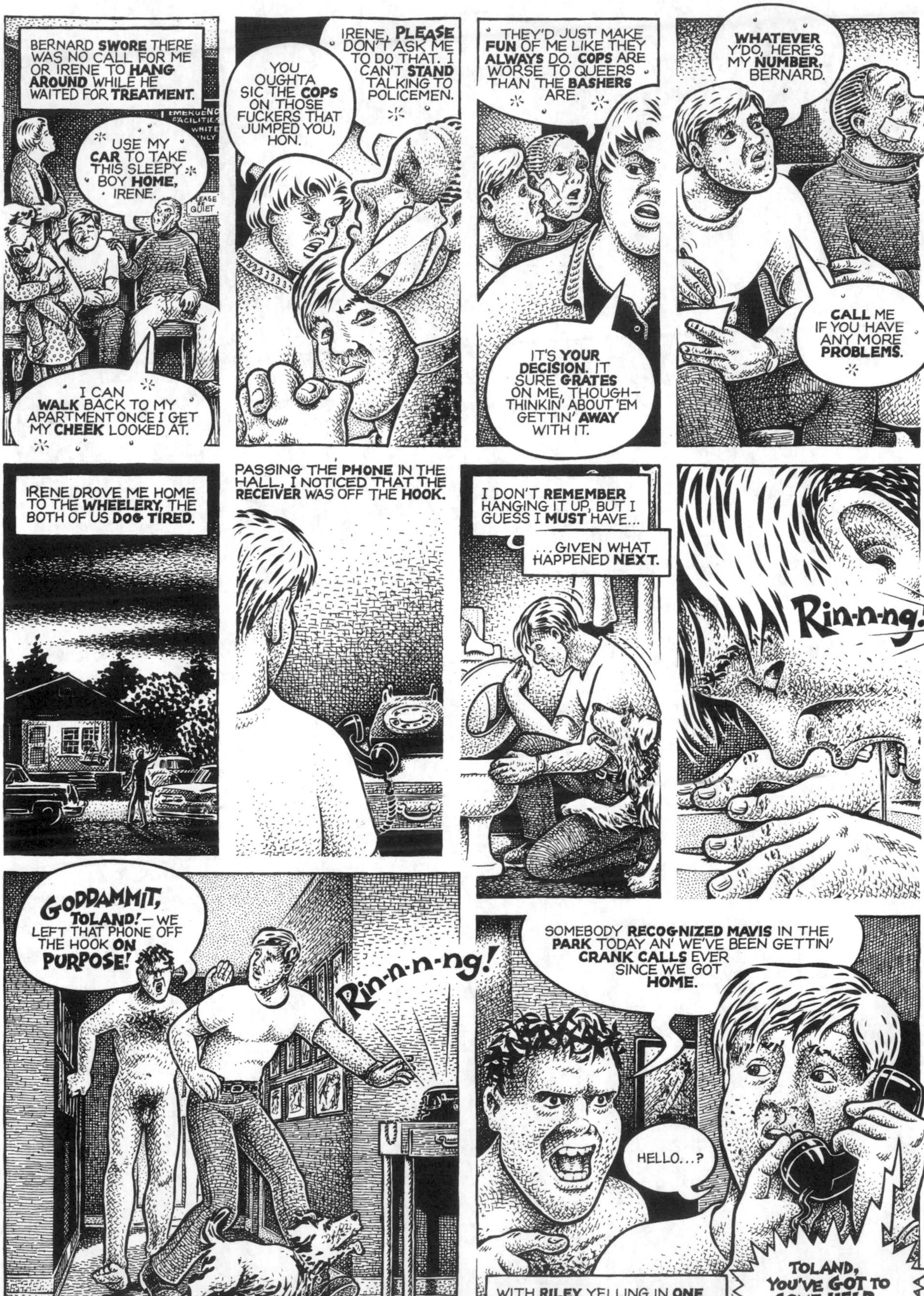
BERNARD SWORE THERE WAS NO CALL FOR ME OR IRENE TO HANG AROUND WHILE HE WAITED FOR TREATMENT.
USE MY CAR TO TAKE THIS SLEEPY BOY HOME, IRENE.
I CAN WALK BACK TO MY APARTMENT ONCE I GET MY CHEEK LOOKED AT.
YOU OUGHTA SIC THE COPS ON THOSE FUCKERS THAT JUMPED YOU, HON.
IRENE, PLEASE DON'T ASK ME TO DO THAT. I CAN'T STAND TALKING TO POLICEMEN.
THEY'D JUST MAKE FUN OF ME LIKE THEY ALWAYS DO. COPS ARE WORSE TO QUEERS THAN THE BASHERS ARE.
IT'S YOUR DECISION. IT SURE GRATES ON ME, THOUGH— THINKIN' ABOUT 'EM GETTIN' AWAY WITH IT.
WHATEVER Y'DO, HERE'S MY NUMBER, BERNARD.
CALL ME IF YOU HAVE ANY MORE PROBLEMS.
IRENE DROVE ME HOME TO THE WHEELERY, THE BOTH OF US DOG TIRED.
PASSING THE PHONE IN THE HALL, I NOTICED THAT THE RECEIVER WAS OFF THE HOOK.
I DON'T REMEMBER HANGING IT UP, BUT I GUESS I MUST HAVE...
...GIVEN WHAT HAPPENED NEXT.
Rin-n-ng!
GODDAMMIT, TOLAND!—WE LEFT THAT PHONE OFF THE HOOK ON PURPOSE!
Rin-n-n-ng!
SOMEBODY RECOGNIZED MAVIS IN THE PARK TODAY AN' WE'VE BEEN GETTIN' CRANK CALLS EVER SINCE WE GOT HOME.
HELLO...?
WITH RILEY YELLING IN ONE OF MY EARS, I HAD BERNARD HALF-HYSTERICAL IN THE OTHER.
TOLAND, YOU'VE GOT TO COME HELP ME!

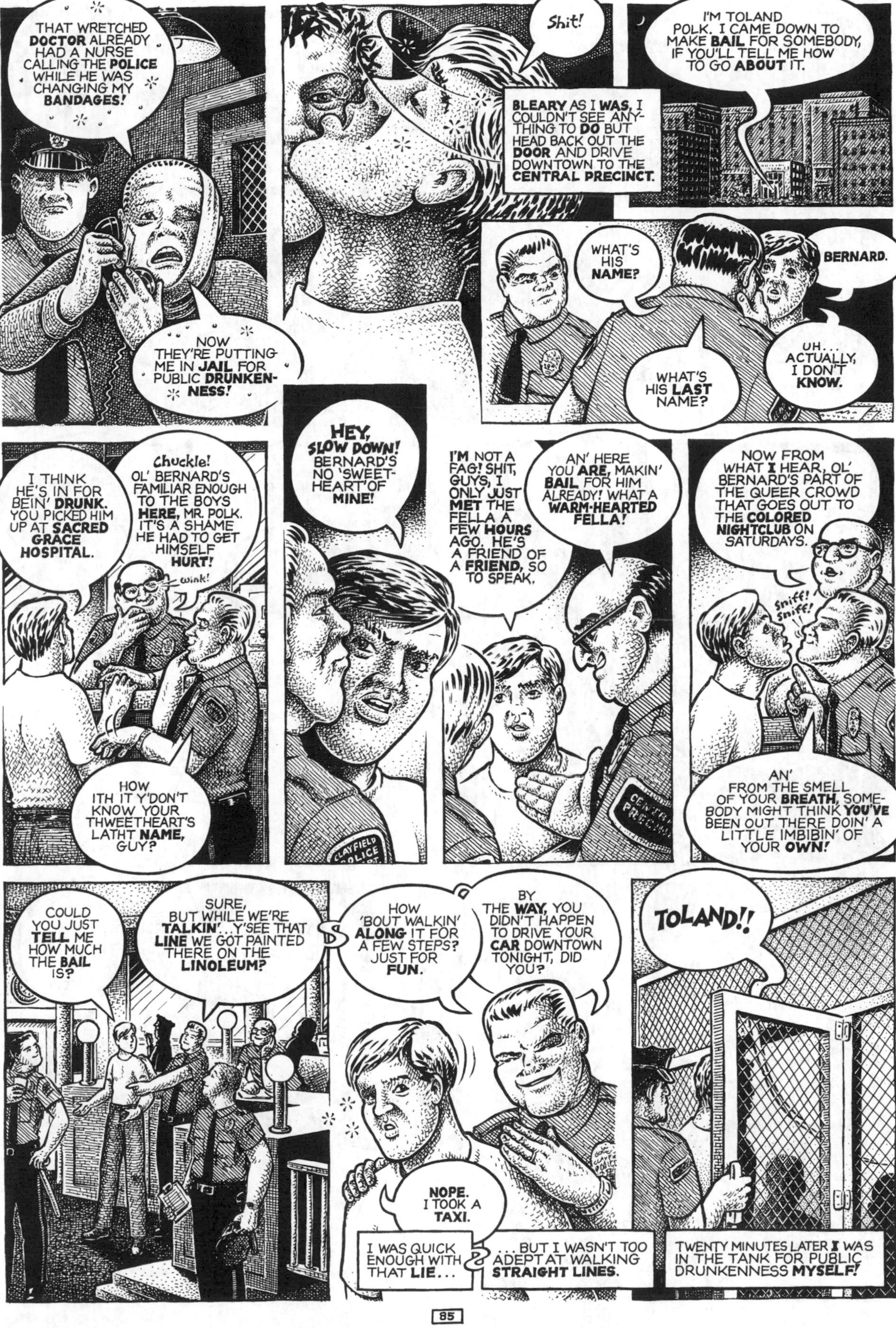

THAT WRETCHED DOCTOR ALREADY HAD A NURSE CALLING THE POLICE WHILE HE WAS CHANGING MY BANDAGES!
NOW THEY'RE PUTTING ME IN JAIL FOR PUBLIC DRUNKENNESS!
Shit!
BLEARY AS I WAS, I COULDN'T SEE ANYTHING TO DO BUT HEAD BACK OUT THE DOOR AND DRIVE DOWNTOWN TO THE CENTRAL PRECINCT.
I'M TOLAND POLK. I CAME DOWN TO MAKE BAIL FOR SOMEBODY, IF YOU'LL TELL ME HOW TO GO ABOUT IT.
WHAT'S HIS NAME?
BERNARD.
WHAT'S HIS LAST NAME?
UH... ACTUALLY, I DON'T KNOW.
I THINK HE'S IN FOR BEIN' DRUNK. YOU PICKED HIM UP AT SACRED GRACE HOSPITAL.
Chuckle! OL' BERNARD'S FAMILIAR ENOUGH TO THE BOYS HERE, MR. POLK. IT'S A SHAME HE HAD TO GET HIMSELF HURT!
wink!
HOW ITH IT Y'DON'T KNOW YOUR THWEETHEART'S LATHT NAME, GUY?
HEY, SLOW DOWN! BERNARD'S NO 'SWEETHEART' OF MINE!
I'M NOT A FAG! SHIT, GUYS, I ONLY JUST MET THE FELLA A FEW HOURS AGO. HE'S A FRIEND OF A FRIEND, SO TO SPEAK.
AN' HERE YOU ARE, MAKIN' BAIL FOR HIM ALREADY! WHAT A WARM-HEARTED FELLA!
NOW FROM WHAT I HEAR, OL' BERNARD'S PART OF THE QUEER CROWD THAT GOES OUT TO THE COLORED NIGHTCLUB ON SATURDAYS.
Sniff! Sniff!
AN' FROM THE SMELL OF YOUR BREATH, SOMEBODY MIGHT THINK YOU'VE BEEN OUT THERE DOIN' A LITTLE IMBIBIN' OF YOUR OWN!
COULD YOU JUST TELL ME HOW MUCH THE BAIL IS?
SURE, BUT WHILE WE'RE TALKIN'... Y'SEE THAT LINE WE GOT PAINTED THERE ON THE LINOLEUM?
HOW 'BOUT WALKIN' ALONG IT FOR A FEW STEPS? JUST FOR FUN.
BY THE WAY, YOU DIDN'T HAPPEN TO DRIVE YOUR CAR DOWNTOWN TONIGHT, DID YOU?
NOPE. I TOOK A TAXI.
I WAS QUICK ENOUGH WITH THAT LIE...
...BUT I WASN'T TOO ADEPT AT WALKING STRAIGHT LINES.
TOLAND!!
TWENTY MINUTES LATER I WAS IN THE TANK FOR PUBLIC DRUNKENNESS MYSELF!

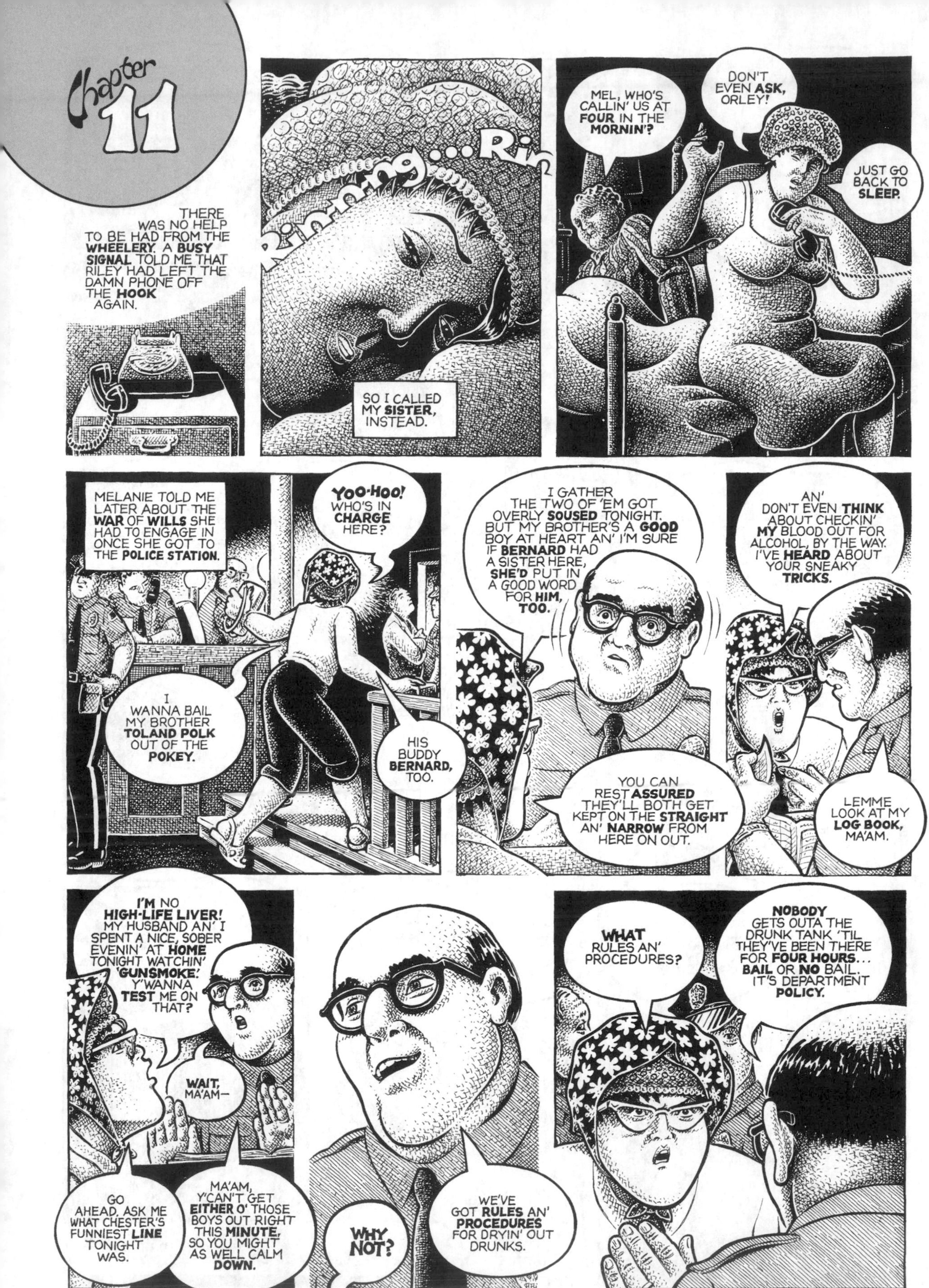
Chapter 11
THERE WAS NO HELP TO BE HAD FROM THE WHEELERY. A BUSY SIGNAL TOLD ME THAT RILEY HAD LEFT THE DAMN PHONE OFF THE HOOK AGAIN.
Rinnng...Rin
SO I CALLED MY SISTER, INSTEAD.
MEL, WHO'S CALLIN' US AT FOUR IN THE MORNIN'?
DON'T EVEN ASK, ORLEY!
JUST GO BACK TO SLEEP.
MELANIE TOLD ME LATER ABOUT THE WAR OF WILLS SHE HAD TO ENGAGE IN ONCE SHE GOT TO THE POLICE STATION.
YOO-HOO! WHO'S IN CHARGE HERE?
I WANNA BAIL MY BROTHER TOLAND POLK OUT OF THE POKEY.
HIS BUDDY BERNARD, TOO.
I GATHER THE TWO OF 'EM GOT OVERLY SOUSED TONIGHT. BUT MY BROTHER'S A GOOD BOY AT HEART AN' I'M SURE IF BERNARD HAD A SISTER HERE, SHE'D PUT IN A GOOD WORD FOR HIM, TOO.
YOU CAN REST ASSURED THEY'LL BOTH GET KEPT ON THE STRAIGHT AN' NARROW FROM HERE ON OUT.
AN' DON'T EVEN THINK ABOUT CHECKIN' MY BLOOD OUT FOR ALCOHOL, BY THE WAY. I'VE HEARD ABOUT YOUR SNEAKY TRICKS.
LEMME LOOK AT MY LOG BOOK, MA'AM.
I'M NO HIGH-LIFE LIVER! MY HUSBAND AN' I SPENT A NICE, SOBER EVENIN' AT HOME TONIGHT WATCHIN' 'GUNSMOKE.' Y'WANNA TEST ME ON THAT?
WAIT, MA'AM—
GO AHEAD. ASK ME WHAT CHESTER'S FUNNIEST LINE TONIGHT WAS.
MA'AM, Y'CAN'T GET EITHER O' THOSE BOYS OUT RIGHT THIS MINUTE, SO YOU MIGHT AS WELL CALM DOWN.
WHY NOT?
WE'VE GOT RULES AN' PROCEDURES FOR DRYIN' OUT DRUNKS.
WHAT RULES AN' PROCEDURES?
NOBODY GETS OUTA THE DRUNK TANK 'TIL THEY'VE BEEN THERE FOR FOUR HOURS... BAIL OR NO BAIL. IT'S DEPARTMENT POLICY.

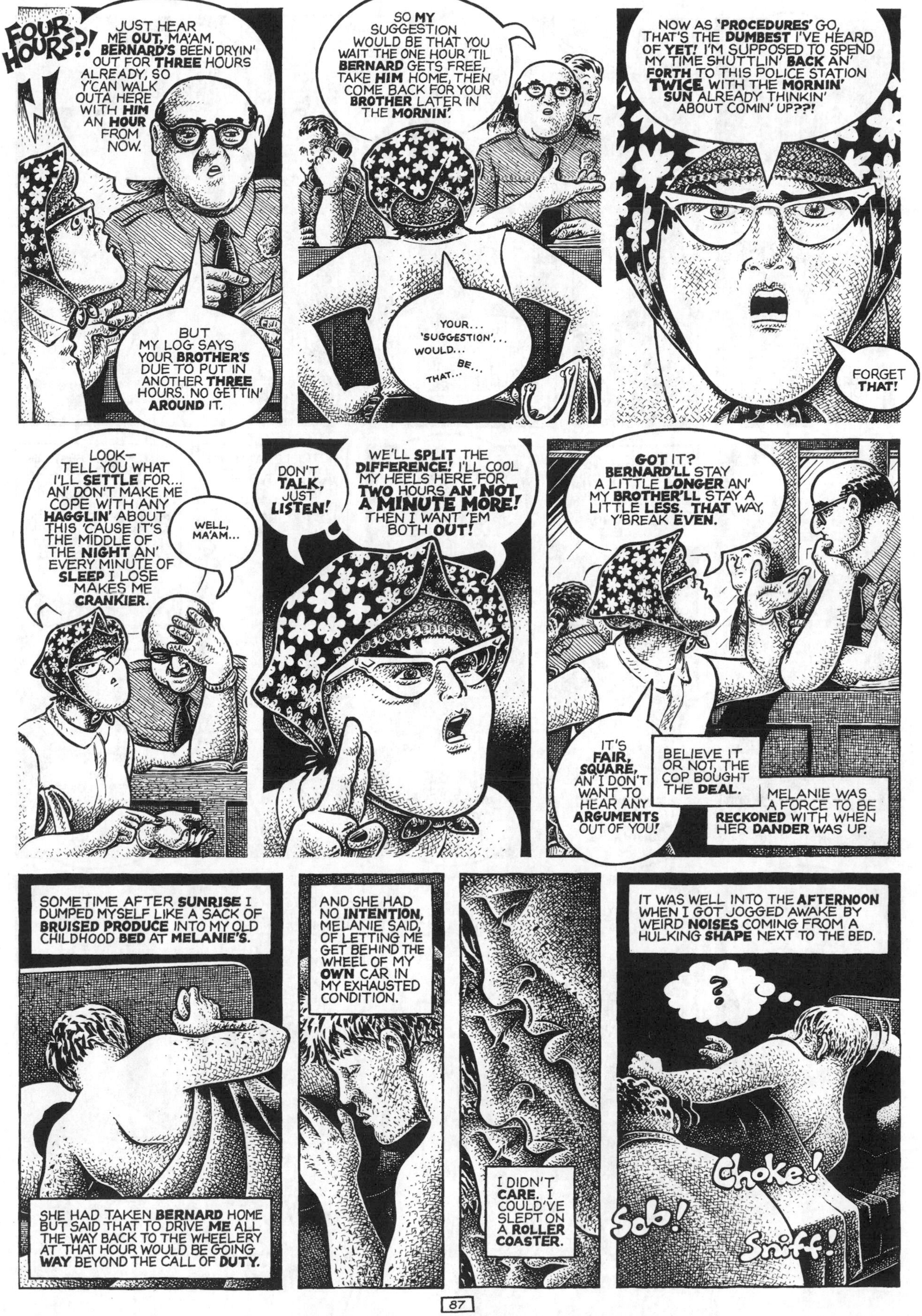
FOUR HOURS?!
JUST HEAR ME OUT, MA'AM. BERNARD'S BEEN DRYIN' OUT FOR THREE HOURS ALREADY, SO Y'CAN WALK OUTA HERE WITH HIM AN HOUR FROM NOW.
BUT MY LOG SAYS YOUR BROTHER'S DUE TO PUT IN ANOTHER THREE HOURS. NO GETTIN' AROUND IT.
SO MY SUGGESTION WOULD BE THAT YOU WAIT THE ONE HOUR 'TIL BERNARD GETS FREE, TAKE HIM HOME, THEN COME BACK FOR YOUR BROTHER LATER IN THE MORNIN'.
YOUR... 'SUGGESTION'... WOULD... BE... THAT...
NOW AS 'PROCEDURES' GO, THAT'S THE DUMBEST I'VE HEARD OF YET! I'M SUPPOSED TO SPEND MY TIME SHUTTLIN' BACK AN' FORTH TO THIS POLICE STATION TWICE WITH THE MORNIN' SUN ALREADY THINKIN' ABOUT COMIN' UP??!
FORGET THAT!
LOOK— TELL YOU WHAT I'LL SETTLE FOR... AN' DON'T MAKE ME COPE WITH ANY HAGGLIN' ABOUT THIS 'CAUSE IT'S THE MIDDLE OF THE NIGHT AN' EVERY MINUTE OF SLEEP I LOSE MAKES ME CRANKIER.
WELL, MA'AM...
DON'T TALK, JUST LISTEN!
WE'LL SPLIT THE DIFFERENCE! I'LL COOL MY HEELS HERE FOR TWO HOURS AN' NOT A MINUTE MORE! THEN I WANT 'EM BOTH OUT!
GOT IT? BERNARD'LL STAY A LITTLE LONGER AN' MY BROTHER'LL STAY A LITTLE LESS. THAT WAY, Y'BREAK EVEN.
IT'S FAIR, SQUARE, AN' I DON'T WANT TO HEAR ANY ARGUMENTS OUT OF YOU!
BELIEVE IT OR NOT, THE COP BOUGHT THE DEAL.
MELANIE WAS A FORCE TO BE RECKONED WITH WHEN HER DANDER WAS UP.
SOMETIME AFTER SUNRISE I DUMPED MYSELF LIKE A SACK OF BRUISED PRODUCE INTO MY OLD CHILDHOOD BED AT MELANIE'S.
SHE HAD TAKEN BERNARD HOME BUT SAID THAT TO DRIVE ME ALL THE WAY BACK TO THE WHEELERY AT THAT HOUR WOULD BE GOING WAY BEYOND THE CALL OF DUTY.
AND SHE HAD NO INTENTION, MELANIE SAID, OF LETTING ME GET BEHIND THE WHEEL OF MY OWN CAR IN MY EXHAUSTED CONDITION.
I DIDN'T CARE. I COULD'VE SLEPT ON A ROLLER COASTER.
IT WAS WELL INTO THE AFTERNOON WHEN I GOT JOGGED AWAKE BY WEIRD NOISES COMING FROM A HULKING SHAPE NEXT TO THE BED.
?
Choke!
Sob!
Sniff!

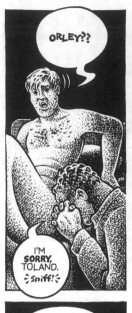

ORLEY??

I'M SORRY, TOLAND. ~*Sniff!*~

I SHOULDN'T OF BEEN **IN** HERE WITH YOU **ASLEEP**.

I WAS **INTENDIN'** TO SAY A LITTLE BEDSIDE **PRAYER** ...BUT THEN I JUST STARTED **CRYIN'**.

ORLEY, WHAT'VE **YOU** GOT TO FRET ABOUT? **I'M** THE ONE WITH THE **HANGOVER!**

THAT'S RIGHT, PAL. BE **FLIP**. NEVER ACT LIKE THERE MIGHT BE ANYTHING OF **IMPORTANCE** GOIN' ON IN THE MIND OF A DUMB OL' GUY THAT **LOVES** YOU.

YOU'RE SOMETHIN' **ELSE** TO WAKE **UP** TO... THAT'S FOR **SURE!**

HEY!... ORL!... WHAT'S **BUGGIN'** YOU?

THE **PATH** YOU'RE SHOWIN' SIGNS OF HEADIN' DOWN.

DRINKIN' IN **BARS**...HANGIN' AROUND WITH PEOPLE THAT GET **ARRESTED**...

...IT COULD END UP WITH YOU GOIN' TO **HELL**.

OH, I KNOW YOU'RE THE **LAST** PERSON WHO'D TAKE **THAT** RISK TO HEART. YOU THINK THAT HELL'S SOME **IMAGINARY** CONCEPT!

BUT HELL IS **REAL**. IT'S AN **ACTUAL** PLACE IN THE **UNIVERSE**.

I DON'T WANT YOU TO FIND THAT OUT THE **HARD** WAY. BUT IF YOU DON'T TAKE A CAREFUL **LOOK** AT THE **LIFE** YOU'RE LEADIN'...

PLEASE, TOLAND... **THINK** ABOUT WHAT MIGHT BE IN **STORE** FOR YOU.

HORRIBLE **TORTURE** THAT'LL LAST FOR **EVER** AND **EVER**. THERE'LL BE NO **END** TO IT, TOLAND. NO **RELIEF** FROM THE AGONY.

SMELLY **BOILS** FESTERIN' ALL OVER YOUR **BODY**. **FLAMES** LICKIN' LIKE **ACETYLENE** TORCHES AT YOU WHILE **STINGIN'** PUS OOZES FROM YOUR **PORES** AN' TRICKLES LIKE A RIVER OF **ACID** DOWN EVERY INCH OF YOUR **SKIN**.

AN' THERE WON'T BE ANYTHING YOUR **SISTER** OR I CAN DO TO **HELP**.

WE'LL BE IN **HEAVEN**, LORD WILLIN'. BUT IT'S HARD TO SEE HOW WE CAN BE VERY **HAPPY** THERE, KNOWIN' YOU'RE IN THE PIT SUFFERIN'.

YOU'VE **GOT** TO BE HAPPY IN **HEAVEN**, ORLEY. HOUSE **RULES!**

FLIPPANCY!... FLIPPANCY!...

CUT RIGHT INTO MY **HEART** WITH YOUR FLIPPANCY!

NOTHIN' LEFT FOR ME TO **DO** BUT PRAY FOR YOU A HUNDRED TIMES **HARDER**, JUST TO MAKE UP FOR THE **BLINDNESS** THAT WON'T LET YOU PRAY FOR **YOUR**-SELF.

I'LL TELL MELANIE YOU'RE **AWAKE**. I'VE GOT SOME **WEEDS** TO PULL IN THE YARD.

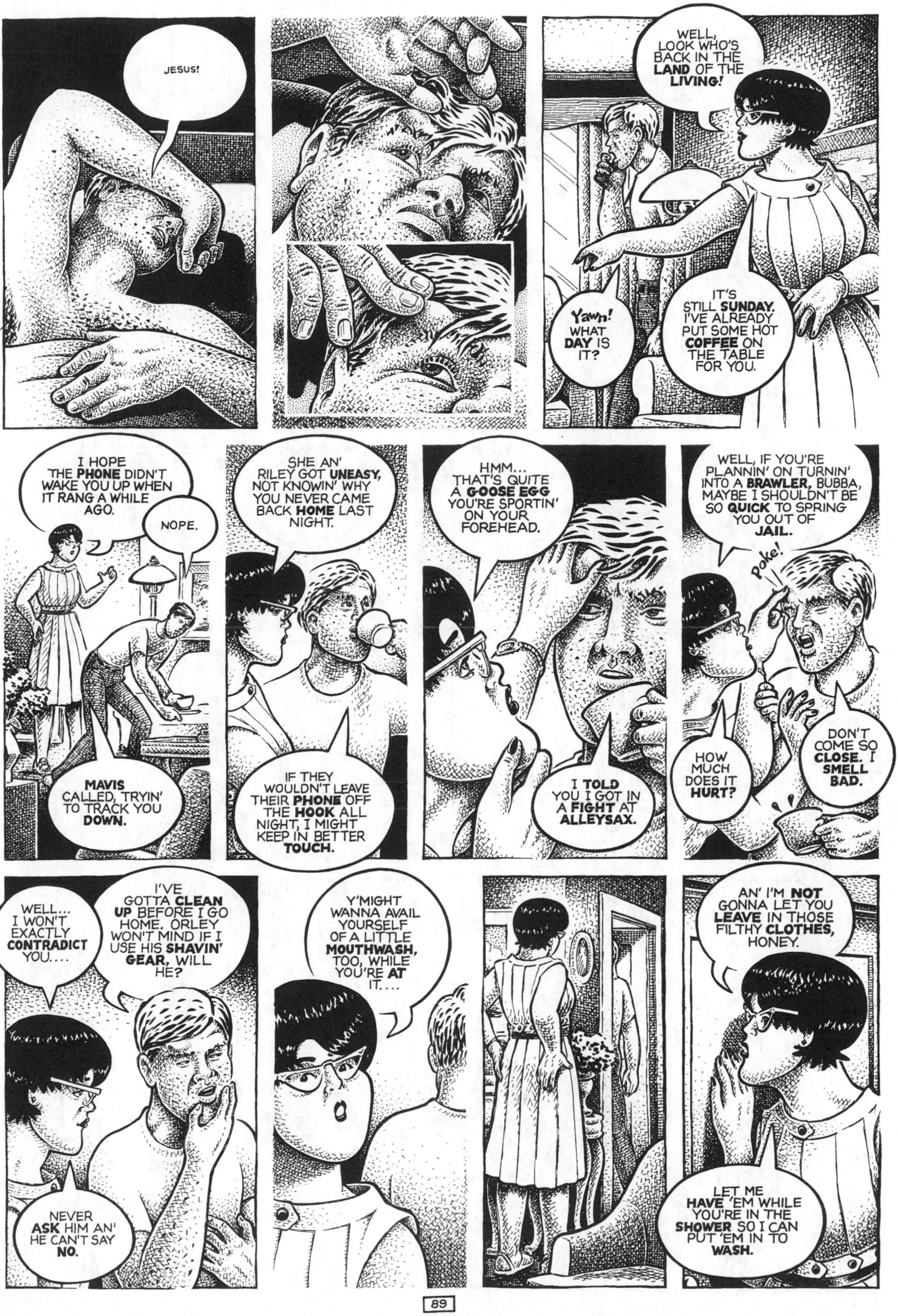
JESUS!
WELL, LOOK WHO'S BACK IN THE LAND OF THE LIVING!
Yawn! WHAT DAY IS IT?
IT'S STILL SUNDAY. I'VE ALREADY PUT SOME HOT COFFEE ON THE TABLE FOR YOU.
I HOPE THE PHONE DIDN'T WAKE YOU UP WHEN IT RANG A WHILE AGO.
NOPE.
MAVIS CALLED, TRYIN' TO TRACK YOU DOWN.
SHE AN' RILEY GOT UNEASY, NOT KNOWIN' WHY YOU NEVER CAME BACK HOME LAST NIGHT.
IF THEY WOULDN'T LEAVE THEIR PHONE OFF THE HOOK ALL NIGHT, I MIGHT KEEP IN BETTER TOUCH.
HMM... THAT'S QUITE A GOOSE EGG YOU'RE SPORTIN' ON YOUR FOREHEAD.
I TOLD YOU I GOT IN A FIGHT AT ALLEYSAX.
WELL, IF YOU'RE PLANNIN' ON TURNIN' INTO A BRAWLER, BUBBA, MAYBE I SHOULDN'T BE SO QUICK TO SPRING YOU OUT OF JAIL.
Poke!
HOW MUCH DOES IT HURT?
DON'T COME SO CLOSE. I SMELL BAD.
WELL... I WON'T EXACTLY CONTRADICT YOU....
I'VE GOTTA CLEAN UP BEFORE I GO HOME. ORLEY WON'T MIND IF I USE HIS SHAVIN' GEAR, WILL HE?
NEVER ASK HIM AN' HE CAN'T SAY NO.
Y'MIGHT WANNA AVAIL YOURSELF OF A LITTLE MOUTHWASH, TOO, WHILE YOU'RE AT IT....
AN' I'M NOT GONNA LET YOU LEAVE IN THOSE FILTHY CLOTHES, HONEY.
LET ME HAVE 'EM WHILE YOU'RE IN THE SHOWER SO I CAN PUT 'EM IN TO WASH.

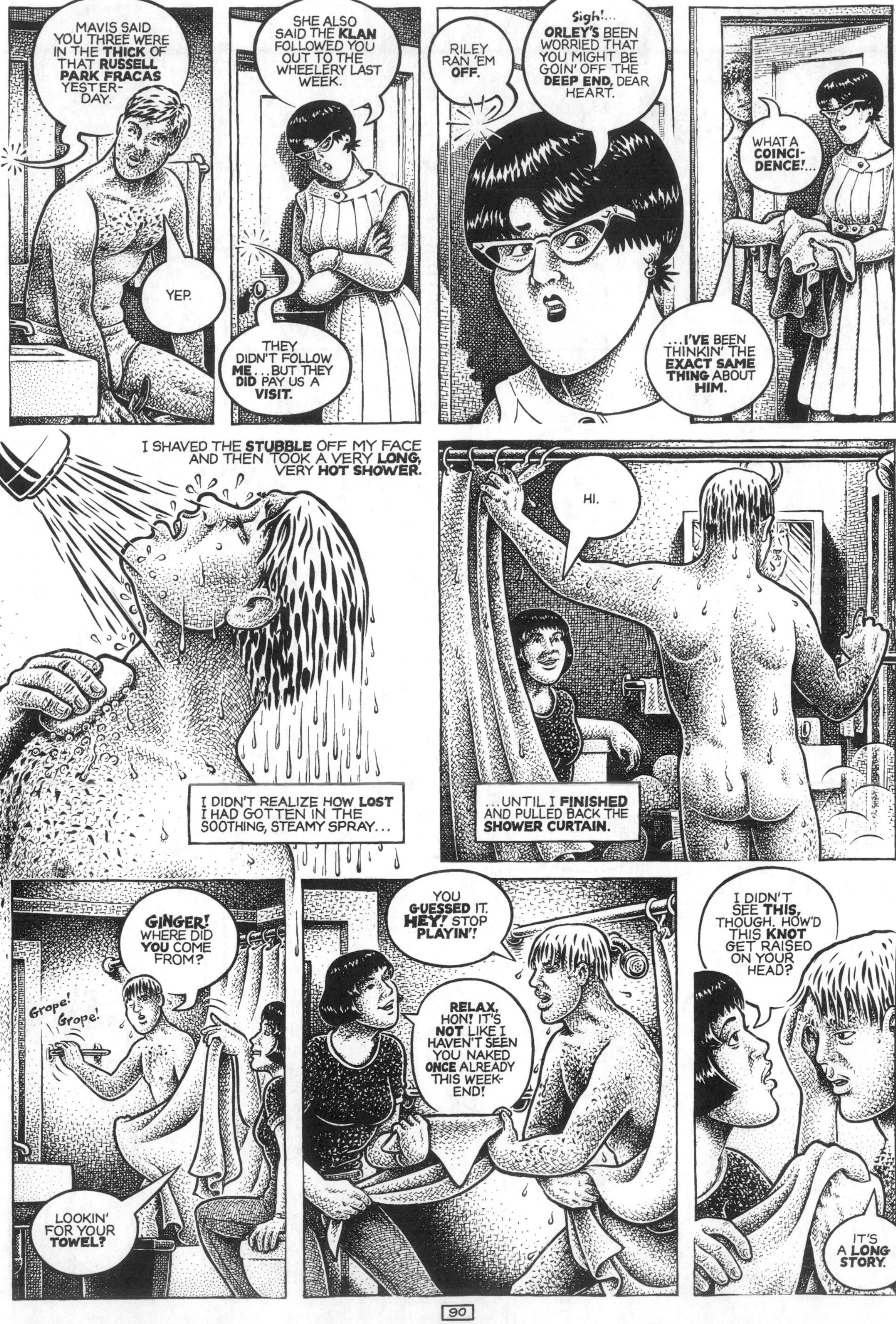

MAVIS SAID YOU THREE WERE IN THE THICK OF THAT RUSSELL PARK FRACAS YESTER-DAY.
YEP.
SHE ALSO SAID THE KLAN FOLLOWED YOU OUT TO THE WHEELERY LAST WEEK.
THEY DIDN'T FOLLOW ME. . . BUT THEY DID PAY US A VISIT.
RILEY RAN 'EM OFF.
Sigh!... ORLEY'S BEEN WORRIED THAT YOU MIGHT BE GOIN' OFF THE DEEP END, DEAR HEART.
WHAT A COINCI-DENCE!...
. . . I'VE BEEN THINKIN' THE EXACT SAME THING ABOUT HIM.
I SHAVED THE STUBBLE OFF MY FACE AND THEN TOOK A VERY LONG, VERY HOT SHOWER.
I DIDN'T REALIZE HOW LOST I HAD GOTTEN IN THE SOOTHING, STEAMY SPRAY. . .
HI.
. . .UNTIL I FINISHED AND PULLED BACK THE SHOWER CURTAIN.
GINGER! WHERE DID YOU COME FROM?
Grope! Grope!
LOOKIN' FOR YOUR TOWEL?
YOU GUESSED IT. HEY! STOP PLAYIN'!
RELAX, HON! IT'S NOT LIKE I HAVEN'T SEEN YOU NAKED ONCE ALREADY THIS WEEK-END!
I DIDN'T SEE THIS, THOUGH. HOW'D THIS KNOT GET RAISED ON YOUR HEAD?
IT'S A LONG STORY.

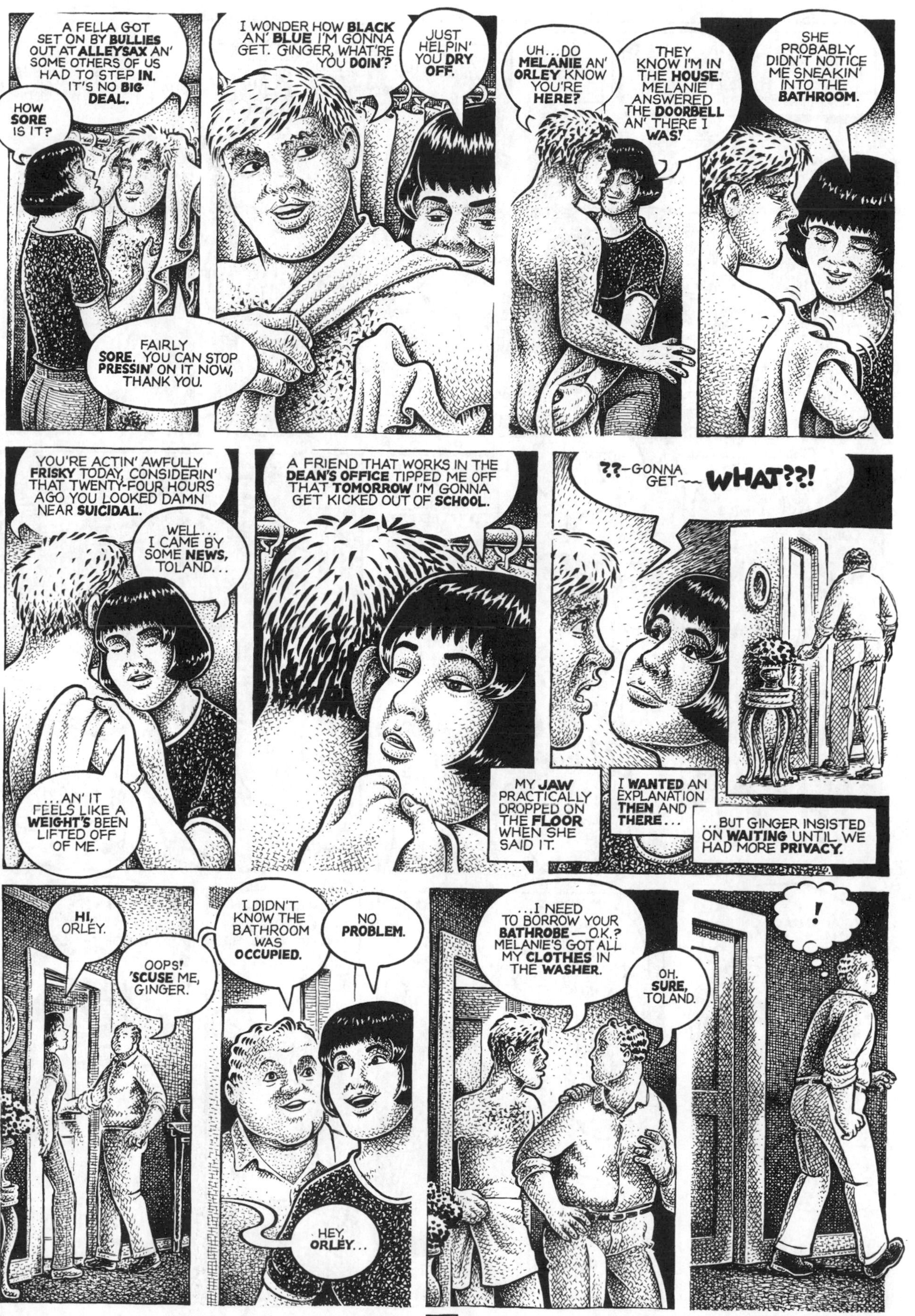
A FELLA GOT SET ON BY BULLIES OUT AT ALLEYSAX AN' SOME OTHERS OF US HAD TO STEP IN. IT'S NO BIG DEAL.
HOW SORE IS IT?
FAIRLY SORE. YOU CAN STOP PRESSIN' ON IT NOW, THANK YOU.
I WONDER HOW BLACK AN' BLUE I'M GONNA GET. GINGER, WHAT'RE YOU DOIN'?
JUST HELPIN' YOU DRY OFF.
UH...DO MELANIE AN' ORLEY KNOW YOU'RE HERE?
THEY KNOW I'M IN THE HOUSE. MELANIE ANSWERED THE DOORBELL AN' THERE I WAS!
SHE PROBABLY DIDN'T NOTICE ME SNEAKIN' INTO THE BATHROOM.
YOU'RE ACTIN' AWFULLY FRISKY TODAY, CONSIDERIN' THAT TWENTY-FOUR HOURS AGO YOU LOOKED DAMN NEAR SUICIDAL.
WELL... I CAME BY SOME NEWS, TOLAND...
...AN' IT FEELS LIKE A WEIGHT'S BEEN LIFTED OFF OF ME.
A FRIEND THAT WORKS IN THE DEAN'S OFFICE TIPPED ME OFF THAT TOMORROW I'M GONNA GET KICKED OUT OF SCHOOL.
??-GONNA GET--- WHAT??!
MY JAW PRACTICALLY DROPPED ON THE FLOOR WHEN SHE SAID IT.
I WANTED AN EXPLANATION THEN AND THERE...
...BUT GINGER INSISTED ON WAITING UNTIL WE HAD MORE PRIVACY.
HI, ORLEY.
OOPS! 'SCUSE ME, GINGER.
I DIDN'T KNOW THE BATHROOM WAS OCCUPIED.
NO PROBLEM.
HEY, ORLEY...
...I NEED TO BORROW YOUR BATHROBE — O.K.? MELANIE'S GOT ALL MY CLOTHES IN THE WASHER.
OH. SURE, TOLAND.
!

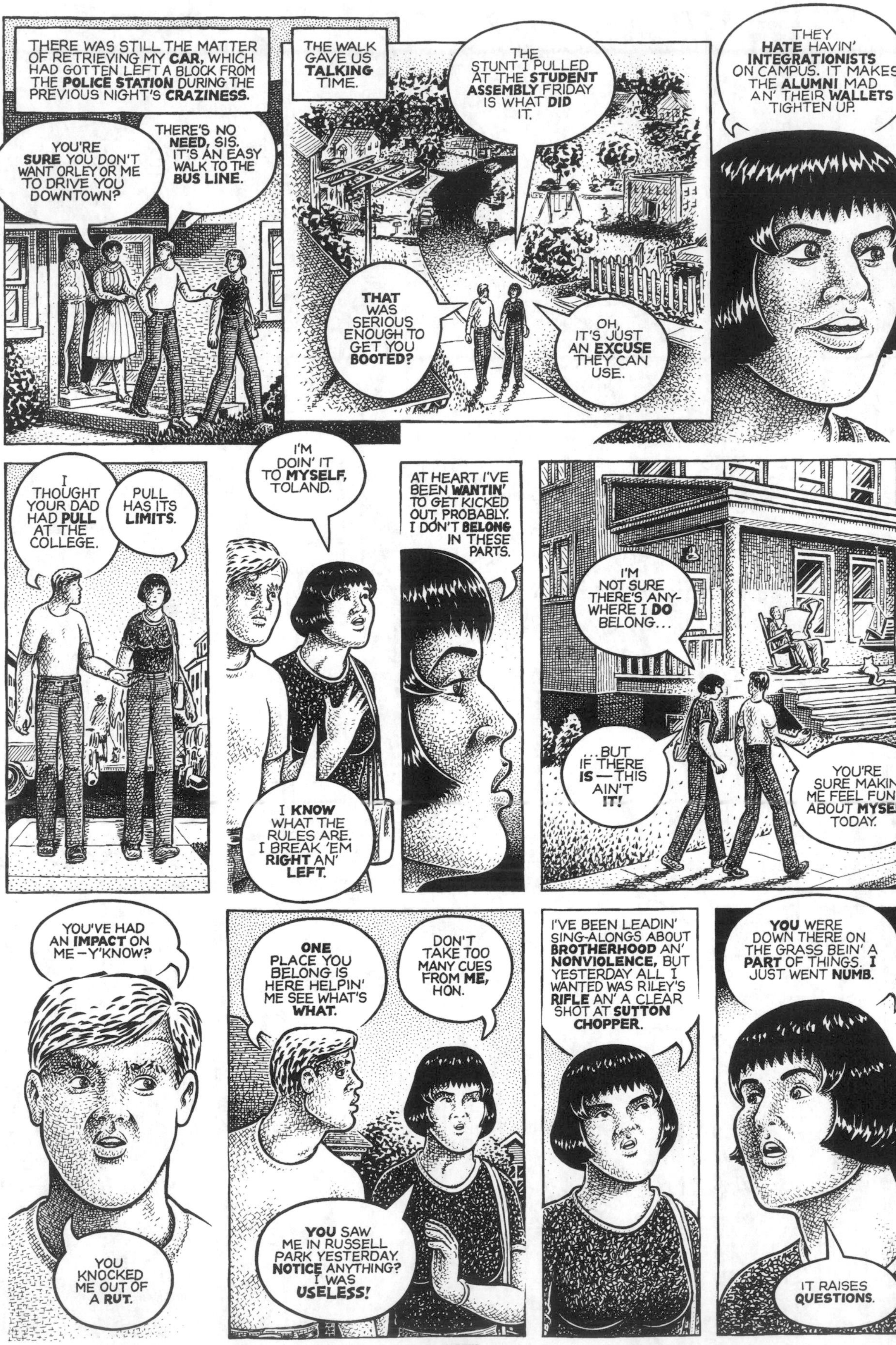
THERE WAS STILL THE MATTER OF RETRIEVING MY CAR, WHICH HAD GOTTEN LEFT A BLOCK FROM THE POLICE STATION DURING THE PREVIOUS NIGHT'S CRAZINESS.
YOU'RE SURE YOU DON'T WANT ORLEY OR ME TO DRIVE YOU DOWNTOWN?
THERE'S NO NEED, SIS. IT'S AN EASY WALK TO THE BUS LINE.
THE WALK GAVE US TALKING TIME.
THE STUNT I PULLED AT THE STUDENT ASSEMBLY FRIDAY IS WHAT DID IT.
THAT WAS SERIOUS ENOUGH TO GET YOU BOOTED?
OH, IT'S JUST AN EXCUSE THEY CAN USE.
THEY HATE HAVIN' INTEGRATIONISTS ON CAMPUS. IT MAKES THE ALUMNI MAD AN' THEIR WALLETS TIGHTEN UP.
I THOUGHT YOUR DAD HAD PULL AT THE COLLEGE.
PULL HAS ITS LIMITS.
I'M DOIN' IT TO MYSELF, TOLAND.
I KNOW WHAT THE RULES ARE. I BREAK 'EM RIGHT AN' LEFT.
AT HEART I'VE BEEN WANTIN' TO GET KICKED OUT, PROBABLY. I DON'T BELONG IN THESE PARTS.
I'M NOT SURE THERE'S ANYWHERE I DO BELONG...
...BUT IF THERE IS—THIS AIN'T IT!
YOU'RE SURE MAKIN' ME FEEL FUNNY ABOUT MYSELF TODAY.
YOU'VE HAD AN IMPACT ON ME—Y'KNOW?
YOU KNOCKED ME OUT OF A RUT.
ONE PLACE YOU BELONG IS HERE HELPIN' ME SEE WHAT'S WHAT.
DON'T TAKE TOO MANY CUES FROM ME, HON.
YOU SAW ME IN RUSSELL PARK YESTERDAY. NOTICE ANYTHING? I WAS USELESS!
I'VE BEEN LEADIN' SING-ALONGS ABOUT BROTHERHOOD AN' NONVIOLENCE, BUT YESTERDAY ALL I WANTED WAS RILEY'S RIFLE AN' A CLEAR SHOT AT SUTTON CHOPPER.
YOU WERE DOWN THERE ON THE GRASS BEIN' A PART OF THINGS. I JUST WENT NUMB.
IT RAISES QUESTIONS.

YOU DID SEEM **UPSET.** I SAW YOU LATER ON AT THE **CHURCH,** GETTIN' SOME COMFORT FROM **SHILOH.**

YOU **SAW** US? WE DIDN'T SEE **YOU.**

YOU SHOULD'VE COME **OVER.**

I DIDN'T WANNA **INTRUDE.**

ARE YOU **JEALOUS** OF SHILOH?

NO. NOT AT **ALL.**

BUT I WISH I COULD BUY A **BOTTLE** OF WHATEVER PEOPLE LIKE SHILOH HAVE.

LOOK HOW HE'S **CHEERED** YOU UP!

I'M NOT **CHEERFUL.** I'M **ADRIFT.**

THERE'S A CERTAIN **GIDDINESS** IN THAT.

WHAT'LL YOU **DO** WITH YOURSELF IF YOU DO GET KICKED OUT OF WESTHILLS?

GO BACK TO **AKRON,** I GUESS.

DO YOU **HAFTA** LEAVE **TOWN...?**

I'LL HAVE SOME **FENCES** TO MEND WITH MY **FOLKS.**

AT TIMES LIKE THAT, THEY TEND TO WANT ME AT **CLOSE RANGE.**

I'M **CONFUSED.** *I* THOUGHT THE LAST FEW MONTHS WERE WHAT YOU'D CALL **HAPPY** TIMES FOR THE TWO OF US.

BUT NOW YOU'RE ACTIN' PLEASED AS **PUNCH** AT THE THOUGHT OF LEAVIN' CLAYFIELD AN' ME **BEHIND.**

ANY CHANCE THE **RELIEF** YOU'RE FEELIN' COMES FROM SHEDDIN' A BOYFRIEND THAT'S GONE **QUEER** ON YOU?

GOD- DAMN IT, TOLAND!

EVERYTHING THAT GOES ON INSIDE OF ME DOESN'T HAVE TO DO WITH **YOU!** QUITE A **LOT** GOES ON THAT DOESN'T HAVE **ANYTHING** TO DO WITH YOU AT **ALL!**

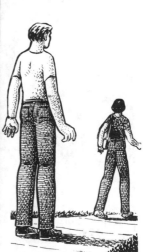

WELL... HERE'S THE **BUS STOP.** SHALL WE **WAIT?**

I DUNNO.

THERE'LL BE **MORE** OF 'EM DOWN THE **ROAD,** Y'KNOW.

THERE'S SOMETHIN' YOU SAID TO ME FRIDAY NIGHT THAT'S BEEN **BOTHERIN'** ME EVER **SINCE,** TOLAND.

YOU SAID THAT **HOMOSEXUALS** DON'T FEEL REAL **LOVE** FOR EACH OTHER.

I DON'T THINK THAT'S **TRUE.**

I woke up this mornin' rememberin' somethin' I haven't thought about in **years.** It happened when I was **six**...

...at a **party** my parents threw at our **home.**

Bein' a **kid,** I couldn't have **alcohol,** of course—but I could get **almost** drunk from soakin' up the **party noise** and **music.**

So I noticed **instantly** when somethin' made everything go **silent** out on the **patio.**

I went to see what was **up.** Everyone was watchin' two **men** who were standin' **facin'** each other. I'd seen 'em at various gatherings before...always **together.**

At first I thought it was an **argument** about to happen.

But they never **spoke.** They just looked with an awful **sadness** into each other's **eyes.**

When my aunt saw that I was about to whisper a **question,** she put a **finger** to her **lips** and looked **away.**

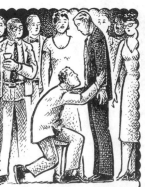

One of the men slid down on his **knees**...

...And pressed his **cheek** against the **leg** of the one still **standing.**

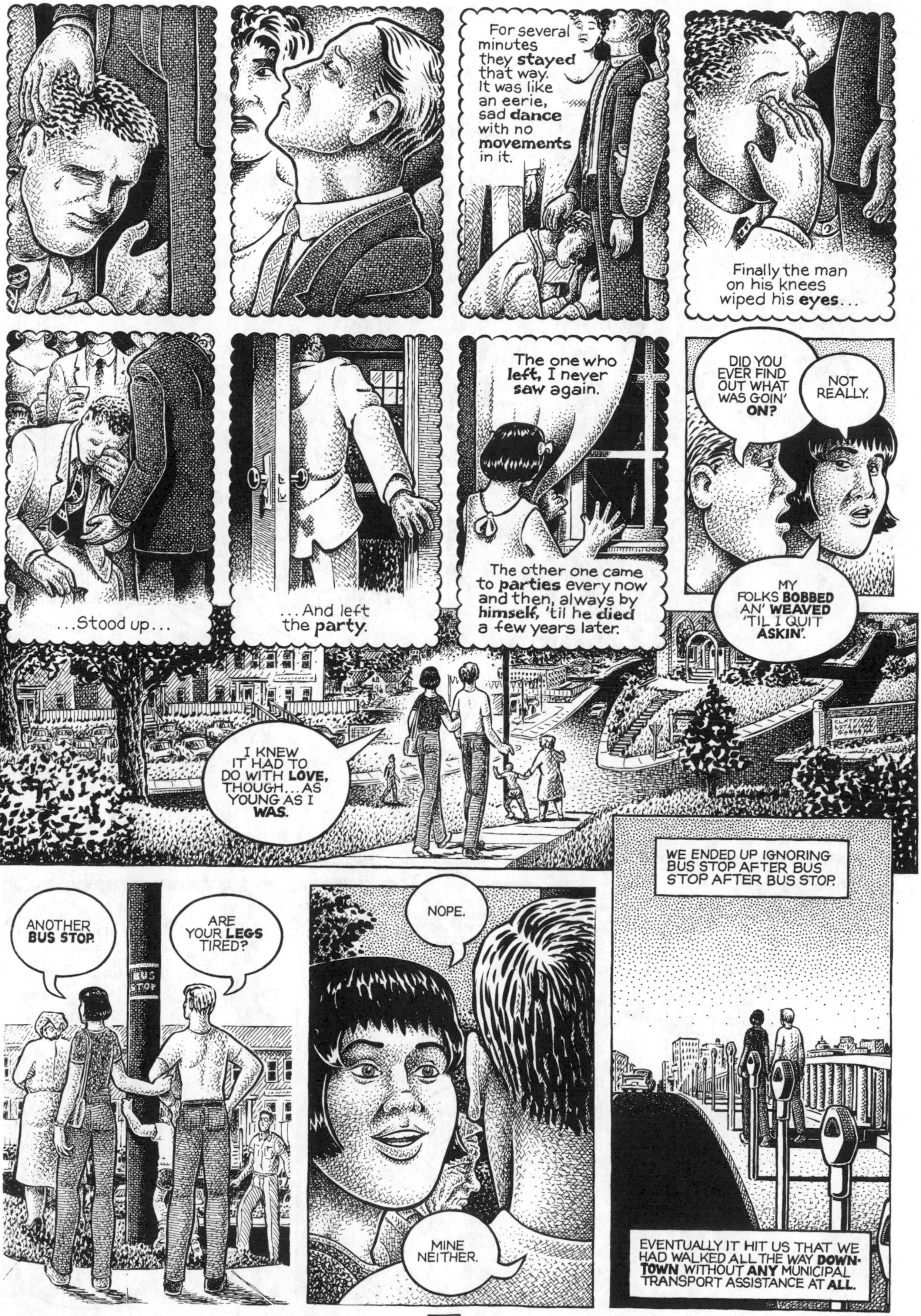
For several minutes they stayed that way. It was like an eerie, sad dance with no movements in it.
Finally the man on his knees wiped his eyes...
...Stood up...
...And left the party.
The one who left, I never saw again.
The other one came to parties every now and then, always by himself, 'til he died a few years later.
DID YOU EVER FIND OUT WHAT WAS GOIN' ON?
NOT REALLY.
MY FOLKS BOBBED AN' WEAVED 'TIL I QUIT ASKIN'.
I KNEW IT HAD TO DO WITH LOVE, THOUGH... AS YOUNG AS I WAS.
ANOTHER BUS STOP.
ARE YOUR LEGS TIRED?
BUS STOP
NOPE.
MINE NEITHER.
WE ENDED UP IGNORING BUS STOP AFTER BUS STOP AFTER BUS STOP.
EVENTUALLY IT HIT US THAT WE HAD WALKED ALL THE WAY DOWNTOWN WITHOUT ANY MUNICIPAL TRANSPORT ASSISTANCE AT ALL.

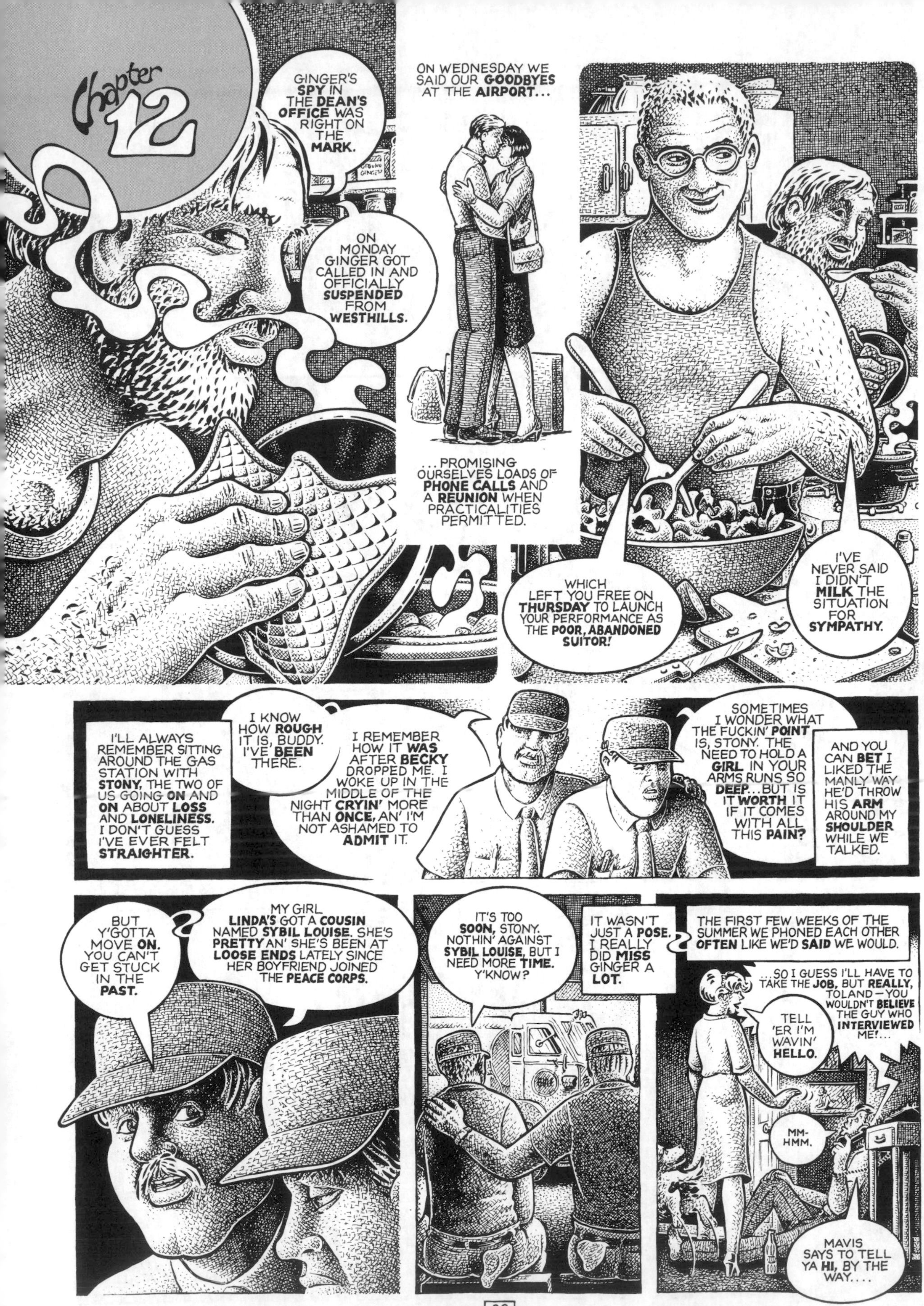

Chapter 12
GINGER'S SPY IN THE DEAN'S OFFICE WAS RIGHT ON THE MARK.
ON MONDAY GINGER GOT CALLED IN AND OFFICIALLY SUSPENDED FROM WESTHILLS.
ON WEDNESDAY WE SAID OUR GOODBYES AT THE AIRPORT...
...PROMISING OURSELVES LOADS OF PHONE CALLS AND A REUNION WHEN PRACTICALITIES PERMITTED.
WHICH LEFT YOU FREE ON THURSDAY TO LAUNCH YOUR PERFORMANCE AS THE POOR, ABANDONED SUITOR!
I'VE NEVER SAID I DIDN'T MILK THE SITUATION FOR SYMPATHY.
I'LL ALWAYS REMEMBER SITTING AROUND THE GAS STATION WITH STONY, THE TWO OF US GOING ON AND ON ABOUT LOSS AND LONELINESS. I DON'T GUESS I'VE EVER FELT STRAIGHTER.
I KNOW HOW ROUGH IT IS, BUDDY. I'VE BEEN THERE.
I REMEMBER HOW IT WAS AFTER BECKY DROPPED ME. I WOKE UP IN THE MIDDLE OF THE NIGHT CRYIN' MORE THAN ONCE, AN' I'M NOT ASHAMED TO ADMIT IT.
SOMETIMES I WONDER WHAT THE FUCKIN' POINT IS, STONY. THE NEED TO HOLD A GIRL IN YOUR ARMS RUNS SO DEEP... BUT IS IT WORTH IT IF IT COMES WITH ALL THIS PAIN?
AND YOU CAN BET I LIKED THE MANLY WAY HE'D THROW HIS ARM AROUND MY SHOULDER WHILE WE TALKED.
BUT Y'GOTTA MOVE ON. YOU CAN'T GET STUCK IN THE PAST.
MY GIRL LINDA'S GOT A COUSIN NAMED SYBIL LOUISE. SHE'S PRETTY AN' SHE'S BEEN AT LOOSE ENDS LATELY SINCE HER BOYFRIEND JOINED THE PEACE CORPS.
IT'S TOO SOON, STONY. NOTHIN' AGAINST SYBIL LOUISE, BUT I NEED MORE TIME. Y'KNOW?
IT WASN'T JUST A POSE. I REALLY DID MISS GINGER A LOT.
THE FIRST FEW WEEKS OF THE SUMMER WE PHONED EACH OTHER OFTEN LIKE WE'D SAID WE WOULD.
...SO I GUESS I'LL HAVE TO TAKE THE JOB, BUT REALLY, TOLAND—YOU WOULDN'T BELIEVE THE GUY WHO INTERVIEWED ME!...
TELL 'ER I'M WAVIN' HELLO.
MM-HMM.
MAVIS SAYS TO TELL YA HI, BY THE WAY....

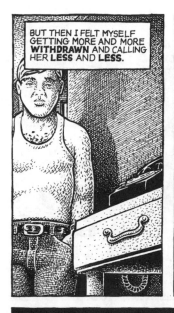

BUT THEN I FELT MYSELF GETTING MORE AND MORE **WITHDRAWN** AND CALLING HER **LESS** AND **LESS**.
IT WASN'T ONLY **GINGER** I WAS PULLING BACK FROM.
The Clayfield Banner
BIRCH SOCIETY CONDEMNS TEST-BAN TREATY TALKS
Resolution Cites High Treason at Presidential Level
I STOPPED SHOWING UP AT **EQUALITY LEAGUE** MEETINGS OR EVEN KEEPING UP WITH HOW REV. PEPPER'S **SKIRMISHES** WITH THE **CITY** WERE FARING.
I EVEN STARTED FEELING PUT **OFF** BY **SAMMY NOONE**.
LOOK, TOLAND! SAMMY'S **CAST** IS OFF.
HEY, THAT'S **GREAT**.
LIKE OUR **LORD** ON **EASTER MORN,** MY HAND IS **RISEN** FROM THE **DEAD!**
FATHER MORRIS—BEING A GOOD **LIBERAL** WHO **APPROVED** OF PROTESTS LIKE THE ONE AT RUSSELL PARK—HAD AVERTED **ONE** POTENTIAL CRISIS BY KEEPING SAMMY ON THE CHURCH **PAYROLL** DURING THE PERIOD WHEN HE COULDN'T **PLAY**.
HOW SOON ARE YA GONNA BE READY TO **PERFORM** AGAIN?
WITH PROPER **PRACTICE** I EXPECT MY TALENTED **DIGITS** TO BE **FULLY REHABILITATED** IN **RECORD TIME!**
I'M SURE **MAVIS** WILL FREELY OFFER UP HER SEMI-VIRGINAL **BODY** FOR MY FIVE-FINGER **EXERCISES!**
NATCH! WHAT'RE FRIENDS **FOR?**
YOU'D THINK I'D HAVE SIMPLY FELT **PLEASED** FOR HIM, BUT FOR SOME REASON SAMMY'S PERPETUAL DEVIL-MAY-CARE **ATTITUDE** HAD BEGUN GETTING ON MY **NERVES**.
SOON I'LL BE TANTALIZING HER TITTIES WITH SHIMMERING TRILL-L-L-LS!...
...VISITING VENTURESOME GLISS-S-SANDOS ON HER QUAKING NETHER-REGIONS!...
...AHH, MAVEEZ... ZEE MACHO PASSION, SHE EEZ RIZEENG...
nibble!
SAMMY, THAT TICKLES!
SPARE US YOUR **STRAIGHT** ACT, SAMMY. IT JUST AIN'T **CONVINCIN'!**
!
?
TOLAND!
BABY, WE'VE BEEN CUTTIN' LOTS OF **SLACK** FOR YOU AN' YOUR **MOODS** LATELY, BUT IF YOU'RE EVER **RUDE** LIKE THAT TO SAMMY **AGAIN,** YOU CAN START LOOKIN' FOR OTHER **QUARTERS!**
MAVIS HAD **NEVER** BLOWN HER **TOP** AT ME LIKE THAT BEFORE. MY STOMACH STILL GETS **WOBBLY** THINKING **BACK** ON IT.
MY SISTER COULD **TELL** I WAS **DEPRESSED**.
TOLAND, IF YOU DON'T AT LEAST MAKE A **STAB** AT SHAKIN' OFF THESE **BLUES**, YOU'RE GONNA DRIVE THE **REST** OF US OUT OF OUR **GOURDS**.
NOW, ORLEY AN' I WANT **YOU** AN **MAVIS** AN' **RILEY** TO COME OVER SUNDAY AFTERNOON FOR A **BARBEQUE**.
AN' IF YOU DON'T BRING A BETTER **DISPOSITION** WITH YOU, IT'S GONNA BE **YOU** THAT GETS **BARBE-QUED!**
AN' FOR GOD'S SAKE, BRING A **DATE**.
I KNOW YOU'D RATHER **GINGER** WAS HERE, BUT YOU **CAN'T** STOP HAVIN' A SOCIAL LIFE **ENTIRELY!**
I TOOK HER **ADVICE**.

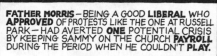

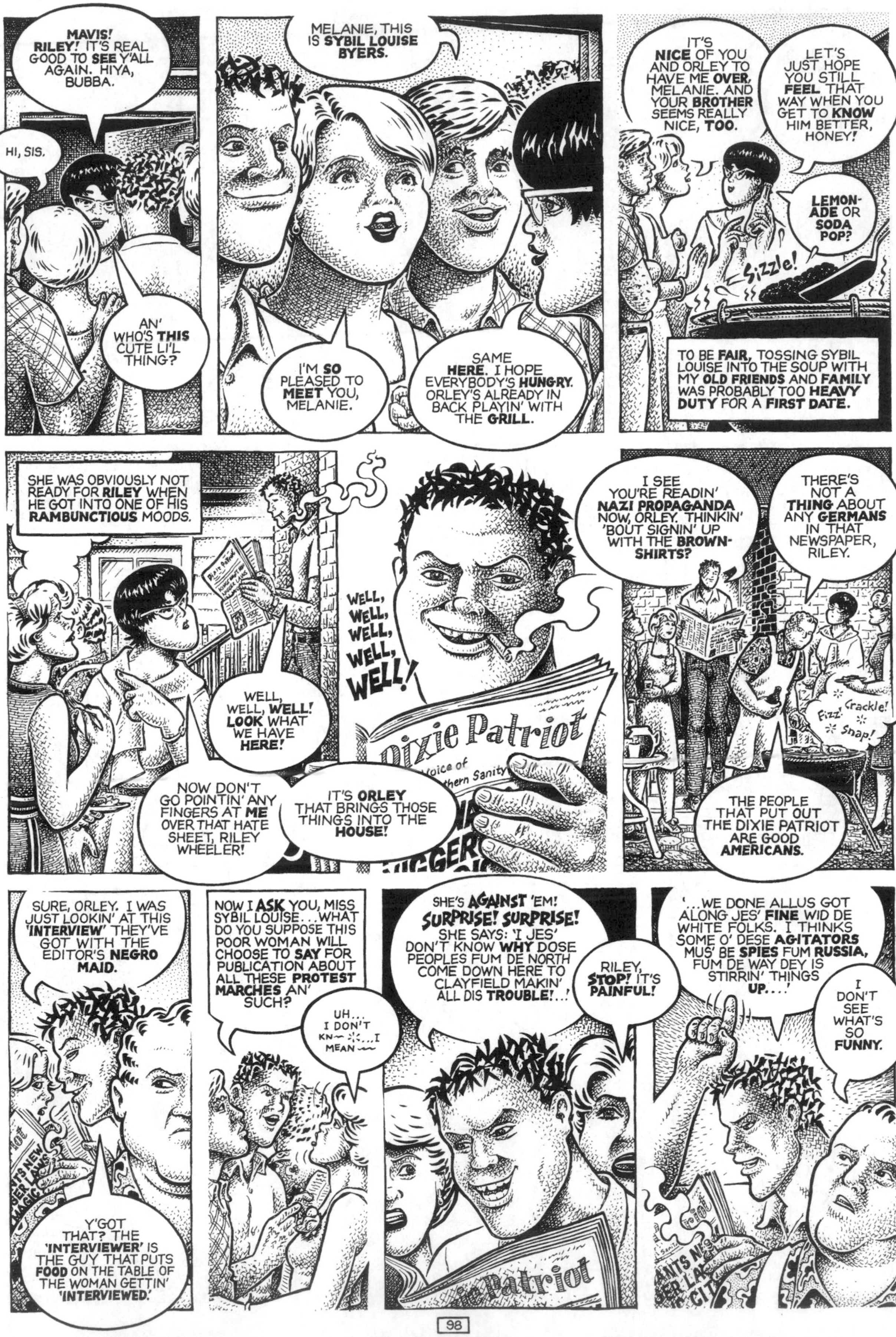
MAVIS! RILEY! IT'S REAL GOOD TO SEE Y'ALL AGAIN. HIYA, BUBBA.
HI, SIS.
AN' WHO'S THIS CUTE LI'L THING?
MELANIE, THIS IS SYBIL LOUISE BYERS.
I'M SO PLEASED TO MEET YOU, MELANIE.
SAME HERE. I HOPE EVERYBODY'S HUNGRY. ORLEY'S ALREADY IN BACK PLAYIN' WITH THE GRILL.
IT'S NICE OF YOU AND ORLEY TO HAVE ME OVER, MELANIE. AND YOUR BROTHER SEEMS REALLY NICE, TOO.
LET'S JUST HOPE YOU STILL FEEL THAT WAY WHEN YOU GET TO KNOW HIM BETTER, HONEY!
LEMON-ADE OR SODA POP?
Sizzle!
TO BE FAIR, TOSSING SYBIL LOUISE INTO THE SOUP WITH MY OLD FRIENDS AND FAMILY WAS PROBABLY TOO HEAVY DUTY FOR A FIRST DATE.
SHE WAS OBVIOUSLY NOT READY FOR RILEY WHEN HE GOT INTO ONE OF HIS RAMBUNCTIOUS MOODS.
WELL, WELL, WELL! LOOK WHAT WE HAVE HERE!
NOW DON'T GO POINTIN' ANY FINGERS AT ME OVER THAT HATE SHEET, RILEY WHEELER!
WELL, WELL, WELL, WELL, WELL!
Dixie Patriot
Voice of Southern Sanity
IT'S ORLEY THAT BRINGS THOSE THINGS INTO THE HOUSE!
I SEE YOU'RE READIN' NAZI PROPAGANDA NOW, ORLEY. THINKIN' 'BOUT SIGNIN' UP WITH THE BROWN-SHIRTS?
THERE'S NOT A THING ABOUT ANY GERMANS IN THAT NEWSPAPER, RILEY.
Fizz! Crackle! Snap!
THE PEOPLE THAT PUT OUT THE DIXIE PATRIOT ARE GOOD AMERICANS.
SURE, ORLEY. I WAS JUST LOOKIN' AT THIS 'INTERVIEW' THEY'VE GOT WITH THE EDITOR'S NEGRO MAID.
Y'GOT THAT? THE 'INTERVIEWER' IS THE GUY THAT PUTS FOOD ON THE TABLE OF THE WOMAN GETTIN' 'INTERVIEWED.'
NOW I ASK YOU, MISS SYBIL LOUISE... WHAT DO YOU SUPPOSE THIS POOR WOMAN WILL CHOOSE TO SAY FOR PUBLICATION ABOUT ALL THESE PROTEST MARCHES AN' SUCH?
UH... I DON'T KN~ ...I MEAN ~
SHE'S AGAINST 'EM! SURPRISE! SURPRISE! SHE SAYS: 'I JES' DON'T KNOW WHY DOSE PEOPLES FUM DE NORTH COME DOWN HERE TO CLAYFIELD MAKIN' ALL DIS TROUBLE!...'
RILEY, STOP! IT'S PAINFUL!
'...WE DONE ALLUS GOT ALONG JES' FINE WID DE WHITE FOLKS. I THINKS SOME O' DESE AGITATORS MUS' BE SPIES FUM RUSSIA, FUM DE WAY DEY IS STIRRIN' THINGS UP....'
I DON'T SEE WHAT'S SO FUNNY.
Patriot

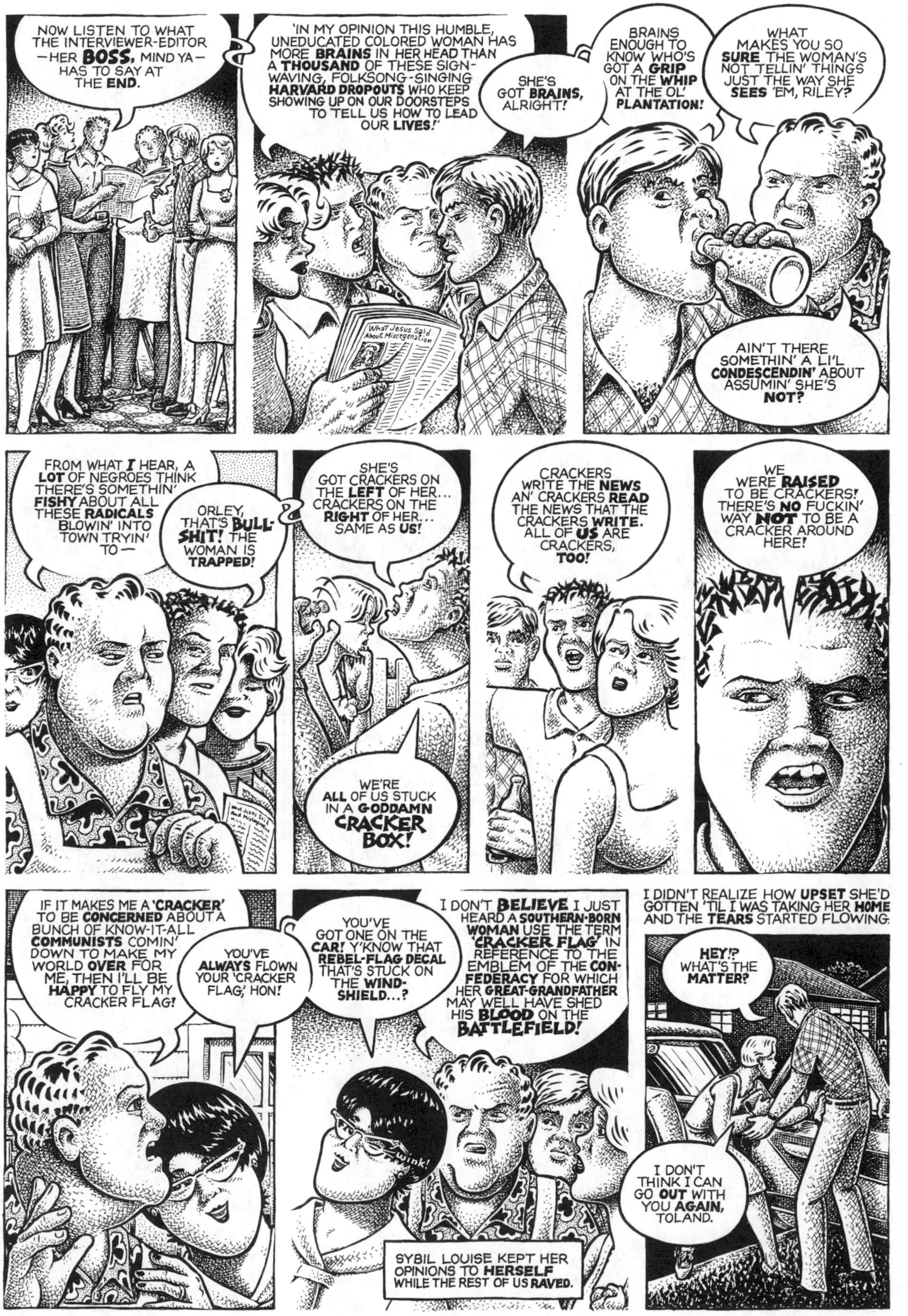
NOW LISTEN TO WHAT THE INTERVIEWER-EDITOR —HER BOSS, MIND YA— HAS TO SAY AT THE END.
'IN MY OPINION THIS HUMBLE, UNEDUCATED COLORED WOMAN HAS MORE BRAINS IN HER HEAD THAN A THOUSAND OF THESE SIGN-WAVING, FOLKSONG-SINGING HARVARD DROPOUTS WHO KEEP SHOWING UP ON OUR DOORSTEPS TO TELL US HOW TO LEAD OUR LIVES!'
SHE'S GOT BRAINS, ALRIGHT!
What Jesus Said About Miscegenation
BRAINS ENOUGH TO KNOW WHO'S GOT A GRIP ON THE WHIP AT THE OL' PLANTATION!
WHAT MAKES YOU SO SURE THE WOMAN'S NOT TELLIN' THINGS JUST THE WAY SHE SEES 'EM, RILEY?
AIN'T THERE SOMETHIN' A LI'L CONDESCENDIN' ABOUT ASSUMIN' SHE'S NOT?
FROM WHAT I HEAR, A LOT OF NEGROES THINK THERE'S SOMETHIN' FISHY ABOUT ALL THESE RADICALS BLOWIN' INTO TOWN TRYIN' TO—
ORLEY, THAT'S BULL-SHIT! THE WOMAN IS TRAPPED!
SHE'S GOT CRACKERS ON THE LEFT OF HER... CRACKERS ON THE RIGHT OF HER... SAME AS US!
WE'RE ALL OF US STUCK IN A GODDAMN CRACKER BOX!
CRACKERS WRITE THE NEWS AN' CRACKERS READ THE NEWS THAT THE CRACKERS WRITE. ALL OF US ARE CRACKERS, TOO!
WE WERE RAISED TO BE CRACKERS! THERE'S NO FUCKIN' WAY NOT TO BE A CRACKER AROUND HERE!
IF IT MAKES ME A 'CRACKER' TO BE CONCERNED ABOUT A BUNCH OF KNOW-IT-ALL COMMUNISTS COMIN' DOWN TO MAKE MY WORLD OVER FOR ME, THEN I'LL BE HAPPY TO FLY MY CRACKER FLAG!
YOU'VE ALWAYS FLOWN YOUR 'CRACKER FLAG,' HON!
YOU'VE GOT ONE ON THE CAR! Y'KNOW THAT REBEL-FLAG DECAL THAT'S STUCK ON THE WIND-SHIELD...?
I DON'T BELIEVE I JUST HEARD A SOUTHERN-BORN WOMAN USE THE TERM 'CRACKER FLAG' IN REFERENCE TO THE EMBLEM OF THE CON-FEDERACY FOR WHICH HER GREAT-GRANDFATHER MAY WELL HAVE SHED HIS BLOOD ON THE BATTLEFIELD!
tink!
SYBIL LOUISE KEPT HER OPINIONS TO HERSELF WHILE THE REST OF US RAVED.
I DIDN'T REALIZE HOW UPSET SHE'D GOTTEN 'TIL I WAS TAKING HER HOME AND THE TEARS STARTED FLOWING.
HEY!? WHAT'S THE MATTER?
I DON'T THINK I CAN GO OUT WITH YOU AGAIN, TOLAND.

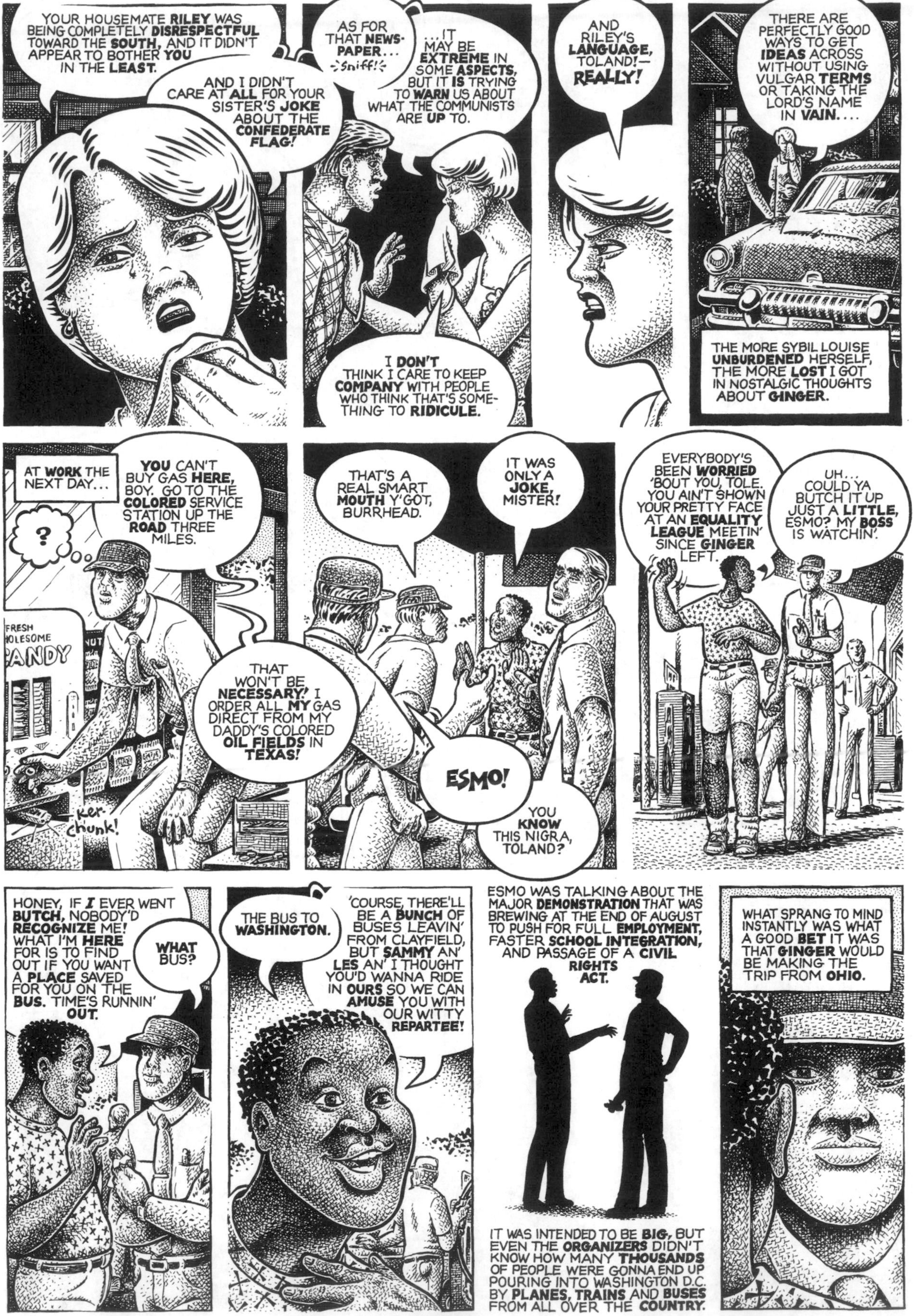
YOUR HOUSEMATE RILEY WAS BEING COMPLETELY DISRESPECTFUL TOWARD THE SOUTH, AND IT DIDN'T APPEAR TO BOTHER YOU IN THE LEAST.
AND I DIDN'T CARE AT ALL FOR YOUR SISTER'S JOKE ABOUT THE CONFEDERATE FLAG!
AS FOR THAT NEWS-PAPER...
-Sniff!-
...IT MAY BE EXTREME IN SOME ASPECTS, BUT IT IS TRYING TO WARN US ABOUT WHAT THE COMMUNISTS ARE UP TO.
I DON'T THINK I CARE TO KEEP COMPANY WITH PEOPLE WHO THINK THAT'S SOME-THING TO RIDICULE.
AND RILEY'S LANGUAGE, TOLAND!— REALLY!
THERE ARE PERFECTLY GOOD WAYS TO GET IDEAS ACROSS WITHOUT USING VULGAR TERMS OR TAKING THE LORD'S NAME IN VAIN....
THE MORE SYBIL LOUISE UNBURDENED HERSELF, THE MORE LOST I GOT IN NOSTALGIC THOUGHTS ABOUT GINGER.
AT WORK THE NEXT DAY...
YOU CAN'T BUY GAS HERE, BOY. GO TO THE COLORED SERVICE STATION UP THE ROAD THREE MILES.
?
FRESH
HOLESOME
ANDY
KER-CHUNK!
THAT WON'T BE NECESSARY! I ORDER ALL MY GAS DIRECT FROM MY DADDY'S COLORED OIL FIELDS IN TEXAS!
THAT'S A REAL SMART MOUTH Y'GOT, BURRHEAD.
IT WAS ONLY A JOKE, MISTER!
ESMO!
YOU KNOW THIS NIGRA, TOLAND?
EVERYBODY'S BEEN WORRIED 'BOUT YOU, TOLE. YOU AIN'T SHOWN YOUR PRETTY FACE AT AN EQUALITY LEAGUE MEETIN' SINCE GINGER LEFT.
UH... COULD YA BUTCH IT UP JUST A LITTLE, ESMO? MY BOSS IS WATCHIN'.
HONEY, IF I EVER WENT BUTCH, NOBODY'D RECOGNIZE ME! WHAT I'M HERE FOR IS TO FIND OUT IF YOU WANT A PLACE SAVED FOR YOU ON THE BUS. TIME'S RUNNIN' OUT.
WHAT BUS?
THE BUS TO WASHINGTON.
'COURSE, THERE'LL BE A BUNCH OF BUSES LEAVIN' FROM CLAYFIELD, BUT SAMMY AN' LES AN' I THOUGHT YOU'D WANNA RIDE IN OURS SO WE CAN AMUSE YOU WITH OUR WITTY REPARTEE!
ESMO WAS TALKING ABOUT THE MAJOR DEMONSTRATION THAT WAS BREWING AT THE END OF AUGUST TO PUSH FOR FULL EMPLOYMENT, FASTER SCHOOL INTEGRATION, AND PASSAGE OF A CIVIL RIGHTS ACT.
IT WAS INTENDED TO BE BIG, BUT EVEN THE ORGANIZERS DIDN'T KNOW HOW MANY THOUSANDS OF PEOPLE WERE GONNA END UP POURING INTO WASHINGTON D.C. BY PLANES, TRAINS AND BUSES FROM ALL OVER THE COUNTRY.
WHAT SPRANG TO MIND INSTANTLY WAS WHAT A GOOD BET IT WAS THAT GINGER WOULD BE MAKING THE TRIP FROM OHIO.

I'LL **THINK** ABOUT IT AN' GIVE YOU A **CALL**.

CALL **ANNA DELLYNE. SHE'S** IN CHARGE OF **BUS** ASSIGNMENTS.

OH!—AN' TOLAND, HONEY, DON'T YOU **DARE** MISS MY **SEPTEMBER SHOW** AT THE **RHOMBUS!** IT'S GONNA BE THE **CROWNIN'** ACHIEVEMENT OF MY **DRAG-QUEEN CAREER!**

I'M DOIN' **MISS DORIS DAY!**

NOW I **ASK** YOU— IS THAT SOME KINDA **STRETCH** OR **WHAT?!**

SORRY 'BOUT THAT **NEGRO,** GLENN. HIS **MOTHER** USED TO CLEAN OUR **HOUSE** FOR US.

HE'S KIND OF A **FAIRY,** BUT I TRY TO BE **NICE** TO HIM FOR **HER** SAKE.

THAT NIGHT I TELEPHONED **GINGER** AND ASKED IF SHE WAS GOING TO THE **MARCH** ON **WASHINGTON.** SHE SAID **YES.**

I TOLD HER I'D BE THERE, **TOO.**

♪ It's a hammer of justice!... ♪

♪ It's a bell of freedom!... ♪

OHIO WAITING STATION

THE**RE** SHE IS!

TO**LAND!**

HIYA, BABE.

...AND **ESMO! LES! SAMMY! SHILOH!**

GINGER, I CAN'T **STAND** YOU HAVIN' MOVED AWAY FROM **TOWN.**

ASIDE FROM MISSIN' **CLAYFIELD'S OTHER** CULTURAL ADVANTAGES, YOU WON'T GET TO SEE MY SPECIAL **TRIBUTE** TO **DORIS DAY** AT THE **RHOMBUS** NEXT MONTH.

OH, BUT I **WILL** GET TO SEE IT, ESMO.

WE **ARCH** FOR **FFECTIVE** CIVIL RIGHTS LAWS

V DE VOT RIG NO

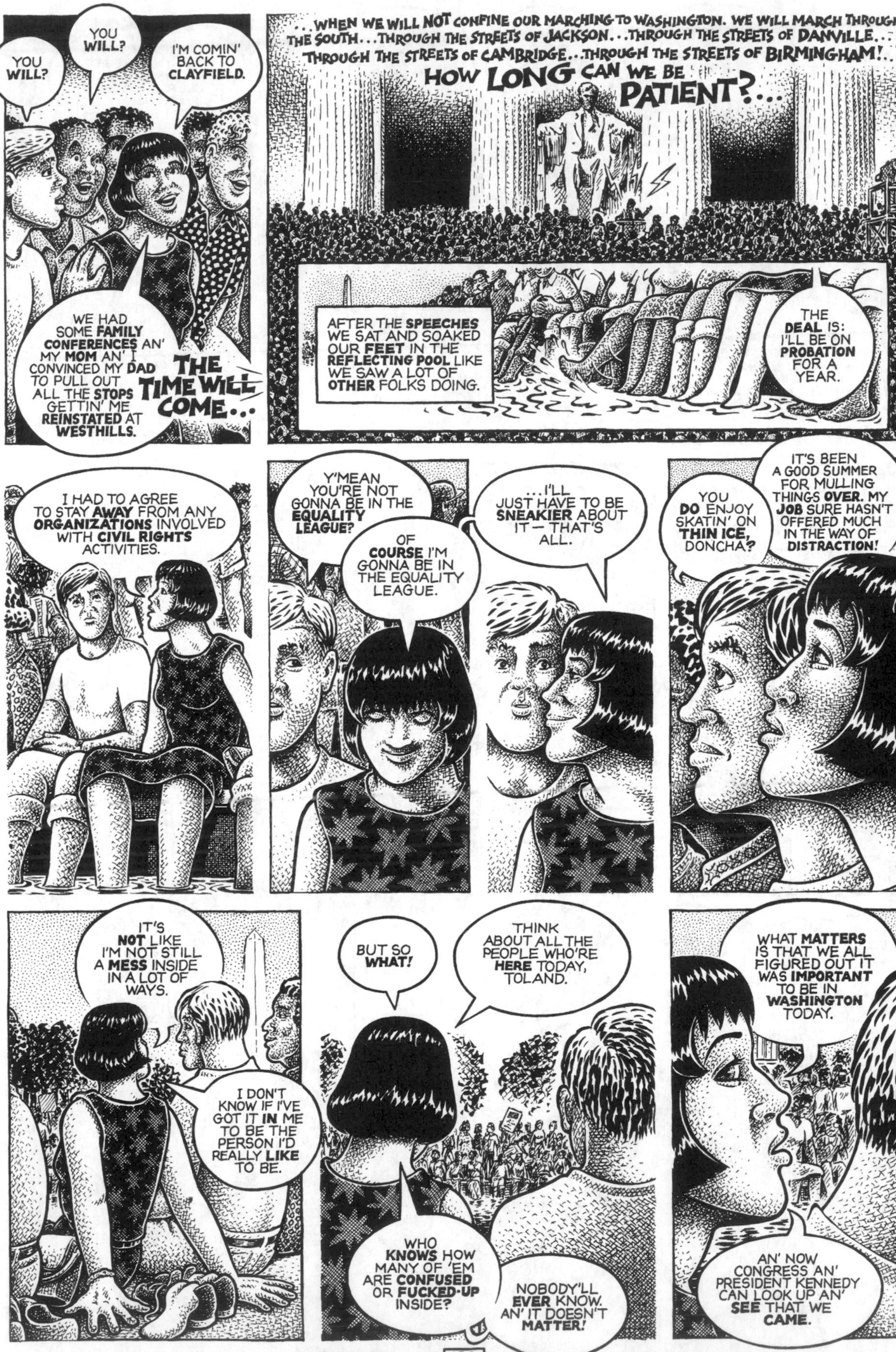
YOU WILL?
YOU WILL?
I'M COMIN' BACK TO CLAYFIELD.
WE HAD SOME FAMILY CONFERENCES AN' MY MOM AN' I CONVINCED MY DAD TO PULL OUT ALL THE STOPS GETTIN' ME REINSTATED AT WESTHILLS.
THE TIME WILL COME...
...WHEN WE WILL NOT CONFINE OUR MARCHING TO WASHINGTON. WE WILL MARCH THROUGH THE SOUTH...THROUGH THE STREETS OF JACKSON...THROUGH THE STREETS OF DANVILLE...THROUGH THE STREETS OF CAMBRIDGE...THROUGH THE STREETS OF BIRMINGHAM!...
HOW LONG CAN WE BE PATIENT?...
AFTER THE SPEECHES WE SAT AND SOAKED OUR FEET IN THE REFLECTING POOL LIKE WE SAW A LOT OF OTHER FOLKS DOING.
THE DEAL IS: I'LL BE ON PROBATION FOR A YEAR.
I HAD TO AGREE TO STAY AWAY FROM ANY ORGANIZATIONS INVOLVED WITH CIVIL RIGHTS ACTIVITIES.
Y'MEAN YOU'RE NOT GONNA BE IN THE EQUALITY LEAGUE?
OF COURSE I'M GONNA BE IN THE EQUALITY LEAGUE.
...I'LL JUST HAVE TO BE SNEAKIER ABOUT IT — THAT'S ALL.
YOU DO ENJOY SKATIN' ON THIN ICE, DONCHA?
IT'S BEEN A GOOD SUMMER FOR MULLING THINGS OVER. MY JOB SURE HASN'T OFFERED MUCH IN THE WAY OF DISTRACTION!
IT'S NOT LIKE I'M NOT STILL A MESS INSIDE IN A LOT OF WAYS.
I DON'T KNOW IF I'VE GOT IT IN ME TO BE THE PERSON I'D REALLY LIKE TO BE.
BUT SO WHAT!
THINK ABOUT ALL THE PEOPLE WHO'RE HERE TODAY, TOLAND.
WHO KNOWS HOW MANY OF 'EM ARE CONFUSED OR FUCKED-UP INSIDE?
NOBODY'LL EVER KNOW. AN' IT DOESN'T MATTER!
WHAT MATTERS IS THAT WE ALL FIGURED OUT IT WAS IMPORTANT TO BE IN WASHINGTON TODAY.
AN' NOW CONGRESS AN' PRESIDENT KENNEDY CAN LOOK UP AN' SEE THAT WE CAME.

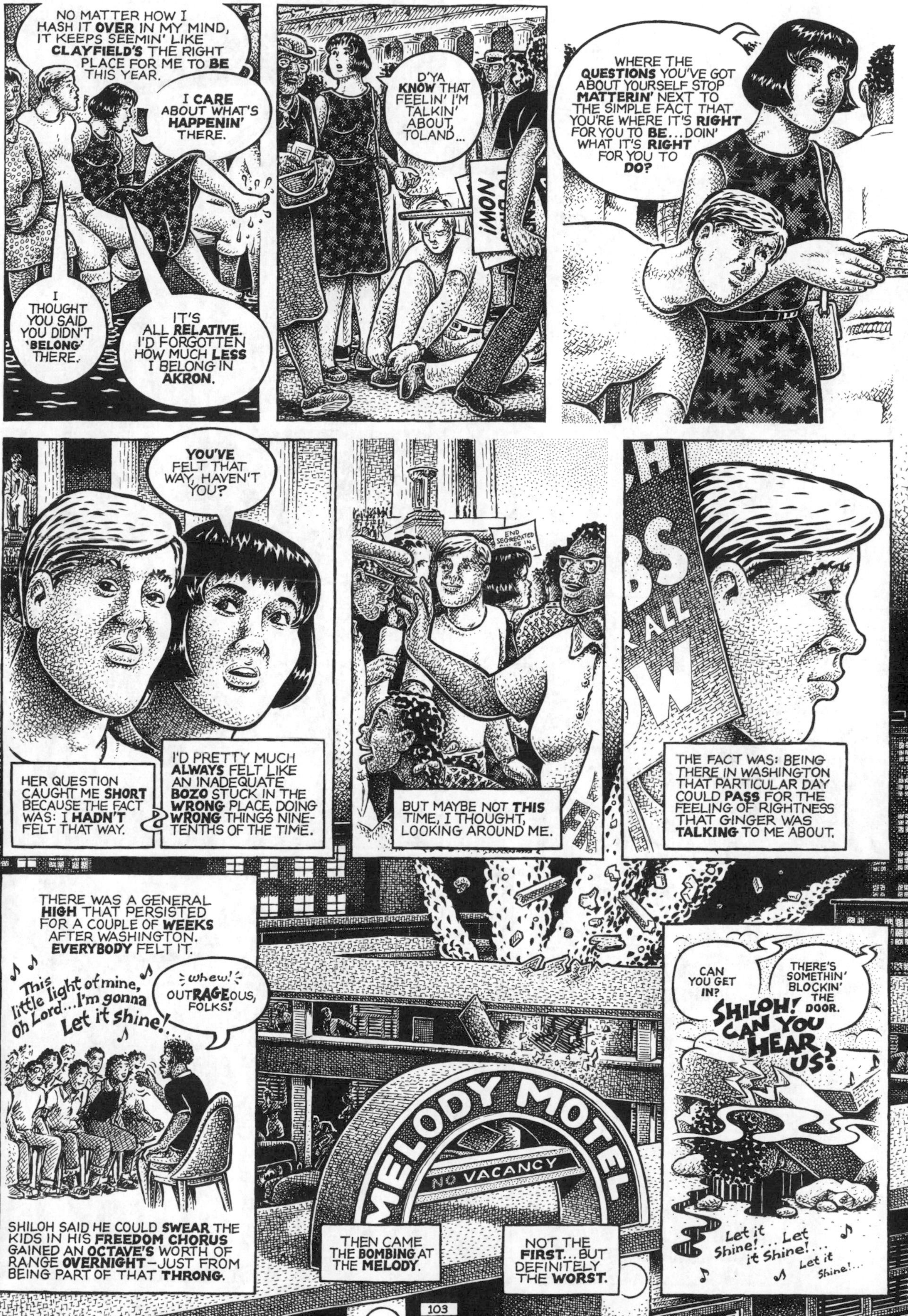
NO MATTER HOW I HASH IT OVER IN MY MIND, IT KEEPS SEEMIN' LIKE CLAYFIELD'S THE RIGHT PLACE FOR ME TO BE THIS YEAR.
I CARE ABOUT WHAT'S HAPPENIN' THERE.
I THOUGHT YOU SAID YOU DIDN'T 'BELONG' THERE.
IT'S ALL RELATIVE. I'D FORGOTTEN HOW MUCH LESS I BELONG IN AKRON.
D'YA KNOW THAT FEELIN' I'M TALKIN' ABOUT, TOLAND...
NOW!
WHERE THE QUESTIONS YOU'VE GOT ABOUT YOURSELF STOP MATTERIN' NEXT TO THE SIMPLE FACT THAT YOU'RE WHERE IT'S RIGHT FOR YOU TO BE... DOIN' WHAT IT'S RIGHT FOR YOU TO DO?
YOU'VE FELT THAT WAY, HAVEN'T YOU?
HER QUESTION CAUGHT ME SHORT BECAUSE THE FACT WAS: I HADN'T FELT THAT WAY.
I'D PRETTY MUCH ALWAYS FELT LIKE AN INADEQUATE BOZO STUCK IN THE WRONG PLACE, DOING WRONG THINGS NINE-TENTHS OF THE TIME.
END SEGREGATED SCHOOLS
BUT MAYBE NOT THIS TIME, I THOUGHT, LOOKING AROUND ME.
THE FACT WAS: BEING THERE IN WASHINGTON THAT PARTICULAR DAY COULD PASS FOR THE FEELING OF RIGHTNESS THAT GINGER WAS TALKING TO ME ABOUT.
THERE WAS A GENERAL HIGH THAT PERSISTED FOR A COUPLE OF WEEKS AFTER WASHINGTON. EVERYBODY FELT IT.
This little light of mine, Oh Lord... I'm gonna Let it shine!...
whew! OUTRAGEOUS, FOLKS!
SHILOH SAID HE COULD SWEAR THE KIDS IN HIS FREEDOM CHORUS GAINED AN OCTAVE'S WORTH OF RANGE OVERNIGHT—JUST FROM BEING PART OF THAT THRONG.
MELODY MOTEL
NO VACANCY
THEN CAME THE BOMBING AT THE MELODY.
NOT THE FIRST... BUT DEFINITELY THE WORST.
CAN YOU GET IN?
THERE'S SOMETHIN' BLOCKIN' THE DOOR.
SHILOH! CAN YOU HEAR US?
Let it Shine!... Let it Shine!... Let it Shine!...

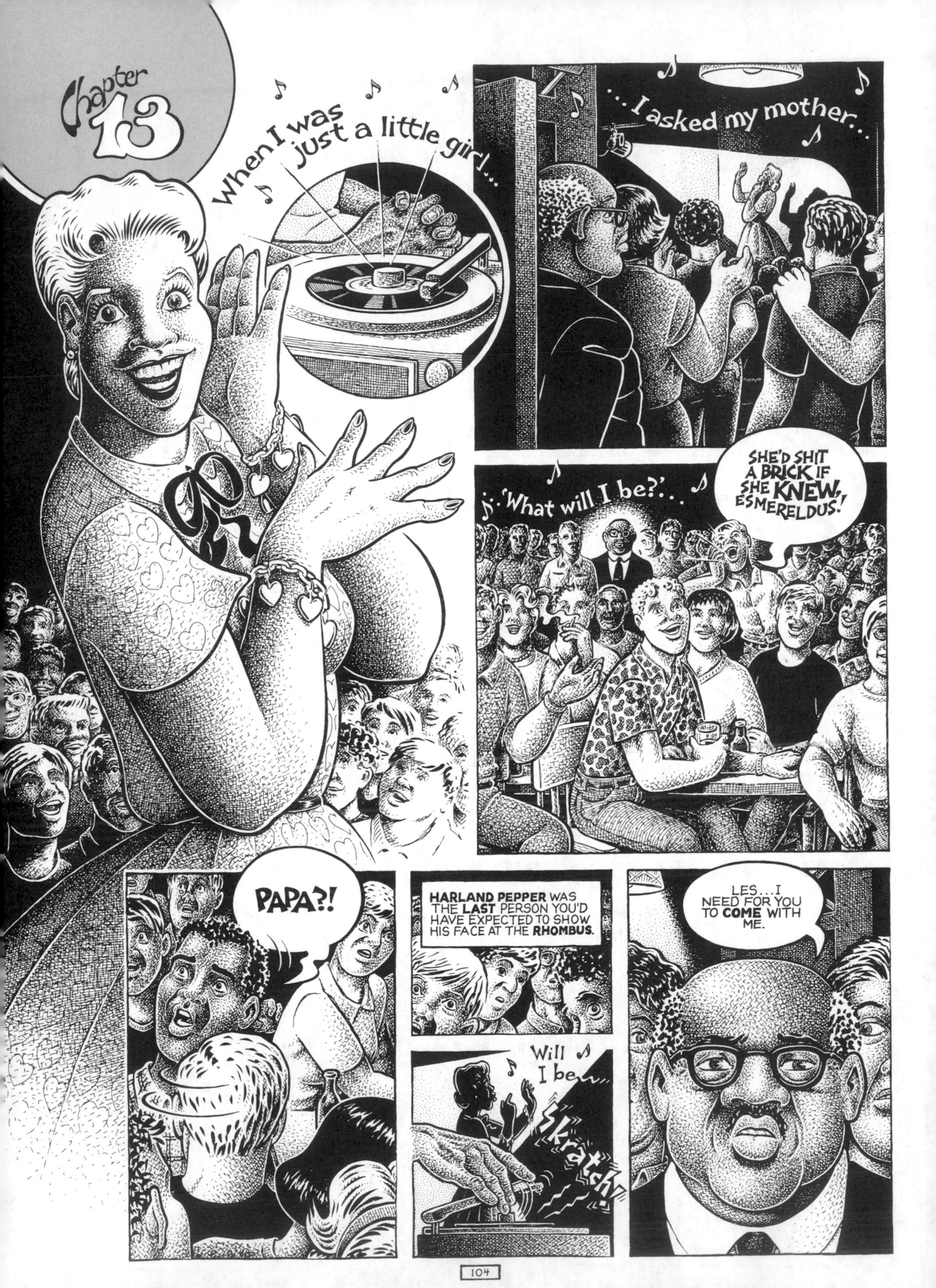
Chapter 13
When I was just a little girl...
...I asked my mother...
'What will I be?'...
SHE'D SHIT A BRICK IF SHE KNEW, ESMERELDUS!
PAPA?!
HARLAND PEPPER WAS THE LAST PERSON YOU'D HAVE EXPECTED TO SHOW HIS FACE AT THE RHOMBUS.
Will I be...
Skratch!
LES...I NEED FOR YOU TO COME WITH ME.

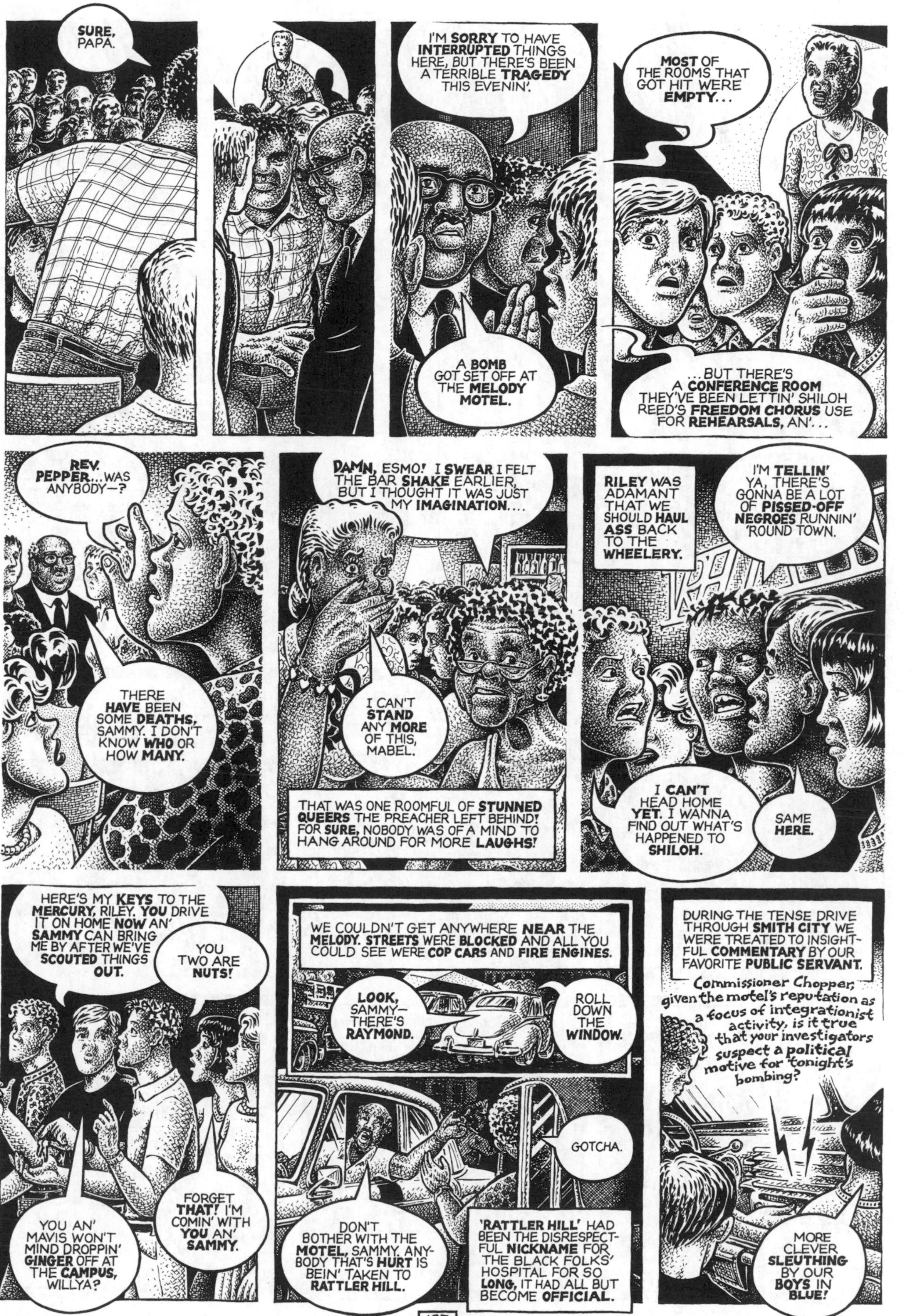
SURE, PAPA.
I'M SORRY TO HAVE INTERRUPTED THINGS HERE, BUT THERE'S BEEN A TERRIBLE TRAGEDY THIS EVENIN'.
A BOMB GOT SET OFF AT THE MELODY MOTEL.
MOST OF THE ROOMS THAT GOT HIT WERE EMPTY...
...BUT THERE'S A CONFERENCE ROOM THEY'VE BEEN LETTIN' SHILOH REED'S FREEDOM CHORUS USE FOR REHEARSALS, AN'...
REV. PEPPER...WAS ANYBODY—?
THERE HAVE BEEN SOME DEATHS, SAMMY. I DON'T KNOW WHO OR HOW MANY.
DAMN, ESMO! I SWEAR I FELT THE BAR SHAKE EARLIER, BUT I THOUGHT IT WAS JUST MY IMAGINATION....
I CAN'T STAND ANY MORE OF THIS, MABEL.
THAT WAS ONE ROOMFUL OF STUNNED QUEERS THE PREACHER LEFT BEHIND! FOR SURE, NOBODY WAS OF A MIND TO HANG AROUND FOR MORE LAUGHS!
RILEY WAS ADAMANT THAT WE SHOULD HAUL ASS BACK TO THE WHEELERY.
I'M TELLIN' YA, THERE'S GONNA BE A LOT OF PISSED-OFF NEGROES RUNNIN' 'ROUND TOWN.
I CAN'T HEAD HOME YET. I WANNA FIND OUT WHAT'S HAPPENED TO SHILOH.
SAME HERE.
HERE'S MY KEYS TO THE MERCURY, RILEY. YOU DRIVE IT ON HOME NOW AN' SAMMY CAN BRING ME BY AFTER WE'VE SCOUTED THINGS OUT.
YOU TWO ARE NUTS!
YOU AN' MAVIS WON'T MIND DROPPIN' GINGER OFF AT THE CAMPUS, WILLYA?
FORGET THAT! I'M COMIN' WITH YOU AN' SAMMY.
WE COULDN'T GET ANYWHERE NEAR THE MELODY. STREETS WERE BLOCKED AND ALL YOU COULD SEE WERE COP CARS AND FIRE ENGINES.
LOOK, SAMMY— THERE'S RAYMOND.
ROLL DOWN THE WINDOW.
GOTCHA.
DON'T BOTHER WITH THE MOTEL, SAMMY. ANYBODY THAT'S HURT IS BEIN' TAKEN TO RATTLER HILL.
'RATTLER HILL' HAD BEEN THE DISRESPECTFUL NICKNAME FOR THE BLACK FOLKS' HOSPITAL FOR SO LONG, IT HAD ALL BUT BECOME OFFICIAL.
DURING THE TENSE DRIVE THROUGH SMITH CITY WE WERE TREATED TO INSIGHTFUL COMMENTARY BY OUR FAVORITE PUBLIC SERVANT.
Commissioner Chopper, given the motel's reputation as a focus of integrationist activity, is it true that your investigators suspect a political motive for tonight's bombing?
MORE CLEVER SLEUTHING BY OUR BOYS IN BLUE!

WHILE THE THREE OF US **LISTENED** AND **GLOWERED**, I GOT LOST IN CONTEMPLATION OF THE **MUSCLES** THAT WERE FLEXING IN SAMMY'S **JAW**.

That's right, Bill... And as shocked as we all are by this deplorable crime, I'm obliged to point out that those sweet children would be alive right now were it not for the inflammatory street demonstrations we've all been subjected to by local malcontents as well as Communistic outside agitators...

EVEN WITH HIS FACE **HIDDEN**, IT WAS CLEAR HIS **BLOOD** WAS **BOILING**.

JEROME RADLER HILL MEMORIAL HOSPITAL FOR NEGROES

AT RATTLER HILL WE HAD TO WEAVE PAST **NEWS CREWS** FROM THE LOCAL **TELEVISION STATIONS**.

THEY WEREN'T BEING ALLOWED **INSIDE**, BUT THAT WASN'T STOPPING THEM FROM ANGLING FOR DRAMATIC FOOTAGE IN THE **PARKING LOT**.

WE SQUEEZED INTO A LOBBY THAT WAS **PACKED** WITH **FRIENDS** AND **RELATIVES** OF THE **BOMB VICTIMS**.

THE REST OF THE HOSPITAL WAS JUST AS **CROWDED**. FISHING AROUND FOR NEWS OF **SHILOH**, WE LEARNED HE WAS **HURT, UNCONSCIOUS** — BUT **ALIVE**.

HARLAND PEPPER WAS A **SIGHT** TO **BEHOLD** AS HE DASHED BACK AND FORTH TENDING TO **FIFTEEN EMOTIONAL CRISES** A MINUTE.

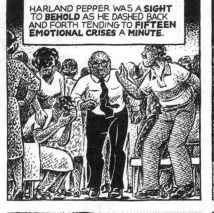

LES STAYED AT HIS DADDY'S **BECK** AND **CALL**. I WAS **IMPRESSED** AT HOW A **PARTYBOY** FROM THE **RHOMBUS** COULD TURN INTO A PERFECT **PREACHER'S KID** AT THE FLICK OF A **SWITCH**.

GINGER NOTICED ANNA DELLYNE COMFORTING A **GAUNT YOUNG WOMAN** IN THE **CORNER**. WE WALKED **OVER**.

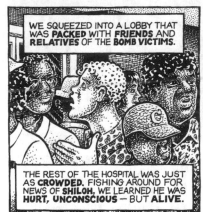

IT WAS **SHILOH'S** WIFE **LOTTIE**, WHOM I'D NEVER **MET**.

IT WAS PROBABLY COMMON **KNOWLEDGE** HOW FAR **GONE** SHE WAS FROM **CANCER**, BUT NOBODY HAD EVER BROUGHT UP THE SUBJECT TO **ME**.

GINGER HUGGED LOTTIE AND ANNA DELLYNE AND THE THREE FEMALES WENT INTO AN INTIMATE **WHISPERING** MODE. I FELT **EXTRANEOUS**.

SAMMY GOT **ANTSY** AND **PEELED OFF** FROM THE GROUP. AFTER EXPRESSING MY **CONCERN** TO **LOTTIE**, I DID, **TOO**.

I WANDERED AROUND, WISHING I HAD SOMEBODY TO **TALK** TO.

I SAW PLENTY OF FAMILIAR **FACES** FROM THE **EQUALITY LEAGUE**. THERE WEREN'T **MANY**, HOWEVER, THAT I'D EVER BOTHERED TO STRIKE UP A REAL **FRIENDSHIP** WITH.

AND **NOW** SEEMED AN AWKWARD TIME TO SET ABOUT **ICE-BREAKING**!

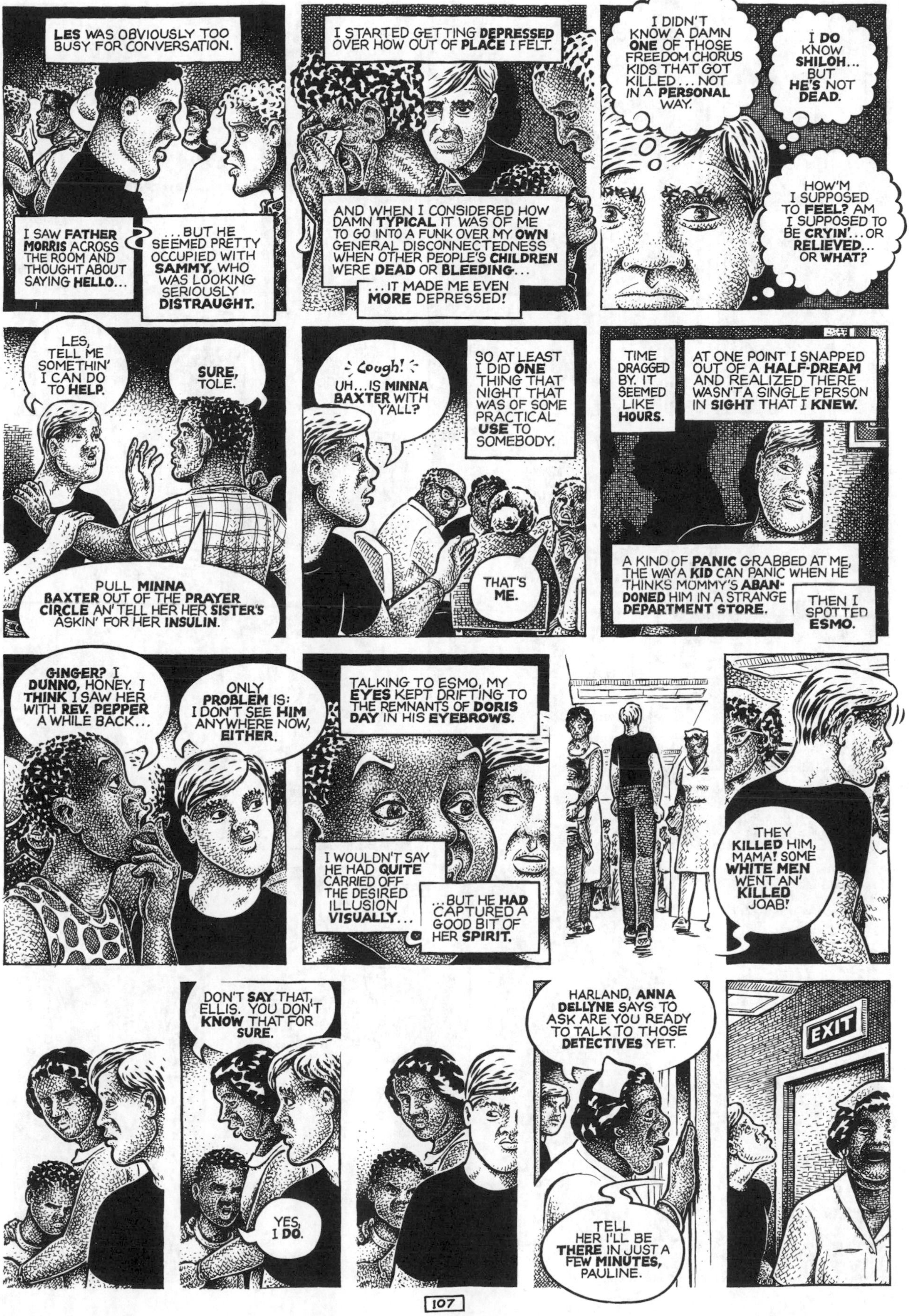
LES WAS OBVIOUSLY TOO BUSY FOR CONVERSATION.
I SAW FATHER MORRIS ACROSS THE ROOM AND THOUGHT ABOUT SAYING HELLO...
...BUT HE SEEMED PRETTY OCCUPIED WITH SAMMY, WHO WAS LOOKING SERIOUSLY DISTRAUGHT.
I STARTED GETTING DEPRESSED OVER HOW OUT OF PLACE I FELT.
AND WHEN I CONSIDERED HOW DAMN TYPICAL IT WAS OF ME TO GO INTO A FUNK OVER MY OWN GENERAL DISCONNECTEDNESS WHEN OTHER PEOPLE'S CHILDREN WERE DEAD OR BLEEDING...
...IT MADE ME EVEN MORE DEPRESSED!
I DIDN'T KNOW A DAMN ONE OF THOSE FREEDOM CHORUS KIDS THAT GOT KILLED... NOT IN A PERSONAL WAY.
I DO KNOW SHILOH... BUT HE'S NOT DEAD.
HOW'M I SUPPOSED TO FEEL? AM I SUPPOSED TO BE CRYIN'... OR RELIEVED... OR WHAT?
LES, TELL ME SOMETHIN' I CAN DO TO HELP.
SURE, TOLE.
PULL MINNA BAXTER OUT OF THE PRAYER CIRCLE AN' TELL HER HER SISTER'S ASKIN' FOR HER INSULIN.
Cough!
UH... IS MINNA BAXTER WITH Y'ALL?
SO AT LEAST I DID ONE THING THAT NIGHT THAT WAS OF SOME PRACTICAL USE TO SOMEBODY.
THAT'S ME.
TIME DRAGGED BY. IT SEEMED LIKE HOURS.
AT ONE POINT I SNAPPED OUT OF A HALF-DREAM AND REALIZED THERE WASN'T A SINGLE PERSON IN SIGHT THAT I KNEW.
A KIND OF PANIC GRABBED AT ME, THE WAY A KID CAN PANIC WHEN HE THINKS MOMMY'S ABANDONED HIM IN A STRANGE DEPARTMENT STORE.
THEN I SPOTTED ESMO.
GINGER? I DUNNO, HONEY. I THINK I SAW HER WITH REV. PEPPER A WHILE BACK...
ONLY PROBLEM IS: I DON'T SEE HIM ANYWHERE NOW, EITHER.
TALKING TO ESMO, MY EYES KEPT DRIFTING TO THE REMNANTS OF DORIS DAY IN HIS EYEBROWS.
I WOULDN'T SAY HE HAD QUITE CARRIED OFF THE DESIRED ILLUSION VISUALLY...
...BUT HE HAD CAPTURED A GOOD BIT OF HER SPIRIT.
THEY KILLED HIM, MAMA! SOME WHITE MEN WENT AN' KILLED JOAB!
DON'T SAY THAT, ELLIS. YOU DON'T KNOW THAT FOR SURE.
YES, I DO.
HARLAND, ANNA DELLYNE SAYS TO ASK ARE YOU READY TO TALK TO THOSE DETECTIVES YET.
TELL HER I'LL BE THERE IN JUST A FEW MINUTES, PAULINE.
EXIT

'SCUSE ME, REV. PEPPER.

ESMO TOLD ME GINGER MIGHT BE WITH YOU.

NO. IT'S JUST ME HERE.

OH. SORRY TO HAVE BOTHERED YOU.

DON'T RUN OFF, THOUGH, TOLAND.

THERE'S SOMETHIN' I'VE BEEN WANTIN' TO ASK YOU ABOUT.

DIDN'T I SEE YOU AT THE SIT-IN THE DAY THEY CLOSED DOWN RUSSELL PARK?

YES, SIR.

I KNEW I REMEMBERED SEEIN' YOU SITTIN' ON THE GRASS. I APPRECIATED YOU AN' YOUR FRIENDS BEIN' THERE.

AN' YOU WERE THERE AT THE BAR WITH LES TONIGHT, WEREN'T YOU...WHEN I CAME TO GET HIM?

UH... YEAH. I WAS.

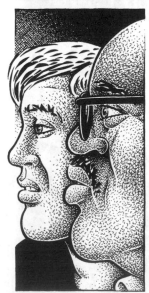

IT WAS DARK, BUT I THOUGHT I RECOGNIZED YOU.

WANT ONE OF THESE?

NO, THANKS, I DON'T SMOKE.

YOU'RE A SMART YOUNG MAN.

108

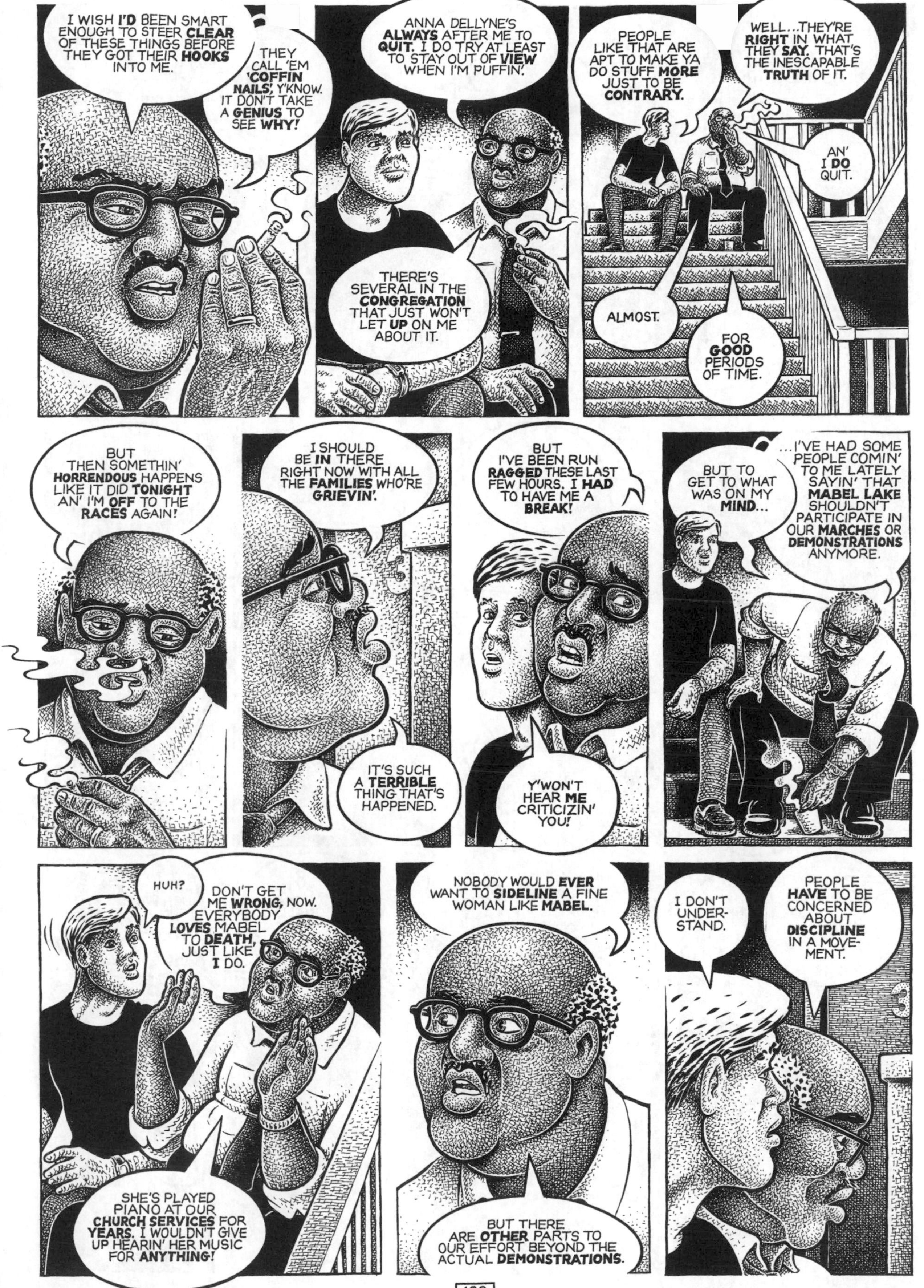
I WISH I'D BEEN SMART ENOUGH TO STEER CLEAR OF THESE THINGS BEFORE THEY GOT THEIR HOOKS INTO ME.
THEY CALL 'EM 'COFFIN NAILS,' Y'KNOW. IT DON'T TAKE A GENIUS TO SEE WHY!
ANNA DELLYNE'S ALWAYS AFTER ME TO QUIT. I DO TRY AT LEAST TO STAY OUT OF VIEW WHEN I'M PUFFIN'.
THERE'S SEVERAL IN THE CONGREGATION THAT JUST WON'T LET UP ON ME ABOUT IT.
PEOPLE LIKE THAT ARE APT TO MAKE YA DO STUFF MORE JUST TO BE CONTRARY.
WELL...THEY'RE RIGHT IN WHAT THEY SAY. THAT'S THE INESCAPABLE TRUTH OF IT.
AN' I DO QUIT.
ALMOST.
FOR GOOD PERIODS OF TIME.
BUT THEN SOMETHIN' HORRENDOUS HAPPENS LIKE IT DID TONIGHT AN' I'M OFF TO THE RACES AGAIN!
I SHOULD BE IN THERE RIGHT NOW WITH ALL THE FAMILIES WHO'RE GRIEVIN'.
IT'S SUCH A TERRIBLE THING THAT'S HAPPENED.
BUT I'VE BEEN RUN RAGGED THESE LAST FEW HOURS. I HAD TO HAVE ME A BREAK!
Y'WON'T HEAR ME CRITICIZIN' YOU!
BUT TO GET TO WHAT WAS ON MY MIND...
...I'VE HAD SOME PEOPLE COMIN' TO ME LATELY SAYIN' THAT MABEL LAKE SHOULDN'T PARTICIPATE IN OUR MARCHES OR DEMONSTRATIONS ANYMORE.
HUH?
DON'T GET ME WRONG, NOW. EVERYBODY LOVES MABEL TO DEATH, JUST LIKE I DO.
SHE'S PLAYED PIANO AT OUR CHURCH SERVICES FOR YEARS. I WOULDN'T GIVE UP HEARIN' HER MUSIC FOR ANYTHING!
NOBODY WOULD EVER WANT TO SIDELINE A FINE WOMAN LIKE MABEL.
BUT THERE ARE OTHER PARTS TO OUR EFFORT BEYOND THE ACTUAL DEMONSTRATIONS.
I DON'T UNDER-STAND.
PEOPLE HAVE TO BE CONCERNED ABOUT DISCIPLINE IN A MOVE-MENT.

PRACTICALLY EVERY **VICTORY** WE'VE **WON** THESE PAST FEW YEARS—IN **CLAYFIELD** OR IN ANY OF THE **OTHER** CITIES WHERE THE BATTLE HAS BEEN JOINED—HAS COME BECAUSE WE ARE A **NONVIOLENT** CRUSADE.

WE **DON'T HIT BACK!**

THAT'S WHERE WE GET OUR MORAL **STRENGTH** AND OUR PSYCHOLOGICAL **LEVERAGE.**

NOW, **SEVERAL** PEOPLE HAVE TOLD ME THAT THEY SAW MABEL HITTIN' A **POLICE DOG** WITH HER **PURSE.**

DID YOU **SEE** HER DO THAT?

WELL... UH...

LEMME SAVE YOU THE TROUBLE OF **HEMMIN'** AN' **HAWIN'.**

WE **KNOW** SHE HIT THAT DOG WITH THAT PURSE.

THERE WERE **MORE** THAN A FEW **PEOPLE** AROUND AN' THEY **ALL** HAD **EYES!**

BUT THERE HAVE **ALSO** BEEN RUMORS THAT MABEL HAD A **BRICK** INSIDE OF THAT PURSE.

AS I **RECALL,** YOU WERE RIGHT THERE **CLOSE** TO HER—

I WAS **THERE,** BUT I DIDN'T SEE A **BRICK.**

NO BRICK.

I DIDN'T **SEE** ONE.

HMM...

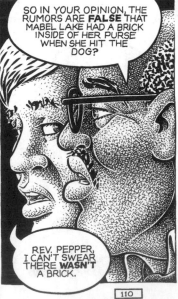

SO IN YOUR OPINION, THE RUMORS ARE **FALSE** THAT MABEL LAKE HAD A BRICK INSIDE OF HER PURSE WHEN SHE HIT THE DOG?

REV. PEPPER, I CAN'T SWEAR THERE **WASN'T** A BRICK.

ALL I CAN SAY IS THAT **I** DIDN'T PERSONALLY **SEE** ONE.

BUT TO TELL THE **TRUTH,** I DON'T SEE MUCH **WRONG** WITH HITTIN' A DOG WHEN IT'S SNAPPIN' ITS **TEETH** AT YOU.

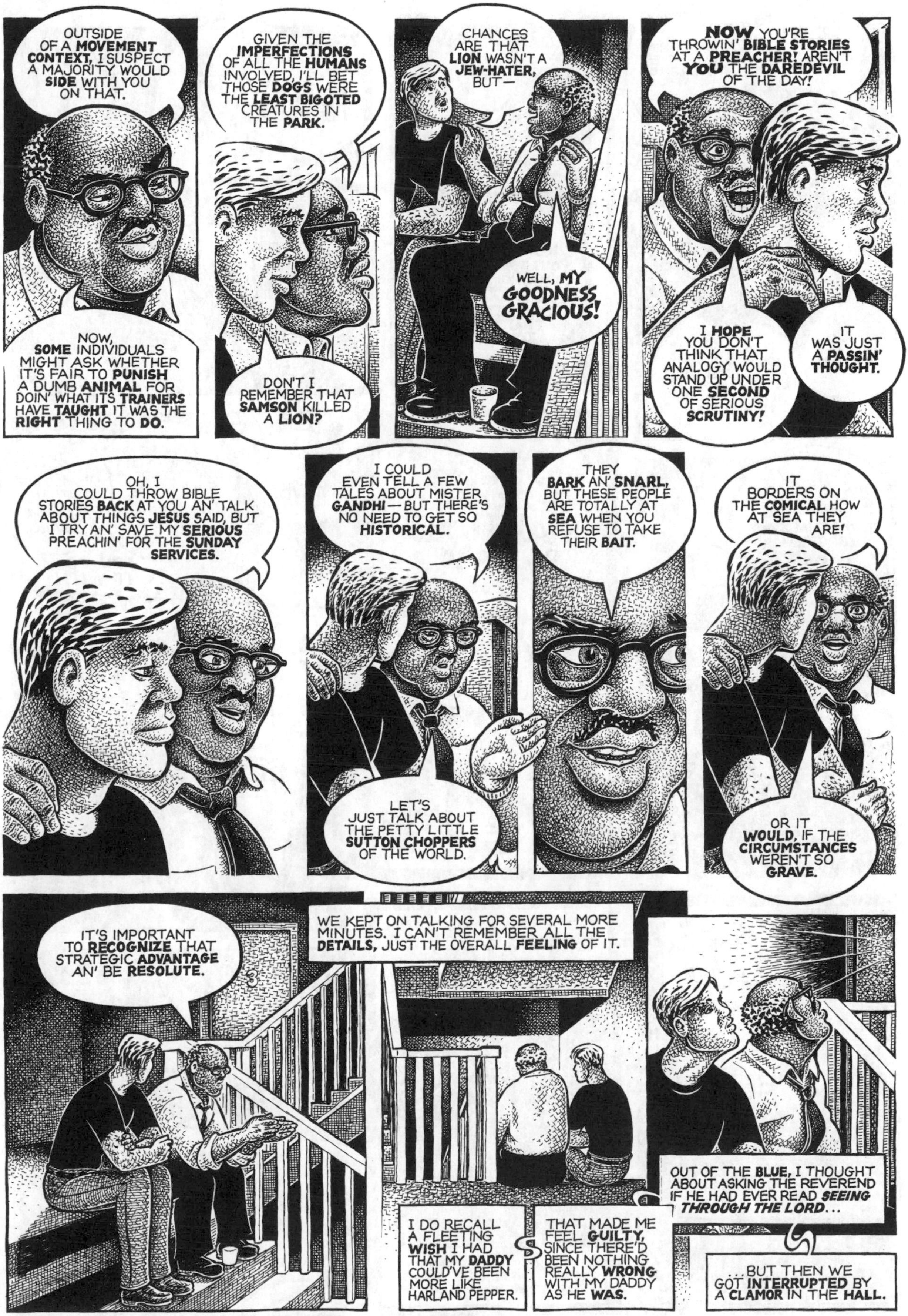
OUTSIDE OF A MOVEMENT CONTEXT, I SUSPECT A MAJORITY WOULD SIDE WITH YOU ON THAT.
NOW, SOME INDIVIDUALS MIGHT ASK WHETHER IT'S FAIR TO PUNISH A DUMB ANIMAL FOR DOIN' WHAT ITS TRAINERS HAVE TAUGHT IT WAS THE RIGHT THING TO DO.
GIVEN THE IMPERFECTIONS OF ALL THE HUMANS INVOLVED, I'LL BET THOSE DOGS WERE THE LEAST BIGOTED CREATURES IN THE PARK.
DON'T I REMEMBER THAT SAMSON KILLED A LION?
CHANCES ARE THAT LION WASN'T A JEW-HATER, BUT—
WELL, MY GOODNESS GRACIOUS!
NOW YOU'RE THROWIN' BIBLE STORIES AT A PREACHER! AREN'T YOU THE DAREDEVIL OF THE DAY!
I HOPE YOU DON'T THINK THAT ANALOGY WOULD STAND UP UNDER ONE SECOND OF SERIOUS SCRUTINY!
IT WAS JUST A PASSIN' THOUGHT.
OH, I COULD THROW BIBLE STORIES BACK AT YOU AN' TALK ABOUT THINGS JESUS SAID, BUT I TRY AN' SAVE MY SERIOUS PREACHIN' FOR THE SUNDAY SERVICES.
I COULD EVEN TELL A FEW TALES ABOUT MISTER GANDHI — BUT THERE'S NO NEED TO GET SO HISTORICAL.
LET'S JUST TALK ABOUT THE PETTY LITTLE SUTTON CHOPPERS OF THE WORLD.
THEY BARK AN' SNARL, BUT THESE PEOPLE ARE TOTALLY AT SEA WHEN YOU REFUSE TO TAKE THEIR BAIT.
IT BORDERS ON THE COMICAL HOW AT SEA THEY ARE!
OR IT WOULD, IF THE CIRCUMSTANCES WEREN'T SO GRAVE.
IT'S IMPORTANT TO RECOGNIZE THAT STRATEGIC ADVANTAGE AN' BE RESOLUTE.
WE KEPT ON TALKING FOR SEVERAL MORE MINUTES. I CAN'T REMEMBER ALL THE DETAILS, JUST THE OVERALL FEELING OF IT.
I DO RECALL A FLEETING WISH I HAD THAT MY DADDY COULD'VE BEEN MORE LIKE HARLAND PEPPER.
THAT MADE ME FEEL GUILTY, SINCE THERE'D BEEN NOTHING REALLY WRONG WITH MY DADDY AS HE WAS.
OUT OF THE BLUE, I THOUGHT ABOUT ASKING THE REVEREND IF HE HAD EVER READ SEEING THROUGH THE LORD...
...BUT THEN WE GOT INTERRUPTED BY A CLAMOR IN THE HALL.

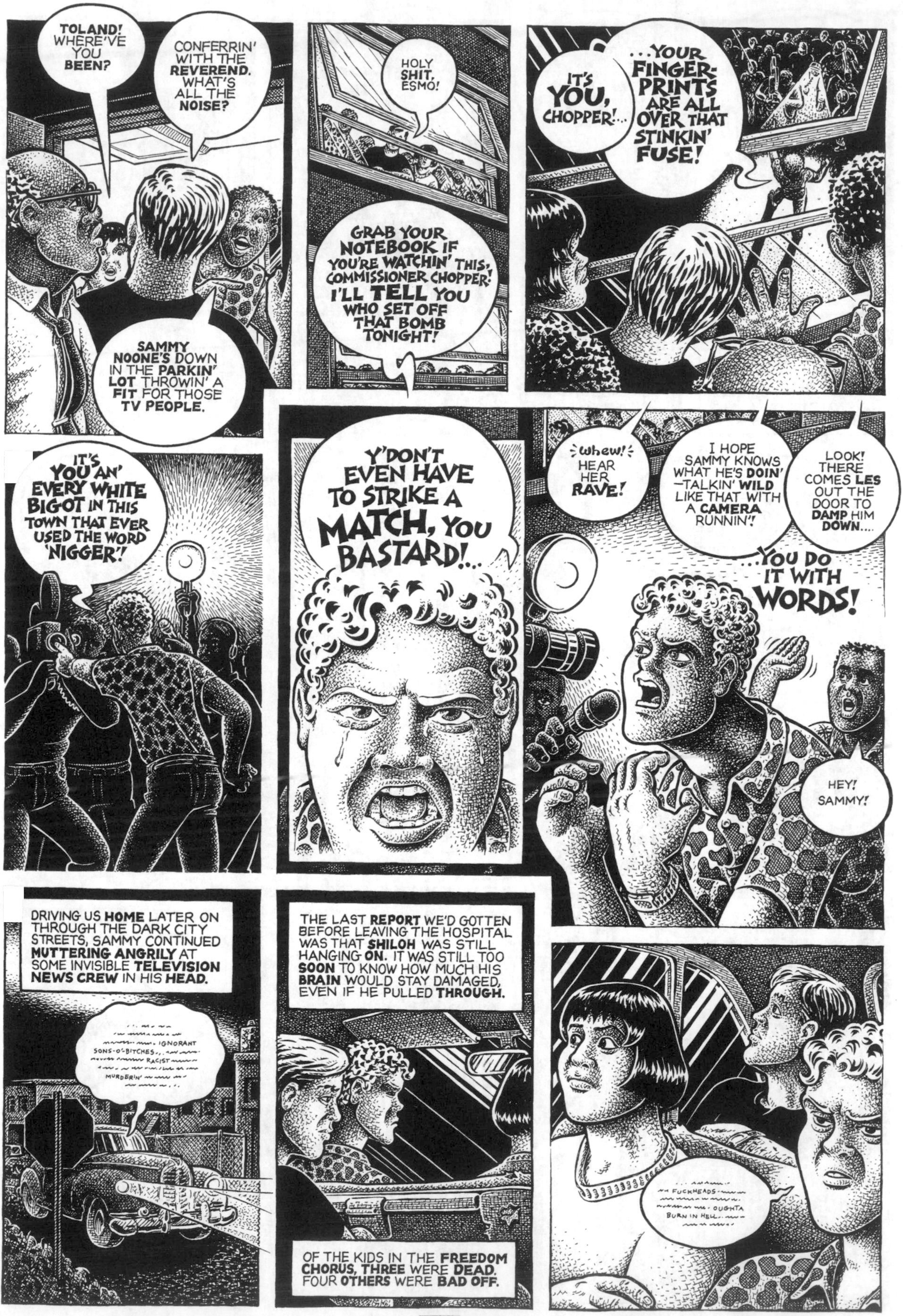
TOLAND! WHERE'VE YOU BEEN?
CONFERRIN' WITH THE REVEREND. WHAT'S ALL THE NOISE?
SAMMY NOONE'S DOWN IN THE PARKIN' LOT THROWIN' A FIT FOR THOSE TV PEOPLE.
HOLY SHIT, ESMO!
GRAB YOUR NOTEBOOK IF YOU'RE WATCHIN' THIS, COMMISSIONER CHOPPER! I'LL TELL YOU WHO SET OFF THAT BOMB TONIGHT!
IT'S YOU, CHOPPER!...
...YOUR FINGER-PRINTS ARE ALL OVER THAT STINKIN' FUSE!
IT'S YOU AN' EVERY WHITE BIGOT IN THIS TOWN THAT EVER USED THE WORD 'NIGGER'!
Y'DON'T EVEN HAVE TO STRIKE A MATCH, YOU BASTARD!...
WHEW! HEAR HER RAVE!
I HOPE SAMMY KNOWS WHAT HE'S DOIN' —TALKIN' WILD LIKE THAT WITH A CAMERA RUNNIN'!
LOOK! THERE COMES LES OUT THE DOOR TO DAMP HIM DOWN....
...YOU DO IT WITH WORDS!
HEY! SAMMY!
DRIVING US HOME LATER ON THROUGH THE DARK CITY STREETS, SAMMY CONTINUED MUTTERING ANGRILY AT SOME INVISIBLE TELEVISION NEWS CREW IN HIS HEAD.
IGNORANT SONS-O'-BITCHES RACIST MURDERIN'
THE LAST REPORT WE'D GOTTEN BEFORE LEAVING THE HOSPITAL WAS THAT SHILOH WAS STILL HANGING ON. IT WAS STILL TOO SOON TO KNOW HOW MUCH HIS BRAIN WOULD STAY DAMAGED, EVEN IF HE PULLED THROUGH.
OF THE KIDS IN THE FREEDOM CHORUS, THREE WERE DEAD. FOUR OTHERS WERE BAD OFF.
FUCKHEADS OUGHTA BURN IN HELL

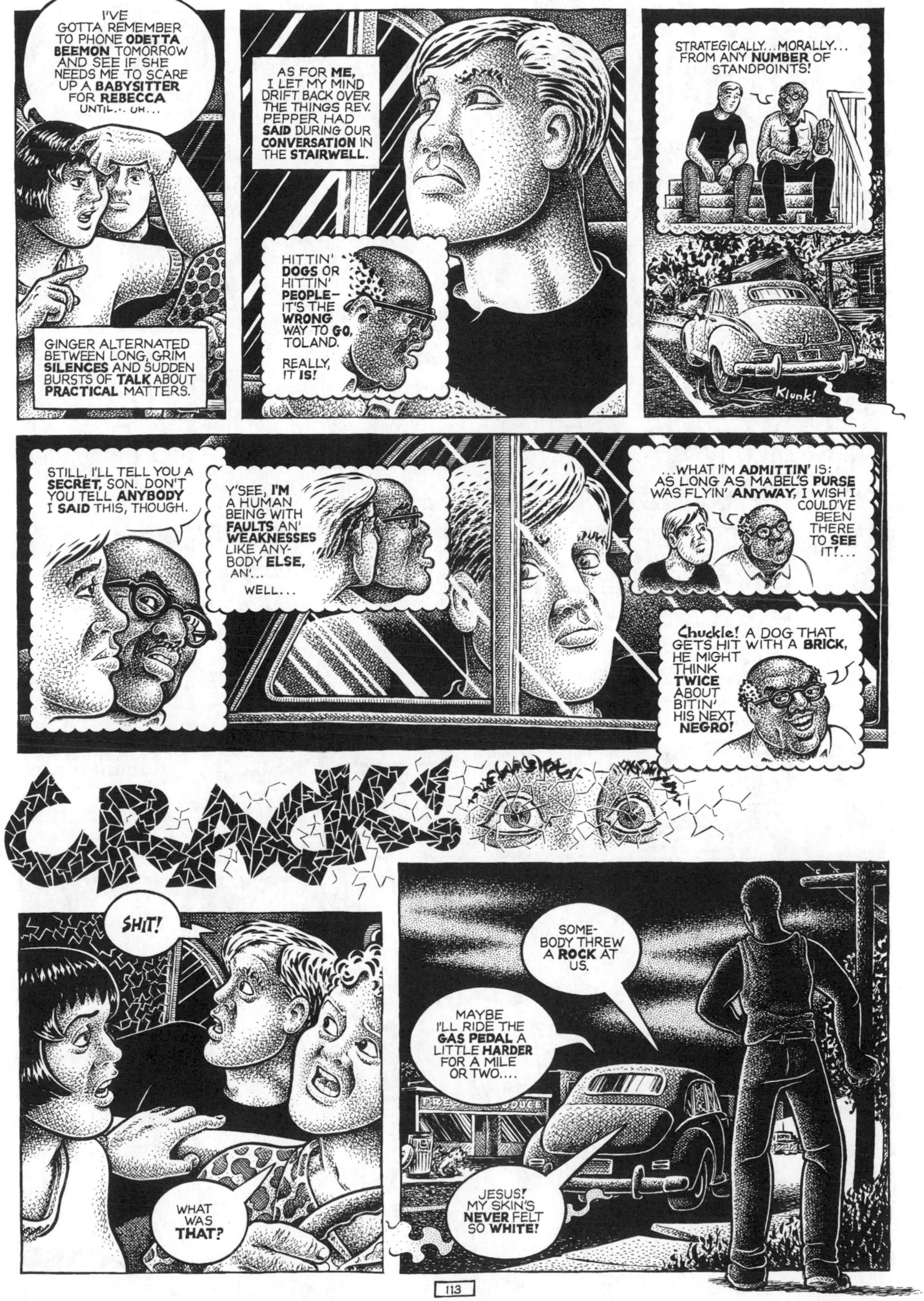
I'VE GOTTA REMEMBER TO PHONE ODETTA BEEMON TOMORROW AND SEE IF SHE NEEDS ME TO SCARE UP A BABYSITTER FOR REBECCA UNTIL... UH...
GINGER ALTERNATED BETWEEN LONG, GRIM SILENCES AND SUDDEN BURSTS OF TALK ABOUT PRACTICAL MATTERS.
AS FOR ME, I LET MY MIND DRIFT BACK OVER THE THINGS REV. PEPPER HAD SAID DURING OUR CONVERSATION IN THE STAIRWELL.
HITTIN' DOGS OR HITTIN' PEOPLE— IT'S THE WRONG WAY TO GO, TOLAND.
REALLY, IT IS!
STRATEGICALLY... MORALLY... FROM ANY NUMBER OF STANDPOINTS!
Klunk!
STILL, I'LL TELL YOU A SECRET, SON. DON'T YOU TELL ANYBODY I SAID THIS, THOUGH.
Y'SEE, I'M A HUMAN BEING WITH FAULTS AN' WEAKNESSES LIKE ANYBODY ELSE, AN'...
WELL...
...WHAT I'M ADMITTIN' IS: AS LONG AS MABEL'S PURSE WAS FLYIN' ANYWAY, I WISH I COULD'VE BEEN THERE TO SEE IT!...
Chuckle! A DOG THAT GETS HIT WITH A BRICK, HE MIGHT THINK TWICE ABOUT BITIN' HIS NEXT NEGRO!
CRACK!
SHIT!
WHAT WAS THAT?
SOME-BODY THREW A ROCK AT US.
MAYBE I'LL RIDE THE GAS PEDAL A LITTLE HARDER FOR A MILE OR TWO....
JESUS! MY SKIN'S NEVER FELT SO WHITE!

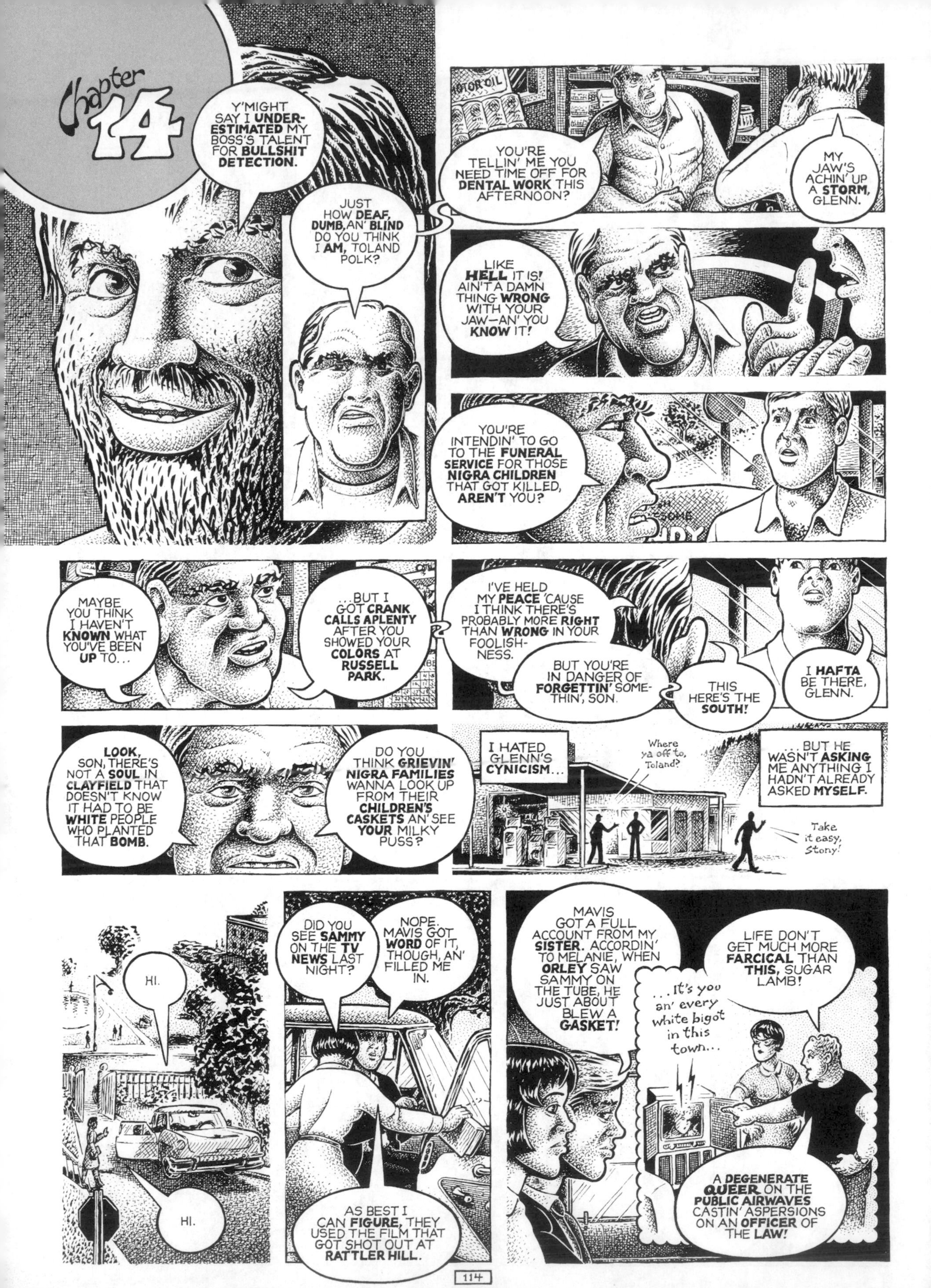

Chapter 14
Y'MIGHT SAY I UNDER-ESTIMATED MY BOSS'S TALENT FOR BULLSHIT DETECTION.
YOU'RE TELLIN' ME YOU NEED TIME OFF FOR DENTAL WORK THIS AFTERNOON?
JUST HOW DEAF, DUMB, AN' BLIND DO YOU THINK I AM, TOLAND POLK?
MY JAW'S ACHIN' UP A STORM, GLENN.
LIKE HELL IT IS! AIN'T A DAMN THING WRONG WITH YOUR JAW—AN' YOU KNOW IT!
YOU'RE INTENDIN' TO GO TO THE FUNERAL SERVICE FOR THOSE NIGRA CHILDREN THAT GOT KILLED, AREN'T YOU?
MAYBE YOU THINK I HAVEN'T KNOWN WHAT YOU'VE BEEN UP TO...
...BUT I GOT CRANK CALLS APLENTY AFTER YOU SHOWED YOUR COLORS AT RUSSELL PARK.
I'VE HELD MY PEACE 'CAUSE I THINK THERE'S PROBABLY MORE RIGHT THAN WRONG IN YOUR FOOLISH-NESS.
BUT YOU'RE IN DANGER OF FORGETTIN' SOME-THIN', SON.
THIS HERE'S THE SOUTH!
I HAFTA BE THERE, GLENN.
LOOK, SON, THERE'S NOT A SOUL IN CLAYFIELD THAT DOESN'T KNOW IT HAD TO BE WHITE PEOPLE WHO PLANTED THAT BOMB.
DO YOU THINK GRIEVIN' NIGRA FAMILIES WANNA LOOK UP FROM THEIR CHILDREN'S CASKETS AN' SEE YOUR MILKY PUSS?
I HATED GLENN'S CYNICISM...
Where ya off to, Toland?
...BUT HE WASN'T ASKING ME ANYTHING I HADN'T ALREADY ASKED MYSELF.
Take it easy, Stony!
HI.
HI.
DID YOU SEE SAMMY ON THE TV NEWS LAST NIGHT?
NOPE. MAVIS GOT WORD OF IT, THOUGH, AN' FILLED ME IN.
AS BEST I CAN FIGURE, THEY USED THE FILM THAT GOT SHOT OUT AT RATTLER HILL.
MAVIS GOT A FULL ACCOUNT FROM MY SISTER. ACCORDIN' TO MELANIE, WHEN ORLEY SAW SAMMY ON THE TUBE, HE JUST ABOUT BLEW A GASKET!
LIFE DON'T GET MUCH MORE FARCICAL THAN THIS, SUGAR LAMB!
...It's you an' every white bigot in this town...
A DEGENERATE QUEER ON THE PUBLIC AIRWAVES CASTIN' ASPERSIONS ON AN OFFICER OF THE LAW!

I'M SURPRISED THEY **RAN** IT. I GUESS THEY THOUGHT SAMMY WAS **COLORFUL!**

GONNA CATCH UP ON YOUR **READIN'** DURIN' THE FUNERAL?

VERY **FUNNY!**

I WAS SO **DISTRACTED** WALKIN' OUT OF THE DORM, I FORGOT THIS WAS IN MY **HAND.**

WOULD YOU BELIEVE I'VE **GOTTA** TAKE A **TEST** ON **NATHANIEL HAWTHORNE** THIS AFTERNOON AT **FIVE?**

I'LL GO YA ONE **BETTER.**

WOULD YOU BELIEVE I GOT MYSELF **FIRED** THIS MORNIN'...?

IF GINGER AND I WERE ENTERTAINING ANY **ILLUSIONS** WHILE DRIVING TO THE CHURCH THAT WE WERE GONNA GET TO **SIT DOWN** DURING THE FUNERAL, WE GOT OVER 'EM **FAST** ONCE WE GOT A LOOK AT THE HUGE **CROWD** THAT WAS GATHERING.

IT WAS OBVIOUS THE **SANCTUARY** WAS ALREADY **FULL** AND THAT YOU COULD'VE FILLED **RUSSELL PARK TWICE** WITH THE **OVERFLOW.**

OF COURSE, SINCE THE **PARK** WAS STILL **FENCED OFF** AND **UNAVAILABLE,** IT WAS THE ADJACENT **STREETS** THAT WERE GETTING SWAMPED WITH **MOURNERS...**

...WHILE AN ARMY OF **COPS** KEPT WATCH, CHARGED WITH MAKING SURE THAT THE **EMOTIONS** OF THE MOMENT DIDN'T START THREATENING **PUBLIC ORDER.**

IN THE COURSE OF THE **SERVICE** WE CAUGHT QUICK GLIMPSES OF **SAMMY** AND A FEW OTHER FRIENDS...

...BUT MOSTLY ALL WE COULD SEE WERE THE **HATS** AND **HEADS** OF THE **STRANGERS** AGAINST WHOM WE WERE BEING PRESSED LIKE **SARDINES.**

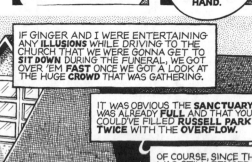

FROM ATOP VARIOUS PERCHES **TV NEWS CREWS** SQUINTED INTO THEIR **VIEWFINDERS** AND PLAYED WITH THEIR **ZOOMS.**

THEY KNEW THE DRAMATIC **FOOTAGE** THEY WERE GETTING WOULD PLAY ON THE TUBE LIKE **GANGBUSTERS.** ESPECIALLY UP **NORTH.**

EVERYONE LISTENED SORROWFULLY TO HARLAND PEPPER'S **EULOGY...**

...WHICH WAS **MOVING** DESPITE THE **CRACKLE** MIXED INTO IT BY THE CHURCH'S **PUBLIC ADDRESS SYSTEM.**

I WAS SURPRISED BY HOW **PERSONALLY** IT WAS HITTING ME, CONSIDERING HOW I'D SCARCELY KNOWN A **ONE** OF THE MURDERED KIDS TO **SPEAK** TO.

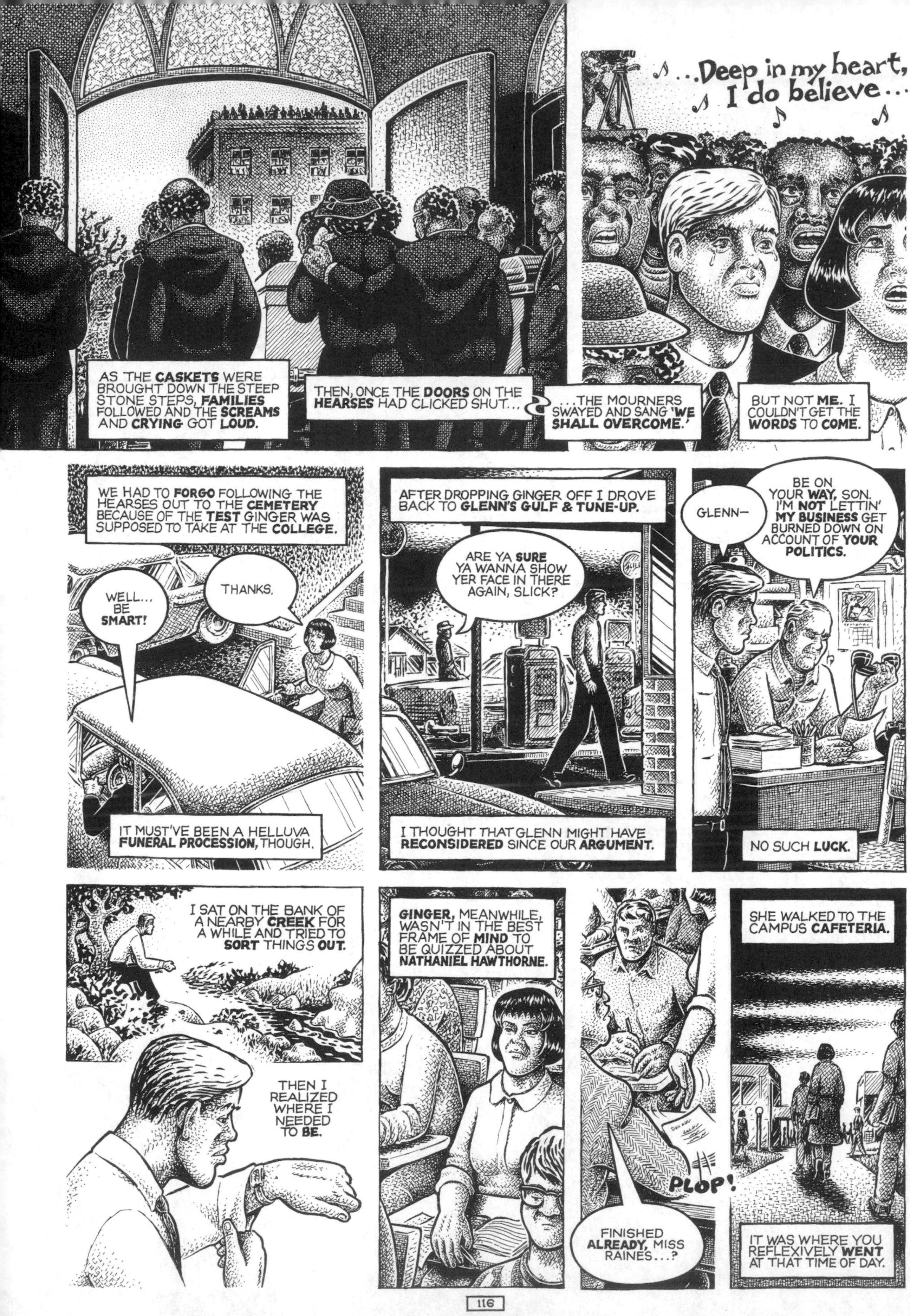
AS THE CASKETS WERE BROUGHT DOWN THE STEEP STONE STEPS, FAMILIES FOLLOWED AND THE SCREAMS AND CRYING GOT LOUD.
THEN, ONCE THE DOORS ON THE HEARSES HAD CLICKED SHUT...
...THE MOURNERS SWAYED AND SANG 'WE SHALL OVERCOME.'
...Deep in my heart, I do believe...
BUT NOT ME. I COULDN'T GET THE WORDS TO COME.
WE HAD TO FORGO FOLLOWING THE HEARSES OUT TO THE CEMETERY BECAUSE OF THE TEST GINGER WAS SUPPOSED TO TAKE AT THE COLLEGE.
WELL... BE SMART!
THANKS.
IT MUST'VE BEEN A HELLUVA FUNERAL PROCESSION, THOUGH.
AFTER DROPPING GINGER OFF I DROVE BACK TO GLENN'S GULF & TUNE-UP.
ARE YA SURE YA WANNA SHOW YER FACE IN THERE AGAIN, SLICK?
I THOUGHT THAT GLENN MIGHT HAVE RECONSIDERED SINCE OUR ARGUMENT.
GLENN—
BE ON YOUR WAY, SON. I'M NOT LETTIN' MY BUSINESS GET BURNED DOWN ON ACCOUNT OF YOUR POLITICS.
NO SUCH LUCK.
I SAT ON THE BANK OF A NEARBY CREEK FOR A WHILE AND TRIED TO SORT THINGS OUT.
THEN I REALIZED WHERE I NEEDED TO BE.
GINGER, MEANWHILE, WASN'T IN THE BEST FRAME OF MIND TO BE QUIZZED ABOUT NATHANIEL HAWTHORNE.
PLOP!
FINISHED ALREADY, MISS RAINES...?
SHE WALKED TO THE CAMPUS CAFETERIA.
IT WAS WHERE YOU REFLEXIVELY WENT AT THAT TIME OF DAY.

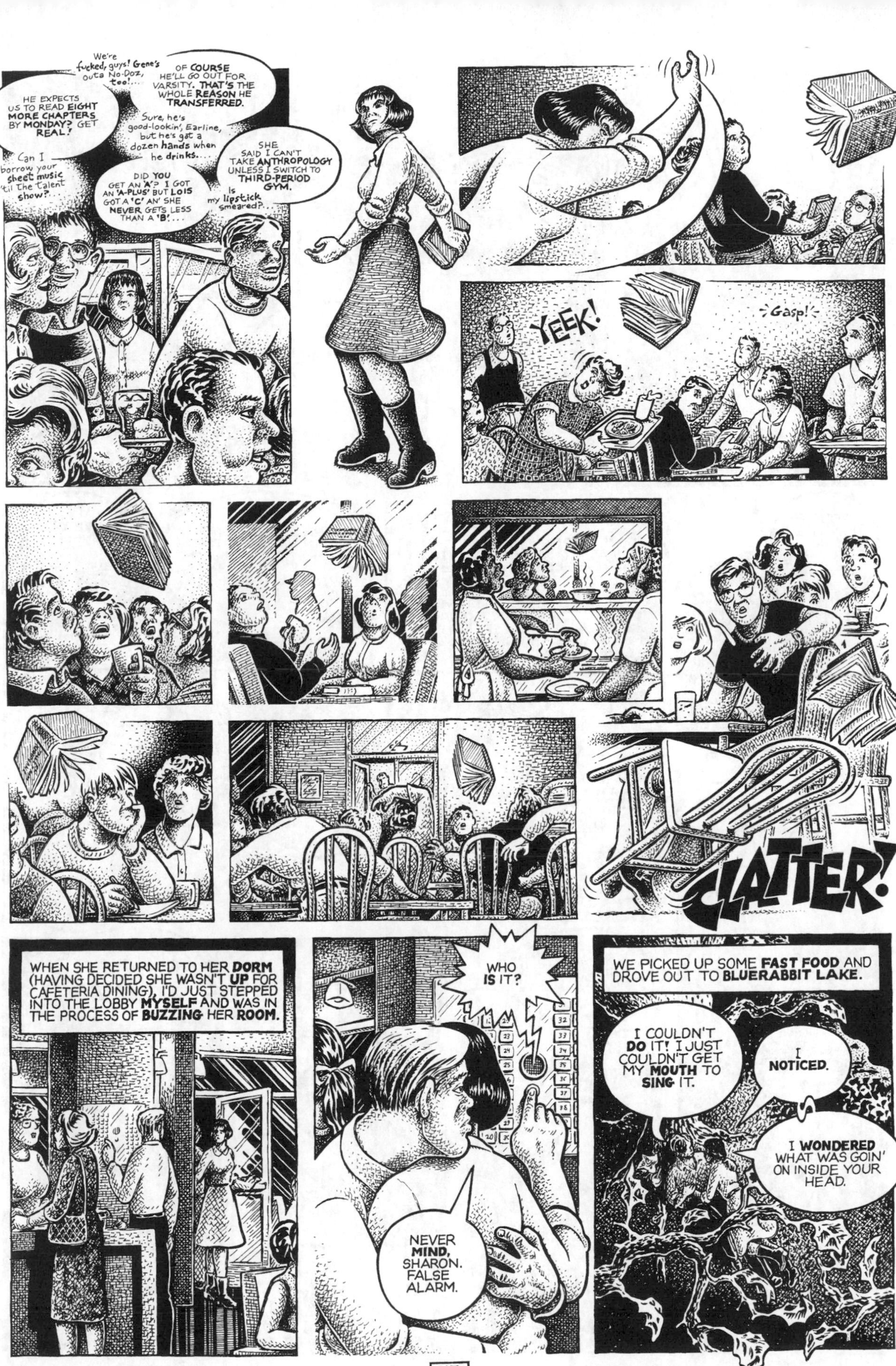
We're fucked, guys! Gene's outa No-Doz, too!...
HE EXPECTS US TO READ EIGHT MORE CHAPTERS BY MONDAY? GET REAL!
OF COURSE HE'LL GO OUT FOR VARSITY. THAT'S THE WHOLE REASON HE TRANSFERRED.
Sure, he's good-lookin', Earline, but he's got a dozen hands when he drinks...
Can I borrow your sheet music 'til the talent show?...
DID YOU GET AN 'A'? I GOT AN 'A-PLUS' BUT LOIS GOT A 'C' AN' SHE NEVER GETS LESS THAN A 'B'...
SHE SAID I CAN'T TAKE ANTHROPOLOGY UNLESS I SWITCH TO THIRD-PERIOD GYM.
Is my lipstick smeared?...
YEEK!
Gasp!
CLATTER!
WHEN SHE RETURNED TO HER DORM (HAVING DECIDED SHE WASN'T UP FOR CAFETERIA DINING), I'D JUST STEPPED INTO THE LOBBY MYSELF AND WAS IN THE PROCESS OF BUZZING HER ROOM.
WHO IS IT?
NEVER MIND, SHARON. FALSE ALARM.
WE PICKED UP SOME FAST FOOD AND DROVE OUT TO BLUERABBIT LAKE.
I COULDN'T DO IT! I JUST COULDN'T GET MY MOUTH TO SING IT.
I NOTICED.
I WONDERED WHAT WAS GOIN' ON INSIDE YOUR HEAD.

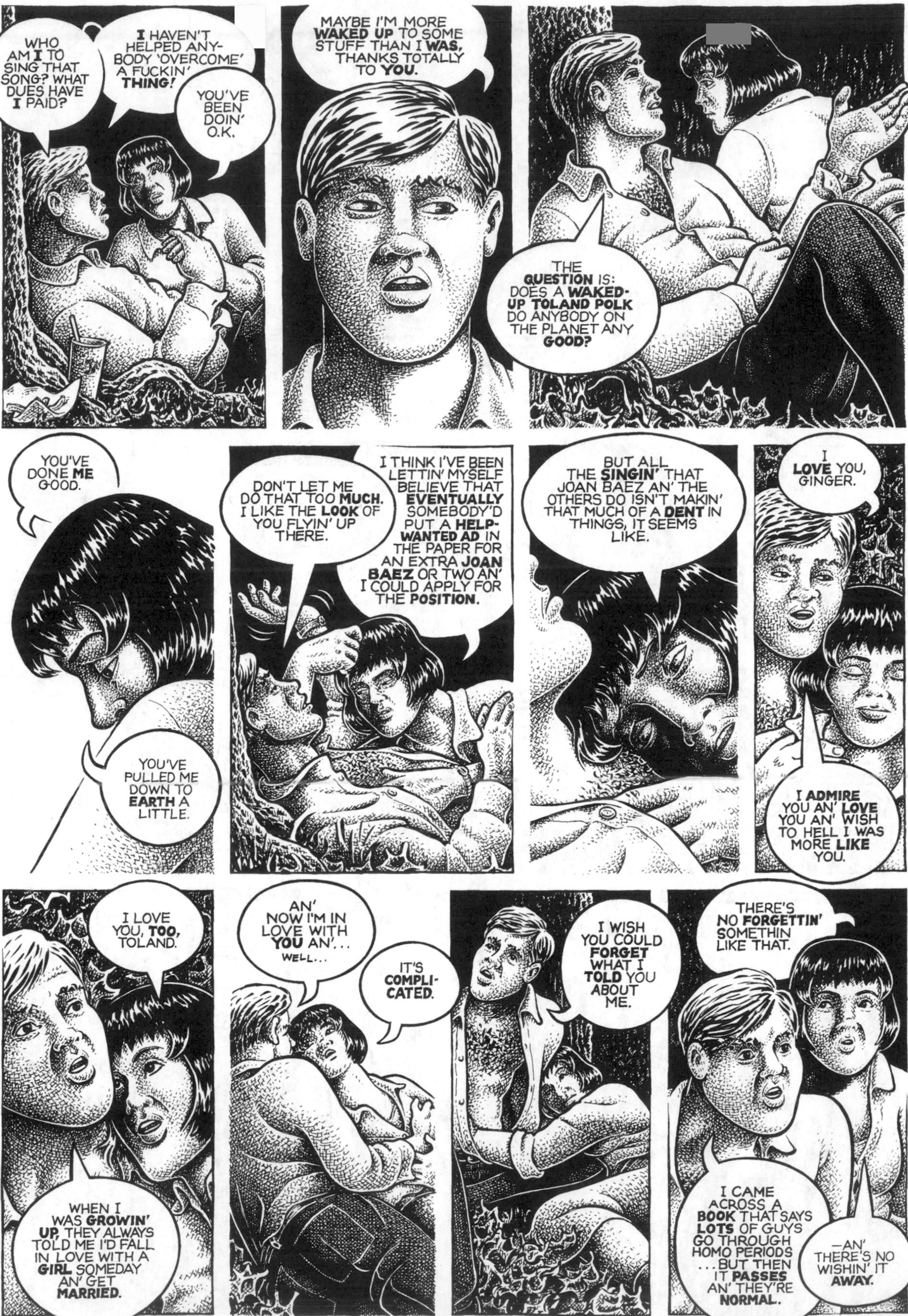
WHO AM I TO SING THAT SONG? WHAT DUES HAVE I PAID?
I HAVEN'T HELPED ANY-BODY 'OVERCOME' A FUCKIN' THING!
YOU'VE BEEN DOIN' O.K.
MAYBE I'M MORE WAKED UP TO SOME STUFF THAN I WAS, THANKS TOTALLY TO YOU.
THE QUESTION IS: DOES A WAKED-UP TOLAND POLK DO ANYBODY ON THE PLANET ANY GOOD?
YOU'VE DONE ME GOOD.
YOU'VE PULLED ME DOWN TO EARTH A LITTLE.
DON'T LET ME DO THAT TOO MUCH. I LIKE THE LOOK OF YOU FLYIN' UP THERE.
I THINK I'VE BEEN LETTIN' MYSELF BELIEVE THAT EVENTUALLY SOMEBODY'D PUT A HELP-WANTED AD IN THE PAPER FOR AN EXTRA JOAN BAEZ OR TWO AN' I COULD APPLY FOR THE POSITION.
BUT ALL THE SINGIN' THAT JOAN BAEZ AN' THE OTHERS DO ISN'T MAKIN' THAT MUCH OF A DENT IN THINGS, IT SEEMS LIKE.
I LOVE YOU, GINGER.
I ADMIRE YOU AN' LOVE YOU AN' WISH TO HELL I WAS MORE LIKE YOU.
I LOVE YOU, TOO, TOLAND.
WHEN I WAS GROWIN' UP, THEY ALWAYS TOLD ME I'D FALL IN LOVE WITH A GIRL SOMEDAY AN' GET MARRIED.
AN' NOW I'M IN LOVE WITH YOU AN'... WELL...
IT'S COMPLI-CATED.
I WISH YOU COULD FORGET WHAT I TOLD YOU ABOUT ME.
THERE'S NO FORGETTIN' SOMETHIN LIKE THAT.
I CAME ACROSS A BOOK THAT SAYS LOTS OF GUYS GO THROUGH HOMO PERIODS ...BUT THEN IT PASSES AN' THEY'RE NORMAL.
—AN' THERE'S NO WISHIN' IT AWAY.

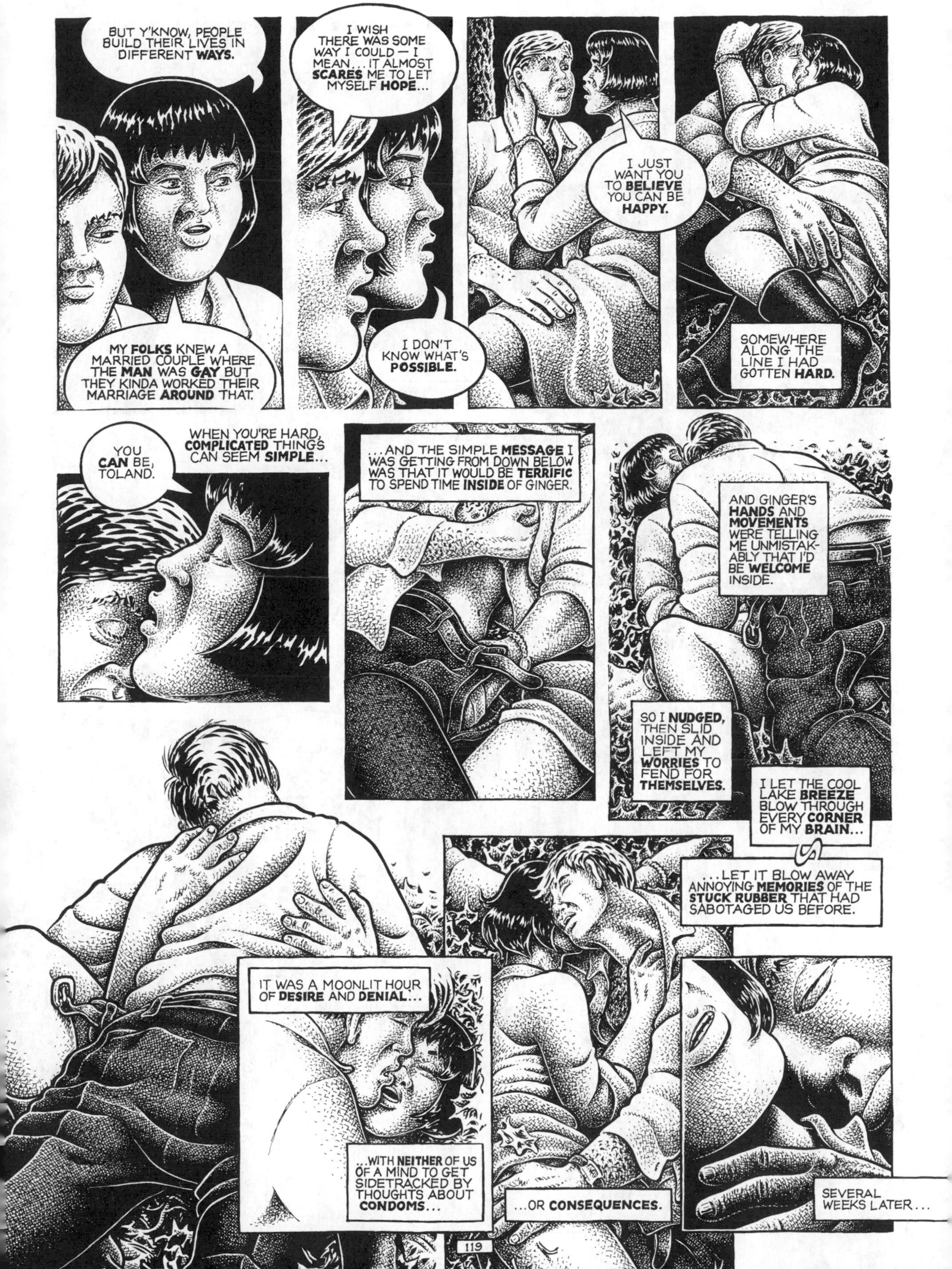

BUT Y'KNOW, PEOPLE BUILD THEIR LIVES IN DIFFERENT **WAYS.**
MY **FOLKS** KNEW A MARRIED COUPLE WHERE THE **MAN** WAS **GAY** BUT THEY KINDA WORKED THEIR MARRIAGE **AROUND** THAT.
I WISH THERE WAS SOME WAY I COULD — I MEAN... IT ALMOST **SCARES** ME TO LET MYSELF **HOPE**...
I DON'T KNOW WHAT'S **POSSIBLE.**
I JUST WANT YOU TO **BELIEVE** YOU CAN BE **HAPPY.**
SOMEWHERE ALONG THE LINE I HAD GOTTEN **HARD.**
YOU **CAN** BE, TOLAND.
WHEN YOU'RE HARD, **COMPLICATED** THINGS CAN SEEM **SIMPLE**...
...AND THE SIMPLE **MESSAGE** I WAS GETTING FROM DOWN BELOW WAS THAT IT WOULD BE **TERRIFIC** TO SPEND TIME **INSIDE** OF GINGER.
AND GINGER'S **HANDS** AND **MOVEMENTS** WERE TELLING ME UNMISTAK-ABLY THAT I'D BE **WELCOME** INSIDE.
SO I **NUDGED,** THEN SLID INSIDE AND LEFT MY **WORRIES** TO FEND FOR **THEMSELVES.**
I LET THE COOL LAKE **BREEZE** BLOW THROUGH EVERY **CORNER** OF MY **BRAIN**...
...LET IT BLOW AWAY ANNOYING **MEMORIES** OF THE **STUCK RUBBER** THAT HAD SABOTAGED US BEFORE.
IT WAS A MOONLIT HOUR OF **DESIRE** AND **DENIAL**...
...WITH **NEITHER** OF US OF A MIND TO GET SIDETRACKED BY THOUGHTS ABOUT **CONDOMS**...
...OR **CONSEQUENCES.**
SEVERAL WEEKS LATER...

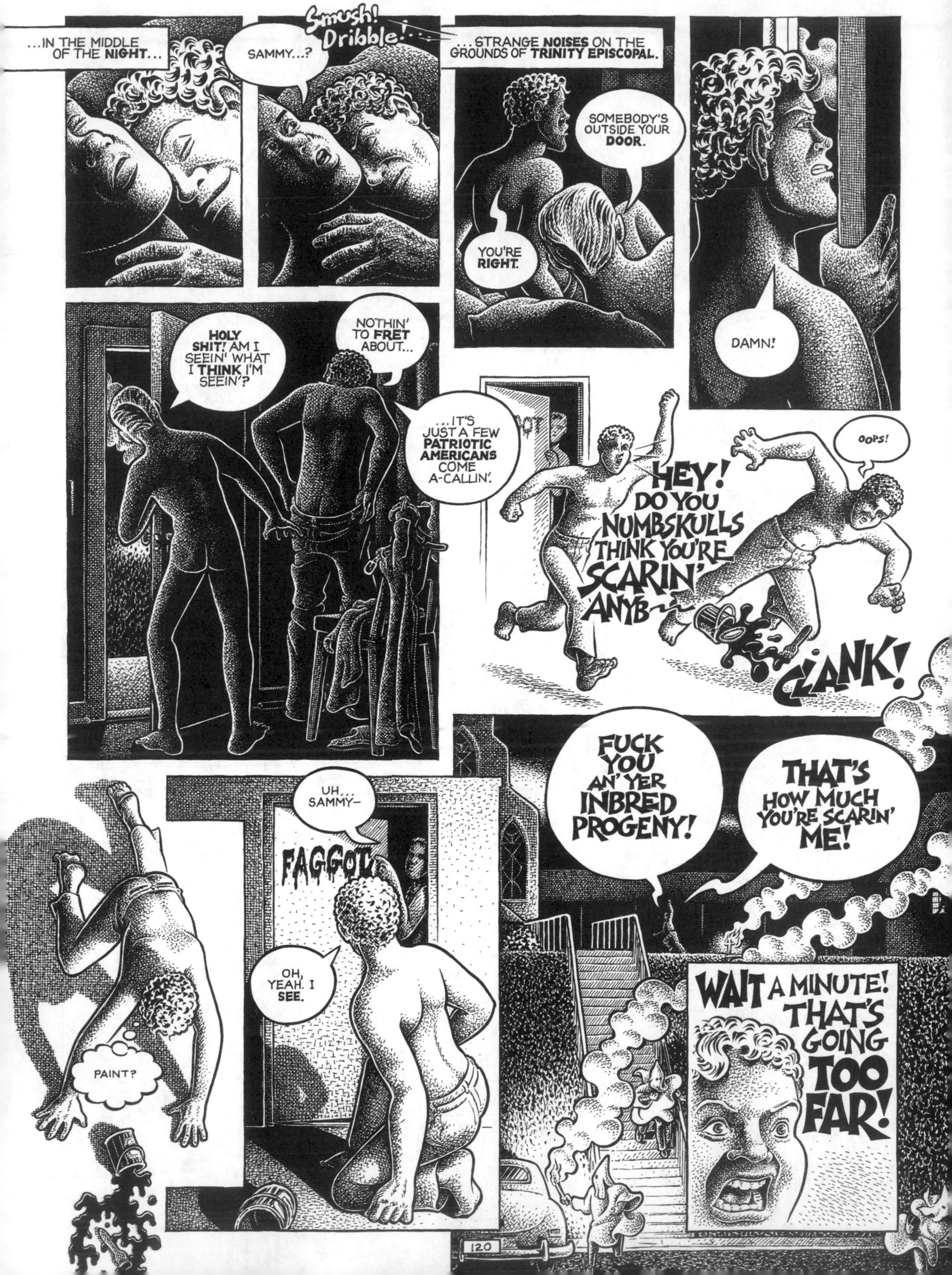

...IN THE MIDDLE OF THE NIGHT...
SAMMY...?
Smush! Dribble!
...STRANGE NOISES ON THE GROUNDS OF TRINITY EPISCOPAL.
SOMEBODY'S OUTSIDE YOUR DOOR.
YOU'RE RIGHT.
DAMN!
HOLY SHIT! AM I SEEIN' WHAT I THINK I'M SEEIN'?
NOTHIN' TO FRET ABOUT...
...IT'S JUST A FEW PATRIOTIC AMERICANS COME A-CALLIN'.
HEY! DO YOU NUMBSKULLS THINK YOU'RE SCARIN' ANYB—
OOPS!
CLANK!
PAINT?
UH... SAMMY—
FAGGOT
OH, YEAH. I SEE.
FUCK YOU AN' YER INBRED PROGENY!
THAT'S HOW MUCH YOU'RE SCARIN' ME!
WAIT A MINUTE! THAT'S GOING TOO FAR!

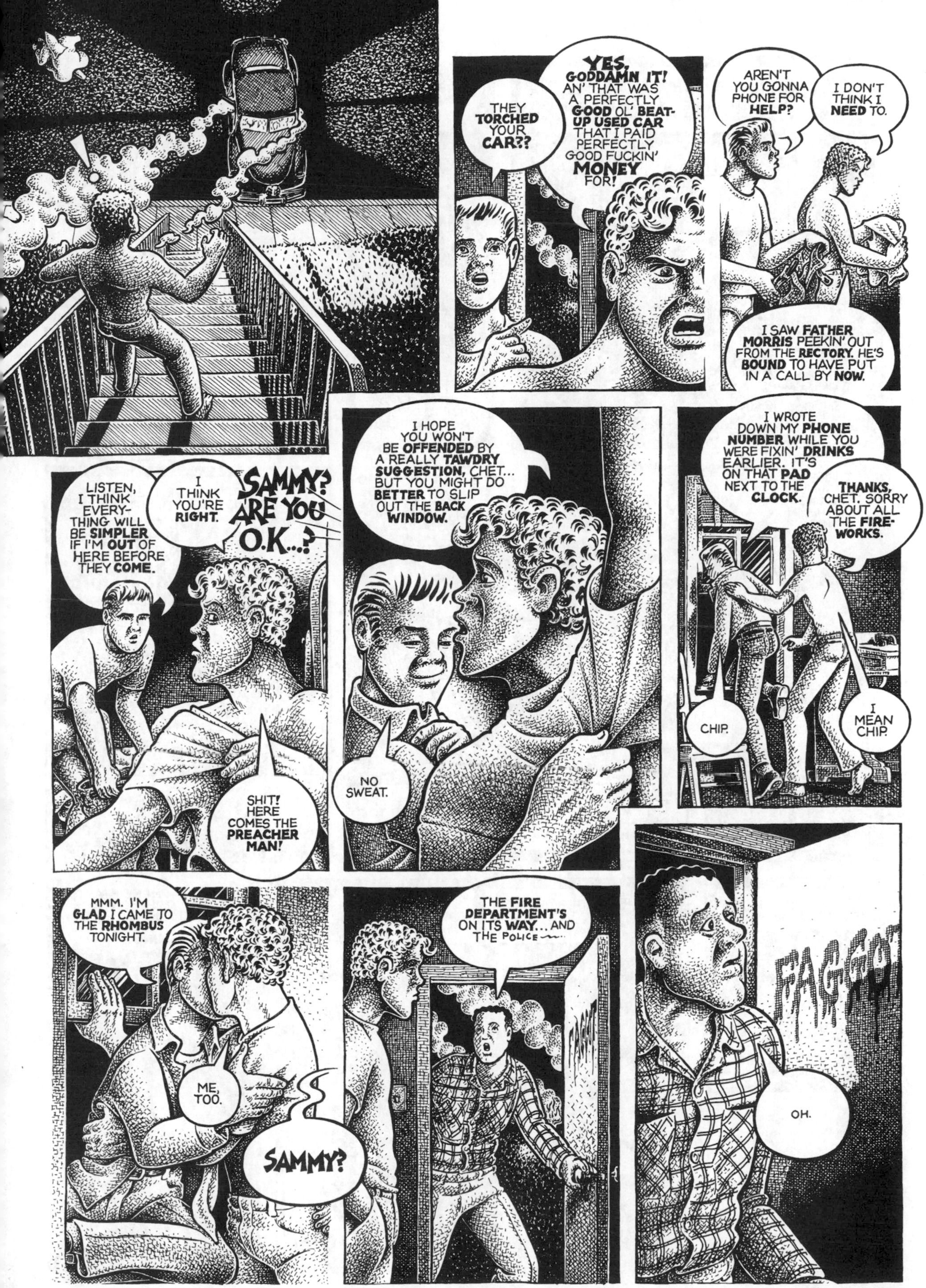
!
THEY TORCHED YOUR CAR??
YES, GODDAMN IT! AN' THAT WAS A PERFECTLY GOOD OL' BEAT-UP USED CAR THAT I PAID PERFECTLY GOOD FUCKIN' MONEY FOR!
AREN'T YOU GONNA PHONE FOR HELP?
I DON'T THINK I NEED TO.
I SAW FATHER MORRIS PEEKIN' OUT FROM THE RECTORY. HE'S BOUND TO HAVE PUT IN A CALL BY NOW.
LISTEN, I THINK EVERY-THING WILL BE SIMPLER IF I'M OUT OF HERE BEFORE THEY COME.
I THINK YOU'RE RIGHT.
SAMMY? ARE YOU O.K...?
SHIT! HERE COMES THE PREACHER MAN!
I HOPE YOU WON'T BE OFFENDED BY A REALLY TAWDRY SUGGESTION, CHET... BUT YOU MIGHT DO BETTER TO SLIP OUT THE BACK WINDOW.
NO SWEAT.
I WROTE DOWN MY PHONE NUMBER WHILE YOU WERE FIXIN' DRINKS EARLIER. IT'S ON THAT PAD NEXT TO THE CLOCK.
THANKS, CHET. SORRY ABOUT ALL THE FIRE-WORKS.
CHIP.
I MEAN CHIP.
MMM. I'M GLAD I CAME TO THE RHOMBUS TONIGHT.
ME, TOO.
SAMMY?
THE FIRE DEPARTMENT'S ON ITS WAY... AND THE POLICE—
FAGGOT
OH.

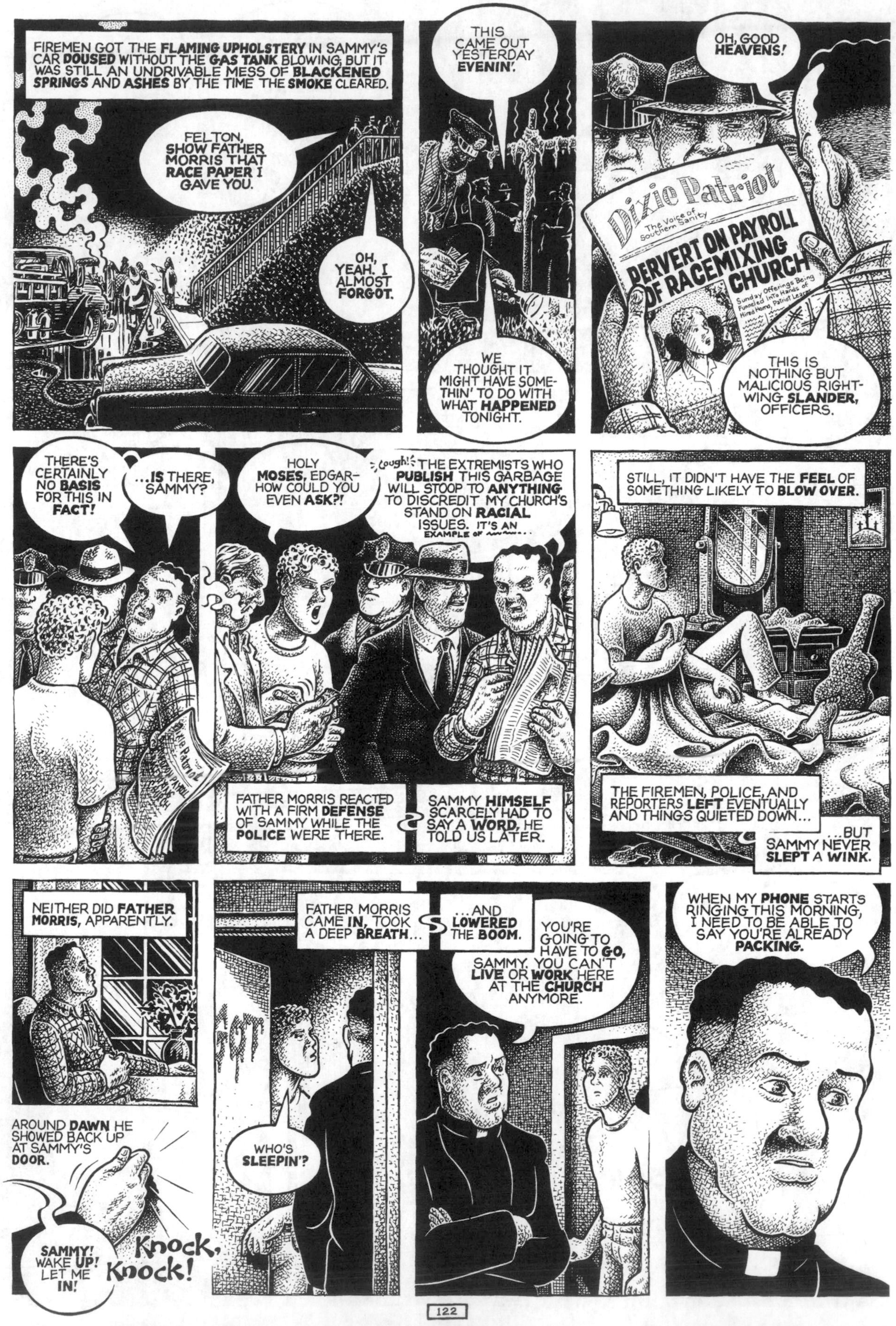

FIREMEN GOT THE FLAMING UPHOLSTERY IN SAMMY'S CAR DOUSED WITHOUT THE GAS TANK BLOWING, BUT IT WAS STILL AN UNDRIVABLE MESS OF BLACKENED SPRINGS AND ASHES BY THE TIME THE SMOKE CLEARED.
FELTON, SHOW FATHER MORRIS THAT RACE PAPER I GAVE YOU.
OH, YEAH. I ALMOST FORGOT.
THIS CAME OUT YESTERDAY EVENIN'.
WE THOUGHT IT MIGHT HAVE SOMETHIN' TO DO WITH WHAT HAPPENED TONIGHT.
OH, GOOD HEAVENS!
Dixie Patriot
The Voice of Southern Sanity
PERVERT ON PAYROLL OF RACEMIXING CHURCH
Sunday Offerings Being Funneled Into Hands of
THIS IS NOTHING BUT MALICIOUS RIGHT-WING SLANDER, OFFICERS.
THERE'S CERTAINLY NO BASIS FOR THIS IN FACT!
...IS THERE, SAMMY?
HOLY MOSES, EDGAR—HOW COULD YOU EVEN ASK?!
cough!
THE EXTREMISTS WHO PUBLISH THIS GARBAGE WILL STOOP TO ANYTHING TO DISCREDIT MY CHURCH'S STAND ON RACIAL ISSUES. IT'S AN EXAMPLE OF
FATHER MORRIS REACTED WITH A FIRM DEFENSE OF SAMMY WHILE THE POLICE WERE THERE.
SAMMY HIMSELF SCARCELY HAD TO SAY A WORD, HE TOLD US LATER.
STILL, IT DIDN'T HAVE THE FEEL OF SOMETHING LIKELY TO BLOW OVER.
THE FIREMEN, POLICE, AND REPORTERS LEFT EVENTUALLY AND THINGS QUIETED DOWN...
...BUT SAMMY NEVER SLEPT A WINK.
NEITHER DID FATHER MORRIS, APPARENTLY.
AROUND DAWN HE SHOWED BACK UP AT SAMMY'S DOOR.
SAMMY! WAKE UP! LET ME IN!
Knock, Knock!
WHO'S SLEEPIN'?
FATHER MORRIS CAME IN, TOOK A DEEP BREATH...
...AND LOWERED THE BOOM.
YOU'RE GOING TO HAVE TO GO, SAMMY. YOU CAN'T LIVE OR WORK HERE AT THE CHURCH ANYMORE.
WHEN MY PHONE STARTS RINGING THIS MORNING, I NEED TO BE ABLE TO SAY YOU'RE ALREADY PACKING.

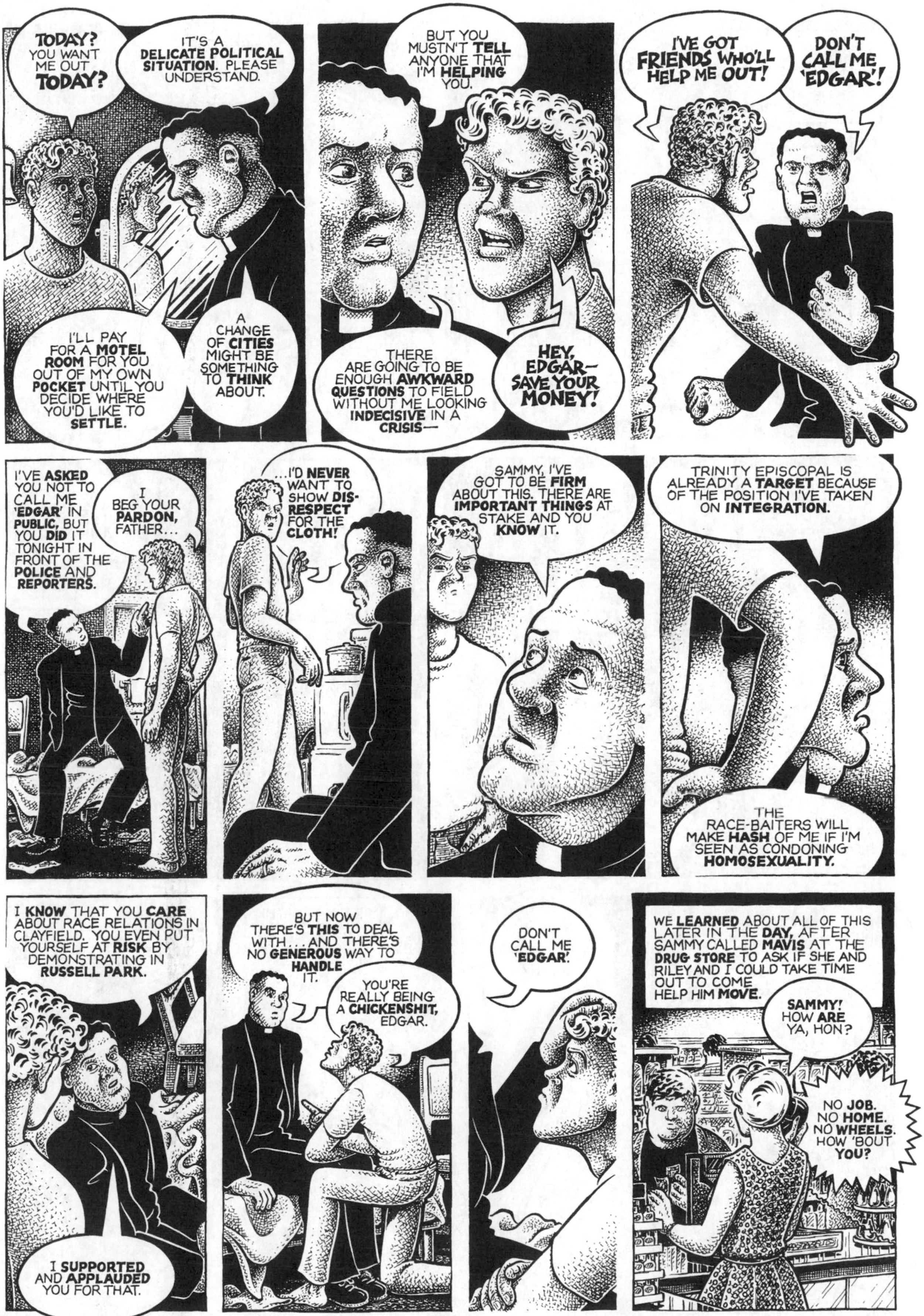
TODAY? YOU WANT ME OUT TODAY?
IT'S A DELICATE POLITICAL SITUATION. PLEASE UNDERSTAND.
I'LL PAY FOR A MOTEL ROOM FOR YOU OUT OF MY OWN POCKET UNTIL YOU DECIDE WHERE YOU'D LIKE TO SETTLE.
A CHANGE OF CITIES MIGHT BE SOMETHING TO THINK ABOUT.
BUT YOU MUSTN'T TELL ANYONE THAT I'M HELPING YOU.
THERE ARE GOING TO BE ENOUGH AWKWARD QUESTIONS TO FIELD WITHOUT ME LOOKING INDECISIVE IN A CRISIS—
HEY, EDGAR— SAVE YOUR MONEY!
I'VE GOT FRIENDS WHO'LL HELP ME OUT!
DON'T CALL ME 'EDGAR'!
I'VE ASKED YOU NOT TO CALL ME 'EDGAR' IN PUBLIC, BUT YOU DID IT TONIGHT IN FRONT OF THE POLICE AND REPORTERS.
I BEG YOUR PARDON, FATHER...
...I'D NEVER WANT TO SHOW DIS-RESPECT FOR THE CLOTH!
SAMMY, I'VE GOT TO BE FIRM ABOUT THIS. THERE ARE IMPORTANT THINGS AT STAKE AND YOU KNOW IT.
TRINITY EPISCOPAL IS ALREADY A TARGET BECAUSE OF THE POSITION I'VE TAKEN ON INTEGRATION.
THE RACE-BAITERS WILL MAKE HASH OF ME IF I'M SEEN AS CONDONING HOMOSEXUALITY.
I KNOW THAT YOU CARE ABOUT RACE RELATIONS IN CLAYFIELD. YOU EVEN PUT YOURSELF AT RISK BY DEMONSTRATING IN RUSSELL PARK.
I SUPPORTED AND APPLAUDED YOU FOR THAT.
BUT NOW THERE'S THIS TO DEAL WITH... AND THERE'S NO GENEROUS WAY TO HANDLE IT.
YOU'RE REALLY BEING A CHICKENSHIT, EDGAR.
DON'T CALL ME 'EDGAR'.
WE LEARNED ABOUT ALL OF THIS LATER IN THE DAY, AFTER SAMMY CALLED MAVIS AT THE DRUG STORE TO ASK IF SHE AND RILEY AND I COULD TAKE TIME OUT TO COME HELP HIM MOVE.
SAMMY! HOW ARE YA, HON?
NO JOB. NO HOME. NO WHEELS. HOW 'BOUT YOU?

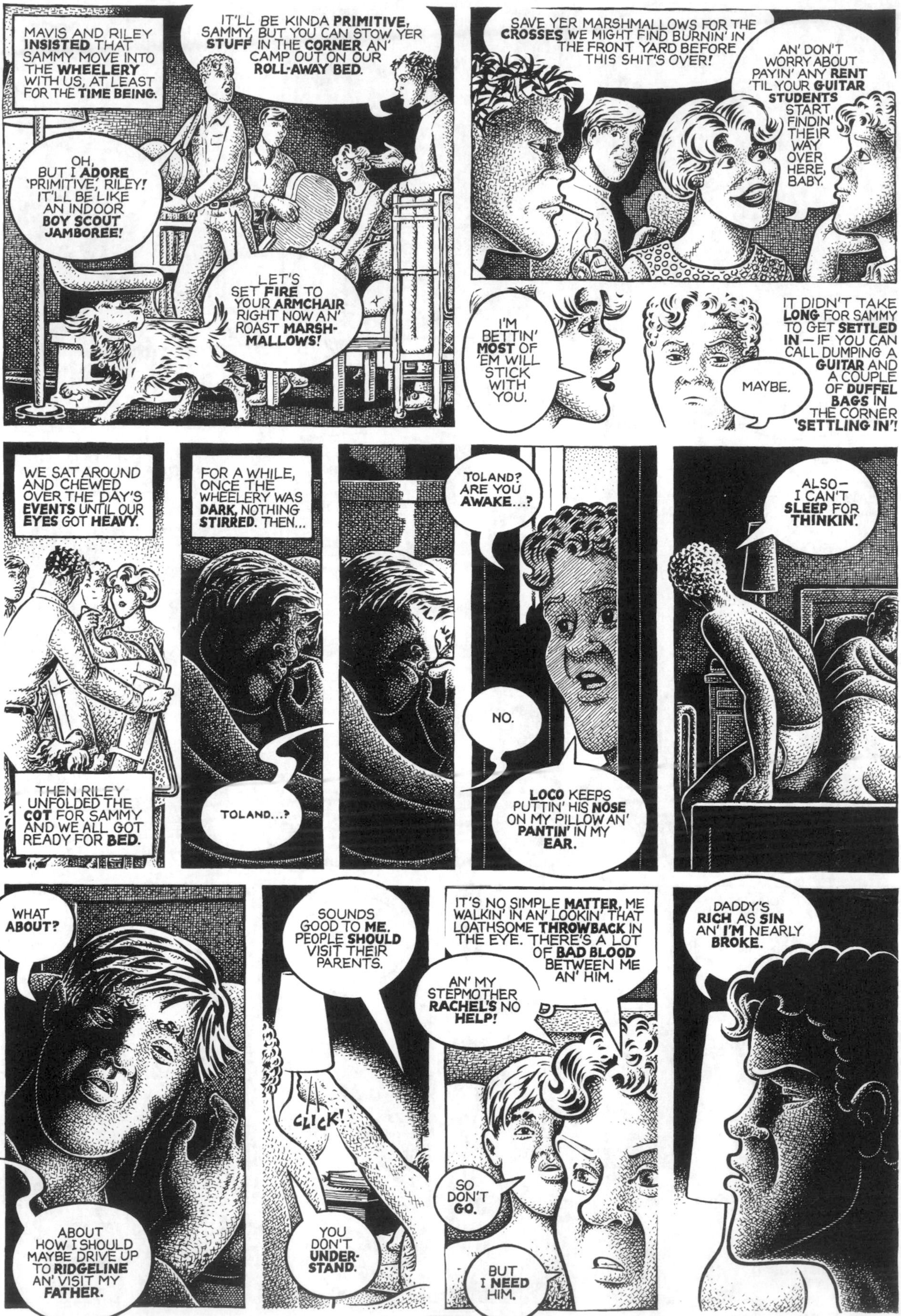
MAVIS AND RILEY INSISTED THAT SAMMY MOVE INTO THE WHEELERY WITH US, AT LEAST FOR THE TIME BEING.
IT'LL BE KINDA PRIMITIVE, SAMMY, BUT YOU CAN STOW YER STUFF IN THE CORNER AN' CAMP OUT ON OUR ROLL-AWAY BED.
OH, BUT I ADORE 'PRIMITIVE,' RILEY! IT'LL BE LIKE AN INDOOR BOY SCOUT JAMBOREE!
LET'S SET FIRE TO YOUR ARMCHAIR RIGHT NOW AN' ROAST MARSH-MALLOWS!
SAVE YER MARSHMALLOWS FOR THE CROSSES WE MIGHT FIND BURNIN' IN THE FRONT YARD BEFORE THIS SHIT'S OVER!
AN' DON'T WORRY ABOUT PAYIN' ANY RENT 'TIL YOUR GUITAR STUDENTS START FINDIN' THEIR WAY OVER HERE, BABY.
I'M BETTIN' MOST OF 'EM WILL STICK WITH YOU.
MAYBE.
IT DIDN'T TAKE LONG FOR SAMMY TO GET SETTLED IN — IF YOU CAN CALL DUMPING A GUITAR AND A COUPLE OF DUFFEL BAGS IN THE CORNER 'SETTLING IN'!
WE SAT AROUND AND CHEWED OVER THE DAY'S EVENTS UNTIL OUR EYES GOT HEAVY.
THEN RILEY UNFOLDED THE COT FOR SAMMY AND WE ALL GOT READY FOR BED.
FOR A WHILE, ONCE THE WHEELERY WAS DARK, NOTHING STIRRED. THEN...
TOLAND...?
TOLAND? ARE YOU AWAKE...?
NO.
LOCO KEEPS PUTTIN' HIS NOSE ON MY PILLOW AN' PANTIN' IN MY EAR.
ALSO— I CAN'T SLEEP FOR THINKIN'.
WHAT ABOUT?
ABOUT HOW I SHOULD MAYBE DRIVE UP TO RIDGELINE AN' VISIT MY FATHER.
SOUNDS GOOD TO ME. PEOPLE SHOULD VISIT THEIR PARENTS.
CLICK!
YOU DON'T UNDER-STAND.
IT'S NO SIMPLE MATTER, ME WALKIN' IN AN' LOOKIN' THAT LOATHSOME THROWBACK IN THE EYE. THERE'S A LOT OF BAD BLOOD BETWEEN ME AN' HIM.
AN' MY STEPMOTHER RACHEL'S NO HELP!
SO DON'T GO.
BUT I NEED HIM.
DADDY'S RICH AS SIN AN' I'M NEARLY BROKE.

HE'S GOT **HOUSES** AN' **CARS** RUNNIN' OUT OF HIS **EARS**... **ACRES** OF **LAND**... HE USED TO RUN OFF TO **EUROPE** WITH RACHEL **ALL** THE TIME...

...'TIL HIS **HEALTH** WENT BAD.

NOW HE'S SO BAD OFF, HE CAN'T **ARCH** HIS **EYEBROW** WITHOUT A **FORKLIFT!**

REALLY?

I'M TALKIN' ABOUT **MAJOR PARALYSIS.**

THAT'S **SAD.**

YEAH. **SEE** SAMMY **CRY.**

SO WHAT **GOOD'S** ALL THAT MONEY TO DADDY **NOW?** THERE'S NOTHIN' LEFT HE CAN **DO** WITH IT BUT **PISS** ON IT JUST TO WATCH IT **DRY!**

MEANWHILE **I'M** GETTIN' VERY **POOR** VERY **QUICK!**

SO GO **SEE** HIM.

BUT HE **HATES** ME.

HE **HATES** THE FACT THAT ONCE UPON SOME ENCHANTED EVENING HE WAS SCREWING MY LOVELY **MOM** AN' A SILLY LITTLE **FAIRY SPERM** CAME WIGGLING OUT OF HIS BIG, BUTCH **DICK.**

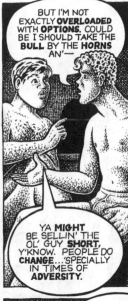

BUT I'M NOT EXACTLY **OVERLOADED** WITH **OPTIONS.** COULD BE I SHOULD TAKE THE **BULL** BY THE **HORNS** AN'—

YA **MIGHT** BE SELLIN' THE OL' GUY **SHORT,** Y'KNOW. PEOPLE **DO CHANGE**...'SPECIALLY IN TIMES OF **ADVERSITY.**

WILL YOU DRIVE ME UP TO **RIDGELINE,** TOLAND? IN **YOUR** CAR?

YOU WANT **ME** TO GO **WITH** YOU?

I'M **NERVOUS** ABOUT GOIN' **ALONE.**

AN' I DON'T THINK **MY** CAR'S SO **ROADWORTHY** SINCE THOSE FELLAS MISTOOK IT FOR A **POTATO** LAST NIGHT AN' TRIED TO **BAKE** IT!

WHEN WOULD YA WANNA **GO?**

I'M NOT **SURE.** IT'LL TAKE ME A **LITTLE** WHILE TO BUILD UP MY **NERVE.**

BUT WE'LL MAKE IT A **WEEK-END,** FOR **SURE,** SO IT WON'T INTERFERE WITH YOUR **JOB.**

WHAT **JOB?**

OOPS! I KEEP **FORGETTIN'** YOU'VE SEVERED YOUR TIES WITH THE **PETROLEUM INDUSTRY!**

HEY, WE'RE **BOTH** OUT OF WORK AT THE **SAME** TIME. LET'S START A **CLUB!**

SERIOUSLY, KID...HOW MUCH OF A **BIND** DOES IT PUT YOU **IN?**

OH, I'M **O.K.** FOR A **WHILE**....

I'VE STILL GOT SOME **SAVINGS** FROM MY FOLKS' **INSURANCE** AN' FROM SELLIN' MELANIE AN' ORLEY MY SHARE OF THE **HOUSE.**

BUT IF YOU **POSTPONE** YOUR LI'L FAMILY REUNION TOO **LONG,** I MIGHT HAFTA TAKE SOME JOB THAT'D **KEEP** ME FROM—

IT'LL BE **SOON.** I'VE JUST GOTTA WORK ON WHAT TO **SAY.**

I'M **SCARED**, TOLAND. I DON'T KNOW WHAT'S GONNA **HAPPEN** TO ME.

I'VE ALWAYS TAKEN **PRIDE** IN MY **CHECKERED HISTORY**, BUT I'VE NEVER GOTTEN MYSELF BRANDED A **PERVERT** ON THE FRONT PAGE OF A **NEWSPAPER** BEFORE!

WHERE'D THAT PHOTO OF YOU **COME** FROM, ANYWAY?

THE **RUSSELL PARK SIT-IN**, AS FAR AS I CAN **TELL**.

MAVIS SAYS I SHOULD POP INTO THE DIXIE PATRIOT **OFFICE** AN' ASK IF THEY'LL SELL ME SOME **EXTRA PRINTS** OF THE PHOTO FOR MY **RELATIVES**!

THE **CLAYFIELD BANNER** IS **ALWAYS** WILLIN' TO DO THAT, Y'KNOW...

...IF THEY PRINT YOUR **PICTURE**, YOU CAN ORDER A **COPY**.

IT'S A REGULAR **SERVICE**.

Chuckle! **THAT'D** BE A SIGHT TO SEE!

I CAN JUST **IMAGINE** THOSE DIXIE PATRIOT WEASELS QUAKIN' IN THEIR **BOOTS**, WATCHIN' ONE OF THE LOCAL **UNDESIRABLES** THEY'VE FINGERED COME SAUNTERIN' UP THE **DRIVEWAY**!

LOOK, PAL, I'LL DRIVE YOU TO RIDGELINE IF YOU **NEED** ME TO. IT WON'T BE MUCH TROUBLE.

THANKS, TOLAND. YOU'RE A REAL **FRIEND**.

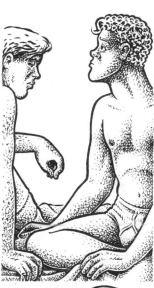

CAN I LIE DOWN **NEXT** TO YOU AN' HOLD **ON** TO YOU FOR JUST A MINUTE?

SAMMY... I WISH YOU WOULDN'T **ASK** THAT.

I'M NOT TALKIN' ABOUT **SEX**.

I JUST WANNA **HOLD ON** TO SOMEBODY FOR **FIVE MINUTES**. I'LL GO AWAY THEN.

THAT'S O.K.— **FORGET** IT.

I JUST REMEMBERED: **LOCO** MIGHT HEAR THE **BEDSPRINGS** CREAKIN' AN' THINK I'M BEIN' **UNFAITHFUL**!

NEVER **TRIFLE** WITH THE AFFECTIONS OF A **CARNIVORE**, IS MY MOTTO!

G'NIGHT.

Chapter 15

SOME DAYS YOU REMEMBER FOR THE **SOUR** NOTES.

Sproioi-n-ng!

THERE WAS NO SHORTAGE OF **THOSE** THE DAY GINGER PHONED TO TELL ME SHE WAS **PREGNANT**.

WE AGREED WE'D MEET TO TALK THINGS **OVER** IN ONE OF THE LITTLE **PRACTICE ROOMS** AT THE COLLEGE **MUSIC BUILDING**.

PRACTICE ROOMS

I WAS SO **AGITATED**, I GOT **LOST** AND WANDERED DOWN EVERY CORRIDOR BUT THE **RIGHT** ONE.

THE PRACTICE ROOM **DOORS** HAD TINY **WINDOWS** IN THEM.

I PEERED INTO **EACH ONE** AS I PASSED **BY**.

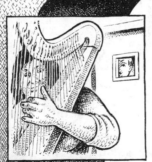

IT SEEMED LIKE **EVERYBODY** IN THE **BUILDING** WAS A FUCKING WHIZ AT DOING **SOMETHING**!

ANY **SECOND** I EXPECTED TO GET ASKED WHAT THE HELL **I** WAS DOING IN A BUILDING LIKE **THAT**!

PRACTICE ROOMS

PRACTICE ROOMS

HEY, **THERE** YOU ARE!

FINALLY I FOUND GINGER.

I ALMOST COULDN'T **SEE** YA, Y'KNOW...

...WITH YOU DOWN ON THE **FLOOR** LIKE THAT.

SO... Y'WANNA GET **MARRIED**?

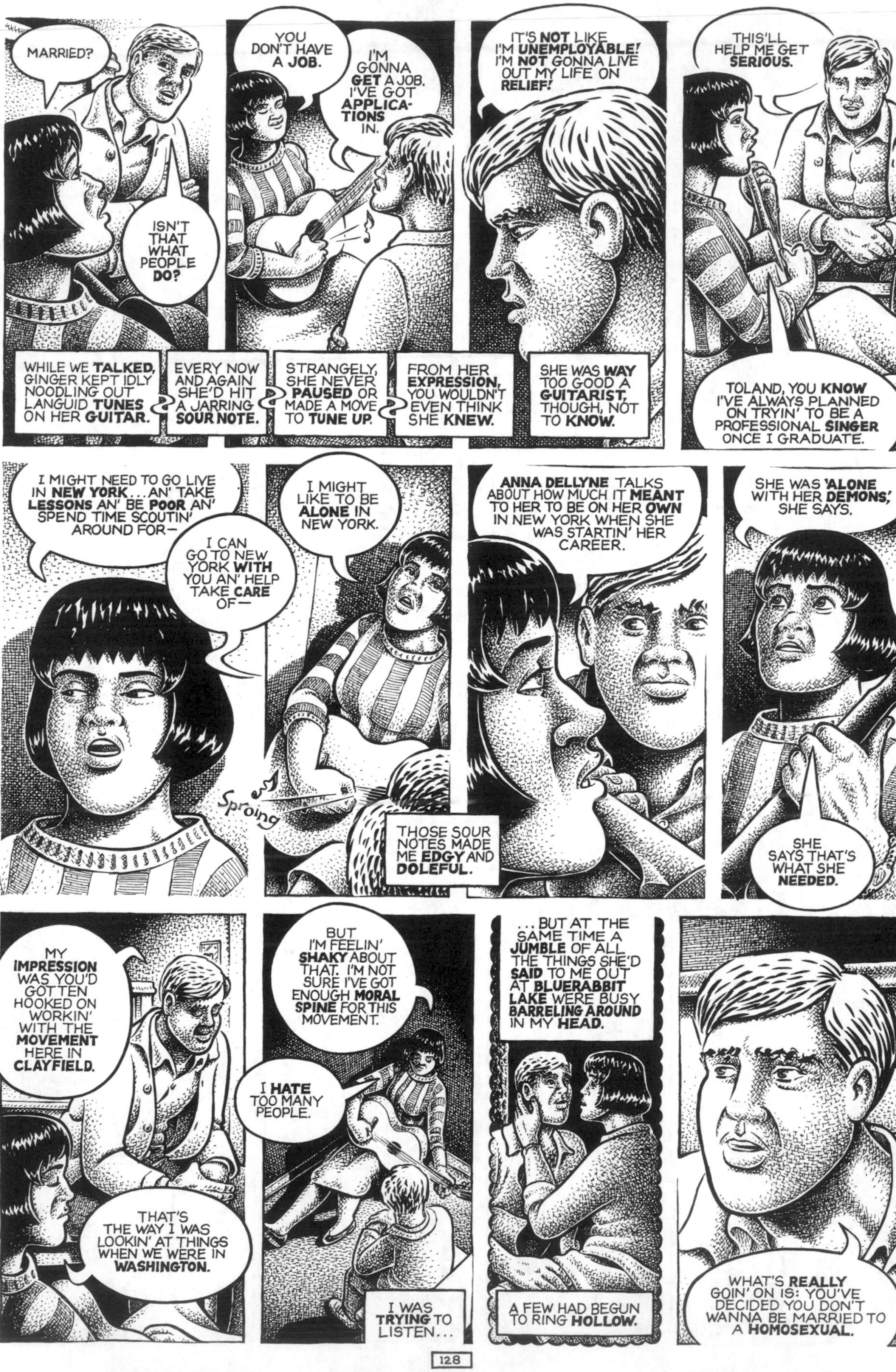
MARRIED?
ISN'T THAT WHAT PEOPLE DO?
YOU DON'T HAVE A JOB.
I'M GONNA GET A JOB. I'VE GOT APPLICATIONS IN.
IT'S NOT LIKE I'M UNEMPLOYABLE! I'M NOT GONNA LIVE OUT MY LIFE ON RELIEF!
THIS'LL HELP ME GET SERIOUS.
WHILE WE TALKED, GINGER KEPT IDLY NOODLING OUT LANGUID TUNES ON HER GUITAR.
EVERY NOW AND AGAIN SHE'D HIT A JARRING SOUR NOTE.
STRANGELY, SHE NEVER PAUSED OR MADE A MOVE TO TUNE UP.
FROM HER EXPRESSION, YOU WOULDN'T EVEN THINK SHE KNEW.
SHE WAS WAY TOO GOOD A GUITARIST, THOUGH, NOT TO KNOW.
TOLAND, YOU KNOW I'VE ALWAYS PLANNED ON TRYIN' TO BE A PROFESSIONAL SINGER ONCE I GRADUATE.
I MIGHT NEED TO GO LIVE IN NEW YORK... AN' TAKE LESSONS AN' BE POOR AN' SPEND TIME SCOUTIN' AROUND FOR—
I CAN GO TO NEW YORK WITH YOU AN' HELP TAKE CARE OF—
I MIGHT LIKE TO BE ALONE IN NEW YORK.
Sproing
THOSE SOUR NOTES MADE ME EDGY AND DOLEFUL.
ANNA DELLYNE TALKS ABOUT HOW MUCH IT MEANT TO HER TO BE ON HER OWN IN NEW YORK WHEN SHE WAS STARTIN' HER CAREER.
SHE WAS 'ALONE WITH HER DEMONS,' SHE SAYS.
SHE SAYS THAT'S WHAT SHE NEEDED.
MY IMPRESSION WAS YOU'D GOTTEN HOOKED ON WORKIN' WITH THE MOVEMENT HERE IN CLAYFIELD.
THAT'S THE WAY I WAS LOOKIN' AT THINGS WHEN WE WERE IN WASHINGTON.
BUT I'M FEELIN' SHAKY ABOUT THAT. I'M NOT SURE I'VE GOT ENOUGH MORAL SPINE FOR THIS MOVEMENT.
I HATE TOO MANY PEOPLE.
I WAS TRYING TO LISTEN...
...BUT AT THE SAME TIME A JUMBLE OF ALL THE THINGS SHE'D SAID TO ME OUT AT BLUERABBIT LAKE WERE BUSY BARRELING AROUND IN MY HEAD.
A FEW HAD BEGUN TO RING HOLLOW.
WHAT'S REALLY GOIN' ON IS: YOU'VE DECIDED YOU DON'T WANNA BE MARRIED TO A HOMOSEXUAL.

TOLAND...

...DO YOU FIND THAT SO **STRANGE**??

SO...LIKE, WHAT AM I SUPPOSED TO **DO**?

WHAT ARE THE **RULES**?

DO I PAY FOR AN **ABORTION**? IS **THAT** WHAT HAPPENS?

ANNA DELLYNE SAYS SHE KNOWS SOMEONE I CAN **TALK** TO... ABOUT THAT.

THAT'S WHEN A WHITE **RAGE** SWELLED UP INSIDE OF ME.

SHE'D TALKED IT ALL OVER WITH **ANNA DELLYNE**... ...EVEN **BEFORE** SHE'D SAID ANYTHING TO **ME**!

DO YOU REALLY **WANT** AN ABORTION?

NO.

BUT I WANT MY **LIFE**.

I DON'T WANNA ABORT MY **OWN** LIFE, EITHER.

I DON'T WANNA GET **STUCK**—ALONE OR WITH **YOU**—JUST BARELY SCRAPIN' **BY**... GIVIN' UP ON BEIN' WHO I **WANT** TO BE.

I GOTTA GO THINK.

MAYBE IF **YOU** HAD SOMEBODY **YOU** REALLY WANTED TO BE, YOU'D UNDERSTAND.

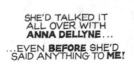

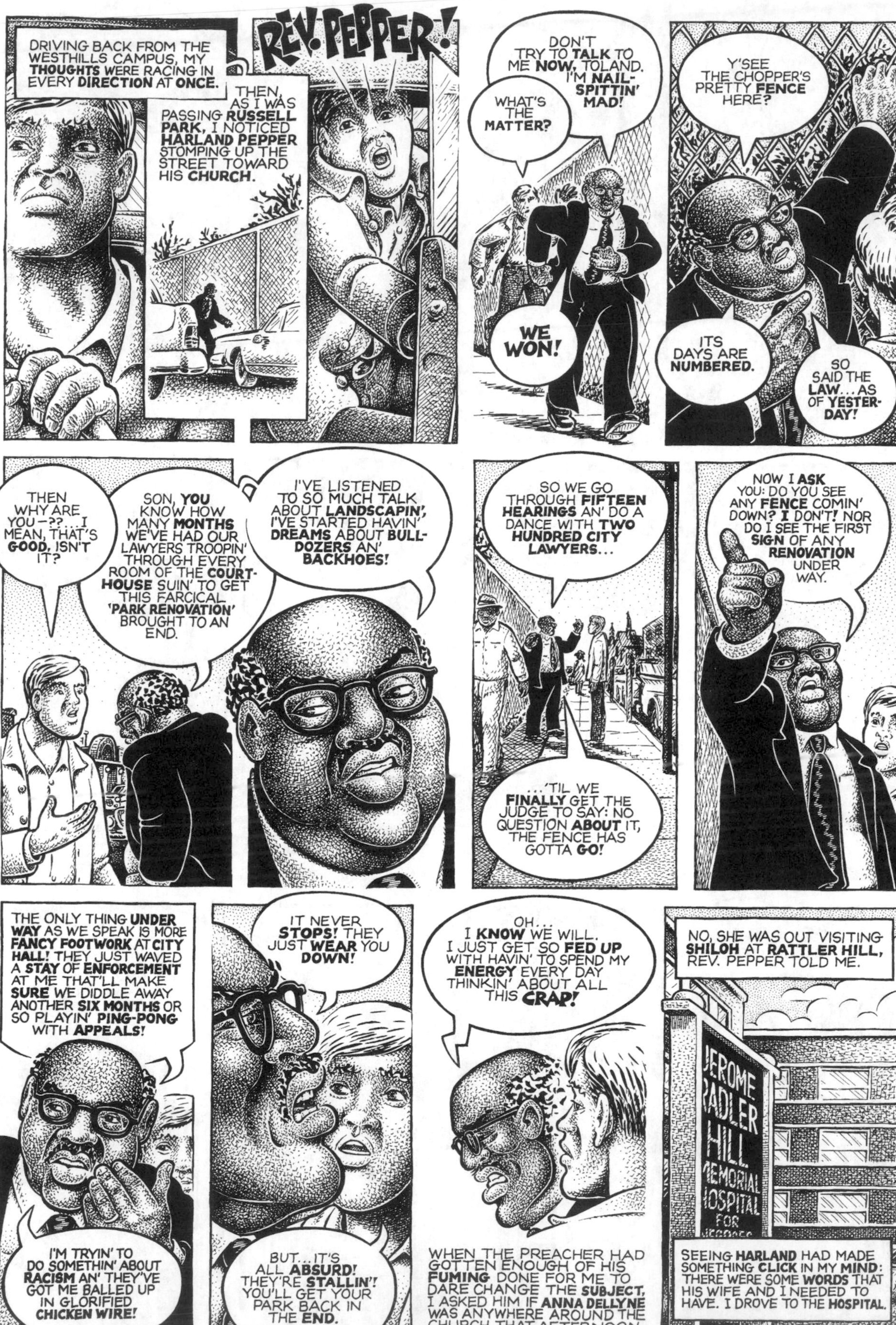

DRIVING BACK FROM THE WESTHILLS CAMPUS, MY THOUGHTS WERE RACING IN EVERY DIRECTION AT ONCE.
THEN, AS I WAS PASSING RUSSELL PARK, I NOTICED HARLAND PEPPER STOMPING UP THE STREET TOWARD HIS CHURCH.
REV. PEPPER!
WHAT'S THE MATTER?
DON'T TRY TO TALK TO ME NOW, TOLAND. I'M NAIL-SPITTIN' MAD!
WE WON!
Y'SEE THE CHOPPER'S PRETTY FENCE HERE?
ITS DAYS ARE NUMBERED.
SO SAID THE LAW... AS OF YESTERDAY!
THEN WHY ARE YOU—??... I MEAN, THAT'S GOOD, ISN'T IT?
SON, YOU KNOW HOW MANY MONTHS WE'VE HAD OUR LAWYERS TROOPIN' THROUGH EVERY ROOM OF THE COURTHOUSE SUIN' TO GET THIS FARCICAL 'PARK RENOVATION' BROUGHT TO AN END.
I'VE LISTENED TO SO MUCH TALK ABOUT LANDSCAPIN', I'VE STARTED HAVIN' DREAMS ABOUT BULLDOZERS AN' BACKHOES!
SO WE GO THROUGH FIFTEEN HEARINGS AN' DO A DANCE WITH TWO HUNDRED CITY LAWYERS...
...'TIL WE FINALLY GET THE JUDGE TO SAY: NO QUESTION ABOUT IT, THE FENCE HAS GOTTA GO!
NOW I ASK YOU: DO YOU SEE ANY FENCE COMIN' DOWN? I DON'T! NOR DO I SEE THE FIRST SIGN OF ANY RENOVATION UNDER WAY.
THE ONLY THING UNDER WAY AS WE SPEAK IS MORE FANCY FOOTWORK AT CITY HALL! THEY JUST WAVED A STAY OF ENFORCEMENT AT ME THAT'LL MAKE SURE WE DIDDLE AWAY ANOTHER SIX MONTHS OR SO PLAYIN' PING-PONG WITH APPEALS!
I'M TRYIN' TO DO SOMETHIN' ABOUT RACISM AN' THEY'VE GOT ME BALLED UP IN GLORIFIED CHICKEN WIRE!
IT NEVER STOPS! THEY JUST WEAR YOU DOWN!
BUT... IT'S ALL ABSURD! THEY'RE STALLIN'! YOU'LL GET YOUR PARK BACK IN THE END.
OH... I KNOW WE WILL. I JUST GET SO FED UP WITH HAVIN' TO SPEND MY ENERGY EVERY DAY THINKIN' ABOUT ALL THIS CRAP!
WHEN THE PREACHER HAD GOTTEN ENOUGH OF HIS FUMING DONE FOR ME TO DARE CHANGE THE SUBJECT, I ASKED HIM IF ANNA DELLYNE WAS ANYWHERE AROUND THE CHURCH THAT AFTERNOON.
NO, SHE WAS OUT VISITING SHILOH AT RATTLER HILL, REV. PEPPER TOLD ME.
JEROME RADLER HILL MEMORIAL HOSPITAL FOR
SEEING HARLAND HAD MADE SOMETHING CLICK IN MY MIND: THERE WERE SOME WORDS THAT HIS WIFE AND I NEEDED TO HAVE. I DROVE TO THE HOSPITAL.

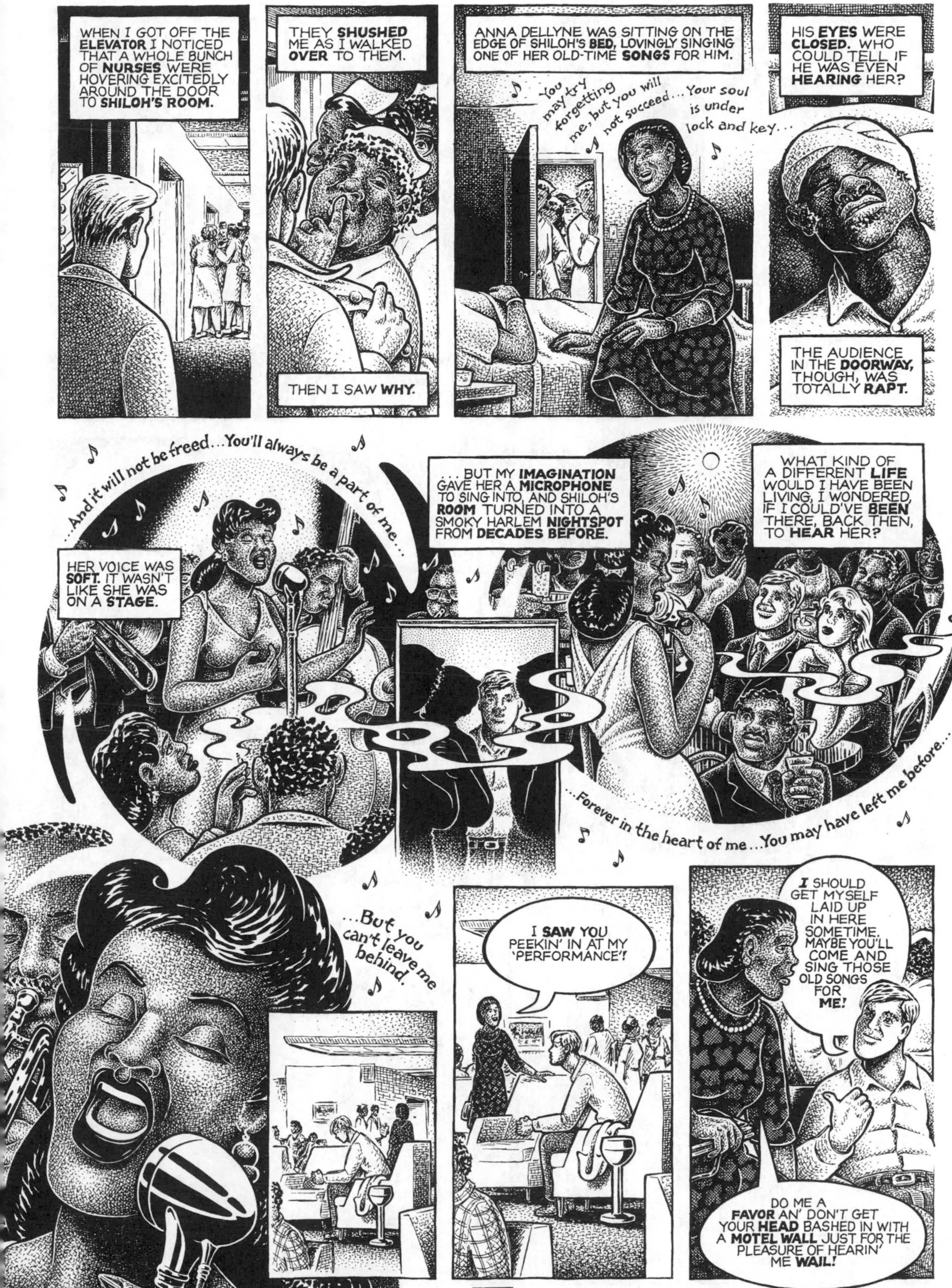

WHEN I GOT OFF THE ELEVATOR I NOTICED THAT A WHOLE BUNCH OF NURSES WERE HOVERING EXCITEDLY AROUND THE DOOR TO SHILOH'S ROOM.
THEY SHUSHED ME AS I WALKED OVER TO THEM.
THEN I SAW WHY.
ANNA DELLYNE WAS SITTING ON THE EDGE OF SHILOH'S BED, LOVINGLY SINGING ONE OF HER OLD-TIME SONGS FOR HIM.
You may try forgetting me, but you will not succeed... Your soul is under lock and key...
HIS EYES WERE CLOSED. WHO COULD TELL IF HE WAS EVEN HEARING HER?
THE AUDIENCE IN THE DOORWAY, THOUGH, WAS TOTALLY RAPT.
...And it will not be freed... You'll always be a part of me...
HER VOICE WAS SOFT. IT WASN'T LIKE SHE WAS ON A STAGE.
...BUT MY IMAGINATION GAVE HER A MICROPHONE TO SING INTO, AND SHILOH'S ROOM TURNED INTO A SMOKY HARLEM NIGHTSPOT FROM DECADES BEFORE.
WHAT KIND OF A DIFFERENT LIFE WOULD I HAVE BEEN LIVING, I WONDERED, IF I COULD'VE BEEN THERE, BACK THEN, TO HEAR HER?
...Forever in the heart of me... You may have left me before...
...But you can't leave me behind.
I SAW YOU PEEKIN' IN AT MY 'PERFORMANCE'!
I SHOULD GET MYSELF LAID UP IN HERE SOMETIME. MAYBE YOU'LL COME AND SING THOSE OLD SONGS FOR ME!
DO ME A FAVOR AN' DON'T GET YOUR HEAD BASHED IN WITH A MOTEL WALL JUST FOR THE PLEASURE OF HEARIN' ME WAIL!

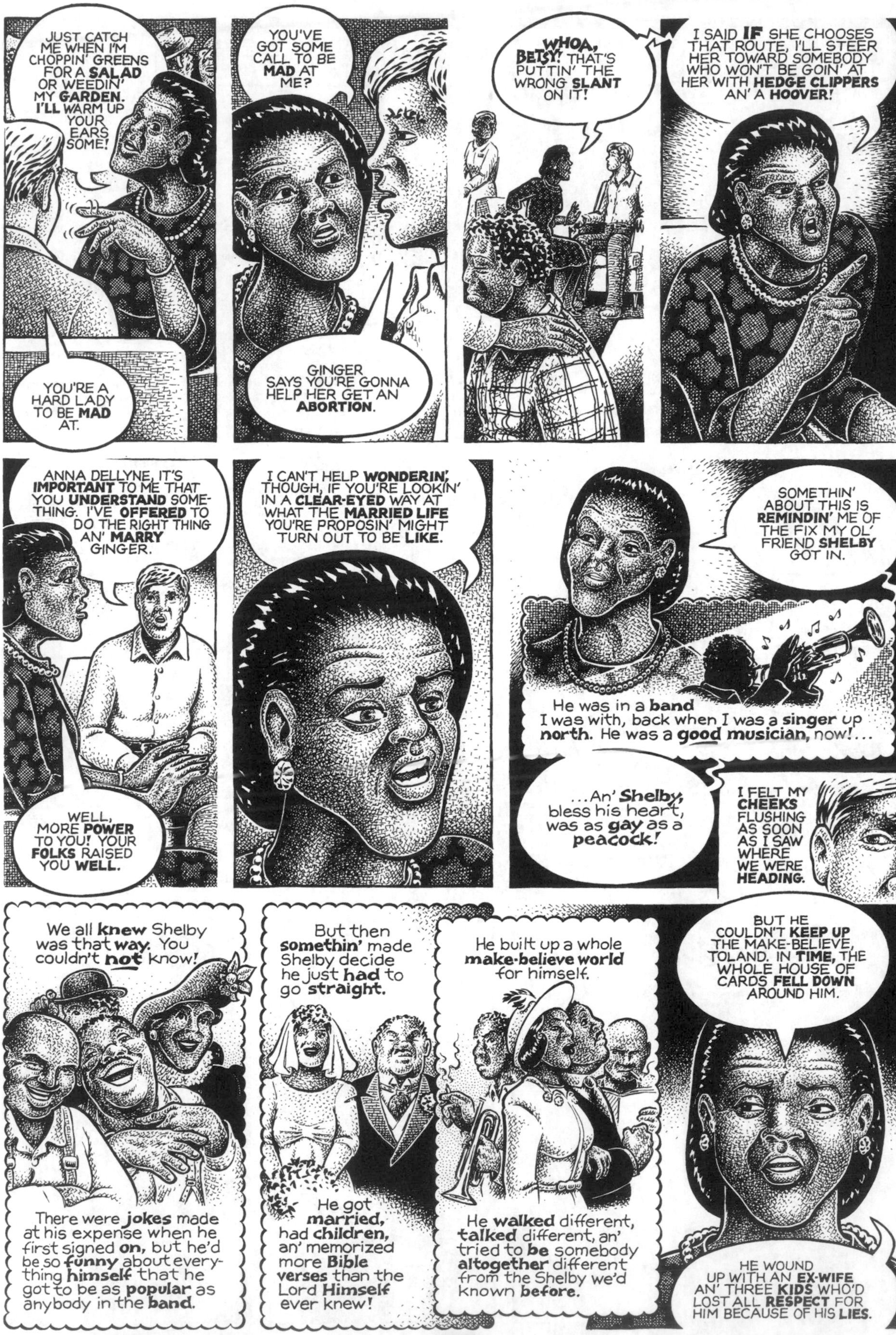
JUST CATCH ME WHEN I'M CHOPPIN' GREENS FOR A SALAD OR WEEDIN' MY GARDEN. I'LL WARM UP YOUR EARS SOME!
YOU'RE A HARD LADY TO BE MAD AT.
YOU'VE GOT SOME CALL TO BE MAD AT ME?
GINGER SAYS YOU'RE GONNA HELP HER GET AN ABORTION.
WHOA, BETSY! THAT'S PUTTIN' THE WRONG SLANT ON IT!
I SAID IF SHE CHOOSES THAT ROUTE, I'LL STEER HER TOWARD SOMEBODY WHO WON'T BE GOIN' AT HER WITH HEDGE CLIPPERS AN' A HOOVER!
ANNA DELLYNE, IT'S IMPORTANT TO ME THAT YOU UNDERSTAND SOMETHING. I'VE OFFERED TO DO THE RIGHT THING AN' MARRY GINGER.
WELL, MORE POWER TO YOU! YOUR FOLKS RAISED YOU WELL.
I CAN'T HELP WONDERIN', THOUGH, IF YOU'RE LOOKIN' IN A CLEAR-EYED WAY AT WHAT THE MARRIED LIFE YOU'RE PROPOSIN' MIGHT TURN OUT TO BE LIKE.
SOMETHIN' ABOUT THIS IS REMINDIN' ME OF THE FIX MY OL' FRIEND SHELBY GOT IN.
He was in a band I was with, back when I was a singer up north. He was a good musician, now!...
...An' Shelby, bless his heart, was as gay as a peacock!
I FELT MY CHEEKS FLUSHING AS SOON AS I SAW WHERE WE WERE HEADING.
We all knew Shelby was that way. You couldn't not know!
There were jokes made at his expense when he first signed on, but he'd be so funny about everything himself that he got to be as popular as anybody in the band.
But then somethin' made Shelby decide he just had to go straight.
He got married, had children, an' memorized more Bible verses than the Lord Himself ever knew!
He built up a whole make-believe world for himself.
He walked different, talked different, an' tried to be somebody altogether different from the Shelby we'd known before.
BUT HE COULDN'T KEEP UP THE MAKE-BELIEVE, TOLAND. IN TIME, THE WHOLE HOUSE OF CARDS FELL DOWN AROUND HIM.
HE WOUND UP WITH AN EX-WIFE AN' THREE KIDS WHO'D LOST ALL RESPECT FOR HIM BECAUSE OF HIS LIES.

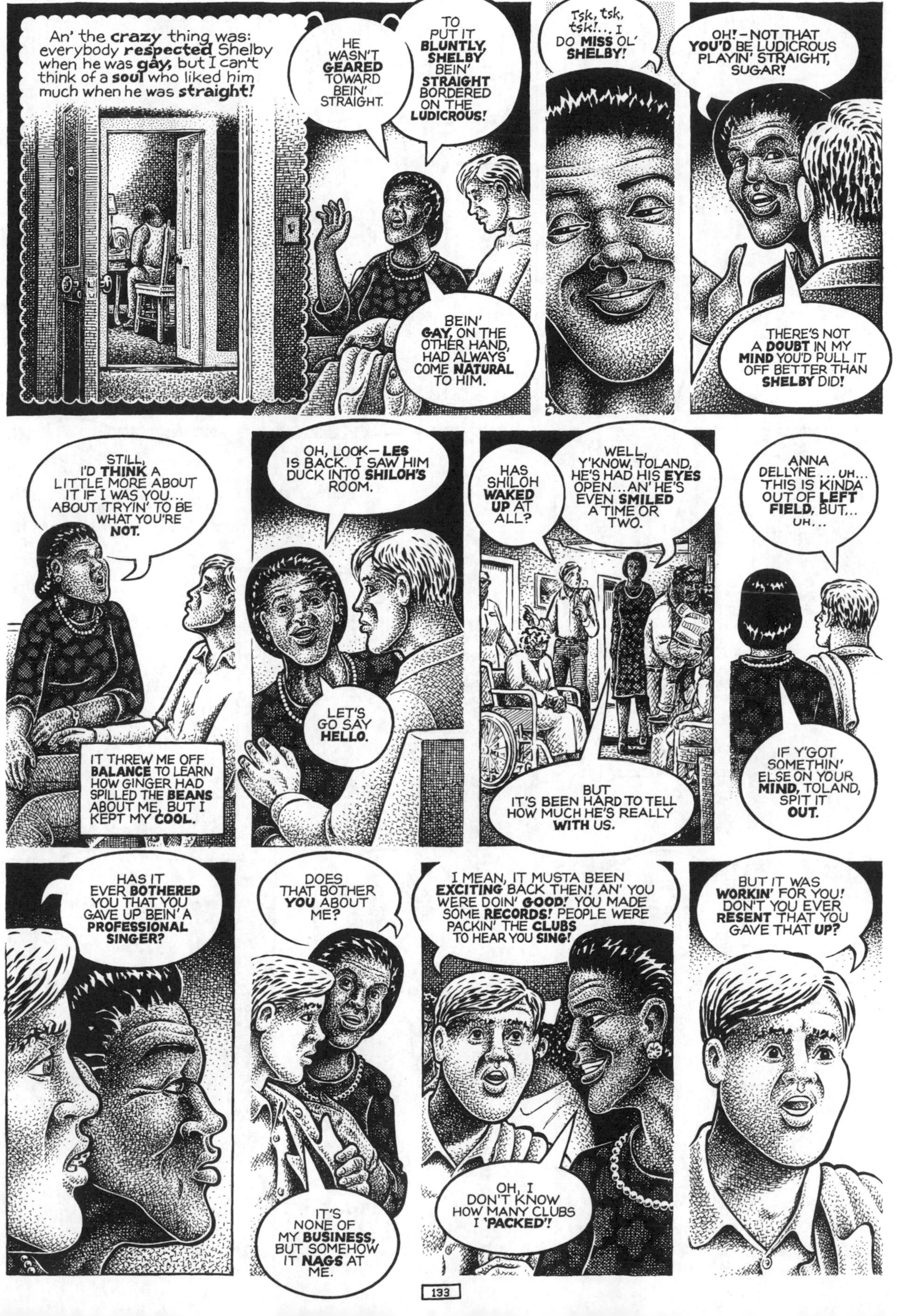

An' the **crazy** thing was: everybody **respected** Shelby when he was **gay,** but I can't think of a **soul** who liked him much when he was **straight!**
HE WASN'T **GEARED** TOWARD BEIN' STRAIGHT.
TO PUT IT **BLUNTLY, SHELBY** BEIN' **STRAIGHT** BORDERED ON THE **LUDICROUS!**
BEIN' **GAY,** ON THE OTHER HAND, HAD ALWAYS COME **NATURAL** TO HIM.
Tsk, tsk, tsk!... I DO **MISS** OL' **SHELBY!**
OH! —NOT THAT **YOU'D** BE LUDICROUS PLAYIN' STRAIGHT, SUGAR!
THERE'S NOT A **DOUBT** IN MY **MIND** YOU'D PULL IT OFF BETTER THAN **SHELBY** DID!
STILL, I'D **THINK** A LITTLE MORE ABOUT IT IF I WAS YOU... ABOUT TRYIN' TO BE WHAT YOU'RE **NOT.**
IT THREW ME OFF **BALANCE** TO LEARN HOW GINGER HAD SPILLED THE **BEANS** ABOUT ME, BUT I KEPT MY **COOL.**
OH, LOOK— **LES** IS BACK. I SAW HIM DUCK INTO **SHILOH'S** ROOM.
LET'S GO SAY **HELLO.**
HAS SHILOH **WAKED UP** AT ALL?
WELL, Y'KNOW, TOLAND, HE'S HAD HIS **EYES** OPEN... AN' HE'S EVEN **SMILED** A TIME OR TWO.
BUT IT'S BEEN HARD TO TELL HOW MUCH HE'S REALLY **WITH US.**
ANNA DELLYNE... UH... THIS IS KINDA OUT OF **LEFT FIELD,** BUT... UH...
IF Y'GOT SOMETHIN' ELSE ON YOUR **MIND,** TOLAND, SPIT IT **OUT.**
HAS IT EVER **BOTHERED** YOU THAT YOU GAVE UP BEIN' A **PROFESSIONAL SINGER?**
DOES THAT BOTHER **YOU** ABOUT ME?
IT'S NONE OF MY **BUSINESS,** BUT SOMEHOW IT **NAGS** AT ME.
I MEAN, IT MUSTA BEEN **EXCITING** BACK THEN! AN' YOU WERE DOIN' **GOOD!** YOU MADE SOME **RECORDS!** PEOPLE WERE PACKIN' THE **CLUBS** TO HEAR YOU **SING!**
OH, I DON'T KNOW HOW MANY CLUBS I **'PACKED'!**
BUT IT WAS **WORKIN'** FOR YOU! DON'T YOU EVER **RESENT** THAT YOU GAVE THAT **UP?**

'CAUSE YOU'RE ENCOURAGIN' **GINGER** TO GO TO NEW YORK BY HERSELF LIKE **YOU** DID.

BUT WHEN ALL WAS SAID AN' DONE, **YOU** CAME BACK **HOME**.

WHAT IF NEW YORK DOESN'T WORK FOR **HER**...AN' **SHE** COMES BACK?

THEN **SHE** WON'T HAVE WHAT **SHE** WENT UP THERE LOOKIN' FOR...

...AN' MEAN-WHILE, THE ONLY **CHILD** I'M EVER LIKELY TO **HAVE** WILL BE **GONE FOREVER!**

I CAN'T CUT A PATH THROUGH **THAT** THICKET FOR YOU.

YOU AN' GINGER HAFTA FIND YOUR **OWN** RIGHT WAY TO GO.

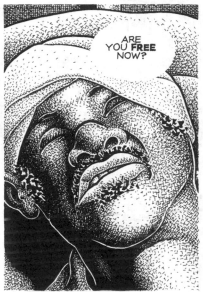

ARE YOU **FREE** NOW?

HUH?

ARE YOU **FREE** NOW?

OH. YEAH.

Y'GOT YOUR OWN **WHEELS** HERE?

YEAH.

MAMA, THE CAR'S **YOURS** TONIGHT. ME AN' TOLAND ARE GONNA GO CATCH A **BITE.**

C'MON. LET'S GET THE HELL **OUTA** HERE.

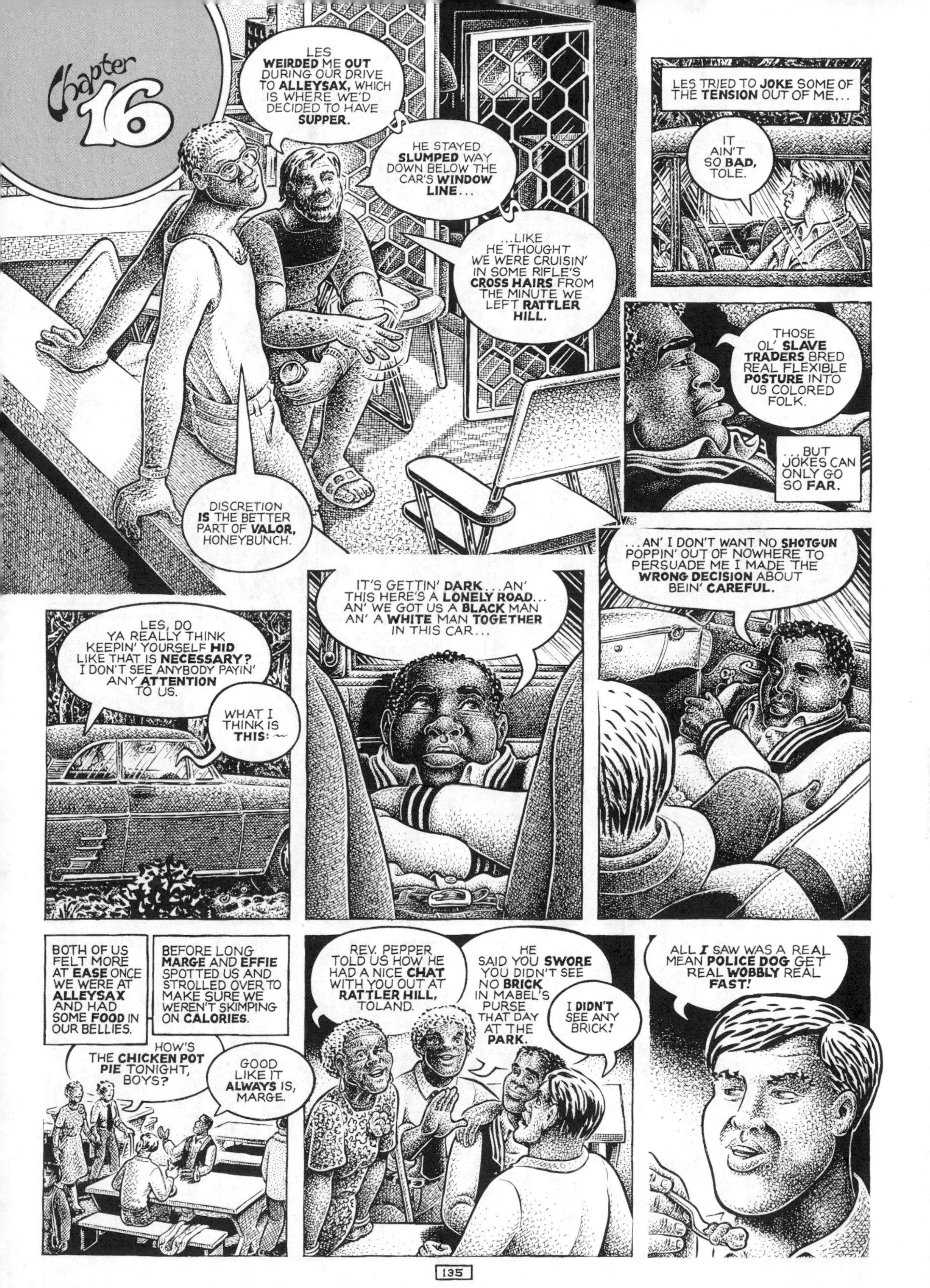
Chapter 16
LES WEIRDED ME OUT DURING OUR DRIVE TO ALLEYSAX, WHICH IS WHERE WE'D DECIDED TO HAVE SUPPER.
HE STAYED SLUMPED WAY DOWN BELOW THE CAR'S WINDOW LINE...
...LIKE HE THOUGHT WE WERE CRUISIN' IN SOME RIFLE'S CROSS HAIRS FROM THE MINUTE WE LEFT RATTLER HILL.
DISCRETION IS THE BETTER PART OF VALOR, HONEYBUNCH.
LES TRIED TO JOKE SOME OF THE TENSION OUT OF ME...
IT AIN'T SO BAD, TOLE.
THOSE OL' SLAVE TRADERS BRED REAL FLEXIBLE POSTURE INTO US COLORED FOLK.
...BUT JOKES CAN ONLY GO SO FAR.
LES, DO YA REALLY THINK KEEPIN' YOURSELF HID LIKE THAT IS NECESSARY? I DON'T SEE ANYBODY PAYIN' ANY ATTENTION TO US.
WHAT I THINK IS THIS: ~
IT'S GETTIN' DARK... AN' THIS HERE'S A LONELY ROAD... AN' WE GOT US A BLACK MAN AN' A WHITE MAN TOGETHER IN THIS CAR...
...AN' I DON'T WANT NO SHOTGUN POPPIN' OUT OF NOWHERE TO PERSUADE ME I MADE THE WRONG DECISION ABOUT BEIN' CAREFUL.
BOTH OF US FELT MORE AT EASE ONCE WE WERE AT ALLEYSAX AND HAD SOME FOOD IN OUR BELLIES.
BEFORE LONG MARGE AND EFFIE SPOTTED US AND STROLLED OVER TO MAKE SURE WE WEREN'T SKIMPING ON CALORIES.
HOW'S THE CHICKEN POT PIE TONIGHT, BOYS?
GOOD LIKE IT ALWAYS IS, MARGE.
REV. PEPPER TOLD US HOW HE HAD A NICE CHAT WITH YOU OUT AT RATTLER HILL, TOLAND.
HE SAID YOU SWORE YOU DIDN'T SEE NO BRICK IN MABEL'S PURSE THAT DAY AT THE PARK.
I DIDN'T SEE ANY BRICK!
ALL I SAW WAS A REAL MEAN POLICE DOG GET REAL WOBBLY REAL FAST!

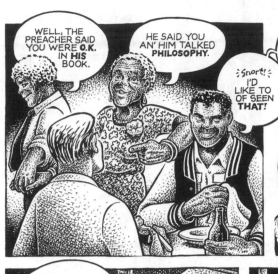
WELL, THE PREACHER SAID YOU WERE **O.K.** IN **HIS** BOOK.

HE SAID YOU AN' HIM TALKED **PHILOSOPHY.**

¿Snort! I'D LIKE TO OF SEEN **THAT!**

I'LL BET THAT WAS A REAL **TWO-WAY CONVERSATION,** WASN'T IT, TOLE!

CORRECT ME IF I'M **WRONG,** BUT 'TALKING PHILOSOPHY' WITH MY PAPA **USUALLY** MEANS DOIN' LOTSA **SMILIN'** AN' **NODDIN'** WHILE HE PREACHES A **SERMON** AT YOU.

I GOT SOME **WORDS** IN.

Y'KNOW, LES, THIS PLACE IS **DIFFERENT** WHEN IT'S **QUIET.** THERE'S ALWAYS BEEN A **BAND** PLAYIN' WHEN I'VE BEEN HERE BEFORE.

Y'GOTTA BE HERE **LATE** AT **NIGHT** TO GET **LIVE** MUSIC.

THERE'S SOME NICE COZY TUNES ON THE **JUKEBOX,** THOUGH.

WHY DON'T I GO PUT ONE OF 'EM **ON** SO YOU AN' ME CAN **DANCE?**

BUT DONCHA THINK I CAN **SEE** WHICH WAY YOUR **EYEBALLS** DRIFT EVERY TIME A HANDSOME **MAN** PASSES BY?

LES~

C'MON. GIVE **IN** A LITTLE. I CAN READ YOUR **BEADS.**

DID YOUR **MOTHER** TALK TO YOU ABOUT ME?

MY MOTHER AIN'T SAID A FUCKIN' **WORD** ABOUT YOU.

C'MON, BABY. LET'S DO THE **SCARY** THING.

I'M GONNA GO PUT MY **MONEY** IN THE SLOT. THEN I WANT YOU TO COME **OVER** TO ME.

♪ Give me just one minute... ♪

♪ ...of the Love of a Lifetime... ♪

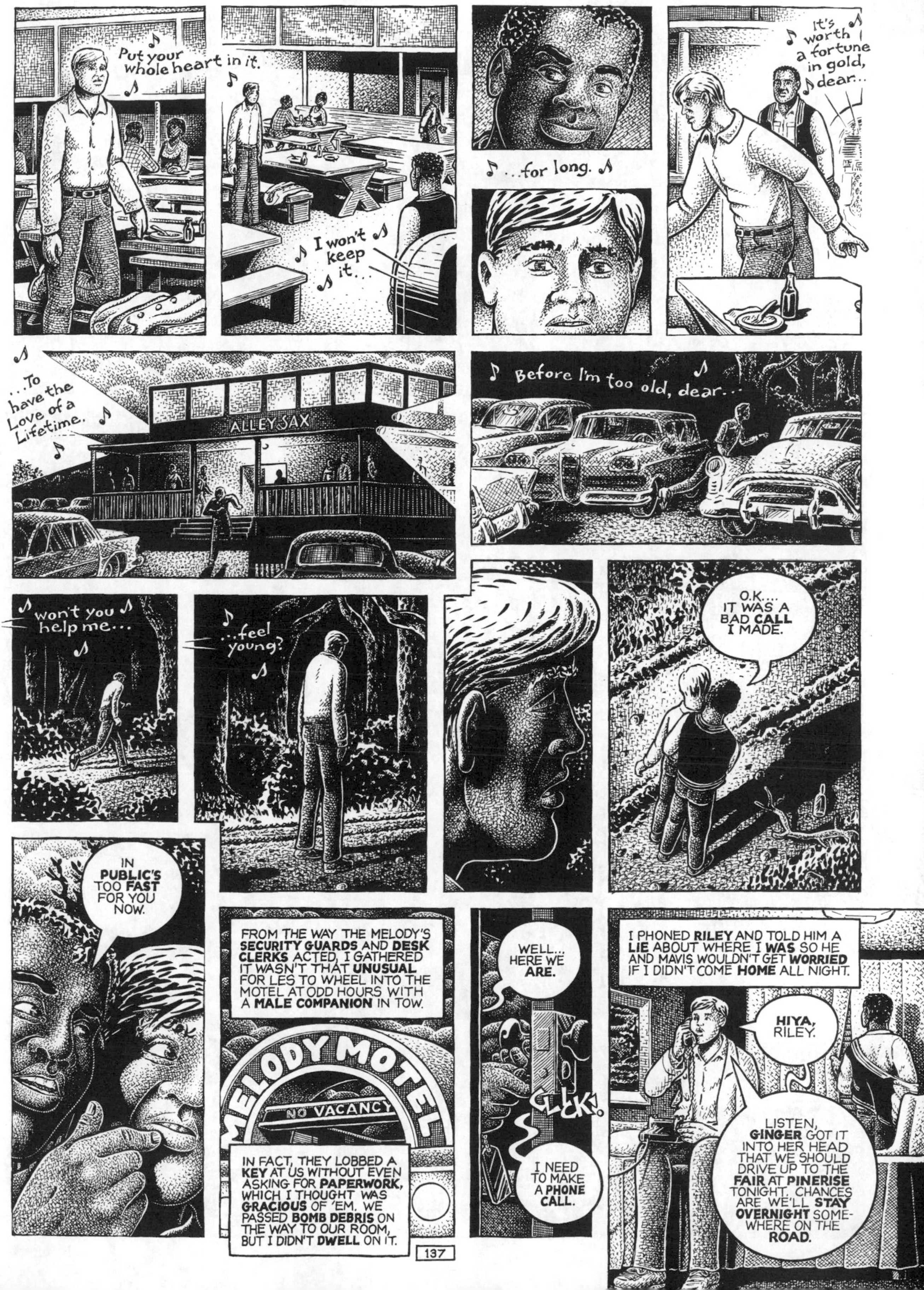
Put your whole heart in it.
I won't keep it...
...for long.
It's worth a fortune in gold, dear...
...To have the Love of a Lifetime.
ALLEY SAX
Before I'm too old, dear...
won't you help me...
...feel young?
O.K.... IT WAS A BAD CALL I MADE.
IN PUBLIC'S TOO FAST FOR YOU NOW.
FROM THE WAY THE MELODY'S SECURITY GUARDS AND DESK CLERKS ACTED, I GATHERED IT WASN'T THAT UNUSUAL FOR LES TO WHEEL INTO THE MOTEL AT ODD HOURS WITH A MALE COMPANION IN TOW.
MELODY MOTEL
NO VACANCY
IN FACT, THEY LOBBED A KEY AT US WITHOUT EVEN ASKING FOR PAPERWORK, WHICH I THOUGHT WAS GRACIOUS OF 'EM. WE PASSED BOMB DEBRIS ON THE WAY TO OUR ROOM, BUT I DIDN'T DWELL ON IT.
WELL... HERE WE ARE.
CLICK!
I NEED TO MAKE A PHONE CALL.
I PHONED RILEY AND TOLD HIM A LIE ABOUT WHERE I WAS SO HE AND MAVIS WOULDN'T GET WORRIED IF I DIDN'T COME HOME ALL NIGHT.
HIYA, RILEY.
LISTEN, GINGER GOT IT INTO HER HEAD THAT WE SHOULD DRIVE UP TO THE FAIR AT PINERISE TONIGHT. CHANCES ARE WE'LL STAY OVERNIGHT SOME-WHERE ON THE ROAD.

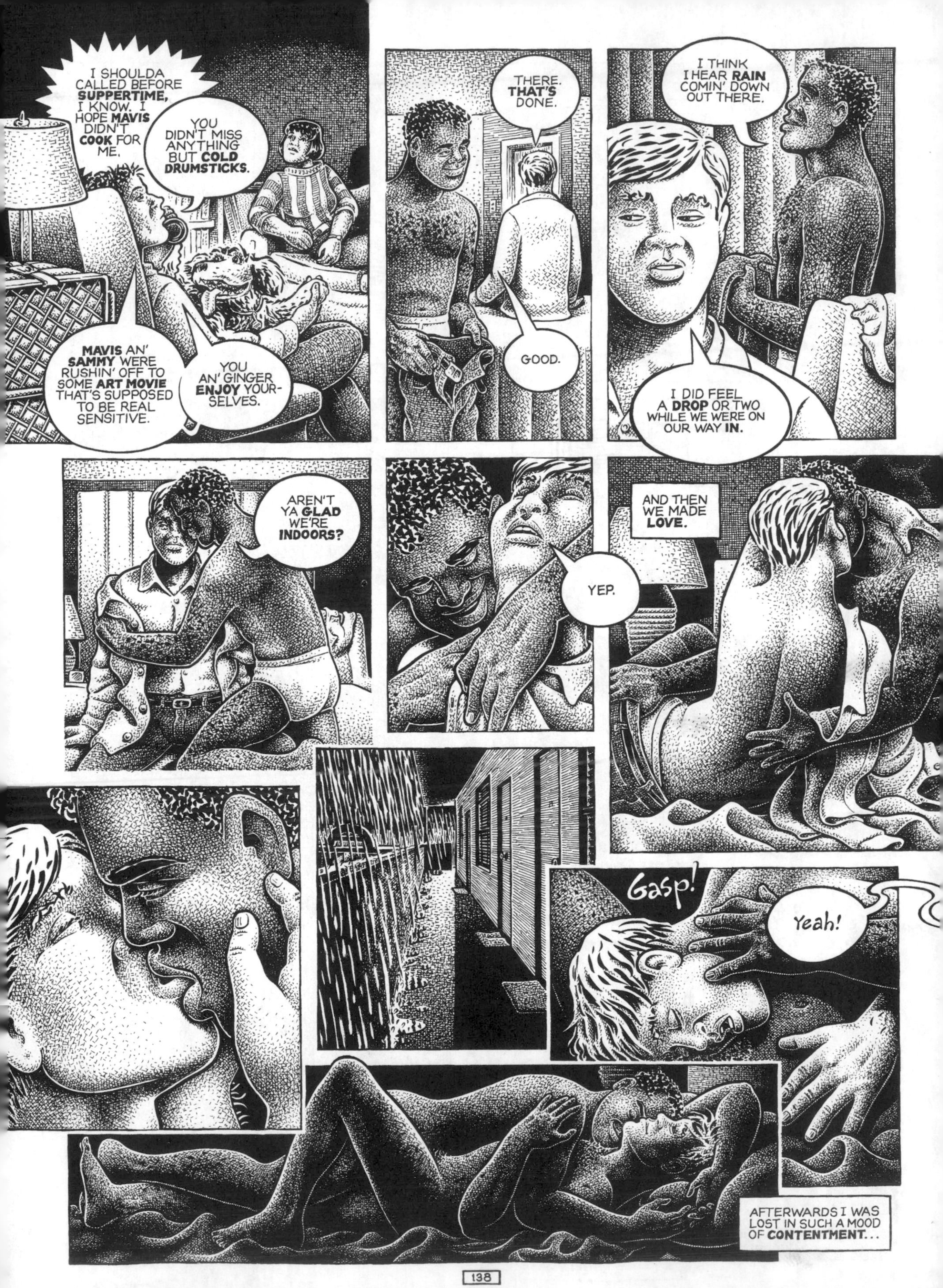

I SHOULDA CALLED BEFORE SUPPERTIME, I KNOW. I HOPE MAVIS DIDN'T COOK FOR ME.
YOU DIDN'T MISS ANYTHING BUT COLD DRUMSTICKS.
MAVIS AN' SAMMY WERE RUSHIN' OFF TO SOME ART MOVIE THAT'S SUPPOSED TO BE REAL SENSITIVE.
YOU AN' GINGER ENJOY YOURSELVES.
THERE. THAT'S DONE.
GOOD.
I THINK I HEAR RAIN COMIN' DOWN OUT THERE.
I DID FEEL A DROP OR TWO WHILE WE WERE ON OUR WAY IN.
AREN'T YA GLAD WE'RE INDOORS?
YEP.
AND THEN WE MADE LOVE.
Gasp!
Yeah!
AFTERWARDS I WAS LOST IN SUCH A MOOD OF CONTENTMENT...

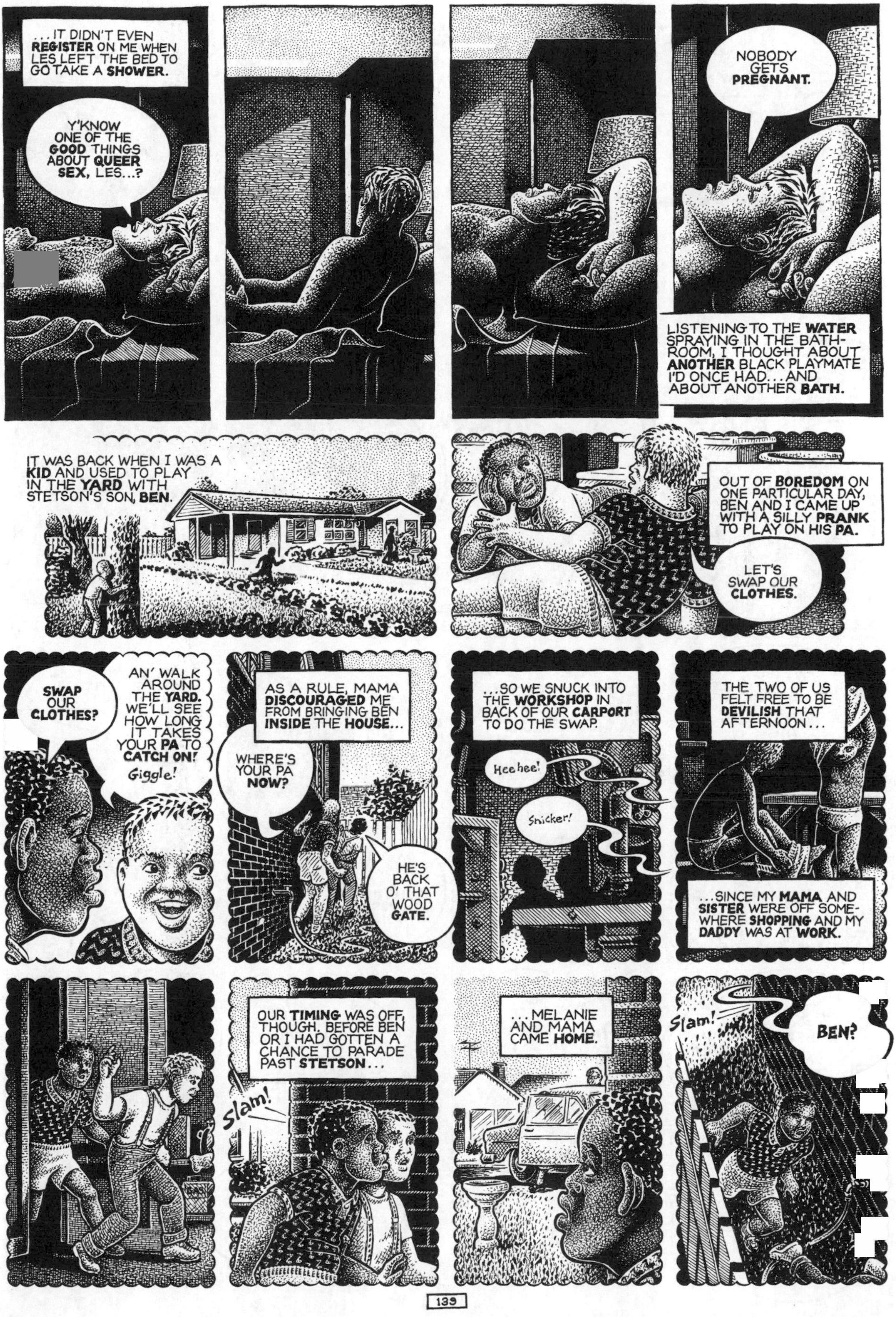
...IT DIDN'T EVEN REGISTER ON ME WHEN LES LEFT THE BED TO GO TAKE A SHOWER.
Y'KNOW ONE OF THE GOOD THINGS ABOUT QUEER SEX, LES...?
NOBODY GETS PREGNANT.
LISTENING TO THE WATER SPRAYING IN THE BATH-ROOM, I THOUGHT ABOUT ANOTHER BLACK PLAYMATE I'D ONCE HAD... AND ABOUT ANOTHER BATH.
IT WAS BACK WHEN I WAS A KID AND USED TO PLAY IN THE YARD WITH STETSON'S SON, BEN.
OUT OF BOREDOM ON ONE PARTICULAR DAY, BEN AND I CAME UP WITH A SILLY PRANK TO PLAY ON HIS PA.
LET'S SWAP OUR CLOTHES.
SWAP OUR CLOTHES?
AN' WALK AROUND THE YARD. WE'LL SEE HOW LONG IT TAKES YOUR PA TO CATCH ON! Giggle!
AS A RULE, MAMA DISCOURAGED ME FROM BRINGING BEN INSIDE THE HOUSE...
WHERE'S YOUR PA NOW?
HE'S BACK O' THAT WOOD GATE.
...SO WE SNUCK INTO THE WORKSHOP IN BACK OF OUR CARPORT TO DO THE SWAP.
Hee hee!
Snicker!
THE TWO OF US FELT FREE TO BE DEVILISH THAT AFTERNOON...
...SINCE MY MAMA AND SISTER WERE OFF SOME-WHERE SHOPPING AND MY DADDY WAS AT WORK.
OUR TIMING WAS OFF, THOUGH. BEFORE BEN OR I HAD GOTTEN A CHANCE TO PARADE PAST STETSON...
Slam!
...MELANIE AND MAMA CAME HOME.
Slam!
BEN?

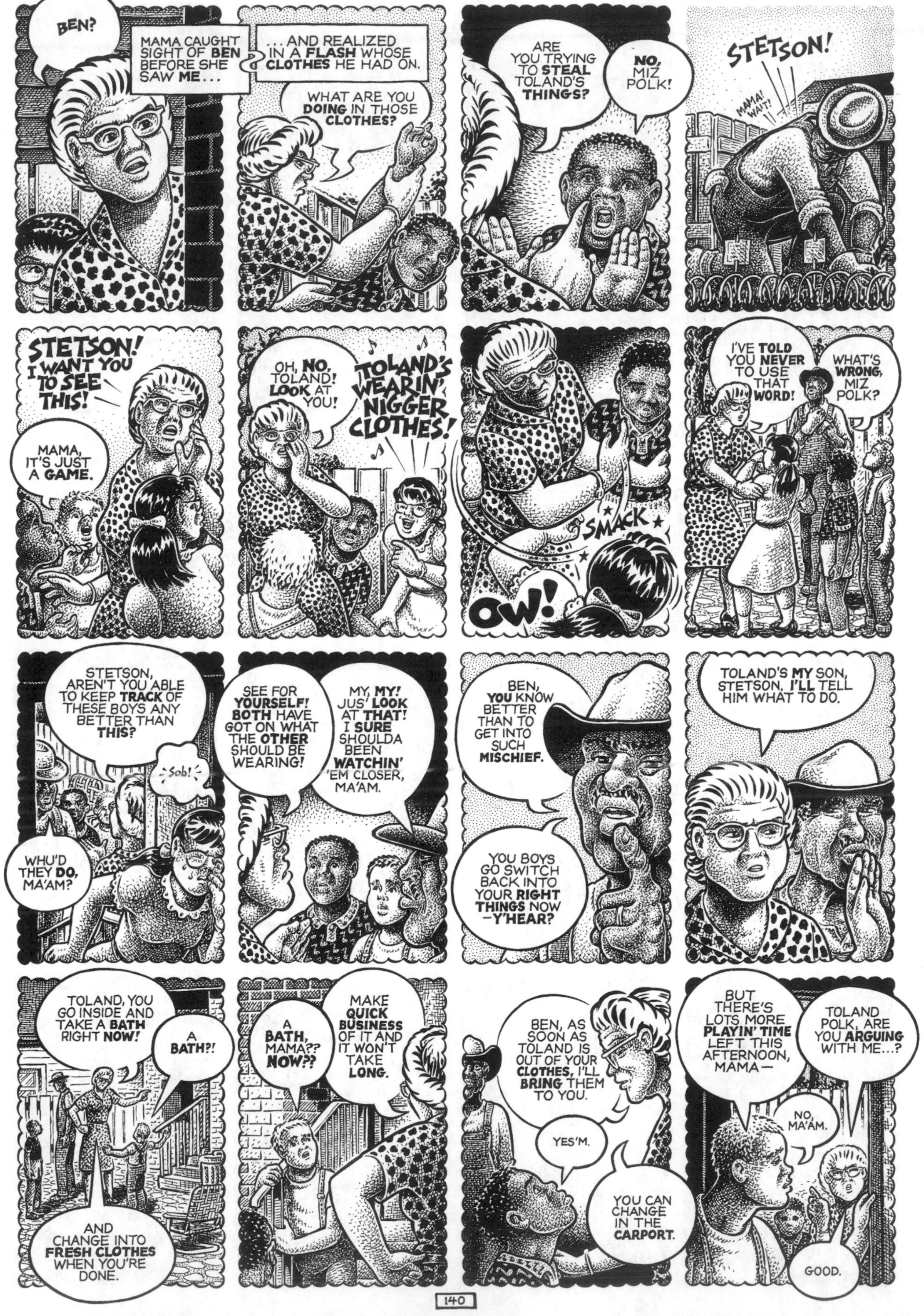

BEN?
MAMA CAUGHT SIGHT OF BEN BEFORE SHE SAW ME . . .
. . . AND REALIZED IN A FLASH WHOSE CLOTHES HE HAD ON.
WHAT ARE YOU DOING IN THOSE CLOTHES?
ARE YOU TRYING TO STEAL TOLAND'S THINGS?
NO, MIZ POLK!
STETSON!
MAMA! WAIT!
STETSON! I WANT YOU TO SEE THIS!
MAMA, IT'S JUST A GAME.
OH, NO, TOLAND! LOOK AT YOU!
TOLAND'S WEARIN' NIGGER CLOTHES!
SMACK
OW!
I'VE TOLD YOU NEVER TO USE THAT WORD!
WHAT'S WRONG, MIZ POLK?
STETSON, AREN'T YOU ABLE TO KEEP TRACK OF THESE BOYS ANY BETTER THAN THIS?
Sob!
WHU'D THEY DO, MA'AM?
SEE FOR YOURSELF! BOTH HAVE GOT ON WHAT THE OTHER SHOULD BE WEARING!
MY, MY! JUS' LOOK AT THAT! I SURE SHOULDA BEEN WATCHIN' 'EM CLOSER, MA'AM.
BEN, YOU KNOW BETTER THAN TO GET INTO SUCH MISCHIEF.
YOU BOYS GO SWITCH BACK INTO YOUR RIGHT THINGS NOW —Y'HEAR?
TOLAND'S MY SON, STETSON. I'LL TELL HIM WHAT TO DO.
TOLAND, YOU GO INSIDE AND TAKE A BATH RIGHT NOW!
A BATH?!
AND CHANGE INTO FRESH CLOTHES WHEN YOU'RE DONE.
A BATH, MAMA?? NOW??
MAKE QUICK BUSINESS OF IT AND IT WON'T TAKE LONG.
BEN, AS SOON AS TOLAND IS OUT OF YOUR CLOTHES, I'LL BRING THEM TO YOU.
YES'M.
YOU CAN CHANGE IN THE CARPORT.
BUT THERE'S LOTS MORE PLAYIN' TIME LEFT THIS AFTERNOON, MAMA—
TOLAND POLK, ARE YOU ARGUING WITH ME...?
NO, MA'AM.
GOOD.

SCRUB YOURSELF GOOD. THEN YOU CAN PLAY WITH BEN SOME MORE.
IT WAS CONFUSING.
I COULDN'T SEE WHERE ALL THE URGENCY WAS COMING FROM.
WHY DID I HAVE TO TAKE A BATH THAT VERY MINUTE?
WHY WAS IT SO IMPORTANT?
MAMA....
SSSSSSSSSSSSSSSSSSSSSS...
WELL... LOOK WHO'S HERE.
LET'S RUB A LITTLE SOAP ON THIS WHITE BOY'S SKIN.

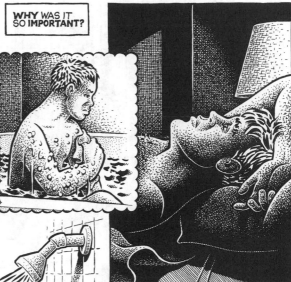

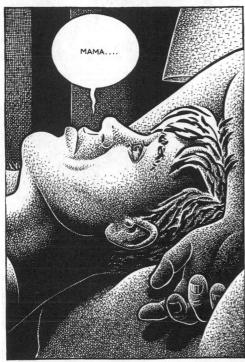

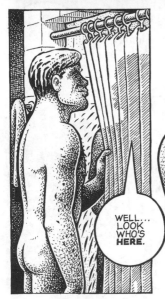

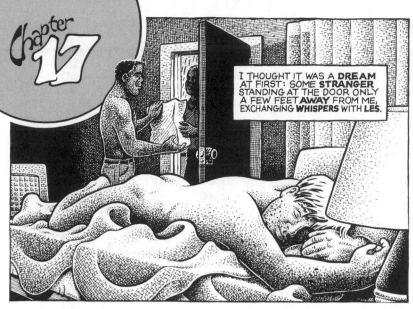

I THOUGHT IT WAS A **DREAM** AT FIRST: SOME **STRANGER** STANDING AT THE DOOR ONLY A FEW FEET **AWAY** FROM ME, EXCHANGING **WHISPERS** WITH **LES.**

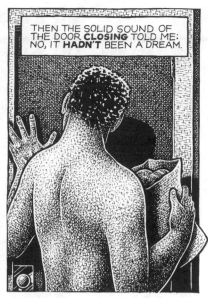

THEN THE SOLID SOUND OF THE DOOR **CLOSING** TOLD ME: NO, IT **HADN'T** BEEN A DREAM.

I WAS **EMBARRASSED,** REALIZING I'D BEEN RIGHT THERE IN FULL **VIEW** THE WHOLE **TIME,** NAKED ON A CLUMP OF TANGLED **BEDSHEETS.**

BUT IT DIDN'T SEEM TO HAVE BOTHERED **LES,** SO I FIGURED, WHAT THE **HELL!**

MORNING **LIGHT** WAS WARMING MY **EYELIDS,** BUT I KEPT THEM SHUT AND TRIED TO GO BACK TO **SLEEP.** I WANTED MORE OF THE DREAMS I'D BEEN HAVING **EARLIER.**

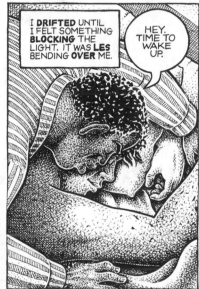

I **DRIFTED** UNTIL I FELT SOMETHING **BLOCKING** THE LIGHT. IT WAS **LES** BENDING **OVER** ME.

HEY. TIME TO WAKE UP.

Whoops!

C'MERE. BACK TO **BED.**

MAN! LOOK AT SLEEPIN' BEAUTY GET WIDE AWAKE **FAST!**

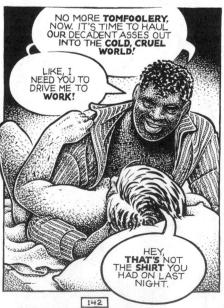

NO MORE **TOMFOOLERY,** NOW. IT'S TIME TO HAUL OUR DECADENT ASSES OUT INTO THE **COLD, CRUEL WORLD!**

LIKE, I NEED YOU TO DRIVE ME TO **WORK!**

HEY, **THAT'S** NOT THE **SHIRT** YOU HAD ON LAST NIGHT.

WHERE'D YOU GET A CHANGE OF **CLOTHES?**

MY FRIEND **RUPE** WAS JUST HERE.

HE LOOKS **OUT** FOR ME WHEN THESE **'SPECIAL OCCASIONS'** ARISE.

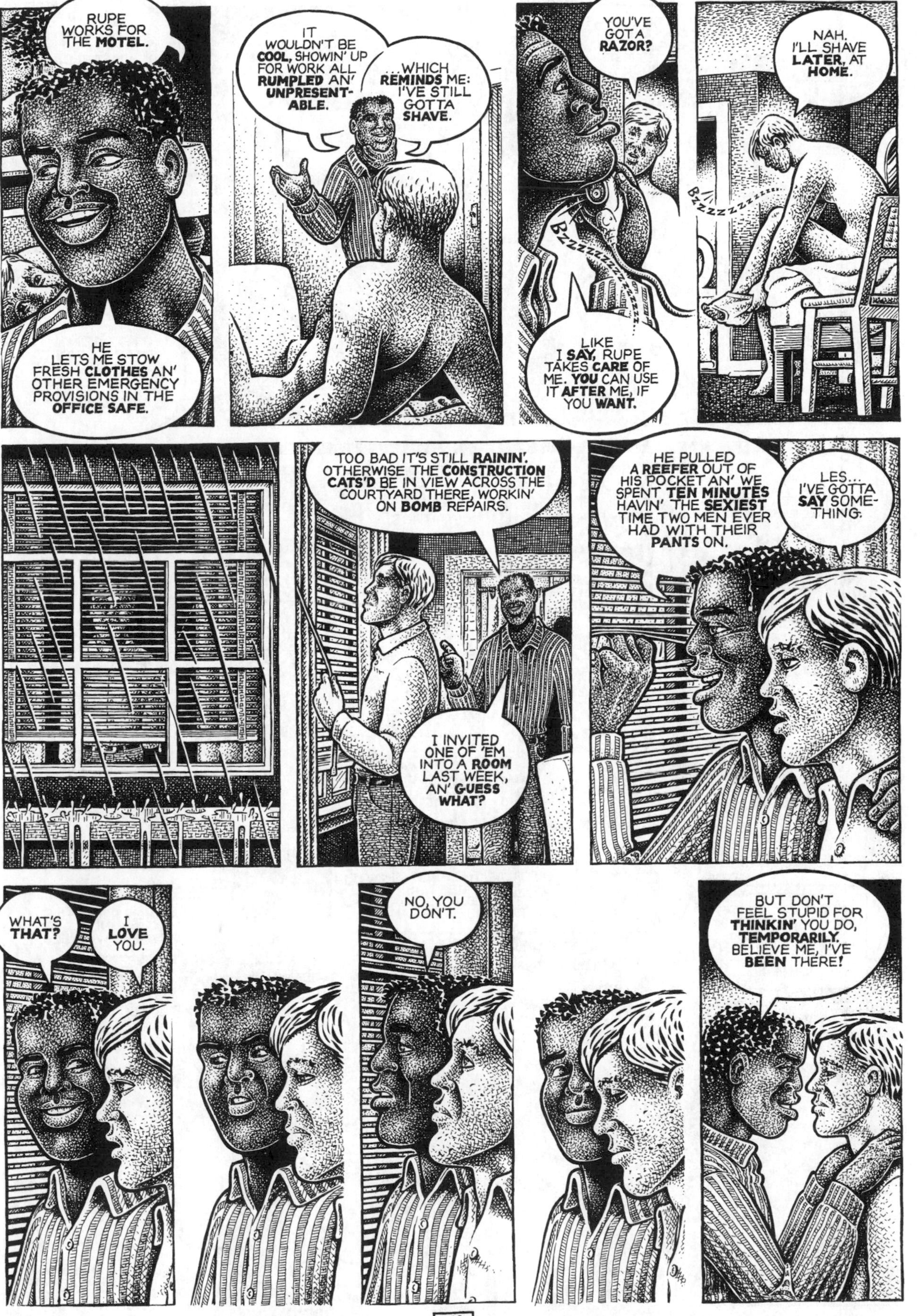

RUPE WORKS FOR THE MOTEL.
HE LETS ME STOW FRESH CLOTHES AN' OTHER EMERGENCY PROVISIONS IN THE OFFICE SAFE.
IT WOULDN'T BE COOL, SHOWIN' UP FOR WORK ALL RUMPLED AN' UNPRESENT-ABLE.
...WHICH REMINDS ME: I'VE STILL GOTTA SHAVE.
YOU'VE GOT A RAZOR?
BZZZZZZZZZZZZZZ
LIKE I SAY, RUPE TAKES CARE OF ME. YOU CAN USE IT AFTER ME, IF YOU WANT.
NAH. I'LL SHAVE LATER, AT HOME.
BZZZZZZZZ
TOO BAD IT'S STILL RAININ'. OTHERWISE THE CONSTRUCTION CATS'D BE IN VIEW ACROSS THE COURTYARD THERE, WORKIN' ON BOMB REPAIRS.
I INVITED ONE OF 'EM INTO A ROOM LAST WEEK, AN' GUESS WHAT?
HE PULLED A REEFER OUT OF HIS POCKET AN' WE SPENT TEN MINUTES HAVIN' THE SEXIEST TIME TWO MEN EVER HAD WITH THEIR PANTS ON.
LES... I'VE GOTTA SAY SOME-THING.
WHAT'S THAT?
I LOVE YOU.
NO, YOU DON'T.
BUT DON'T FEEL STUPID FOR THINKIN' YOU DO, TEMPORARILY. BELIEVE ME, I'VE BEEN THERE!

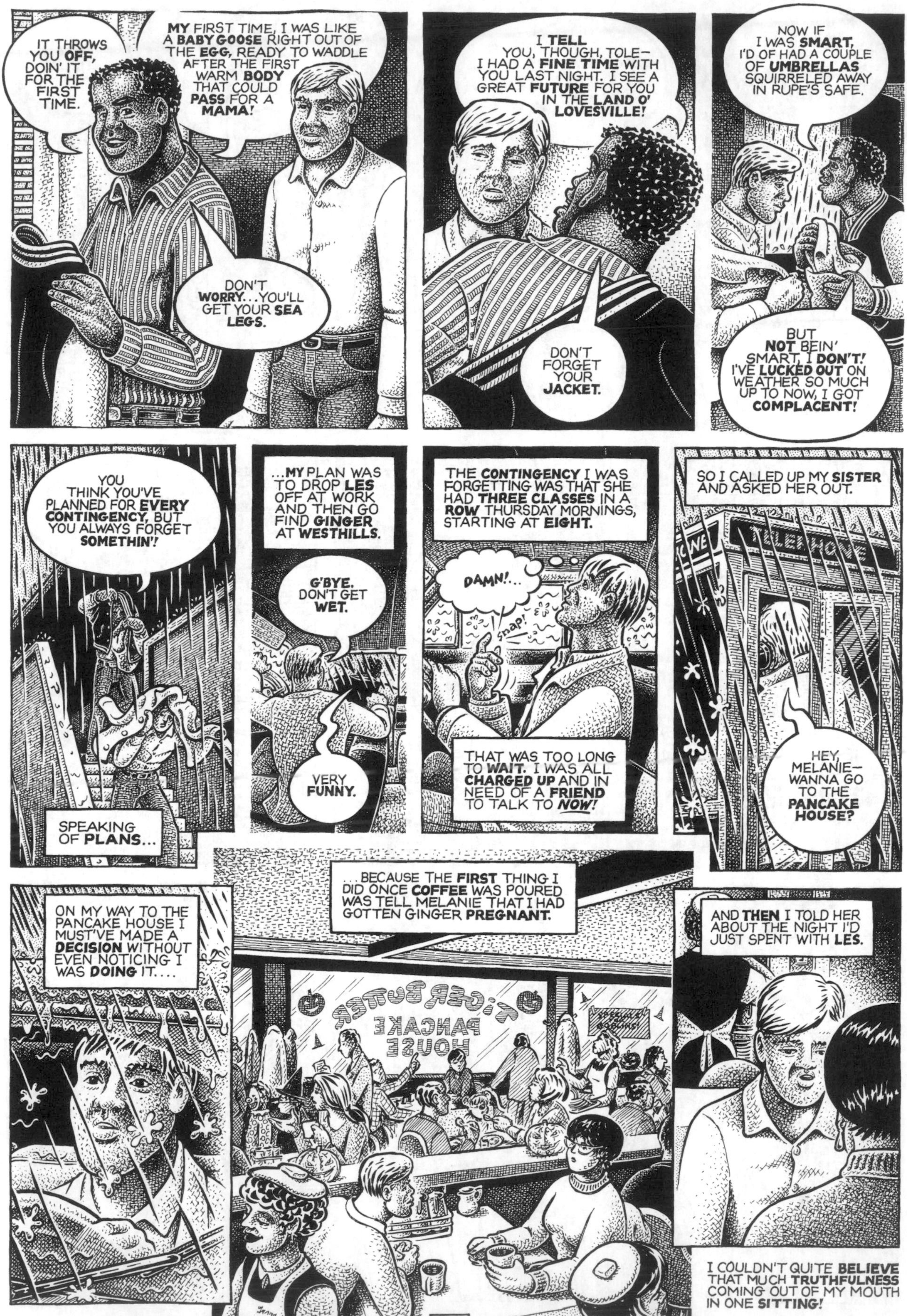
IT THROWS YOU OFF, DOIN' IT FOR THE FIRST TIME.
MY FIRST TIME, I WAS LIKE A BABY GOOSE RIGHT OUT OF THE EGG, READY TO WADDLE AFTER THE FIRST WARM BODY THAT COULD PASS FOR A MAMA!
DON'T WORRY... YOU'LL GET YOUR SEA LEGS.
I TELL YOU, THOUGH, TOLE— I HAD A FINE TIME WITH YOU LAST NIGHT. I SEE A GREAT FUTURE FOR YOU IN THE LAND O' LOVESVILLE!
DON'T FORGET YOUR JACKET.
NOW IF I WAS SMART, I'D OF HAD A COUPLE OF UMBRELLAS SQUIRRELED AWAY IN RUPE'S SAFE.
BUT NOT BEIN' SMART, I DON'T! I'VE LUCKED OUT ON WEATHER SO MUCH UP TO NOW, I GOT COMPLACENT!
YOU THINK YOU'VE PLANNED FOR EVERY CONTINGENCY, BUT YOU ALWAYS FORGET SOMETHIN'!
SPEAKING OF PLANS...
...MY PLAN WAS TO DROP LES OFF AT WORK AND THEN GO FIND GINGER AT WESTHILLS.
G'BYE. DON'T GET WET.
VERY FUNNY.
THE CONTINGENCY I WAS FORGETTING WAS THAT SHE HAD THREE CLASSES IN A ROW THURSDAY MORNINGS, STARTING AT EIGHT.
DAMN!...
SNAP!
THAT WAS TOO LONG TO WAIT. I WAS ALL CHARGED UP AND IN NEED OF A FRIEND TO TALK TO NOW!
SO I CALLED UP MY SISTER AND ASKED HER OUT.
TELEPHONE
HEY, MELANIE— WANNA GO TO THE PANCAKE HOUSE?
ON MY WAY TO THE PANCAKE HOUSE I MUST'VE MADE A DECISION WITHOUT EVEN NOTICING I WAS DOING IT....
...BECAUSE THE FIRST THING I DID ONCE COFFEE WAS POURED WAS TELL MELANIE THAT I HAD GOTTEN GINGER PREGNANT.
TIGER BUTTER PANCAKE HOUSE
AND THEN I TOLD HER ABOUT THE NIGHT I'D JUST SPENT WITH LES.
I COULDN'T QUITE BELIEVE THAT MUCH TRUTHFULNESS COMING OUT OF MY MOUTH IN ONE SITTING!

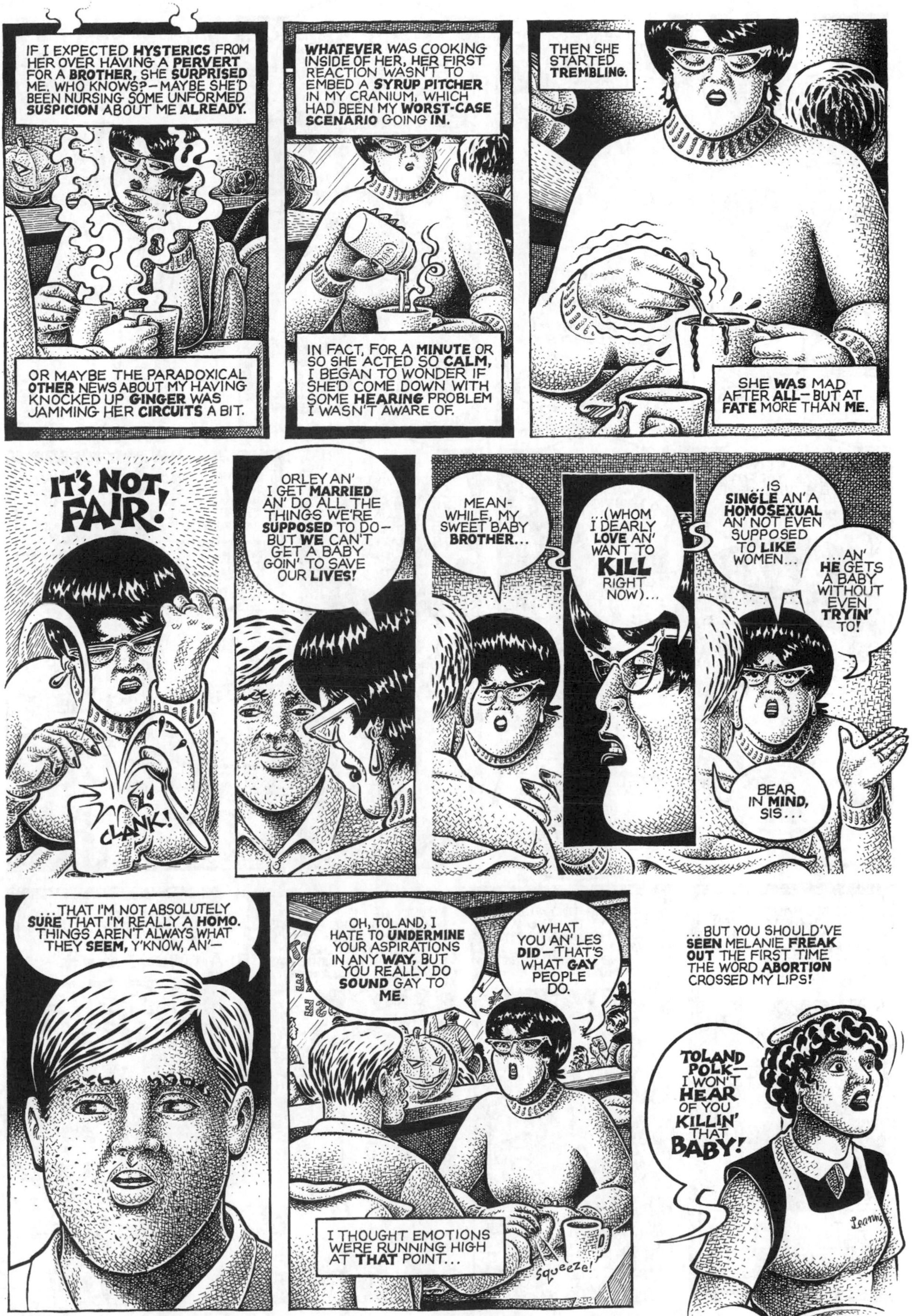

IF I EXPECTED **HYSTERICS** FROM HER OVER HAVING A **PERVERT** FOR A **BROTHER**, SHE **SURPRISED** ME. WHO KNOWS?—MAYBE SHE'D BEEN NURSING SOME UNFORMED **SUSPICION** ABOUT ME **ALREADY.**
OR MAYBE THE PARADOXICAL **OTHER** NEWS ABOUT MY HAVING KNOCKED UP **GINGER** WAS JAMMING HER **CIRCUITS** A BIT.
WHATEVER WAS COOKING INSIDE OF HER, HER FIRST REACTION WASN'T TO EMBED A **SYRUP PITCHER** IN MY CRANIUM, WHICH HAD BEEN MY **WORST-CASE SCENARIO** GOING **IN.**
IN FACT, FOR A **MINUTE** OR SO SHE ACTED SO **CALM**, I BEGAN TO WONDER IF SHE'D COME DOWN WITH SOME **HEARING** PROBLEM I WASN'T AWARE OF.
THEN SHE STARTED **TREMBLING.**
SHE **WAS** MAD AFTER **ALL**—BUT AT **FATE** MORE THAN **ME.**
IT'S NOT FAIR!
CLANK!
ORLEY AN' I GET **MARRIED** AN' DO ALL THE THINGS WE'RE **SUPPOSED** TO DO—BUT **WE** CAN'T GET A BABY GOIN' TO SAVE OUR **LIVES!**
MEAN-WHILE, MY SWEET BABY **BROTHER...**
...(WHOM I DEARLY **LOVE** AN' WANT TO **KILL** RIGHT NOW)...
...IS **SINGLE** AN' A **HOMOSEXUAL** AN' NOT EVEN SUPPOSED TO **LIKE** WOMEN...
...AN' **HE** GETS A BABY WITHOUT EVEN **TRYIN'** TO!
BEAR IN **MIND,** SIS...
...THAT I'M NOT ABSOLUTELY **SURE** THAT I'M REALLY A **HOMO.** THINGS AREN'T ALWAYS WHAT THEY **SEEM,** Y'KNOW, AN'—
OH, TOLAND, I HATE TO **UNDERMINE** YOUR ASPIRATIONS IN ANY **WAY,** BUT YOU REALLY DO **SOUND** GAY TO **ME.**
WHAT YOU AN' LES **DID**—THAT'S WHAT **GAY** PEOPLE DO.
I THOUGHT EMOTIONS WERE RUNNING HIGH AT **THAT** POINT...
squeeze!
...BUT YOU SHOULD'VE **SEEN** MELANIE **FREAK OUT** THE FIRST TIME THE WORD **ABORTION** CROSSED MY LIPS!
TOLAND POLK—I WON'T **HEAR** OF YOU **KILLIN'** THAT **BABY!**

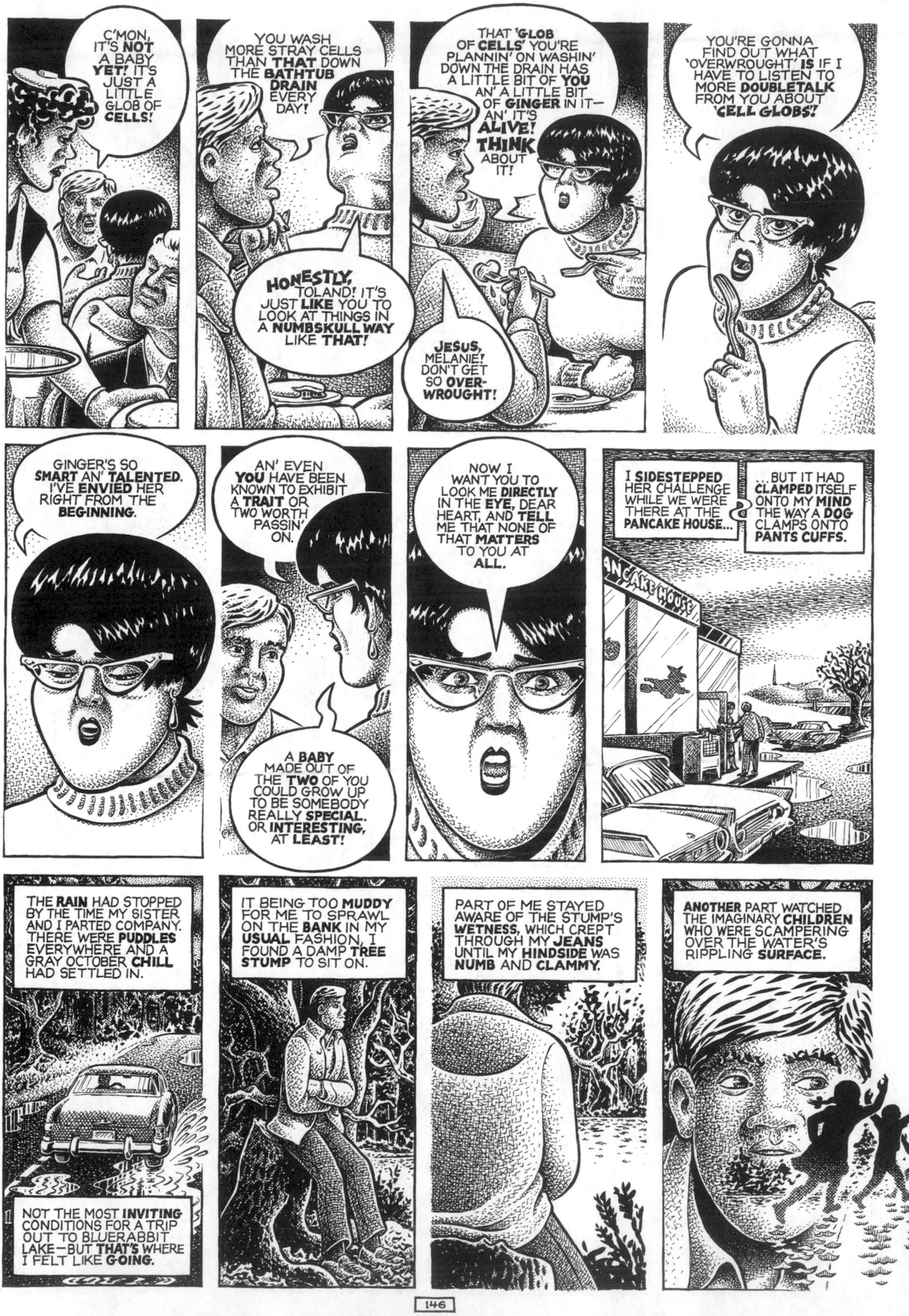

C'MON, IT'S NOT A BABY YET! IT'S JUST A LITTLE GLOB OF CELLS!
YOU WASH MORE STRAY CELLS THAN THAT DOWN THE BATHTUB DRAIN EVERY DAY!
HONESTLY, TOLAND! IT'S JUST LIKE YOU TO LOOK AT THINGS IN A NUMBSKULL WAY LIKE THAT!
THAT 'GLOB OF CELLS' YOU'RE PLANNIN' ON WASHIN' DOWN THE DRAIN HAS A LITTLE BIT OF YOU AN' A LITTLE BIT OF GINGER IN IT— AN' IT'S ALIVE! THINK ABOUT IT!
JESUS, MELANIE! DON'T GET SO OVERWROUGHT!
YOU'RE GONNA FIND OUT WHAT 'OVERWROUGHT' IS IF I HAVE TO LISTEN TO MORE DOUBLETALK FROM YOU ABOUT 'CELL GLOBS'!
GINGER'S SO SMART AN' TALENTED. I'VE ENVIED HER RIGHT FROM THE BEGINNING.
AN' EVEN YOU HAVE BEEN KNOWN TO EXHIBIT A TRAIT OR TWO WORTH PASSIN' ON.
A BABY MADE OUT OF THE TWO OF YOU COULD GROW UP TO BE SOMEBODY REALLY SPECIAL. OR INTERESTING, AT LEAST!
NOW I WANT YOU TO LOOK ME DIRECTLY IN THE EYE, DEAR HEART, AND TELL ME THAT NONE OF THAT MATTERS TO YOU AT ALL.
I SIDESTEPPED HER CHALLENGE WHILE WE WERE THERE AT THE PANCAKE HOUSE...
&
...BUT IT HAD CLAMPED ITSELF ONTO MY MIND THE WAY A DOG CLAMPS ONTO PANTS CUFFS.
ANCAKE HOUSE
THE RAIN HAD STOPPED BY THE TIME MY SISTER AND I PARTED COMPANY. THERE WERE PUDDLES EVERYWHERE AND A GRAY OCTOBER CHILL HAD SETTLED IN.
NOT THE MOST INVITING CONDITIONS FOR A TRIP OUT TO BLUERABBIT LAKE—BUT THAT'S WHERE I FELT LIKE GOING.
IT BEING TOO MUDDY FOR ME TO SPRAWL ON THE BANK IN MY USUAL FASHION, I FOUND A DAMP TREE STUMP TO SIT ON.
PART OF ME STAYED AWARE OF THE STUMP'S WETNESS, WHICH CREPT THROUGH MY JEANS UNTIL MY HINDSIDE WAS NUMB AND CLAMMY.
ANOTHER PART WATCHED THE IMAGINARY CHILDREN WHO WERE SCAMPERING OVER THE WATER'S RIPPLING SURFACE.

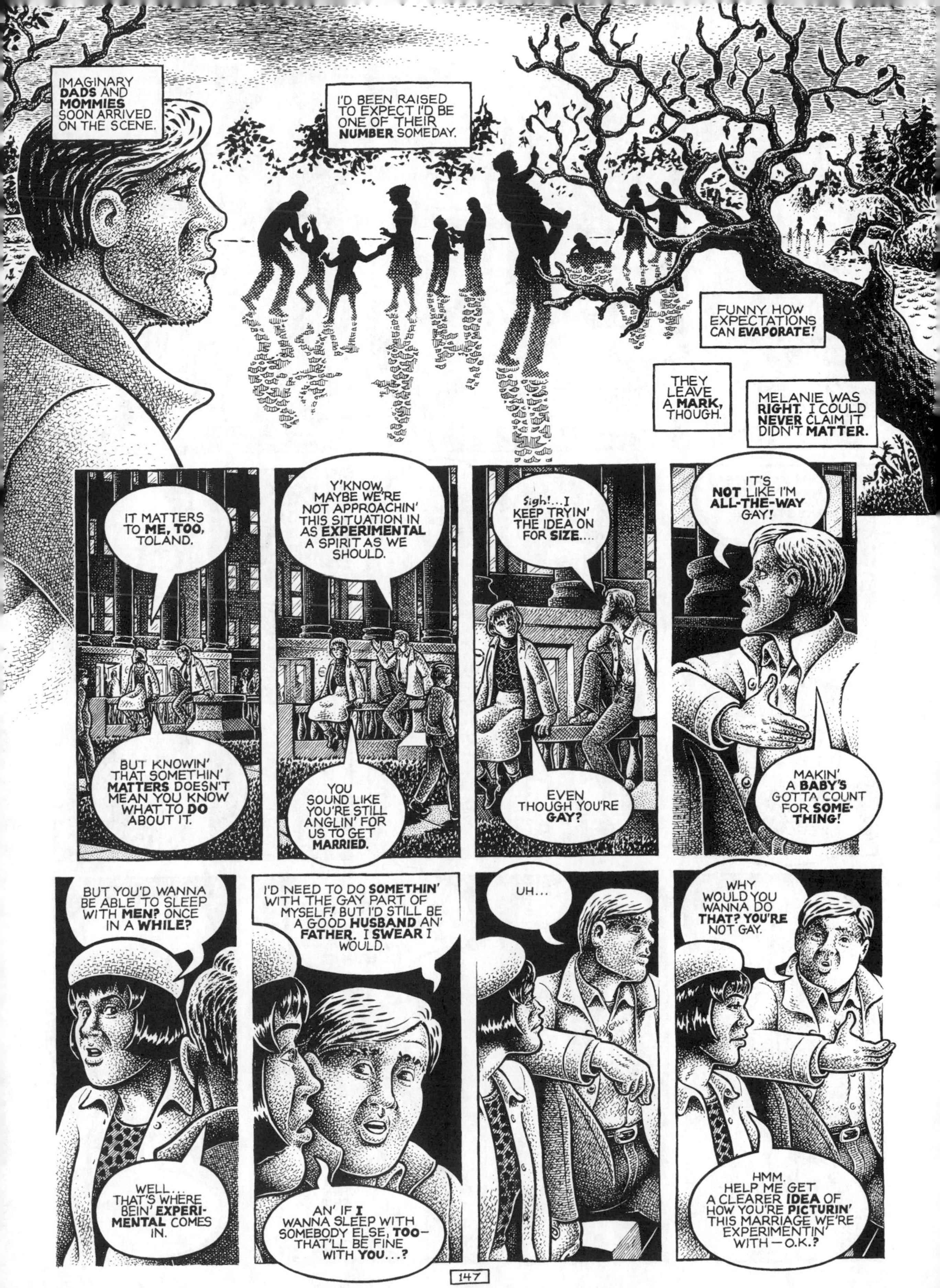

IMAGINARY DADS AND MOMMIES SOON ARRIVED ON THE SCENE.
I'D BEEN RAISED TO EXPECT I'D BE ONE OF THEIR NUMBER SOMEDAY.
FUNNY HOW EXPECTATIONS CAN EVAPORATE!
THEY LEAVE A MARK, THOUGH.
MELANIE WAS RIGHT. I COULD NEVER CLAIM IT DIDN'T MATTER.
IT MATTERS TO ME, TOO, TOLAND.
BUT KNOWIN' THAT SOMETHIN' MATTERS DOESN'T MEAN YOU KNOW WHAT TO DO ABOUT IT.
Y'KNOW, MAYBE WE'RE NOT APPROACHIN' THIS SITUATION IN AS EXPERIMENTAL A SPIRIT AS WE SHOULD.
YOU SOUND LIKE YOU'RE STILL ANGLIN' FOR US TO GET MARRIED.
Sigh!... I KEEP TRYIN' THE IDEA ON FOR SIZE...
EVEN THOUGH YOU'RE GAY?
IT'S NOT LIKE I'M ALL-THE-WAY GAY!
MAKIN' A BABY'S GOTTA COUNT FOR SOME-THING!
BUT YOU'D WANNA BE ABLE TO SLEEP WITH MEN? ONCE IN A WHILE?
WELL... THAT'S WHERE BEIN' EXPERI-MENTAL COMES IN.
I'D NEED TO DO SOMETHIN' WITH THE GAY PART OF MYSELF! BUT I'D STILL BE A GOOD HUSBAND AN' FATHER. I SWEAR I WOULD.
AN' IF I WANNA SLEEP WITH SOMEBODY ELSE, TOO— THAT'LL BE FINE WITH YOU...?
UH...
WHY WOULD YOU WANNA DO THAT? YOU'RE NOT GAY.
HMM. HELP ME GET A CLEARER IDEA OF HOW YOU'RE PICTURIN' THIS MARRIAGE WE'RE EXPERIMENTIN' WITH — O.K.?

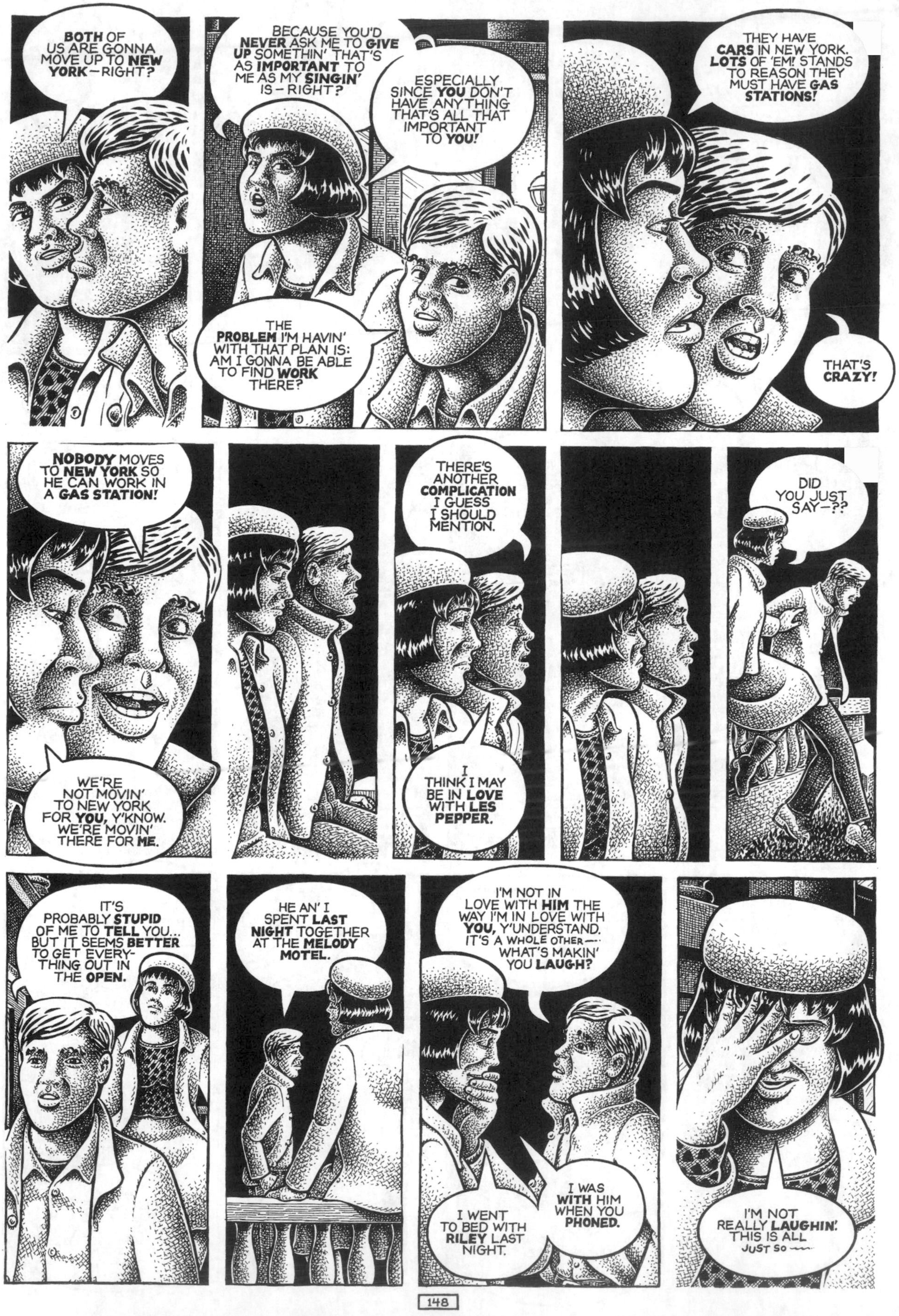
BOTH OF US ARE GONNA MOVE UP TO NEW YORK—RIGHT?
BECAUSE YOU'D NEVER ASK ME TO GIVE UP SOMETHIN' THAT'S AS IMPORTANT TO ME AS MY SINGIN' IS—RIGHT?
ESPECIALLY SINCE YOU DON'T HAVE ANYTHING THAT'S ALL THAT IMPORTANT TO YOU!
THE PROBLEM I'M HAVIN' WITH THAT PLAN IS: AM I GONNA BE ABLE TO FIND WORK THERE?
THEY HAVE CARS IN NEW YORK. LOTS OF 'EM! STANDS TO REASON THEY MUST HAVE GAS STATIONS!
THAT'S CRAZY!
NOBODY MOVES TO NEW YORK SO HE CAN WORK IN A GAS STATION!
WE'RE NOT MOVIN' TO NEW YORK FOR YOU, Y'KNOW. WE'RE MOVIN' THERE FOR ME.
THERE'S ANOTHER COMPLICATION I GUESS I SHOULD MENTION.
I THINK I MAY BE IN LOVE WITH LES PEPPER.
DID YOU JUST SAY—??
IT'S PROBABLY STUPID OF ME TO TELL YOU... BUT IT SEEMS BETTER TO GET EVERY-THING OUT IN THE OPEN.
HE AN' I SPENT LAST NIGHT TOGETHER AT THE MELODY MOTEL.
I'M NOT IN LOVE WITH HIM THE WAY I'M IN LOVE WITH YOU, Y'UNDERSTAND. IT'S A WHOLE OTHER— WHAT'S MAKIN' YOU LAUGH?
I WENT TO BED WITH RILEY LAST NIGHT.
I WAS WITH HIM WHEN YOU PHONED.
I'M NOT REALLY LAUGHIN'. THIS IS ALL JUST SO—

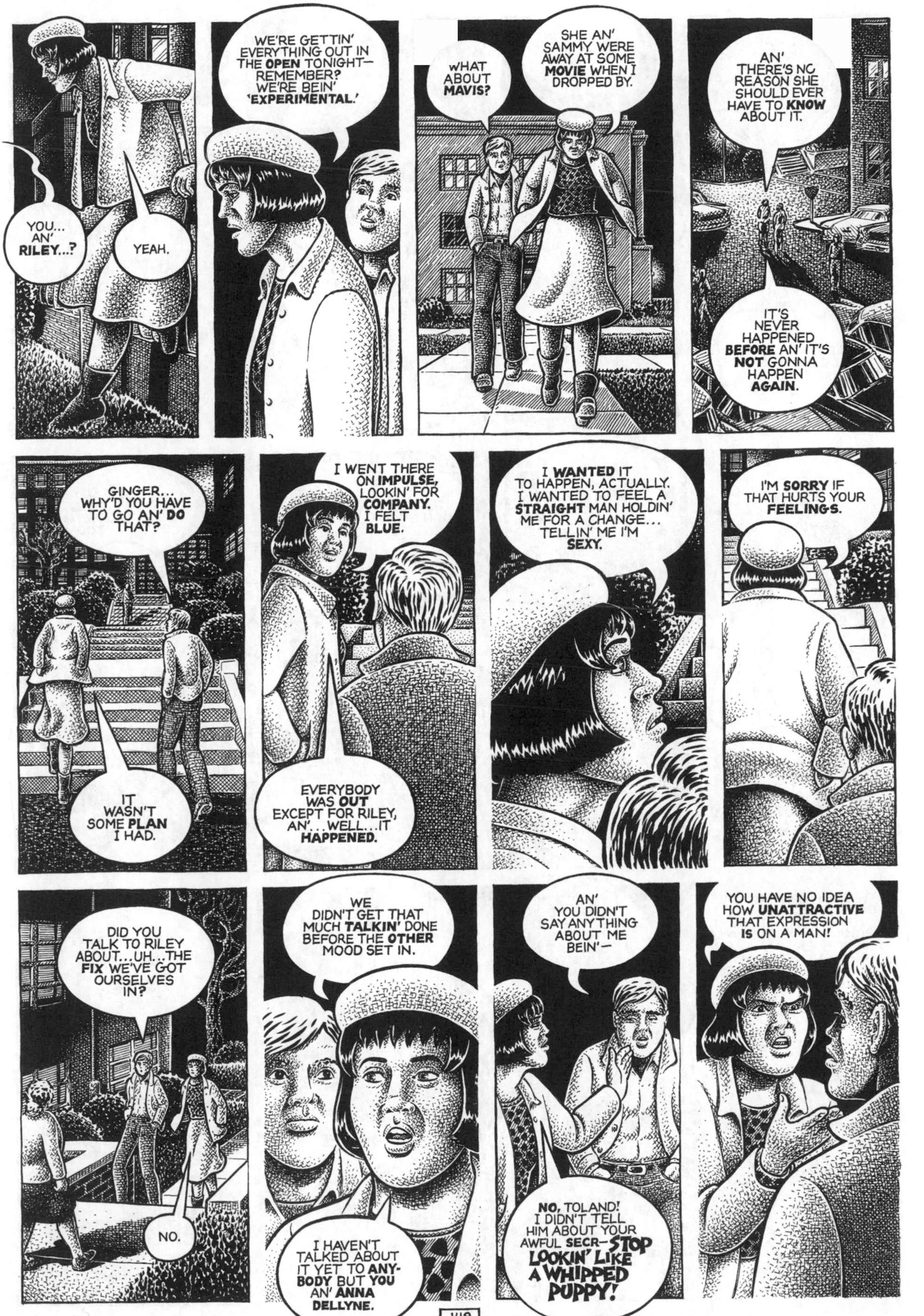
YOU... AN' RILEY...?
YEAH.
WE'RE GETTIN' EVERYTHING OUT IN THE OPEN TONIGHT— REMEMBER? WE'RE BEIN' 'EXPERIMENTAL.'
WHAT ABOUT MAVIS?
SHE AN' SAMMY WERE AWAY AT SOME MOVIE WHEN I DROPPED BY.
AN' THERE'S NO REASON SHE SHOULD EVER HAVE TO KNOW ABOUT IT.
IT'S NEVER HAPPENED BEFORE AN' IT'S NOT GONNA HAPPEN AGAIN.
GINGER... WHY'D YOU HAVE TO GO AN' DO THAT?
IT WASN'T SOME PLAN I HAD.
I WENT THERE ON IMPULSE, LOOKIN' FOR COMPANY. I FELT BLUE.
EVERYBODY WAS OUT EXCEPT FOR RILEY, AN'...WELL...IT HAPPENED.
I WANTED IT TO HAPPEN, ACTUALLY. I WANTED TO FEEL A STRAIGHT MAN HOLDIN' ME FOR A CHANGE... TELLIN' ME I'M SEXY.
I'M SORRY IF THAT HURTS YOUR FEELINGS.
DID YOU TALK TO RILEY ABOUT...UH...THE FIX WE'VE GOT OURSELVES IN?
NO.
WE DIDN'T GET THAT MUCH TALKIN' DONE BEFORE THE OTHER MOOD SET IN.
I HAVEN'T TALKED ABOUT IT YET TO ANY-BODY BUT YOU AN' ANNA DELLYNE.
AN' YOU DIDN'T SAY ANYTHING ABOUT ME BEIN'—
NO, TOLAND! I DIDN'T TELL HIM ABOUT YOUR AWFUL SECR—STOP LOOKIN' LIKE A WHIPPED PUPPY!
YOU HAVE NO IDEA HOW UNATTRACTIVE THAT EXPRESSION IS ON A MAN!

YOU WERE OUT WARMIN' THE BEDSPRINGS WITH **LES** LAST NIGHT. WHAT'VE **YOU** GOT TO COMPLAIN ABOUT?

RILEY'S MY **BEST FRIEND!**

AN' **LES** IS ONE OF **MY** BEST FRIENDS!

SO IS **MAVIS!**

AN' **SAMMY!**

WE'RE **ALL** OF US 'BEST FRIENDS' AROUND HERE!

I'M GOIN' **IN.**

GINGER— **WAIT.**

DO YOU **MIND** IF I...?

IT'S TOO **SOON** BY A **LONG** SHOT TO FEEL ANYTHING **KICKIN'.**

I KNOW. HE PROBABLY HASN'T EVEN FIGURED OUT FOR **HIMSELF** YET THAT HE **EXISTS!** OR **SHE** EXISTS.

STILL—

GO AHEAD AN' **FEEL.** WHOEVER'S **IN** THERE IS YOURS, **TOO.**

WHAT IT **REMINDS** ME OF IS TIMES I'VE LAID ON THE **GROUND** AT NIGHT, LOOKIN' UP AT THE **STARS** AN' WONDERIN' IF THERE ARE ANY **LITTLE GREEN PEOPLE** FROM **OTHER PLANETS** UP THERE.

COULD BE YOU'RE LOOKIN' ONE OF 'EM RIGHT IN THE **EYE**—BUT HE'S SO **FAR AWAY** AN' **TINY,** THERE'S NO WAY OF **KNOWIN'.**

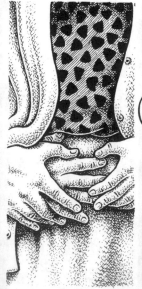

COMIN' FROM THE TWO OF **US,** THIS ONE MIGHT JUST AS **WELL** BE FROM ANOTHER PLANET!

WE'RE A **PAIR,** ALL RIGHT!

Chapter 18

THE NEXT DAY WAS A **FRIDAY,** I REMEMBER.

I WAS SITTING IN SOME MUSTY **OFFICE** WAITING FOR A **JOB INTERVIEW**...

...WHEN ALL OF A SUDDEN VARIOUS **NEURONS** FROM ASSORTED SECTORS OF MY **BRAIN** OPENED **FIRE** ON EACH OTHER....

AND I KNEW THAT LES WAS **RIGHT:** I **WASN'T** IN LOVE WITH HIM.

NOT **HIM** IN PARTICULAR!

SOME **EMOTIONS** I DIDN'T **UNDERSTAND** TOOK HOLD OF ME...

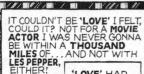

MR. POLK...?

...AND I **BOLTED** OUT THE **DOOR.**

THE **MAGAZINE** I'D BEEN LEAFING THROUGH HAD HAD A PHOTOGRAPH OF **SAL MINEO** IN IT.

WHICH REMINDED ME OF THE NIGHT I'D GONE TO SEE **'REBEL WITHOUT A CAUSE'** A FEW YEARS BACK...

...AND COME HOME UNABLE TO THINK ABOUT **ANYTHING** EXCEPT WANTING TO HOLD JAMES DEAN'S DARK-EYED FRIEND IN MY **ARMS** AND **COMFORT** HIM.

IT COULDN'T BE **'LOVE'** I FELT, COULD IT? NOT FOR A **MOVIE ACTOR** I WAS NEVER GONNA BE WITHIN A **THOUSAND MILES** OF... AND NOT WITH **LES PEPPER,** EITHER!

'LOVE' HAD TO BE SOME-THING **ELSE!**

SOMETHING YOU COULD FIT INTO **SONG** LYRICS AND **DANCE** TO!

WHAT I WAS FEELING WAS A YEARNING **ACHE** THAT HAD TO DO WITH **MORE** THAN SOME **ONE GUY** I'D HAD MY ARMS AROUND IN A **MOTEL.**

I SAT ON MY **CAR FENDER** AND WATCHED THE RUSH HOUR **TRAFFIC** BUILD.

A PERSON COULD **HOP** RIGHT OUT INTO THE **MIDDLE** OF IT IF HE WANTED TO.

ONE WELL-TIMED **CARTWHEEL** AND IT'D BE: **HELLO-O-O, OBLIVION!**

I WASN'T LOOKING **FORWARD** TO DRIVING BACK TO THE **WHEELERY.**

NOTHING THERE WAS THE WAY IT **USED** TO BE ANYMORE.

SINCE **WEDNESDAY**, RILEY AND I HAD BEEN **DODGING** EACH OTHER'S **GLANCES** WHEN WE PASSED.

AND THERE WERE **OTHER** TENSIONS BUILDING AS **WELL**...

NOONE, KICK THE **REST** OF YER USED CLOTHES BEHIND MY CHAIR IF YA **GOTTA**, BUT **NOT** YER FUCKIN' **UNDERWEAR!**

...TENSIONS THAT DIDN'T INVOLVE **ME.**

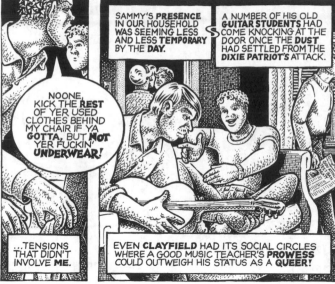

SAMMY'S **PRESENCE** IN OUR HOUSEHOLD WAS SEEMING LESS AND LESS **TEMPORARY** BY THE **DAY.**

A NUMBER OF HIS OLD **GUITAR STUDENTS** HAD COME KNOCKING AT THE DOOR ONCE THE **DUST** HAD SETTLED FROM THE **DIXIE PATRIOT'S** ATTACK.

EVEN **CLAYFIELD** HAD ITS SOCIAL CIRCLES WHERE A GOOD MUSIC TEACHER'S **PROWESS** COULD OUTWEIGH HIS STATUS AS A **QUEER!**

BEFORE **LONG**, SAMMY WAS FANTASIZING ABOUT SAVING UP FOR AN **ORGAN** TO PUT IN THE CORNER.

IT'S MY AREA OF GREATEST **EXPERTISE.**

I COULD **DOUBLE** MY **STUDENT LOAD** IN A **MONTH.**

AREN'T ORGANS **EXPENSIVE,** SAMMY...?

THE **EDGE** THAT WOULD CREEP INTO RILEY'S VOICE WHEN SAMMY TALKED LIKE THAT **SCARED** ME.

I GET **MORE'N** ENOUGH **ORGAN NOISE** TO SUIT ME WALKIN' PAST THE **METHODIST CHURCH** ON SUNDAYS.

chuckle!

OR MAYBE I WAS JUST SPOOKED BY THE WAY **EVERYTHING** THAT HAD SEEMED **STABLE** IN MY LIFE WAS COMING **UNHINGED** ALL AT **ONCE.**

SOME **VOICE** FROM A CORNER OF MY BRAIN WAS REMINDING ME THAT THE WHEELERY WASN'T LIKELY TO **KEEP ON** BEING **HOME** FOR ME **FOREVER.**

ON **SATURDAY** GINGER BIT THE **BULLET** AND TELEPHONED HER **PARENTS** IN **OHIO** TO TELL THEM SHE WAS **PREGNANT.**

SHE USED THE **PAY PHONE** IN A **LAUNDROMAT** SEVERAL MILES FROM THE COLLEGE, NOT WANTING ANY **DORMMATES** TO WANDER BY UNEXPECTEDLY.

SHE ASKED ME TO STAY **NEXT** TO HER FOR **MORAL SUPPORT.**

FROM WHAT I COULD TELL OF THE CONVERSATION'S **DRIFT**, THEY WEREN'T GIVING HER AS **HARD** A TIME AS YOU MIGHT HAVE **EXPECTED.**

Ker- Chunk!
Ker- Chunk!
Ker- chunk!

DAD WANTS TO **SPEAK** TO YOU.

ME?! YOU **TOLD** HIM I WAS **HERE?!**

HE **GUESSED.**

H'LO, MR. RAINES. UH...

HELLO, TOLAND. IT'S GOOD TO **TALK** TO YOU AT **LAST**. GINGER'S TOLD US A LOT **ABOUT** YOU, SON, AND YOU'VE ALWAYS SOUNDED LIKE A **RESPONSIBLE** KIND OF FELLOW WHO'D WANT TO DO THE **RIGHT THING**...

Ker- chunk!
Ker- chunk!!

CONSIDERING THE **CIRCUMSTANCES,** I GIVE THE OL' GUY CREDIT FOR **FORBEARANCE** ABOVE AND BEYOND THE CALL OF **DUTY!**

YESSIR.

YESSIR.

THAT SOUNDS GOOD TO **ME,** SIR.

HE SAID THAT HE AND GINGER'S MOTHER WOULD MAKE A **TRIP SOUTH** VERY SHORTLY SO THAT WE COULD ALL **STRATEGIZE** TOGETHER ABOUT WHAT TO DO **NEXT.**

THEN ON **MONDAY**, AS IF THINGS HADN'T BEEN **STIRRED UP** ENOUGH YET, MY **SISTER** HAD HER **BRAINSTORM**.

MELANIE! ORLEY! WHAT A NICE **SURPRISE**!

DIDN'T MY BROTHER TELL YOU TO **EXPECT** US?

WE'RE A **SURPRISE**?

UH... NO.

ₛsigh!ₛ TYPICAL!

I TALKED TO HIM **EARLIER** TODAY AN' **SAID** WE'D BE COMIN' OVER TONIGHT WITH SOMETHIN' **IMPORTANT** TO DISCUSS.

I TOLD HIM TO PRY HIS **GIRLFRIEND** AWAY FROM HER BOOKS AN' GET **HER** OVER HERE, **TOO**. I NEED TO TALK TO **BOTH** OF 'EM.

WELL, COME ON **INSIDE**. THEY'RE NOT **HERE** YET, BUT CHANCES ARE THEY'RE ON THEIR **WAY**.

YOU CAN KEEP ME **COMPANY** WHILE I FINISH DRYIN' SOME **DISHES**.

RILEY! SAMMY! SAY HELLO TO MELANIE AN' **ORLEY**.

HI, ORLEY.

HI, MELANIE.

DON'T EXPECT **THOSE TWO** TO SHOW ANY **MANNERS**! THEY'RE TOO WRAPPED UP IN THEIR **CHESS GAME**!

WHAT'S THE **CHURCH-MUSIC GUY** DOIN' HERE?

SAMMY'S BEEN LIVIN' HERE AT THE **WHEELERY** SINCE THAT **DIXIE PATRIOT** STORY LOST HIM HIS **JOB**.

ORLEY, DON'T GET US **SIDETRACKED** ONTO **SAMMY NOONE**.

I WANNA HEAR WHAT MAVIS THINKS OF OUR **PLAN**.

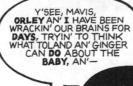

Y'SEE, MAVIS, **ORLEY** AN' I HAVE BEEN WRACKIN' OUR BRAINS FOR **DAYS**, TRYIN' TO THINK WHAT TOLAND AN' GINGER CAN **DO** ABOUT THE **BABY**, AN'—

ABOUT THE...

THE BABY??

!

YOU DIDN'T KNOW...?

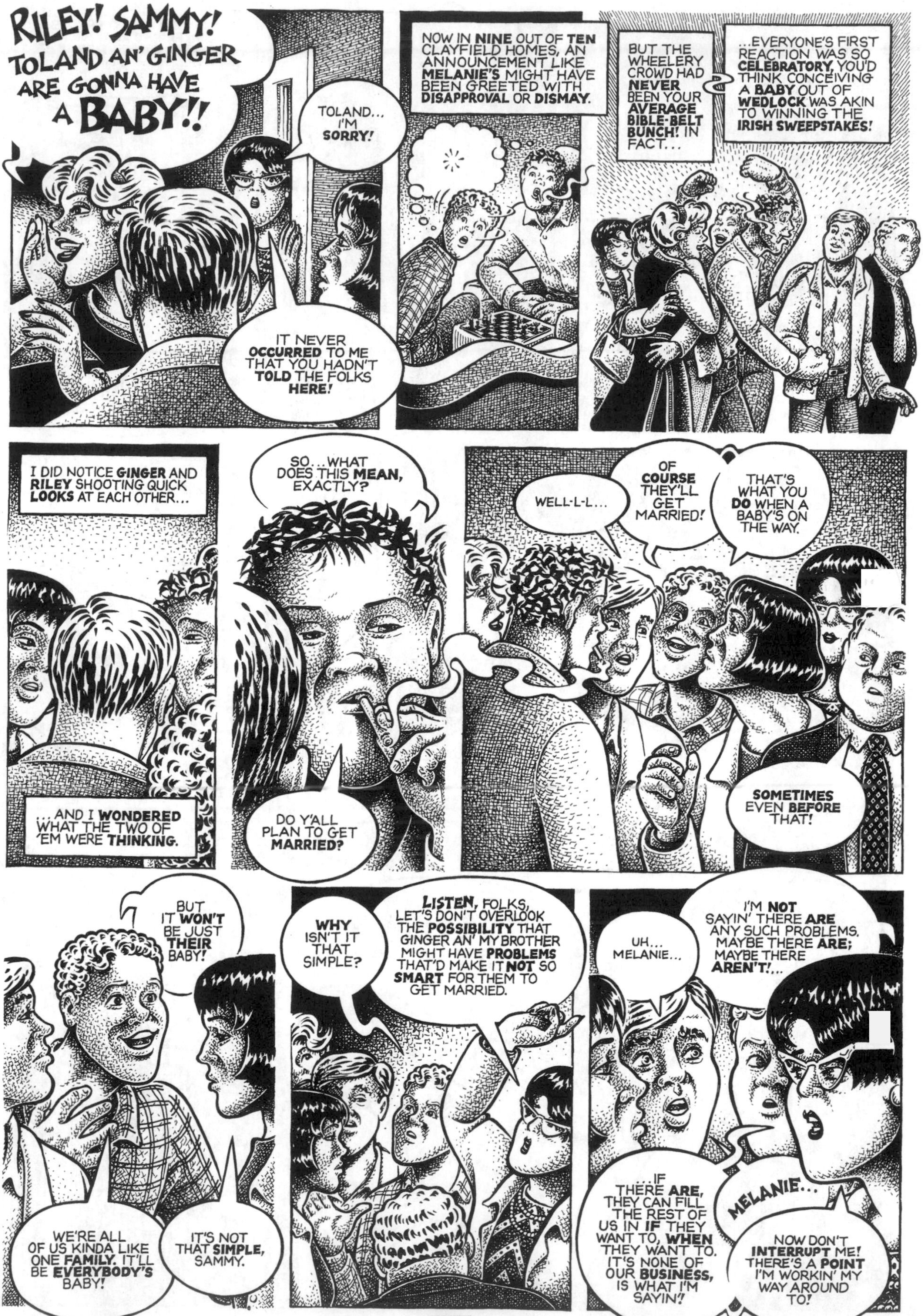
RILEY! SAMMY! TOLAND AN' GINGER ARE GONNA HAVE A BABY!!
TOLAND... I'M SORRY!
IT NEVER OCCURRED TO ME THAT YOU HADN'T TOLD THE FOLKS HERE!
NOW IN NINE OUT OF TEN CLAYFIELD HOMES, AN ANNOUNCEMENT LIKE MELANIE'S MIGHT HAVE BEEN GREETED WITH DISAPPROVAL OR DISMAY.
BUT THE WHEELERY CROWD HAD NEVER BEEN YOUR AVERAGE BIBLE-BELT BUNCH! IN FACT...
...EVERYONE'S FIRST REACTION WAS SO CELEBRATORY, YOU'D THINK CONCEIVING A BABY OUT OF WEDLOCK WAS AKIN TO WINNING THE IRISH SWEEPSTAKES!
I DID NOTICE GINGER AND RILEY SHOOTING QUICK LOOKS AT EACH OTHER...
...AND I WONDERED WHAT THE TWO OF 'EM WERE THINKING.
SO...WHAT DOES THIS MEAN, EXACTLY?
DO Y'ALL PLAN TO GET MARRIED?
WELL-L-L...
OF COURSE THEY'LL GET MARRIED!
THAT'S WHAT YOU DO WHEN A BABY'S ON THE WAY.
SOMETIMES EVEN BEFORE THAT!
BUT IT WON'T BE JUST THEIR BABY!
WE'RE ALL OF US KINDA LIKE ONE FAMILY. IT'LL BE EVERYBODY'S BABY!
IT'S NOT THAT SIMPLE, SAMMY.
WHY ISN'T IT THAT SIMPLE?
LISTEN, FOLKS, LET'S DON'T OVERLOOK THE POSSIBILITY THAT GINGER AN' MY BROTHER MIGHT HAVE PROBLEMS THAT'D MAKE IT NOT SO SMART FOR THEM TO GET MARRIED.
UH... MELANIE...
I'M NOT SAYIN' THERE ARE ANY SUCH PROBLEMS. MAYBE THERE ARE; MAYBE THERE AREN'T!...
...IF THERE ARE, THEY CAN FILL THE REST OF US IN IF THEY WANT TO, WHEN THEY WANT TO. IT'S NONE OF OUR BUSINESS, IS WHAT I'M SAYIN'!
MELANIE...
NOW DON'T INTERRUPT ME! THERE'S A POINT I'M WORKIN' MY WAY AROUND TO!

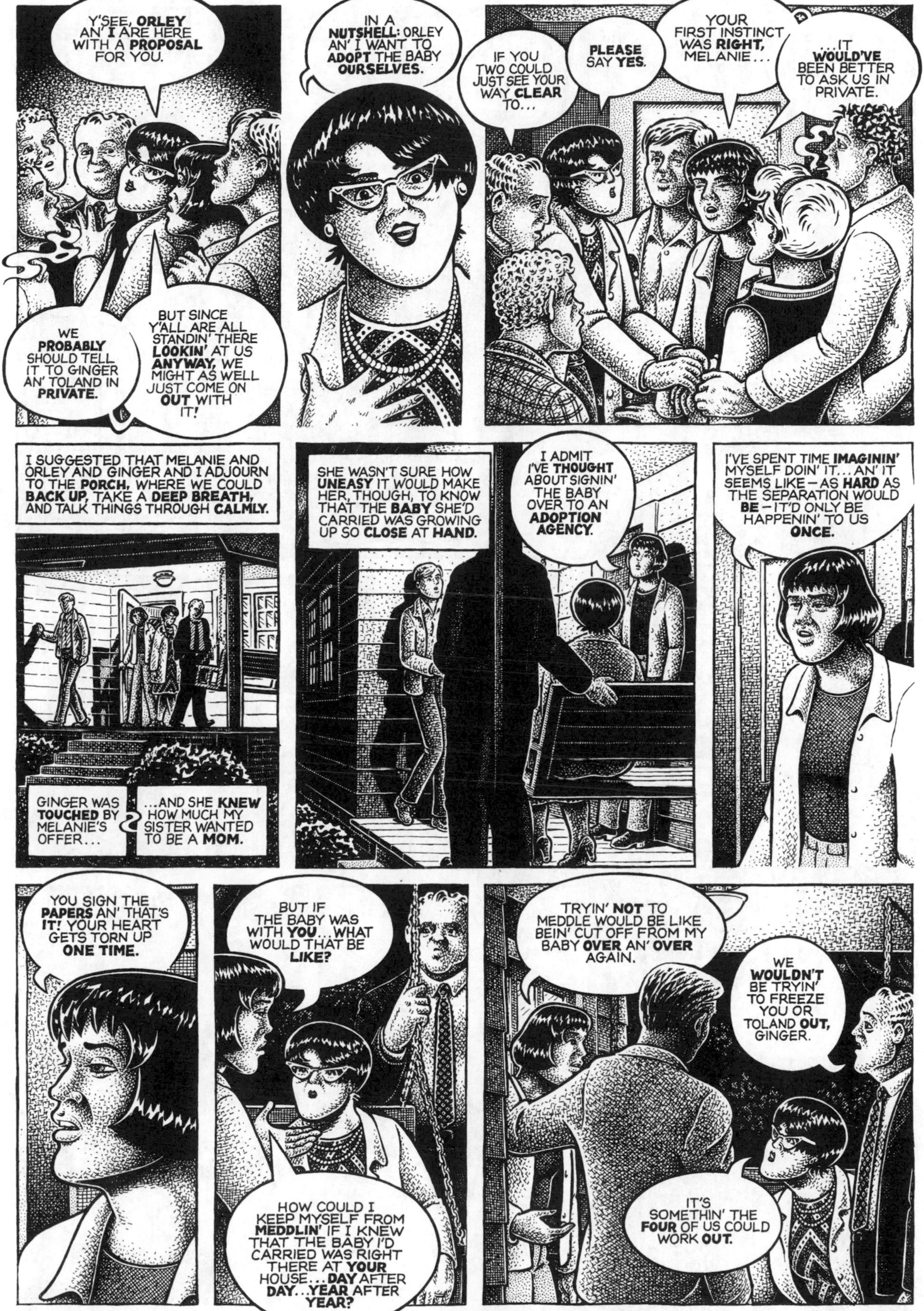
Y'SEE, ORLEY AN' I ARE HERE WITH A PROPOSAL FOR YOU.
WE PROBABLY SHOULD TELL IT TO GINGER AN' TOLAND IN PRIVATE.
BUT SINCE Y'ALL ARE ALL STANDIN' THERE LOOKIN' AT US ANYWAY, WE MIGHT AS WELL JUST COME ON OUT WITH IT!
IN A NUTSHELL: ORLEY AN' I WANT TO ADOPT THE BABY OURSELVES.
IF YOU TWO COULD JUST SEE YOUR WAY CLEAR TO...
PLEASE SAY YES.
YOUR FIRST INSTINCT WAS RIGHT, MELANIE...
...IT WOULD'VE BEEN BETTER TO ASK US IN PRIVATE.
I SUGGESTED THAT MELANIE AND ORLEY AND GINGER AND I ADJOURN TO THE PORCH, WHERE WE COULD BACK UP, TAKE A DEEP BREATH, AND TALK THINGS THROUGH CALMLY.
GINGER WAS TOUCHED BY MELANIE'S OFFER...
...AND SHE KNEW HOW MUCH MY SISTER WANTED TO BE A MOM.
SHE WASN'T SURE HOW UNEASY IT WOULD MAKE HER, THOUGH, TO KNOW THAT THE BABY SHE'D CARRIED WAS GROWING UP SO CLOSE AT HAND.
I ADMIT I'VE THOUGHT ABOUT SIGNIN' THE BABY OVER TO AN ADOPTION AGENCY.
I'VE SPENT TIME IMAGININ' MYSELF DOIN' IT... AN' IT SEEMS LIKE—AS HARD AS THE SEPARATION WOULD BE—IT'D ONLY BE HAPPENIN' TO US ONCE.
YOU SIGN THE PAPERS AN' THAT'S IT! YOUR HEART GETS TORN UP ONE TIME.
BUT IF THE BABY WAS WITH YOU... WHAT WOULD THAT BE LIKE?
HOW COULD I KEEP MYSELF FROM MEDDLIN' IF I KNEW THAT THE BABY I'D CARRIED WAS RIGHT THERE AT YOUR HOUSE... DAY AFTER DAY... YEAR AFTER YEAR?
TRYIN' NOT TO MEDDLE WOULD BE LIKE BEIN' CUT OFF FROM MY BABY OVER AN' OVER AGAIN.
WE WOULDN'T BE TRYIN' TO FREEZE YOU OR TOLAND OUT, GINGER.
IT'S SOMETHIN' THE FOUR OF US COULD WORK OUT.

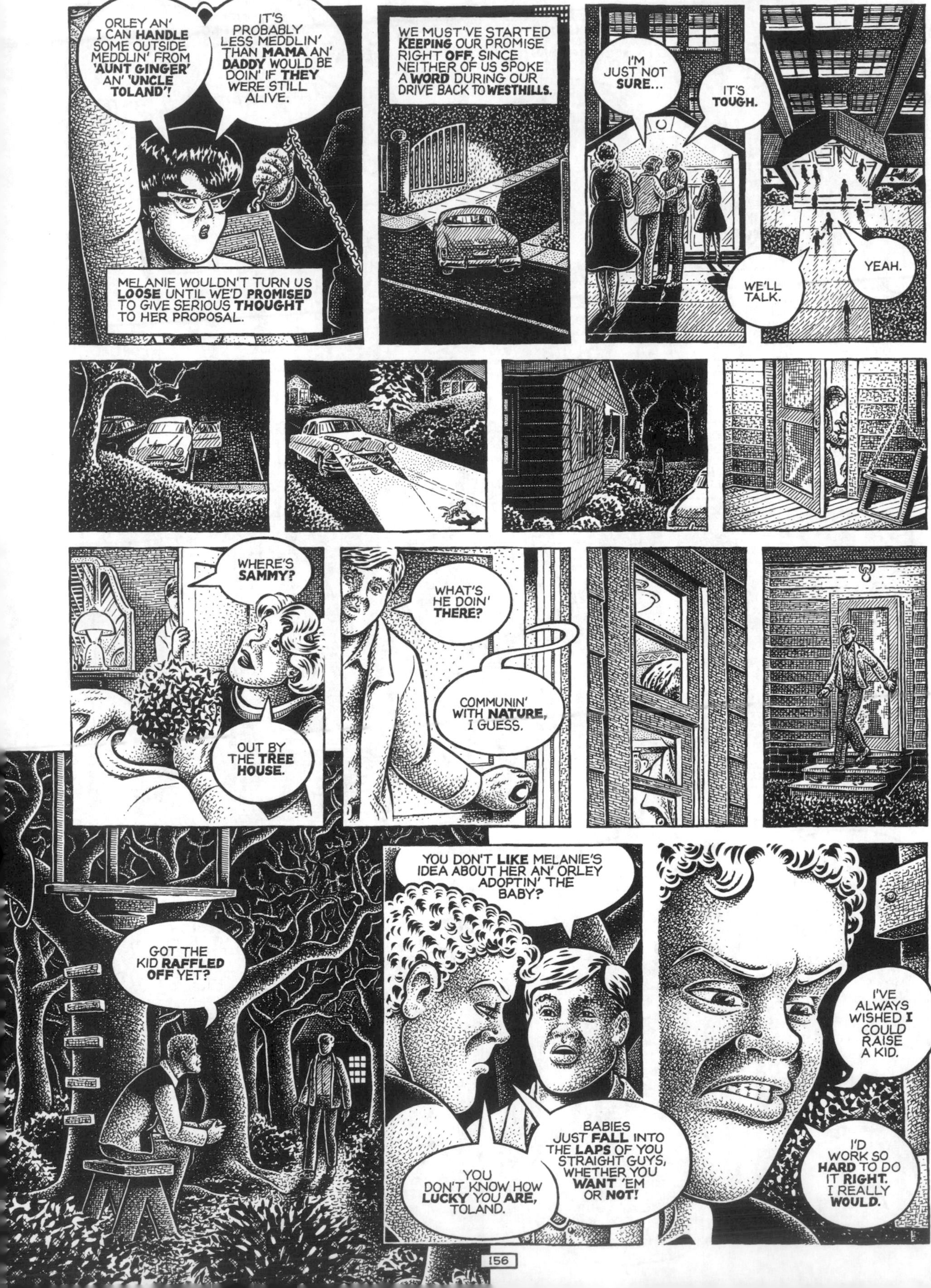
ORLEY AN' I CAN HANDLE SOME OUTSIDE MEDDLIN' FROM 'AUNT GINGER' AN' 'UNCLE TOLAND'!
IT'S PROBABLY LESS MEDDLIN' THAN MAMA AN' DADDY WOULD BE DOIN' IF THEY WERE STILL ALIVE.
MELANIE WOULDN'T TURN US LOOSE UNTIL WE'D PROMISED TO GIVE SERIOUS THOUGHT TO HER PROPOSAL.
WE MUST'VE STARTED KEEPING OUR PROMISE RIGHT OFF, SINCE NEITHER OF US SPOKE A WORD DURING OUR DRIVE BACK TO WESTHILLS.
I'M JUST NOT SURE...
IT'S TOUGH.
WE'LL TALK.
YEAH.
WHERE'S SAMMY?
OUT BY THE TREE HOUSE.
WHAT'S HE DOIN' THERE?
COMMUNIN' WITH NATURE, I GUESS.
GOT THE KID RAFFLED OFF YET?
YOU DON'T LIKE MELANIE'S IDEA ABOUT HER AN' ORLEY ADOPTIN' THE BABY?
YOU DON'T KNOW HOW LUCKY YOU ARE, TOLAND.
BABIES JUST FALL INTO THE LAPS OF YOU STRAIGHT GUYS, WHETHER YOU WANT 'EM OR NOT!
I'VE ALWAYS WISHED I COULD RAISE A KID.
I'D WORK SO HARD TO DO IT RIGHT. I REALLY WOULD.

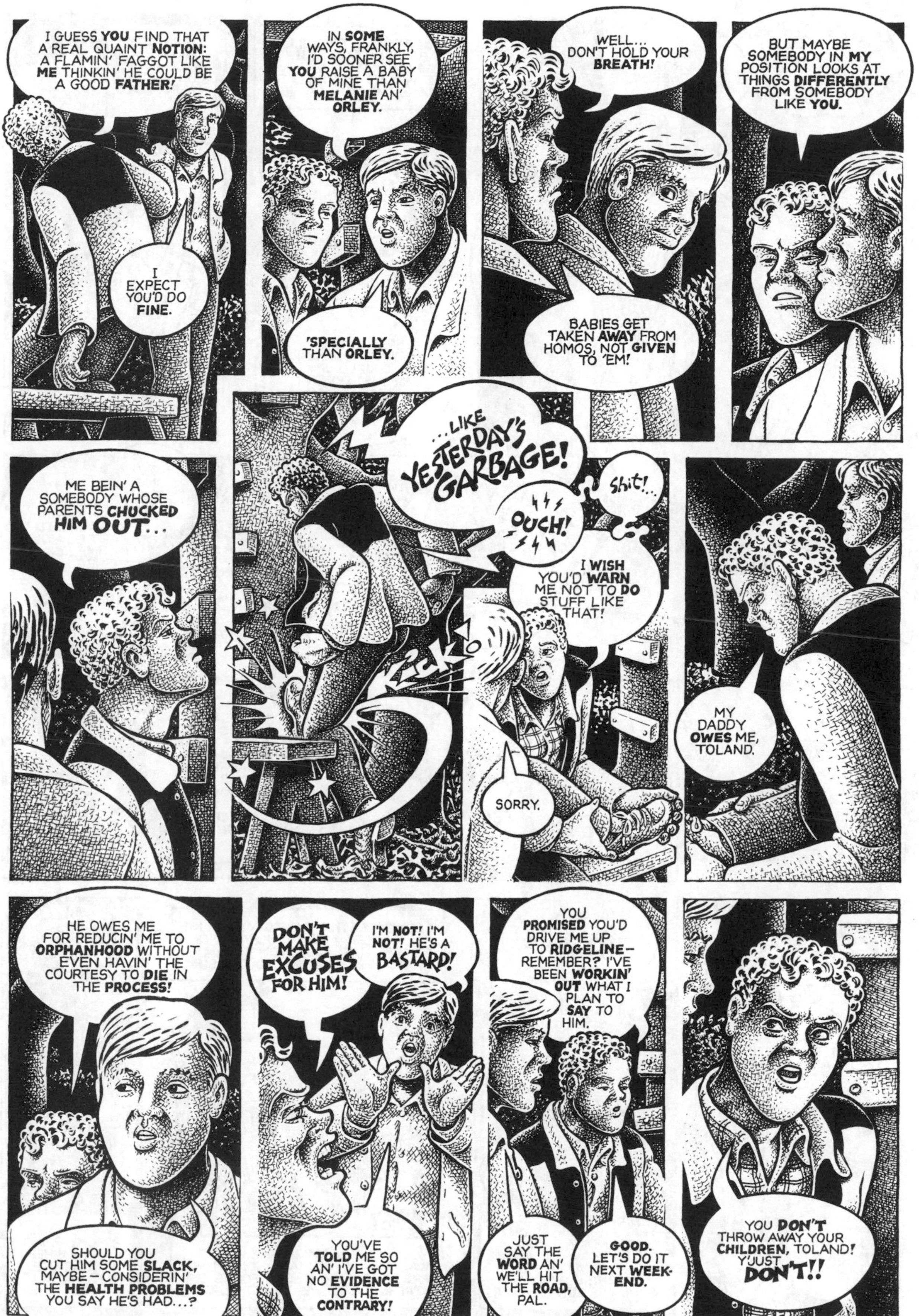
I GUESS YOU FIND THAT A REAL QUAINT NOTION: A FLAMIN' FAGGOT LIKE ME THINKIN' HE COULD BE A GOOD FATHER!
I EXPECT YOU'D DO FINE.
IN SOME WAYS, FRANKLY, I'D SOONER SEE YOU RAISE A BABY OF MINE THAN MELANIE AN' ORLEY.
'SPECIALLY THAN ORLEY.
WELL... DON'T HOLD YOUR BREATH!
BABIES GET TAKEN AWAY FROM HOMOS, NOT GIVEN TO 'EM!
BUT MAYBE SOMEBODY IN MY POSITION LOOKS AT THINGS DIFFERENTLY FROM SOMEBODY LIKE YOU.
ME BEIN' A SOMEBODY WHOSE PARENTS CHUCKED HIM OUT...
...LIKE YESTERDAY'S GARBAGE!
KICK
OUCH!
Shit!...
I WISH YOU'D WARN ME NOT TO DO STUFF LIKE THAT!
SORRY.
MY DADDY OWES ME, TOLAND.
HE OWES ME FOR REDUCIN' ME TO ORPHANHOOD WITHOUT EVEN HAVIN' THE COURTESY TO DIE IN THE PROCESS!
SHOULD YOU CUT HIM SOME SLACK, MAYBE—CONSIDERIN' THE HEALTH PROBLEMS YOU SAY HE'S HAD...?
DON'T MAKE EXCUSES FOR HIM!
I'M NOT! I'M NOT! HE'S A BASTARD!
YOU'VE TOLD ME SO AN' I'VE GOT NO EVIDENCE TO THE CONTRARY!
YOU PROMISED YOU'D DRIVE ME UP TO RIDGELINE—REMEMBER? I'VE BEEN WORKIN' OUT WHAT I PLAN TO SAY TO HIM.
JUST SAY THE WORD AN' WE'LL HIT THE ROAD, PAL.
GOOD. LET'S DO IT NEXT WEEK-END.
YOU DON'T THROW AWAY YOUR CHILDREN, TOLAND! Y'JUST DON'T!!

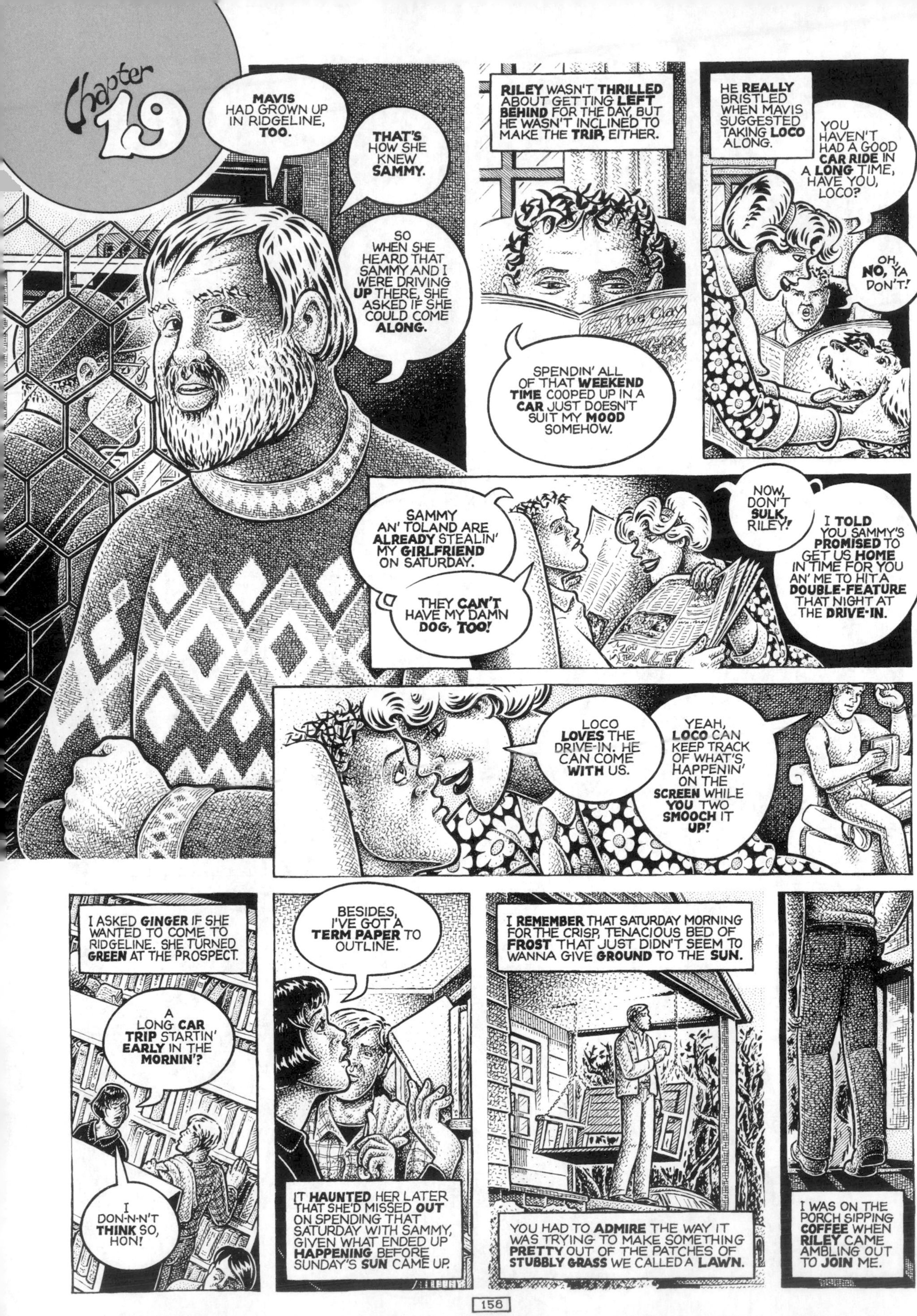

Chapter 19
MAVIS HAD GROWN UP IN RIDGELINE, TOO.
THAT'S HOW SHE KNEW SAMMY.
SO WHEN SHE HEARD THAT SAMMY AND I WERE DRIVING UP THERE, SHE ASKED IF SHE COULD COME ALONG.
RILEY WASN'T THRILLED ABOUT GETTING LEFT BEHIND FOR THE DAY, BUT HE WASN'T INCLINED TO MAKE THE TRIP, EITHER.
SPENDIN' ALL OF THAT WEEKEND TIME COOPED UP IN A CAR JUST DOESN'T SUIT MY MOOD SOMEHOW.
HE REALLY BRISTLED WHEN MAVIS SUGGESTED TAKING LOCO ALONG.
YOU HAVEN'T HAD A GOOD CAR RIDE IN A LONG TIME, HAVE YOU, LOCO?
OH, NO, YA DON'T!
SAMMY AN' TOLAND ARE ALREADY STEALIN' MY GIRLFRIEND ON SATURDAY.
THEY CAN'T HAVE MY DAMN DOG, TOO!
NOW, DON'T SULK, RILEY!
I TOLD YOU SAMMY'S PROMISED TO GET US HOME IN TIME FOR YOU AN' ME TO HIT A DOUBLE-FEATURE THAT NIGHT AT THE DRIVE-IN.
LOCO LOVES THE DRIVE-IN. HE CAN COME WITH US.
YEAH, LOCO CAN KEEP TRACK OF WHAT'S HAPPENIN' ON THE SCREEN WHILE YOU TWO SMOOCH IT UP!
I ASKED GINGER IF SHE WANTED TO COME TO RIDGELINE. SHE TURNED GREEN AT THE PROSPECT.
A LONG CAR TRIP STARTIN' EARLY IN THE MORNIN'?
I DON-N-N'T THINK SO, HON!
BESIDES, I'VE GOT A TERM PAPER TO OUTLINE.
IT HAUNTED HER LATER THAT SHE'D MISSED OUT ON SPENDING THAT SATURDAY WITH SAMMY, GIVEN WHAT ENDED UP HAPPENING BEFORE SUNDAY'S SUN CAME UP.
I REMEMBER THAT SATURDAY MORNING FOR THE CRISP, TENACIOUS BED OF FROST THAT JUST DIDN'T SEEM TO WANNA GIVE GROUND TO THE SUN.
YOU HAD TO ADMIRE THE WAY IT WAS TRYING TO MAKE SOMETHING PRETTY OUT OF THE PATCHES OF STUBBLY GRASS WE CALLED A LAWN.
I WAS ON THE PORCH SIPPING COFFEE WHEN RILEY CAME AMBLING OUT TO JOIN ME.

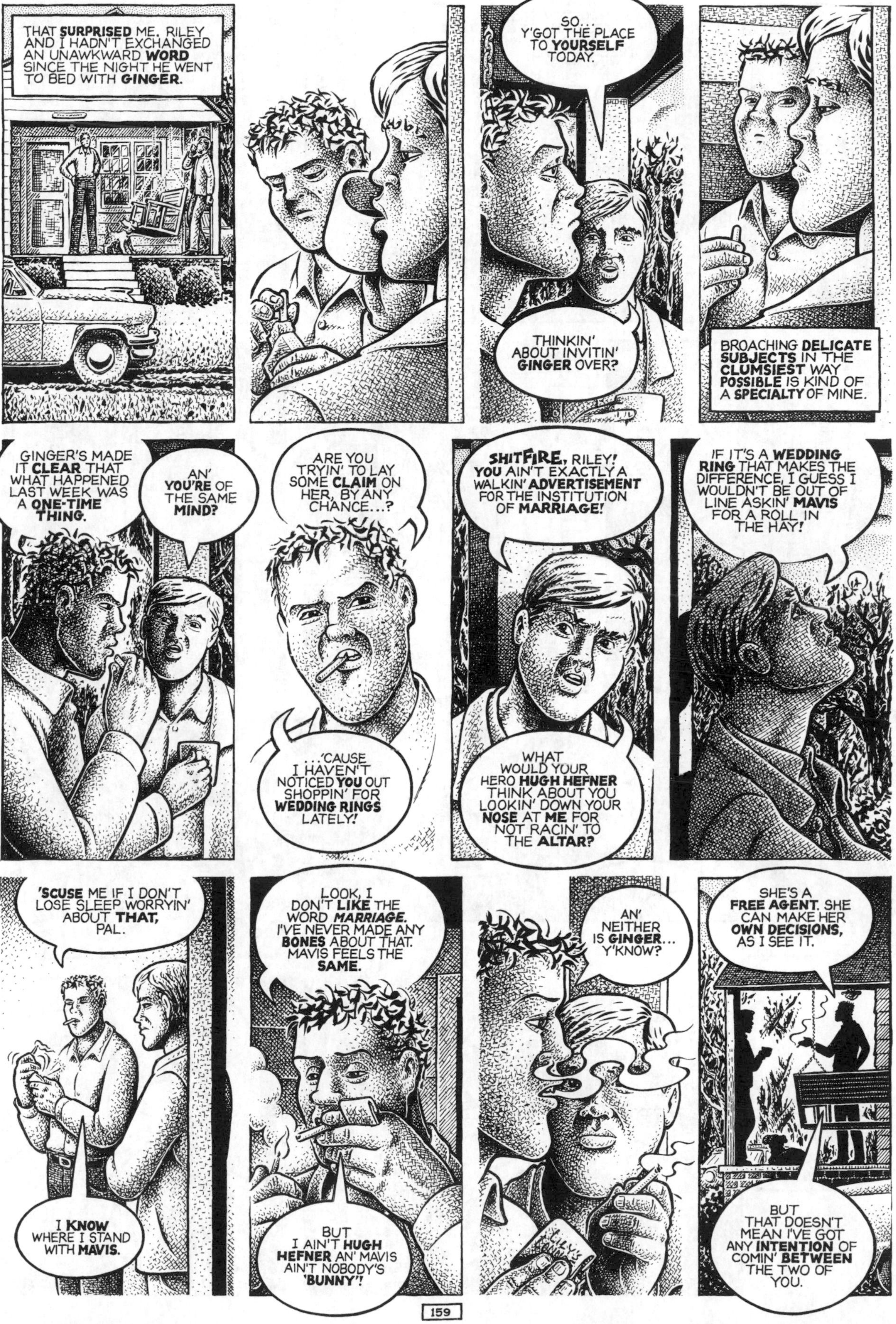
THAT SURPRISED ME. RILEY AND I HADN'T EXCHANGED AN UNAWKWARD WORD SINCE THE NIGHT HE WENT TO BED WITH GINGER.
SO... Y'GOT THE PLACE TO YOURSELF TODAY.
THINKIN' ABOUT INVITIN' GINGER OVER?
BROACHING DELICATE SUBJECTS IN THE CLUMSIEST WAY POSSIBLE IS KIND OF A SPECIALTY OF MINE.
GINGER'S MADE IT CLEAR THAT WHAT HAPPENED LAST WEEK WAS A ONE-TIME THING.
AN' YOU'RE OF THE SAME MIND?
ARE YOU TRYIN' TO LAY SOME CLAIM ON HER, BY ANY CHANCE...?
...'CAUSE I HAVEN'T NOTICED YOU OUT SHOPPIN' FOR WEDDING RINGS LATELY!
SHITFIRE, RILEY! YOU AIN'T EXACTLY A WALKIN' ADVERTISEMENT FOR THE INSTITUTION OF MARRIAGE!
WHAT WOULD YOUR HERO HUGH HEFNER THINK ABOUT YOU LOOKIN' DOWN YOUR NOSE AT ME FOR NOT RACIN' TO THE ALTAR?
IF IT'S A WEDDING RING THAT MAKES THE DIFFERENCE, I GUESS I WOULDN'T BE OUT OF LINE ASKIN' MAVIS FOR A ROLL IN THE HAY!
'SCUSE ME IF I DON'T LOSE SLEEP WORRYIN' ABOUT THAT, PAL.
I KNOW WHERE I STAND WITH MAVIS.
LOOK, I DON'T LIKE THE WORD MARRIAGE. I'VE NEVER MADE ANY BONES ABOUT THAT. MAVIS FEELS THE SAME.
BUT I AIN'T HUGH HEFNER AN' MAVIS AIN'T NOBODY'S 'BUNNY'!
AN' NEITHER IS GINGER... Y'KNOW?
SHE'S A FREE AGENT. SHE CAN MAKE HER OWN DECISIONS, AS I SEE IT.
BUT THAT DOESN'T MEAN I'VE GOT ANY INTENTION OF COMIN' BETWEEN THE TWO OF YOU.

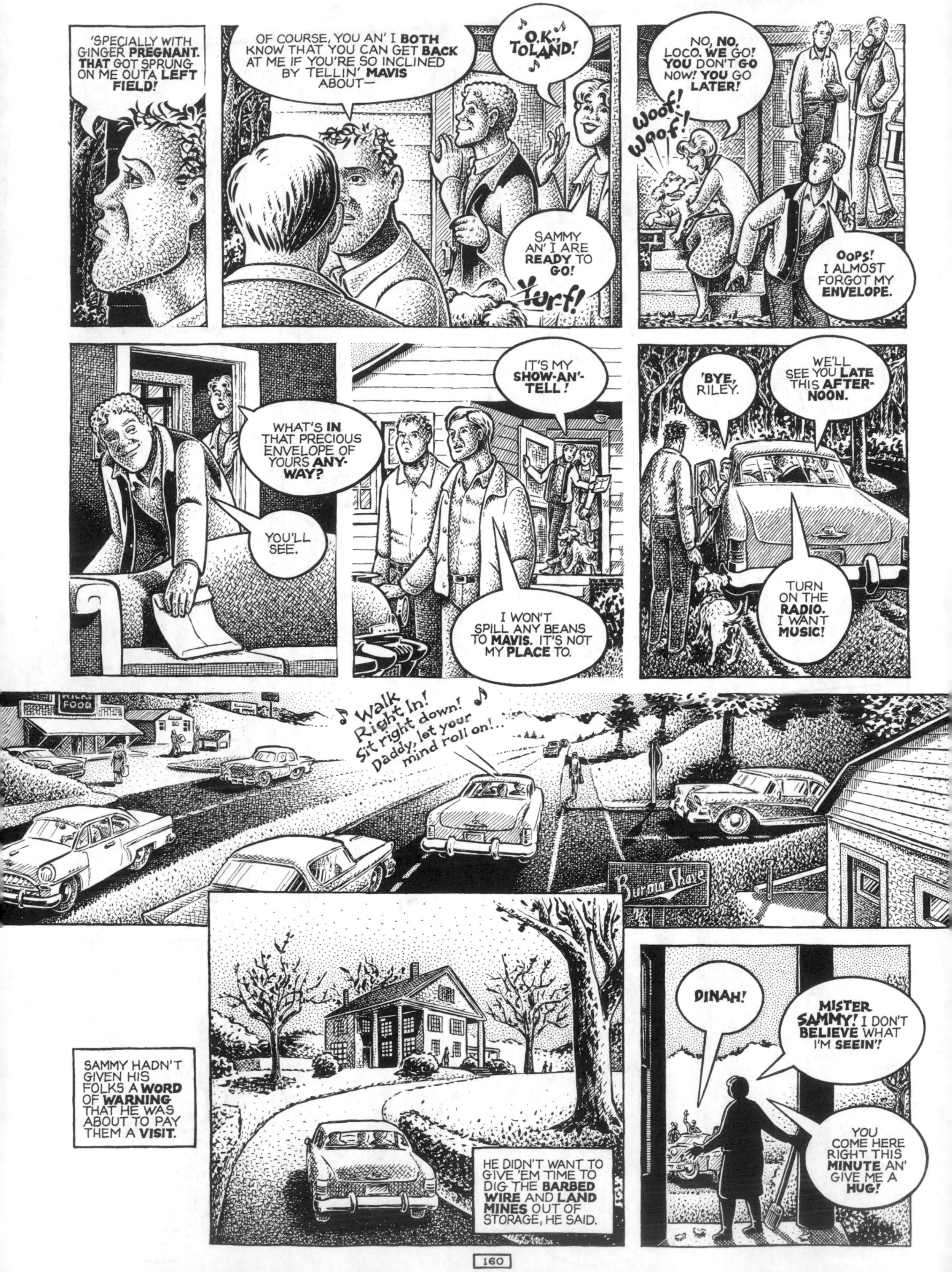
'SPECIALLY WITH GINGER PREGNANT. THAT GOT SPRUNG ON ME OUTA LEFT FIELD!
OF COURSE, YOU AN' I BOTH KNOW THAT YOU CAN GET BACK AT ME IF YOU'RE SO INCLINED BY TELLIN' MAVIS ABOUT—
O.K., TOLAND!
SAMMY AN' I ARE READY TO GO!
Yurf!
NO, NO, LOCO. WE GO! YOU DON'T GO NOW! YOU GO LATER!
Woof! Woof!
OOPS! I ALMOST FORGOT MY ENVELOPE.
WHAT'S IN THAT PRECIOUS ENVELOPE OF YOURS ANYWAY?
YOU'LL SEE.
IT'S MY SHOW-AN'-TELL!
I WON'T SPILL ANY BEANS TO MAVIS. IT'S NOT MY PLACE TO.
'BYE, RILEY.
WE'LL SEE YOU LATE THIS AFTERNOON.
TURN ON THE RADIO. I WANT MUSIC!
FOOD
Walk Right In! Sit right down! Daddy, let your mind roll on!...
Burma Shave
SAMMY HADN'T GIVEN HIS FOLKS A WORD OF WARNING THAT HE WAS ABOUT TO PAY THEM A VISIT.
HE DIDN'T WANT TO GIVE 'EM TIME TO DIG THE BARBED WIRE AND LAND MINES OUT OF STORAGE, HE SAID.
DINAH!
MISTER SAMMY! I DON'T BELIEVE WHAT I'M SEEIN'!
YOU COME HERE RIGHT THIS MINUTE AN' GIVE ME A HUG!

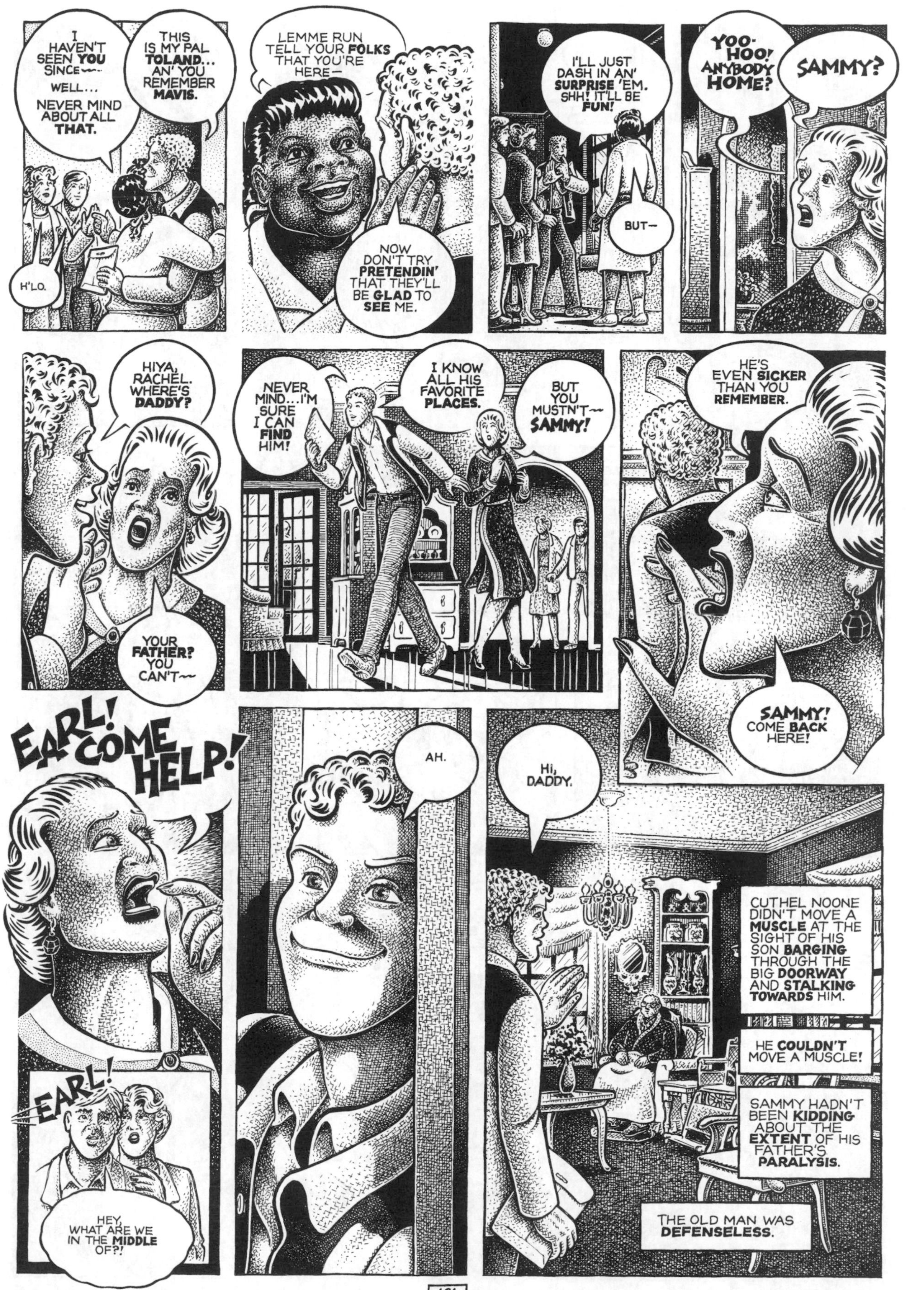

I HAVEN'T SEEN YOU SINCE— WELL... NEVER MIND ABOUT ALL THAT.
THIS IS MY PAL TOLAND... AN' YOU REMEMBER MAVIS.
H'LO.
LEMME RUN TELL YOUR FOLKS THAT YOU'RE HERE—
NOW DON'T TRY PRETENDIN' THAT THEY'LL BE GLAD TO SEE ME.
I'LL JUST DASH IN AN' SURPRISE 'EM. SHH! IT'LL BE FUN!
BUT—
YOO-HOO! ANYBODY HOME?
SAMMY?
HIYA, RACHEL. WHERE'S DADDY?
YOUR FATHER? YOU CAN'T—
NEVER MIND...I'M SURE I CAN FIND HIM!
I KNOW ALL HIS FAVORITE PLACES.
BUT YOU MUSTN'T— SAMMY!
HE'S EVEN SICKER THAN YOU REMEMBER.
SAMMY! COME BACK HERE!
EARL! COME HELP!
EARL!
HEY, WHAT ARE WE IN THE MIDDLE OF?!
AH.
Hi, DADDY.
CUTHEL NOONE DIDN'T MOVE A MUSCLE AT THE SIGHT OF HIS SON BARGING THROUGH THE BIG DOORWAY AND STALKING TOWARDS HIM.
HE COULDN'T MOVE A MUSCLE!
SAMMY HADN'T BEEN KIDDING ABOUT THE EXTENT OF HIS FATHER'S PARALYSIS.
THE OLD MAN WAS DEFENSELESS.

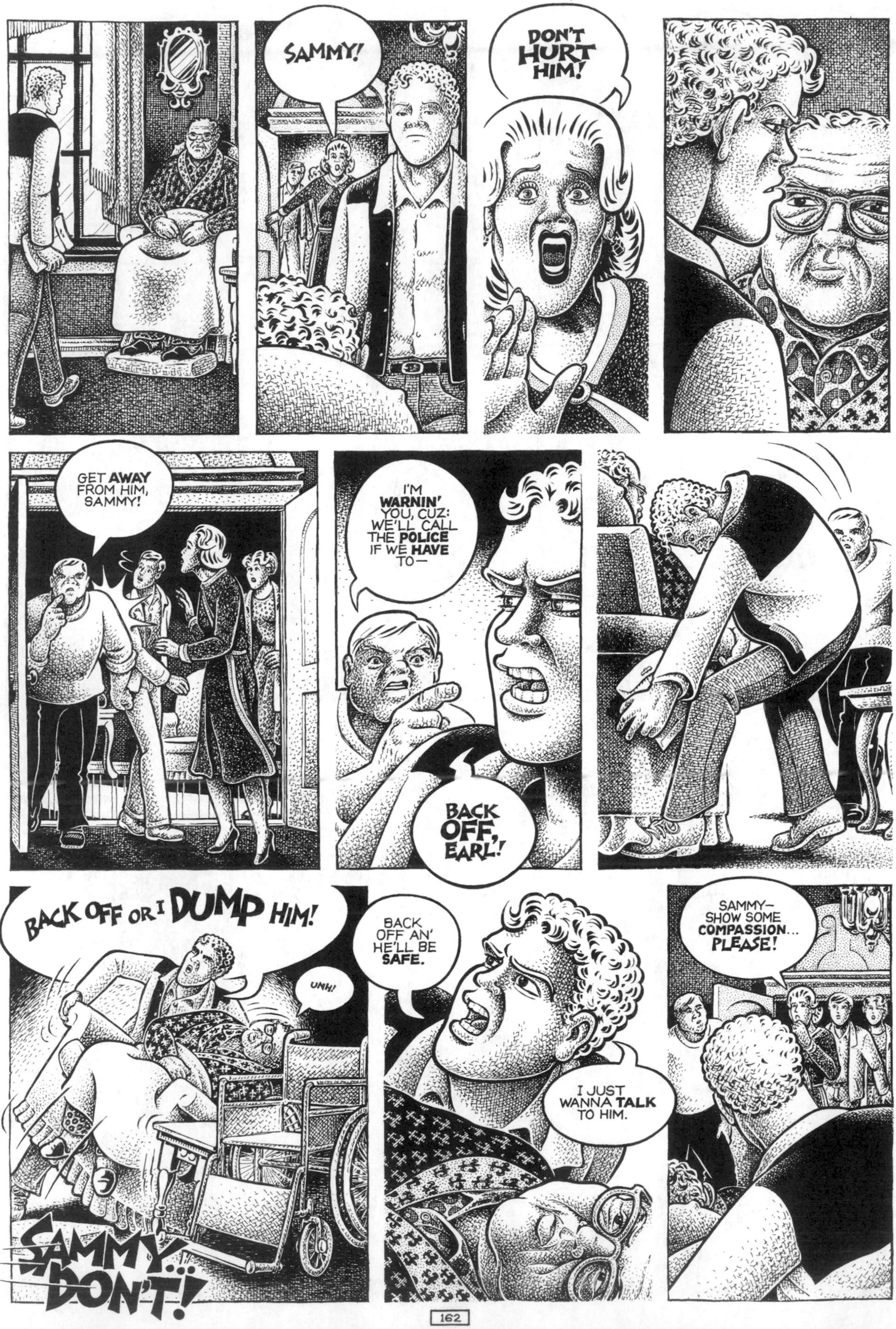
SAMMY!
DON'T HURT HIM!
GET AWAY FROM HIM, SAMMY!
I'M WARNIN' YOU, CUZ: WE'LL CALL THE POLICE IF WE HAVE TO—
BACK OFF, EARL!
BACK OFF OR I DUMP HIM!
UNH!
SAMMY... DON'T!
BACK OFF AN' HE'LL BE SAFE.
I JUST WANNA TALK TO HIM.
SAMMY— SHOW SOME COMPASSION... PLEASE!

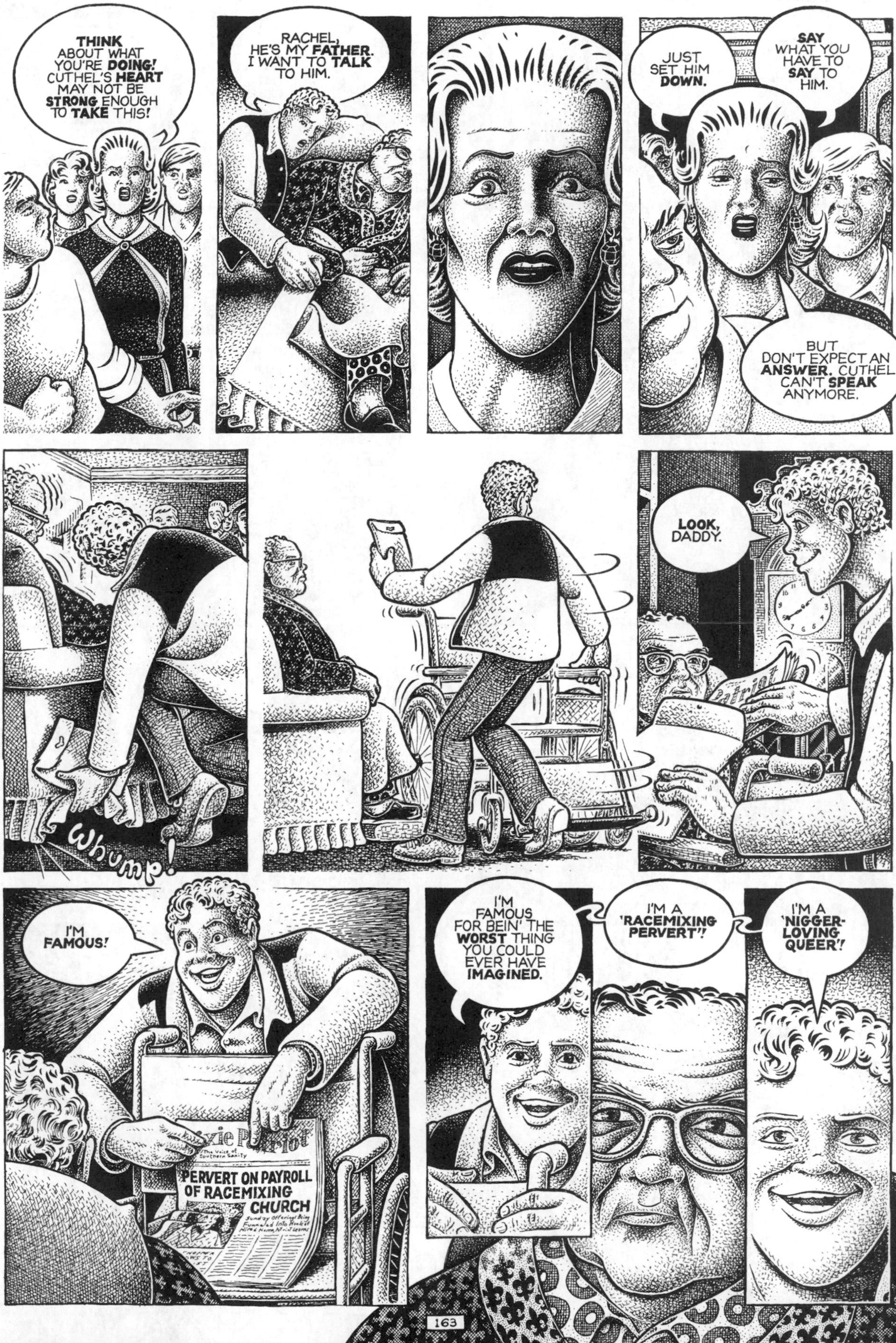
THINK ABOUT WHAT YOU'RE DOING! CUTHEL'S HEART MAY NOT BE STRONG ENOUGH TO TAKE THIS!
RACHEL, HE'S MY FATHER. I WANT TO TALK TO HIM.
JUST SET HIM DOWN.
SAY WHAT YOU HAVE TO SAY TO HIM.
BUT DON'T EXPECT AN ANSWER. CUTHEL CAN'T SPEAK ANYMORE.
Whump!
LOOK, DADDY.
Patriot
I'M FAMOUS!
The Voice of Southern Sanity
PERVERT ON PAYROLL OF RACEMIXING CHURCH
I'M FAMOUS FOR BEIN' THE WORST THING YOU COULD EVER HAVE IMAGINED.
I'M A 'RACEMIXING PERVERT'!
I'M A 'NIGGER-LOVING QUEER'!

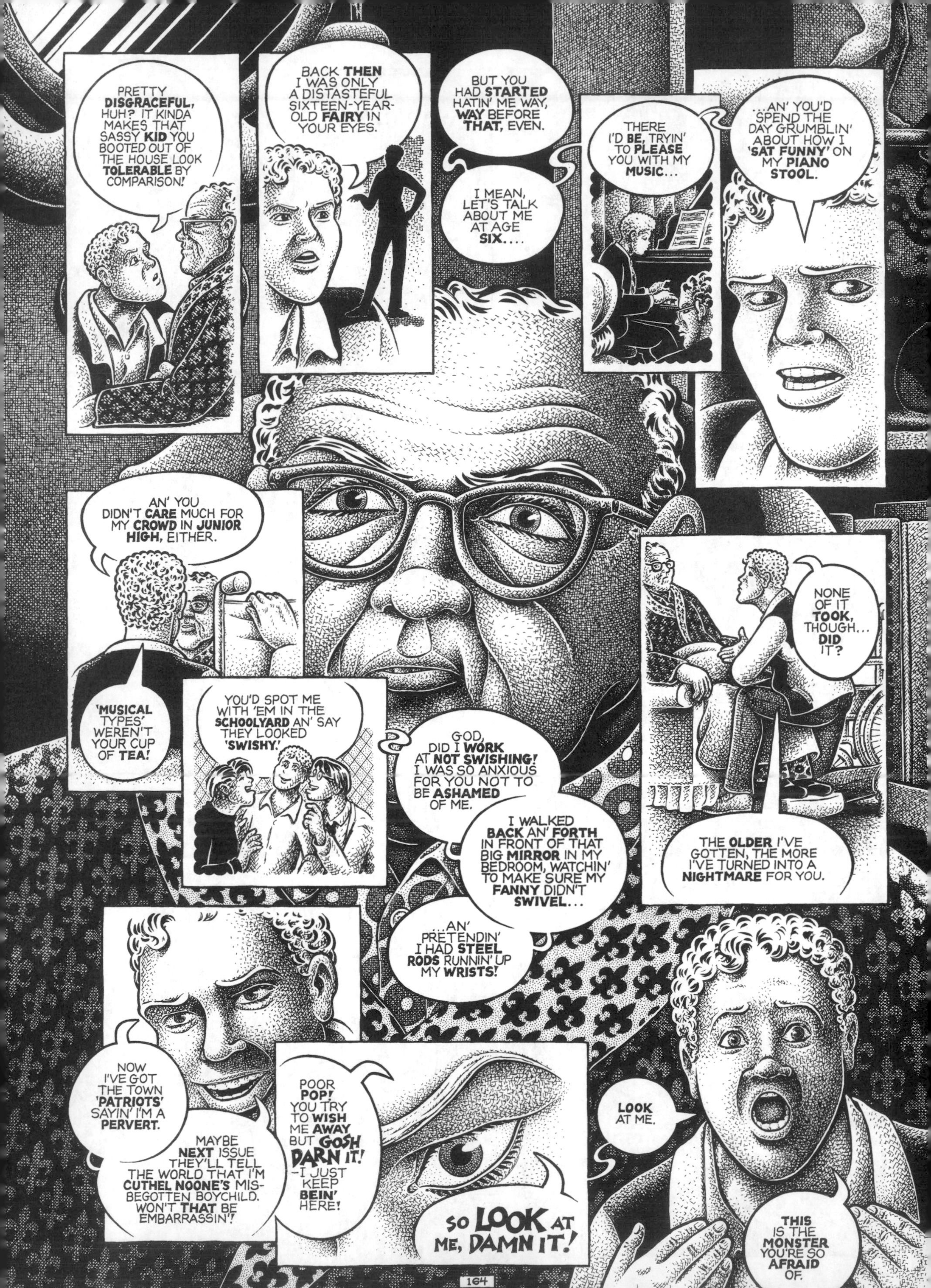
PRETTY DISGRACEFUL, HUH? IT KINDA MAKES THAT SASSY KID YOU BOOTED OUT OF THE HOUSE LOOK TOLERABLE BY COMPARISON!
BACK THEN I WAS ONLY A DISTASTEFUL SIXTEEN-YEAR-OLD FAIRY IN YOUR EYES.
BUT YOU HAD STARTED HATIN' ME WAY, WAY BEFORE THAT, EVEN.
I MEAN, LET'S TALK ABOUT ME AT AGE SIX....
THERE I'D BE, TRYIN' TO PLEASE YOU WITH MY MUSIC...
...AN' YOU'D SPEND THE DAY GRUMBLIN' ABOUT HOW I 'SAT FUNNY' ON MY PIANO STOOL.
AN' YOU DIDN'T CARE MUCH FOR MY CROWD IN JUNIOR HIGH, EITHER.
'MUSICAL TYPES' WEREN'T YOUR CUP OF TEA!
YOU'D SPOT ME WITH 'EM IN THE SCHOOLYARD AN' SAY THEY LOOKED 'SWISHY.'
GOD, DID I WORK AT NOT SWISHING! I WAS SO ANXIOUS FOR YOU NOT TO BE ASHAMED OF ME.
I WALKED BACK AN' FORTH IN FRONT OF THAT BIG MIRROR IN MY BEDROOM, WATCHIN' TO MAKE SURE MY FANNY DIDN'T SWIVEL...
...AN' PRETENDIN' I HAD STEEL RODS RUNNIN' UP MY WRISTS!
NONE OF IT TOOK, THOUGH... DID IT?
THE OLDER I'VE GOTTEN, THE MORE I'VE TURNED INTO A NIGHTMARE FOR YOU.
NOW I'VE GOT THE TOWN 'PATRIOTS' SAYIN' I'M A PERVERT.
MAYBE NEXT ISSUE THEY'LL TELL THE WORLD THAT I'M CUTHEL NOONE'S MIS-BEGOTTEN BOYCHILD. WON'T THAT BE EMBARRASSIN'?
POOR POP! YOU TRY TO WISH ME AWAY BUT GOSH DARN IT! -I JUST KEEP BEIN' HERE!
LOOK AT ME.
SO LOOK AT ME, DAMN IT!
THIS IS THE MONSTER YOU'RE SO AFRAID OF.

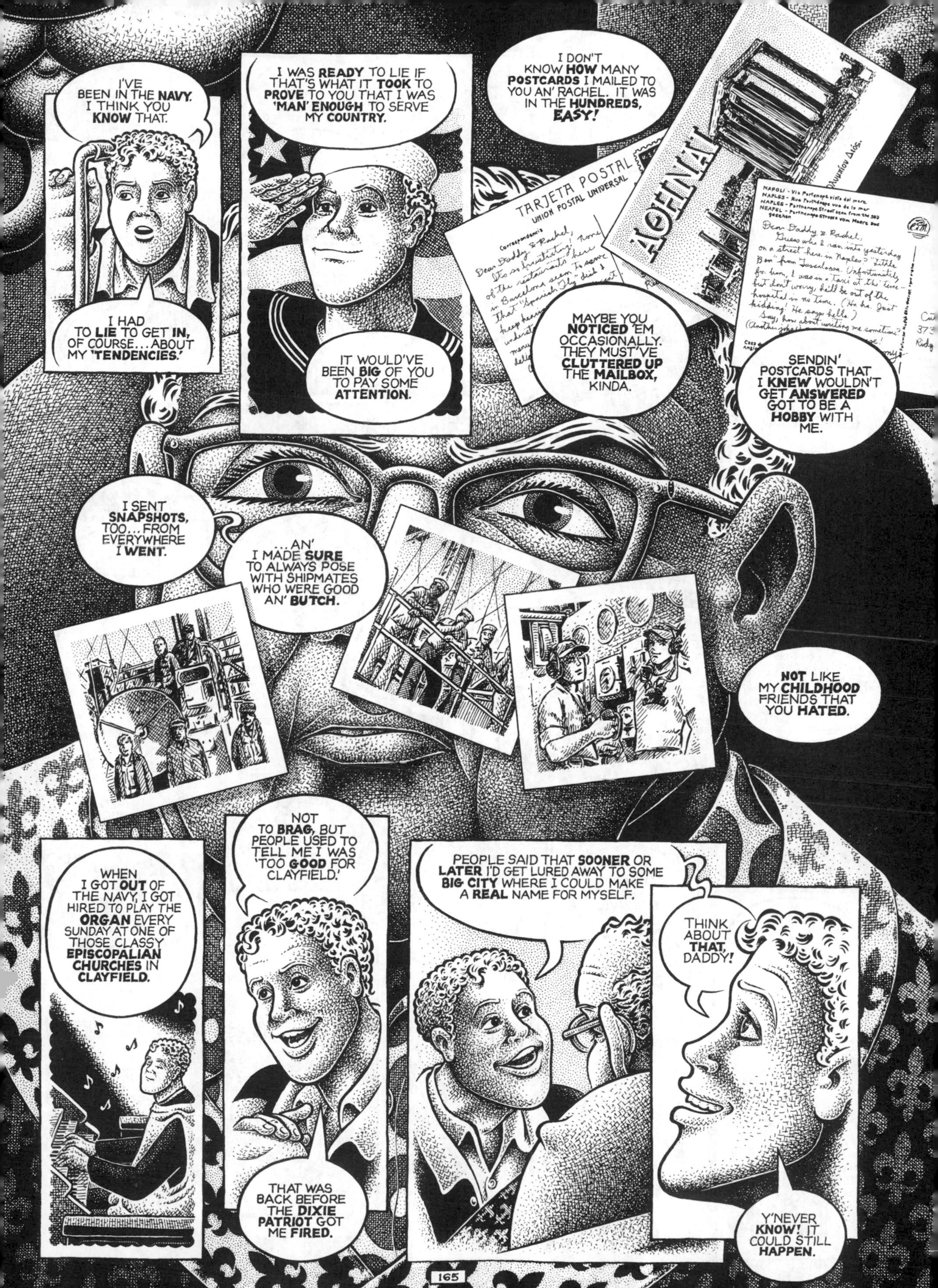
I'VE BEEN IN THE NAVY. I THINK YOU KNOW THAT.
I HAD TO LIE TO GET IN, OF COURSE... ABOUT MY 'TENDENCIES.'
I WAS READY TO LIE IF THAT'S WHAT IT TOOK TO PROVE TO YOU THAT I WAS 'MAN' ENOUGH TO SERVE MY COUNTRY.
IT WOULD'VE BEEN BIG OF YOU TO PAY SOME ATTENTION.
I DON'T KNOW HOW MANY POSTCARDS I MAILED TO YOU AN' RACHEL. IT WAS IN THE HUNDREDS, EASY!
TARJETA POSTAL
UNION POSTAL UNIVERSAL
NAPOLI - Via Partenope vista dal mare
NAPLES - Rue Parthénope vue de la mer
NAPLES - Parthenope Street seen from the sea
NEAPEL - Parthenope Strasse vom Meere aus gesehen
Dear Daddy & Rachel, Guess who I ran into yesterday on a street here in Naples? "Little Ben" from Tuscaloosa. Unfortunately for him, I was in a taxi at the time — but don't worry, he'll be out of the hospital in no time. (Ha ha. Just kidding! He says hello.) Say, how about writing me sometime?
MAYBE YOU NOTICED 'EM OCCASIONALLY. THEY MUST'VE CLUTTERED UP THE MAILBOX, KINDA.
SENDIN' POSTCARDS THAT I KNEW WOULDN'T GET ANSWERED GOT TO BE A HOBBY WITH ME.
I SENT SNAPSHOTS, TOO... FROM EVERYWHERE I WENT.
...AN' I MADE SURE TO ALWAYS POSE WITH SHIPMATES WHO WERE GOOD AN' BUTCH.
NOT LIKE MY CHILDHOOD FRIENDS THAT YOU HATED.
WHEN I GOT OUT OF THE NAVY, I GOT HIRED TO PLAY THE ORGAN EVERY SUNDAY AT ONE OF THOSE CLASSY EPISCOPALIAN CHURCHES IN CLAYFIELD.
NOT TO BRAG, BUT PEOPLE USED TO TELL ME I WAS 'TOO GOOD FOR CLAYFIELD.'
THAT WAS BACK BEFORE THE DIXIE PATRIOT GOT ME FIRED.
PEOPLE SAID THAT SOONER OR LATER I'D GET LURED AWAY TO SOME BIG CITY WHERE I COULD MAKE A REAL NAME FOR MYSELF.
THINK ABOUT THAT, DADDY!
Y'NEVER KNOW! IT COULD STILL HAPPEN.

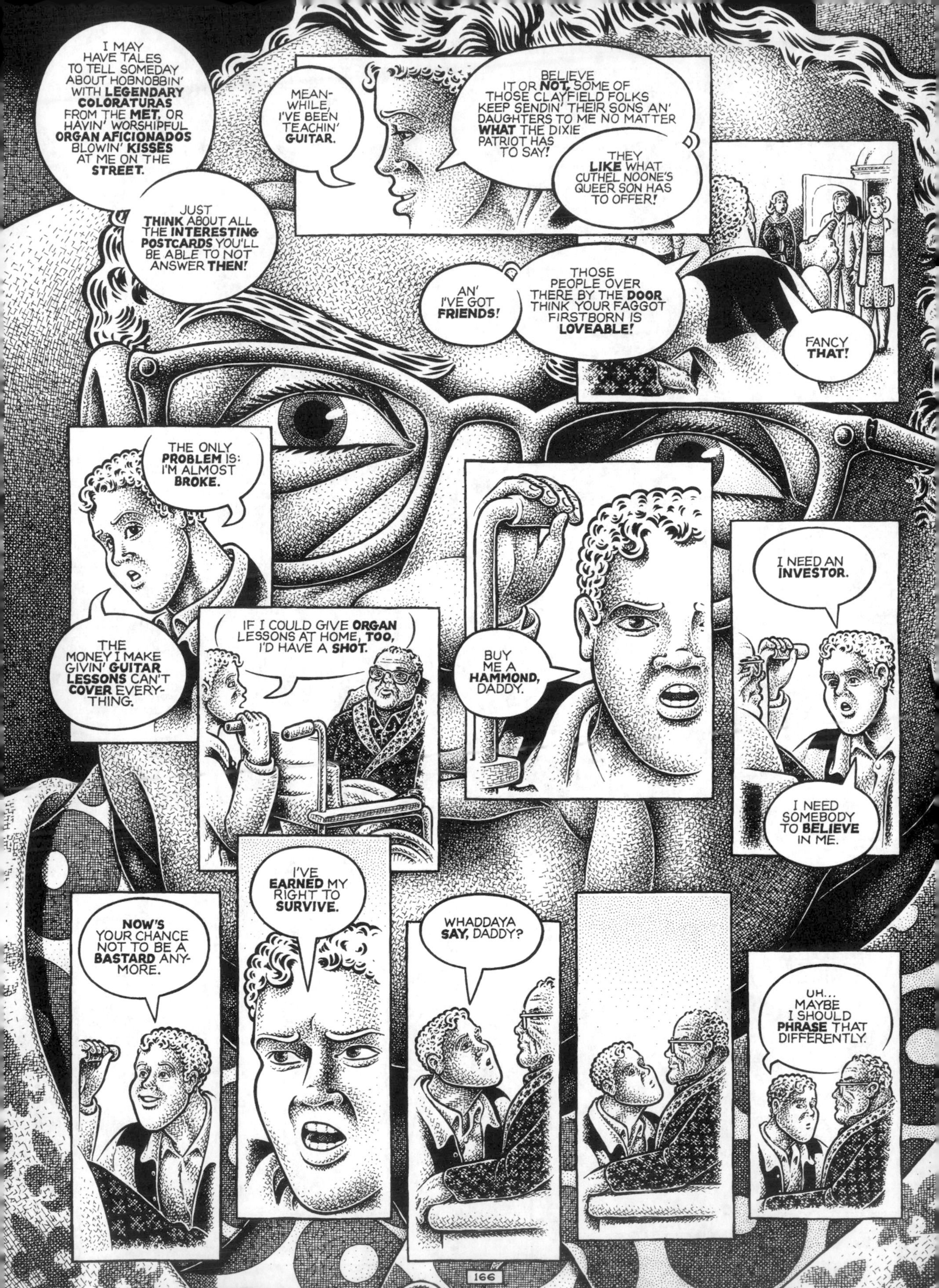
I MAY HAVE TALES TO TELL SOMEDAY ABOUT HOBNOBBIN' WITH LEGENDARY COLORATURAS FROM THE MET, OR HAVIN' WORSHIPFUL ORGAN AFICIONADOS BLOWIN' KISSES AT ME ON THE STREET.
JUST THINK ABOUT ALL THE INTERESTING POSTCARDS YOU'LL BE ABLE TO NOT ANSWER THEN!
MEAN-WHILE, I'VE BEEN TEACHIN' GUITAR.
BELIEVE IT OR NOT, SOME OF THOSE CLAYFIELD FOLKS KEEP SENDIN' THEIR SONS AN' DAUGHTERS TO ME NO MATTER WHAT THE DIXIE PATRIOT HAS TO SAY!
THEY LIKE WHAT CUTHEL NOONE'S QUEER SON HAS TO OFFER!
AN' I'VE GOT FRIENDS!
THOSE PEOPLE OVER THERE BY THE DOOR THINK YOUR FAGGOT FIRSTBORN IS LOVEABLE!
FANCY THAT!
THE ONLY PROBLEM IS: I'M ALMOST BROKE.
THE MONEY I MAKE GIVIN' GUITAR LESSONS CAN'T COVER EVERY-THING.
IF I COULD GIVE ORGAN LESSONS AT HOME, TOO, I'D HAVE A SHOT.
BUY ME A HAMMOND, DADDY.
I NEED AN INVESTOR.
I NEED SOMEBODY TO BELIEVE IN ME.
NOW'S YOUR CHANCE NOT TO BE A BASTARD ANY-MORE.
I'VE EARNED MY RIGHT TO SURVIVE.
WHADDAYA SAY, DADDY?
UH... MAYBE I SHOULD PHRASE THAT DIFFERENTLY.

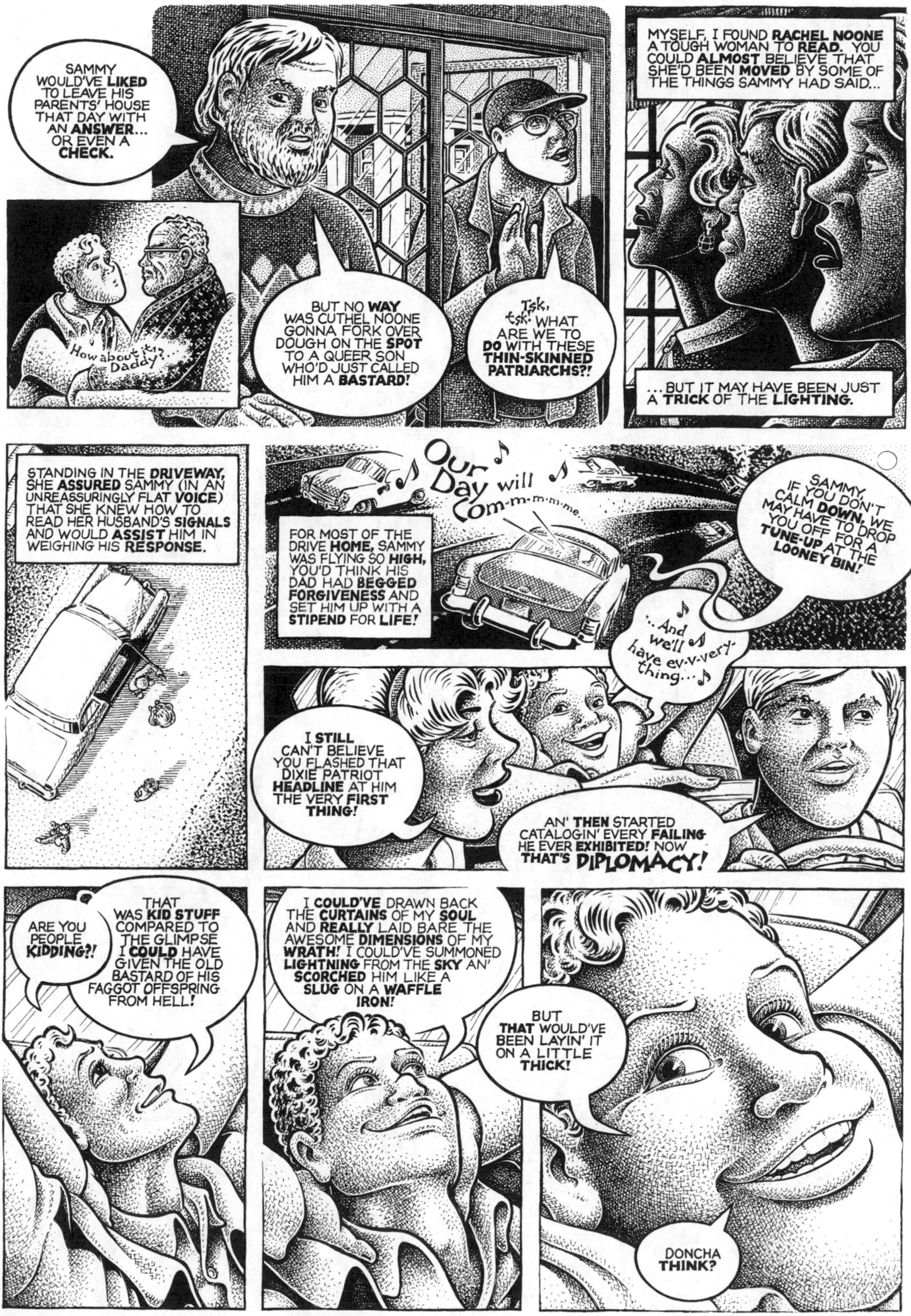

SAMMY WOULD'VE LIKED TO LEAVE HIS PARENTS' HOUSE THAT DAY WITH AN ANSWER... OR EVEN A CHECK.
How about it, Daddy?
BUT NO WAY WAS CUTHEL NOONE GONNA FORK OVER DOUGH ON THE SPOT TO A QUEER SON WHO'D JUST CALLED HIM A BASTARD!
Tsk, tsk. WHAT ARE WE TO DO WITH THESE THIN-SKINNED PATRIARCHS?!
MYSELF, I FOUND RACHEL NOONE A TOUGH WOMAN TO READ. YOU COULD ALMOST BELIEVE THAT SHE'D BEEN MOVED BY SOME OF THE THINGS SAMMY HAD SAID...
...BUT IT MAY HAVE BEEN JUST A TRICK OF THE LIGHTING.
STANDING IN THE DRIVEWAY, SHE ASSURED SAMMY (IN AN UNREASSURINGLY FLAT VOICE) THAT SHE KNEW HOW TO READ HER HUSBAND'S SIGNALS AND WOULD ASSIST HIM IN WEIGHING HIS RESPONSE.
Our Day will com-m-m-m-me...
FOR MOST OF THE DRIVE HOME, SAMMY WAS FLYING SO HIGH, YOU'D THINK HIS DAD HAD BEGGED FORGIVENESS AND SET HIM UP WITH A STIPEND FOR LIFE!
SAMMY, IF YOU DON'T CALM DOWN, WE MAY HAVE TO DROP YOU OFF FOR A TUNE-UP AT THE LOONEY BIN!
...And we'll have ev-v-very-thing...
I STILL CAN'T BELIEVE YOU FLASHED THAT DIXIE PATRIOT HEADLINE AT HIM THE VERY FIRST THING!
AN' THEN STARTED CATALOGIN' EVERY FAILING HE EVER EXHIBITED! NOW THAT'S DIPLOMACY!
ARE YOU PEOPLE KIDDING?!
THAT WAS KID STUFF COMPARED TO THE GLIMPSE I COULD HAVE GIVEN THE OLD BASTARD OF HIS FAGGOT OFFSPRING FROM HELL!
I COULD'VE DRAWN BACK THE CURTAINS OF MY SOUL AND REALLY LAID BARE THE AWESOME DIMENSIONS OF MY WRATH! I COULD'VE SUMMONED LIGHTNING FROM THE SKY AN' SCORCHED HIM LIKE A SLUG ON A WAFFLE IRON!
BUT THAT WOULD'VE BEEN LAYIN' IT ON A LITTLE THICK!
DONCHA THINK?

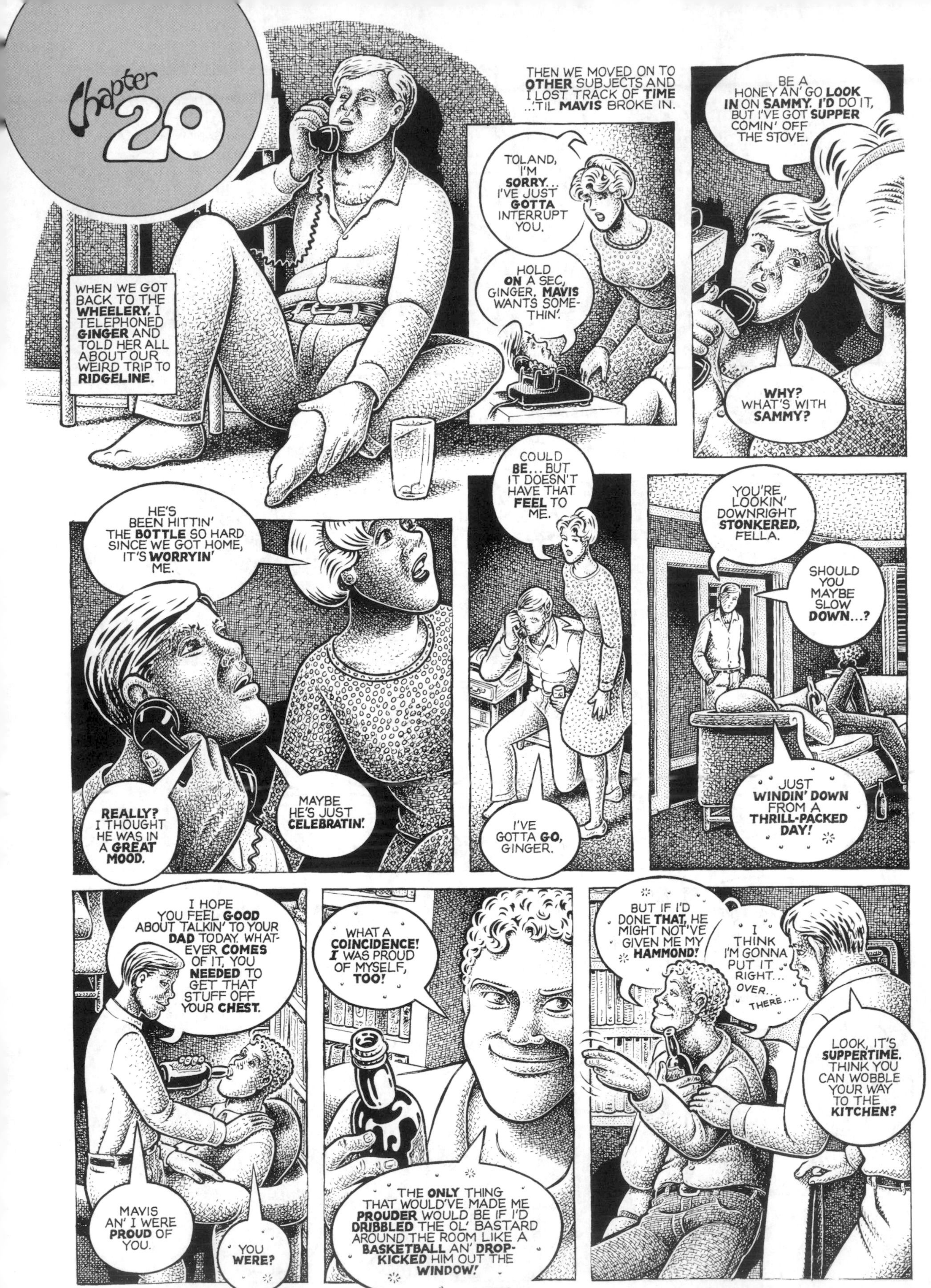
Chapter 20
WHEN WE GOT BACK TO THE WHEELERY, I TELEPHONED GINGER AND TOLD HER ALL ABOUT OUR WEIRD TRIP TO RIDGELINE.
THEN WE MOVED ON TO OTHER SUBJECTS AND I LOST TRACK OF TIME ...'TIL MAVIS BROKE IN.
TOLAND, I'M SORRY... I'VE JUST GOTTA INTERRUPT YOU.
HOLD ON A SEC, GINGER. MAVIS WANTS SOMETHIN'.
BE A HONEY AN' GO LOOK IN ON SAMMY. I'D DO IT, BUT I'VE GOT SUPPER COMIN' OFF THE STOVE.
WHY? WHAT'S WITH SAMMY?
HE'S BEEN HITTIN' THE BOTTLE SO HARD SINCE WE GOT HOME, IT'S WORRYIN' ME.
REALLY? I THOUGHT HE WAS IN A GREAT MOOD.
MAYBE HE'S JUST CELEBRATIN'.
COULD BE... BUT IT DOESN'T HAVE THAT FEEL TO ME.
I'VE GOTTA GO, GINGER.
YOU'RE LOOKIN' DOWNRIGHT STONKERED, FELLA.
SHOULD YOU MAYBE SLOW DOWN...?
JUST WINDIN' DOWN FROM A THRILL-PACKED DAY!
I HOPE YOU FEEL GOOD ABOUT TALKIN' TO YOUR DAD TODAY. WHATEVER COMES OF IT, YOU NEEDED TO GET THAT STUFF OFF YOUR CHEST.
MAVIS AN' I WERE PROUD OF YOU.
YOU WERE?
WHAT A COINCIDENCE! I WAS PROUD OF MYSELF, TOO!
THE ONLY THING THAT WOULD'VE MADE ME PROUDER WOULD BE IF I'D DRIBBLED THE OL' BASTARD AROUND THE ROOM LIKE A BASKETBALL AN' DROP-KICKED HIM OUT THE WINDOW!
BUT IF I'D DONE THAT, HE MIGHT NOT'VE GIVEN ME MY HAMMOND!
I THINK I'M GONNA PUT IT RIGHT... OVER... THERE....
LOOK, IT'S SUPPERTIME. THINK YOU CAN WOBBLE YOUR WAY TO THE KITCHEN?

SAMMY MADE IT TO THE **TABLE** AND MANAGED TO STAY PRETTY NEAR **VERTICAL**, GIVE OR TAKE A **FEW** DEGREES.

...BUT WITH HIM **RAVING** AND **FLAILING** THE WHOLE TIME, IT WAS ONE OF THE **LEAST RELAXING** MEALS IN HUMAN **HISTORY.**

YOU COULD **SEE** THAT **RILEY** WAS GETTING MORE AND MORE **PISSED.**

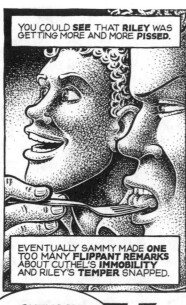

EVENTUALLY SAMMY MADE **ONE** TOO MANY **FLIPPANT** REMARKS ABOUT CUTHEL'S **IMMOBILITY** AND RILEY'S **TEMPER** SNAPPED.

THIS IS ALL GETTIN' TO BE **JUST A BIT MUCH!**

THE MAN IS **PARALYZED!**

THAT **AIN'T** NO FUCKIN' **JOKE!**

YOU EXPECT THE **REST** OF US TO SIT AROUND AN' **DESPISE** YOUR **FATHER** RIGHT **ALONG** WITH YOU, BUT— **MY GOD,** SAMMY!...

...BASTARD OR **NOT,** IT SOUNDS LIKE THE GUY'S BEIN' PUT THROUGH A PRETTY HEFTY **WRINGER** FOR HIS **SINS!**

NOT HEFTY ENOUGH TO SUIT **ME!**

WELL, **LET'S** JUST MAKE SAMMY NOONE **JUDGE OF THE UNIVERSE,** THEN!

HOW WOULD **YOU** LIKE TO GET STUCK IN A BODY LIKE YOUR OL' MAN'S?

tap, tap!

IT COULD **HAPPEN.** SOME DISEASES GET **INHERITED.**

AN' HERE COMES SOME **WILD MAN** STORMIN' INTO YOUR HOUSE, SCREAMIN' 'BOUT WHAT A **SHITHEAD** YOU ARE!

Y'GOT NO **WAY** TO SAY YOU'RE **SORRY!** Y'GOT NO WAY TO GIVE HIM THE **FINGER!**

YOU'RE **WAY** PAST BEIN' ABLE TO MAKE **AMENDS** FOR PAST **FAILINGS!**

DAMN IF I CAN'T MUSTER SOME **SYMPATHY** FOR A MAN IN THAT **FIX!**

Y'KNOW, I **WASN'T** JUST SOME **STRAY PSYCHO** BARGIN' IN ON HIM TODAY!

I'M HIS **SON!** ...AN' I'VE GOT AMPLE **CAUSE** TO BE MAD AT HIM!

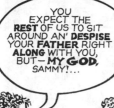

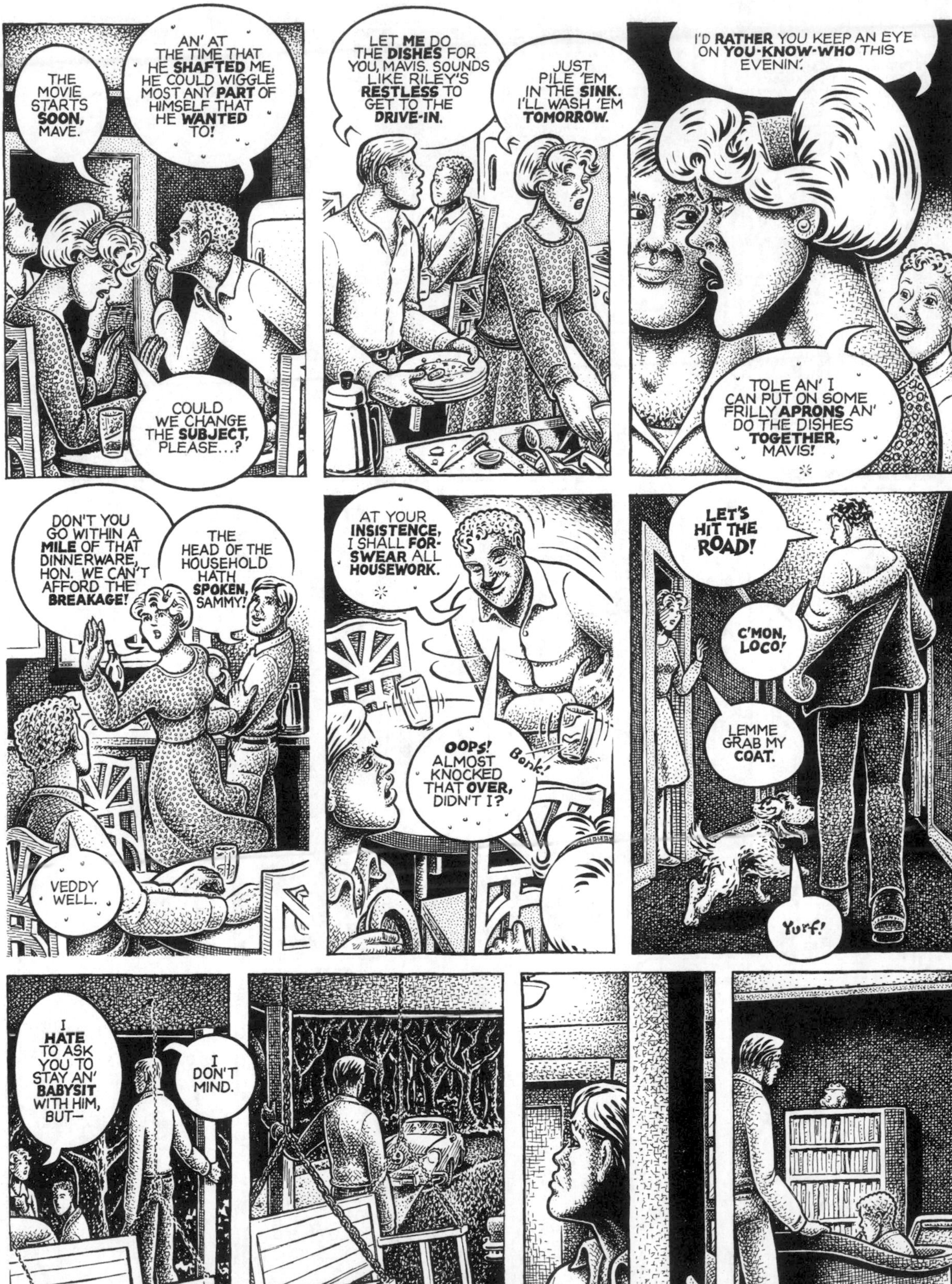

THE MOVIE STARTS SOON, MAVE.
AN' AT THE TIME THAT HE SHAFTED ME, HE COULD WIGGLE MOST ANY PART OF HIMSELF THAT HE WANTED TO!
COULD WE CHANGE THE SUBJECT, PLEASE...?
LET ME DO THE DISHES FOR YOU, MAVIS. SOUNDS LIKE RILEY'S RESTLESS TO GET TO THE DRIVE-IN.
JUST PILE 'EM IN THE SINK. I'LL WASH 'EM TOMORROW.
I'D RATHER YOU KEEP AN EYE ON YOU-KNOW-WHO THIS EVENIN'.
TOLE AN' I CAN PUT ON SOME FRILLY APRONS AN' DO THE DISHES TOGETHER, MAVIS!
DON'T YOU GO WITHIN A MILE OF THAT DINNERWARE, HON. WE CAN'T AFFORD THE BREAKAGE!
THE HEAD OF THE HOUSEHOLD HATH SPOKEN, SAMMY!
VEDDY WELL.
AT YOUR INSISTENCE, I SHALL FORSWEAR ALL HOUSEWORK.
OOPS! ALMOST KNOCKED THAT OVER, DIDN'T I?
Bonk!
LET'S HIT THE ROAD!
C'MON, LOCO!
LEMME GRAB MY COAT.
Yurf!
I HATE TO ASK YOU TO STAY AN' BABYSIT WITH HIM, BUT—
I DON'T MIND.

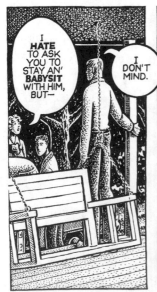

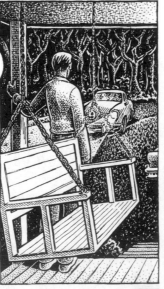

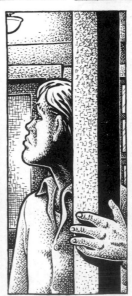

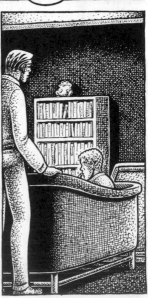

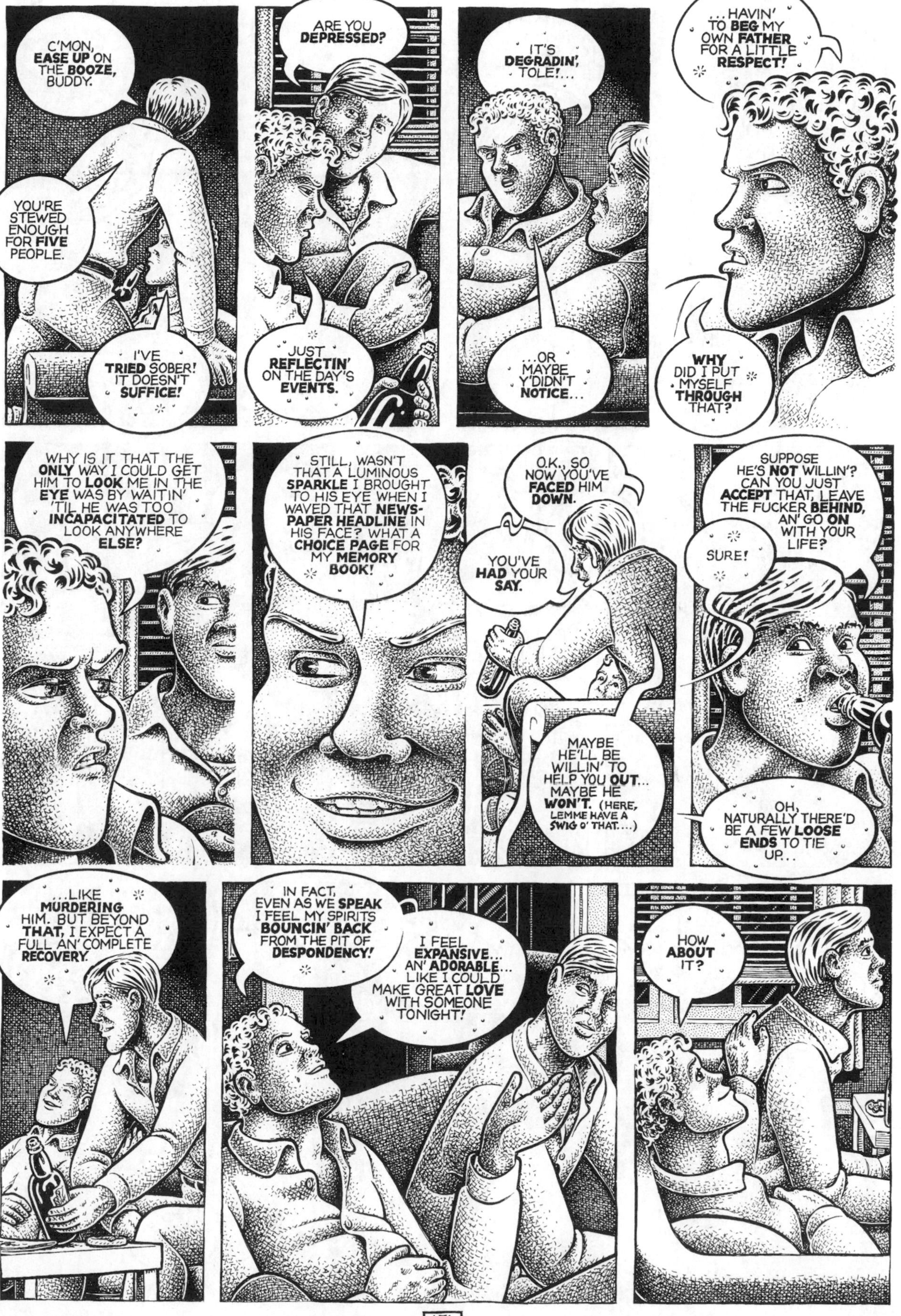
C'MON, EASE UP ON THE BOOZE, BUDDY.
YOU'RE STEWED ENOUGH FOR FIVE PEOPLE.
I'VE TRIED SOBER! IT DOESN'T SUFFICE!
ARE YOU DEPRESSED?
JUST REFLECTIN' ON THE DAY'S EVENTS.
IT'S DEGRADIN', TOLE!...
...OR MAYBE Y'DIDN'T NOTICE...
...HAVIN' TO BEG MY OWN FATHER FOR A LITTLE RESPECT!
WHY DID I PUT MYSELF THROUGH THAT?
WHY IS IT THAT THE ONLY WAY I COULD GET HIM TO LOOK ME IN THE EYE WAS BY WAITIN' 'TIL HE WAS TOO INCAPACITATED TO LOOK ANYWHERE ELSE?
STILL, WASN'T THAT A LUMINOUS SPARKLE I BROUGHT TO HIS EYE WHEN I WAVED THAT NEWS-PAPER HEADLINE IN HIS FACE? WHAT A CHOICE PAGE FOR MY MEMORY BOOK!
O.K., SO NOW YOU'VE FACED HIM DOWN.
YOU'VE HAD YOUR SAY.
MAYBE HE'LL BE WILLIN' TO HELP YOU OUT... MAYBE HE WON'T. (HERE, LEMME HAVE A SWIG O' THAT....)
SUPPOSE HE'S NOT WILLIN'? CAN YOU JUST ACCEPT THAT, LEAVE THE FUCKER BEHIND, AN' GO ON WITH YOUR LIFE?
SURE!
OH, NATURALLY THERE'D BE A FEW LOOSE ENDS TO TIE UP..
...LIKE MURDERING HIM. BUT BEYOND THAT, I EXPECT A FULL AN' COMPLETE RECOVERY.
IN FACT, EVEN AS WE SPEAK I FEEL MY SPIRITS BOUNCIN' BACK FROM THE PIT OF DESPONDENCY!
I FEEL EXPANSIVE... AN' ADORABLE... LIKE I COULD MAKE GREAT LOVE WITH SOMEONE TONIGHT!
HOW ABOUT IT?

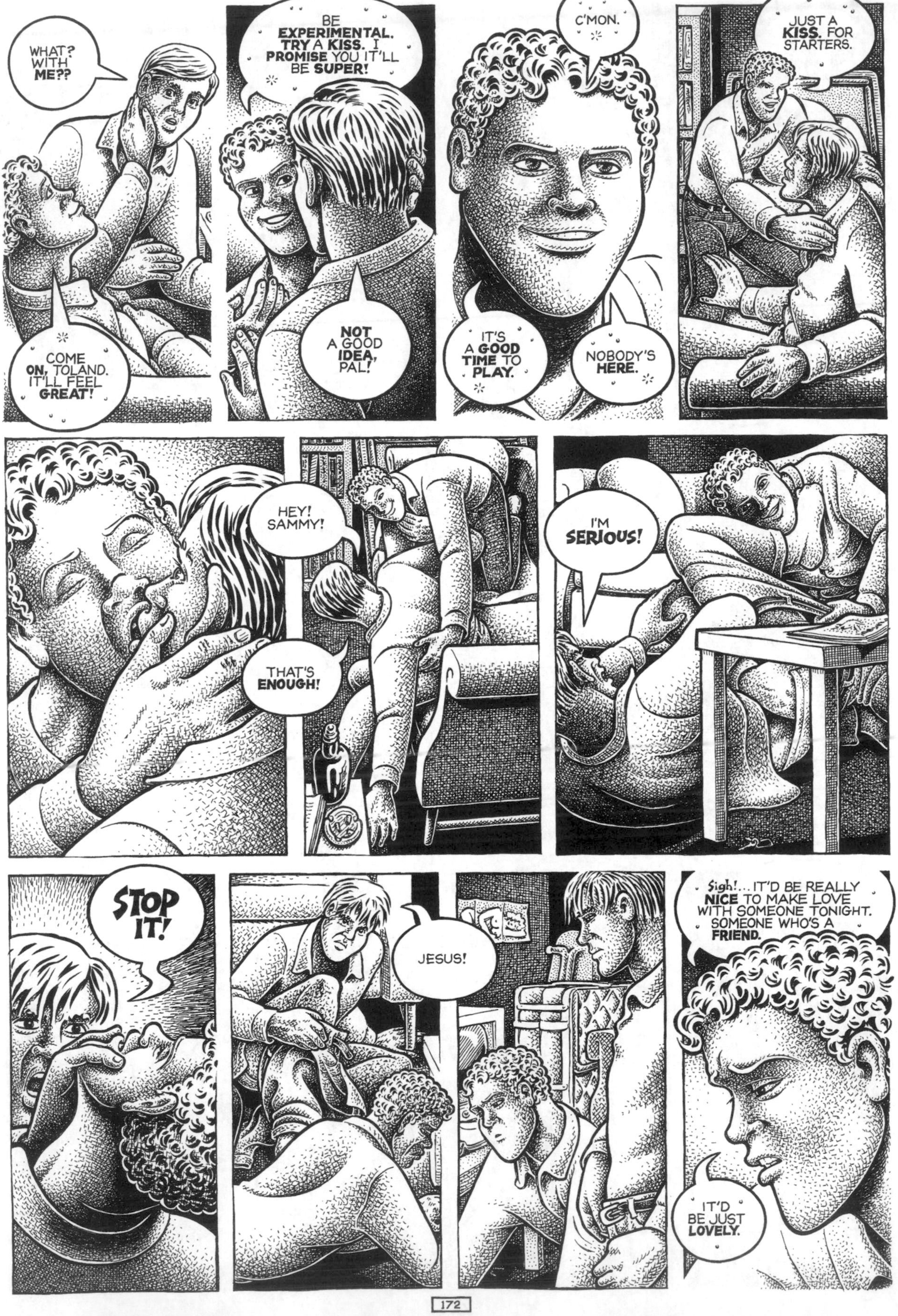
WHAT? WITH ME??
COME ON, TOLAND. IT'LL FEEL GREAT!
BE EXPERIMENTAL. TRY A KISS. I PROMISE YOU IT'LL BE SUPER!
NOT A GOOD IDEA, PAL!
C'MON.
IT'S A GOOD TIME TO PLAY.
NOBODY'S HERE.
JUST A KISS, FOR STARTERS.
HEY! SAMMY!
THAT'S ENOUGH!
I'M SERIOUS!
STOP IT!
JESUS!
Sigh!... IT'D BE REALLY NICE TO MAKE LOVE WITH SOMEONE TONIGHT. SOMEONE WHO'S A FRIEND.
IT'D BE JUST LOVELY.

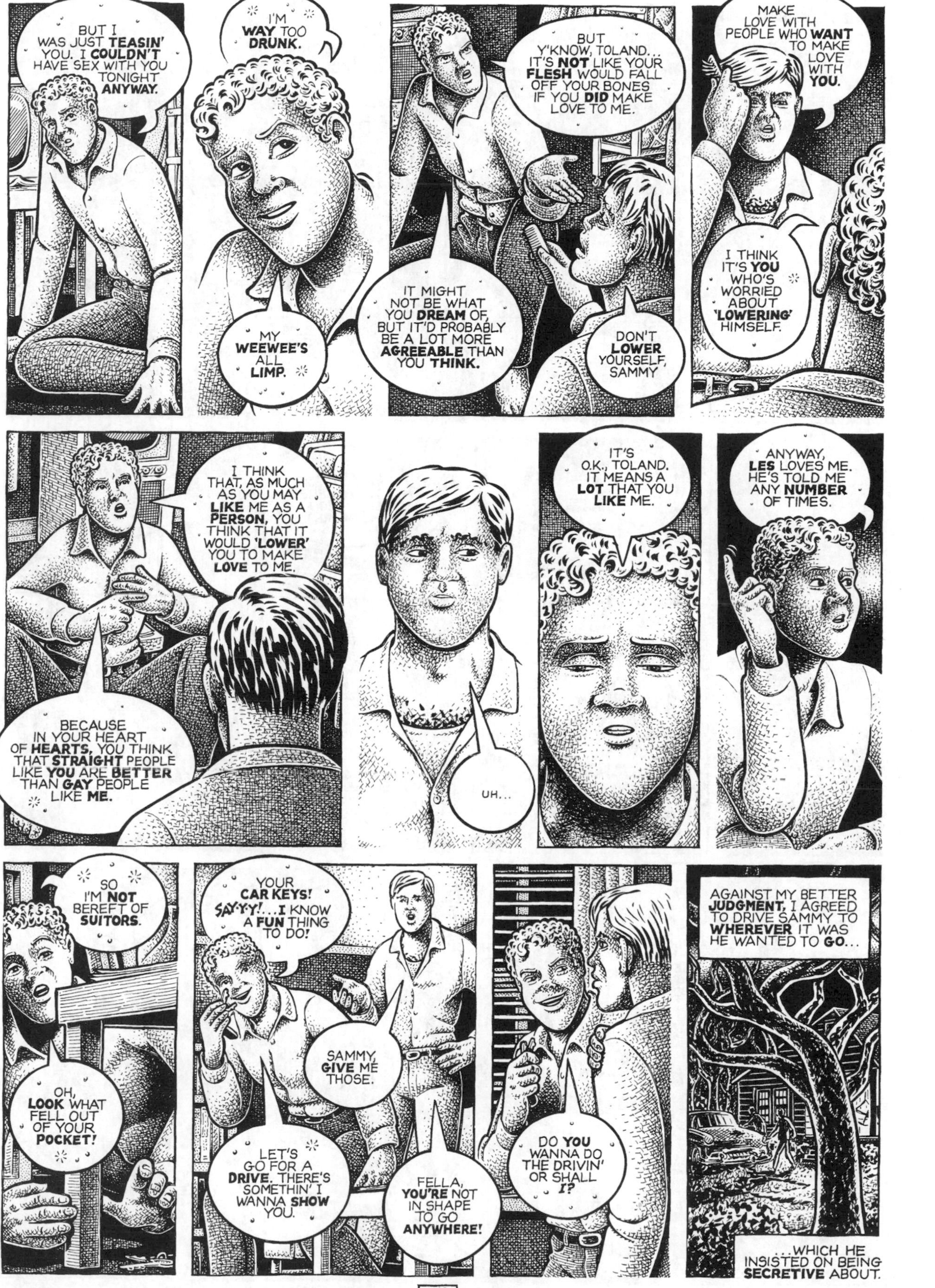
BUT I WAS JUST **TEASIN'** YOU. I **COULDN'T** HAVE SEX WITH YOU TONIGHT **ANYWAY**.
I'M **WAY** TOO **DRUNK**.
MY **WEEWEE'S** ALL **LIMP**.
BUT Y'KNOW, TOLAND... IT'S **NOT** LIKE YOUR **FLESH** WOULD FALL OFF YOUR BONES IF YOU **DID** MAKE LOVE TO ME.
IT MIGHT NOT BE WHAT YOU **DREAM** OF, BUT IT'D PROBABLY BE A LOT MORE **AGREEABLE** THAN YOU **THINK**.
DON'T **LOWER** YOURSELF, SAMMY
MAKE LOVE WITH PEOPLE WHO **WANT** TO MAKE LOVE WITH **YOU**.
I THINK IT'S **YOU** WHO'S WORRIED ABOUT **'LOWERING'** HIMSELF.
I THINK THAT, AS MUCH AS YOU MAY **LIKE** ME AS A **PERSON**, YOU THINK THAT IT WOULD **'LOWER'** YOU TO MAKE **LOVE** TO ME.
BECAUSE IN YOUR HEART OF **HEARTS**, YOU THINK THAT **STRAIGHT** PEOPLE LIKE **YOU** ARE **BETTER** THAN **GAY** PEOPLE LIKE **ME**.
UH...
IT'S O.K., TOLAND. IT MEANS A **LOT** THAT YOU **LIKE** ME.
ANYWAY, **LES** LOVES ME. HE'S TOLD ME ANY **NUMBER** OF TIMES.
SO I'M **NOT** BEREFT OF **SUITORS**.
OH, **LOOK** WHAT FELL OUT OF YOUR **POCKET!**
YOUR **CAR KEYS!** *SAY-Y-Y!*... I KNOW A **FUN** THING TO DO!
SAMMY, **GIVE** ME THOSE.
LET'S GO FOR A **DRIVE**. THERE'S SOMETHIN' I WANNA **SHOW** YOU.
FELLA, **YOU'RE** NOT IN SHAPE TO GO **ANYWHERE!**
DO **YOU** WANNA DO THE DRIVIN' OR SHALL ***I?***
AGAINST MY BETTER **JUDGMENT**, I AGREED TO DRIVE SAMMY TO **WHEREVER** IT WAS HE WANTED TO **GO**...
...WHICH HE INSISTED ON BEING **SECRETIVE** ABOUT.

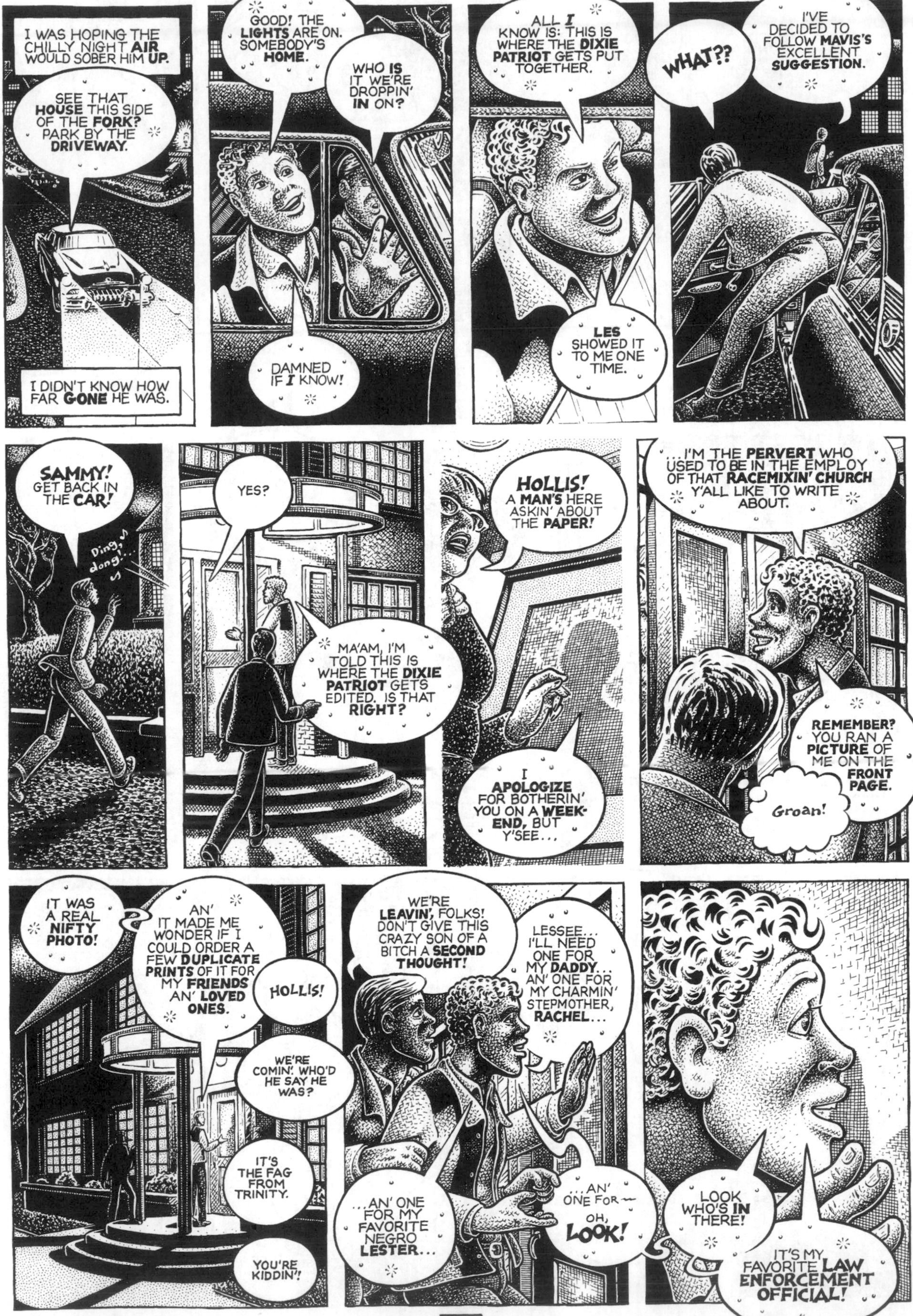

I WAS HOPING THE CHILLY NIGHT AIR WOULD SOBER HIM UP.
SEE THAT HOUSE THIS SIDE OF THE FORK? PARK BY THE DRIVEWAY.
I DIDN'T KNOW HOW FAR GONE HE WAS.
GOOD! THE LIGHTS ARE ON. SOMEBODY'S HOME.
WHO IS IT WE'RE DROPPIN' IN ON?
DAMNED IF I KNOW!
ALL I KNOW IS: THIS IS WHERE THE DIXIE PATRIOT GETS PUT TOGETHER.
LES SHOWED IT TO ME ONE TIME.
WHAT??
I'VE DECIDED TO FOLLOW MAVIS'S EXCELLENT SUGGESTION.
SAMMY! GET BACK IN THE CAR!
Ding dong
YES?
MA'AM, I'M TOLD THIS IS WHERE THE DIXIE PATRIOT GETS EDITED. IS THAT RIGHT?
HOLLIS! A MAN'S HERE ASKIN' ABOUT THE PAPER!
I APOLOGIZE FOR BOTHERIN' YOU ON A WEEK-END, BUT Y'SEE...
...I'M THE PERVERT WHO USED TO BE IN THE EMPLOY OF THAT RACEMIXIN' CHURCH Y'ALL LIKE TO WRITE ABOUT.
REMEMBER? YOU RAN A PICTURE OF ME ON THE FRONT PAGE.
Groan!
IT WAS A REAL NIFTY PHOTO!
AN' IT MADE ME WONDER IF I COULD ORDER A FEW DUPLICATE PRINTS OF IT FOR MY FRIENDS AN' LOVED ONES.
HOLLIS!
WE'RE COMIN'. WHO'D HE SAY HE WAS?
IT'S THE FAG FROM TRINITY.
YOU'RE KIDDIN'!
WE'RE LEAVIN', FOLKS! DON'T GIVE THIS CRAZY SON OF A BITCH A SECOND THOUGHT!
LESSEE... I'LL NEED ONE FOR MY DADDY... AN' ONE FOR MY CHARMIN' STEPMOTHER, RACHEL...
...AN' ONE FOR MY FAVORITE NEGRO LESTER...
...AN' ONE FOR— OH, LOOK!
LOOK WHO'S IN THERE!
IT'S MY FAVORITE LAW ENFORCEMENT OFFICIAL!

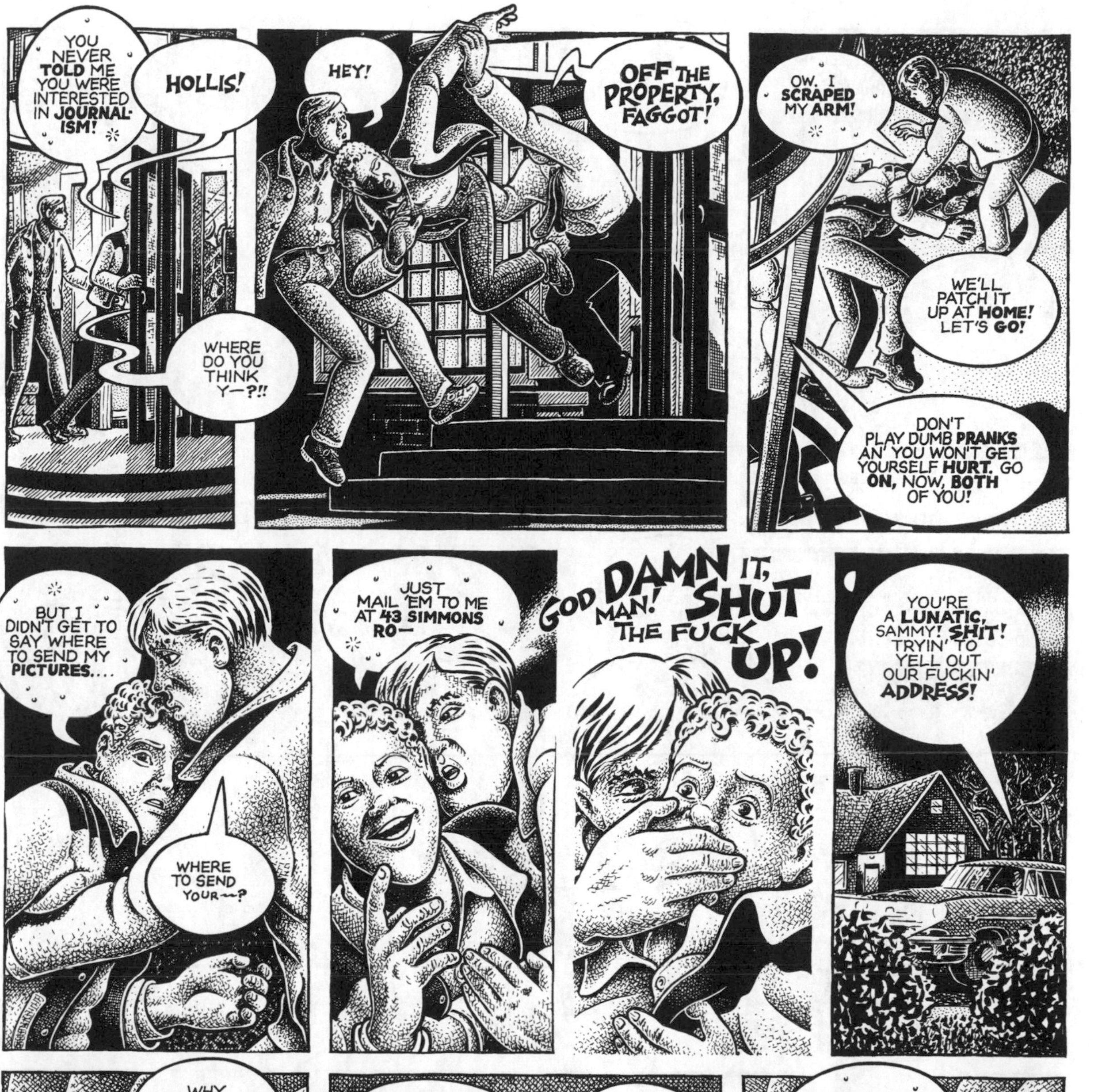
YOU NEVER TOLD ME YOU WERE INTERESTED IN JOURNALISM!
HOLLIS!
WHERE DO YOU THINK Y—?!!
HEY!
OFF THE PROPERTY, FAGGOT!
OW. I SCRAPED MY ARM!
WE'LL PATCH IT UP AT HOME! LET'S GO!
DON'T PLAY DUMB PRANKS AN' YOU WON'T GET YOURSELF HURT. GO ON, NOW, BOTH OF YOU!
BUT I DIDN'T GET TO SAY WHERE TO SEND MY PICTURES....
WHERE TO SEND YOUR—?
JUST MAIL 'EM TO ME AT 43 SIMMONS RO—
GOD DAMN IT, MAN! SHUT THE FUCK UP!
YOU'RE A LUNATIC, SAMMY! SHIT! TRYIN' TO YELL OUT OUR FUCKIN' ADDRESS!
WHY DIDN'T YOU STOP AN' SKETCH OUT A MAP FOR 'EM WHILE YOU WERE AT IT?
OH, THEY ALL KNOW WHERE WE LIVE.
THEY'VE STOPPED BY THE WHEELERY BEFORE! RILEY SAID SO!
THAT WAS THE KKK, MORE'N LIKELY—NOT THIS CROWD!
THEY'RE ALL THE SAME!
DONCHA THINK THEY KEEP EACH OTHER ABREAST OF OUR LI'L OL' WHEREABOUTS?
THEY'RE SUCH GOSSIPS, HONEY—IT'S A SCANDAL! AN' THEY ALL GO TO THE SAME CONCERTS AN' BABY SHOWERS!
YOU'VE HAD YOUR LAST DRINK FOR TONIGHT, PAL—THAT'S FOR SURE!
I MEANT IT!

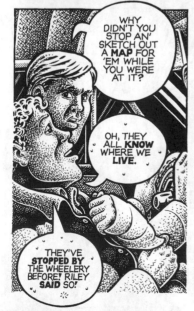

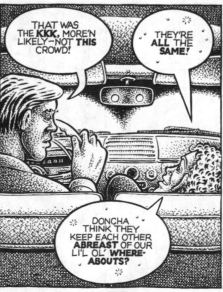

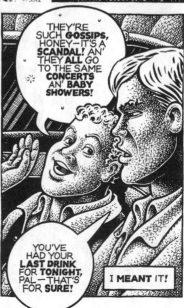

WHEN WE GOT **HOME**, I SET ABOUT CONFISCATING EVERY DROP OF **ALCOHOL** ON THE **PREMISES**...

* DON'T PUT YOURSELF **OUT** SO, TOLAND. *

...EXCEPT FOR THE **'RUBBING'** KIND WE DOUSED ON SAMMY'S **SCRAPES**.

I SHOVED THE JUMBLE OF **CANS** AND **BOTTLES** UNDER MY **BED**, SO SAMMY COULDN'T GET **AT** 'EM EVEN AFTER I'D GONE TO **SLEEP**.

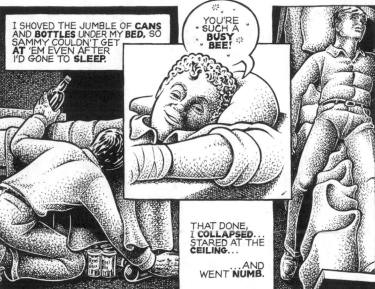

* YOU'RE SUCH A **BUSY BEE**! *

THAT DONE, I **COLLAPSED**... STARED AT THE **CEILING**... AND WENT **NUMB**.

MY MIND **DRIFTED** AND **SPUN**...

...'TIL I HEARD A **NOISE**...

...WHICH I TOOK TO BE SAMMY **BARFING** OUT IN THE **YARD**.

SAMMY...?

I WALKED OUT THE **BACK DOOR** TO MAKE SURE HE FELT **STEADY** ENOUGH TO GET BACK **INSIDE**.

AND THAT'S ALL I **REMEMBER**.

KRAK

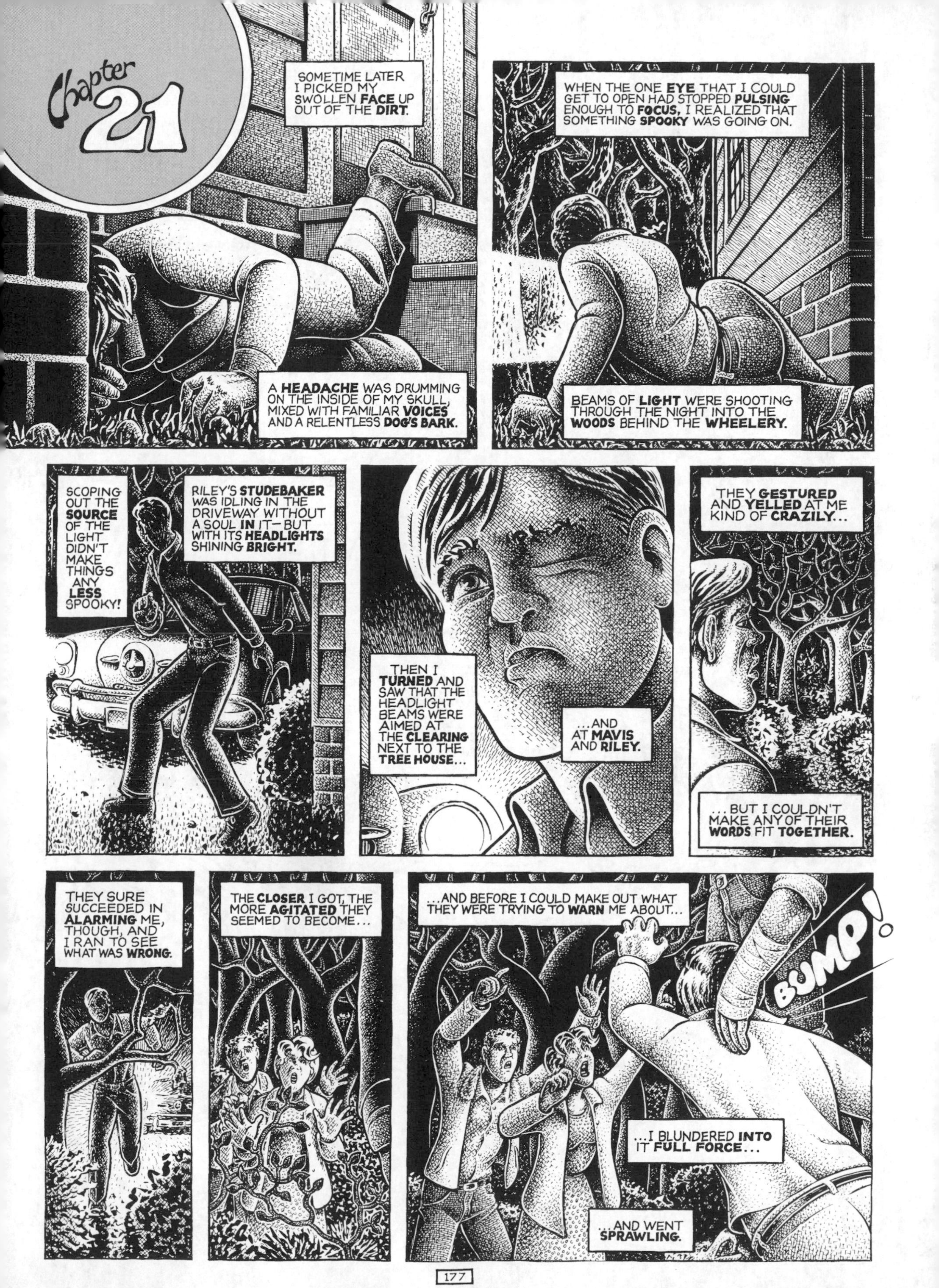
Chapter 21
SOMETIME LATER I PICKED MY SWOLLEN FACE UP OUT OF THE DIRT.
A HEADACHE WAS DRUMMING ON THE INSIDE OF MY SKULL, MIXED WITH FAMILIAR VOICES AND A RELENTLESS DOG'S BARK.
WHEN THE ONE EYE THAT I COULD GET TO OPEN HAD STOPPED PULSING ENOUGH TO FOCUS, I REALIZED THAT SOMETHING SPOOKY WAS GOING ON.
BEAMS OF LIGHT WERE SHOOTING THROUGH THE NIGHT INTO THE WOODS BEHIND THE WHEELERY.
SCOPING OUT THE SOURCE OF THE LIGHT DIDN'T MAKE THINGS ANY LESS SPOOKY!
RILEY'S STUDEBAKER WAS IDLING IN THE DRIVEWAY WITHOUT A SOUL IN IT—BUT WITH ITS HEADLIGHTS SHINING BRIGHT.
THEN I TURNED AND SAW THAT THE HEADLIGHT BEAMS WERE AIMED AT THE CLEARING NEXT TO THE TREE HOUSE...
...AND AT MAVIS AND RILEY.
THEY GESTURED AND YELLED AT ME KIND OF CRAZILY...
... BUT I COULDN'T MAKE ANY OF THEIR WORDS FIT TOGETHER.
THEY SURE SUCCEEDED IN ALARMING ME, THOUGH, AND I RAN TO SEE WHAT WAS WRONG.
THE CLOSER I GOT, THE MORE AGITATED THEY SEEMED TO BECOME...
...AND BEFORE I COULD MAKE OUT WHAT THEY WERE TRYING TO WARN ME ABOUT...
BUMP!
...I BLUNDERED INTO IT FULL FORCE...
...AND WENT SPRAWLING.

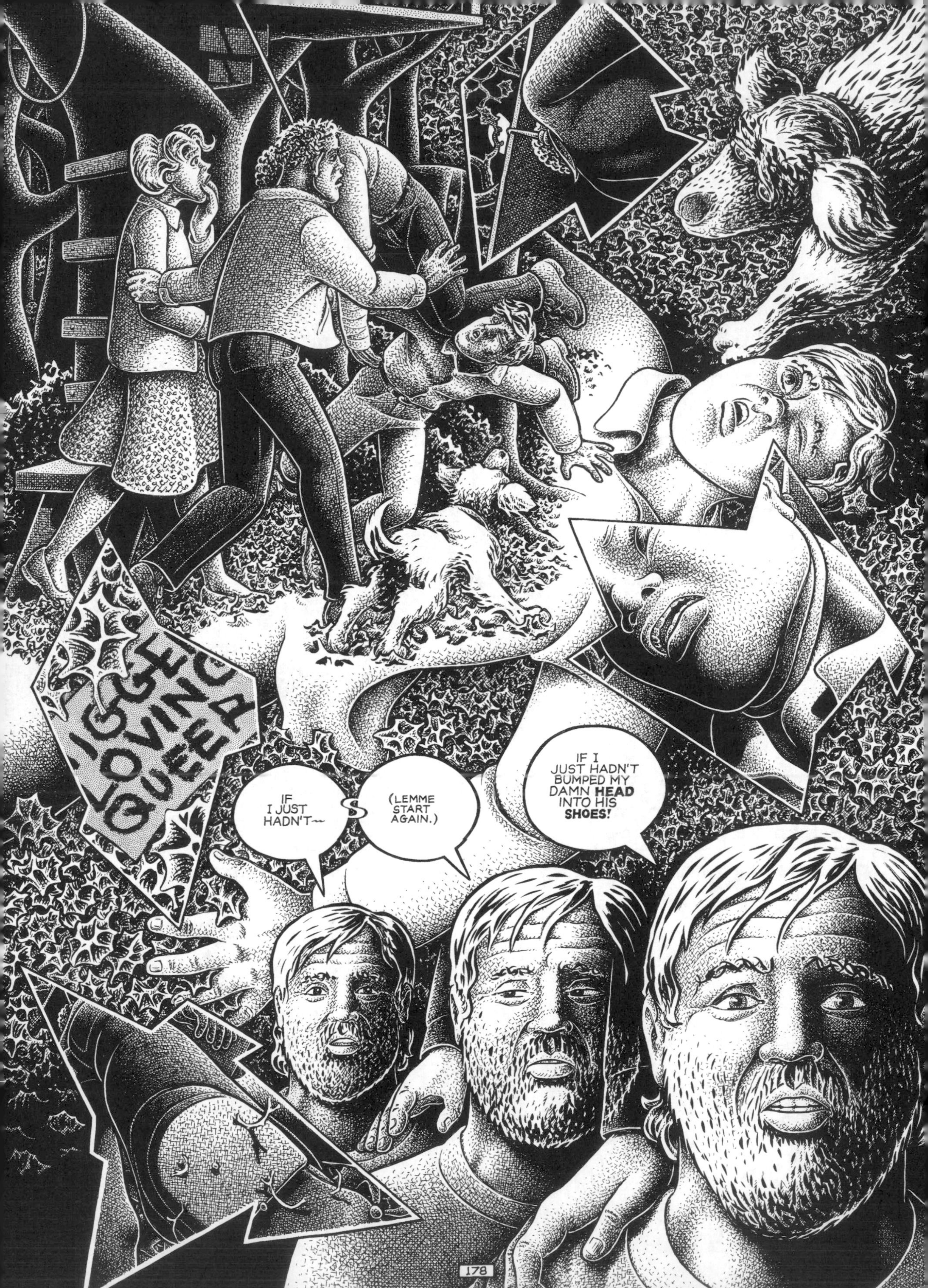
NIGGER LOVING QUEER
IF I JUST HADN'T--
(LEMME START AGAIN.)
IF I JUST HADN'T BUMPED MY DAMN HEAD INTO HIS SHOES!

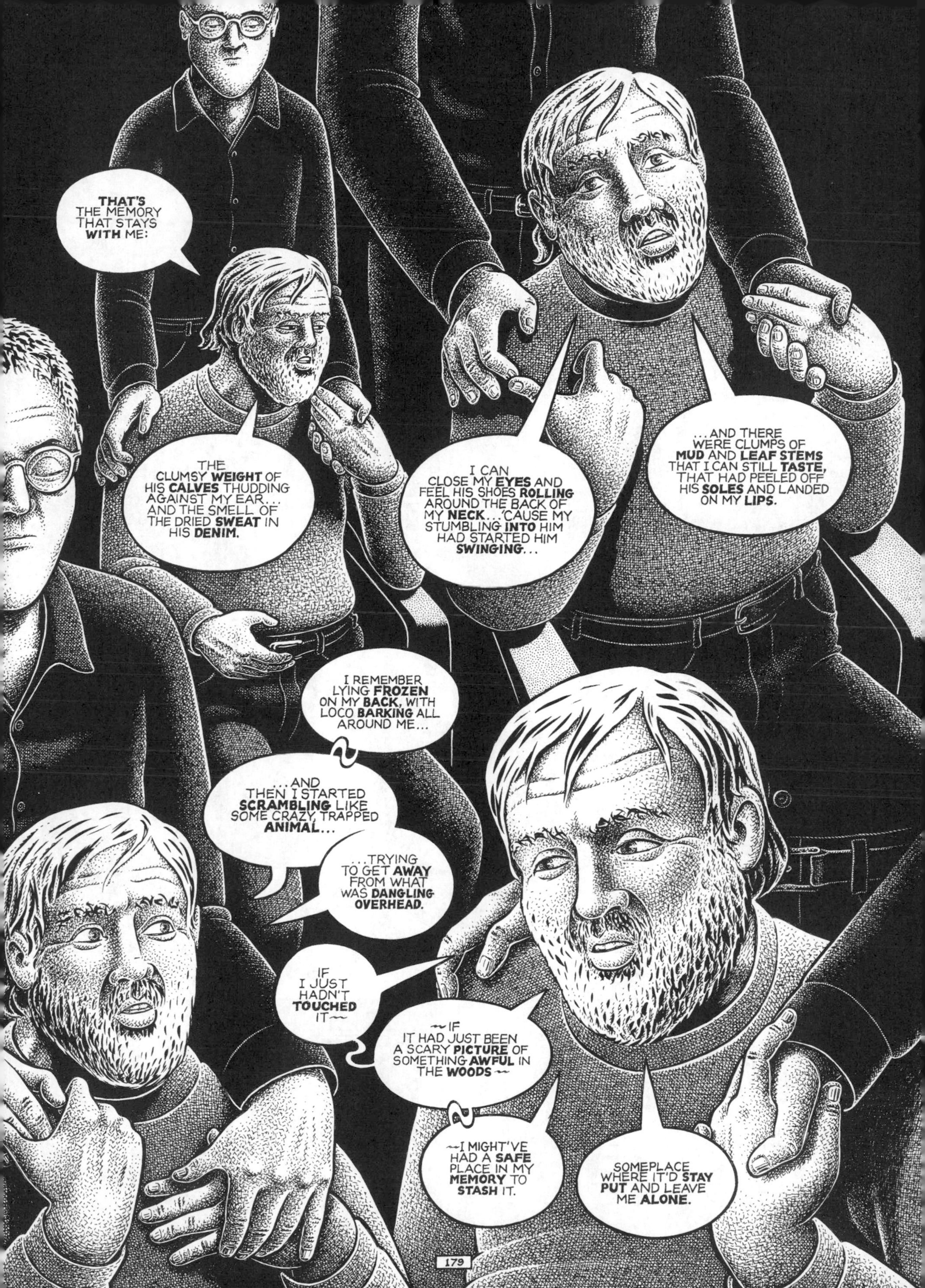
THAT'S THE MEMORY THAT STAYS WITH ME:
THE CLUMSY WEIGHT OF HIS CALVES THUDDING AGAINST MY EAR... AND THE SMELL OF THE DRIED SWEAT IN HIS DENIM.
I CAN CLOSE MY EYES AND FEEL HIS SHOES ROLLING AROUND THE BACK OF MY NECK... 'CAUSE MY STUMBLING INTO HIM HAD STARTED HIM SWINGING...
...AND THERE WERE CLUMPS OF MUD AND LEAF STEMS THAT I CAN STILL TASTE, THAT HAD PEELED OFF HIS SOLES AND LANDED ON MY LIPS.
I REMEMBER LYING FROZEN ON MY BACK, WITH LOCO BARKING ALL AROUND ME...
...AND THEN I STARTED SCRAMBLING LIKE SOME CRAZY, TRAPPED ANIMAL...
...TRYING TO GET AWAY FROM WHAT WAS DANGLING OVERHEAD.
IF I JUST HADN'T TOUCHED IT~
~IF IT HAD JUST BEEN A SCARY PICTURE OF SOMETHING AWFUL IN THE WOODS~
~I MIGHT'VE HAD A SAFE PLACE IN MY MEMORY TO STASH IT.
SOMEPLACE WHERE IT'D STAY PUT AND LEAVE ME ALONE.

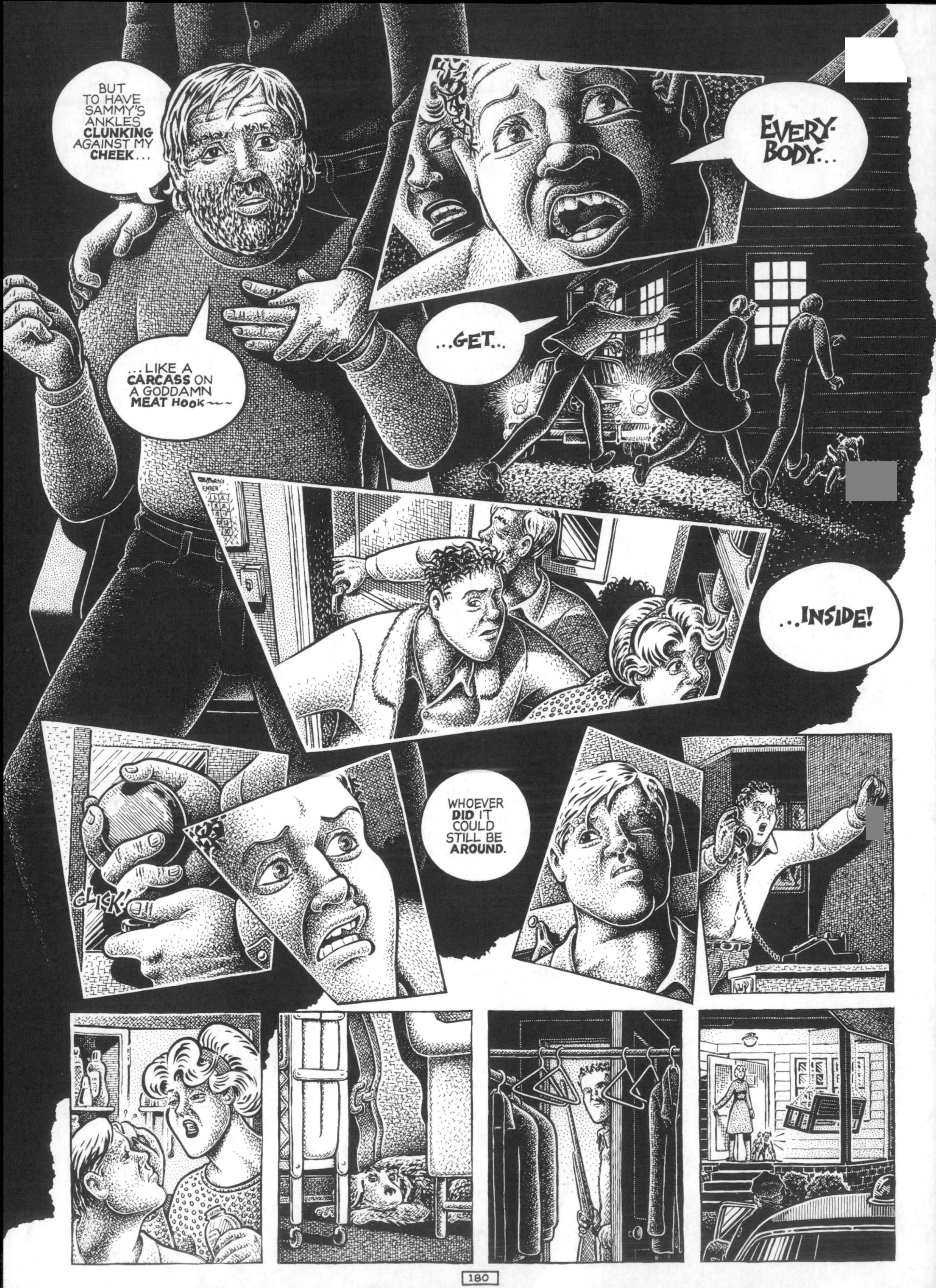
BUT TO HAVE SAMMY'S ANKLES CLUNKING AGAINST MY CHEEK...
...LIKE A CARCASS ON A GODDAMN MEAT HOOK~~~
EVERY-BODY...
...GET...
...INSIDE!
CLICK!
WHOEVER DID IT COULD STILL BE AROUND.

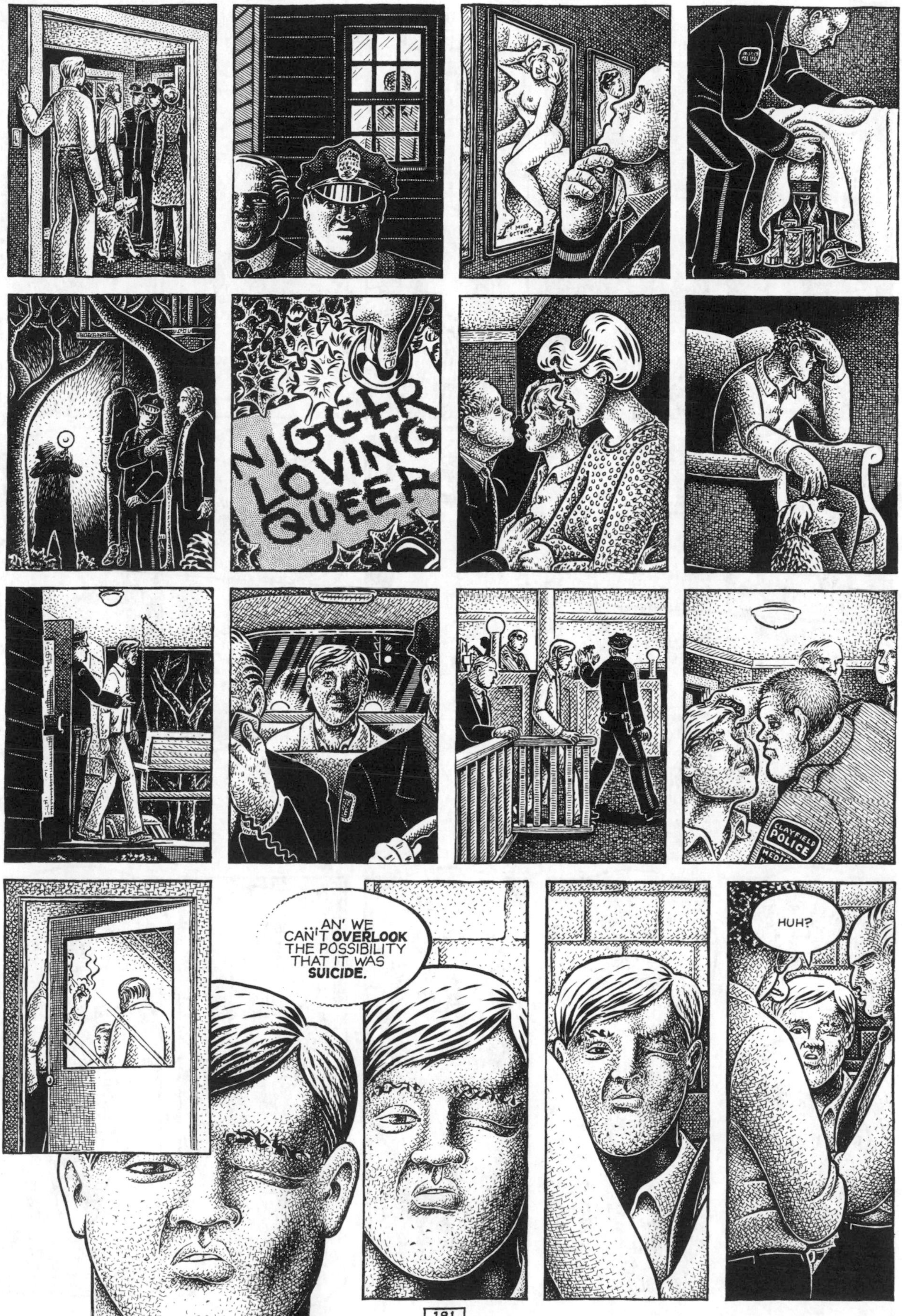
MISS OCTOBER
NIGGER LOVING QUEER
CLAYFIELD POLICE
... AN' WE CAN'T OVERLOOK THE POSSIBILITY THAT IT WAS SUICIDE.
HUH?

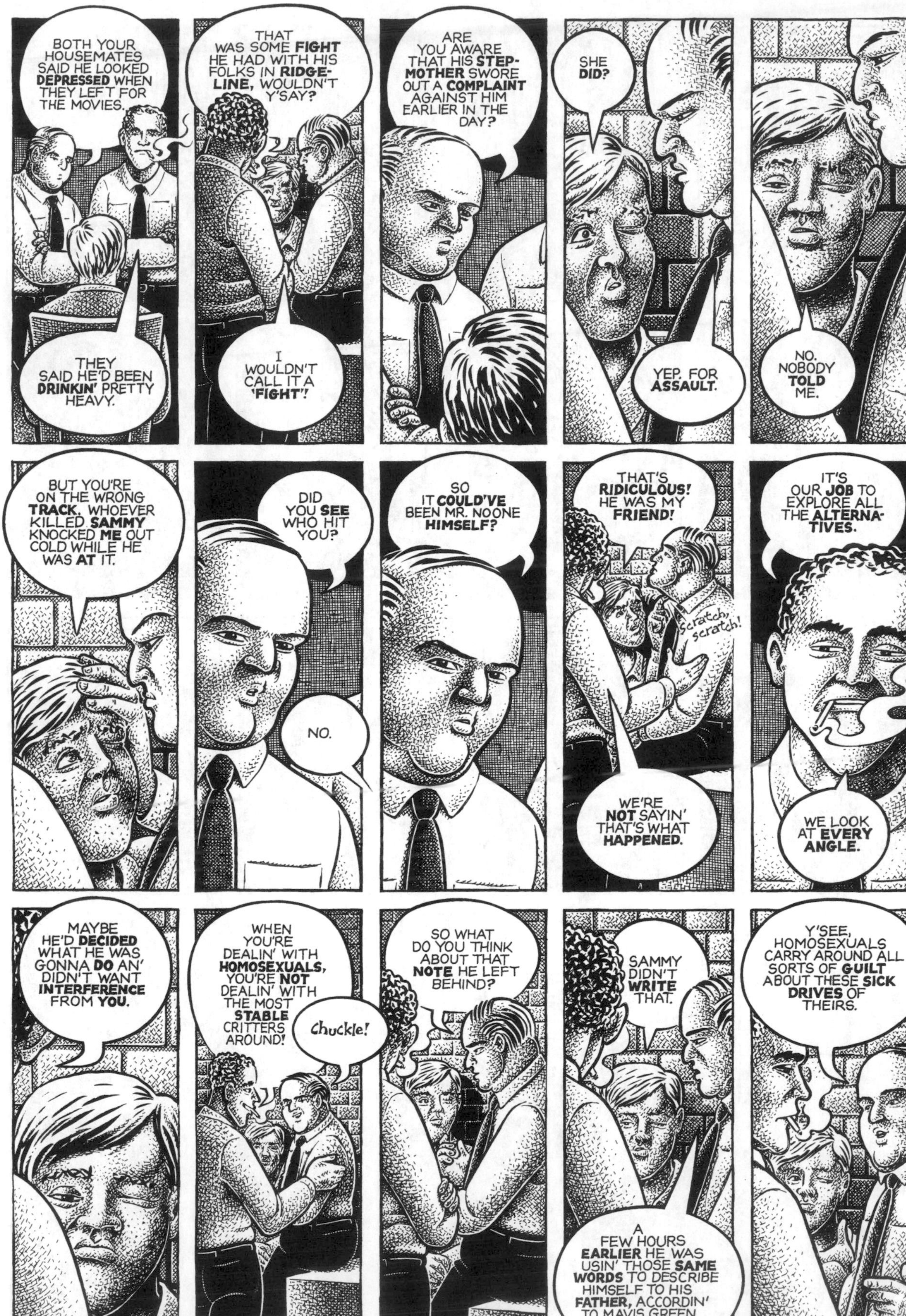
BOTH YOUR HOUSEMATES SAID HE LOOKED DEPRESSED WHEN THEY LEFT FOR THE MOVIES.
THEY SAID HE'D BEEN DRINKIN' PRETTY HEAVY.
THAT WAS SOME FIGHT HE HAD WITH HIS FOLKS IN RIDGE-LINE, WOULDN'T Y'SAY?
I WOULDN'T CALL IT A 'FIGHT'!
ARE YOU AWARE THAT HIS STEP-MOTHER SWORE OUT A COMPLAINT AGAINST HIM EARLIER IN THE DAY?
SHE DID?
YEP. FOR ASSAULT.
NO. NOBODY TOLD ME.
BUT YOU'RE ON THE WRONG TRACK. WHOEVER KILLED SAMMY KNOCKED ME OUT COLD WHILE HE WAS AT IT.
DID YOU SEE WHO HIT YOU?
NO.
SO IT COULD'VE BEEN MR. NOONE HIMSELF?
THAT'S RIDICULOUS! HE WAS MY FRIEND!
Scratch, scratch!
WE'RE NOT SAYIN' THAT'S WHAT HAPPENED.
IT'S OUR JOB TO EXPLORE ALL THE ALTERNA-TIVES.
WE LOOK AT EVERY ANGLE.
MAYBE HE'D DECIDED WHAT HE WAS GONNA DO AN' DIDN'T WANT INTERFERENCE FROM YOU.
WHEN YOU'RE DEALIN' WITH HOMOSEXUALS, YOU'RE NOT DEALIN' WITH THE MOST STABLE CRITTERS AROUND!
Chuckle!
SO WHAT DO YOU THINK ABOUT THAT NOTE HE LEFT BEHIND?
SAMMY DIDN'T WRITE THAT.
A FEW HOURS EARLIER HE WAS USIN' THOSE SAME WORDS TO DESCRIBE HIMSELF TO HIS FATHER, ACCORDIN' TO MAVIS GREEN.
Y'SEE, HOMOSEXUALS CARRY AROUND ALL SORTS OF GUILT ABOUT THESE SICK DRIVES OF THEIRS.

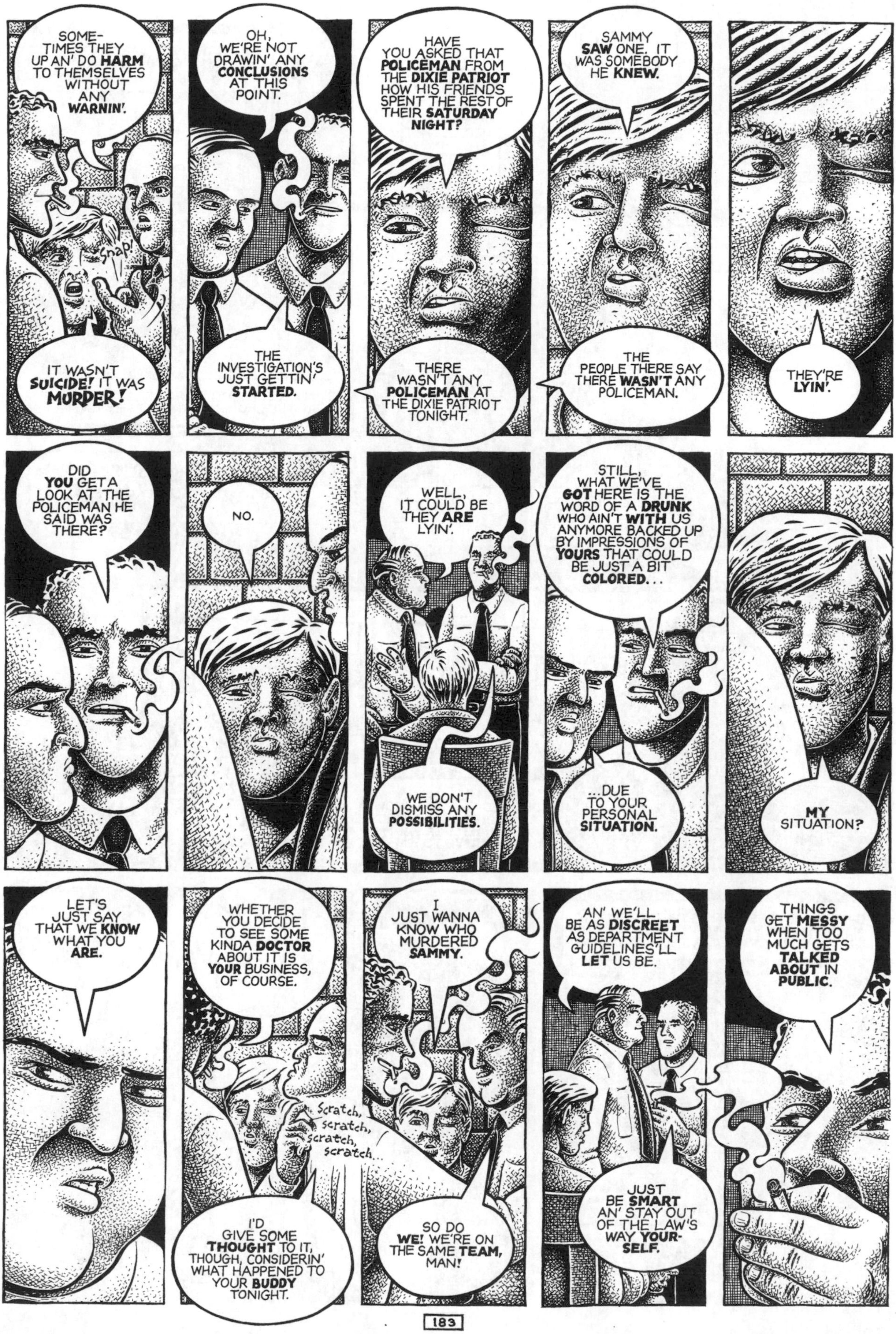
SOME-TIMES THEY UP AN' DO HARM TO THEMSELVES WITHOUT ANY WARNIN'.
Snap!
IT WASN'T SUICIDE! IT WAS MURDER!
OH, WE'RE NOT DRAWIN' ANY CONCLUSIONS AT THIS POINT.
THE INVESTIGATION'S JUST GETTIN' STARTED.
HAVE YOU ASKED THAT POLICEMAN FROM THE DIXIE PATRIOT HOW HIS FRIENDS SPENT THE REST OF THEIR SATURDAY NIGHT?
THERE WASN'T ANY POLICEMAN AT THE DIXIE PATRIOT TONIGHT.
SAMMY SAW ONE. IT WAS SOMEBODY HE KNEW.
THE PEOPLE THERE SAY THERE WASN'T ANY POLICEMAN.
THEY'RE LYIN'.
DID YOU GET A LOOK AT THE POLICEMAN HE SAID WAS THERE?
NO.
WELL, IT COULD BE THEY ARE LYIN'.
WE DON'T DISMISS ANY POSSIBILITIES.
STILL, WHAT WE'VE GOT HERE IS THE WORD OF A DRUNK WHO AIN'T WITH US ANYMORE BACKED UP BY IMPRESSIONS OF YOURS THAT COULD BE JUST A BIT COLORED...
...DUE TO YOUR PERSONAL SITUATION.
MY SITUATION?
LET'S JUST SAY THAT WE KNOW WHAT YOU ARE.
WHETHER YOU DECIDE TO SEE SOME KINDA DOCTOR ABOUT IT IS YOUR BUSINESS, OF COURSE.
Scratch, scratch, scratch, scratch...
I'D GIVE SOME THOUGHT TO IT, THOUGH, CONSIDERIN' WHAT HAPPENED TO YOUR BUDDY TONIGHT.
I JUST WANNA KNOW WHO MURDERED SAMMY.
SO DO WE! WE'RE ON THE SAME TEAM, MAN!
AN' WE'LL BE AS DISCREET AS DEPARTMENT GUIDELINES'LL LET US BE.
JUST BE SMART AN' STAY OUT OF THE LAW'S WAY YOURSELF.
THINGS GET MESSY WHEN TOO MUCH GETS TALKED ABOUT IN PUBLIC.

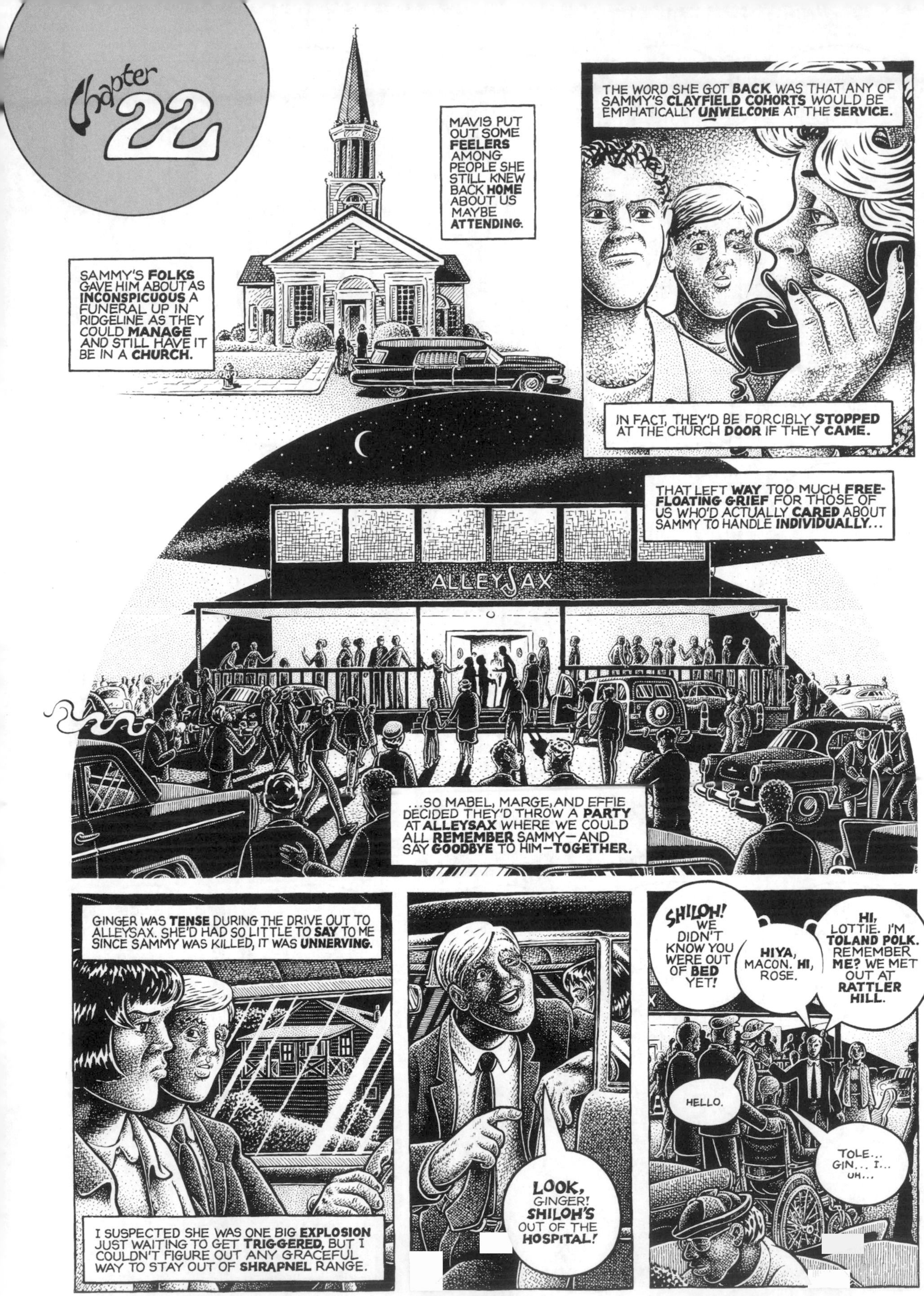
Chapter 22
SAMMY'S FOLKS GAVE HIM ABOUT AS INCONSPICUOUS A FUNERAL UP IN RIDGELINE AS THEY COULD MANAGE AND STILL HAVE IT BE IN A CHURCH.
MAVIS PUT OUT SOME FEELERS AMONG PEOPLE SHE STILL KNEW BACK HOME ABOUT US MAYBE ATTENDING.
THE WORD SHE GOT BACK WAS THAT ANY OF SAMMY'S CLAYFIELD COHORTS WOULD BE EMPHATICALLY UNWELCOME AT THE SERVICE.
IN FACT, THEY'D BE FORCIBLY STOPPED AT THE CHURCH DOOR IF THEY CAME.
THAT LEFT WAY TOO MUCH FREE-FLOATING GRIEF FOR THOSE OF US WHO'D ACTUALLY CARED ABOUT SAMMY TO HANDLE INDIVIDUALLY...
ALLEYSAX
...SO MABEL, MARGE, AND EFFIE DECIDED THEY'D THROW A PARTY AT ALLEYSAX WHERE WE COULD ALL REMEMBER SAMMY—AND SAY GOODBYE TO HIM—TOGETHER.
GINGER WAS TENSE DURING THE DRIVE OUT TO ALLEYSAX. SHE'D HAD SO LITTLE TO SAY TO ME SINCE SAMMY WAS KILLED, IT WAS UNNERVING.
I SUSPECTED SHE WAS ONE BIG EXPLOSION JUST WAITING TO GET TRIGGERED, BUT I COULDN'T FIGURE OUT ANY GRACEFUL WAY TO STAY OUT OF SHRAPNEL RANGE.
LOOK, GINGER! SHILOH'S OUT OF THE HOSPITAL!
SHILOH! WE DIDN'T KNOW YOU WERE OUT OF BED YET!
HIYA, MACON. HI, ROSE.
HI, LOTTIE. I'M TOLAND POLK. REMEMBER ME? WE MET OUT AT RATTLER HILL.
HELLO.
TOLE... GIN... I... UH...

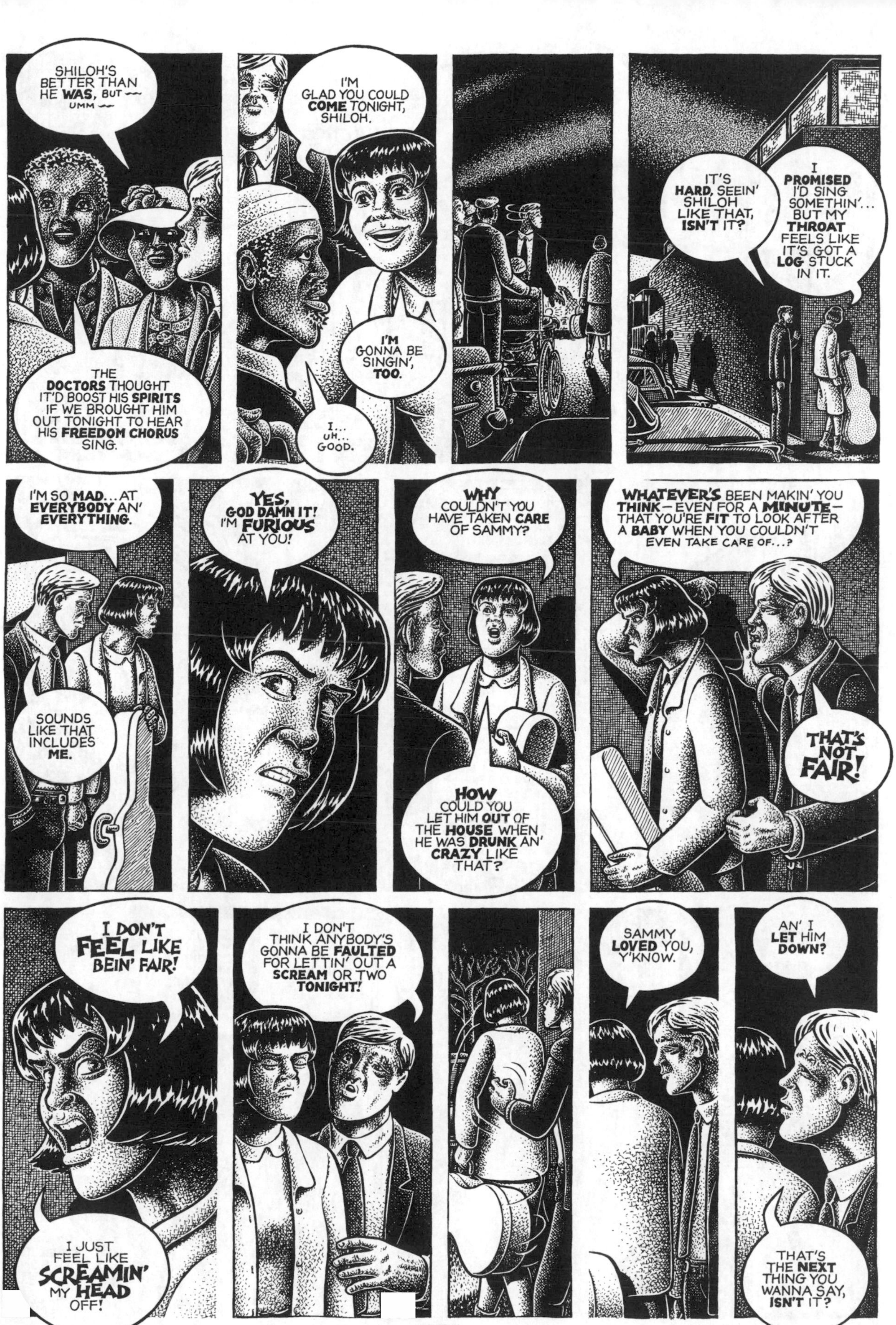

SHILOH'S BETTER THAN HE WAS, BUT ~~ UMM ~~
THE DOCTORS THOUGHT IT'D BOOST HIS SPIRITS IF WE BROUGHT HIM OUT TONIGHT TO HEAR HIS FREEDOM CHORUS SING.
I'M GLAD YOU COULD COME TONIGHT, SHILOH.
I'M GONNA BE SINGIN', TOO.
I... UH... GOOD.
IT'S HARD, SEEIN' SHILOH LIKE THAT, ISN'T IT?
I PROMISED I'D SING SOMETHIN'... BUT MY THROAT FEELS LIKE IT'S GOT A LOG STUCK IN IT.
I'M SO MAD... AT EVERYBODY AN' EVERYTHING.
SOUNDS LIKE THAT INCLUDES ME.
YES, GOD DAMN IT! I'M FURIOUS AT YOU!
WHY COULDN'T YOU HAVE TAKEN CARE OF SAMMY?
HOW COULD YOU LET HIM OUT OF THE HOUSE WHEN HE WAS DRUNK AN' CRAZY LIKE THAT?
WHATEVER'S BEEN MAKIN' YOU THINK—EVEN FOR A MINUTE—THAT YOU'RE FIT TO LOOK AFTER A BABY WHEN YOU COULDN'T EVEN TAKE CARE OF...?
THAT'S NOT FAIR!
I DON'T FEEL LIKE BEIN' FAIR!
I JUST FEEL LIKE SCREAMIN' MY HEAD OFF!
I DON'T THINK ANYBODY'S GONNA BE FAULTED FOR LETTIN' OUT A SCREAM OR TWO TONIGHT!
SAMMY LOVED YOU, Y'KNOW.
AN' I LET HIM DOWN?
THAT'S THE NEXT THING YOU WANNA SAY, ISN'T IT?

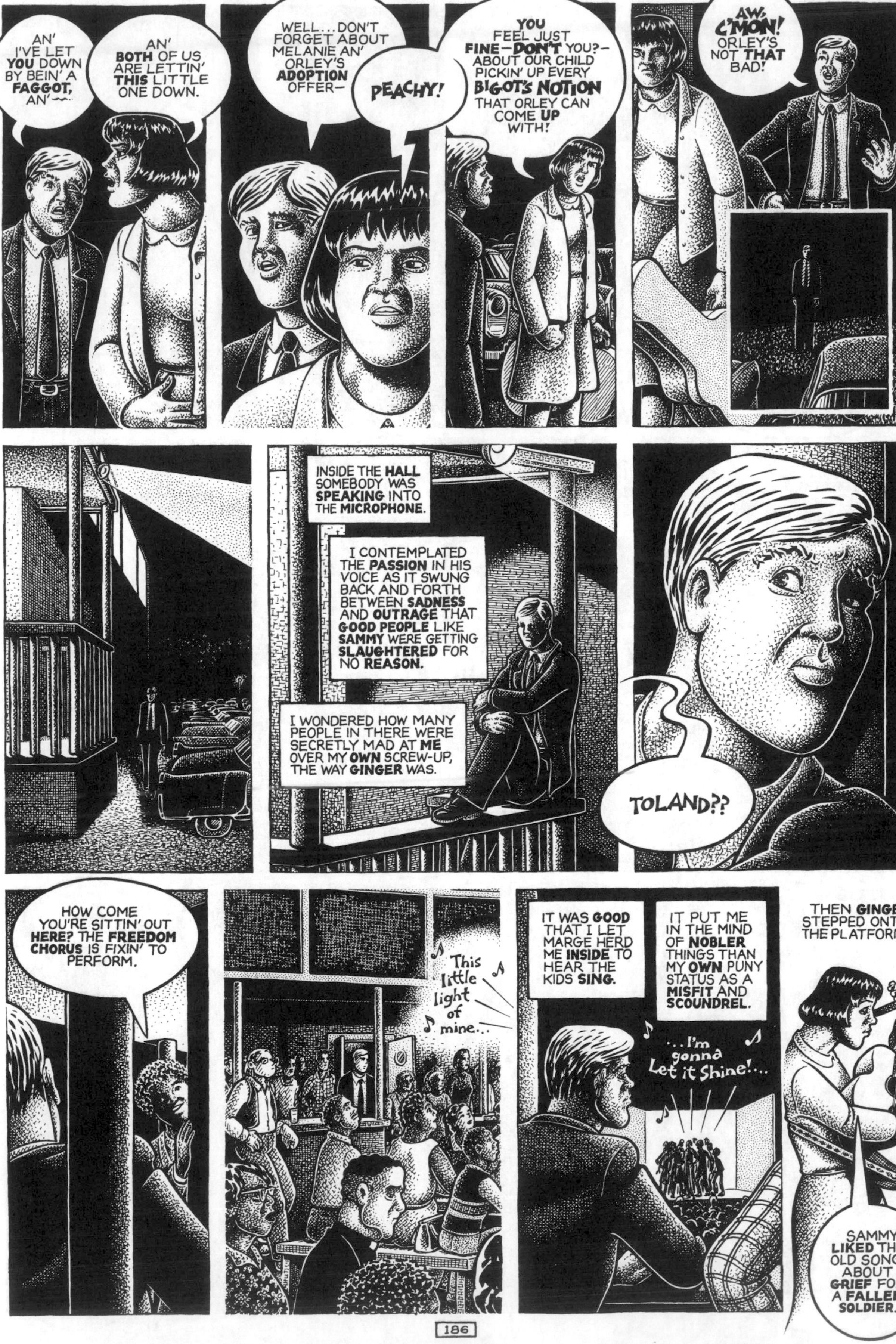

AN' I'VE LET YOU DOWN BY BEIN' A FAGGOT, AN'~~
AN' BOTH OF US ARE LETTIN' THIS LITTLE ONE DOWN.
WELL... DON'T FORGET ABOUT MELANIE AN' ORLEY'S ADOPTION OFFER—
PEACHY!
YOU FEEL JUST FINE—DON'T YOU?—ABOUT OUR CHILD PICKIN' UP EVERY BIGOT'S NOTION THAT ORLEY CAN COME UP WITH!
AW, C'MON! ORLEY'S NOT THAT BAD!
INSIDE THE HALL SOMEBODY WAS SPEAKING INTO THE MICROPHONE.
I CONTEMPLATED THE PASSION IN HIS VOICE AS IT SWUNG BACK AND FORTH BETWEEN SADNESS AND OUTRAGE THAT GOOD PEOPLE LIKE SAMMY WERE GETTING SLAUGHTERED FOR NO REASON.
I WONDERED HOW MANY PEOPLE IN THERE WERE SECRETLY MAD AT ME OVER MY OWN SCREW-UP, THE WAY GINGER WAS.
TOLAND??
HOW COME YOU'RE SITTIN' OUT HERE? THE FREEDOM CHORUS IS FIXIN' TO PERFORM.
This little light of mine...
IT WAS GOOD THAT I LET MARGE HERD ME INSIDE TO HEAR THE KIDS SING.
IT PUT ME IN THE MIND OF NOBLER THINGS THAN MY OWN PUNY STATUS AS A MISFIT AND SCOUNDREL.
...I'm gonna Let it Shine!...
THEN GINGER STEPPED ONTO THE PLATFORM.
SAMMY LIKED THIS OLD SONG ABOUT GRIEF FOR A FALLEN SOLDIER.

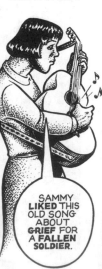

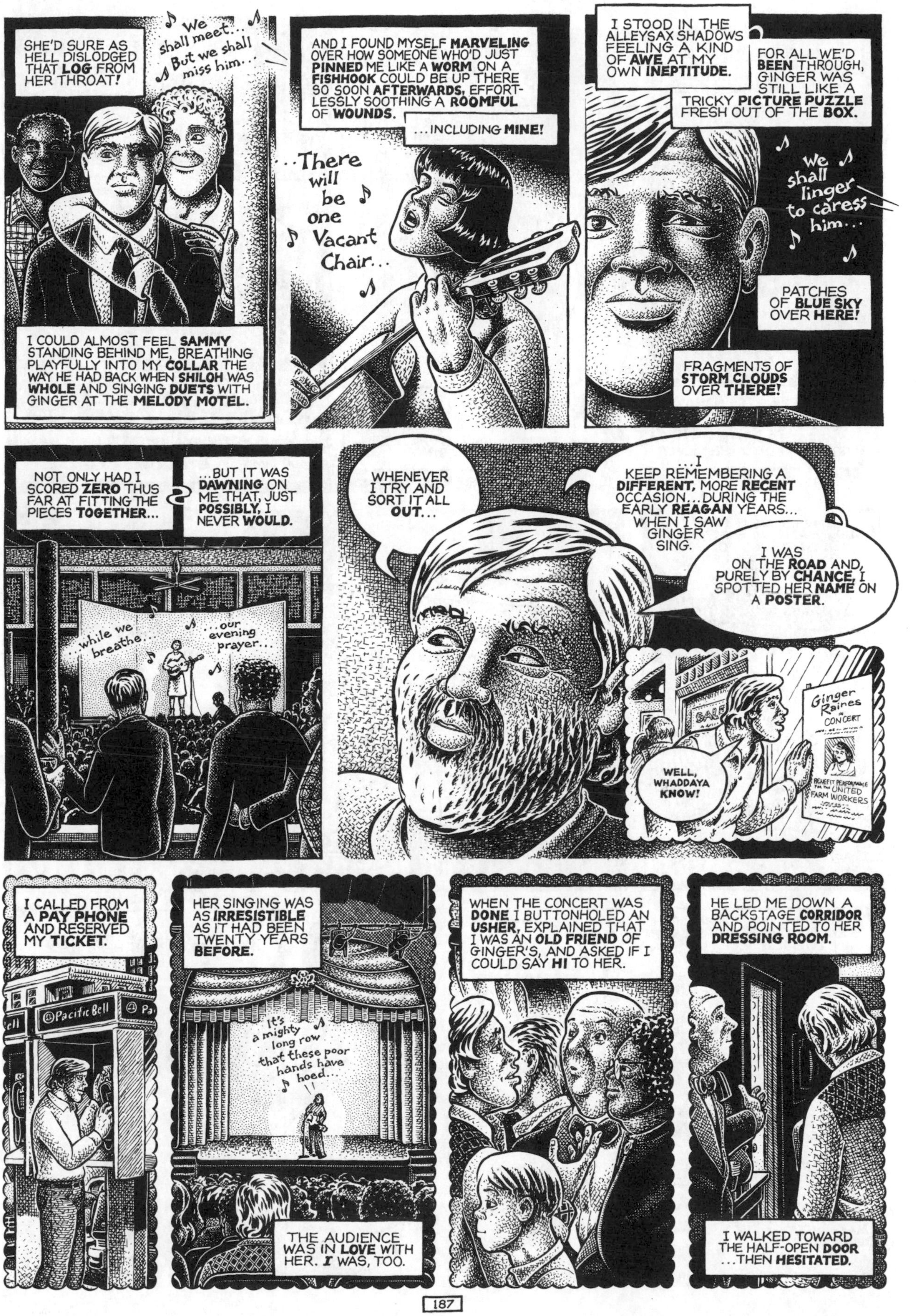
SHE'D SURE AS HELL DISLODGED THAT LOG FROM HER THROAT!
We shall meet... But we shall miss him...
I COULD ALMOST FEEL SAMMY STANDING BEHIND ME, BREATHING PLAYFULLY INTO MY COLLAR THE WAY HE HAD BACK WHEN SHILOH WAS WHOLE AND SINGING DUETS WITH GINGER AT THE MELODY MOTEL.
AND I FOUND MYSELF MARVELING OVER HOW SOMEONE WHO'D JUST PINNED ME LIKE A WORM ON A FISHHOOK COULD BE UP THERE SO SOON AFTERWARDS, EFFORTLESSLY SOOTHING A ROOMFUL OF WOUNDS.
...INCLUDING MINE!
...There will be one Vacant Chair...
I STOOD IN THE ALLEYSAX SHADOWS FEELING A KIND OF AWE AT MY OWN INEPTITUDE.
FOR ALL WE'D BEEN THROUGH, GINGER WAS STILL LIKE A TRICKY PICTURE PUZZLE FRESH OUT OF THE BOX.
We shall linger to caress him...
PATCHES OF BLUE SKY OVER HERE!
FRAGMENTS OF STORM CLOUDS OVER THERE!
NOT ONLY HAD I SCORED ZERO THUS FAR AT FITTING THE PIECES TOGETHER...
...BUT IT WAS DAWNING ON ME THAT, JUST POSSIBLY, I NEVER WOULD.
...while we breathe...
...our evening prayer...
WHENEVER I TRY AND SORT IT ALL OUT...
...I KEEP REMEMBERING A DIFFERENT, MORE RECENT OCCASION...DURING THE EARLY REAGAN YEARS... WHEN I SAW GINGER SING.
I WAS ON THE ROAD AND, PURELY BY CHANCE, I SPOTTED HER NAME ON A POSTER.
WELL, WHADDAYA KNOW!
Ginger Raines in CONCERT
BENEFIT PERFORMANCE FOR THE UNITED FARM WORKERS
I CALLED FROM A PAY PHONE AND RESERVED MY TICKET.
Pacific Bell
HER SINGING WAS AS IRRESISTIBLE AS IT HAD BEEN TWENTY YEARS BEFORE.
It's a mighty long row that these poor hands have hoed...
THE AUDIENCE WAS IN LOVE WITH HER. I WAS, TOO.
WHEN THE CONCERT WAS DONE I BUTTONHOLED AN USHER, EXPLAINED THAT I WAS AN OLD FRIEND OF GINGER'S, AND ASKED IF I COULD SAY HI TO HER.
HE LED ME DOWN A BACKSTAGE CORRIDOR AND POINTED TO HER DRESSING ROOM.
I WALKED TOWARD THE HALF-OPEN DOOR ...THEN HESITATED.

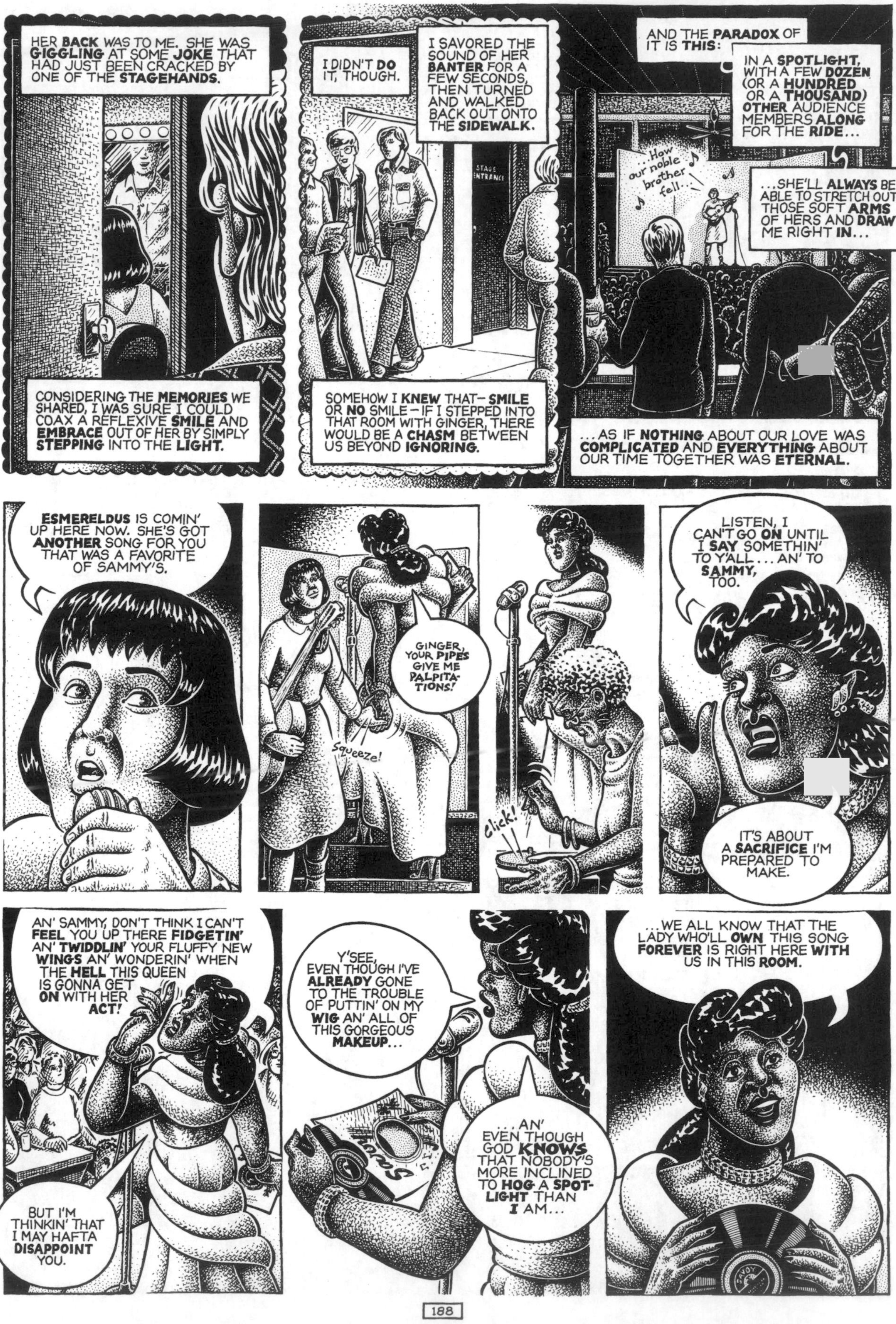
HER BACK WAS TO ME. SHE WAS GIGGLING AT SOME JOKE THAT HAD JUST BEEN CRACKED BY ONE OF THE STAGEHANDS.
CONSIDERING THE MEMORIES WE SHARED, I WAS SURE I COULD COAX A REFLEXIVE SMILE AND EMBRACE OUT OF HER BY SIMPLY STEPPING INTO THE LIGHT.
I DIDN'T DO IT, THOUGH.
I SAVORED THE SOUND OF HER BANTER FOR A FEW SECONDS, THEN TURNED AND WALKED BACK OUT ONTO THE SIDEWALK.
STAGE ENTRANCE
SOMEHOW I KNEW THAT— SMILE OR NO SMILE — IF I STEPPED INTO THAT ROOM WITH GINGER, THERE WOULD BE A CHASM BETWEEN US BEYOND IGNORING.
AND THE PARADOX OF IT IS THIS:
IN A SPOTLIGHT, WITH A FEW DOZEN (OR A HUNDRED OR A THOUSAND) OTHER AUDIENCE MEMBERS ALONG FOR THE RIDE...
...How our noble brother fell...
...SHE'LL ALWAYS BE ABLE TO STRETCH OUT THOSE SOFT ARMS OF HERS AND DRAW ME RIGHT IN...
...AS IF NOTHING ABOUT OUR LOVE WAS COMPLICATED AND EVERYTHING ABOUT OUR TIME TOGETHER WAS ETERNAL.
ESMERELDUS IS COMIN' UP HERE NOW. SHE'S GOT ANOTHER SONG FOR YOU THAT WAS A FAVORITE OF SAMMY'S.
GINGER, YOUR PIPES GIVE ME PALPITATIONS!
Squeeze!
Click!
LISTEN, I CAN'T GO ON UNTIL I SAY SOMETHIN' TO Y'ALL... AN' TO SAMMY, TOO.
IT'S ABOUT A SACRIFICE I'M PREPARED TO MAKE.
AN' SAMMY, DON'T THINK I CAN'T FEEL YOU UP THERE FIDGETIN' AN' TWIDDLIN' YOUR FLUFFY NEW WINGS AN' WONDERIN' WHEN THE HELL THIS QUEEN IS GONNA GET ON WITH HER ACT!
BUT I'M THINKIN' THAT I MAY HAFTA DISAPPOINT YOU.
Y'SEE, EVEN THOUGH I'VE ALREADY GONE TO THE TROUBLE OF PUTTIN' ON MY WIG AN' ALL OF THIS GORGEOUS MAKEUP...
...AN' EVEN THOUGH GOD KNOWS THAT NOBODY'S MORE INCLINED TO HOG A SPOT-LIGHT THAN I AM...
...WE ALL KNOW THAT THE LADY WHO'LL OWN THIS SONG FOREVER IS RIGHT HERE WITH US IN THIS ROOM.

EVERYBODY **KNOWS** WHO I'M **TALKIN'** ABOUT.

IF **SHE'D** BE WILLIN' TO COME UP HERE AN' PERFORM THIS SONG **INSTEAD** OF ME...

...**SHE** WOULDN'T EVEN HAVE TO **LIP-SYNC!**

COME ON AN' **DO** IT, ANNA DELLYNE. EVERY-BODY WOULD **LOVE** FOR YOU TO.

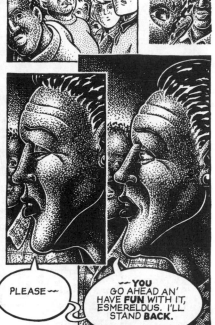

PLEASE --

--**YOU** GO AHEAD AN' HAVE **FUN** WITH IT, ESMERELDUS. I'LL STAND **BACK.**

O.K., HONEY.

EFFIE, STRIKE UP THE **BAND!**

♪ Got a feeling there's a Secret in the Air... ♪

♪ Nods and whispers among my sisters here and there... ♪

Awkward pauses... Eyes averted... Little warnings, oddly worded... ♪

♪ Can the truth be all that hard to bear..? ♪

AND THEN CAME THE TIME WHEN SEVERAL OF SAMMY'S **FRIENDS** WERE SLATED TO SHARE **PERSONAL REMINISCENCES** ABOUT HIM.

OTHERS WENT **AHEAD** OF ME.

IT WAS **HOPELESS** TRYING TO LISTEN TO WHAT **THEY** WERE SAYING WITH MY **OWN** TURN COMING UP.

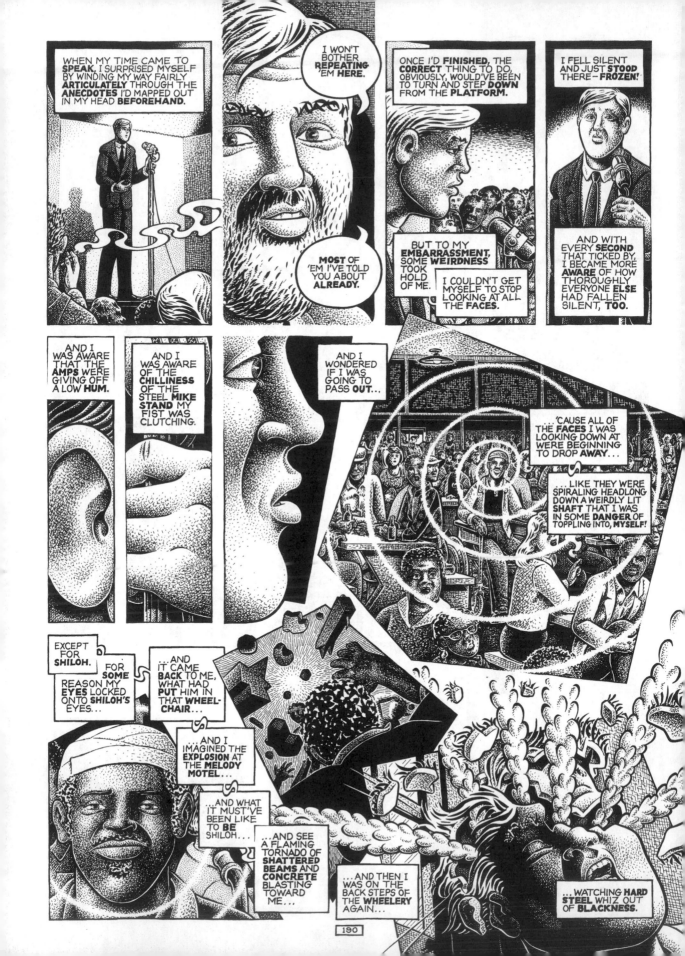

WHEN MY TIME CAME TO **SPEAK**, I SURPRISED MYSELF BY WINDING MY WAY FAIRLY **ARTICULATELY** THROUGH THE **ANECDOTES** I'D MAPPED OUT IN MY HEAD **BEFOREHAND**.

I WON'T BOTHER **REPEATING** 'EM **HERE**.

MOST OF 'EM I'VE TOLD YOU ABOUT **ALREADY**.

ONCE I'D **FINISHED**, THE **CORRECT** THING TO DO, OBVIOUSLY, WOULD'VE BEEN TO TURN AND STEP **DOWN** FROM THE **PLATFORM**.

I FELL SILENT AND JUST **STOOD** THERE – **FROZEN!**

BUT TO MY **EMBARRASSMENT**, SOME **WEIRDNESS** TOOK HOLD OF ME.

I COULDN'T GET MYSELF TO STOP LOOKING AT ALL THE **FACES**.

AND WITH EVERY **SECOND** THAT TICKED BY, I BECAME MORE **AWARE** OF HOW THOROUGHLY EVERYONE **ELSE** HAD FALLEN SILENT, **TOO**.

AND I WAS AWARE THAT THE **AMPS** WERE GIVING OFF A LOW **HUM**.

AND I WAS AWARE OF THE **CHILLINESS** OF THE STEEL **MIKE STAND** MY FIST WAS CLUTCHING.

AND I WONDERED IF I WAS GOING TO PASS **OUT**...

...'CAUSE ALL OF THE **FACES** I WAS LOOKING DOWN AT WERE BEGINNING TO DROP **AWAY**...

...LIKE THEY WERE SPIRALING HEADLONG DOWN A WEIRDLY LIT **SHAFT** THAT I WAS IN SOME **DANGER** OF TOPPLING INTO, **MYSELF!**

EXCEPT FOR **SHILOH**.

FOR **SOME** REASON MY **EYES** LOCKED ONTO SHILOH'S EYES...

...AND IT CAME **BACK** TO ME, WHAT HAD **PUT** HIM IN THAT **WHEEL-CHAIR**...

...AND I IMAGINED THE **EXPLOSION** AT THE **MELODY MOTEL**...

...AND WHAT IT MUST'VE BEEN LIKE TO **BE** SHILOH...

...AND SEE A FLAMING **TORNADO** OF **SHATTERED** BEAMS AND **CONCRETE** BLASTING TOWARD ME...

...AND THEN I WAS ON THE **BACK** STEPS OF THE **WHEELERY** AGAIN...

...WATCHING **HARD STEEL** WHIZ OUT OF **BLACKNESS**.

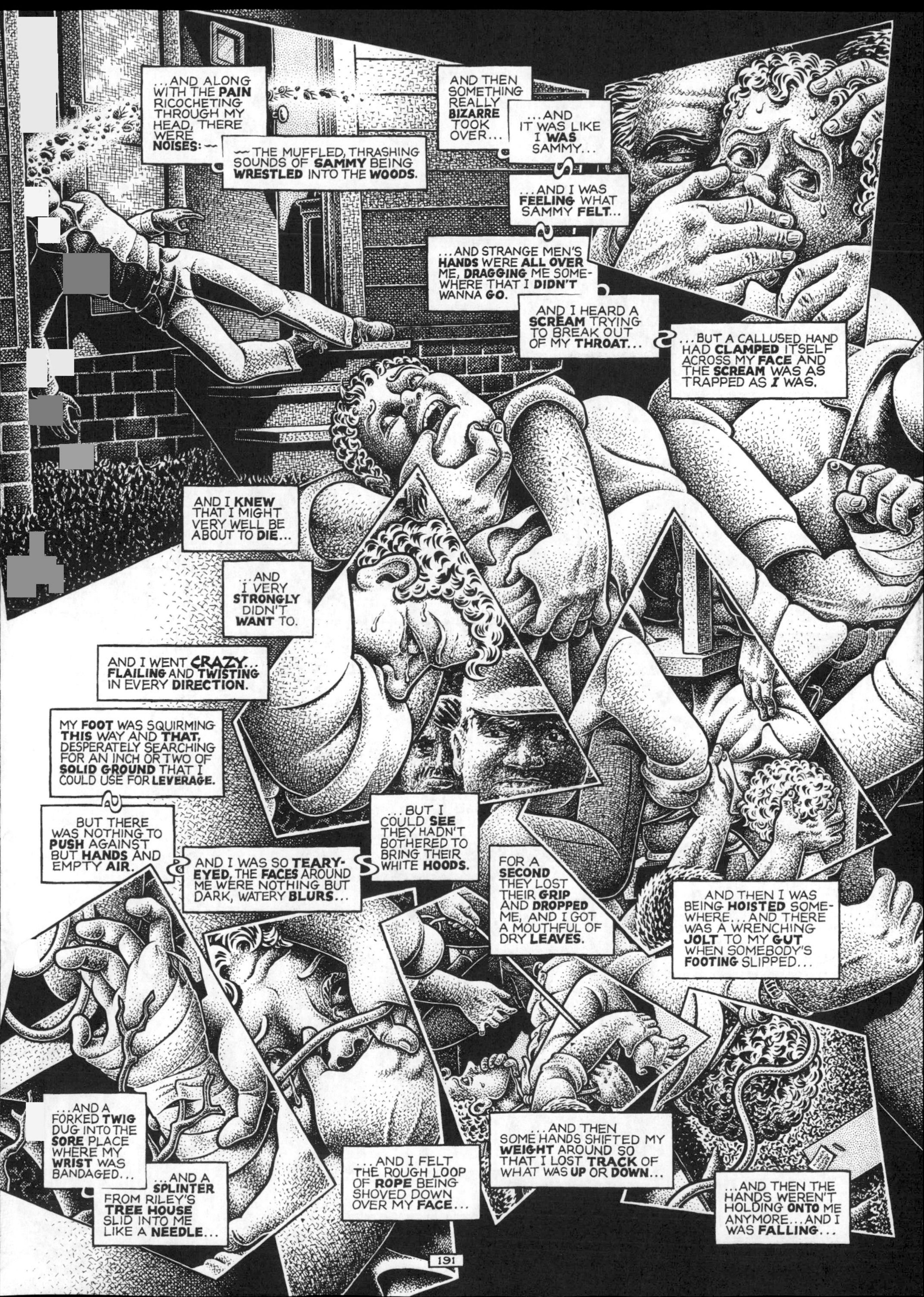
...AND ALONG WITH THE PAIN RICOCHETING THROUGH MY HEAD, THERE WERE NOISES: —
— THE MUFFLED, THRASHING SOUNDS OF SAMMY BEING WRESTLED INTO THE WOODS.
AND THEN SOMETHING REALLY BIZARRE TOOK OVER...
...AND IT WAS LIKE I WAS SAMMY...
...AND I WAS FEELING WHAT SAMMY FELT...
...AND STRANGE MEN'S HANDS WERE ALL OVER ME, DRAGGING ME SOMEWHERE THAT I DIDN'T WANNA GO.
AND I HEARD A SCREAM TRYING TO BREAK OUT OF MY THROAT...
...BUT A CALLUSED HAND HAD CLAMPED ITSELF ACROSS MY FACE AND THE SCREAM WAS AS TRAPPED AS I WAS.
AND I KNEW THAT I MIGHT VERY WELL BE ABOUT TO DIE...
...AND I VERY STRONGLY DIDN'T WANT TO.
AND I WENT CRAZY... FLAILING AND TWISTING IN EVERY DIRECTION.
MY FOOT WAS SQUIRMING THIS WAY AND THAT, DESPERATELY SEARCHING FOR AN INCH OR TWO OF SOLID GROUND THAT I COULD USE FOR LEVERAGE.
BUT THERE WAS NOTHING TO PUSH AGAINST BUT HANDS AND EMPTY AIR.
AND I WAS SO TEARY-EYED, THE FACES AROUND ME WERE NOTHING BUT DARK, WATERY BLURS...
...BUT I COULD SEE THEY HADN'T BOTHERED TO BRING THEIR WHITE HOODS.
FOR A SECOND THEY LOST THEIR GRIP AND DROPPED ME, AND I GOT A MOUTHFUL OF DRY LEAVES.
AND THEN I WAS BEING HOISTED SOMEWHERE... AND THERE WAS A WRENCHING JOLT TO MY GUT WHEN SOMEBODY'S FOOTING SLIPPED...
...AND A FORKED TWIG DUG INTO THE SORE PLACE WHERE MY WRIST WAS BANDAGED...
...AND A SPLINTER FROM RILEY'S TREE HOUSE SLID INTO ME LIKE A NEEDLE...
...AND I FELT THE ROUGH LOOP OF ROPE BEING SHOVED DOWN OVER MY FACE...
...AND THEN SOME HANDS SHIFTED MY WEIGHT AROUND SO THAT I LOST TRACK OF WHAT WAS UP OR DOWN...
...AND THEN THE HANDS WEREN'T HOLDING ONTO ME ANYMORE... AND I WAS FALLING...

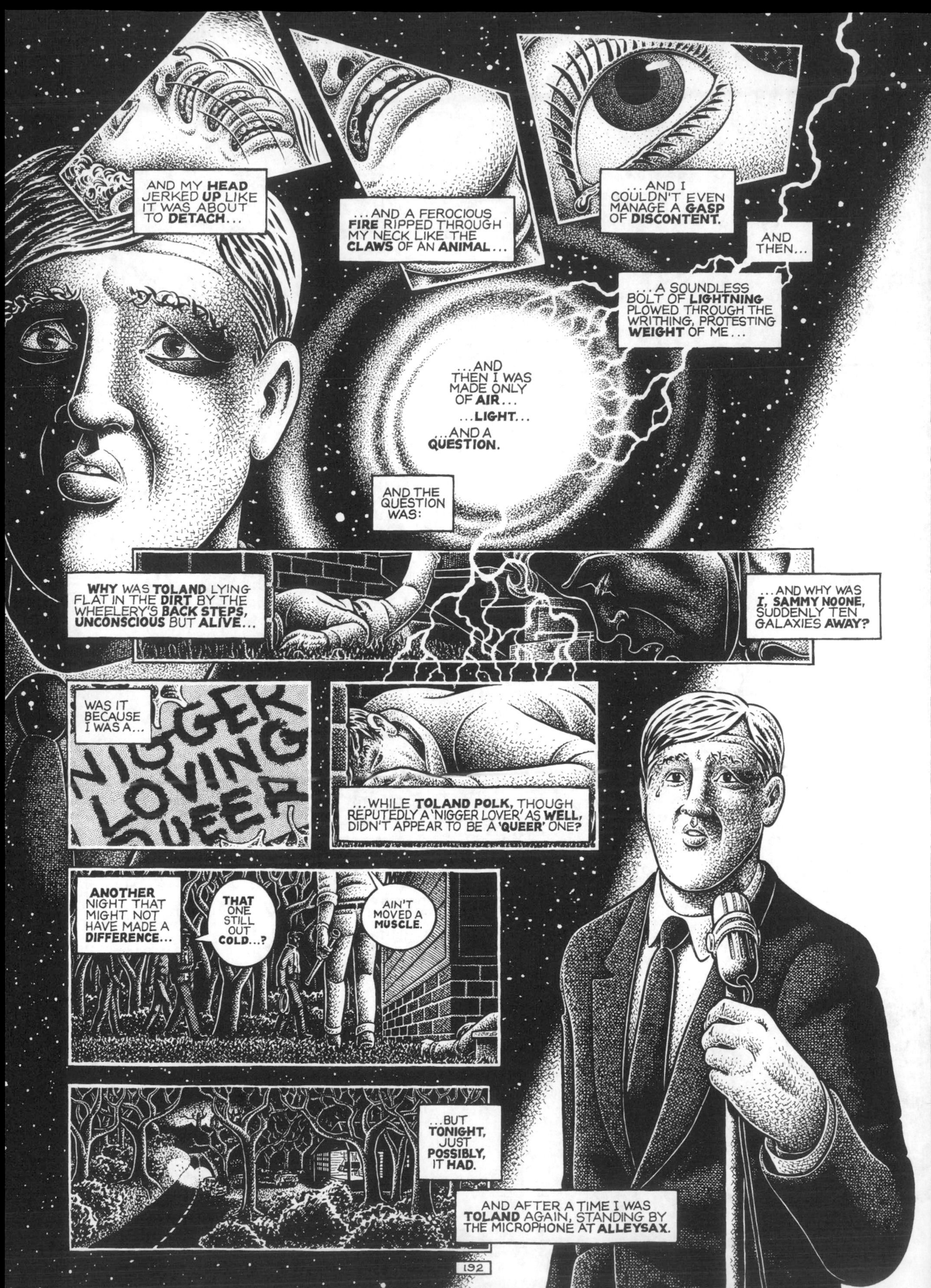
AND MY **HEAD** JERKED **UP** LIKE IT WAS ABOUT TO **DETACH**...
...AND A FEROCIOUS **FIRE** RIPPED THROUGH MY NECK LIKE THE **CLAWS** OF AN **ANIMAL**...
...AND I COULDN'T EVEN MANAGE A **GASP** OF **DISCONTENT**.
AND THEN...
...A SOUNDLESS BOLT OF **LIGHTNING** PLOWED THROUGH THE WRITHING, PROTESTING **WEIGHT** OF ME...
...AND THEN I WAS MADE ONLY OF **AIR**...
...**LIGHT**...
...AND A **QUESTION**.
AND THE QUESTION WAS:
WHY WAS **TOLAND** LYING FLAT IN THE **DIRT** BY THE WHEELERY'S **BACK STEPS**, **UNCONSCIOUS** BUT **ALIVE**...
...AND WHY WAS ***I***, **SAMMY NOONE**, SUDDENLY TEN GALAXIES **AWAY**?
WAS IT BECAUSE I WAS A...
NIGGER LOVING QUEER
...WHILE **TOLAND POLK**, THOUGH REPUTEDLY A 'NIGGER LOVER' AS **WELL**, DIDN'T APPEAR TO BE A **'QUEER'** ONE?
ANOTHER NIGHT THAT MIGHT NOT HAVE MADE A **DIFFERENCE**...
THAT ONE STILL OUT **COLD**...?
AIN'T MOVED A **MUSCLE**.
...BUT **TONIGHT**, JUST **POSSIBLY**, IT **HAD**.
AND AFTER A TIME I WAS **TOLAND** AGAIN, STANDING BY THE MICROPHONE AT **ALLEYSAX**.

AND LIKE A **FOOL** I WAS UP THERE **SOBBING** IN FRONT OF **EVERYBODY.**

I **DOUBT** ANYBODY THOUGHT **LESS** OF ME FOR IT, OF COURSE.

IT **WAS** A NIGHT FOR **GRIEVING,** AFTER ALL.

BUT I DIDN'T **DARE** LEAVE PEOPLE THINKING THAT MY TEARS HAD BEEN FLOWING FOR A **MURDERED** FRIEND AND NOTHING **MORE.**

'CAUSE I **KNEW** THAT, IF I **DIDN'T** SAY THE WORDS **RIGHT THEN**—

—(AND I'M TALKING ABOUT THE REALLY **FRIGHTENING** WORDS THAT ALL THE **HABITS** OF A LIFETIME WERE **SCREAMING** AT ME TO HOLD **BACK** AND LEAVE **UNSAID**)—

—I MIGHT JUST **CONTINUE** ON MY COWARD'S WAY THE **NEXT** DAY AND THE **NEXT**... AND THE DAY AFTER **THAT**...

...AND **ALL** THE DAYS THEREAFTER.

SO I **SAID** THE **WORDS.**

AND THERE WERE **LOTS** OF THEM!

I **KNOW** THAT I DID 'CAUSE I CAN STILL REMEMBER THE STAMMERING, GULPING **SOUND** OF THEM TUMBLING OUT OF MY **MOUTH.**

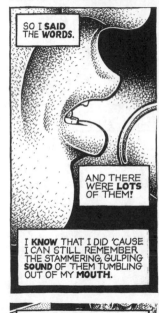

AND I'LL BE **DAMNED** IF I CAN RECALL WHAT ANY OF THEM **WERE** IN PARTICULAR —EXCEPT FOR THESE **FOUR:**

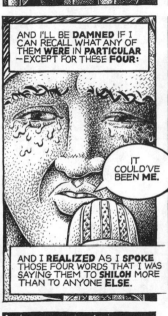

IT COULD'VE BEEN **ME.**

AND I **REALIZED** AS I **SPOKE** THOSE FOUR WORDS THAT I WAS SAYING THEM TO **SHILOH** MORE THAN TO ANYONE **ELSE.**

I KNEW I'D FIND **UNDERSTANDING** IN SHILOH'S **EYES.**

EVENTUALLY A POINT CAME WHEN I KNEW I WAS **DONE** TALKING.

I'D **SAID** WHAT NEEDED **SAYING.**

AND PART OF ME WAS **EMBARRASSED** BY THE **WETNESS** OF MY **CHEEKS** AND BY THE EMOTIONAL **EXCESSES** I KNEW I'D PROBABLY COMMITTED...

...BUT **ANOTHER** PART OF ME WAS LEFT WITH AN ALMOST GIDDY **SERENITY.**

IN THE DAYS THAT **FOLLOWED,** THE DELICATE SUBJECT OF MY ALLEY-SAX **OUTBURST** GOT **RAISED** A FEW TIMES BY FRIENDS WHO'D **WITNESSED** IT.

I DIDN'T **SAY** TOO MUCH, FIGURING THAT THE MORE I WENT **INTO** IT, THE **CRAZIER** I'D SEEM.

I'M **STILL** NOT A HUNDRED PERCENT **SURE** WHAT REALLY **HAPPENED** THAT NIGHT...

SAY IT **ONCE** IN **PUBLIC** AND THE **GRAPEVINE'LL** TAKE IT FROM **THERE!**

...BUT THE CLEAR **EFFECT** OF IT WAS TO PUT TO **REST** ANY **MISIMPRESSIONS** I'D FOSTERED THAT **TOLAND POLK** WAS ANY **STRAIGHTER** THAN **SAMMY NOONE** HAD BEEN!

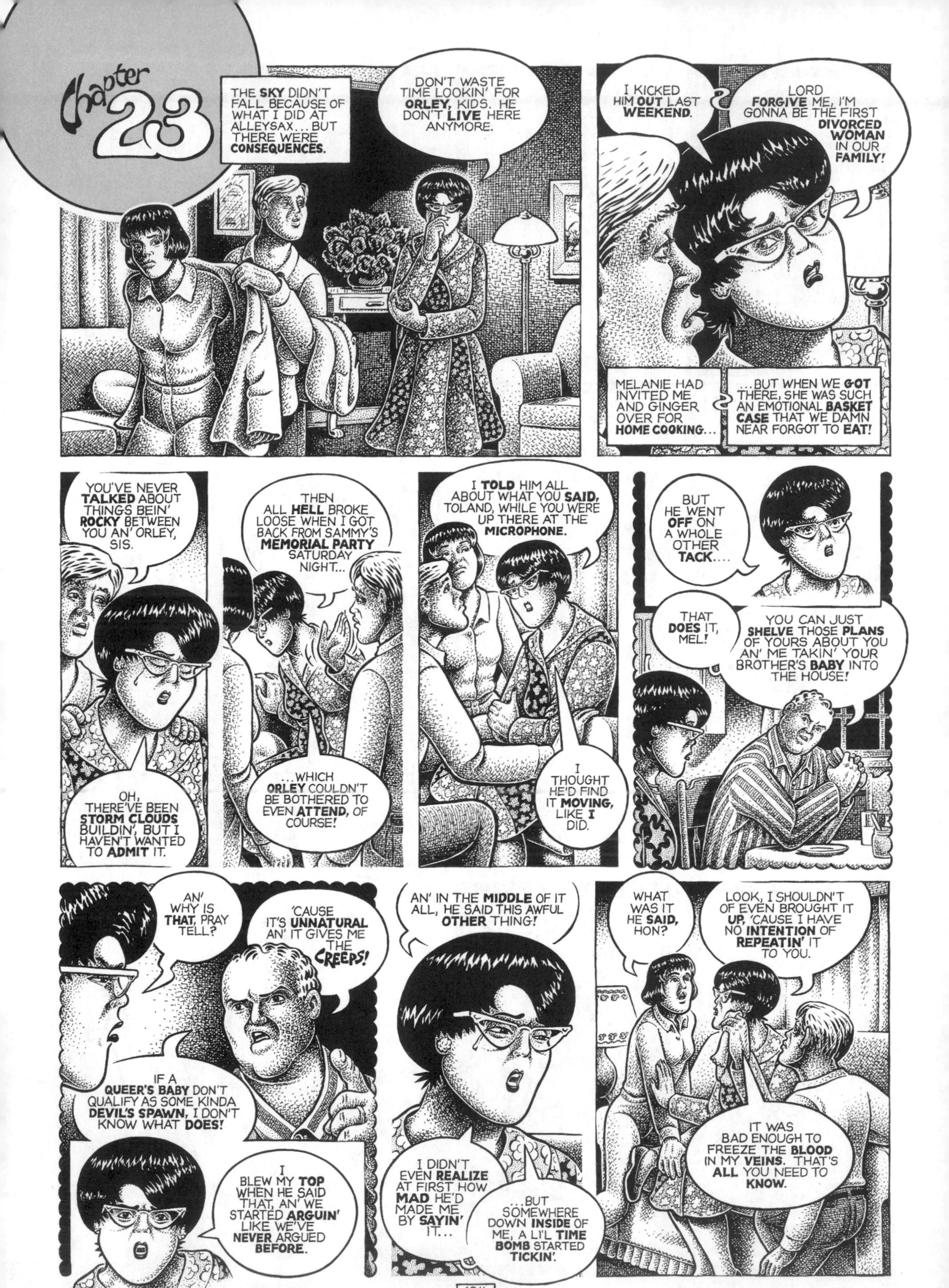
Chapter 23
THE SKY DIDN'T FALL BECAUSE OF WHAT I DID AT ALLEYSAX... BUT THERE WERE CONSEQUENCES.
DON'T WASTE TIME LOOKIN' FOR ORLEY, KIDS. HE DON'T LIVE HERE ANYMORE.
I KICKED HIM OUT LAST WEEKEND.
LORD FORGIVE ME, I'M GONNA BE THE FIRST DIVORCED WOMAN IN OUR FAMILY!
MELANIE HAD INVITED ME AND GINGER OVER FOR HOME COOKING...
...BUT WHEN WE GOT THERE, SHE WAS SUCH AN EMOTIONAL BASKET CASE THAT WE DAMN NEAR FORGOT TO EAT!
YOU'VE NEVER TALKED ABOUT THINGS BEIN' ROCKY BETWEEN YOU AN' ORLEY, SIS.
OH, THERE'VE BEEN STORM CLOUDS BUILDIN', BUT I HAVEN'T WANTED TO ADMIT IT.
THEN ALL HELL BROKE LOOSE WHEN I GOT BACK FROM SAMMY'S MEMORIAL PARTY SATURDAY NIGHT...
...WHICH ORLEY COULDN'T BE BOTHERED TO EVEN ATTEND, OF COURSE!
I TOLD HIM ALL ABOUT WHAT YOU SAID, TOLAND, WHILE YOU WERE UP THERE AT THE MICROPHONE.
I THOUGHT HE'D FIND IT MOVING, LIKE I DID.
BUT HE WENT OFF ON A WHOLE OTHER TACK....
THAT DOES IT, MEL!
YOU CAN JUST SHELVE THOSE PLANS OF YOURS ABOUT YOU AN' ME TAKIN' YOUR BROTHER'S BABY INTO THE HOUSE!
AN' WHY IS THAT, PRAY TELL?
'CAUSE IT'S UNNATURAL AN' IT GIVES ME THE CREEPS!
IF A QUEER'S BABY DON'T QUALIFY AS SOME KINDA DEVIL'S SPAWN, I DON'T KNOW WHAT DOES!
I BLEW MY TOP WHEN HE SAID THAT, AN' WE STARTED ARGUIN' LIKE WE'VE NEVER ARGUED BEFORE.
AN' IN THE MIDDLE OF IT ALL, HE SAID THIS AWFUL OTHER THING!
I DIDN'T EVEN REALIZE AT FIRST HOW MAD HE'D MADE ME BY SAYIN' IT...
...BUT SOMEWHERE DOWN INSIDE OF ME, A LI'L TIME BOMB STARTED TICKIN'.
WHAT WAS IT HE SAID, HON?
LOOK, I SHOULDN'T OF EVEN BROUGHT IT UP, 'CAUSE I HAVE NO INTENTION OF REPEATIN' IT TO YOU.
IT WAS BAD ENOUGH TO FREEZE THE BLOOD IN MY VEINS. THAT'S ALL YOU NEED TO KNOW.

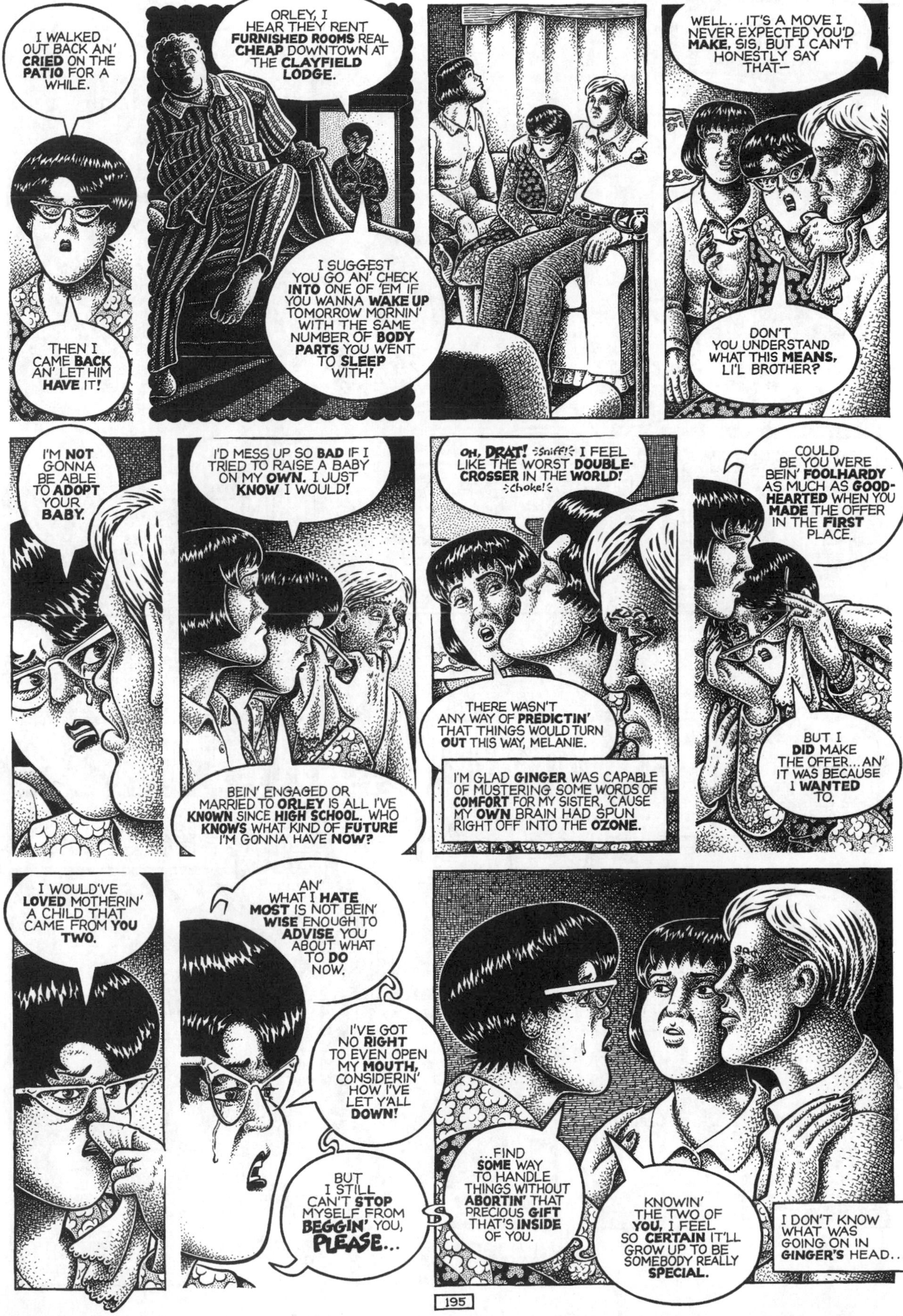
I WALKED OUT BACK AN' CRIED ON THE PATIO FOR A WHILE.
THEN I CAME BACK AN' LET HIM HAVE IT!
ORLEY, I HEAR THEY RENT FURNISHED ROOMS REAL CHEAP DOWNTOWN AT THE CLAYFIELD LODGE.
I SUGGEST YOU GO AN' CHECK INTO ONE OF 'EM IF YOU WANNA WAKE UP TOMORROW MORNIN' WITH THE SAME NUMBER OF BODY PARTS YOU WENT TO SLEEP WITH!
WELL... IT'S A MOVE I NEVER EXPECTED YOU'D MAKE, SIS, BUT I CAN'T HONESTLY SAY THAT—
DON'T YOU UNDERSTAND WHAT THIS MEANS, LI'L BROTHER?
I'M NOT GONNA BE ABLE TO ADOPT YOUR BABY.
I'D MESS UP SO BAD IF I TRIED TO RAISE A BABY ON MY OWN. I JUST KNOW I WOULD!
BEIN' ENGAGED OR MARRIED TO ORLEY IS ALL I'VE KNOWN SINCE HIGH SCHOOL. WHO KNOWS WHAT KIND OF FUTURE I'M GONNA HAVE NOW?
OH, DRAT! *SNIFF!* I FEEL LIKE THE WORST DOUBLE-CROSSER IN THE WORLD! *CHOKE!*
THERE WASN'T ANY WAY OF PREDICTIN' THAT THINGS WOULD TURN OUT THIS WAY, MELANIE.
I'M GLAD GINGER WAS CAPABLE OF MUSTERING SOME WORDS OF COMFORT FOR MY SISTER, 'CAUSE MY OWN BRAIN HAD SPUN RIGHT OFF INTO THE OZONE.
COULD BE YOU WERE BEIN' FOOLHARDY AS MUCH AS GOOD-HEARTED WHEN YOU MADE THE OFFER IN THE FIRST PLACE.
BUT I DID MAKE THE OFFER... AN' IT WAS BECAUSE I WANTED TO.
I WOULD'VE LOVED MOTHERIN' A CHILD THAT CAME FROM YOU TWO.
AN' WHAT I HATE MOST IS NOT BEIN' WISE ENOUGH TO ADVISE YOU ABOUT WHAT TO DO NOW.
I'VE GOT NO RIGHT TO EVEN OPEN MY MOUTH, CONSIDERIN' HOW I'VE LET Y'ALL DOWN!
BUT I STILL CAN'T STOP MYSELF FROM BEGGIN' YOU, PLEASE...
...FIND SOME WAY TO HANDLE THINGS WITHOUT ABORTIN' THAT PRECIOUS GIFT THAT'S INSIDE OF YOU.
KNOWIN' THE TWO OF YOU, I FEEL SO CERTAIN IT'LL GROW UP TO BE SOMEBODY REALLY SPECIAL.
I DON'T KNOW WHAT WAS GOING ON IN GINGER'S HEAD...

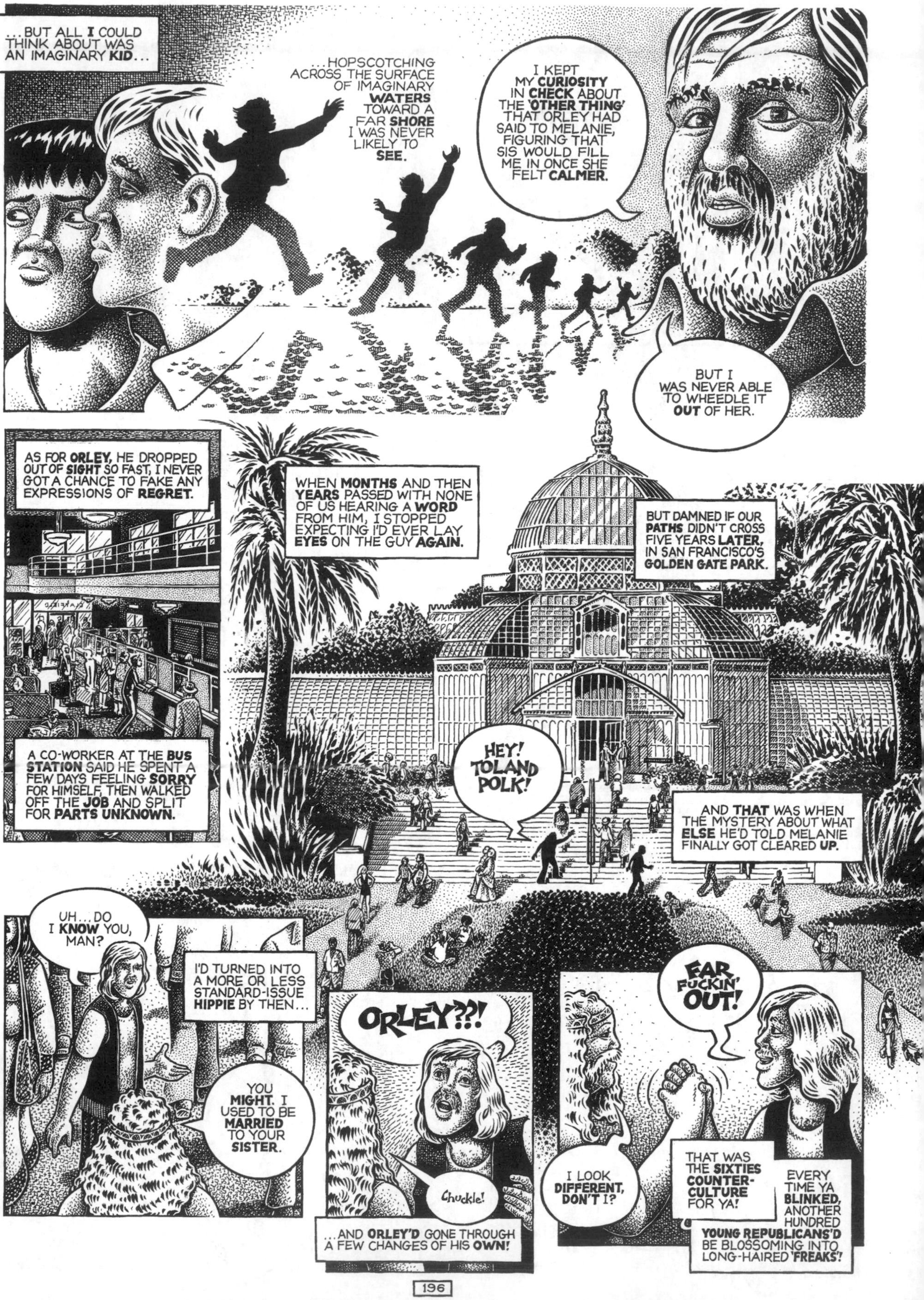
...BUT ALL I COULD THINK ABOUT WAS AN IMAGINARY KID...
...HOPSCOTCHING ACROSS THE SURFACE OF IMAGINARY WATERS TOWARD A FAR SHORE I WAS NEVER LIKELY TO SEE.
I KEPT MY CURIOSITY IN CHECK ABOUT THE 'OTHER THING' THAT ORLEY HAD SAID TO MELANIE, FIGURING THAT SIS WOULD FILL ME IN ONCE SHE FELT CALMER.
BUT I WAS NEVER ABLE TO WHEEDLE IT OUT OF HER.
AS FOR ORLEY, HE DROPPED OUT OF SIGHT SO FAST, I NEVER GOT A CHANCE TO FAKE ANY EXPRESSIONS OF REGRET.
A CO-WORKER AT THE BUS STATION SAID HE SPENT A FEW DAYS FEELING SORRY FOR HIMSELF, THEN WALKED OFF THE JOB AND SPLIT FOR PARTS UNKNOWN.
WHEN MONTHS AND THEN YEARS PASSED WITH NONE OF US HEARING A WORD FROM HIM, I STOPPED EXPECTING I'D EVER LAY EYES ON THE GUY AGAIN.
BUT DAMNED IF OUR PATHS DIDN'T CROSS FIVE YEARS LATER, IN SAN FRANCISCO'S GOLDEN GATE PARK.
HEY! TOLAND POLK!
AND THAT WAS WHEN THE MYSTERY ABOUT WHAT ELSE HE'D TOLD MELANIE FINALLY GOT CLEARED UP.
UH... DO I KNOW YOU, MAN?
I'D TURNED INTO A MORE OR LESS STANDARD-ISSUE HIPPIE BY THEN...
YOU MIGHT. I USED TO BE MARRIED TO YOUR SISTER.
ORLEY??!
Chuckle!
...AND ORLEY'D GONE THROUGH A FEW CHANGES OF HIS OWN!
FAR FUCKIN' OUT!
I LOOK DIFFERENT, DON'T I?
THAT WAS THE SIXTIES COUNTER-CULTURE FOR YA!
EVERY TIME YA BLINKED, ANOTHER HUNDRED YOUNG REPUBLICANS'D BE BLOSSOMING INTO LONG-HAIRED 'FREAKS'!

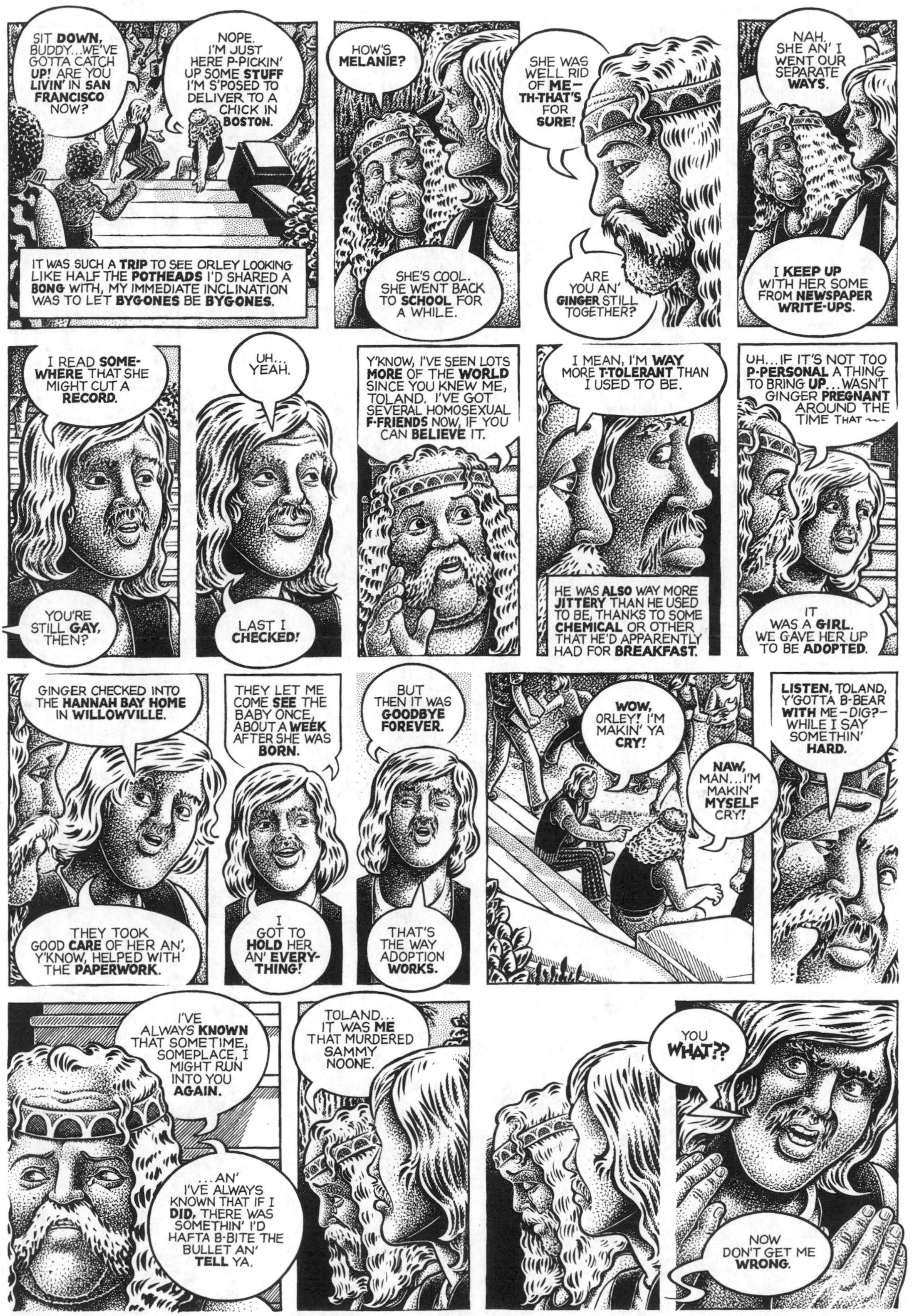
SIT DOWN, BUDDY... WE'VE GOTTA CATCH UP! ARE YOU LIVIN' IN SAN FRANCISCO NOW?
NOPE. I'M JUST HERE P-PICKIN' UP SOME STUFF I'M S'POSED TO DELIVER TO A CHICK IN BOSTON.
IT WAS SUCH A TRIP TO SEE ORLEY LOOKING LIKE HALF THE POTHEADS I'D SHARED A BONG WITH, MY IMMEDIATE INCLINATION WAS TO LET BYGONES BE BYGONES.
HOW'S MELANIE?
SHE'S COOL. SHE WENT BACK TO SCHOOL FOR A WHILE.
SHE WAS WELL RID OF ME— TH-THAT'S FOR SURE!
ARE YOU AN' GINGER STILL TOGETHER?
NAH. SHE AN' I WENT OUR SEPARATE WAYS.
I KEEP UP WITH HER SOME FROM NEWSPAPER WRITE-UPS.
I READ SOME-WHERE THAT SHE MIGHT CUT A RECORD.
YOU'RE STILL GAY, THEN?
UH... YEAH.
LAST I CHECKED!
Y'KNOW, I'VE SEEN LOTS MORE OF THE WORLD SINCE YOU KNEW ME, TOLAND. I'VE GOT SEVERAL HOMOSEXUAL F-FRIENDS NOW, IF YOU CAN BELIEVE IT.
I MEAN, I'M WAY MORE T-TOLERANT THAN I USED TO BE.
HE WAS ALSO WAY MORE JITTERY THAN HE USED TO BE, THANKS TO SOME CHEMICAL OR OTHER THAT HE'D APPARENTLY HAD FOR BREAKFAST.
UH... IF IT'S NOT TOO P-PERSONAL A THING TO BRING UP... WASN'T GINGER PREGNANT AROUND THE TIME THAT ~~
IT WAS A GIRL. WE GAVE HER UP TO BE ADOPTED.
GINGER CHECKED INTO THE HANNAH BAY HOME IN WILLOWVILLE.
THEY TOOK GOOD CARE OF HER AN', Y'KNOW, HELPED WITH THE PAPERWORK.
THEY LET ME COME SEE THE BABY ONCE, ABOUT A WEEK AFTER SHE WAS BORN.
I GOT TO HOLD HER AN' EVERY-THING!
BUT THEN IT WAS GOODBYE FOREVER.
THAT'S THE WAY ADOPTION WORKS.
WOW, ORLEY! I'M MAKIN' YA CRY!
NAW, MAN... I'M MAKIN' MYSELF CRY!
LISTEN, TOLAND, Y'GOTTA B-BEAR WITH ME—DIG?— WHILE I SAY SOMETHIN' HARD.
I'VE ALWAYS KNOWN THAT SOMETIME, SOMEPLACE, I MIGHT RUN INTO YOU AGAIN.
...AN' I'VE ALWAYS KNOWN THAT IF I DID, THERE WAS SOMETHIN' I'D HAFTA B-BITE THE BULLET AN' TELL YA.
TOLAND... IT WAS ME THAT MURDERED SAMMY NOONE.
YOU WHAT??
NOW DON'T GET ME WRONG.

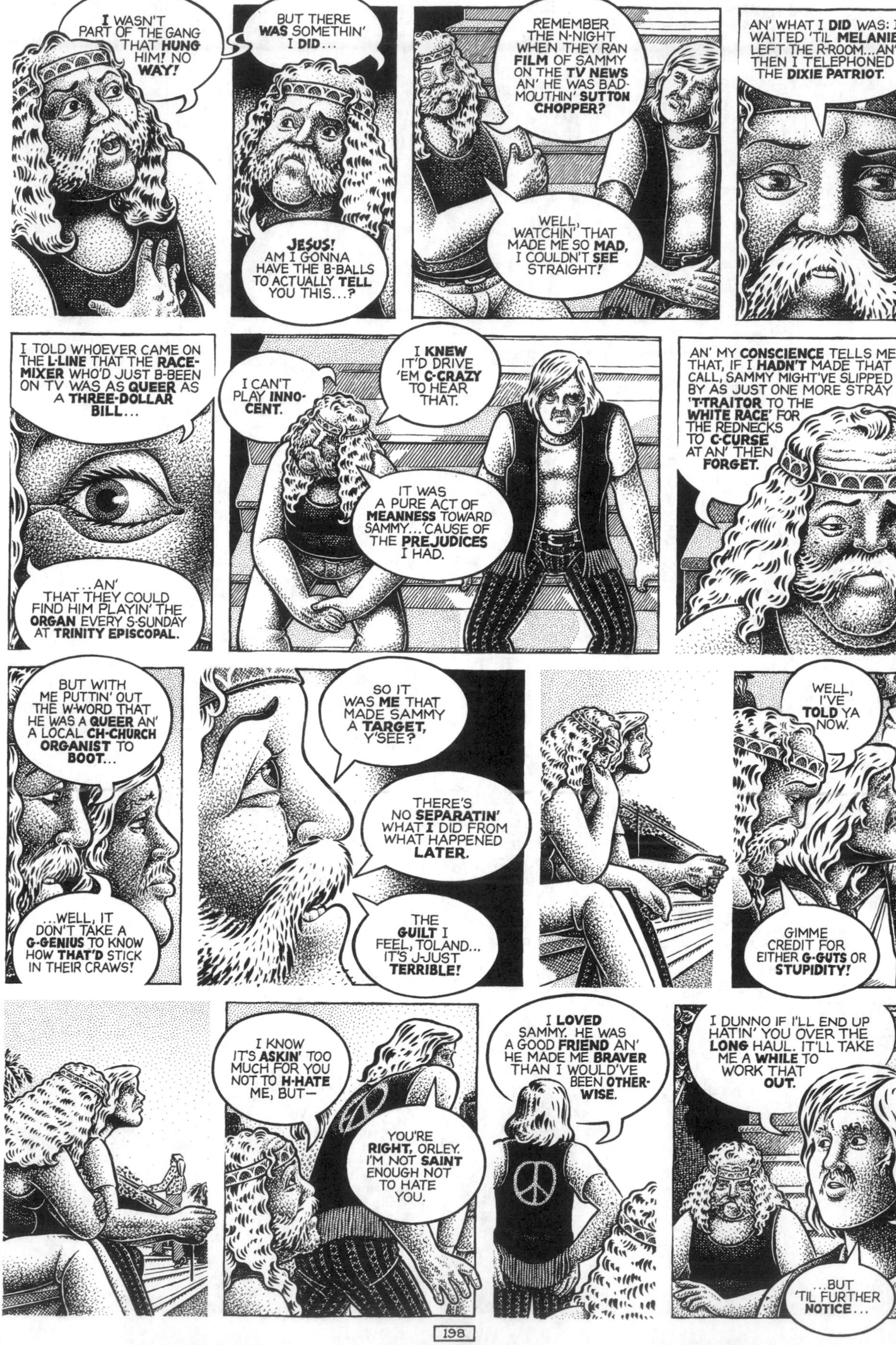
I WASN'T PART OF THE GANG THAT HUNG HIM! NO WAY!
BUT THERE WAS SOMETHIN' I DID...
JESUS! AM I GONNA HAVE THE B-BALLS TO ACTUALLY TELL YOU THIS...?
REMEMBER THE N-NIGHT WHEN THEY RAN FILM OF SAMMY ON THE TV NEWS AN' HE WAS BAD-MOUTHIN' SUTTON CHOPPER?
WELL, WATCHIN' THAT MADE ME SO MAD, I COULDN'T SEE STRAIGHT!
AN' WHAT I DID WAS: I WAITED 'TIL MELANIE LEFT THE R-ROOM...AN' THEN I TELEPHONED THE DIXIE PATRIOT.
I TOLD WHOEVER CAME ON THE L-LINE THAT THE RACE-MIXER WHO'D JUST B-BEEN ON TV WAS AS QUEER AS A THREE-DOLLAR BILL...
...AN' THAT THEY COULD FIND HIM PLAYIN' THE ORGAN EVERY S-SUNDAY AT TRINITY EPISCOPAL.
I CAN'T PLAY INNO-CENT.
I KNEW IT'D DRIVE 'EM C-CRAZY TO HEAR THAT.
IT WAS A PURE ACT OF MEANNESS TOWARD SAMMY...'CAUSE OF THE PREJUDICES I HAD.
AN' MY CONSCIENCE TELLS ME THAT, IF I HADN'T MADE THAT CALL, SAMMY MIGHT'VE SLIPPED BY AS JUST ONE MORE STRAY 'T-TRAITOR TO THE WHITE RACE' FOR THE REDNECKS TO C-CURSE AT AN' THEN FORGET.
BUT WITH ME PUTTIN' OUT THE W-WORD THAT HE WAS A QUEER AN' A LOCAL CH-CHURCH ORGANIST TO BOOT...
...WELL, IT DON'T TAKE A G-GENIUS TO KNOW HOW THAT'D STICK IN THEIR CRAWS!
SO IT WAS ME THAT MADE SAMMY A TARGET, Y'SEE?
THERE'S NO SEPARATIN' WHAT I DID FROM WHAT HAPPENED LATER.
THE GUILT I FEEL, TOLAND... IT'S J-JUST TERRIBLE!
WELL, I'VE TOLD YA NOW.
GIMME CREDIT FOR EITHER G-GUTS OR STUPIDITY!
I KNOW IT'S ASKIN' TOO MUCH FOR YOU NOT TO H-HATE ME, BUT—
YOU'RE RIGHT, ORLEY. I'M NOT SAINT ENOUGH NOT TO HATE YOU.
I LOVED SAMMY. HE WAS A GOOD FRIEND AN' HE MADE ME BRAVER THAN I WOULD'VE BEEN OTHER-WISE.
I DUNNO IF I'LL END UP HATIN' YOU OVER THE LONG HAUL. IT'LL TAKE ME A WHILE TO WORK THAT OUT.
...BUT 'TIL FURTHER NOTICE...

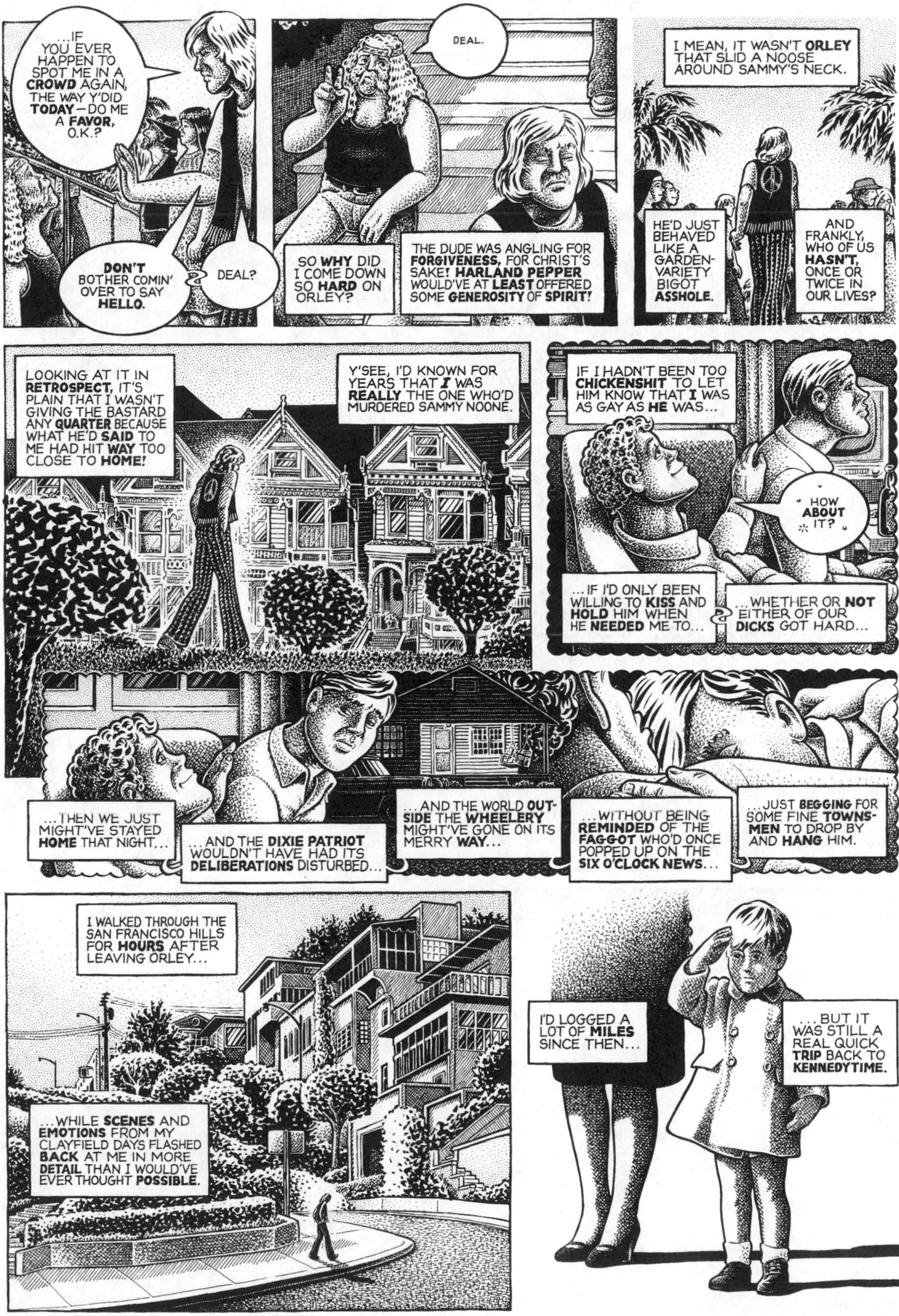
...IF YOU EVER HAPPEN TO SPOT ME IN A CROWD AGAIN, THE WAY Y'DID TODAY—DO ME A FAVOR, O.K.?
DON'T BOTHER COMIN' OVER TO SAY HELLO.
DEAL?
DEAL.
SO WHY DID I COME DOWN SO HARD ON ORLEY?
THE DUDE WAS ANGLING FOR FORGIVENESS, FOR CHRIST'S SAKE! HARLAND PEPPER WOULD'VE AT LEAST OFFERED SOME GENEROSITY OF SPIRIT!
I MEAN, IT WASN'T ORLEY THAT SLID A NOOSE AROUND SAMMY'S NECK.
HE'D JUST BEHAVED LIKE A GARDEN-VARIETY BIGOT ASSHOLE.
AND FRANKLY, WHO OF US HASN'T, ONCE OR TWICE IN OUR LIVES?
LOOKING AT IT IN RETROSPECT, IT'S PLAIN THAT I WASN'T GIVING THE BASTARD ANY QUARTER BECAUSE WHAT HE'D SAID TO ME HAD HIT WAY TOO CLOSE TO HOME!
Y'SEE, I'D KNOWN FOR YEARS THAT I WAS REALLY THE ONE WHO'D MURDERED SAMMY NOONE.
IF I HADN'T BEEN TOO CHICKENSHIT TO LET HIM KNOW THAT I WAS AS GAY AS HE WAS...
HOW ABOUT IT?
...IF I'D ONLY BEEN WILLING TO KISS AND HOLD HIM WHEN HE NEEDED ME TO...
...WHETHER OR NOT EITHER OF OUR DICKS GOT HARD...
...THEN WE JUST MIGHT'VE STAYED HOME THAT NIGHT...
...AND THE DIXIE PATRIOT WOULDN'T HAVE HAD ITS DELIBERATIONS DISTURBED...
...AND THE WORLD OUTSIDE THE WHEELERY MIGHT'VE GONE ON ITS MERRY WAY...
...WITHOUT BEING REMINDED OF THE FAGGOT WHO'D ONCE POPPED UP ON THE SIX O'CLOCK NEWS...
...JUST BEGGING FOR SOME FINE TOWNSMEN TO DROP BY AND HANG HIM.
I WALKED THROUGH THE SAN FRANCISCO HILLS FOR HOURS AFTER LEAVING ORLEY...
...WHILE SCENES AND EMOTIONS FROM MY CLAYFIELD DAYS FLASHED BACK AT ME IN MORE DETAIL THAN I WOULD'VE EVER THOUGHT POSSIBLE.
I'D LOGGED A LOT OF MILES SINCE THEN...
...BUT IT WAS STILL A REAL QUICK TRIP BACK TO KENNEDYTIME.

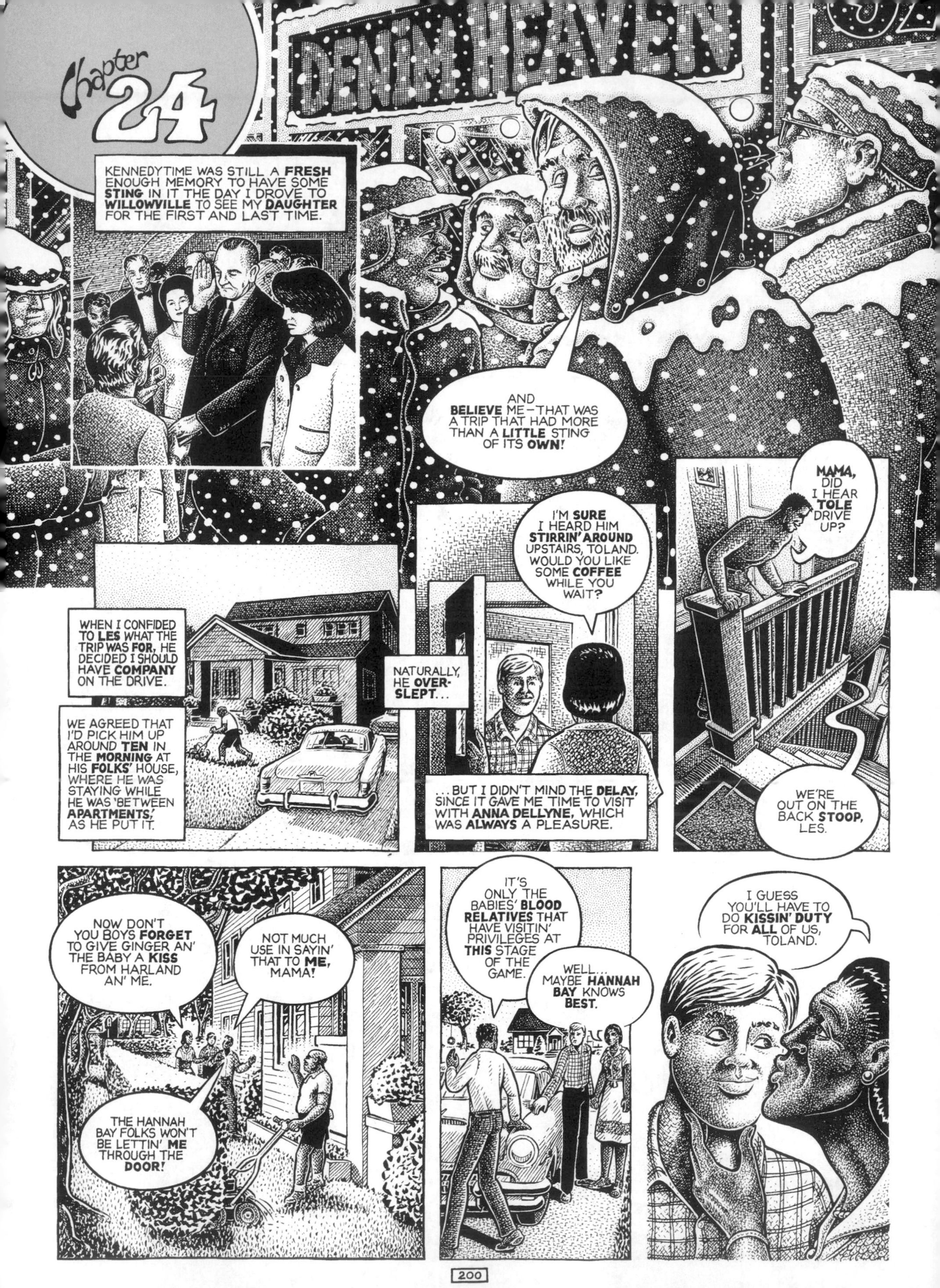
Chapter 24
DENIM HEAVEN
KENNEDYTIME WAS STILL A FRESH ENOUGH MEMORY TO HAVE SOME STING IN IT THE DAY I DROVE TO WILLOWVILLE TO SEE MY DAUGHTER FOR THE FIRST AND LAST TIME.
AND BELIEVE ME—THAT WAS A TRIP THAT HAD MORE THAN A LITTLE STING OF ITS OWN!
WHEN I CONFIDED TO LES WHAT THE TRIP WAS FOR, HE DECIDED I SHOULD HAVE COMPANY ON THE DRIVE.
WE AGREED THAT I'D PICK HIM UP AROUND TEN IN THE MORNING AT HIS FOLKS' HOUSE, WHERE HE WAS STAYING WHILE HE WAS 'BETWEEN APARTMENTS,' AS HE PUT IT.
NATURALLY, HE OVER-SLEPT...
I'M SURE I HEARD HIM STIRRIN' AROUND UPSTAIRS, TOLAND. WOULD YOU LIKE SOME COFFEE WHILE YOU WAIT?
...BUT I DIDN'T MIND THE DELAY, SINCE IT GAVE ME TIME TO VISIT WITH ANNA DELLYNE, WHICH WAS ALWAYS A PLEASURE.
MAMA, DID I HEAR TOLE DRIVE UP?
WE'RE OUT ON THE BACK STOOP, LES.
NOW DON'T YOU BOYS FORGET TO GIVE GINGER AN' THE BABY A KISS FROM HARLAND AN' ME.
NOT MUCH USE IN SAYIN' THAT TO ME, MAMA!
THE HANNAH BAY FOLKS WON'T BE LETTIN' ME THROUGH THE DOOR!
IT'S ONLY THE BABIES' BLOOD RELATIVES THAT HAVE VISITIN' PRIVILEGES AT THIS STAGE OF THE GAME.
WELL... MAYBE HANNAH BAY KNOWS BEST.
I GUESS YOU'LL HAVE TO DO KISSIN' DUTY FOR ALL OF US, TOLAND.

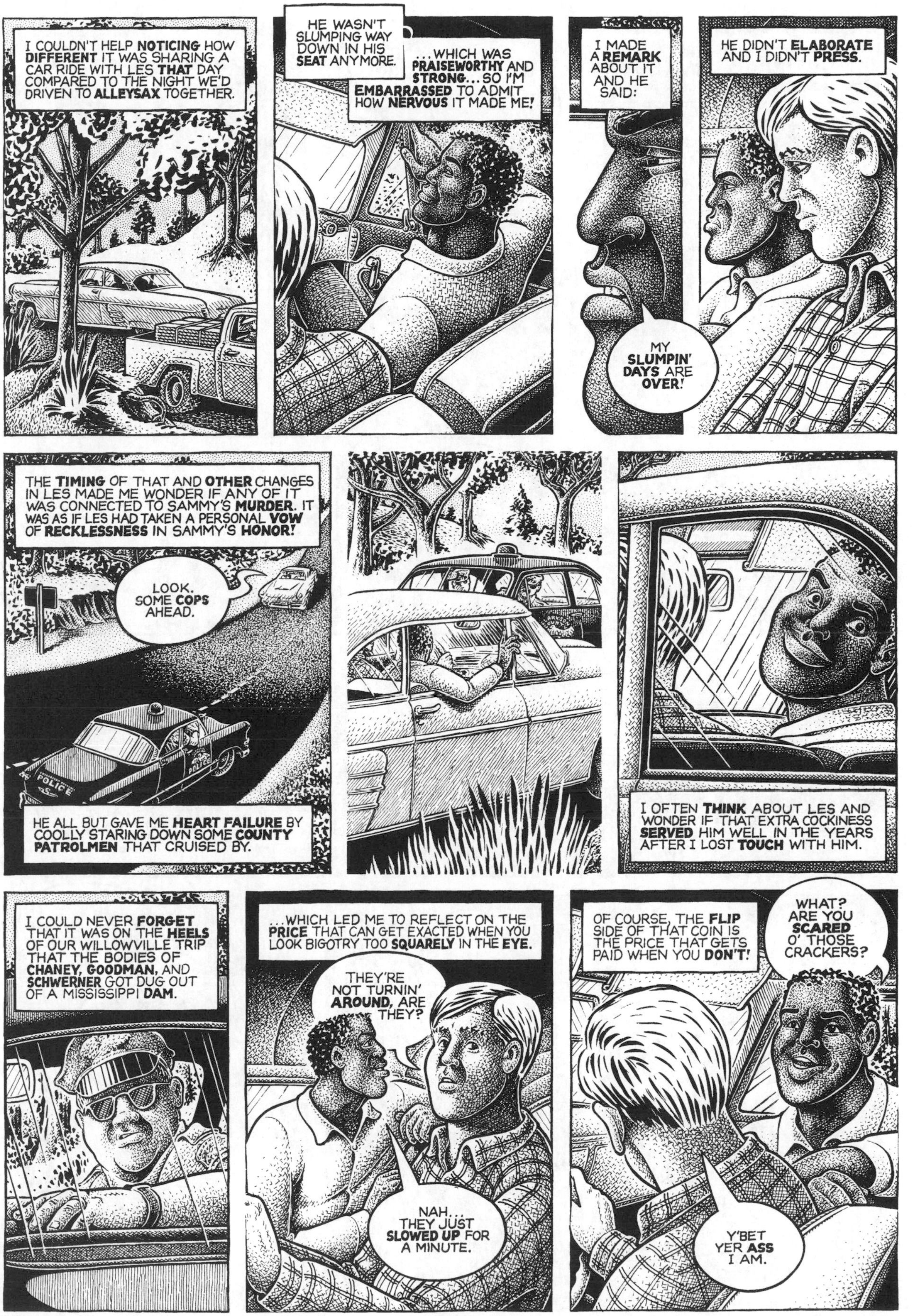

I COULDN'T HELP NOTICING HOW DIFFERENT IT WAS SHARING A CAR RIDE WITH LES THAT DAY COMPARED TO THE NIGHT WE'D DRIVEN TO ALLEYSAX TOGETHER.
HE WASN'T SLUMPING WAY DOWN IN HIS SEAT ANYMORE.
...WHICH WAS PRAISEWORTHY AND STRONG... SO I'M EMBARRASSED TO ADMIT HOW NERVOUS IT MADE ME!
I MADE A REMARK ABOUT IT AND HE SAID:
MY SLUMPIN' DAYS ARE OVER!
HE DIDN'T ELABORATE AND I DIDN'T PRESS.
THE TIMING OF THAT AND OTHER CHANGES IN LES MADE ME WONDER IF ANY OF IT WAS CONNECTED TO SAMMY'S MURDER. IT WAS AS IF LES HAD TAKEN A PERSONAL VOW OF RECKLESSNESS IN SAMMY'S HONOR!
LOOK. SOME COPS AHEAD.
POLICE
HE ALL BUT GAVE ME HEART FAILURE BY COOLLY STARING DOWN SOME COUNTY PATROLMEN THAT CRUISED BY.
I OFTEN THINK ABOUT LES AND WONDER IF THAT EXTRA COCKINESS SERVED HIM WELL IN THE YEARS AFTER I LOST TOUCH WITH HIM.
I COULD NEVER FORGET THAT IT WAS ON THE HEELS OF OUR WILLOWVILLE TRIP THAT THE BODIES OF CHANEY, GOODMAN, AND SCHWERNER GOT DUG OUT OF A MISSISSIPPI DAM.
...WHICH LED ME TO REFLECT ON THE PRICE THAT CAN GET EXACTED WHEN YOU LOOK BIGOTRY TOO SQUARELY IN THE EYE.
THEY'RE NOT TURNIN' AROUND, ARE THEY?
NAH... THEY JUST SLOWED UP FOR A MINUTE.
OF COURSE, THE FLIP SIDE OF THAT COIN IS THE PRICE THAT GETS PAID WHEN YOU DON'T!
WHAT? ARE YOU SCARED O' THOSE CRACKERS?
Y'BET YER ASS I AM.

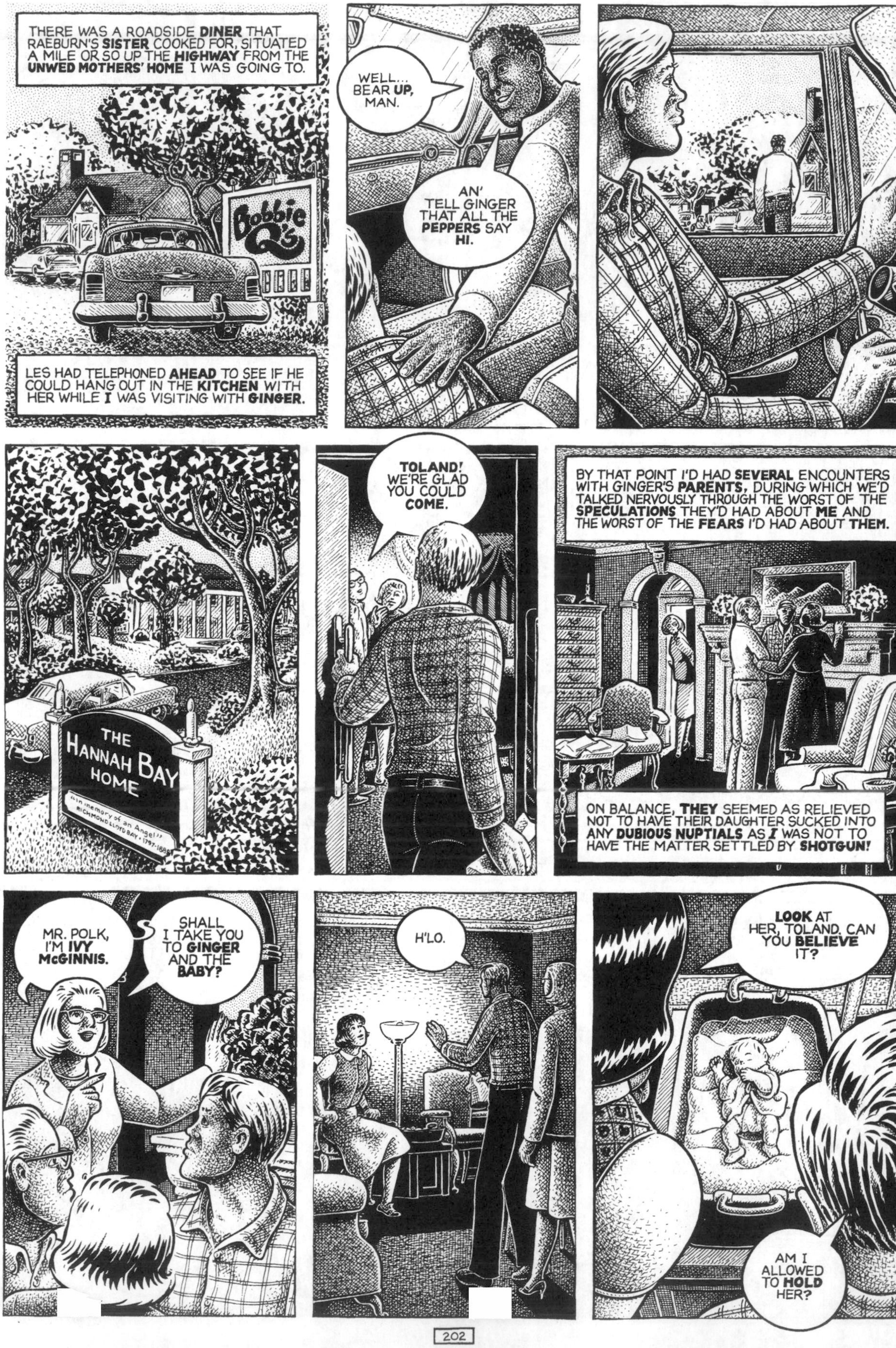
THERE WAS A ROADSIDE DINER THAT RAEBURN'S SISTER COOKED FOR, SITUATED A MILE OR SO UP THE HIGHWAY FROM THE UNWED MOTHERS' HOME I WAS GOING TO.
Bobbie Q's
LES HAD TELEPHONED AHEAD TO SEE IF HE COULD HANG OUT IN THE KITCHEN WITH HER WHILE I WAS VISITING WITH GINGER.
WELL... BEAR UP, MAN.
AN' TELL GINGER THAT ALL THE PEPPERS SAY HI.
THE HANNAH BAY HOME
"In memory of an Angel" RICHMOND LLOYD BAY • 1797-1888
TOLAND! WE'RE GLAD YOU COULD COME.
BY THAT POINT I'D HAD SEVERAL ENCOUNTERS WITH GINGER'S PARENTS, DURING WHICH WE'D TALKED NERVOUSLY THROUGH THE WORST OF THE SPECULATIONS THEY'D HAD ABOUT ME AND THE WORST OF THE FEARS I'D HAD ABOUT THEM.
ON BALANCE, THEY SEEMED AS RELIEVED NOT TO HAVE THEIR DAUGHTER SUCKED INTO ANY DUBIOUS NUPTIALS AS I WAS NOT TO HAVE THE MATTER SETTLED BY SHOTGUN!
MR. POLK, I'M IVY McGINNIS.
SHALL I TAKE YOU TO GINGER AND THE BABY?
H'LO.
LOOK AT HER, TOLAND. CAN YOU BELIEVE IT?
AM I ALLOWED TO HOLD HER?

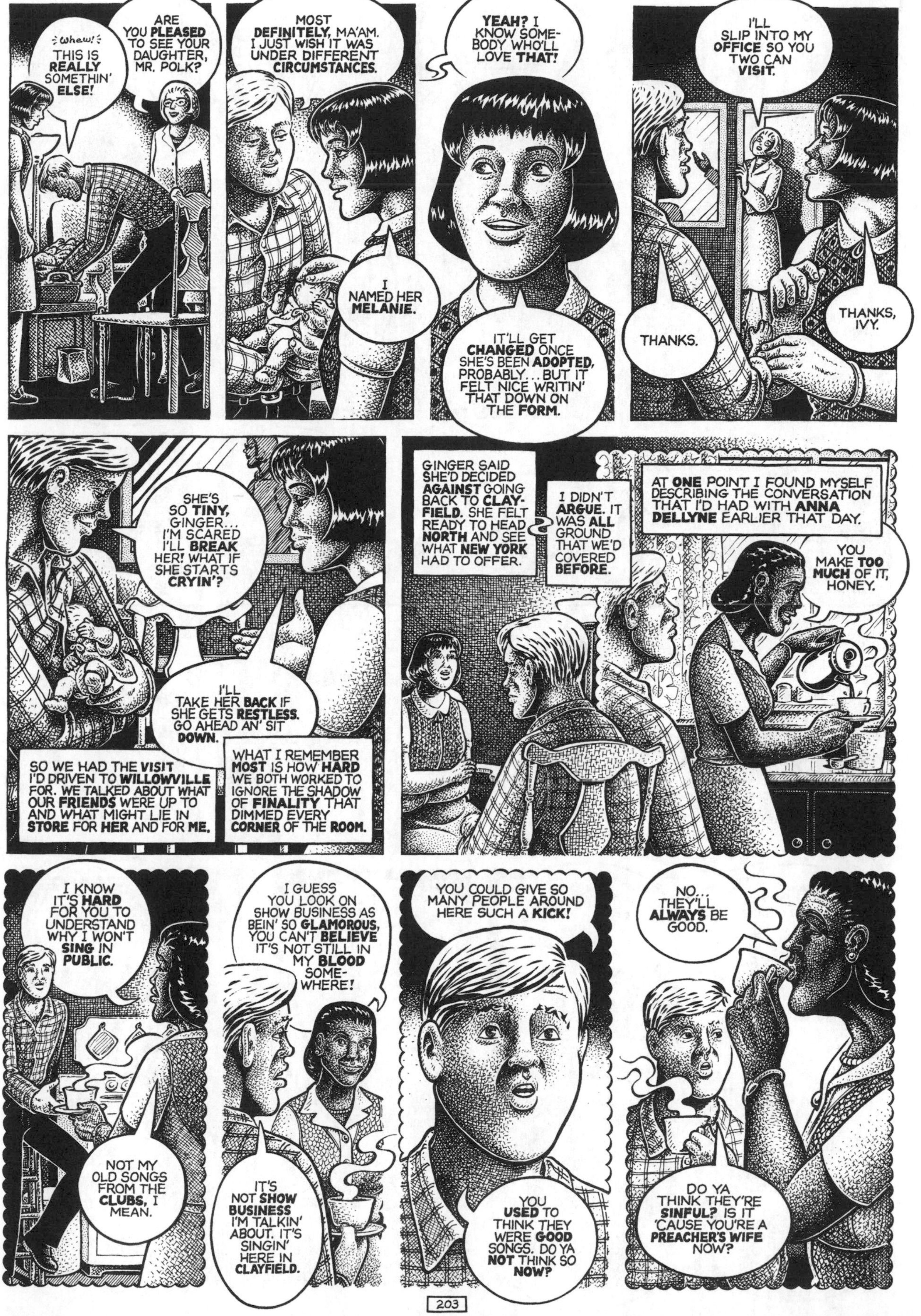

ARE YOU PLEASED TO SEE YOUR DAUGHTER, MR. POLK?
WHEW! THIS IS REALLY SOMETHIN' ELSE!
MOST DEFINITELY, MA'AM. I JUST WISH IT WAS UNDER DIFFERENT CIRCUMSTANCES.
I NAMED HER MELANIE.
YEAH? I KNOW SOMEBODY WHO'LL LOVE THAT!
IT'LL GET CHANGED ONCE SHE'S BEEN ADOPTED, PROBABLY... BUT IT FELT NICE WRITIN' THAT DOWN ON THE FORM.
I'LL SLIP INTO MY OFFICE SO YOU TWO CAN VISIT.
THANKS.
THANKS, IVY.
SHE'S SO TINY, GINGER... I'M SCARED I'LL BREAK HER! WHAT IF SHE STARTS CRYIN'?
I'LL TAKE HER BACK IF SHE GETS RESTLESS. GO AHEAD AN' SIT DOWN.
SO WE HAD THE VISIT I'D DRIVEN TO WILLOWVILLE FOR. WE TALKED ABOUT WHAT OUR FRIENDS WERE UP TO AND WHAT MIGHT LIE IN STORE FOR HER AND FOR ME.
WHAT I REMEMBER MOST IS HOW HARD WE BOTH WORKED TO IGNORE THE SHADOW OF FINALITY THAT DIMMED EVERY CORNER OF THE ROOM.
GINGER SAID SHE'D DECIDED AGAINST GOING BACK TO CLAYFIELD. SHE FELT READY TO HEAD NORTH AND SEE WHAT NEW YORK HAD TO OFFER.
I DIDN'T ARGUE. IT WAS ALL GROUND THAT WE'D COVERED BEFORE.
AT ONE POINT I FOUND MYSELF DESCRIBING THE CONVERSATION THAT I'D HAD WITH ANNA DELLYNE EARLIER THAT DAY.
YOU MAKE TOO MUCH OF IT, HONEY.
I KNOW IT'S HARD FOR YOU TO UNDERSTAND WHY I WON'T SING IN PUBLIC.
NOT MY OLD SONGS FROM THE CLUBS, I MEAN.
I GUESS YOU LOOK ON SHOW BUSINESS AS BEIN' SO GLAMOROUS, YOU CAN'T BELIEVE IT'S NOT STILL IN MY BLOOD SOMEWHERE!
IT'S NOT SHOW BUSINESS I'M TALKIN' ABOUT. IT'S SINGIN' HERE IN CLAYFIELD.
YOU COULD GIVE SO MANY PEOPLE AROUND HERE SUCH A KICK!
YOU USED TO THINK THEY WERE GOOD SONGS. DO YA NOT THINK SO NOW?
NO... THEY'LL ALWAYS BE GOOD.
DO YA THINK THEY'RE SINFUL? IS IT 'CAUSE YOU'RE A PREACHER'S WIFE NOW?

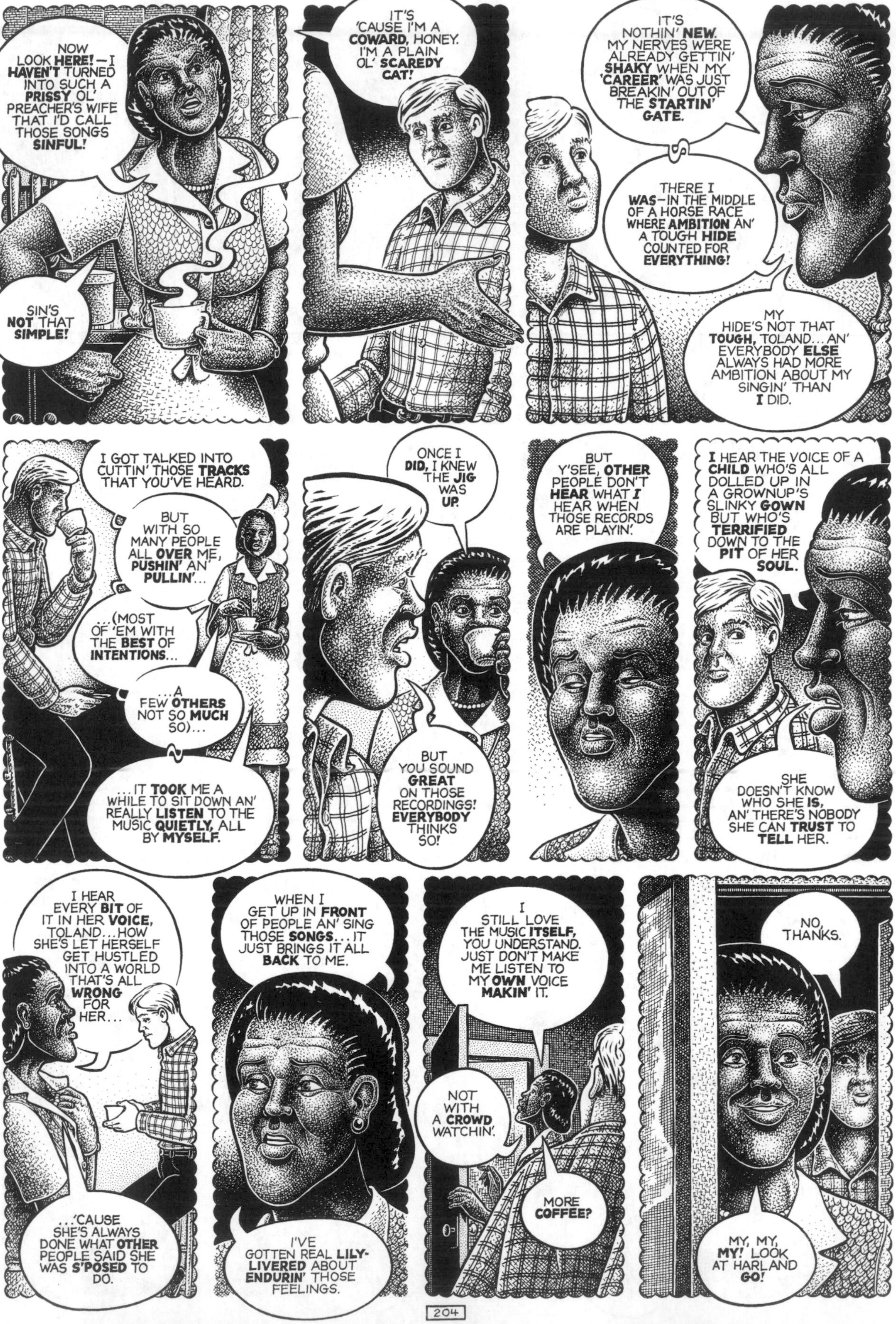
NOW LOOK HERE! —I HAVEN'T TURNED INTO SUCH A PRISSY OL' PREACHER'S WIFE THAT I'D CALL THOSE SONGS SINFUL!
SIN'S NOT THAT SIMPLE!
IT'S 'CAUSE I'M A COWARD, HONEY. I'M A PLAIN OL' SCAREDY CAT!
IT'S NOTHIN' NEW. MY NERVES WERE ALREADY GETTIN' SHAKY WHEN MY 'CAREER' WAS JUST BREAKIN' OUT OF THE STARTIN' GATE.
THERE I WAS—IN THE MIDDLE OF A HORSE RACE WHERE AMBITION AN' A TOUGH HIDE COUNTED FOR EVERYTHING!
MY HIDE'S NOT THAT TOUGH, TOLAND... AN' EVERYBODY ELSE ALWAYS HAD MORE AMBITION ABOUT MY SINGIN' THAN I DID.
I GOT TALKED INTO CUTTIN' THOSE TRACKS THAT YOU'VE HEARD.
BUT WITH SO MANY PEOPLE ALL OVER ME, PUSHIN' AN' PULLIN'...
...(MOST OF 'EM WITH THE BEST OF INTENTIONS...
...A FEW OTHERS NOT SO MUCH SO)...
...IT TOOK ME A WHILE TO SIT DOWN AN' REALLY LISTEN TO THE MUSIC QUIETLY, ALL BY MYSELF.
ONCE I DID, I KNEW THE JIG WAS UP.
BUT YOU SOUND GREAT ON THOSE RECORDINGS! EVERYBODY THINKS SO!
BUT Y'SEE, OTHER PEOPLE DON'T HEAR WHAT I HEAR WHEN THOSE RECORDS ARE PLAYIN'.
I HEAR THE VOICE OF A CHILD WHO'S ALL DOLLED UP IN A GROWNUP'S SLINKY GOWN BUT WHO'S TERRIFIED DOWN TO THE PIT OF HER SOUL.
SHE DOESN'T KNOW WHO SHE IS, AN' THERE'S NOBODY SHE CAN TRUST TO TELL HER.
I HEAR EVERY BIT OF IT IN HER VOICE, TOLAND...HOW SHE'S LET HERSELF GET HUSTLED INTO A WORLD THAT'S ALL WRONG FOR HER...
...'CAUSE SHE'S ALWAYS DONE WHAT OTHER PEOPLE SAID SHE WAS S'POSED TO DO.
WHEN I GET UP IN FRONT OF PEOPLE AN' SING THOSE SONGS... IT JUST BRINGS IT ALL BACK TO ME.
I'VE GOTTEN REAL LILY-LIVERED ABOUT ENDURIN' THOSE FEELINGS.
I STILL LOVE THE MUSIC ITSELF, YOU UNDERSTAND. JUST DON'T MAKE ME LISTEN TO MY OWN VOICE MAKIN' IT.
NOT WITH A CROWD WATCHIN'.
MORE COFFEE?
NO, THANKS.
MY, MY, MY! LOOK AT HARLAND GO!

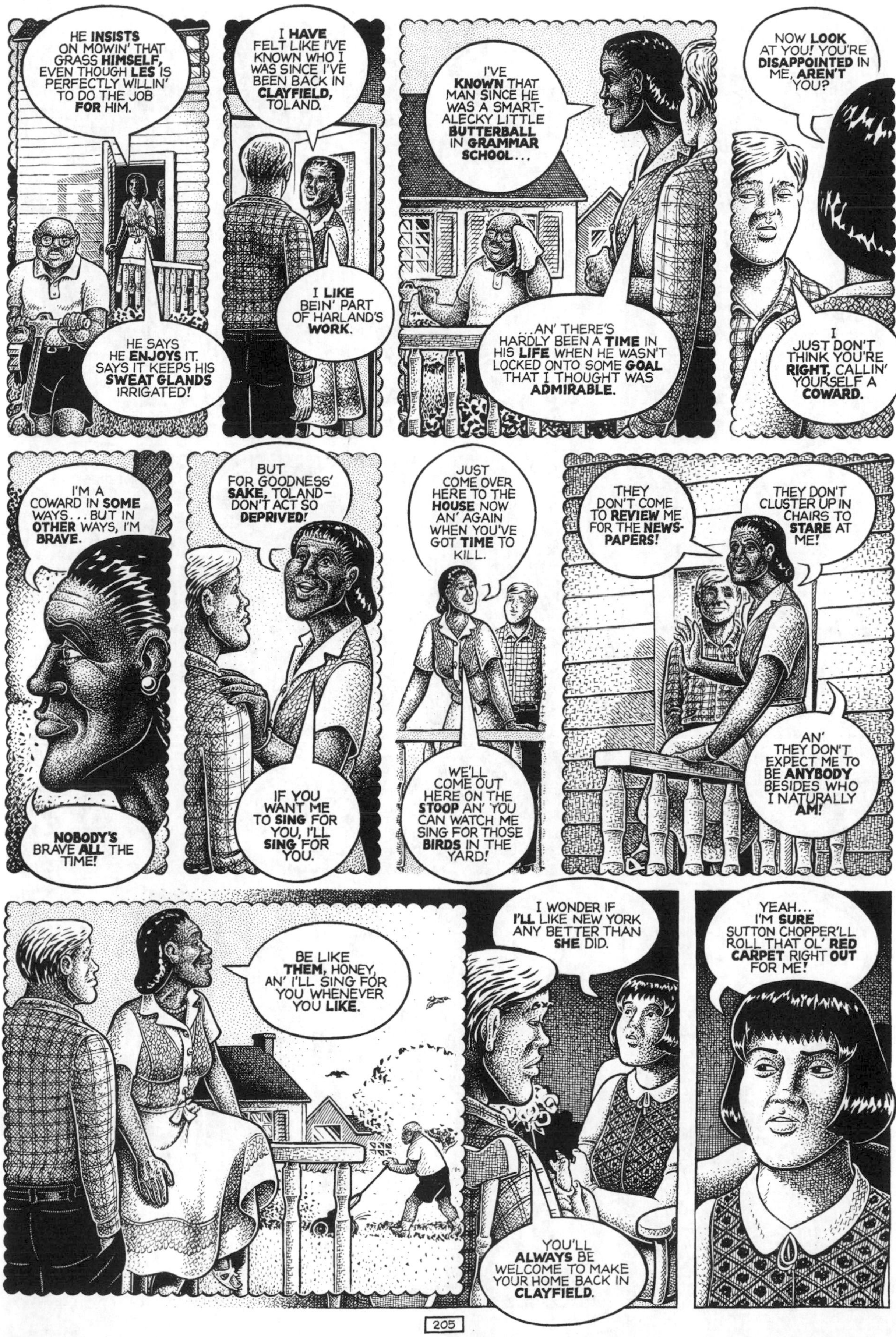

HE INSISTS ON MOWIN' THAT GRASS HIMSELF, EVEN THOUGH LES IS PERFECTLY WILLIN' TO DO THE JOB FOR HIM.
HE SAYS HE ENJOYS IT. SAYS IT KEEPS HIS SWEAT GLANDS IRRIGATED!
I HAVE FELT LIKE I'VE KNOWN WHO I WAS SINCE I'VE BEEN BACK IN CLAYFIELD, TOLAND.
I LIKE BEIN' PART OF HARLAND'S WORK.
I'VE KNOWN THAT MAN SINCE HE WAS A SMART-ALECKY LITTLE BUTTERBALL IN GRAMMAR SCHOOL...
...AN' THERE'S HARDLY BEEN A TIME IN HIS LIFE WHEN HE WASN'T LOCKED ONTO SOME GOAL THAT I THOUGHT WAS ADMIRABLE.
NOW LOOK AT YOU! YOU'RE DISAPPOINTED IN ME, AREN'T YOU?
I JUST DON'T THINK YOU'RE RIGHT, CALLIN' YOURSELF A COWARD.
I'M A COWARD IN SOME WAYS... BUT IN OTHER WAYS, I'M BRAVE.
NOBODY'S BRAVE ALL THE TIME!
BUT FOR GOODNESS' SAKE, TOLAND-DON'T ACT SO DEPRIVED!
IF YOU WANT ME TO SING FOR YOU, I'LL SING FOR YOU.
JUST COME OVER HERE TO THE HOUSE NOW AN' AGAIN WHEN YOU'VE GOT TIME TO KILL.
WE'LL COME OUT HERE ON THE STOOP AN' YOU CAN WATCH ME SING FOR THOSE BIRDS IN THE YARD!
THEY DON'T COME TO REVIEW ME FOR THE NEWS-PAPERS!
THEY DON'T CLUSTER UP IN CHAIRS TO STARE AT ME!
AN' THEY DON'T EXPECT ME TO BE ANYBODY BESIDES WHO I NATURALLY AM!
BE LIKE THEM, HONEY, AN' I'LL SING FOR YOU WHENEVER YOU LIKE.
I WONDER IF I'LL LIKE NEW YORK ANY BETTER THAN SHE DID.
YOU'LL ALWAYS BE WELCOME TO MAKE YOUR HOME BACK IN CLAYFIELD.
YEAH... I'M SURE SUTTON CHOPPER'LL ROLL THAT OL' RED CARPET RIGHT OUT FOR ME!

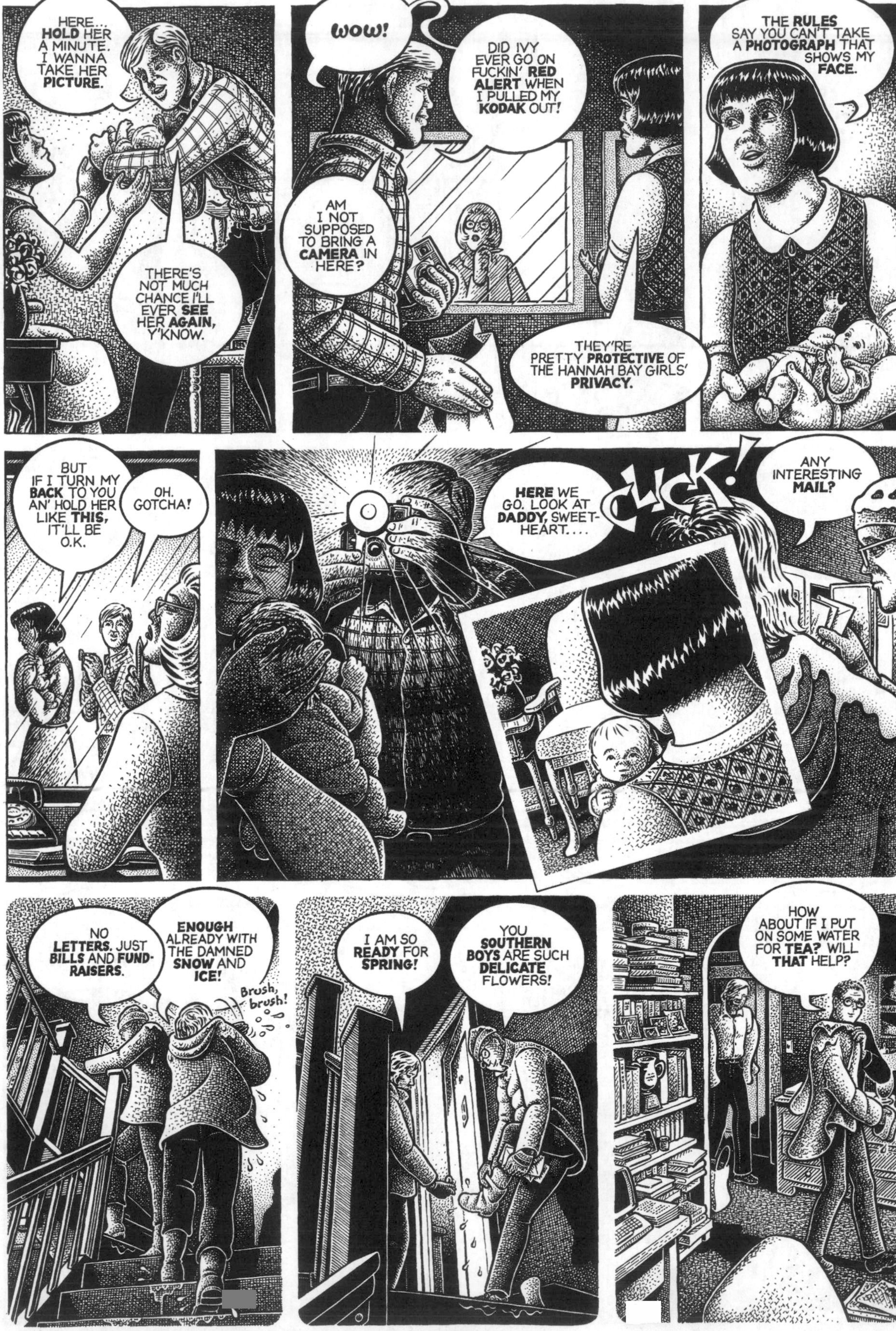
HERE... HOLD HER A MINUTE. I WANNA TAKE HER PICTURE.
THERE'S NOT MUCH CHANCE I'LL EVER SEE HER AGAIN, Y'KNOW.
WOW!
DID IVY EVER GO ON FUCKIN' RED ALERT WHEN I PULLED MY KODAK OUT!
AM I NOT SUPPOSED TO BRING A CAMERA IN HERE?
THEY'RE PRETTY PROTECTIVE OF THE HANNAH BAY GIRLS' PRIVACY.
THE RULES SAY YOU CAN'T TAKE A PHOTOGRAPH THAT SHOWS MY FACE.
BUT IF I TURN MY BACK TO YOU AN' HOLD HER LIKE THIS, IT'LL BE O.K.
OH. GOTCHA!
HERE WE GO. LOOK AT DADDY, SWEET-HEART....
CLICK!
ANY INTERESTING MAIL?
NO LETTERS. JUST BILLS AND FUND-RAISERS.
ENOUGH ALREADY WITH THE DAMNED SNOW AND ICE!
Brush, brush!
I AM SO READY FOR SPRING!
YOU SOUTHERN BOYS ARE SUCH DELICATE FLOWERS!
HOW ABOUT IF I PUT ON SOME WATER FOR TEA? WILL THAT HELP?

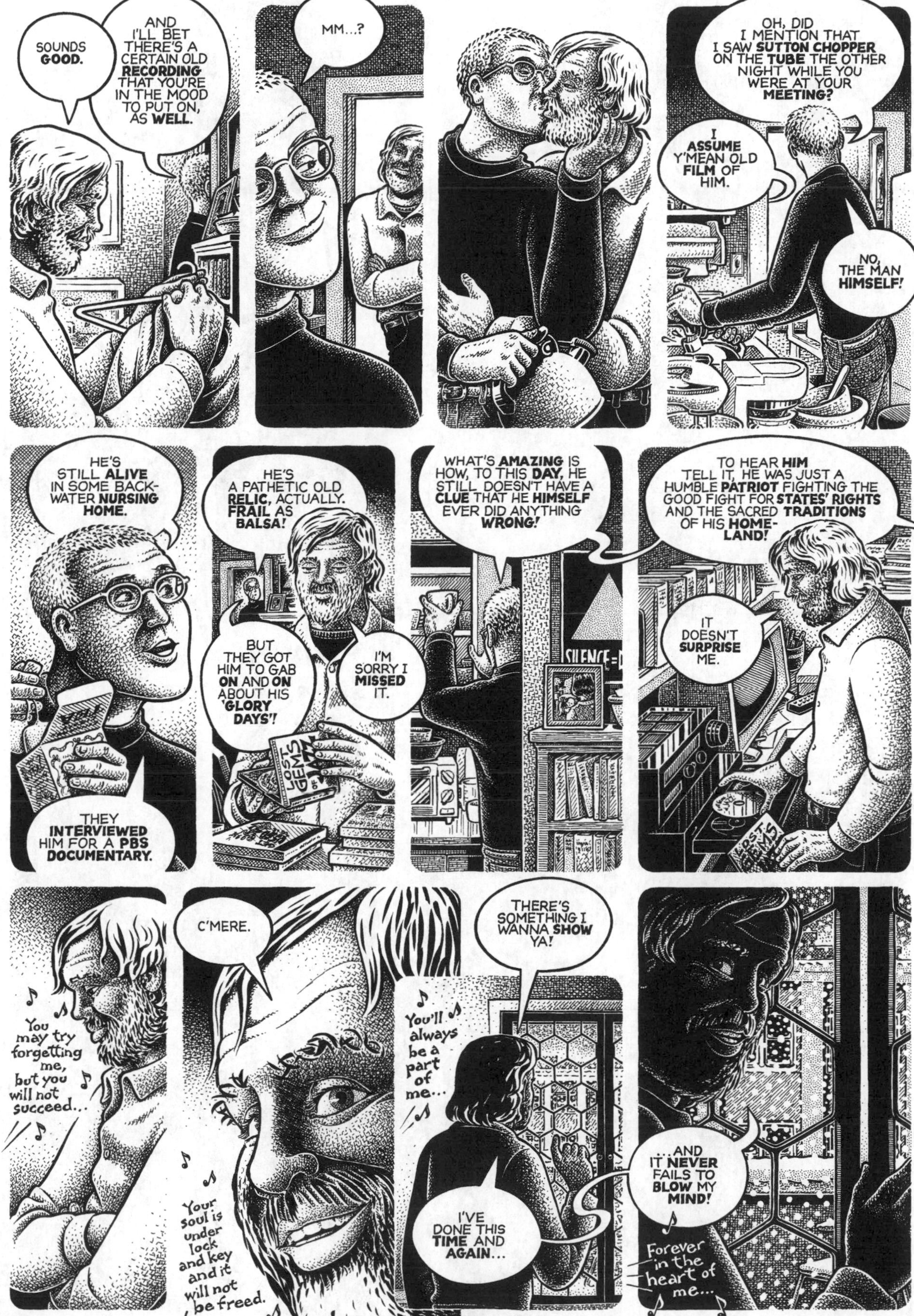
SOUNDS GOOD.
AND I'LL BET THERE'S A CERTAIN OLD RECORDING THAT YOU'RE IN THE MOOD TO PUT ON, AS WELL.
MM...?
OH, DID I MENTION THAT I SAW SUTTON CHOPPER ON THE TUBE THE OTHER NIGHT WHILE YOU WERE AT YOUR MEETING?
I ASSUME Y'MEAN OLD FILM OF HIM.
NO, THE MAN HIMSELF!
HE'S STILL ALIVE IN SOME BACK-WATER NURSING HOME.
THEY INTERVIEWED HIM FOR A PBS DOCUMENTARY.
HE'S A PATHETIC OLD RELIC, ACTUALLY. FRAIL AS BALSA!
BUT THEY GOT HIM TO GAB ON AND ON ABOUT HIS 'GLORY DAYS'!
I'M SORRY I MISSED IT.
LOST GEMS OF JAZZ
WHAT'S AMAZING IS HOW, TO THIS DAY, HE STILL DOESN'T HAVE A CLUE THAT HE HIMSELF EVER DID ANYTHING WRONG!
SILENCE=
TO HEAR HIM TELL IT, HE WAS JUST A HUMBLE PATRIOT FIGHTING THE GOOD FIGHT FOR STATES' RIGHTS AND THE SACRED TRADITIONS OF HIS HOME-LAND!
IT DOESN'T SURPRISE ME.
LOST GEMS
You may try forgetting me, but you will not succeed...
C'MERE.
Your soul is under lock and key and it will not be freed.
THERE'S SOMETHING I WANNA SHOW YA!
You'll always be a part of me...
I'VE DONE THIS TIME AND AGAIN...
...AND IT NEVER FAILS TO BLOW MY MIND!
Forever in the heart of me...

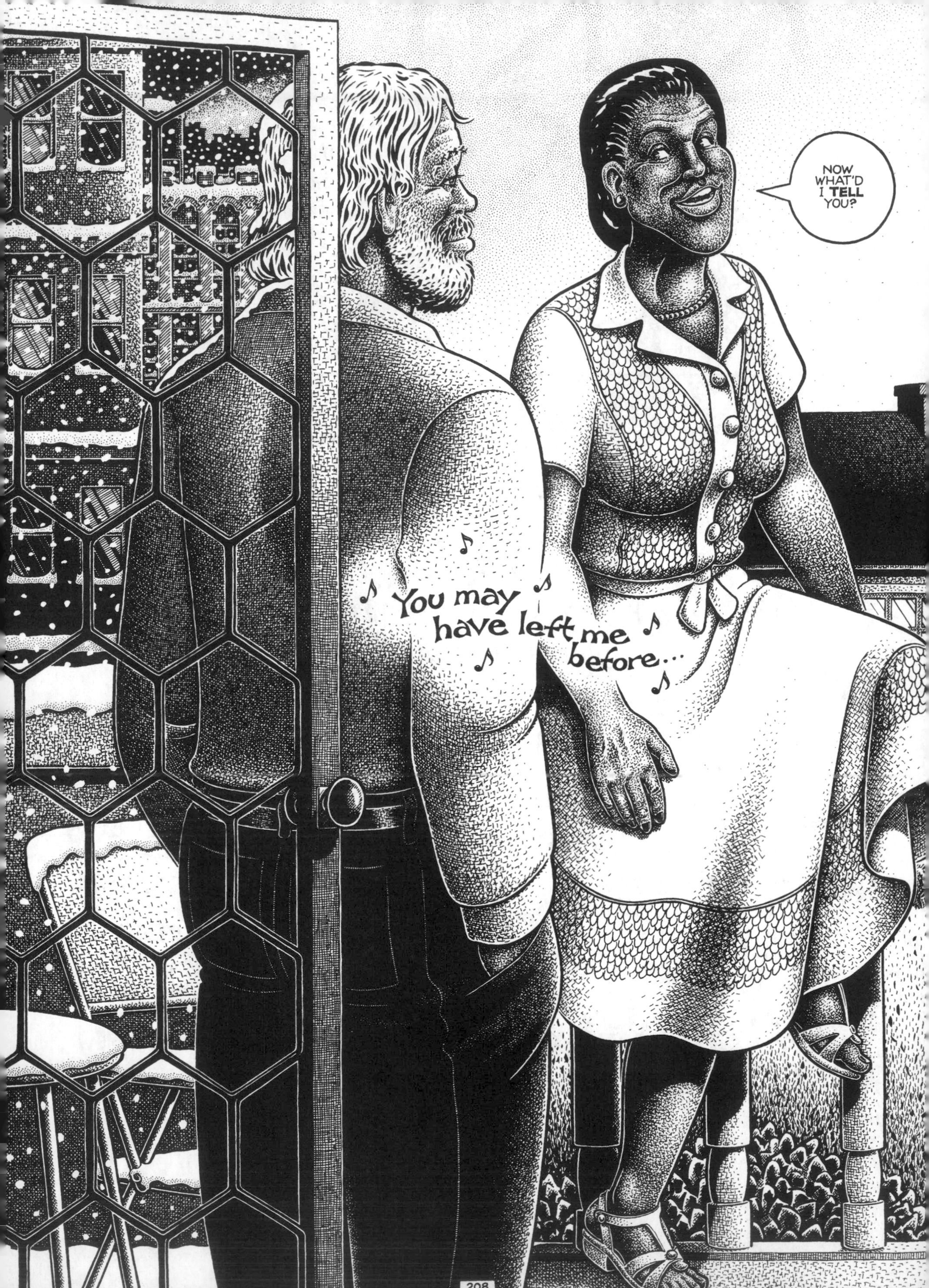
NOW WHAT'D I **TELL** YOU?
♪ You may have left me before... ♪

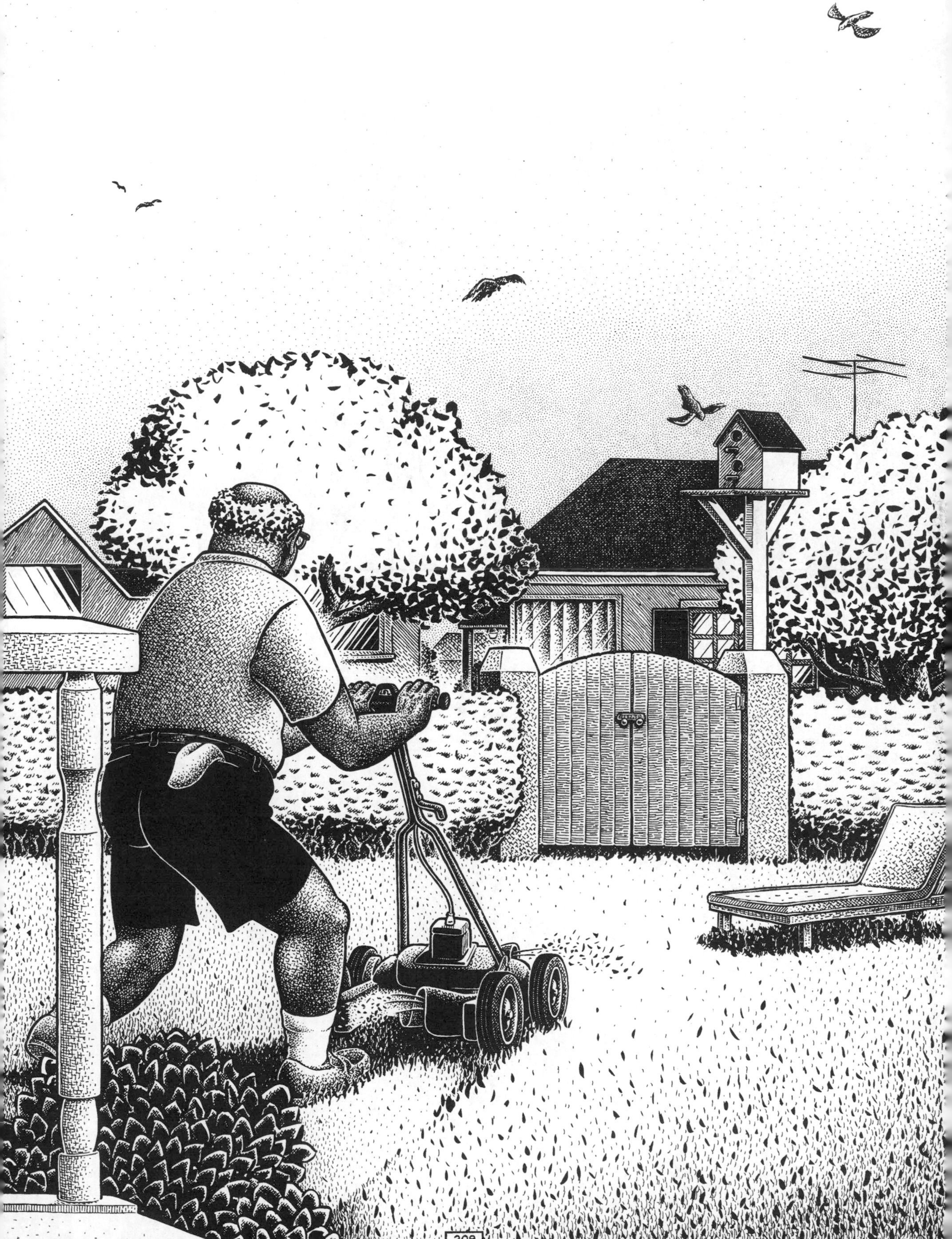

♪ ♪

. . . But you can't leave me behind. ♪

♪

♪

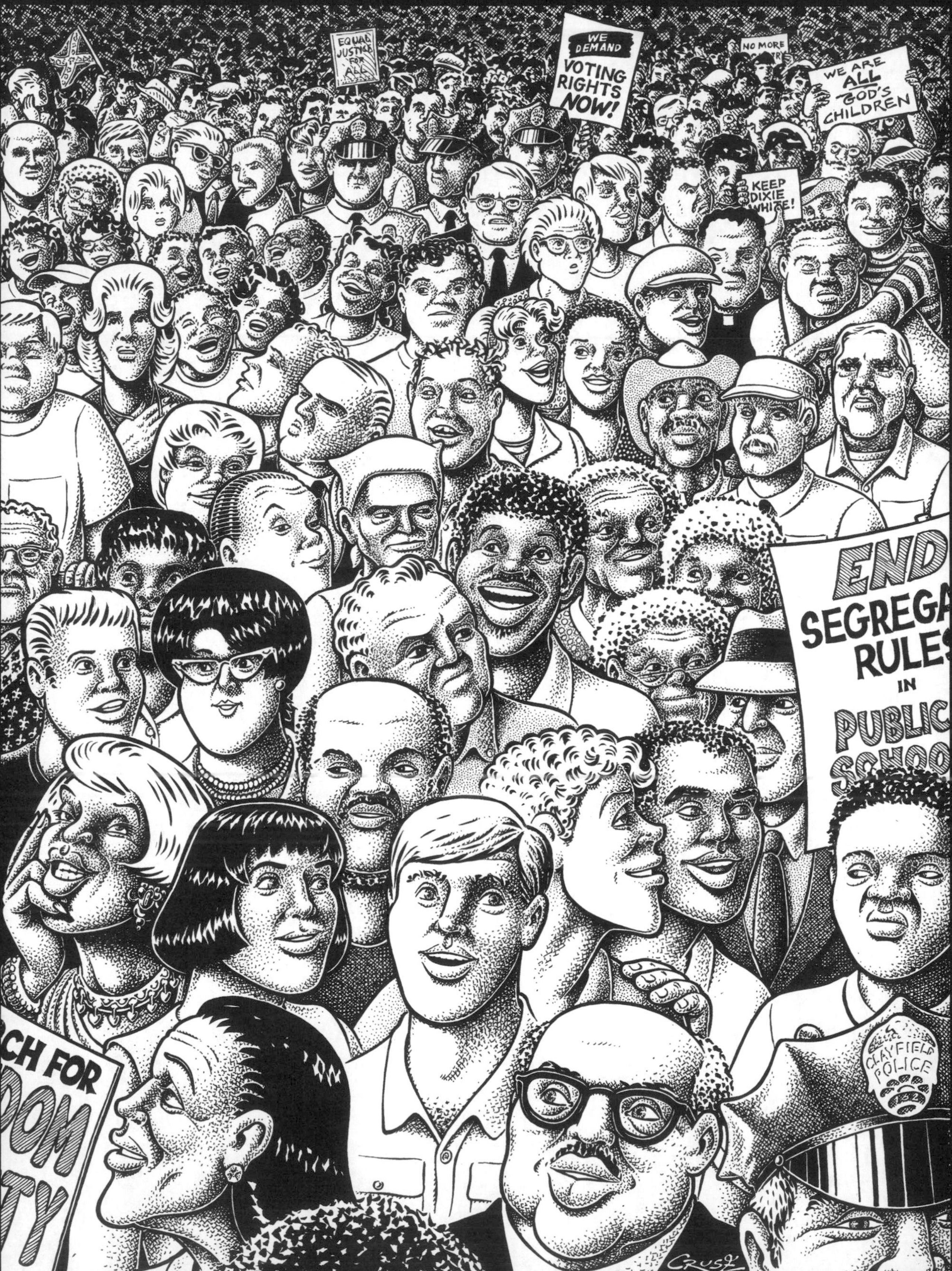
EQUAL JUSTICE FOR ALL
WE DEMAND
VOTING RIGHTS NOW!
NO MORE
WE ARE ALL GOD'S CHILDREN
KEEP DIXIE WHITE!
END
SEGREGA
RULES
IN
PUBLIC
CH FOR
CLAYFIELD POLICE
CRUSE

AFTERWORD

Stuck Rubber Baby is a work of fiction, not autobiography. Its characters are inventions of mine, and Clayfield is a make-believe city.

That said, it's doubtful I'd have been moved to write and draw this graphic novel if I hadn't come of age in Birmingham, Alabama, during the early '60s, and significant episodes from my own youth are undeniably woven, in fictionalized form, throughout the fabric of Toland Polk's story. But my own limited history as a white Southerner is far from the only resource I've drawn on in creating this book. Toland's story is equally shaped by potent memories that were generously shared with me by others who behaved with far more valor than I ever did when the struggle against racial segregation was transforming the streets of Birmingham into a morality play in real time.

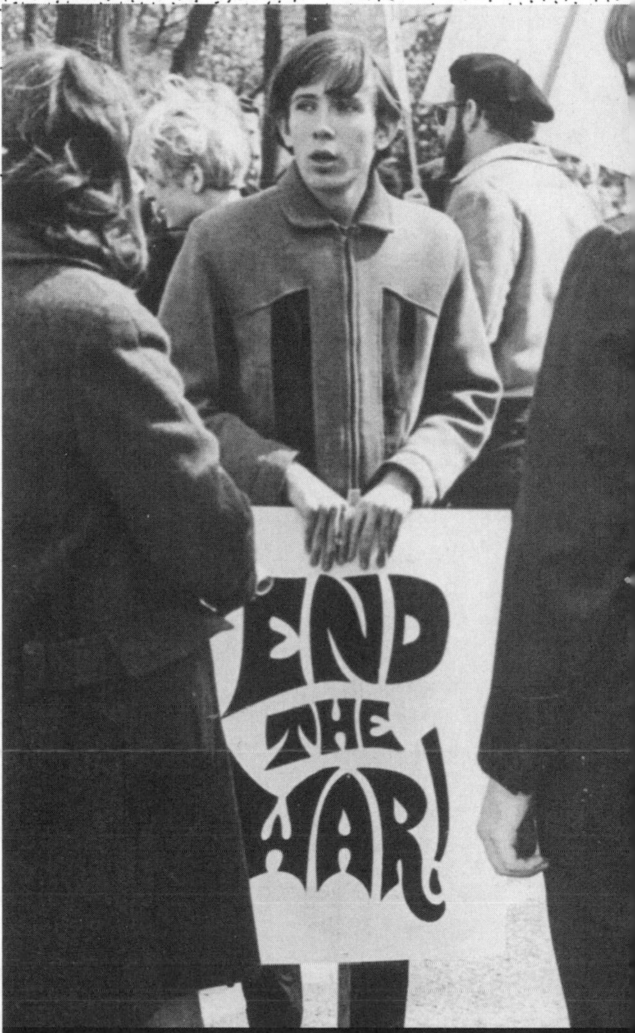
END THE WAR!
Howard Cruse at an anti-war demonstration, 1968

The germinal idea for *Stuck Rubber Baby* sprang from my youthful closetedness. Dishonesty with oneself often has unfortunate consequences, and in my case the fear of my gayness seduced me into believing the ill-informed therapist who told me that if I went to a co-ed college and dated girls, I would discover that in actuality I was as heterosexual as any red-blooded male could ask to be. I took his advice, enrolled at Birmingham-Southern College, and soon fell into a genuinely affectionate relationship with a classmate named Pam. Our romance became complicated, though, when Pam and I discovered that we had inadvertently conceived a child.

Viewed from a distance of decades, that youthful contretemps struck me as a promising premise for a graphic novel. A closeted gay man becomes an accidental father. How could dramatic complications not ensue?

Editor Mark Nevelow at Piranha Press, an experimental offshoot of DC Comics that was later renamed Paradox Press, saw my idea's potential and encouraged me to submit a formal proposal. But the process of fleshing out my premise laid bare the inherent slenderness of a narrative thread that didn't venture beyond the boundaries of Toland and Ginger's personal difficulties. In fact, it could easily become just another of the numerous "coming-out novels" that were then filling bookstore shelves, thanks to the new permission that gay and lesbian novelists were feeling to reflect their own lives honestly and unambiguously in works of fiction.

Many of those novels were excellent and stirring, but if I was going to spend years crafting a 200-page book, I wanted it to cover ground that wasn't already being exhaustively covered—to keep things interesting for me, if for no other reason. This led me to remember the richness of the cultural change that was surrounding Pam and me while we were trying to find our way through our comparatively small dilemma.

My concept of the graphic novel quickly expanded. Its real-life roots were in the early 1960s struggles that I had observed firsthand: the tumultuous and often dangerous engagement between racial segregationists and integrationists. Etched just as strongly in my memory was the widespread homophobia that would have made it hazardous for a secretly gay man like Toland to step into the line of fire by being honest about himself.

I began envisioning Ginger as a fascinating and multifaceted character. She could be more than Toland's girlfriend; she could serve as a crucial mentor to him by opening his eyes to moral issues he had grown up ignoring. This was the role that Pam had played in my life, so I knew those interpersonal dynamics well.

As I set about writing a working draft, the projected book's circle of characters kept growing, each of them an analogue to individuals who had been part of my life in Birmingham. It became a thrill to live in their company, day after day, for what ended up being a four-year creative marathon.

And throughout those years, in the back of my mind was an extra motivating factor. I wanted to tell a story that pushed back against the cynical "greed is good" ethos that had become dominant in 1980s America. Long before I began *Stuck Rubber Baby*, I had watched grassroots activists alter the trajectory of the hidebound South with their fearless idealism. It rankled me when many Americans began viewing the 1960s as a guitar-strumming, bell-bottomed hippie caricature of what it had really been.

I had viewed at close range the heroism of many who dreamed that the longstanding bigotries that had become commonplace in the South could actually be overcome. They inspired me then and my respect for them has never waned since. They deserved more than condescension from a morally brittle American culture that was in danger of becoming all about money. And that danger is still with us today, for that matter.

Howard Cruse
June 2019

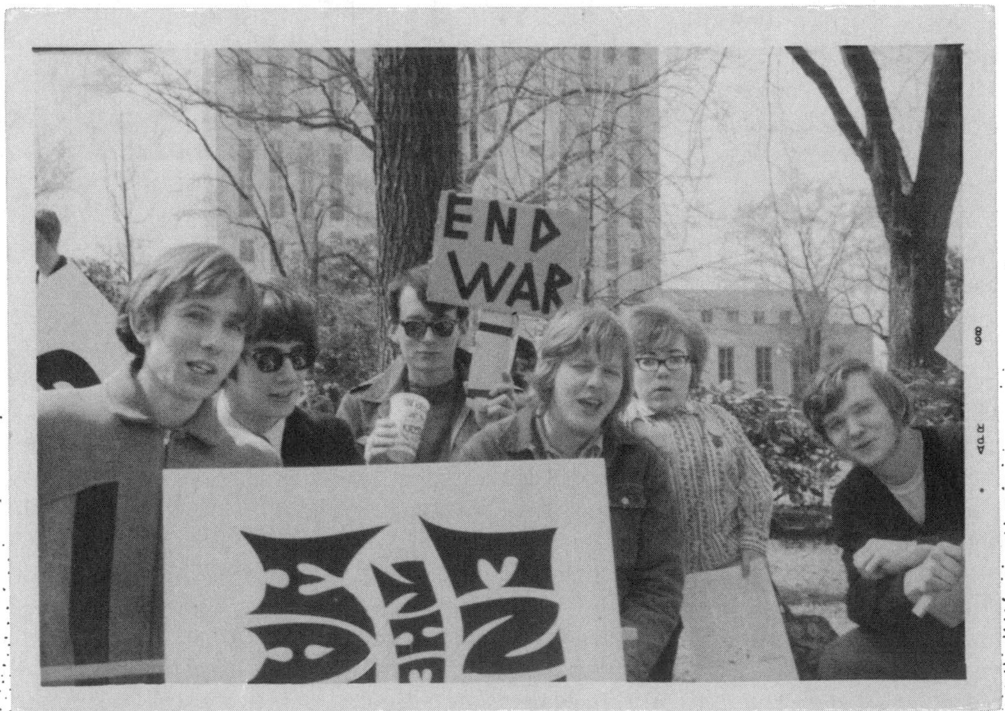
END
WAR

LETTER FROM KIM VENTER

I'm Howard Cruse's daughter—the baby in *Stuck Rubber Baby*.

I feel touched and honored to be a part of this 25th anniversary edition. It's bittersweet, however, as my children and I were looking forward to joining Howard and Eddie for the book's debut at the 2020 Toronto Comics Arts Festival. When I spoke to Howard a couple of weeks before his passing, he shared that he was at peace, whatever the outcome of his fight with cancer might be, but he had hoped to get a bit more time to enjoy the relaunch and to work on some other creative initiatives. A few hours before he passed on from this life, Pam, my birth mother, whom Howard based the character of Ginger on, held the phone up to his ear. I was able to tell him I loved him and would miss him, and that he was the best birth dad ever.

Our family is a unique one, and there are many members of it. First there were Howard and Pam, two beautiful people in their early years of college. They were young actors starring in a play together who were drawn to each other in a deeply connected way at that moment in time. Then, unexpectedly, there was me. After months spent considering what was best for everyone involved under many different circumstances, it was decided I would be given up for adoption. I was raised by two wonderful people, who, I might add, have been married sixty-seven years and are still alive today. Then, at age twenty-two, I was able to uncover Pam's and Howard's names—and proceeded to contact them both.

I can't recall all the details of my first conversation with Howard, but I'll never forget the loving acceptance he exemplified right from the beginning, as that part is etched in my heart. Howard and Eddie have been in my life for longer than Howard was out of my life: thirty-three years. Their grandchildren, Emily and Ethan, have known them their entire lives. I remember Emily used to say to her friends, "I have four grandfathers. How can that be?" Her young friends would scratch their heads. And she would say, "I have Oupa and Oupa and Howard and Eddie."

What I have realized over the years is that if you are openhearted, you can make anything work. Love wins. Howard always gave me the space to live my life, and out of respect for my adoptive parents, didn't share information openly about me. He never wanted to take the chance that it might negatively affect my adoptive parents and our lives here in Atlanta. And I always respected the life he had with Eddie in Williamstown, Massachusetts. I enjoyed our visits over the years and was appreciative of Eddie sharing him with me.

At the same time, Howard and I had planned that one day, when the time was right, I would be more of a part of his art, his engagements, and his pursuits. And that time would have been now—I so wanted to stand by his side as he enjoyed this rerelease of *Stuck Rubber Baby*.

Even though Howard is not here on Earth in his physical body, I have no question that he is with us all in spirit. For me this may even mean he can get to know me better in my day-to-day life, since the distance between Atlanta and Williamstown doesn't matter when you are no longer bound by this world. So I'm not going to let his transition alter our plans. And, for this rerelease, I am happy to be a part of his pursuit and happy to share in this exciting new chapter of his life. I love you, Howard.

Kim Venter
December 2019

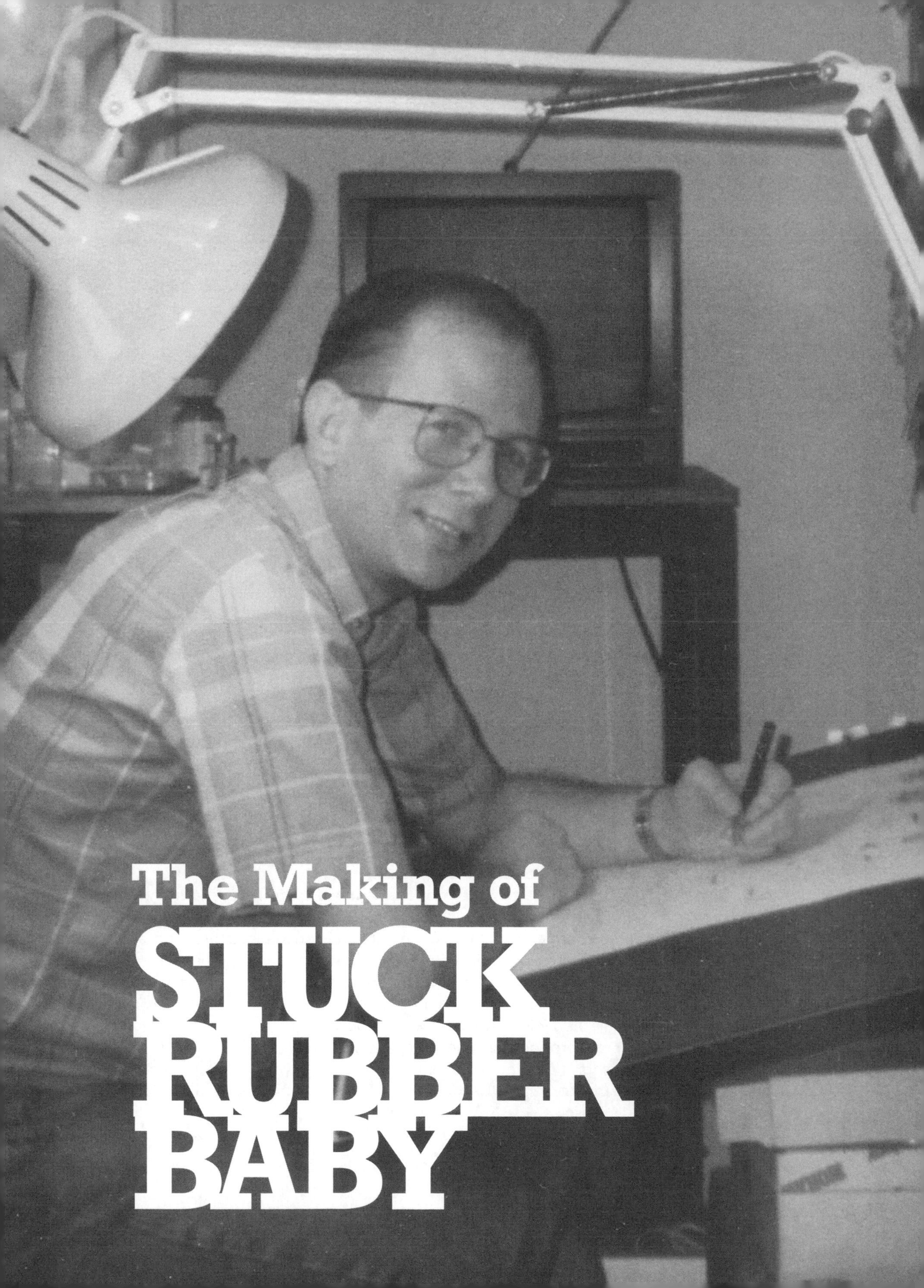

The Making of STUCK RUBBER BABY

The Proposal

"If you were to create a graphic novel," Mark Nevelow asked me in 1990, "what would it be like?"

His question caught me by surprise. Mark was the editor at Piranha Press, an innovative new imprint of DC Comics, whom I had never met before. I found myself in his office having what I had expected to be nothing more than a get-acquainted meeting. I certainly hadn't arrived with a pitch in hand. But then he sprang that question on me, and all I could do was dredge up a half-formed idea that had been clinging to the back of my brain for a few years but that I could never imagine having enough money to undertake. Graphic novelizing is an all-consuming activity that doesn't leave much time in the day for earning a living.

But DC was a major corporation with deep pockets, so maybe creating a graphic novel on their dime wasn't as far outside the realm of possibility as I had assumed. So I shared my idea—a story based on my accidental impregnation of my college girlfriend in 1963, back when I thought I could will myself into being straight.

Mark was intrigued enough to urge me to go home and work up a formal proposal that he could pass around to the publisher and his fellow editors. I reminded him that any plotline I came up with would have to incorporate several central characters, including the protagonist, who were gay. Otherwise I would be viewed as a sellout to the movement for LGBTQ visibility that had been a central political concern of mine for a couple of decades by then.

Mark was fine with that, but he also wanted to be sure there were strong heterosexual characters in the book as well so that straight readers would be able to have a comfortable entry point into Toland Polk's world.

I also reminded Mark that, thanks to my history in underground comix and drawing my *Wendel* series for the *Advocate*, I had developed my own peculiar process for drawing comics. I won't take up space describing those peculiarities here, but the upshot of this was that I have always done my best work when I can create in solitude with minimal editorial oversight and maximum artistic freedom. In other words, my editors would only see a chapter's pages *after* they were completed; I wouldn't be running any pencils by the office for approval. "Take a look at the books I've already published and decide if you can trust me to provide professional-level work," I suggested. "Because if you're not confident about that, we'll do better to scrap the idea of me drawing a graphic novel for Piranha. I just can't work the normal DC way." Mark was reassuringly open to that unusual provision, and I left his office with the expectation that I would return soon with a proposal in hand.

When I had completed a first draft of the proposal I showed it to Mike Friedrich, a comics writer and the publisher turned agent who had offered to help me navigate DC's long and formidable contract. He made some valuable suggestions. Most notable was his observation that I was exhibiting a common blind spot among male comics creators. Practically all of my main characters were men, with Ginger and Anna Dellyne being the only exceptions. Before I handed over my proposal to Mark, Mavis and Toland's sister, Melanie, had joined the cast with important roles to play.

Mark felt good about my proposal and set about drumming up support for it at DC. It took many months for a contract to be inked and signed, but that time finally arrived and I was at last free to begin writing the working script that Mark wanted to look at before I started drawing.

The Characters

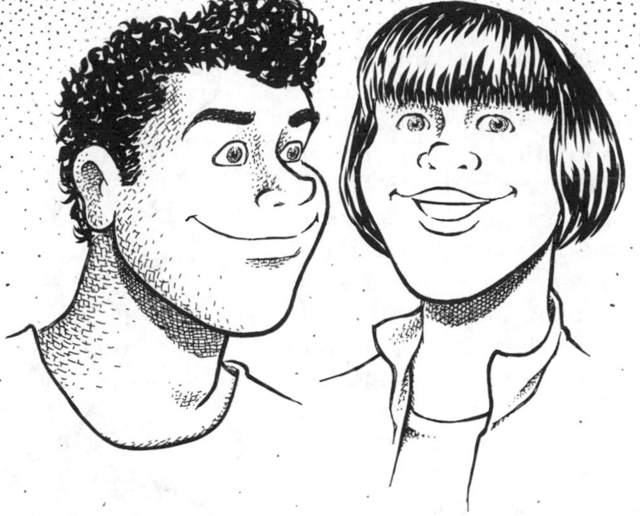

When the time came to submit my proposal for *Stuck Rubber Baby* to DC Comics, I didn't yet have a clue what my characters were going to look like. Still, I knew that including some provisional renditions of the main characters in the proposal couldn't be avoided. So I punted with the images of Toland and Ginger that you see above, which obviously owe a debt to the simpler style I had previously used in my *Wendel* comic

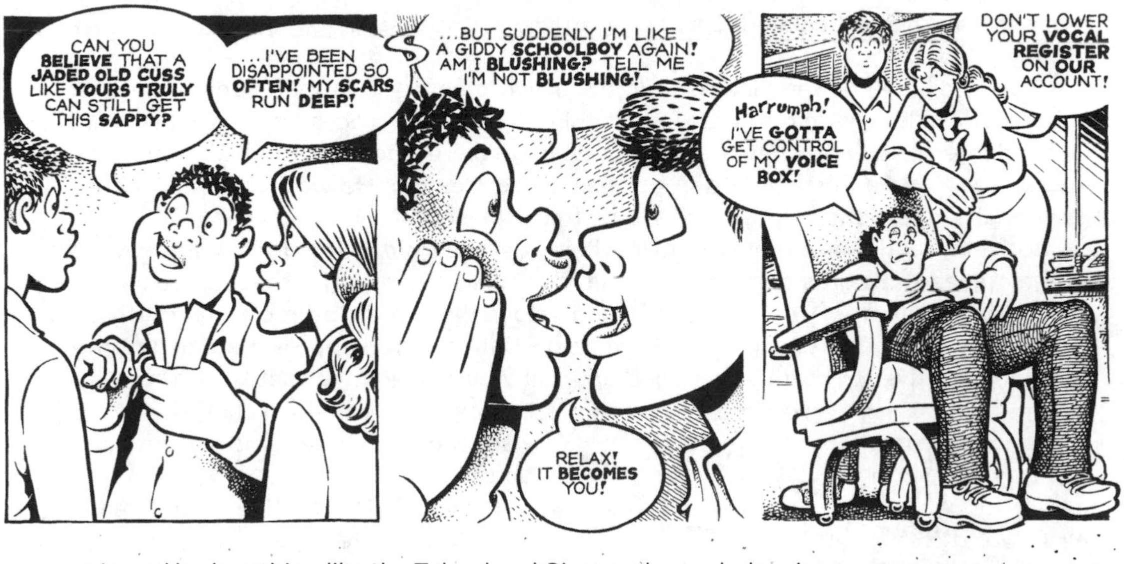

CAN YOU BELIEVE THAT A JADED OLD CUSS LIKE YOURS TRULY CAN STILL GET THIS SAPPY?
...I'VE BEEN DISAPPOINTED SO OFTEN! MY SCARS RUN DEEP!
...BUT SUDDENLY I'M LIKE A GIDDY SCHOOLBOY AGAIN! AM I BLUSHING? TELL ME I'M NOT BLUSHING!
RELAX! IT BECOMES YOU!
DON'T LOWER YOUR VOCAL REGISTER ON OUR ACCOUNT!
Harrumph! I'VE GOTTA GET CONTROL OF MY VOICE BOX!

strip and look nothing like the Toland and Ginger who ended up in the finished book. I also experimented with a more extensive use of crosshatched shading than I had ever undertaken before. You won't see the crosshatched character on the right anywhere in the finished book. He was just a random face that I invented to test my ability to use the technique effectively before I committed myself to drawing the graphic novel for real.

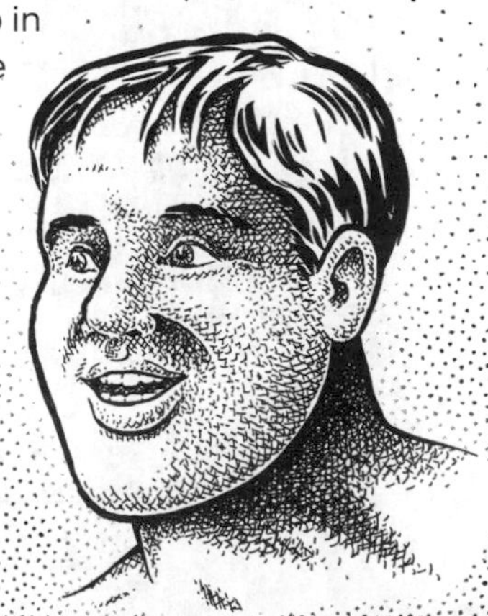

The Writing Process

NO, TOLAND, I HAVE NO IDEA WHAT YOU'RE TALKING ABOUT.
IT'S WEIRD. MAMA LOOKS DEAD THE WAY A STORE MANEQUIN LOOKS DEAD -- LIKE SHE NEVER SPENT ANY TIME ALIVE.
YOU AN' I KNOW THAT'S NOT THE CASE, OF COURSE...

How was I going to put together a plotline for a book that would be more than ten times as long as any story I had drawn before? I tried several strategies, like drawing a couple of pages in a quick, sketchy style and using typewritten text to fill the word balloons and narration blocks. That seemed simple in theory, but it wasn't simple enough. It became increasingly clear that scripting out my story with no pictures at all, as if it were a theatrical script, would be the only practical way to go. And even coming up with that working script meant going through several stages of writing. First came roughing out potential text in pencil scrawls—meant for my eyes only. Next came refining and revising those pencil scribblings with a typewriter while figuring out how the events I was imagining could be broken up into panels and pages. Lots of scenes got scrapped along the way, but better ones got inserted. And eventually I was able to assemble the sturdier parts of my first two drafts into a working script ready to be submitted to DC for approval.

It took me five months and several drafts to come up with my working script—much longer than I had anticipated. But I finally arrived at a script that felt ready to hand over to my editor.

To my relief Mark was enthusiastic about what he saw. He made some editorial suggestions that made good sense and pointed out some places where scenes could unfold more briskly or where transitions could go more smoothly. But he honored the agreement we had established in our first office meeting: He was welcome to offer editorial suggestions, but I would also be free to reject them.

Both Mark and I knew that I would inevitably deviate from the script in many ways as better ideas and words occurred to me in the course of drawing the book. I've always revised my comics as I went along. Mark understood that I would be implementing those changes without first asking for his permission. But having an approximate beginning-to-end narrative structure established up front would guarantee that I wouldn't start improvising in inadvisable ways and wander off onto dead-end narrative cul-de-sacs.

IT WAS THE NEXT-DOO
WHO HAD BABY-SAT WITH ME
MY SISTER SINCE WE WERE
SHE HAD A HEART ATTACK.
SEVEN.
(PAGE TWO)
(1)
The first human corpse I saw was Miss Violet, the old lady next door who'd always babysat with me. She had a heart attack in her bathtub when I was seven.
She was all dressed up and powdered by the time they had her in a casket, of course, which presumably she hadn't been at the time of her demise.
(2)
We had some cats and dogs that died,
PANEL #4
(TOLAND STARES AT A BODY AT AN OPEN-CASKET FUNERAL.)
As a rule, the busy hands of our best local morticians had already spruced up the remains by the time I got a look at whoever was "lying in state." So there was never anything to gory about the display.
PANEL #5
(MISS VIOLET PERISHES IN HER GARDEN.)
The first human corpse I saw was Miss Violet, the old lady ne door who babysat with me. She had a heart attack in the gard but was dressed up and powdered by the time I saw her in a casket.
PANEL #6
(YOUNG TOLAND STARES IN SHOCK AT A PET FATALITY.)
We had a cat that got run over.

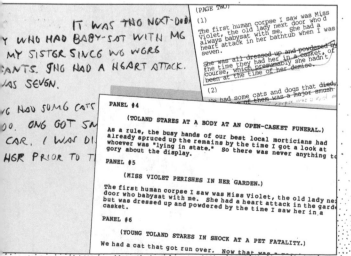

Mark left DC in 1991 and Piranha Press folded a few years later, to be replaced by the imprint Paradox Press, which would ultimately be the publisher of *Stuck Rubber Baby*. Other editors took the helm after Mark's departure, but I'm happy to say that all of them respected the commitment that he had made. I was allowed to exercise *almost* the level of creative freedom that had made underground comix such a comfortable art form for me.

Then came the drawing part.

Underground Comix vs. Graphic Novels

I was savvy enough by then to know the difference between creating an underground comic and a graphic novel to be sold in mainstream bookstores. My story would include sexy moments, but I would need to approach those moments differently than I would if I were drawing an underground comic book. Undergrounds were famous for their total lack of censorship. No manifestation of sexuality was too explicit to shove in the target audiences' faces; indeed, many readers of the UGs were disappointed if their comic didn't gross them out at least a little. It was the "Adults Only" labels on their covers that (largely) protected them from prosecution for obscenity.

There would be no such labels on the copies of *Stuck Rubber Baby* that would be sold at, say, Barnes & Noble bookstores. So I knew that I would need to show more restraint than was my habit. I adopted the maxim that *Playboy* magazine had provided me when I was drawing cartoons for them. To be acceptable for street-vendor display, the rule for cartoonists was "No erections; no penetration." You will find no drawings of either in *Stuck Rubber Baby*.

The Art Revisions

Even after I had begun drawing finished art for the book, I would notice errors that I knew I would need to revisit and correct later. For example, the first page of the book is dominated by a large portrait of the "present-day" Toland Polk. But in the course of drawing my character over and over again for years on end, my perception of his appearance changed. So if you happen to cross paths with the original art for page one someday, you'll notice that a revised rendition of Toland's face has been patched in, one that's friendlier to look at and bears less resemblance to a Cro-Magnon human from prehistory.

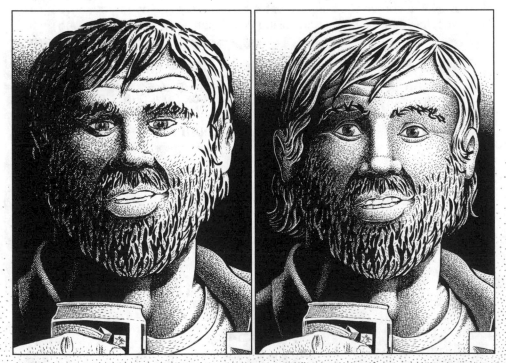

Reference Material

During a trip to visit my mother in Alabama one Christmas, I set aside time to stroll around Birmingham's old neighborhoods, snapping pictures of any interesting houses I saw that would have been around in Toland Polk's day for potential use as photo reference.

I'M NOT SURE THERE'S ANY-WHERE I **DO** BELONG...
...BUT IF THERE **IS**—THIS AIN'T **IT!**
YOU'RE SURE MAKIN' ME FEEL FUNNY ABOUT **MYSELF** TODAY.

Drawing houses derived from those that I photographed often added valuable background texture to a scene. An embarrassing thing I've learned about myself is that, left to my own devices, I'm unlikely to coax dwellings from my imagination that resemble anything human beings occupy in the real world. Put more bluntly, any house I draw without access to photo reference will probably look like it was drawn by a first-grader.

My husband, Eddie, played guitar when he was young, and even though he had left that hobby behind by the time we moved in together, his abandoned instrument remained tucked away in a corner of our apartment, ready to be seized on for reference by a cartoonist who was bent on presenting Toland Polk's girlfriend, Ginger, as a skilled guitarist.

AND I FOUND MYSELF **MARVELING** OVER HOW SOMEONE WHO'D JUST **PINNED** ME LIKE A **WORM** ON A **FISHHOOK** COULD BE UP THERE SO SOON **AFTERWARDS**, EFFORT-LESSLY SOOTHING A **ROOMFUL** OF **WOUNDS**.
...INCLUDING **MINE!**
There will be one Vacant Chair...

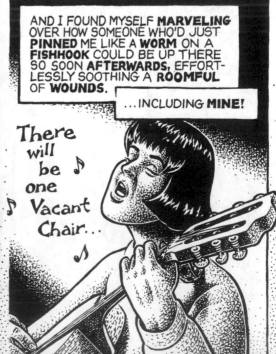

Common manual activities can seem totally uncomplicated—until the time comes to draw them. That's when you wish you had paid closer attention the last time you saw someone pour sugar into a cup of coffee. How exactly were they clasping the sugar container while they poured? How many fingers of their opposing hand did they insert into the coffee mug's handle? There was always a quick and easy way to answer such questions while I was drawing *Stuck Rubber Baby*, since Eddie and I both worked at home during my book's creation. "Eddie, can you come and do some hand modeling?" was my frequent call for help. There's scarcely a character of any importance in *Stuck Rubber Baby* whose hands weren't played at some time or other by the hands of Ed Sedarbaum.

EDDIE AS MELANIE
P. 145

WHATEVER WAS COOKING INSIDE OF HER, HER FIRST REACTION WASN'T TO EMBED A SYRUP PITCHER IN MY CRANIUM, WHICH HAD BEEN MY WORST-CASE SCENARIO GOING IN.
IN FACT, FOR A MINUTE OR SO SHE ACTED SO CALM, I BEGAN TO WONDER IF SHE'D COME DOWN WITH SOME HEARING PROBLEM I WASN'T AWARE OF.

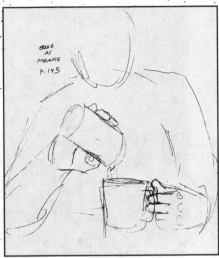

I don't know how I could have drawn *Stuck Rubber Baby* without the New York Public Library's massive Picture Collection, whose folders were stuffed with images of just about anything that had been clipped from magazines over many decades. As a general source of photo reference for artists (as well as Broadway and film designers and costumers), it has been matchless for years. Unfortunately, the collection was uncharacteristically limited when it came to showing me how to dress my characters in clothes appropriate for the early sixties. The reason? The clothing folders consisted primarily of garb for fashion models and otherwise extraordinary people, and I needed to put clothes on characters who were comparatively ordinary.

Sears
ALIVE LOOK
for
PETITE JUNIORS
Proportioned for you who are
5 ft. 1 in. or less
1
2
1 Fashionable High Waist ringed by bands of color. Dress with

WELL, LOOK WHO'S BACK IN THE LAND OF THE LIVING!
Yawn! WHAT DAY IS IT?
IT'S STILL SUNDAY. I'VE ALREADY PUT SOME HOT COFFEE ON THE TABLE FOR YOU.

What saved the day for me was the shelves of old Sears catalogs that resided in the archives at the Fashion Institute of Technology in Manhattan. Not only was the 1962 Sears catalog filled with ads for clothing worn by everyday folks of that era, but elsewhere in its pages were useful ads depicting the period lawn mowers, television

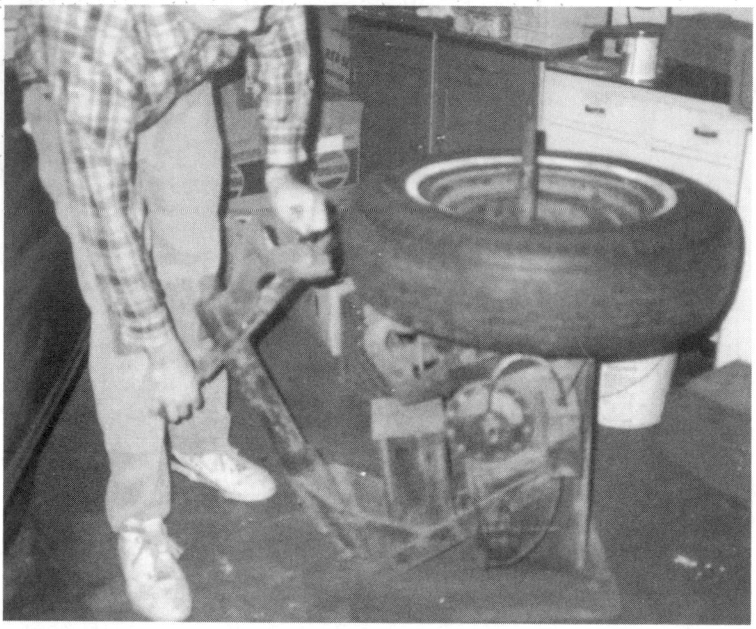

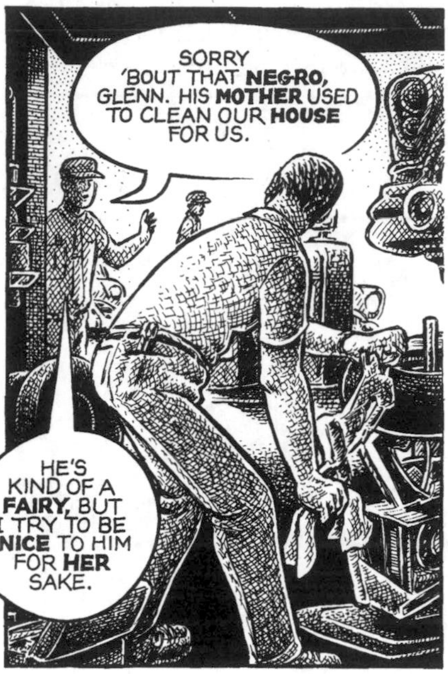
SORRY 'BOUT THAT **NEGRO,** GLENN. HIS **MOTHER** USED TO CLEAN OUR **HOUSE** FOR US.
HE'S KIND OF A **FAIRY,** BUT I TRY TO BE **NICE** TO HIM FOR **HER** SAKE.

sets, rollaway beds, coffee makers, and other mundane items that would most likely have a presence in my characters' homes or toolsheds.

During the time I was gathering photo reference for *Stuck Rubber Baby,* Leonard Shiller ran the Antique Automobile Association of Brooklyn, and in that capacity he oversaw dozens of period cars from the fifties and sixties, which were stashed away inconspicuously in an array of private garages throughout the borough. His normal business was leasing out period automobiles to filmmakers who needed them as props, but he generously devoted a Saturday afternoon to escorting me to several of those garages. As I described my characters to him, he led me to the cars that they would most likely have driven and allowed me to take snapshots of both the outsides and the interiors. Along the way he showed me other related artifacts, such as period gas pumps, period fire engines, and a period device for balancing wheels, taking time to demonstrate how the latter was operated. I snapped a photo, and Len's wheel-balancing expertise subsequently made a cameo appearance on page 101 of my book.

I asked my comics colleague Harvey Pekar, an aficionado of classic jazz recordings, which record label would most likely have signed Anna Dellyne during her youthful flirtation with jazz stardom. He suggested Savoy, and told me about a classic vinyl records shop in Manhattan called Records Revisited, where I might find one of the company's old labels to use as reference. The proprietor of the shop, Morton Savada, not only showed me several rare items from Savoy that he had in stock, but graciously allowed me to photocopy one of the labels and even take home an empty Savoy sleeve that I could copy at my leisure.

"IF IT'S A HIT....IT'S A SAVOY"
Savoy
SAVOY
MANUFACTURED BY
SAVOY RECORD CO.
NEWARK 1, N.J.
SERIES 500 and 1000 — 75c

YOU'VE STILL GOT THE **RECORD** I GAVE YOU.
"IF IT'S A HIT.... IT'S A SAVOY"
Savoy
SAVOY
OF **COURSE,** DUMBBELL!

The complex geometry of apartment-building stairwells can be hard to visualize unless you're an architect. However, once my working draft for *Stuck Rubber Baby* was approved, I knew the time would come to tackle chapter 24, when drawing such a stairwell from several vantage points would be vital to my story. The chapter closes with a "magic realism" moment in which the present-day Toland steps onto the balcony of his apartment in an unspecified city during a snowstorm and finds himself unexpectedly on the sunbathed backyard stoop of Harland and Anna Dellyne Pepper's 1960s home down South. This emotional plunge into the past will only catch readers by surprise if I've made it clear that the apartment is located in a multistory walk-up. Hence the conversation between Toland and his lover, which otherwise could easily have taken place anywhere, needed to take place while the two step in from the snow and trudge up a long set of stairs. The stairs being ascended by my pal Howie Katz in the photo here were just the reference I needed.

Brush, brush!

NO **LETTERS.** JUST **BILLS** AND **FUND-RAISERS.**
ENOUGH ALREADY WITH THE DAMNED **SNOW** AND **ICE!**
Brush, brush!

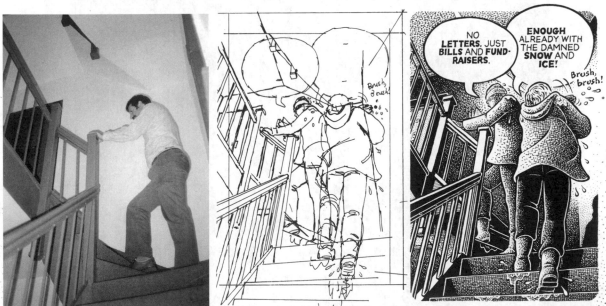

The Funeral Scene

I wanted to avoid slipping into autopilot mode while drawing this overhead view of funeral attendees, aware that the throng could easily turn into a field of undifferentiated ovals if I didn't pay attention. My strategy was to slow down and feel the grief of each individual as I drew them, as small as they were. This took intense concentration, more than I could manage if I tried to spend more than a half hour in one sitting. So to keep the process fresh I adopted a special routine. For the week or so it took to complete this panel, I spent the first thirty minutes of each working day drawing head after head after head, trying to give each an individual touch. After that I would give myself permission to draw less demanding portions of page 115.

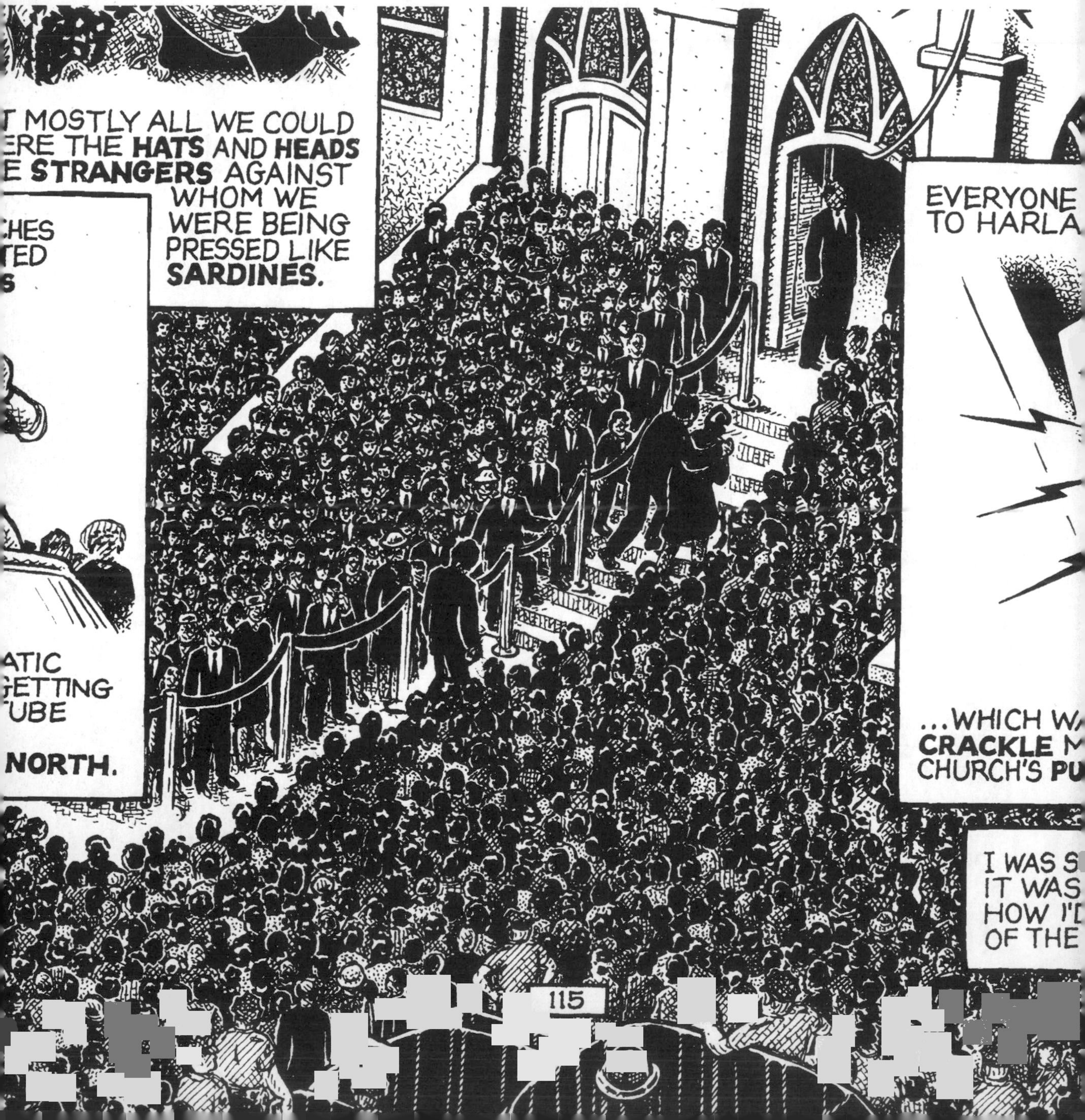

T MOSTLY ALL WE COULD
ERE THE **HATS** AND **HEADS**
E **STRANGERS** AGAINST
WHOM WE
WERE BEING
PRESSED LIKE
SARDINES.
HES
TED
ATIC
ETTING
UBE
NORTH.
EVERYONE
TO HARLA
...WHICH W
CRACKLE M
CHURCH'S **PU**
I WAS S
IT WAS
HOW I'
OF THE
115

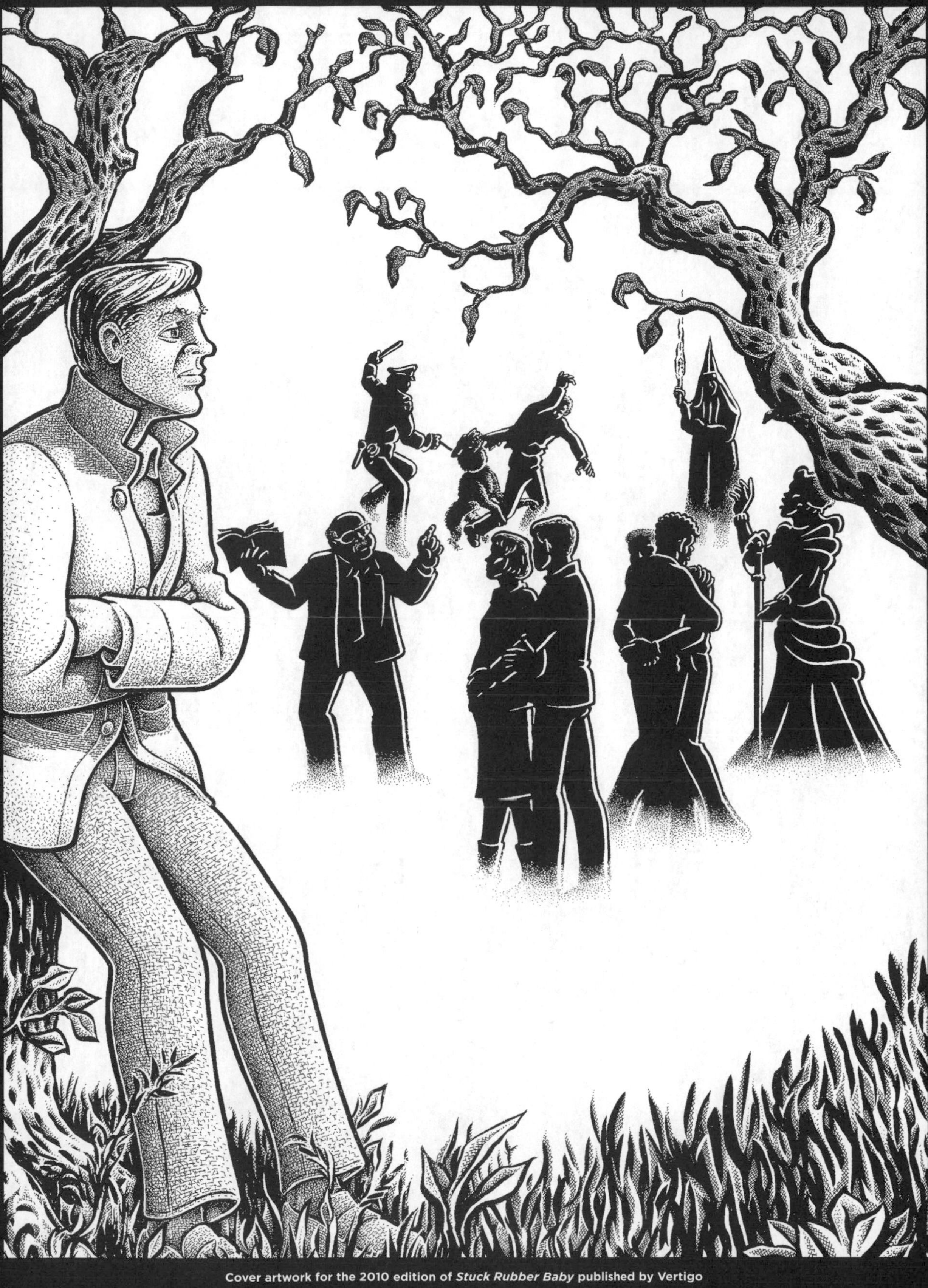

Cover artwork for the 2010 edition of *Stuck Rubber Baby* published by Vertigo

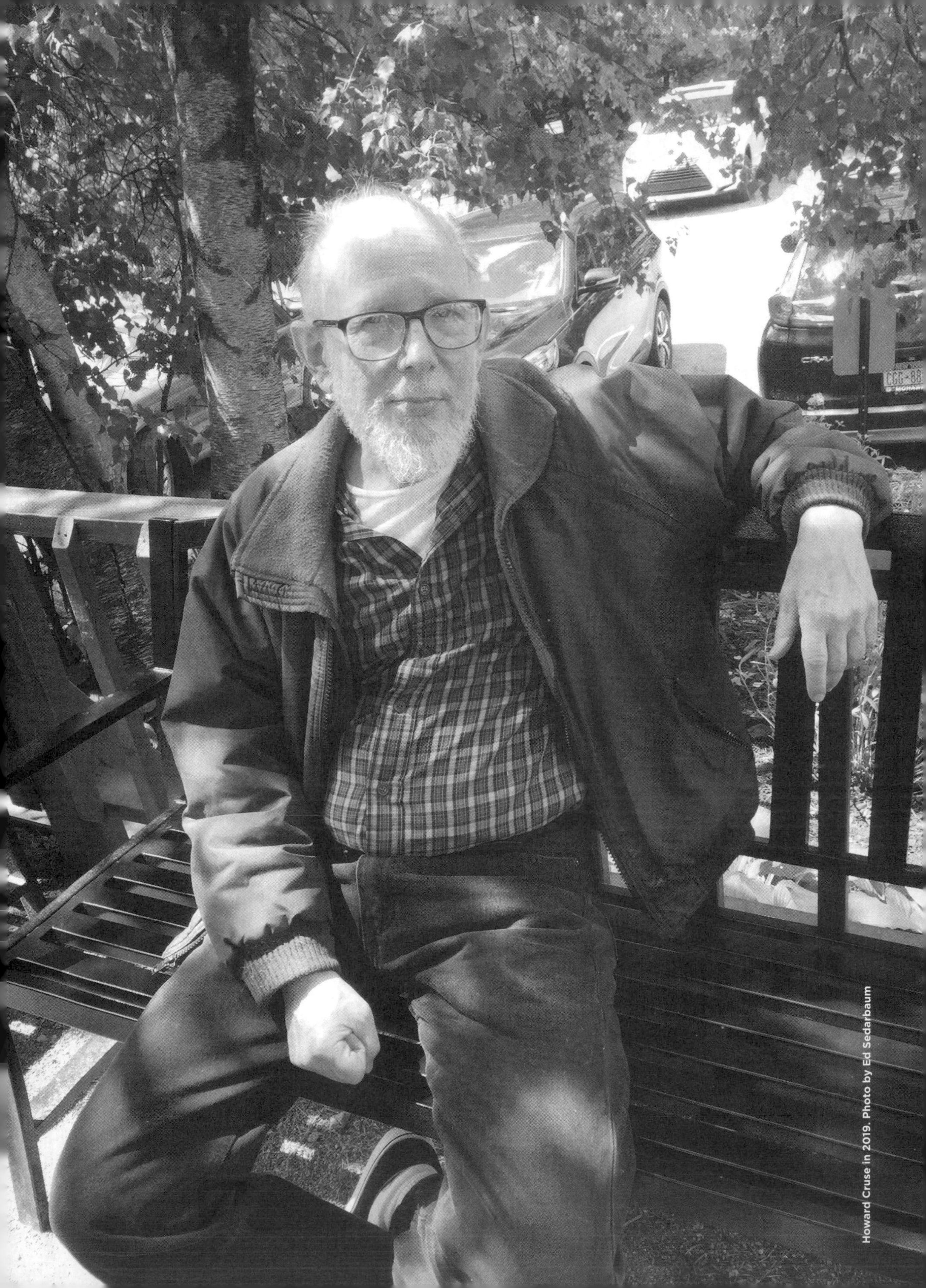

Howard Cruse in 2019. Photo by Ed Sedarbaum

HOWARD CRUSE was an Alabama native

whose concerns about racism and systemic inequality were shaped by witnessing at close quarters the civil rights conflicts that unfolded in downtown Birmingham in the early '60s, only blocks away from the campus of Birmingham-Southern College, where he was a drama major specializing in playwriting. The plays he wrote and directed during his student years led to his acceptance in 1968 as a Shubert Playwriting Fellow at Penn State University.

Feeling temperamentally unsuited for graduate school life, though, Cruse moved to New York City after only a single term, where his focus shifted from theater to cartooning, a childhood ambition that had been honed by the Famous Artists Cartoon Course, the three-year correspondence course that he completed while in high school.

Scattered examples of his cartoons saw publication in regional and national magazines while he was still in high school and college, but Cruse's more serious cartooning career dates from 1970, when he launched the two-year run of his daily cartoon panel *Tops & Button* in the pages of the *Birmingham Post-Herald*. Simultaneously with that venture he created a weekly comic strip called *Barefootz* for the *Crimson White*, the student newspaper at the University of Alabama in Tuscaloosa.

After its *Crimson White* run, Cruse shepherded his *Barefootz* feature into Birmingham-based underground and alternative newspapers before finding a national audience for his characters in 1972 in underground comic books published by Kitchen Sink Press.

Although cartooning would remain a constant in his creative life during the subsequent decades, Cruse also spent time as a professional actor at the Atlanta Children's Theatre, an art director and children's show puppeteer at a Birmingham

Howard Cruse at his college graduation in 1968, coming down from the LSD trip he experienced the night before. Photo by Irma Cruse

television station, and a paste-up artist for a Birmingham advertising agency. After moving to New York City in 1977, he served as the art director of *Starlog* and *Future Life* magazines until he felt ready to become a full-time freelancer. Even so, he frequently wrote and illustrated for *Starlog* and its sister magazines, penning a regular column about cartooning called *Loose Cruse* for early issues of *Comics Scene* magazine and creating the comic strip *Count Fangor* for *Fangoria*. On another front during the 1980s he illustrated the comic strip *Doctor Duck* for *Bananas* magazine, bringing to life scripts written by that periodical's then-editor, now celebrated as R. L. Stine, author of the Goosebumps series of horror novels for kids. Cruse maintained a presence in Kitchen Sink's line of underground comic books, culminating in his founding editorship beginning in 1980 of the groundbreaking *Gay Comix* series, created as a platform for LGBTQ comics creators to portray their lives more honestly in their chosen medium than had been possible before. His bread-and-butter income during this period came from providing humorous illustrations and comic strips for *Playboy*, *The Village Voice*, *Heavy Metal*, *American Health*, and other mainstream American magazines.

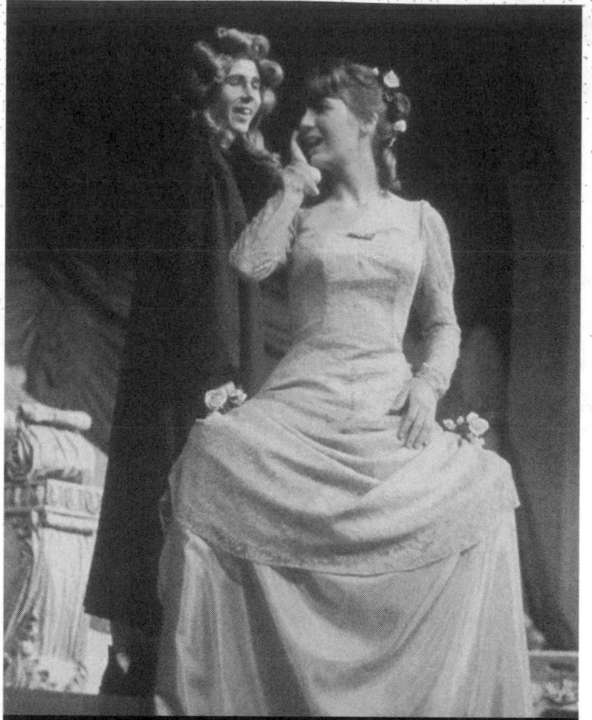

Howard Cruse playing Thomas Diaforus in Birmingham-Southern College's production of Moliere's *The Imaginary Invalid*. Alongside him playing Angelique is Pamela Montanaro, the inspiration for the character Ginger Raines in *Stuck Rubber Baby*.

In 1983 Cruse launched *Wendel*, his comic strip about a circle of LGBTQ friends that was serialized in the *Advocate* through much of the 1980s. *Wendel*'s final episode appeared in 1989, with the feature's strips ultimately being compiled in four books, the most recent being *The Complete Wendel*, published in 2011 by Universe Books, an imprint of Rizzoli International. A Spanish translation of the full *Wendel* series was published in companion editions by Ediciones La Cupula in Barcelona in 2004 and 2005.

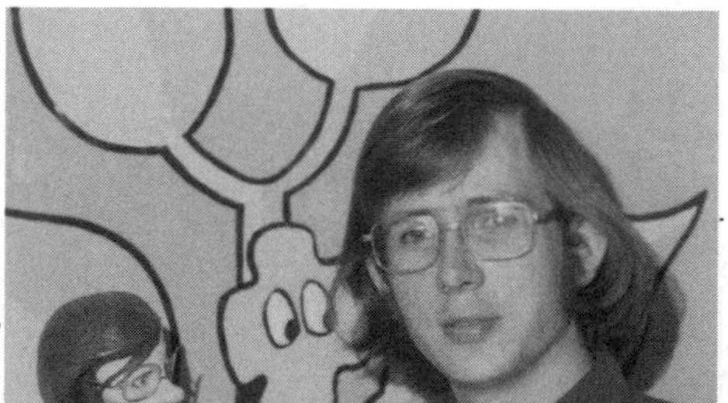

Howard Cruse in 1972 on the set of a UHF television station in Birmingham where he worked as the art director. Photo by Bob Carney

Stuck Rubber Baby, Cruse's most widely known work, was first published in 1995 by DC Comics under its Paradox Press imprint and later translated into Spanish, French, German, Italian, and Polish. Immediate critical response to the book was enthusiastic, and the graphic novel promptly won both Eisner and Harvey Awards in the U.S. and a UK

Comic Art Award for best original graphic novel. Translations of *Stuck Rubber Baby* have earned a Comics Critics Award in Spain, a Luchs Award in Germany, and a Prix de la critique at the International Comics Festival in Angoulême, France. Because the book's themes touch on a wide range of ongoing issues, it has been adopted for classroom use at various colleges and universities in disciplines such as gender studies, ethnicity and race studies, fine art, and cartooning.

BAREFOOTZ
by HOWARD CRUSE
SOMETIMES I WONDER IF I'M SCHIZOPHRENIC!
I MEAN, SOMETIMES I SEEM TO BE ONE PERSON
AND SOMETIMES I FEEL LIKE ANOTHER PERSON ENTIRELY!
WHAT DO YOU THINK ABOUT THAT?
I THINK YOU TWO WORRY TOO MUCH!
CRUSE

A 1971 episode of Howard Cruse's comic strip *Barefootz*, originally published in the University of Alabama student newspaper, *Crimson White*

Book-length compilations of Cruse's comics include *From Headrack to Claude*, *Early Barefootz*, and *The Other Sides of Howard Cruse*. Stand-alone books include Cruse's illustrated adaptation of a fable by Jeanne E. Shaffer, *The Swimmer with a Rope in His Teeth*, and a mock kid's book titled *Felix's Friends: A Story for Grown-ups and Unpleasant Children*. He also taught cartooning to undergraduates at the School of Visual Arts in New York and, after moving with his husband, Ed Sedarbaum, to the Berkshires in 2003, at the Massachusetts College of Liberal Arts.

Cruse's theatrical roots occasionally reasserted themselves nonprofessionally, as when his one-act play "Three Clowns on a Journey," which originated as a student production at Penn State, was subsequently performed at the Academy Theatre in Atlanta, broadcast in a television adaptation at WBIQ-TV in Birmingham, and staged in New York as part of the 2002 Chip Deffaa Invitational Theatre Festival.

In November of 2019, Howard Cruse died after a brief battle with lymphoma. For more about his life and work, visit howardcruse.com.

ADULTS ONLY
GAY
COMIX
NO. 1
KITCHEN SINK COMIX
$1.50
GASP!
..OHMYGHOD!
...CHOKE...
Lesbians and Gay Men
Put It On Paper!
Rand Holmes © 1980

The first issue of *Gay Comix*, published in 1980 by Kitchen Sink Press. Cover art by Rand Holmes

ACKNOWLEDGMENTS

I'm grateful to the following individuals for setting aside time to tell me tales: Bob Bailey, Irene Beavers, Clyde and Linda Buzzard, Nina Cain, Dr. Dodson Curry, William A. Dry, John Fuller, Harry Garwood, Mary Larsen, Bill Miller, Linda Miller, Bertram N. Perry, Cora Pitt, Perry Schwartz, Jim and Eileen Walbert, Jack Williamson, and Thomas E. Wrenn.

Let me emphasize that none of the individuals cited above had any hand in the actual development of my storyline nor any opportunity to evaluate the liberties I've taken in bringing my own point of view to the fictional incidents loosely inspired by their accounts. Any errors of history or perceived wrong-headedness of interpretation should be laid at my door, not theirs.

Others have aided me, too, in varying ways. Much help was provided at the outset by Marvin Whiting, who was the Birmingham Public Library's distinguished archivist when my book was taking form. I have turned for enlightenment on technical points of law to David Fleischer and to David Hansell. Ed Still provided background on the history of Jim Crow laws. John Gillick helped me with guns; Diana Arecco provided architectural reference; and Murdoch Matthew and Gary Gilbert instructed me on Episcopalian matters. Mary McClain, Stephen Solomita, Dennis O'Neil, and John Townsend also provided important nuggets of information.

I'm grateful to the late Harvey Pekar for answering my questions about jazz lore and to Wade Black of Bozart Mountain/Jade Films for letting me photograph his old movie cameras for reference. And it's by the good graces of Morton J. Savada of Records Revisited in Manhattan that Anna Dellyne's record labels and sleeves have a touch of authenticity.

I'm especially indebted to Leonard Shiller of the Antique Automobile Association of Brooklyn, Inc., for cheerfully escorting me from garage to garage in his borough as I photographed not only classic cars but also his fascinating cache of gas pumps, washing machines, vacuum cleaners, scooters, bicycles, beverage trucks, fire engines, and other collectibles from a bygone era.

I owe thanks to those who admitted me into their private domains so I could snap reference photos of old furniture, appliances, and representative bits of architecture: Arthur Davis and Ellen Elliott; David Nimmons and David Fleischer; Howie Katz; Elyse Taylor and Leonard Shiller; and Tony Ward and Richard Goldstein. And I'm grateful as well for the special contributions of Grady Clarkson, Tim J. Luddy, and David Hutchison.

I'm indebted to Robyn Chapman for welcoming *Stuck Rubber Baby* into the fold of First Second Books and engineering this 25th Anniversary Edition of the book, to Mindy Rosenkrantz for ironing out the contract, and to Kirk Benshoff for art directing its interior pages and designing the cover.

Stuck Rubber Baby was originally published in 1995 by DC Comics (now DC Entertainment) under the company's Paradox Press imprint. Editors Mark Nevelow, Andrew Helfer, Margaret Clark, and Bronwyn Taggart supported *Stuck Rubber Baby* unwaveringly during its extended incubation and allowed me broad artistic autonomy in its execution. I deeply appreciate their willingness to stand behind a graphic novel that embodied themes that might have tempted less adventurous editors to step back. Their collective feedback contributed significantly to a sturdier narrative. Mike Friedrich of Star*Reach Productions, Inc., who served as my agent during the book's inception, was an effective problem solver and a valued advisor with regard to both pictures and text while I was drawing it. And I'm especially grateful to my longtime friend Martha Thomases, then the publicity manager of DC Comics, for the help she provided on too many fronts to mention here, as well as for her seminal insistence, in the face of my initial skepticism, that space might exist at the House of Superman for an underground cartoonist's pursuit of a labor of love.

In 2015 representation of the book passed from Star*Reach to Kitchen, Lind &

Associates, with Mike Friedrich's blessing. This was a change that felt especially felicitous because of my long history with my friend Denis Kitchen, who first began publishing my underground comix in 1972. The change made sense because Kitchen, Lind had been representing all my other books since 2011. I have great confidence in this agency and am grateful to Denis and his partner, John Lind, for taking me under their wing.

When I started *Stuck Rubber Baby,* I thought I could do it in two years. It took four. Thus was precipitated a personal budgetary crisis of unnerving proportions, one that forced an unwelcome diversion of energy into the search for enough supplemental funds to cover two unanticipated years of full-time drawing.

Accustomed as I have always been to creating art in relative solitude, it was disorienting to find myself so dependent on assistance from others. But dependent I was, and it's with deep gratitude that I catalog here the varied ways that friends and creative colleagues went to bat for me during difficult times.

Most of the forms I filled out in applying for foundation grants while I was drawing *Stuck Rubber Baby* asked for letters of endorsement from individuals of creative accomplishment. The following people wrote such letters on my behalf: Stephen R. Bissette; Martin Duberman; Will Eisner; Harvey Fierstein; Richard Goldstein; Maurice Horn; Scott McCloud; Ida Panicelli; and Harvey Pekar.

When things seemed most precarious, a fundraising tactic was devised by which individuals could become "sponsors" of this book through the purchase of original artwork from it at higher-than-market value and in advance of its even being drawn. In support of this tactic, a letter of endorsement for *Stuck Rubber Baby* was drafted and signed by fifteen writers, artists, film and TV producers, and other cultural leaders. Those who signed that letter were: Michael Feingold; Matt Foreman; David Frankel; Richard Goldstein; Arnie Kantrowitz; Tony Kushner; Harvey Marks; Lawrence D. Mass; Jed Mattes; Armistead Maupin; Michael Musto; Robert Newman; John Scagliotti; Randy Shilts; and John Wessel. Crucial technical tasks related to fundraising were performed by Tony Ward, Jennifer Camper, Robert Hanna, and Suk Choi of Box Graphics, Inc. I appreciate the willingness of Paul Levitz, then the executive vice president and publisher of DC Comics, to sanction the bending of some normal company practices in the assembly of our fundraising prospectus.

I am deeply grateful to the individual sponsors themselves, whose advance purchases of original art from this graphic novel made the completion of *Stuck Rubber Baby* possible. They are:

Fred Adams   **Tony Kushner**
Allan Cruse   **Stanley Reed**
Kevin Eastman   **Martha Thomases and John R. Tebbel**
Richard Goldstein   **Bob Wingate**

Additional financial support for this project was provided by:

Joan Cullman   **Chopeta Lyons**
Glenn Izutsu   **The Anderson Prize Foundation**

Let me finish by thanking Ed Sedarbaum, my companion of forty-plus years and since 2004 my legal husband, for his unshakable belief in me and in the merits of this graphic novel; for the concrete help he offered when practical problems loomed; and for the encouragement and thoughtful feedback he provided as successive chapters were offered for his assessment.

Howard Cruse
July 1995
Updated in June 2019

:01

First Second

Stuck Rubber Baby. Copyright © 1995 by Howard Cruse
Introduction copyright © 2020 by Alison Bechdel
Afterword, biography, and "The Making of Stuck Rubber Baby" copyright © 2020 by The Estate of Howard Cruse
Jackie Estrada's photo of Howard Cruse copyright © 2020 by Jackie Estrada
Ed Sedarbaum's tribute to Howard Cruse copyright © 2020 by Edward Sedarbaum
Kim Venter's tribute to Howard Cruse copyright © 2020 by Kimberly Kolze Venter

Published by First Second
First Second is an imprint of Roaring Brook Press,
a division of Holtzbrinck Publishing Holdings Limited Partnership
120 Broadway, New York, NY 10271

Don't miss your next favorite book from First Second!
For the latest updates go to firstsecondnewsletter.com and sign up for our enewsletter.

Library of Congress Control Number: 2019903653
ISBN: 978-1-250-24948-7

Our books may be purchased in bulk for promotional, educational, or business use.
Please contact your local bookseller or the Macmillan Corporate and Premium Sales
Department at (800) 221-7945 ext. 5442 or by email at
MacmillanSpecialMarkets@macmillan.com.

Stuck Rubber Baby was originally published in 1995 by Paradox Press, an imprint of DC Comics.
It was republished in 2010 by Vertigo, also an imprint of DC Comics.

First Second would like to thank the Rare Book and Manuscript Library at Columbia University,
which houses Howard Cruse's papers, for opening its collection to us.

25th Anniversary Edition edited by Robyn Chapman
Cover and interior book design by Kirk Benshoff
Printed in the United States of America

Penciled on 2-ply Strathmore smooth illustration board with a #2 HB graphite pencil.
Inked with Koh-i-noor Rapidograph pens (assorted tip sizes), augmented
with Winsor & Newton red sable brushwork and Japanese brush pens.
All lettering done by hand with the exception of the typeset newspaper copy on page 50.
The endpapers feature preliminary sketches drawn in ink on tracing vellum.

1 3 5 7 9 10 8 6 4 2

BY ART
WE LIVE

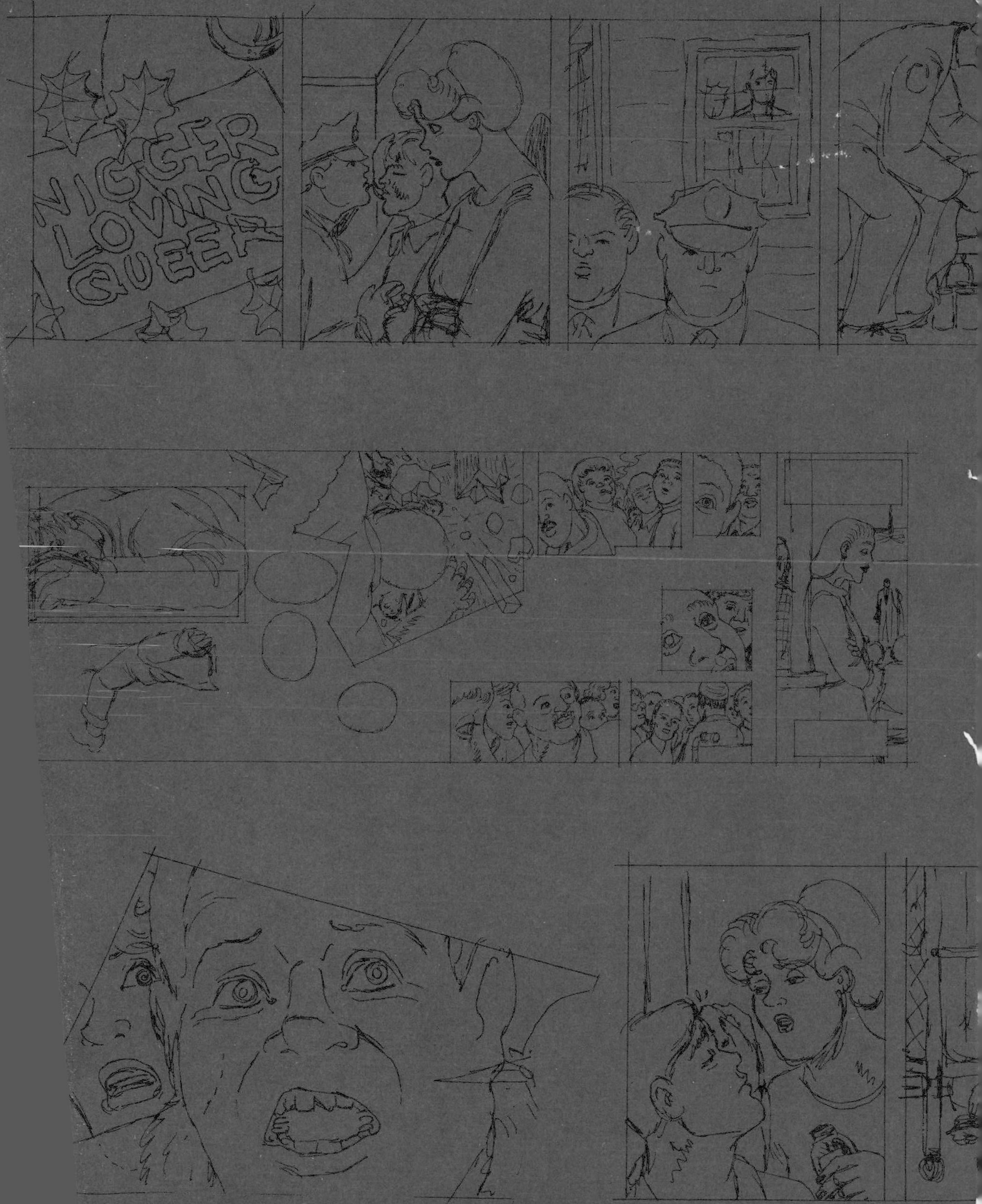
NIGGER LOVING QUEER